A DISTANT RIDGE

A Novel of the Northern Plains in the 1870s

James W McDonough

Ranger Creek Publishing

RANGER CREEK
PUBLISHING

ISBN-13: 9798402958340
ISBN-10: 1477123456

Library of Congress Control Number: 2018675309
Printed in the United States of America

For my wife, Sharon, thanks for your patience and understanding while I stumbled my way through this process, and to my friends Stan Ternes and Richard Lutz, for their encouragement and feedback. Special thanks to my 'Ace' proof reader and sister, Patty Evatt.

Finally, in special appreciation to all of the NCOs and enlisted men of the US military forces down through the years, that were tasked with converting orders into action, be they right or wrong.

CONTENTS

INTRODUCTION

My first exposure, to the controversies surrounding any of the events in this book, was while on a Boy Scout field trip to the Old Cowtown Museum in Wichita, Kansas. Displayed on a wall in the renovated Railroad Depot, was a copy of a lithograph titled "Custer's Last Fight". The Anheuser-Busch Brewery commissioned it back in the late 1880s, and it was widely distributed across the country. It's vivid colors portrayed Custer standing bravely in the middle of his men, brandishing a saber while clad in buckskins and with a scarlet scarf flowing around his neck. Fierce visaged Indian warriors surrounding him and the soldiers are attacking on all sides, while in the foreground several of the troopers are being stabbed, scalped and mutilated. My youthful imagination soared and now, 60 years later I'm still intrigued!

Over the years, my interest ebbed and flowed about Custer and the Battle of the Little Big Horn, usually peeking again whenever a new book came out. After retirement, with new found time on my hands, I committed to write a book about it. But there are already a myriad of books about it. So, I decided to expand beyond the events of June 1876. In doing so, I discovered that this battle was not a culmination of the frontier conflicts of that period, but merely a waypoint in the timeline of the events of that decade, albeit a significant one.

After the end of the Civil War, the relentless push of what was termed 'Manifest Destiny" resumed. By the early 1870s, it paused briefly due to the Panic of '73. But eventually, between the continuing influx of immigrants from Europe seeking land, and the Railroads pushing to expand their lines and acquire the land grants that came with the right-of-ways, it soon resumed. There was a problem though, most of the land out west was Indian land, granted in treaties to the various tribes.

Little attention has been paid to the 1873/74 US Boundary Commission Survey and the two companies, D & I, of the 7th Cavalry that served as part of the military escort. I decided to use this as a backdrop to introduce the fictional characters, Jake Rogers, and Pat Morse into my story as members of Company D. All the other 7th Cavalry characters were real people, and the events that take place are based on historical research. I did decide to take a few liberties with Lt. Bell and the men of his supply detail, by placing them on a riverboat. But I wanted to introduce early on the importance of these crude steamships and the critical logistical role they played throughout the decade. After the departure from Fort Stevenson, every other occurrence and timeline is as historically accurate as I could make it.

The two years covered by the Boundary Survey reveal the complex nature of the Northern Plains and the tribes that lived there. The Lakota Sioux and Northern Cheyenne tribes were prominent, but the Crow, Blackfeet, Gross Ventre, Assinibone, Chippewa, Arikara, Mandan, Hidatsa, Arapaho, Dakota Sioux, Nez Perce, and the relatively obscure bands of Métis were all impacted by the encroachment of white settlers advancing from all directions. Exacerbating the situation was the beginning of the methodical decimation of the northern buffalo herd. The character, Val Wheeler, was a real life mixed blood scout working for the Survey. His foray into ranching is a product of my imagination, but it serves to illustrate that cattle ranching in Montana was a growing industry, even in 1874, and before. The Nelson Story cattle drive that inspired "Lonesome Dove" is a case in point.

The 7th Cavalry that fought at the Little Big Horn was not the elite unit that some accounts would lead us to believe. It was the only time, in its then brief existance, that the entire Regiment was assembled as a tactical unit. Prior to that, the various companies had been parceled between multiple Kansas military posts, and then posted to Reconstruction Duty and scattered across the South. The majority of the regiment had been gathered for both the Yellowstone Expedition of "73, and the Black Hills Expedition of '74, but then quickly re-dispersed. Rarely posted with more than a few of his companies, Custer was frequently absent on trips. In fact, he returned to assume command of the regiment just a week before it took the field. One third of the 7th's officers were on detached duty, or leave when it marched out of Fort Abraham Lincoln that May. Most of the individual company rolls were only 60-70% full, and of those, close to 20% had less than a year in service. Many had no horses and over 160 troopers had to be left at the Powder River depot, including the band.

The officers of the 7th were a mixed bag of experienced, ex-Civil War veterans and some newer West Point graduates. The Frontier Army had a complex system of Brevet Ranking left over from the War, (i.e. Custer had been a Major General during the War) and the use of the higher rank was an honorific. However, I elected to use the actual rank of each officer to simplify things. Advancement took years, and was primarily dependent on the retirements and deaths of those senior. Custer played favorites and surrounded himself with them, while making sure that most of his detractors were posted elsewhere

The post-Civil War Army was perilously underfunded and many of it's supplies were outdated war surplus. There was no budget for advanced training such as marksmanship, and the weaponry was kept simplistic, barring the Colt 45 pistol. This in itself, handicapped the troops when they were confronted by the unconventional tactics of the Indians, who favored repeating rifles purchased with treaty monies.

I made a concentrated effort to to adhere to historical accuracy and timelines of the campaigns, before, during, and after the Little Big Horn. The defeat at the hands of the Sioux and their Cheyenne allies served as a catalyst for changing the Army's strategy towards them, forcing the adaption of a policy of total submission.

My research into the post-Custer 7th Cavalry led me to the Nez Perce Campaign the following year. Although it doesn't have the quite the same notoriety of the Sioux War of 1876, I found that the 7th Cavalry's role was still significant. With the assistance of some military registers, I was able to piece together the fates of most of the Company D veterans.

This project was like those puzzle boxes that once opened, reveal another inside. When I tried to focus on a single event I found it was impossible to isolate it and take it out of context. The five years covered in this novel cannot fully illustrate the magnitude of the changes precipitated on the Indian tribes of the Northern Plains. Many of the repercussions are still felt there to this day.

Some of the fictional characters I introduced into the story lines were to pull in elements of related non military events. Jake's family and friends, the civilian women, and the railroad agents fall in this category. The post traders that are named were actually in business at the forts where they are mentioned.

This book is work of historical fiction, based on multiple sources. I elected not to burden readers with footnotes. I wanted to come up with a different perspective of these events that occurred almost 150 years ago. Hopefully, I have!

James W McDonough
Fort Gibson Lake, Oklahoma
Illinois District - Cherokee Nation

FICTIONAL CHARACTERS

Jacob Rogers
Zeb & Sarah Rogers
Frank and Colleen Armstrong
Pat Morse
Val Wheeler
Murray Johnson - NPRR agent
Holly Walker
Kate Seip
Vanessa Blake
Jack Ward - Wagoneer & Packer
Joe Martin - Wagoneer & Packer
Mark Walsh - M K & T RR agent
Bill Byrne- St. Paul HQ sergeant
Danny Foster- New York Artillery sergeant
Bernie Braun- Arsenal Clerk
Dan Fuss - Training sergeant
Ned Walkingstick - Cherokee trail guide

These characters and several other minor ones are all fictional and some may represent an amalgamation of undocumented real life individuals

MAP OF THE WESTERN US - CIRCA LATE 1870S

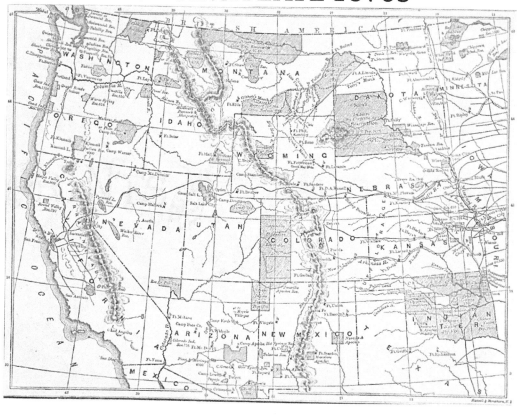

CHAPTER 1

The brilliant blue sky was in stark contrast with the rich green hues of tree covered hillsides as a wagon lurched slowly along a rutted trail, following a lone horseman. The driver was dark haired and wore a straw hat and plaid shirt with the sleeves rolled up. He tossed the reins and called out. "Yo Hector! Yo Paris! Git along there! I want to get to town today."

The horses seemed indifferent to his cries, as they plodded along at a steady pace, raising little spurts of dust when their hoofs struck the dirt track. They flicked their tails, and snorted, as flies swarmed about their ears. The late morning sun was beating down and the lack of any breeze promised another sweltering spring afternoon, in the humid Ozark foothills.

"Hey Jake, where'd you ever come up with such dumb names for those horses?" asked another young man, as he clung to the bouncing wooden seat on the wagon. He was smaller of the two and had reddish hair with a freckled complexion. He was dressed similarly to his friend.

"Oh, my Ma used to read me this story about a war in a place called Troy. It was a long, long time ago. Hector and Paris were the names of the sons of the king of Troy. It was always one of my favorites, so when we got these horses as foals, I named them after them." answered the driver.

"You're lucky, my Ma only reads me the Bible."

"Well, your Ma ain't a school teacher either, Frank," he replied. "And you didn't get schooled at home like I did. I'd had rather been fishing. That would have been lucky."

The horseman dropped back and pulled abreast. as they moved down the road

"I'm going to ride on ahead into town." he called out. "I've got your Ma's list. I'll get with Mr. Jackson at the general store, and give it to him. Save us some time. You take the wagon on up by Division Street to our regular spot, and get them horses watered and fed. I'll meet up with you there and we'll go find some supper. I want to be ready to load up and head back first thing in the morning"

"Come on Pa! At least let us have enough time to wander around a little, and see the local sights." Jake exclaimed. "We don't get to come to town that much. Besides, we want to go up to the rail yards and see that new roundhouse that I heard they're building. And, Frank here has never seen a train up close."

"More like you boys want to go sneak a beer, and ogle some of the local pretty girls" the rider chuckled. "Well, I guess I don't blame you. I was your age once myself"

"I'm twenty, and Frank's almost. We're a little old for sarsaparilla and candy."

"I tell you what, you boys go do your sight seeing then get everything settled in. Then I'll come get you and we'll go down to the town square, and I'll treat you to a beer. But just remember if I want your Ma to know about it, I'll tell her!" Zeb called, as he turned his horse to ride away.

Zeb Rogers had served in the Union Army during the recent war. He had been wounded in the leg and still had a slight limp that showed when he was tired. He'd been taken to a hospital in Springfield, and while recuperating, he had made friends with some of the locals. When he was well enough to get around, they had shown him the area and he'd found a place in a small valley, with a clear rock bottom creek running through it. As soon as he received his discharge, he went back to Pike County, Missouri, and fetched his wife, Sarah, and son Jake, who was twelve at the time. Pike County was up north of St.Louis, close on the Mississippi River. It was named after Zebulon Pike, the famous western explorer, as was Zeb. It was said that Pike had spent time in that area, before he took off on his expedition to find the headwaters of the Arkansas River, back in '06. The abundance of fish and game, along with the more temperate climate, compared with northern Missouri, were the main reasons Zeb wanted to the move south. Having endured Zeb's absence during the war, Sarah was not inclined to argue about it, so the family pulled up stakes. Henderson, a little community of three hundred, welcomed them with open arms and were very pleased to be adding a school teacher to their ranks. Eventually, the productivity of the new farm, along with Sarah's teachers earnings which mostly came in form of barter, allowed them to live in relative comfort. Zeb was an avid hunter and fisherman, and Jake, following in his footsteps, was becoming a crack shot and excellent horseman.

As Jake watched his father head off towards town, he thought about all of the other times he'd made the trip over the last several years. It was a full day's wagon ride from their place just outside of Henderson, sixteen miles southeast of Springfield. At fifteen, his father had declared him old enough to accompany him on his infrequent trips, to Springfield. This was the first time that his friend Frank had tagged along with them, though. Frank Armstrong was Jake's best friend, and the son of a neighboring farm family. Slightly built, red headed, with a pale complexion and lots of freckles, Frank was quick witted, and fairly high strung. In contrast with Jake, who had dark hair and a lithe build, and was deliberate in his speech and actions.

"Do you think really think we'll get to see a train while we're in town ?" Frank asked

The Atlantic and Pacific Railway Company had completed their rail line, through Springfield just over two years previously, and trains were still quite a novelty to most of the rural population of southern Missouri.

"We should be able to see one, they come through everyday, we'll hear them coming." Jake answered.

"Man, I'd give my left nut to ride on one." Frank proclaimed.

"I don't think you have any nuts left. As many times as you've offered out the left one, I'm sure someone has claimed the right one, too." Jake jibed

Frank jabbed Jake in the ribs and grinned.

Springfield had started out as a way stop on the 'The Military Road' that ran from St.Louis, to Ft. Smith, Arkansas in the late 1830s, the principal portion of the town had been founded on a hilltop above Jordan Creek, a spring-fed, clear flowing stream, that had also been a stop on the "Trail of Tears" for the Cherokee Indians as they followed it during their forced relocation from the Southeastern US, to Indian Territory. The telegraph also followed, and by 1860 the route was referred to as 'The Wire Road'. The town had also been the scene of several battles and skirmishes during the recent war. In 1861, the Battle of Wilson's Creek was the first battle fought west of the Mississippi, and was won by the Southern forces. Springfield had been occupied briefly by the Confederates, in early 1862. After the Union army re-occupied, it served as a major Union supply depot and hospital center. Another attempt to capture and raid the town was made by the Confederates, in January 1863. They were repulsed and Springfield remained in Union hands the rest of the war. The area around Springfield, and the rest of Southwest Missouri, had been contested since the earliest days of the war. Partisan bushwackers and irregular troops from both sides had conducted guerrilla raids. The town had also attracted a few unsavory businesses that catered to the military troops that were stationed there, and others passing through, so the city had served as a focal point for all of the combatants. After the war, these elements combined to create a period of lawlessness, that took several years to settle down. It was a combination of the influx of ex-Union troops, such as Zeb and other Northerners that had spurred post war growth. That, along with the arrival of the railroads, finally brought a calmer aspect to the community. In fact, the arrival of the trains had spawned a new city, North Springfield, which was still in its infancy. Located a mile north of Springfield, it built up around the new railroad depot, and it's accompanying rail and stockyards. Division Street was the dividing line between the two cities. South of Division, was "Old Town', whose occupants referred to the new city derisively, as 'Moon City'. The area between the two, was rapidly becoming the nexus of growth for both communities. There were still patches of woods and vacant lots where visitors, mostly local farmers, could camp out if they didn't want to pay for the cost of lodging and livery stables. Jordan Creek was still handy for watering the horses.That was where the Rogers usually parked their wagon and overnighted.

Late that afternoon, Jake and Frank were just finishing up with the wagon and horses when Zeb Rogers rode up.

'Hey, boys! It looks like you're about settled in. Help me get Ol' Ulysses here unsaddled and fed. Then we'll get cleaned up and go down to the square."

"I can't believe you named your horse after the President." Frank laughed.

"Actually, we didn't." Jake replied, "He's named after a famous Greek hero. It's from that Trojan War story I was telling you about. There's actually a whole other story based on him. The stories are called the Iliad and the Odyssey. Actually, my mother made me read both of them"

"Boy, I'm glad it was you instead of me, reading makes my head hurt." Frank opined. "I'd just as soon take an ass whuppin!"

"That's almost the way I feel too." said Zeb, "But Jake here takes after his Ma when it comes to learnin'. She taught him to read when he was just a little tyke. It's just as well, though, the way things are changing so fast. You bear that in mind, Frank. A man needs to have some education if he wants to get ahead in these times."

"Don't worry Frank. Ma says they'll always need ditch diggers, so you'll always have a job!" exclaimed Jake with a grin.

The smaller lad bent to pick up a dirt clod, and tossed it at his friend. "Here study on this." he said as Jake ducked. "Bet all your fancy reading comes in handy when you're writing love letters to your girl friend, Colleen."

"I don't write her love letters. She's just a friend"

"Yeh! Well you always seem to be studying her real close when ever she comes around"

"Mind your own business you little red-headed peckerwood!" said Jake, as he tossed a stick back at Frank.

"Hey, you boys hurry up ,and quit foolin 'around!" Zeb exclaimed, "I want to get down to the Lyon House soon. My old friend, Pat Morse, is supposed to be around town. I haven't seen him in years. He sent me a letter a while back letting me know he might be in Springfield this month. You remember him don't you Jake?"

"Yes, sir, you were in the War with him. I remember him visiting us. He gave me a pocket knife.

"Good ol' Pat!" Zeb stated.

Pat Morse and Zeb had both joined the 4th Missouri State Militia Cavalry, at St. Joseph, Missouri back in early1862. Zeb, the older by four years, was appointed a sergeant, and Pat a corporal. They became fast friends and had fought together, at the Battle of Springfield, back in January of 1863, where Zeb was wounded. After Zeb recovered, he rejoined the unit and they had fought skirmishes up and down the Kansas/Missouri border the rest of the war, culminating in the Battle of Westport, and the subsequent route of the General Sterling Price's Confederates back down to Arkansas. When the unit was mustered out, in St. Louis, in mid-1865, Zeb had fetched his family, and headed back to Springfield and settled in. Pat had accompanied the Rogers, and even helped build their place. But Pat had taken to the military life, and in mid 1866, he'd heard that the Army was raising four new Cavalry regiments. He went out to Ft. Riley, Kansas and joined the 7th Cavalry. Over the years, he'd stayed in touch with Zeb, through letters, and had even come back to visit them when on leave, on occasion. His wild stories of the western plains, and chasing Indians, were always entertaining, and never failed to enthrall the Rogers and their neighbors. Pat's storytelling was always very enthusiastic, and most probably embellished a bit, but that was just Pat's nature. It would be good to see him again.

One of the latest signs of urbanization, was the horse drawn trolley line that ran between the two cities. Zeb and the boys caught it at Division Street and rode it down to the Springfield town square. They walked across the square, to the south side. The Lyon House was a hotel, located on South

Street where it met the square. It also had a saloon and had been a favorite watering hole, and gambling place, for many years. The large covered front porch of the hotel provided an excellent vantage point for the three acre public square, which served as a gathering place for many public functions. There were men lounging in chairs ranged around the porch, enjoying the shade in the late spring afternoon. As they approached, Jake noticed that several were wearing old Army caps, and uniform jackets. Some of them had sleeves, or pant legs pinned up, denoting various missing appendages. There seemed to be about an even mix between Union Blue and Confederate Gray, in apparel. The rest were wearing various types of civilian clothes ranging from black suits to homespun pants and shirts. Most of them grasped mugs of beer, and a dense cloud of cigar smoke hung in the air surrounding them. As Zeb and the boys approached, one of them called out.

"Well, lookee there, here comes Zeb Rogers. He's just in time to buy me a fresh beer!"

The speaker was a burly, mustached man with dark hair, wearing a blue forage cap, tilted back on his head. A dark blue Army coat with chevrons on the sleeves, over sky blue pants with a vertical yellow stripes, that were tucked into black leather knee-high boots. He had bright blue eyes, and a big smile on his ruddy face. He hoisted a large mug and quickly drained it, then swiped the back of one hand across his mouth.

"Hello Pat!" exclaimed Zeb. "You're looking good."

Pat grasped Zeb by the hand, and said. "Always good when I see you hale and hearty my friend. He glanced over at Jake and Frank. "And I see you brought some pups with you. This can't be little Jake. He was just this tall last time I saw him." He held out his hand about level with Jake's shoulder.

"Ma's been feeding me good, sir!" Jake said grinning. "And the hunting has been good this spring."

"Don't call me sir." he said, pointing at the chevrons on his jacket sleeve. "I've got too much common sense to be an officer. Just call me Pat."

"Yes sir! I mean Pat. This is my friend, Frank." he said nodding towards Frank, who was clearly impressed by the soldier.

"Well, Pat, I see that you're empty there." said Zeb, "Let's get you a fresh mug, and some for us as well. The lads say they're old enough, and they assure me that they'll not mention it to their Mas. Lead the way and I'll buy."

"I'll blaze a trail for us." replied Pat, and he proceeded to usher them through the front doors, towards the long bar inside. After securing a round of beers, they went back out front, and found some chairs.

"How long you in town for?" asked Pat

"Just for the night, I'm getting supplies, and picking up some things for Sarah. How about you?"

"Oh, another couple of days, or so."

"Well, maybe you can find time to come and visit, I know Sarah would like to see you."

Pat and Zeb fired up cigars, and leaned back. Pat gestured out towards the square

"You remember what this place looked like during the Battle?" queried Pat.

"Not likely to forget it." answered Zeb, "This place and the courthouse were both being used as hospitals, and the square was covered with tents, wagons, and horses were everywhere. I remember the chaos that erupted when we heard that General Marmaduke was spotted heading this way, with Jo Shelby's cavalry. You and I escorted the walking wounded that volunteered to fight down to Fort #4, just three blocks south of here. They mounted a couple of old cannons on wagon frames, that was all the artillery we had."

Jake and Frank leaned forward in their chairs listening intently. Pat noticed and pointed down South Street.

"The forts are gone now, but there were several around town. #4 was 3 blocks down that way. The Rebs were coming up from the south, from the direction of Ozark. General Brown had the houses south of the fort burned down to clear fields of fire. The 4th Missouri Cavalry, our unit, was sent to scout their advance. We skirmished with Shelby's troopers, and fell back to our lines. They had a couple of field pieces, and started shelling us." Pat pointed straight up, They hit the Lyon House, and several other buildings, and sent balls in to the square, fortunately they didn't have any shells that exploded. We dismounted and helped hold the lines. That's when Zeb got hit in the leg. I helped him back here to the square and the doctor's worked on him right over there." he pointed. "We fought until dark, among the houses and buildings, then Marmaduke withdrew, so we won the battle. Funny thing was, if he'd swung around to the east side of town, the Rebs would have been in to the square in 10 minutes, and we wouldn't have been able to stop them. Goes to show's you the importance of good scouts."

Zeb just nodded his head in agreement, as he gazed out on the square, reliving that wild day, in his mind. Smoke, from the burning houses, and gunfire had obscured everything. The sound of the screaming horses, gunfire, the moans of wounded men, and shouts. The shock of his wound and the ringing in his ears had made it all so surreal.

"Hard to believe it was right here." he commented. "Every thing is so clean and peaceful." He puffed on his cigar.

Jake looked at his father and said, "How long were you in the hospital, Pa?"

"Oh, about 6 weeks, fortunately the bullet didn't shatter any bone, or they would've taken my leg off . Damn lucky."

"Yeh, we were lucky the rest of the war." chimed in Pat, "Neither one of us got wounded. Even at the Battle of Westport, which made Springfield look like a skirmish. There were over 30,000 men fought in that one. It's been called the Gettysburg of the West. For a week afterward, we chased the Rebs all the way back to Arkansas. That's where your Pa and I met Wild Bill."

"Wild Bill Hickok? exclaimed Frank, "The Wild Bill Hickok! I've got books about him."

"Sure enough!" Pat answered, "Well, we met him when he was scouting for General Curtis. After the war was over, some of us weren't sure what we wanted to do. Wild Bill was that way. He came back here to Springfield after the war, and just hung around town. He stayed here at the Lyon House, quite a bit. In fact, I watched him shoot Dave Tutt, right over there." He pointed out at the square. "If you believe Harper's Magazine and your dime novels, it was the first Wild West gunfight."

"Frank and I have read most of em." said Jake. "Will you tell us the real story about it, Pat?"

Zeb looked over at Pat and rolled his eyes. "You may as well get on with it, you got these boys hooked, now" he exclaimed.

Pat took a big pull on his beer, and grinned. "Well!" he began, "Your Pa had gone up north to fetch you, and your Ma, back down here. So, left to my own devices, I spent a lot of time hanging around downtown here. This was in July of '65. You have to understand that, during the war, Springfield was a major supply and troop replacement depot, and there were a lot of businesses, saloons and such, that catered to all of the men that were here, and passing through. After the war they were still mostly open for business. Now Ol 'Bill worked for the Provost Marshall, back in '63, before he left to go scouting, and they say he did a little spying on the side, too. There were quite a few "irregulars" in these parts that played on both sides during the war. They liked to hang out around Springfield, mostly in the saloons. Bill got to know who they were, and pumped them for information. He also developed a taste for card playing. When he came back after the war, he re-acquainted himself with these places, and quickly gained a reputation as a gambler and sporting man. One of these"irregulars", was an Arkansawyer by the name of Davis Tutt. He and Hickock were friendly at one point, but eventually had a falling out. Some said it was over Bill's woman, at that time, Susanna Moore. It got so bad between them, that Hickock wouldn't play cards if Tutt was at a table."

Pat paused for another drink of his beer and puffed his cigar. "I came in here one evening, towards the end of July, and saw Wild Bill at a table playing poker. He appeared to be winning. I sat down a table with some acquaintances and was pursuing a friendly game of chance. After a while, I noticed a man, standing off to the side of where Bill was at. I would later find out he was Davis Tutt. He was loaning money to a couple of the players, and encouraging them to raise their bets against Hickock. Bill continued to win, and Tutt suddenly announced, "Hickock, you still owe me $40 for that horse I traded you." Bill looked up at him, then counted out the money and tossed it to him. "There we are even." he stated, and began to shuffle the deck. Tutt reached over and snatched a gold pocket watch of the table where it had been laying, and said, "You still owe me $35 from that poker game a couple of weeks ago, too." Hickock turned to look at Tutt. "It is $25, and I still have your marker in my pocket." he replied, cooly. "Well, I'll just keep this watch until you pay me the $35," Tutt said. I can tell you that things started to get a little tense right then. The room went totally silent, and I started looking around, and saw that everyone in the place was watching. Hickok rose from his chair. "That gold watch is worth a hell of a lot more than that." he stated. Two of the men that had been playing, and had received money from Tutt, pushed back their chairs, and a couple of other men walked over and stood next to Tutt. "This Yankee giving you some grief, Dave?" one of them asked. Tutt smiled and said, "No problem. Wild Bill, here, owes me some money and I'm just going to hold on to this fancy watch of his, until he pays me." Well, Ol 'Bill took in the situation, and said stone-faced to Tutt. "I only owe you $25. But seeing that your memory out numbers mine right now, we'll let this rest for now. But, don't let me catch you wearing that watch." Tutt chuckled and replied, "I just may try it out tomorrow, show it off out on the town square!" Hickock gathered up his winnings, and turned to leave. He locked eyes with Tutt, as he passed him and stated flatly, "You wear that watch out on the square tomorrow, and I'll kill you." Then walked away. Well, that was all for the night for me, and I decided to call it in early, I intended to be up and around the next day early, to see how it played out.

Zeb glanced over at the two younger men and saw the rapt

expressions on their faces as Pat regaled them with his tale.

"The next morning, which was a Friday, I showed up here for breakfast at about 9:00 in the morning. Wild Bill was also here, calmly having his coffee. At about 10:00, Tutt came out on the square wearing Hickok's watch. There were several people that ran in to tell Wild Bill. With several bystander's in tow, Bill came out of the Lyon House, and went over and sat down on a bench with Tutt. One of them, a fellow that I knew, by the name of Orr, told me later what transpired. Bill offered up the $25, and asked for his watch back. Dave replied that the debt was now $45, and waved the watch in front of Hickock. Bill was adamant that he would not pay more than the $25. After some further attempts to negotiate, Tutt walked off with some friends to get a drink, and told Wild Bill he would be at the livery stable, that afternoon. Bill walked off towards his lodgings, south of the square. Well, I can tell you that everyone knew that wasn't the end of it, and the saloons and shops did a brisk business that day as everyone hung around to see what was going to happen. I got me a perch right here where we're sitting, so I had a front row seat for the whole thing. About 6:00 O'clock, Hickok comes walking up South Street on to the square, right over there." Pat said pointing. "He stopped and as the people around him saw he was toting his "Navy Colt" in hand, they scattered." Pat pointed again, indicating a building across the square to the northwest. "Dave Tutt was sitting over there by the livery stable. When he noticed the crowd moving, and saw Bill walking in his direction, he stood up. Wild Bill called out to him, "Dave, here I am!" Tutt started walking across, and Bill called out again, "Don't cross over here wearing that watch!" Hickok then cocked his revolver and placed it in his belt holster. They were about 75-100 feet apart at that point. Now some say that Tutt was the better shot of the two, Wild Bill didn't have much of a reputation, other than being an Army scout back then, so it was pretty brave of him to stand out in the open like that. At any rate, they both turned sideways, and drew their pistols. Bill took the time to brace his on his left forearm, and they both fired at about the same time. At first we thought they'd both missed, but then Dave staggered over towards the courthouse steps, crying out, "Boys, I'm killed!" and then fell on to the street dead. Bill had shot him clean through the chest, then he walked over, calm as you please, and got his watch back"

"Wow." Both boys said in unison. "What happened to Wild Bill afterwards?"

"He was arrested, two days later, stood trial. He was found not guilty, and in August, ran for and lost the election for City Marshall. He left town shortly after that and headed out to Fort Riley Kansas, about he same time I did. They were forming a new Cavalry regiment, and I went out there to join up. I saw him once or twice over the years. He scouted for the Army, and Custer, for a while, then bounced around the Kansas cowtowns for several years. I'm sure you boys know more about his exploits than I do. Last I heard he was headed back east, with Buffalo Bill Cody, and they're performing in a show called "Scouts of the Plains".

Zeb and Pat had kept in touch over the years, and Zeb knew that he had a wealth of stories that he could regale the two boys with, and would, if he wasn't reigned in shortly.

"Come on Pat, let's go on and get these boys some dinner. They've got a full day ahead of them, tomorrow."

Pat drained his mug and slammed it down. "By God that sounds good to me. As I recall they used to cook a damn good steak here. Come on lads, your Pa's buying!" he exclaimed and winked at Zeb.

After eating they re-adjourned to the porch. As the evening quiet settled around the square, whip-or-wills could be heard sounding their plaintive refrain.

"I see you're still with Custer." said Zeb, eyeing the brass crossed sabers under the numeral 7, on Pat's kepi."

At the mention of the name, Custer, again, both Jake, and Frank, looked up with awe.

"You're in the 7th Cavalry, with General Custer?" exclaimed Frank wide eyed. "Have you fought any wild Indians?"

Pat sat back and chuckled, "The closest I've been to an Indian in the last couple of years, is a wooden Indian outside a cigar store, in Kentucky. The Army has had the 7th Cavalry spread across seven different Southern states. We've been chasing moonshiners and Ku Klux Klansmen for the last two years."

"So how'd you end up here, in Springfield?" asked Zeb.

"They started reassembling the regiment over in Memphis, back in February. Then in March, sent it up to Fort Rice, in the Dakota Territory. They are finishing Fort Abraham Lincoln, farther up the Missouri River, across from the new town of Bismarck. That's where the Northern Pacific Railroad stopped building tracks. The Regiment is going to be moving there. We're supposed to protect the survey and railroad construction crews from the Sioux. I'm part of a recruiting force, left down south to find bodies to help get us up to full strength. I was up at Jefferson Barracks, in St. Louis, so I grabbed a train to come down here. You know the railroads let us soldiers ride for free. Of course we can't be picky about the seats. But it's a good way to see some country, beats horseback. I'll get enough of that when I get out back out west. It'll be the first time the Regiment has been together in several years and Custer will be itching to do something."

A thrill went through Jake, as he had a vision of himself clad in a uniform like Pat, and imagined himself mounted on horseback, with saber drawn, charging headlong against fierce horde of howling savages.

Zeb noticed Jake's rapt attention focused on every word coming out of Pat's mouth. He felt a little twinge of alarm. He suddenly remembered the siren call to arms from back in his youth, and immediately thought to himself that he needed to inject a little reality into the conversation.

"What's the pay rate for an enlistee these days, Pat? He asked.

"We pay our new lads a whopping $13 a month!" Pat replied, grinning. "Of course, most of them have been living hand to mouth, anyway. They're likely one step from the poorhouse, or jail, so they don't tend to focus much on the pay anyway. We get our share of pilgrims from over the water, too. There's lot's of Irish and Germans, a few Brits too."

"I don't imagine you tell them about the shitty weather or the mud, dust, and saddle sores, either." said Zeb, "Let alone the chance that they're apt to get their scalps lifted."

"Well, there's that too." Pat stated. "In all reality it's a mostly a lot of drudgery. Daily drills and training, work details, stable duty and standing guard. Pretty much 5 years of Ho Hum unless the Indians act up. But we don't like to advertise the negative. Join the Cavalry! See the West! That's my line."

Jake nodded his head, He was thinking that it didn't sound much different from the confines and tedium of the daily farm routine that he went through.

Zeb stood up exclaiming, "Well, my line is that it's late, and these lads have a full day in front of them starting early in the morning. Time for us to head back to the wagon, and bed down. How many days you staying here Pat? You have time to ride over and see Sarah? She always enjoys your tales, too. She may even fix you up with some fresh strawberries and cream. We just started picking them, last week."

"That sounds great, Zeb. I'm due to take the train out in a couple of days. I think I might go ride over with you boys, tomorrow. Then come back the next day, and see if I can gather up some recruits. I'll meet up with you in the morning."

"We'll be loading up at Jackson's store, right after breakfast. We're camped up on Jordan Creek if you want coffee." Zeb stated. "Let's go boys!"

They next day as they were loading up to head out of town, Pat rode up on large black horse with a shiny coat. It tossed its dark mane and snorted as he reigned it in. Pat was dressed in civilian clothes except for his boots and a wide brimmed slouch hat with yellow braid and crossed sabers, a 7 above and a D below.

"Top o' the morning to you, lads!" he exclaimed.

Jake, who was lashing boxes to the wagon bed, looked up and replied. "That's a good looking horse!"

Zeb walked over and ran a hand over the horses's flank. "Fine piece of horse flesh, Pat. I'm surprised that the Army is mounting troops this well."

Pat stated, "This here's Gus. One benefit of spending the last two years down South was that we were able to find some prime mounts for our boys. I don't reckon that there's a better mounted cavalry unit in the Army right now than the 7th. Custer kept his headquarters in Elizabethtown, Kentucky right outside Louisville. That's horse country don't you know! I'll let you boys ride him later on, if you want."

Both boy's beamed and exclaimed, "You bet!"

That evening Pat and Zeb were sitting out on the front porch watching the sunset. Jake was out in the barn grooming Gus.

"Well, Pat, It's good that you're still content to stay in the Army. I guess you're going to make it full ride?"

"I suppose so Zeb, I just signed on again back in November. I don't know what else I'd be doing, and I'm seeing a lot of this country. Been all over Kansas, the Colorado and Indian Territories, and now we're heading up to the Dakota Territory, and probably Wyoming . Maybe I'll find me a place somewhere like you did. Of course it'd help if I met a fine woman like your Sarah. Kind of hard to do that in those parts right now, but there's lot's of people following the railroads. I guess when I quit wondering what's over the next horizon I'll start looking"

"Yeh well, I think Jake is coming down with same wanderlust. He devours books about history and travels. His Mother keeps encouraging him to go away to college, but he likes the outdoors too much. I think you're being here stokes his imagination."

"Well, there's worse ways for young men like Jake to spend time. You know he'd make a fine trooper, just like his Pa!" Pat exclaimed.

Zeb nodded his head thoughtfully, "I suppose so."

"You suppose so about what?" questioned his wife, Sarah, who had just stepped out on to the porch. She looked quizzically at Zeb.

"Pat and I were just discussing the possibility that Jake may want to join up in the cavalry."

Sarah paused, regarding both of them with a frown. "Well, I suppose that would not be my first choice, but it has becoming plain to me that Jake is getting more restless by the day. He needs to get out and experience some of the country besides Henderson and Springfield. He doesn't seem to be inclined towards more school. Don't you be asking him though Pat. If he asks, I'll not stand in his way. But I will task you to watch over him, if you can."

"I'll do that for you Sarah, if he goes. I'm heading up to Jefferson Barracks, in St. Louis, with some other recruits. That's where we put them through some training before sending them on to the Regiment. A friend of my does the postings and I can have him assigned to be in my Company"

She and Zeb held each others gaze for a second and he nodded.

Jake finished up currying Gus, Pat had allowed to ride him earlier in exchange for Jake putting him up in the barn. He walked over to where Pat's saddle and harness sat balanced on a bale of hay. It was a McClellan with a rawhide covered tree and long black skirts and stirrup hoods, there were steel rings, on each side just in front the rounded pommel that had a slot in the middle and, on the front, a metal bracket on each side. Behind the tall, rounded cantle which was pierced with three slots, there were also steel rings. Leather straps were neatly coiled through the slots. Jake was pretty familiar with the saddle, as his Pa had one similar to it. He knew you could hang a lot of gear off it. The rawhide on Pat's though, looked almost polished and seemed to glow. He guessed it was from continuous use compared to what little theirs got used. He admired the dark blue horse blanket with its yellow trim and numeral 7 in the lower rear corner. The whole rig sure looked good on Gus. He'd ridden over to show off Gus to some of his friends, particularly Colleen. She'd smiled at his enthusiasm, but didn't seem particularly impressed. She'd wanted more to discuss local gossip and events that he was only vaguely aware of, and really didn't care much about anyway.

"I wonder what it would be like to spend days and even weeks at a time on horseback? " Jake wondered. "And, what about the sights he'd see?"

He loved to ride, but had never been more than a day's worth away from home. He and Frank camped out some times while out hunting, and they had talked for hours around the fire about what adventures they would have when they grew up. Well, mostly he talked and Frank listened.

"Not much for adventures around Henderson. I ought to talk with Pa about joining up, maybe going with Pat. His mother would have a fit though." He thought to himself.

And he thought briefly about his friend Colleen, not sure what she would think about it either He liked her fine, and had even gotten a kiss, or two, from her. She listened, patiently as he told her stories, and about places that he had read about in books, nodding her head now and then and laughing at his enthusiasm. But she seemed content with the occasional trip to Springfield, or the neighboring small towns. He supposed that if he left, she wouldn't have a hard time finding her a new boy to flirt with, maybe even Frank, he liked everything around here. He put his hand on the McClellan, rubbing the pommel, then headed out the door to the house. As he got closer to the porch, he saw that his parents, and Pat were all watching him. Suddenly, he made up his mind. He'd go with Pat and join the cavalry!

CHAPTER 2

Sioux City, Iowa - July 6, 1873, on the Missouri River

Missouri Riverboats - Circa 1870s

The sternwheeler *Western* nosed into the landing, jockeying in the Missouri River current allowing it, and momentum, to push the shallow draft hull around so it ended up pointing upstream, then engaged the paddlewheel to ease forward so the crew could toss lines to secure the boat to massive wood pilings that had been driven into the riverbank. A long landing stage was then lowered from the bow of the boat to the sprawling boardwalk that served as a wharf. Stacks of cargo, lumber, chords of split wood, horses and livestock were all staged ready to be loaded aboard. A crowd of onlookers waved as the boat's steam whistle sounded. There were also several groups of soldiers sprawled on their packs, under the few shade trees in the area.

Jake Rogers watched in fascination as the riverboat was made fast. The last couple of months since leaving home had been a whirlwind of new experiences, and sights. On May the 3rd, he had signed his enlistment papers and taken the oath, at Jefferson Barracks, also known as the U. S. Army's St. Louis Depot, and home to the Cavalry Recruit and Training Center. Originally built on a bluff overlooking the Mississippi south of St. Louis in 1826, it served as a major post during the Mexican War. Back then it was home to the 1st US Dragoons, the original permanent cavalry of the US Army. During the Civil War, it was a major recruit training center for the Western Theater, and a large hospital was built on the grounds. It was turned over to the Cavalry in 1871, and was tasked with supplying enlisted manpower to the various cavalry regiments scattered across the West. His first weeks there were a jumble of frenzied activity; getting uniforms, learning military etiquette, enduring the shouting sergeants, who cursed them as they stumbled through basic drills. He hadn't had any problems, but some of the other men did, particularly a couple of a Germans who didn't speak much English had a tough time. After a couple weeks though, it became more of a routine and when they finally got to mount up on horses Jake was in his element. The old tired training horses were a snap for him. He just had to learn the commands and bugle calls, and how to respond. It was the same when they started with firearms instruction. The old Civil War vintage weapons were pretty worn out, and more attention was paid to cleaning them, then using them. The training sergeants eased up when they saw that he was already pretty proficient. In fact, he had reached out to some of the other trainees to help them. There were several from several eastern cities, and others that came from Europe. One thing that they all shared equally was the terrible food that they were forced to eat, and the continuous fatigue details that they were assigned to. They were told that most of the training would be completed after they reached their company assignments.

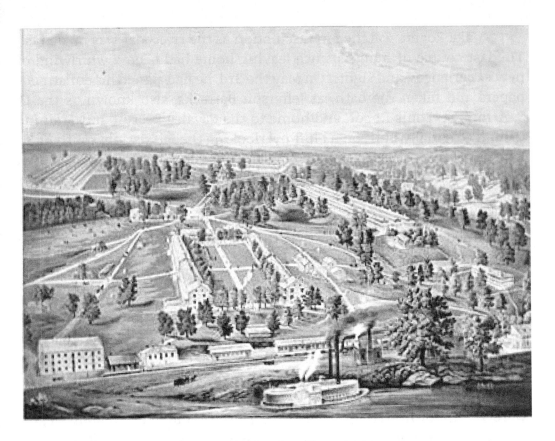

Jefferson Barracks near St. Louis - Circa 1870s

They all looked forward to leaving the recruit depot. Occasionally he had noticed Pat, whom he now had to remember as Sgt. Morse when around others, watching from a distance, and jawing with the NCO trainers. On one occasion he made eye contact and nodded his head in Jake's direction. Then towards the end of June, Sgt. Morse had called him aside.

"Jake m'boy, I've just gotten orders to take eight of you lads and head west to the Missouri River, then board a supply boat to go up to Fort Stevenson, in the Dakotas. We're going to join up with a resupply column. General Terry, the commander of the Department of Dakota, has detached Companies D and I, of the 7th Cavalry, to provide a military escort for the upcoming Border Survey. I'm going to pull a few strings and get you in Company D with me. Are you ready to see how big this country is?"

Jake nodded his head. "When do we leave?"

"Oh, in a few days! We need to be there by July 20. You lads need to buy yourself some extra socks and whatever sundries you can afford. You won't need much money where we're headed. We'll be up north by the border and will be heading west towards the Montana Territory. It'll probably be fall when we get back anywhere close to a trading post. Your Da gave me some money for you. We need to get you into a decent pair of boots before we leave here. Those issue ones won't last. There should be some money left over, too. I know it's half pay while you're here."

"Pa gave me $20 dollars before I left, and I still have most of it."

"Good! Spend it wisely. Better take this opportunity to write to your folks and let them know."

Jake grinned and replied, "Thanks for the heads up, Pat. I appreciate you looking out for me. I'll pass the advice on. Who else is going with us?"

"O'Brien, Dunn, Hunt, Korn, Welch, Braun, and Driscoll are coming with us."

"Okay, Welch and I have gotten to be pretty good friends. Can you get him in Company D too?

"Well, I suppose I can try, but don't say anything yet. We've a ways to go before we get to that point."

Sgt. Morse had herded him, and the other privates, through various railroad depots, cheap hotels, and onto trains. They had pulled into Sioux City, Iowa this morning, and were told that they would embark on the *Western* as soon as it was loaded and provisioned with wood. They were headed upstream to Fort Rice, then on to Ft. Stephenson, both forts were built next to the Missouri River. Jake and the other recruits were dressed in cavalry issue, enlisted uniforms. Sky blue woolen trousers held up by a black leather belt and suspenders, with double fabric inside the legs and tucked into black leather cavalry boots. Gray flannel shirts, and dark blue woolen blouses which because of the heat they had rolled and tied to their haversacks. Their hats were the new style wide brimmed dark felt campaign style which had hooks to secure the sides when folded up. The rest of their uniforms, and the issue gear was packed in wooden footlockers that they were sitting on.. They'd been told that they would not receive any weapons or field gear until they caught up with the regimental quartermaster. Morse had gathered them off to the side of the bustling activity.

"You lads sit tight right here, and stay out of the way! I'll come get you when it's time to load up."

He approached a knot of uniformed officers, who were watching the proceedings.

"Beg your pardon, sirs." He intoned as he saluted. "Sgt. Morse, reporting with replacements! Ah, Lt. Bell, I'm surprised to see you here. I thought you'd be out with the company."

The officer he'd addressed looked over at him, "Hello, Sgt. Morse,

I see you've brought us a gaggle of newbies. They look a bit raw don't you think?"

"Aye, they are that." Morse replied. "I couldn't afford to be too choosy, especially if I wanted to catch up with the outfit this season. I've just brought them over from Jefferson Barracks and was instructed to bring these lads straight through to the Regiment. We can finish up training them ourselves." He replied smiling. "That way we get ta break'm in the way we want. Sink or swim you might say, Sir"

"Any likely prospects among them?" Bell asked as he looked over towards them.

"Yes, the young man standing. He's the son of an old friend of mine from the war, who served in the 4th Missouri Cavalry with me. He's already a fair shot, and sits a horse well. He'll not take much to make in him into a decent trooper"

"Indeed? Well, grab him up. I know we're short a couple of men. Pick of the litter, so to speak."

"I'd appreciate it, Sir. I told his Da that I'd look out for him. You'll not be disappointed, I think. He's a sharp lad, he can read, write, and cypher numbers, too."

"Well, now I'm intrigued. Consider him in Company D. What's his name?"

"Jacob Rogers, I'll let him know. Thank you, Sir."

"Yes, do that. As for the rest of them, we can always use some strong backs. They can pitch in and help to get us loaded. We need to pull out as soon as we can. I'm told it's at least a two week run up to Fort Stevenson, depending on the weather and river conditions. Capt. Weir and the rest of company are supposed to meet us there for supplies and they should be getting there about the same time. We'll be out all summer from what I hear. We're tasked to escort the Northern Boundary Survey of the 49th parallel." You might work with them on the way up. They'll probably get pack train duty, but it won't hurt to train them up a bit before Reno sets eyes on them."

"Reno, Sir? I thought the Major was back east serving on some Army Board."

"Well, not anymore. He's in command of the escort. He's got Keogh and Company I, also. I just got a telegram that they left Ft. Pembina, earlier this week. Major Reno assigned me as quartermaster and commissary officer for the expedition. He sent me to see that our supplies make it up there, timely and intact. So, it's fortuitous that you showed up with extra manpower." He said smiling.

"What about the rest of the Regiment?'

" Well, I'm told that Custer and the rest of the Regiment are off with General Stanley's Yellowstone Survey Expedition, exploring the best route for the Northern Pacific tracks. They left Ft. Rice a few weeks back. It promises to be an interesting summer. Better start sorting out your new men, they will be seeing a lot of country."

"I intend to Lieutenant, but we just arrived this morning. I need to see to my mount, and I need to kit these boys out with bedrolls and some slickers, for the trip upriver. Who's acting as your supply sergeant?"

"Sgt. Rush, he's over watching the stores being loaded. We'll be stopping at Ft. Rice on the way up, we'll see about mounts and weapons for your men, also. I've got a dozen or so remounts being loaded onto the lower deck, if you want to look them over. There's several likely three year old black geldings that I have earmarked for D. You might see about getting young Pvt. Rogers mounted on one of them. They're the last ones that we acquired down in Kentucky"

"Yes, Sir! I'll get with Sgt. Rush. Tom and I go back aways." Morse replied, then saluted and made his way back to the wharf.

****

1st Lieutenant James Montgomery Bell

Bell had served in the 13th Pennsylvania Cavalry as a Captain. After the war He was then assigned to the new 7th Cavalry, forming up at Ft Riley, KS. He served as Regimental Quartermaster for two years, and was cited for heroism at the Battle of the Washita for resupplying ammunition at a critical point in the conflict. He became a friend and frequent guest of the Custer's. The 7th was already considered the finest cavalry regiment in the Army. He was reassigned to Company D under Capt. Thomas Weir, who had been on Custer's staff down in Texas, after the war. He was also one of the first officers assigned to the regiment when it was formed. Weir and Company D had been with Custer at the Washita. When the Regiment was assigned to Reconstruction duty, Company D was sent to Chester, South Carolina. The rest of the 7th was scattered across South Carolina, Mississippi, Georgia, and Tennessee, assisting authorities in chasing Ku Klux Klansmen and raiding stills for the last two years. Initially, Custer took his wife Libbie on a nine month leave up to New York, before returning to Regimental Headquarters, in Elizabethtown, Kentucky. The garrison there had a rather tame time. The officers and men enjoyed the amenities of the small town, and nearby Louisville. Custer, an avid hunter, roamed the countryside with his pack of wolfhounds and staghounds. He, and Libbie, had a house right next to the 7th's HQ where they entertained frequently, including many of the local politicians. General Sheridan ordered him to serve as escort to the Grand Duke of Russia, along with Buffalo Bill, on a hunting trip out of Ft. McPherson up in the Nebraska Territory, in early 1873. He also found time to dabble in horses, acquiring a nice string of thoroughbred horses to race. When the Regiment was reunited in Memphis, then on to Ft. Rice, Companies D and I had been selected, and gone on by train, to Fort Snelling, Minnesota. They were being sent up to the US/Canada border where they would serve as escort for the surveying teams who were marking the boundary line.

Lt. James Bell had married a pretty, vivacious English woman, Emilie, last year, and was disappointed that he would be separated from her. He'd sent her back to Pittsburgh, until he was sure where the Company would be stationed later. He hoped that their continued separation from the rest of the regiment, would end. He knew Weir and Keogh well enough, but Major Reno hadn't joined the 7th until Dec '69. He had mostly been stationed at Ft. Hayes, so Bell hadn't served with him before. He knew that Reno had acquired a reputation for being pushy, and had had several confrontations with other officers. But, all in all, Bell was looking forward to getting back out west. He'd never volunteered to be a policeman. He was enthused about the new duty assignment and looking forward to the trip upriver.

****

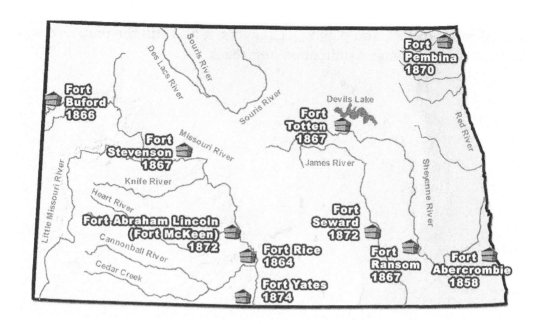

Missouri River Forts

Beginning in the early 1860s, the Army had built a series of forts along the Lower and Upper Missouri River, starting with Ft. Randall just over the territory line from Nebraska, to Ft. Benton in the Montana territory. The Minnesota Sioux uprising had been the first instance of the Army utilizing riverboats. The various troops stationed at the distant forts depended on the riverboats for resupply and communications. They could also be used to shuttle soldiers to other forts, or ferry troops across a mostly unfordable river. They were also used to deliver the yearly treaty annuities to the various tribes. The steamers usually tied up at night, as they stopped at each fort or Indian agency, or anchored mid-stream or on a sandbar if in unfriendly territory. Since the decline of the Fur trade, and as the Montana gold fields had played out back in late 1860s, the number of boats on the river had been greatly reduced. With the advent of the railroad reaching Bismarck, only the forts north on the Missouri towards Ft. Benton, and Ft. Buford were still logistically dependent on the boats. The typical sternwheeler could carry 200-330 tons of cargo and consumed roughly 25-30 cords of wood per day. They were dependent on private wood cutters called 'Woodhawks' for fuel, and it took around 2-3 hours to take on full load of wood. Some boats carried sawmills, so that whole trees could be dragged aboard and cut up by crew and soldier work details. The constantly changing contours of the river, high winds, and shifting sandbars and snags dictated a herky jerky pace to most upstream journeys. After August when river levels were lowest, the pace was even worse. But for officers, officials, and paying passengers, it was still the preferred way to travel versus a wagon train or on horseback.

CHAPTER 3

Fort Rice, Dakota Territory - July 15, 1873

The *Western* nosed into the bank just south of Fort Rice. The fort was located on the west side of the Missouri River, near the mouth of Long Knife Creek, and was originally surrounded by a ten foot tall stockade, with two blockhouses. The northern stockade wall had since been taken down. Built originally as an Infantry fort by Ex-Confederate US Volunteers towards the end of the War, it was expanded in 1868 and recently modified to accommodate several companies of the 7th Cavalry.

Jake and the other bedraggled recruits stood watching, anxiously waiting for the riverboat to tie up. It had been an exhausting trip upriver. They had to help cut the wood and stack it on board every day, which was necessary to keep the fires stoked for the steam engine. When they weren't doing that, they had to help shift the load, and livestock whenever the *Western* ran aground on a sand bar, which was also a daily, if not more frequent occurrence. Their uniforms were filthy, and ripped. They had washed them out in the river water when possible, which only added to the sour smell of sweat, horses, and cattle that had been their other main task, feeding and caring for the livestock on the lower deck. Sleep and food had not been plentiful commodities. Early on, near Ft. Randall, they had seen a few Indians along the eastern riverbank, and were told that they were Yankton Sioux, generally considered friendly Indians. The following week, after passing Ft. Sully, they saw a large village of tepees with a nearby pony herd. They were told that these were Blackfeet Sioux Indians and advised that while they weren't necessarily considered hostile, they had no love for the white man.

"I'll be damn glad to get off this tub!" exclaimed Charlie Welch.

"Amen, brother," replied Jake. The other new men nodded their heads in agreement.

"You men!" shouted Sgt. Rush, coming up from behind them, "Get ready to help offload the livestock! The Regiment is out in the field, along with most of the infantry that is stationed here, so there's a barracks for us to use. The sooner you get done, the sooner you'll can wash up and get some hot chow. Tomorrow, I'll be issuing your field gear, saddles, and weapons. Then Sgt. Morse and I will be showing you how to stow everything. We'll get you mounted and spend a little time at the rifle range, too. The plan is to be leaving here in three days for Ft. Stevenson, which is another two-three day run upriver. Better enjoy having a barracks roof over your head. You'll not have one again for a while."

"Okay Sarge." they replied nodding, then plodded along towards the lower deck that also served as stables.

At Pat's suggestion, Jake had already picked out one of the black horses, and had been treating him with snacks and brushing him. He'd already decided to name him 'Ajax.' Sgt. Morse had confirmed that he, Charlie Welch, George Hunt, & George Dann were all assigned to Company D. Welch and Dann were from New York, while Hunt was from Boston. The other new men; Gustav Korn, a Pole from Prussia, and John O'Brien from Pennsylvania, were assigned to I Company along with Braun, from Germany, and Ed Driscoll, from Ireland. Sgt. Milton DeLacy, from Company I, had gathered them up. Morse had told him that all of the 7th Cavalry Companies were assigned horses by color. Company D rode Bays and Blacks, I Company rode Bays only. So all of the horses and remounts Lt. Bell had brought along were of those types. There were also numerous oxen and mules to help haul the barrels of salt pork and bacon, crates of hardtack, and bagged salt, sugar and coffee beans that would constitute the bulk of the field rations for the troops. This would all be off loaded when they got to Ft Stephenson farther upriver where wagons were waiting.

Fort Rice, Dakota Territory - 1870s

The barracks at Fort Rice were four long buildings made from cottonwood lumber that faced west along the central parade ground inside the stockade walls. They had attached kitchens and were normally assigned to to individual companies. There were detached privies and bathhouses. There were also seven officers quarters across the parade ground to the west. There were also low clapboard covered, log storehouses on the north and south sides of the parade ground. The 17th Infantry Regiment was currently headquartered there, but three companies were accompanying the Yellowstone Expedition. A detachment remained behind to guard the fort, tend the vegetable gardens and livestock, and monitor the riverboats coming and going. There was a small group of 7th Cavalry troops remaining also.They were commanded by Quartermaster 2nd Lt. Henry Nowlan, and Commissary Sgt. Charles Brown. They had been left behind to watch over the regimental stores and equipment that had been left at the fort. The 7th's contingent was assigned the South Barracks which was closest to the stables and corral which were directly south of the stockade

The following morning after roll call, Sergeants Morse and De Lacy gathered up the D and I company recruits and took them over to storehouses that served as a warehouse and ordinance building. Sgt. Rush was already there talking with the Sgt. Brown and consulting some paperwork. Brown nodded his head, and Rush went behind a counter made from board planks laid across upright wooden barrels.

"Okay men, we are going to issue you your gear and weapons. Then, Sgt. Morse and Sgt. De Lacy, will show you how to get all of it ready for the field. Forget everything you might have been told at your recruit depot, if they bothered to even show you." He turned towards a rack on the wall that held cavalry sabers grabbed several of them and laid them on the counter.

"These are M1860, light cavalry sabers. Not a lot of use for them against Mr. Lo, but we are the cavalry so we carry them unless ordered otherwise. You'll strap these to your saddles instead of your belts."

Jake, seeing the puzzled looks on his companions faces raised his hand and asked, "Who's Mr. Lo, Sarge?"

Rush laughed and replied. "That's our nickname for the Indians out here. Some philosophers back east describe them as "Lo, the poor Indian! Or Lo, the noble savage! Obviously they've never met a Sioux or Cheyenne warrior in full war paint. You'll know what I mean when you meet one, if you get to see one. They're sneaky little bastards."

Sgt. Morse stepped forwards and went over to a rifle rack, hefted one and turned back towards them.

"This is a Spencer Model 1865 repeating carbine. When I say repeating, I mean that you can shoot seven times before reloading. It's effective range is advertised as 500 yards, but you'll probably never have to try a shot that far. As Sgt. Rush just said, Mr. Lo is not one to stand and fight. He likes to sneak up, hit, and run." He worked the lever beneath the trigger. "It's fed by a tube in the butt holding seven .52 caliber copper rimfire cartridges. This gun will be your primary weapon in the field." He paused to grab a wide leather sling with a swivel attachment on the end. "You wear this around your shoulder and hook it to the ring on the stock, so you can get to it quickly when necessary. It can also be stowed in this rifle scabbard ring strapped to your saddle. He laid several more on the counter, then turned and started piling items next to them.

"These are Blakeslee quick loader cases and slings, you wear them over your other shoulder. They hold tubes of bullets for quick reloading of the Spencer. The belts hold your pistol holsters, on the right side butts facing forwards, cartridge boxes on front, and on the left side are hooks for the saber when you need it"

In the mean time, Sgt. Rush had retrieved some pistols from another box and laid them next to the holsters.

"These are your pistols, Model 1860 U.S. Army Colt 44 caliber revolvers. These are powerful handguns, and effective out to 75 yards in the hands of an experienced soldier. These are what you will depend on if you get up close with Mr. Lo. I guarantee you they will put a hurt on him! Over the next couple of days you will get an opportunity to fire these guns, after that you will need to focus on keeping them cleaned, oiled and ready should you need them. Don't expect to be shooting them on a regular basis."

"Now, we still have field gear for you. Canteens, mess kits, blankets and ground cloths, and other items. But we might as well wait until you get your mounts, saddles, and tack. We need to show you how to stow everything away, and how to attach everything. When we're in the field, your horse is pretty much your home." Sgt. Morse explained, "And, I strongly suggest that when we give you some time, you go over to the sutlers store and get yourself a wide brim hat, preferably a light color. Buy a good sharp 6-7" belt knife along with whetstone, too. You'll use it more than anything else you'll be carrying. Let me know if you need money and I can get it drawn against your pay. You will be required to sign for all of this equipment, and will be held responsible for it. Sgt. Brown has the paperwork. So take care of it. Sgt. Morse will take those assigned to Company D, and DeLacy will take those of you assigned to Company I.

After lunch Morse took them outside the stockade walls to where the corrals and stables were located. They went to the tack room where McClellen saddles, blankets, straps, reins, rope and picket pins were issued to each man. They quizzed them about their riding capabilities and inspected the available horses, assigning them as they saw fit.

Sgt. Morse announced "We're going to split you up in pairs, or bunkmates when we're lucky enough to be in a barracks. When we're in the field you will be 'bunkies'. You will ride, eat, and sleep together, sharing food and blankets. I'm sure they explained at the recruit depot, that you will be assigned to a 'Set-of-four'. It's similar to an infantry squad. Two sets-of-four make up a 'Section', two sections make up a platoon. We'll try and pair you up with another more experienced 'Set of four'. Welch and Rogers you're together, Hunt and Dann same for you. Since you're all new, Rogers will No.1 as he's the senior private by his date of enlistment, so he will be in charge of your set. Welch is No.2, Hunt is No. 3, and Dann is No.4. Over the next couple of days we're going to show you how that works within the company and how to function on a daily basis. You'd better pay attention, it's going to be a long couple months if you don't."

Later that evening, in the barracks, the four men gathered around sitting on a pair of wooden bunks. They had been adjusting their belts, sling and holsters and were beginning to clean and examine their weapons. There were four other Company D privates in the barracks. They had been traveling with Lt. Bell, Sgt. Rush, and the supplies on the *Western*, and had worked along side them, but really hadn't much of an opportunity to talk without the officers and NCOs around. The previous night everyone had been so weary from the boat trip and off-loading the livestock, that they'd just washed up, grabbed some stew and biscuits in the kitchen, then thrown their bed rolls on the bunks that were empty. But this evening, two of the younger men came over and approached to where Jake and Charlie were laying out everything. They were both short, with dark-hair and mustaches.

"Where do you lads hail from?" asked one of them, with a distinct Irish brogue. He held out his hand and stated "I'm Pat Golden, and this is my mate Joe Green also known as Biscuit." he pointed at the fellow next to him.

Jake and Charlie introduced themselves and took turns shaking hands, then George Dann and George Hunt did the same.

"What! Two more Georges, that'll never do. We'll have to give you nicknames."

"No need, just call me Big, because I'm taller than Little George here" Said Dann.

Pat laughed. "That'll work for now!" he said looking at Dann, who was the taller by an inch, or two. "Of course those names might change when we get to know you better." He motioned for them to follow him over to where the other two men were sitting.

"This is George Horn, he's from Spain. We call him Hurry, cause he never does and it sounds a little like the way you say George in Spanish." He said, "And this old bastard here is Henry Holden. We call him Sage, because he's so wise. He's a Brit, and a professional Private. He got tired of walking in the Infantry though, so he signed on with the 7th. He fought in the War. He's adopted us, ain't that right Da?"

Holden offered his hand. He was of medium height with light hair and grey eyes and appeared several years older than the rest of them.

"Don't pay any attention to my young Mick friend here. Sgt. Rush put me in with them as a baby sitter, so he wouldn't have to dress them in the mornings. They keep trying to put their pants on backwards." He said smiling.

"Nice to meet you Henry. I'm from Missouri and Charlie here is from New York. We already learned how to dress, so you don't have to worry about that. But we'd appreciate any other pointers you can give us." Jake stated.

George Dann said, "I'm from New York, and the other George is from Boston."

Holden said, "The ship I was on from England landed in Boston. I joined the Massachusetts Infantry Volunteers back in '64, right after I got to the States. Nice city if you have money. But cold in December if you don't. I saw a little fighting towards the end of the War. Also spent some time in New York, on Davids Island, when I re-enlisted and was with the 8th Infantry. Then, we were posted in Chicago right after the Great Fire. My enlistment was up and the 7th was doing some recruiting there. They told me the regiment was going down south. I had spent several years down in South Carolina back in the late Sixties while on Reconstruction duty, and liked the weather. That was main reason that I volunteered to re-enlist with them. Riding instead of walking was just a bonus. So, I'm guessing you boys just came out from Jefferson Barracks?"

They all nodded their heads. Jake said, "And we were glad to leave. We came out with Sgt. Morse. So, how did you guys end up here?"

"Well, we were all down South, in Alabama, with the Company. When it was reassigned, Lt. Bell, and Sgt. Rush needed men to help with moving the extra gear and supplies. Rooster here," he said, pointing at Golden, "got us volunteered. He got caught trying to romance one of the local young girls. She didn't mind, but her father did. He complained to the Captain, just about the time the 1st Sergeant was making plans to leave. So, he assigned us to Quartermaster Sgt. Rush and we've had to work our way here. We're a 'set-of-four', so we got volunteered. Besides, Rooster and Biscuit cry when they're apart. George and I have to tuck them in at night."

"Sil" I must also help with the ninos." chimed in Hurry, his dark eyes crinkling with humor. He was black haired, but had a fair complexion and was slightly older, though not as old as Holden.

Everyone chuckled and including the two young Irishmen.

"These old geezers have to help and take care of us so we can help them mount their horses!" Rooster exclaimed.

"So, how long have the you guys been in the regiment?" asked Jake.

"We all joined in January last year. Me and Biscuit, left Ireland and came over on a ship together. When we got to New York it was the dead of winter and we had no money, so like Henry said, we volunteered."

"That is my story also, chicos. I was a poor boatman in Andalusia. My father was an English sailor who was stationed at Gibraltar, then stayed in Spain and owned several boats. He and my mother had me late in life, and my older brothers inherited the boats. I got tired of working for them. I knew how to speak English and I read that there was free land in America, so I worked my way on a ship from Seville to New York. Like them I had no money. So, I met all these fellows when I got to Jefferson Barracks." Horn explained. "Our amigo, Henry, took us all under his wing and helped us learn to be soldiers. He's quite experienced."

Charlie asked, "So what were you guys doing down south?"

"Well, mostly we were chasing down Ku Klux Klan night riders and busting bootleggers. We were in Chester, South Carolina when we first got there, last year, then moved down to Opelika, Alabama until we left there in mid-March. That was one wild little railroad town," replied Pat grinning.

"There were several parties vying for control of the town, the Pro-union, the railroad faction, the saloon men, and the pro-KKK. Obviously we were backing the Pro-union people, whose head man just happened to have a pretty daughter." Holden stated.

"Which again is how we ended up here humping barrels." Biscuit added, as he nudged Goldie in the ribs.

"Well, it seems that we're in for quite a change in scenery now, doesn't it? I reckon there'll not be too many places to wet our whistles up north where we're headed. Sgt. Rush said that Lt. Bell told him that we'll be right up on the Canadian border, watching over some surveyors." Rooster sighed.

Henry looked up at all of them and said, "Best all of us pay attention to the sergeants in the morning. They've both been out campaigning against the hostiles. Most everything you own will be on your horse with you, and you won't want it falling off. I've known my share of sergeants and these seem to know their stuff."

Jake nodded his head and said, "My Pa was in the cavalry with Sgt. Morse during the war, and he told me that I could trust him with my life."

They all turned and looked at him with raised eyebrows, and Pat observed, "Well, Jake here may get us some slack form Sgt. Morse then."

"I wouldn't count on it." he replied, "He's pretty much no nonsense when on duty."

"How's about we show you chicos the easy way too clean your guns and show you how keep them from getting dirty when you're mounted?" asked Hurry.

Sgt. Morse and Sgt. Rush marched them all down to the stables, the following morning, and began issuing saddles, bridles, spurs and tack. They showed the men how they should saddle their mounts, and how to adjust the straps and tack to secure the best fit and comfort for both horse and rider. Then they all mounted up and rode through the surrounding countryside. Jake realized how fortunate that he had gotten Ajax. The horse had an easy gait and disposition. Some of the others, particularly both the new Georges, and his friend Charlie, were having some issues with their mounts. The Irishmen, Rooster and Biscuit sat their horses well. And surprisingly the ex-infantry man, Holden, seemed a natural horseman. Of course they had the advantage of already being familiar with their horses. They returned to the fort and after lunch picketed their mounts outside the storehouse. They made several trips back and forth, and soon had piles of gear in front of the horses. Morse positioned himself in the center and shouted.

"Okay, all of you listen up! Even you jokers from Opelika! This won't be like your little overnight excursions down there. So pay attention. We will be going out in the field for the rest of the summer and early fall. We will very likely be away from our base camp for weeks at a time, and probably not be staying in the same place many nights. That means that you will carry all of your clothing, gear, food, water, ammunition, and feed for your horses. We're going to show you the handiest way to stow and hang everything."

"We'll start from the front of the saddle. First, we'll take our blankets and rubber ground cloth, lay them out and roll then up together. Then we'll bend them into a horseshoe and tie them across, 'U' side down, in front of the pommel. Your picket rope and pin will hang on the left side, looped and tied for quick access. Your spare cartridge box goes on the right side."

"Moving to the rear, behind the cantle is where you'll hang your haversacks and feed sacks. Your canteen goes on the left side, also your mess kit, and cup. Wrap them in towel inside a bag so they don't rattle. Roll up your overcoat and poncho. Yes, it will be cold at night! Tie it behind your cantle. Hang your saber off of the left side, and your carbine goes in the leather scabbard on the right side . You should try and balance out the weight so it's about the same on each side. You'll need to check this daily. Your Set of Four will have a coffee pot, and maybe a skillet and pot. You'll have to work that out between you as to who carries what. Your main diet will consist of salt pork, hardtack, beans, and coffee. I suggest that you all go together and pool some sugar, pepper, spices, and whatever you can afford to buy at the sutlers. The company will have a pack train and you will have a small amount of room to store some gear. A cook wagon and supplies will be at the base camp."

They spent the rest of the day practicing saddling their mounts and hanging their gear. They took another trip outside the fort and were led across a couple of creeks, through some gullies, and varied the horses from a fast walk, to a canter, and then a full gallup. Needless to say, if they hadn't stopped to retrieve the items as they fell off they would have left quite a trail. They learned the best and most efficient knots to secure their gear. They watered the horses upon returning to the fort, then took them to the stables, fed and groomed them. Before dismissing the men so they could head to the mess hall Sgt. Morse gathered the men around and spoke loudly.

"Your horse comes first men! You have to make sure it is fed, watered and groomed every day. Depending on the pace of march, you will lead it every third hour, and make sure it gets to graze at every opportunity. We are never able to carry enough feed out in the field compared to what they are used to. Each company has a farrier and blacksmith who can help you check the shoes, and replace them. Take care of your mount. I can't stress this enough!"

Later that evening in the barracks, Jake was lying on his bunk going over the events of the day in his mind, when Charlie plopped down on his bunk next to him and asked. "What are you thinking about, Jake?"

"Well, I was just thinking that there's a lot more to being a cavalry man than what I expected. But I'm looking forward to getting out in the field. It beats the daily routine that we went through back at Jefferson. Drilling, fatigue details and getting harassed by the old timer sergeants. And the food doesn't sound much worse than that swill we had to choke down there. It's bound to be more interesting than hanging around a fort somewhere, too. I suspect that if you and I stick close to the Georges, and Henry and his crew, that we'll be all right."

"Yeh, you're probably right. Let's go over and get with them to see if they all want to go in together and pick some things up at the sutlers?. I'm sure Henry can help us with a list of things that will be useful. Even though he was in the Infantry, The rations are still the same."

"Okay, let's go over and see them. Grab the Georges."

The Company D men gathered together and Jake explained what they wanted to discuss and asked if everyone was okay with his suggestion. When they all nodded their heads, Jake suggested that since Holden was the most experienced that they should look to him for guidance. They all turned towards Henry who shrugged his shoulders and said.

"Well, first of all we need to establish how much we have to spend. Then we figure out a list of items, and who will be responsible for each one.

We need to go to the kitchen and see what we can scrounge up for free, then see what we need to buy. The best items are spices, preserves, molasses, and anything that can be used to improve salt pork and hardtack. A good coffeepot is a must for boiling water, and a solid pan or two."

Rooster grinned and said, "See I knew Ol' Sage would take care of us.

They spent the next day working with the horses, being drilled in basis cavalry tactics and learning the dozen or so different bugles calls. They practiced a little saber drill and Jake realized that the blades were pretty unwieldy, particularly while trying to control your mount. None the less, they hacked away at some posts anyway. They were issued some ammunition and spent a couple of hours at the rifle range. Jake needed no lessons on the Spencer carbine. He'd learned to shoot with an old cap and ball rifle when he was younger. But Zeb had been able to keep the Spencer that he'd carried in the War, and when Jake got older, he trained Jake how to shoot it. Jake always marveled at the simplicity of firing multiple shots by cocking the lever, and reloading the copper cartridges held in the nifty reloading tubes. His father had worked with him on how to judge distance, and once he figured out how to work the sights, he hit what he aimed at most times. He wasn't quite as proficient with the heavy Colt revolver, it required a two handed grip to attain any accuracy and it had quite a recoil. The others shot with mixed results, generally with a tendency to shoot too high, although Henry proved to be a good shot. He was also the only one that had actually fired in real combat. He took his time and was very deliberate in his aiming. Jake made a mental note to remember that. He had to agree with Sgt. Morse, his first choice would always be the carbine.

When they finished up with the horses that afternoon the sergeants met them outside the stables.

"Men, we'll be getting back on board the *Western* the day after next. So, me and Rush are gonna give you a break." Morse said, "Make sure you clean your weapons, clothes and other gear are sorted out.. Other than caring for your mounts, the day is yours to do with as you please tomorrow. I'd recommend you spend some time enjoying some good food from the kitchen, and visiting the post traders. I spoke with the Lt. Bell and he's not sure how much time we'll have at Ft. Stevenson. From there we will be heading back north, with the Company, to rendezvous with the survey party. Company K 20 Infantry, and Company I are with them. We'll be out for the rest of the summer, then we'll go into winter quarters at Ft. Totten. So enjoy the day tomorrow. If I see you when I'm at the post traders store I'll treat you to a beer."

When they adjourned to the barracks that evening, the Company D privates huddled to together.

"Okay lads." Holden announced. "I suggest that we each put in $5. I checked with the cook and he's going to fix us up with what he can. Extra coffee, sugar, some flour and cornmeal, beans and the like. It's likely that we'll have several wagons to haul company stores, so we'll take a footlocker with us to put it in. A word of advice, don't be bragging about it when we meet up with the rest of the company. The lads have already out several weeks and they'll be competing for what's on hand at Fort Stevenson post traders. We'll wait until we get out in the field to start pulling from it. Make sure you save as much room as you can in your saddle bags, and try to find some canvas bags to carry things in."

"Sounds like a good plan, Sage." Rooster said grinning. "Let's all pitch in and get done as early as we can tomorrow. I'd like to wet my whistle with a few beers before we head out up to the wilderness."

"Yes, indeed!" Charlie said emphatically, and all were in agreement.

The following day they split up after stable call, and hustled around the fort on various errands. They had agreed that Holden and Charlie would make the purchases at the post trader's, with Hurry and Big George along to help tote things. The rest of them took care of stable call duties. Back at the barracks, they helped each other with their gear and had it ready for the morning. Henry volunteered to stay and watch over everything while the rest of them went down to the post traders, which was south of the stockade, in front of the stables. When they got there, there was a brisk trade going on around a beer keg. Jake had just secured a mug of beer when he saw Sgt. Morse sitting, on the porch, at a table with Sgt. Rush, Sgt. DeLacy, and an infantry sergeant that he didn't know. Pat motioned for him to come over.

"Jake my boy! Have a seat!" he exclaimed, "I was telling these gents here about your Pa and I."

Jake nodded at the sergeants and sat down. "Well, I've probably heard some of it before. Although the stories have had a tendency to change with the re-telling." He said with a grin.

Pat laughed and slapped the table, "That they do, Lad, and they'll probably continue to!" He nodded towards the other sergeant, "This is Sgt. Bennett, he's with the 17th Infantry and he's been telling about where we're heading. The 17th is spread out through the line of forts up and down the Missouri River. They've been out here a couple of years, and Pete here has been to most of the forts."

Bennett nodded his head and said, "Well, once you leave Ft. Stevenson it's pretty easy country to cross, mostly flat, a few creeks here and there. It's only 100 miles or so, up to the Northern Boundary. This time of year, once you get to the Mouse River, it's no problem. I can tell you most of the Indians on the east side of the Missouri aren't hostile. The friendliest ones are the Rees, Mandans, and Gros Ventres, they're enemies of the Sioux. Farther north there's a mixed bag of Dakota Sioux, Yakotonai and Santee. Most of them live in semi-permanent villages growing crops, hunting and trading. Then there's the Chippewas who are scattered back towards the Red River. There are also some mixed blood fur trappers and traders called Métis. The Turtle Mountain area has some good hunting and fishing. Ft. Totten is on Devils Lake, which the Indians call Spirit Lake. There's good game and fishing there also. They have established a reservation there for the Sisseton and Wahpeton bands, but I'm not sure how many have settled there. Once you get west of the Mouse River, there's just ain't much up there. That's as far west as the 17th has patrolled. I can tell you that troops from the 6th Infantry are stationed at Fort Buford which is right at the edge of the Dakota Territory. West of there you get into Assiniboine and Blackfoot territory over in Montana. And south of them are the Lakota Sioux, Northern Cheyenne, and Arapahos. They're the ones you need to worry about! But they usually stay down along the Yellowstone,"

"So you don't think we'll have any trouble with any of them?" asked Morse.

"No, but that doesn't mean they won't try and make off with a horse, or two. They have been stealing from each other for generations, It's a game for them." replied Bennett.

"Hmm! Doesn't sound too bad. Beats chasing around Cheyennes like we did down in Kansas." Sgt. Rush stated. "We never would've caught up with them if it wasn't for winter when they went into camps."

"Well, I'll tell you one thing. You'll not want be out in the winter up here. Once September gets here you'd better head somewhere for the winter, quick!" The infantry sergeant exclaimed, "Winter gets here in a hurry! You get caught out on the high plains in a 40 degree below blizzard they'll not find your frozen asses until spring. We're halfway through the summer already. I suppose there's no reason for a civilian survey team to stay out and brave the elements. But you need to bear that in mind in a couple of months."

"Rumor has it that we'll probably be sent to Ft. Totten for the winter." Morse said, Fort Lincoln is still under construction and probably won't be far enough along to have barracks ready for us.

"Ah well, that's as good a place as any up there. It's a bit isolated, I spent a winter up there. Make sure you lay in a good supply of whisky and firewood. Not much to do, although there's some good hunting and ice fishing if you like. It's gets colder than a well digger's ass, and stays that way for several months, better make sure you have winter gear. And if you kill any buffalo while out in the field, save the hides. You can make them into blankets and robes. You can probably trade for some also."

"Thanks for the heads up, Pete. We'll make sure we're ready. Meanwhile, if you gents will pardon me." Morse said, "I need to speak to Private Rogers here, and make sure he gets a letter off to his mother before we shove off. I made her a promise that I'd make him write!"

They wandered off to the side a ways. Jake looked over and saw his guys sitting over by the trading post, watching. He waved at them.

"So what do you think now Jake?" Pat asked.

"It's kind of overwhelming at times, but it's also exciting. I'd rather be here doing this, than picking corn back home." he replied.

"That's the spirit! You and I, and the whole company are about to set off on a journey to parts of this country that most people will never get to see. Now it's going to be monotonous and hard work, and you'll be tired, cold, hot, and hungry at times. But remember, the Company is a unit. We work together to get whatever we're asked to do, done well. Just do your duty and everything works out for the best."

"I will, Pat. Can we stay together as a pair of 'sets of four' when we meet up with the company?' he asked, eyeing Charlie and the others.

"Aye, I suppose can we ask the 1st Sergeant." Morse said smiling, "Maybe you can help keep Gold and Greene in line."

"They're not that bad, besides Sage is good at steering everyone in the right direction. I'm surprised he's still a private after all his time in the Army."

"Holden is a strange one, he's a good soldier, but not interested in taking a promotion. His unit was in some serious fighting in the war. His regiment was at the Battle of the Wilderness, Spotsylvania Courthouse, and Cold Harbor, all bloody fights. It was also at the Battle of the Crater outside Petersburg. Hard to believe, but he came through it all unscathed. A good man to have at your side."

Jake nodded his head in agreement. "Yes, we all listen to him."

"As you should. Okay, we're off tomorrow for Ft Stevenson, to meet up with Capt. Weir and the rest of the company. He's a good officer. I've ridden beside him in combat and many a trail. You'll find that he runs a tight, but fair outfit, and is well respected by all ranks. As for Major Reno, he's a bit of a stickler. He's a West Pointer and a professional, but more of a staff officer type. He was with the regiment at Ft. Hays in Kansas briefly, but I don't know that much about him other than scuttlebutt through the grapevine. I don't expect you'll have much contact with him, but try and look your best when he's around. Now go have a beer with your mates and pass along what you've learned. I always like let the lads know a bit about what the company is up to. I expect they will be glad to have a clue about things." Pat said winking at Jake, "And make sure you write to your mother!"

"Yes, Sgt. Morse, I will. And thanks for everything, I won't disappoint you."

CHAPTER 4

Fort Stevenson Dakota Territory - July 22, 1873

Fort Stevenson - Circa 1873

Fort Stevenson was established in 1867 on the north bank of the Missouri where it turned west. It was a relatively secure outpost, being on the northern fringe of Sioux territory and protected by the swift currents of a wide river. Its main purpose was as a resupply depot for Fort Totten 140 miles to the east, and to provide secure mooring for the riverboats as they journeyed up and down stream.

The *Western* had arrived at Fort Stevenson earlier that day and after helping get everything unloaded, the contingent of the 7th had set up a camp perimeter, in a bivouac area next to a creek near the fort. Some of them were tasked with watering the horses and livestock, then turning them out to graze. The rest were busy erecting tents and gathering firewood. Lt. Bell left the sergeants to get it all organized and had gone to check on the storage of the supplies, and the availability of wagons and teamsters. Fortunately for Jake and the other new men, Henry and the others troopers were adept at setting up camp. They put up Lt. Bell's tent by the bank of the creek, and lined up their two man tents in a straight line away from it using a stretched out picket rope to align them. Within an hour they had it done and stacked their saddles and tack three feet in front of the tents. with their bedrolls inside them. Then the horses were led to the area behind the tents and tied with a lariat and picket rope for grazing. Several pots of coffee were already brewing over a common campfire trench. Stable call was sounded and they all turned out to groom and curry their mounts.

"Well, it looks like we beat the Company here." Sgt. Rush announced with a grin, "I won't have to get an earful from 1st Sgt. Martin about holding up things."

Rush had accompanied Lt. Bell to the fort and returned with a wagonload of forage for the horses and mules. He stood chatting with the other sergeants as the men stood in line to draw their horses oat rations.

"Looks like we'll have plenty of wagons to haul our supplies." he continued.

"How are they fixed for beer here?" Pat Morse asked, "Thought I might let our lads loose to go to the fort tonight. Not much mischief they can get into up here. Is there any news on the rest of the company?"

"They sent a couple of runners in this afternoon. Major Reno and Company D are on their way, along with a few civilians from the survey party. Keogh and I Company were left to escort the survey team and their supply train. They are on the way to establish a supply depot on the Mouse River. The Captain and the rest will be along some time tomorrow I'd guess. We'd best get around in the morning and get the company area policed and ready for them. They've been out several weeks already. Top Martin will expect us to have things all arranged. From what I heard at the fort, it will probably be about a week for all the supplies and teamster arrangements to be sorted out."

"That's good!" Sgt. Morse said, "I'll get with Top and see about a little extra time to work with the new men before we get back on the trail."

"Hey Pat, if you don't mind, I'll tag along with my I Company newbies." queried DeLacy. "That'll help keep them from getting underfoot."

" My thoughts exactly, Milt! It'll give us something to do besides supervising details." Morse replied with a smile.

The next morning after breakfast, roll call, and stable call, Jake and his set saddled their mounts then followed Morse and DeLacy, who had his new set in tow, north along the trail from the fort. They stopped several times, dismounted and practiced handing off their reins to Big George, who was designated as horse holder for Jake's set. They established intervals for a firing line and simulated prone, or kneeling volley fire. They rode in a column of twos, and then swung into line abreast. They varied their pace, and listened intently while the sergeants explained how they would to respond to bugle calls. They were handicapped by the lack of a bugler, but were told that they would get up to speed quickly, just watch what the veterans were doing and copy them.

It was a bright sunny day and warmed up quickly. They stopped by a creek to water their horses. The two sergeants had them remove their tunics, and roll up the sleeves of their gray issue flannel shirts. They dipped their bandannas in the water then tied them around their necks. They were walking their horses when Morse saw a dust cloud in the distance.

That'll be the outfit!" he announced. "Mount up and look sharp. Try and keep your sabers from getting tangled up and make sure your other gear's on straight. Check and see that your carbine swivels are hooked. Let's go make a good first impression with the captain."

They formed up in a column of twos and headed towards the advancing dust cloud. After a couple of minutes they crested a slight rise and could make a line of cavalry and wagons approaching. Out front were several riders, as they got closer one of them spurred his horse forwards.

"By God, lookie here! Ifin' it ain't Ol' Pat comin' up the trail! Figured you'd be along eventually."

Morse grinned and nodded his head towards the speaker, "Men, this here sorry excuse for a sergeant is Tom Harrison. Another smelly son of the Old Sod! I suppose you're in charge of the advance party, scoutin' ahead for trouble in this dangerous territory."

"Aye Morse, but I can see that you've come out to bring us all in safely with this fierce looking lot." Harrison replied, chuckling, "You'd best go ahead and report to the Captain, then. He'll welcome the company, seeing as how he's riding with his friend, Major Reno. Mind your manners when you report. Reno's a stickler on protocol."

"Thanks for the heads up, Tom. I've not had the pleasure of meeting him. He was never at any of the stations that I was at. Turning back to his men he said, "Let's go boys."

****

Major Marcus Albert Reno

Major Marcus Albert Reno was a 39 year old career soldier. Born in Carrollton, Illinois to a local hotelier and mercantile family, he applied to West Point after the death of his father. He entered West Point in 1851, but didn't graduate until 1857 due to excessive demerits. He was twentieth out of a class of thirty-eight. He was assigned as a second lieutenant in the 1st Dragoons and served with them on several frontier posts in the Pacific Northwest. The now 1st Cavalry Regiment was recalled back east after the start of the Civil War. Reno, now a captain commanding Company H, spent most of his time on picket and escort duty in the Washington D.C. area until April, 1862. When McClellan began his Peninsular Campaign, Reno and the 1st were assigned to the cavalry reserve and conducted reconnaissance patrols, escorts, and supporting the artillery. They were peripherally engaged in action during several of the Richmond area battles, and suffered very few casualties. That fall they participated in the campaigns along the Potomac again supporting the artillery, doing picket and escort duty, and the occasional reconnaissance patrol.

In late October, Reno was detailed to Harrisburg, Pennsylvania to procure horses. There he met his future wife, who belonged to one of the areas most prominent families. He remained there until late November, then returned to his company. He had, however, requested to be assigned to the Adjutant Generals Department first. Reno and Company H were again used as escorts and pickets during the Fredericksburg campaign and saw little combat. He took 6 weeks leave following this to return to Harrisburg and court Mary Hannah. In the spring of 1863, he participated in General Averell's 2nd Cavalry division campaign against Confederate General Fitzhugh Lee that culminated in the fighting at Kelly's Ford along the Rappahannock River. His horse went down under him and he suffered a hernia. He was brevetted to Major as a result of this action, and given 30 days leave. He rested and received three separate extensions, and then requested to be assigned recruiting duties which he was granted. He got engaged and was planning a fashionable wedding for early July. However, in late May as Lee began his invasion into Pennsylvania, Reno was reassigned as chief of staff to General "Baldy" Smith, who was assembling an ad hoc force to defend Harrisburg and the region from Confederate General Ewell's II Army Corps. Fortunately Lee recalled Ewell to support his efforts around Gettysburg. Reno was granted a brief leave of absence, and he hurried off to New York, where his fiancé and her family had fled to. He was married on July 1 and returned to Harrisburg that night. Smith attempted to pursue Lee after his defeat at Gettysburg, but bad weather and his disorganized troops were not effective in doing this. In mid-July

Reno was reordered back to recruiting duty in Harrisburg. He stayed there until early October when he returned to the 1st Cavalry and was given command of two squadrons in Calvary Corps Reserve Brigade. His troops spent the next two months patrolling along the Rappahannock, probing towards Culpepper, VA. Reno developed lumbago and sciatica, then spent a month in a Washington DC. hospital, but returned in early February 1864 to command a couple of reconnaissance in force missions. In early March he was ordered to the Cavalry Bureau in Washington DC. He was assigned as the acting assistant inspector general, 1st Division, Cavalry Corps and visited various brigades in that capacity. He was accompanying General Torbert in May, and later in June was present at the battle of Trevillian Station. One of the brigadier generals serving under Tolbert was George Custer. Reno remained with General Torbert, and in early August was appointed his chief of staff. Well liked by Torbert, he was encouraged by him to apply for a volunteer command. Using his wife's family connections in Pennsylvania, he applied for command of the 12th Pennsylvania cavalry. While he was waiting, he was still chief of staff for General Torbert, and in that capacity was at the battle of Cedar Creek, Va.. Torbert recommended that he be brevetted Lieutenant Colonel in November. Reno received another leave of absence in late October and went to Harrisburg. He requested a leave extension until further orders to accept the colonelcy of the 12th Pennsylvania, who's commander had been relieved for incompetency. Finally on January 6, 1865, he assumed command and spent the next several months trying to improve the 12th with mixed results. Based near Charleston, West Virginia they skirmished up and down the Shenandoah Valley where Confederate General John Mosby pretty much conducted raids with impunity, and then disappeared into the countryside. Reno pursued him but was never successful, always seeming to be one step behind. Luckily for Reno the 12th was reassigned to his mentor, General Torbert, in Winchester, VA in early April. He was conducting a reconnaissance in force towards Lynchburg when Lee surrendered.

On June 16th he was informed that he had been brevetted Brigadier General Volunteers and Colonel, US Army on March 13. When the unit was mustered out, in July, he reverted to his regular rank of captain. He was initially going to be assigned to Carlisle Barracks, Pa., but was abruptly reassigned to West Point as an infantry instructor, but on arriving in late August, he found the quarters assigned him unsuitable and filed several protests in writing. The next month he was reassigned to New Orleans, La.. Reno immediately telegraphed the Adjutant Generals office and asked for permission to visit and plead his case. His request was denied. Arriving in New Orleans in late October, he spent time as an adjutant general and provost marshal. The following August 1866 he requested a 90 day leave before he was to rejoin the 1st Cavalry Regiment, out in Oregon. He spent that time traveling to and from Washington lobbying in the hope of advancing his military career. He persuaded the governor of Pennsylvania to write a letter to President Johnson, and he even wrote one directly himself, in December. He bombarded the Adjutant Generals office with requests for changing duty assignments and leave extensions. Reno finally left New York in late February 1867 and reported to Fort Vancouver in early May. He spent the rest of his tour there as acting assistant inspector general and serving on general courts martial duty

In April 1869 he was promoted to fill a vacant majority in the 7th Cavalry created by the death of Major Alfred Gibbs. He joined the 7th at Fort Hays, Kansas and spent the next year and a half roaming Western Kansas and Eastern Colorado, protecting the Kansas Pacific Railroad from Indian raids. In May 1871 Reno and four companies of the 7th (B, E, G, & M) were ordered to Spartanburg, South Carolina for reconstruction duty. He remained there until July 1872 when he was assigned to the US Army Breech Loading Small Arms Board, in New York City. This was the Board that selected the single shot, Model .45 caliber 1873 Springfield Carbine to replace the Spencer carbine. After the Board convened, Reno was ordered to Fort Snelling, to take over as squadron commander of Companies D & I, of the 7th Cavalry, headed up to escort the 49th Parallel Survey party

****

Morse and his troops continued towards the approaching column. As they got nearer, Jake saw two riders side by side, out ahead of the column a few yards. Behind then were two more riders carrying the US Flag Guidon and a red over white company guidon. Jake studied the company as they closed the distance. It was formed up in a column of twos and appeared to be moving a regular walking pace. He noticed several of the troopers pointing at them.

"Okay lads," said Morse as he turned slightly toward them. "Sit up straight and look sharp. He then shouted "Troop Halt!"

He then moved forward towards the lead riders, as one of them held up his hand to signal the column to halt.

Morse saluted and said, "Sgt. Morse reporting sirs. Good to see you again, Captain Weir. And I don't believe I had the pleasure of meeting you before Major Reno."

Both officers had removed their uniform jackets and were wearing checked cotton shirts. Major Reno who was riding on the left, had dark eyes, a plump swarthy face with a small wispy mustache and wore a wide brimmed straw hat. Weir had a wide face with a large drooping mustache and wore a black narrow brimmed campaign hat without braid but had a crossed saber emblem. He had a red bandana around his neck. Weir held up his hand and indicated for the column to halt.

Reno stared at Morse and said, "No, I don't recall seeing you before. What brings you out from the fort, Sergeant, did you ride out here just to greet us?"

"Sgt. DeLacy, from Company I," Morse replied nodding towards the Company I troops, "And myself, are get a little training time in with these replacements. We're drilling them on formations and commands. We just brought them up from Jefferson Barracks and thought we'd best show them how we do things in the 7th, Sir." Morse replied.

Weir nodded his head in approval, but Reno continued to stare at Morse and asked, "Can you tell me if our supplies are waiting at Ft, Stevenson?"

"Yes, sir! Lt. Bell is trying to round up wagon teams, and Sgt. Rush has a nice bivouac area for the company to set up camp."

"Well, we can wait a day or two. No need to be in a big hurry, we haven't encountered any hostiles anyway. Besides Capt. Keogh and Company K of the 20th Infantry are with the Survey team. Captain Weir, I think that I'll just ride on in to the fort and find Lt. Bell. I'll let you see to getting the company the settled in. Make sure my striker gets help with my tent and furnishings. Might as well be comfortable while we're here. Thank you for the information Sergeant Morse. Carry on." With that Reno prodded his horse and moved on towards the fort without looking back.

Jake had been watching the officers, and was close enough to hear the conversation. He thought he detected a brief glimpse of annoyance flicker across Capt.Weir's face. Weir then looked at Sgt. Morse and stated, "Good to see you again Sergeant. I was wondering when you'd turn up. You've missed the beginning of our little summer jaunt."

Meanwhile another rider came up from where he'd been stopped near the guidon bearers behind Weir. He was wearing a gray issue flannel shirt with the sleeves rolled up, and a light gray felt hat. He shouted as he got near.

"About God Damn Time! Tis a wonder that you could find your way. Ya fookin' thick headed Paddy!"

"First Sergeant! Do I sense that you missed me?" asked Morse smiling, "I tried to get back as fast as I could."

"Aye, probably by way of every saloon you rode by."

"Well, I always toasted, 'Here's to you Top!' whenever I took my first sip."

First Sergeant Martin rode close to Morse and leaned out from his saddle and extended his hand who did the same and the shook hands heartily.

"Good to see you, Pat." he said quietly.

"And you also, Mike!"

Capt. Weir who was smiling at the exchange, turned and looked at Jake and the others.

"Well, Sergeant, I assume these four belong to us?" He asked.

"Yes, sir! The other four are with Sgt. DeLacy."

"Very well, have them all fall in at the back of the column and we'll get moving again. You ride up by the First Sergeant, I'm sure he has a few things he'd like to discuss. Sgt. DeLacy you're welcome to ride along"

DeLacy replied. "If it's all the same to you sir, I think I'd like to continue working with my men a while longer. I want to have them a little better up to speed before Captain Keogh lays eyes on them. But we will enjoy tagging along on the way back north."

"Very good Sergeant! Carry on"

"Yes, Sir!" he said and saluted. He turned his mount to the left and called over to his troops. "Follow me men."

Morse looked over to where Jake waited his set. "Private Rogers, take your set of four back to the end of the column and fall in behind the last rank."

Jake nodded his head and said. "Yes, Sergeant! Let's go boys!" He and Charlie turned off to the right and the Georges followed them. Weir waved the column forward and rode ahead.

As the moved off, Sgt. Martin said. "Ride with me Pat, I need to bring you up to speed on current events, and you can tell me about your newbies. Bye the bye, I assume Sgt. Rush has Private Holden and his mates in tow."

"Indeed he does, and I'd like to add them and the new boys, as a section in my platoon if you don't mind."

"No, I don't mind, Holden is a steady influence on our two young Irish lads. We'll put him in charge of the section. I can't understand why he's not been promoted being a seven year man and all. So tell me about our newbies, do I detect that you have young Rogers as a No. 1?"

"I do Top. He's a natural born soldier. I served with his Da in the war, and he was also. Jake's a quick study. Raised on a farm, a good horseman and crack shot. I just need to put a little pressure on him and see how he responds. The others are okay, just city boys from back East. But they're all eager, and follow Rogers lead. I"ll be keeping a close eye on them."

Martin nodded his head, Morse looked ahead toward Captain Weir and asked Martin, "So, tell me about our current enterprise, and Major Reno. I detected that our Capt. Weir is not enamored of the man."

"That's putting it lightly! The Major is a right smug bastard. He's one of those that has a knack for rubbing people the wrong way, particularly if he perceives that he can bully you. The Captain told me that Reno is not happy that he got shunted off to command the military escort for this survey team, and has been quite vocal that he would prefer on some other assignment. He just came from New York where he was on the Ordinance Evaluation Board where he was hobnobbing with General Terry, and other Army brass. I get the impression that he perceives this duty assignment as beneath him. He's been at odds with our medical officer, Doctor Nash, for weeks. No one is entirely sure why, but Reno has it in for him. Apparently Nash has a reputation for tipping the bottle a wee bit. He had him sent back to St.Paul earlier, but was ordered to let him return when we left Ft. Pembina. He's also been arguing with Dr. Coues, the surgeon and naturalist to the Northern Boundary Commission, about how our men are to be utilized. It seems that Coues has been authorized to use them in their spare time to collect specimens. And, he's already butting heads with Commissioner Campbell, who's in charge of the Survey. When Reno set up a supply depot just west of Turtle Mountain two weeks ago, the Commissioner arrived three days later with Dr. Coues, and they told Reno to move the depot 75 miles further west. He wasn't happy about that, and immediately decided to come with us to Fort Stevenson, leaving Keogh and I Company to escort the survey team and supply train to the new location. Poor Capt. Weir's had to listen to his bitching for four days now."

Morse nodded his head in sympathy as Martin continued.

"Both Doctors are riding with us back by the wagons. I think there's more fireworks due between them and Reno when we get to Ft. Stevenson. suspect Reno went ahead to get his messages away first. He seems the vindictive sort."

Morse replied, "He was at Fort Hays for a while back in '70, before we went South. I remember some rumors that he and Capt. Benteen got in a drunken dispute. I heard that Benteen challenged him, then Reno backed down. That Benteen, I remember him from the Washita, shooting it out with that Cheyenne buck. He's a cool customer when it comes to fighting. Reno had a battalion at River Bend, out in Colorado, guarding the Kansas Pacific Railroad crews, and then down at Spartanburg, South Carolina.

Fortunately for us the company was never under him."

Martin stated, "When the Regiment was assembling down in Memphis earlier this year, and I found out we were coming up here, I talked to some of the other First Sergeants that had served under Reno. They told me that he hates it out in the field and is always applying for detached service back East. He's a West Pointer, and is always trying to toady up using that connection to secure a staff position somewhere. Maybe he'll succeed and we'll be rid of him before too long. I've heard this survey could take two to three years."

"Well, Top, let's get these lads into camp and settled down. Then you and I can go find us some beers. I suspect we'll have a hard time finding any the rest of the summer. The first round is on me!"

"You can bet your arse it is, Patrick!" exclaimed Sergeant Martin.

As Jake and his set made their way to the back of the column, he was looking at the other troopers. He noticed that they were wearing a mixed variation in uniforms ranging from faded gray or blue shirts, assorted types and colors of hats and bandannas, pale blue or stained canvas trousers. Most wore ragged beards below dark tan faces. Dust hung in the air, thicker as they rode towards the rear. When they got closer to the last ranks, a sergeant moved towards them from his position on the left flank. He eyed them up and down as he did.

"You lads lost?" He queried, with a sardonic expression on his face.

"Sergeant Morse told us to join the rear." Jake stated.

"I thought I spotted that thick headed Mick bastard. I'm Sergeant Flanagan. Okay, fall in after the last rank. We'll get this sorted out when we get to camp. I assume you boys have just come out of the fort. Is Sgt. Rush there with our supplies.

"Yes, Sergeant, we came up the river on the *Western*, and unloaded them yesterday."

"That's good news!" Flanagan nodded his head and shouted over to the column, "We should eat good tonight, lads! Mind your manners and don't be overstuffing these tenderfoot rookies."

"Aye, Sarge! We'll make sure that they get their fill!" a trooper called out. That produced a few guffaws and chuckles.

Big George commented. "Well, that's mighty nice of these guys. I can always use an extra bite."

"I think that means that they're going to be bullshitting us about Mr. Lo and his friends, Big. No food involved. We're the newbies." Welch replied.

When they arrived at the bivouac near the fort, the company quickly set about making camp. Jake marveled at how quickly it materialized. The troopers set about their duties with very little discussion. He supposed that having to make camp everyday would create a routine where everyone was familiar with what had to be done. Plus, he supposed that there was the added incentive of the camp's proximity to Fort Stevenson and its Trading Post. The headquarters tent had been pitched where Lt. Bell's tent had stood with its back to the creek, and a guard tent in front. Stretching out on each flank, starting with the sergeant's tents were rows of two man tents for the platoons. They faced to the middle, with about 20 yards apart between the rows, and pitched in a line along a picket rope to keep them uniform. The saddles and horse equipage was stacked three yards in front of the tents. A fire trench was dug in along center and the company wagons interspaced along it. The cook wagon was unloaded and set up at the far end. The rest of the trench was being utilized along its length and the smell of coffee soon filled the air. The officers tents were set up 25 yards to the rear of the men's tents facing towards them, and the officer's mess tent and kitchen fifteen yards behind them. The horses were led to be watered, and then lariated and picketed for grazing on both sides behind the tents. The troopers then collected the forage ration in nose bags from the quartermaster sergeant and farrier, to feed them. Then they brushed and curried their mounts while the sergeants strolled around inspecting the animals. Morse had taken them in hand on their return and had assigned Jake and his set to collect more firewood after stable call. Holden and Horn, along with Golden and Green, jumped in and were helping out as they exchanged good natured barbs with the arriving troopers. Rooster was in the thick of things.

"Well, now! While you boys were plodding along on your horses and camping in the woods, we were riding on a riverboat enjoying fine meals and feather mattresses. Too wile away the time we fished and played cards. Ol' Biscuit here was trying to romance a sweet lass that he became smitten with." He said with a grin while elbowing Joe, "Ain't that right Biscuit?"

Joe rolled his eye and replied, "Sure now, I'm not stepping out in the bull shite with you, Pat. These lads will not be understanding how lucky they were to not be crawling around in mud up to your bollocks, humping wood for the fooking boilers, and mucking out the stable deck. Not to mention the sweet lass was a little filly of a mare that hated being on the boat. And if you smelled a fine meal, and saw a featherbed, it were while you were sneaking around up on the cabin deck in officers country, whilst they were playing cards. And the only thing fishy is the smell of your spiel of malarkey!"

"Oh you're a sour one, Joe! "Golden exclaimed, "He just don't care for boats ever since we came across the water down in steerage class."

Jake and Charlie came in with armloads of wood, followed by the Georges. As they dumped their loads Holden motioned for them to come over and he addressed the soldiers nearby.

"Let me introduce our newest D Company troopers. These blokes just came out with Sgt. Morse from Jefferson Barracks. They rode up on the *Western* with us, and have been playing awkward squad with him for a week or so now. In his wisdom, the esteemed Sergeant has seen fit to form them up with our set of four as a section, with yours truly a senior. So, let's welcome them to the outfit. Bye the bye, they shared the same luxury accommodations as the rest of us, contrary to what Rooster would have you believe. From what I've seen they are square lads, not a dead beat among them."

Just then the call went out. "Supper!" A line soon formed as the men grabbed their mess kits and filed towards the troop kitchen. After they got their chow they gravitated back to the vicinity of their tents, filled their coffee cups and lounged by their saddles.

"Beef again, and potatoes!" exclaimed a private, "Cookie's gonna spoil us if he keeps this up"

"Likely as not, he's counting on restocking his larder before we leave. I'll not be complaining though." commented another.

"I heard tell from one of our survey crews that they eat pretty damn good. And they said the Brits and Canadian survey crews eat even better. Supposed to be a lot of wild game, even buffalos, where we're headed." another stated.

"This trip may not be so bad after all. Although I heard it gets colder than a witch's tit up here. Surely we'll not stay out much past the end if the summer."

Jake and the other new men sat silently off to the side, taking in the conversation. Henry had told him these troopers were in one the other sections, that made up the platoon. Sergeant Flanagan had been in charge of them in Morse's absence. He noticed one of the men watching his group intently. When Jake made eye contact, the trooper got up and walked over.

"I be bettin' these damnt rookies got some money. Hasn't anyone told them that it's customary for them to buy a round for the old hands?" he asked as he looked down at Jake challengingly, "Is bad enough that Morse is shakin' up the section order, to keep these recruits together."

"Now Smiley, you haven't even introduced yourself and you're asking my boys to buy you a drink. Where's your manners?" Holden asked.

"Vell, some of us don't fancy ourselves as gents like you, Henry." he replied, looking over at Holden.

"Then let me do the introductions for you. Lads, this is Charlie Sanders, better know as "Smiley" He's a grouchy old Deutcher who's reenlisted like I did. He's got a couple of New Yorkers in his set, John Hager and Elwyn Reid. Plus, a token southern lad from down North Carolina way who fell for Lt. Bell's recruiting spiel, Harvey Fox."

As Henry was talking the men got up and came over to introduce themselves. Welsh and Big were immediately questioned by the other New York men as to the location they were from back home. Hager and Reid appeared to be in their mid twenties, while Sanders and Fox were a few years older.

"Just my luck, more damn Yankees." Fox drawled, "You ain't got no southern boys?"

Jake stated, "Well, I'm from Missouri, if that helps."

Fox stared at him for a second and said. "Ah Hell! Now I'll have to' show you' to boot." Then held out his hand, grinning. "I'm Harvey Fox."

"Jake Rogers."

"I think I'll just call you Show. You can call me Quick. Fortunately for me, there's Kentuckians in the other set of four in our section. He pointed over to where they were sitting sipping coffee. The sandy haired is, Jimmy Hurd the #1, just finishing up his beef, we call him Peaches, next to him is Tommy Stivers also known as Stiff, Billy Harris, his cousin, and the other is George Scott."

"Uh Oh, we have two Georges. Hunt from Boston, we call him 'Small'. As opposed to him over there, pointing at George Dann. We just call him 'Big'." said Jake.

"That's okay, we call ours, Jocko."

They all waved back and forth. Just then 1st Sgt. Martin, followed by Sgt. Morse and Flanagan, came from the direction of the HQ tent.

"Just the men we were looking for. Holden, your section is up for guard duty tonight. Get them ready and report to the guard tent in 20 minutes. Since we're in close to the fort, this will be a good opportunity for you lads to see what it's like on guard out here after dark. Sgt. Rush will be Sergeant of the Guard." Sgt. Flanagan said. "The rest of you can wander over to the Post Traders if you'd like."

"I was just told me we're having a down day tomorrow." 1st Sgt. Martin announced, "Just normal stable call, so have a good time. Capt.

Weir is also going to see about getting a Paymaster here before we go back out. He's going to let the trader know. We'll know more about things after tomorrow."

The men were all grinning and hurried to get their mess gear cleaned up. Holden walked over and patted Sanders on the shoulder.

"Well, Smiley I guess your free beer will have to wait." Holden said smiling, "Come on lads, I'll show you how to get ready for guard duty."

After guard posts were assigned, Jake and the others were escorted to their posts by the sergeant of the guard. Given the proximity to the fort, and the area being considered secure, the horses remained on pickets and lariats to the rear of the company area. Guards were posted at all four corners and a roving post between them, one of which was assigned to Jake. He was to patrol the area from near the creek, out to the middle where the officers tents and mess were located. It was just dusk, and as Jake approached the officers area he saw Capt. Weir step out from under his tent flap, lighting a pipe and looking towards the Headquarters tent. He puffed to get the pipe going, then turned and noticed Jake. Jake was unsure whether to address the officer, so he just stopped and saluted.

****

Captain Thomas Benton Weir

Weir was a 37 year old career officer. He was born in Ohio, and raised in Upper Michigan. He graduated from the University of Michigan then enlisted in the 3rd Michigan Volunteer Cavalry in August 1861, and by October had been commissioned as a 2nd Lieutenant. He spent most of his time with the Union Army campaigning along the Mississippi River, participated in the Siege of Corinth, and was promoted to 1st Lt., in June of 1862, shortly after which he was captured by the Confederates. He was promoted to Captain in November while still a prisoner of war, was exchanged in January 1863 and returned to his unit. A promotion to Major came in early 1865, and he was a brevetted as a Lt. Colonel for gallantry, before the end of the War. After the war, he served as a brevet Major in the Regular Army, while on Reconstruction Duty in Texas, where he first met General Custer and was assigned to his staff. He was mustered out of the Army, in San Antonio, on Feb, 1866. In November of that year he was appointed as a 1st Lieutenant in the newly formed 7th Cavalry, and reported for duty in February1867 at Fort Riley, Ks. He then served in various staff positions for Colonel A. J. Smith, the original commander of the 7th, spending most of his time at Fort Hays, Ks. He was promoted by seniority to Captain in July, and in September 1867 he assumed command of Company D, which he would command the rest of his career. A veteran of the 1868 winter campaign and the Washita Fight, he had assumed command of the battalion Capt. Hamilton was leading, after he was killed. Weir was a popular officer with both the rank and file. Known for his intelligence, quick wit, and gentlemanly demeanor, Weir was considered a member of the "Custer Clique". He was a particular favorite of Libby Custer, although she disapproved of his tendency to over indulge on occasion. His reputation for being intemperate, almost got him removed by the Hancock Boards, but Brig. Gen. Pope, the Department commander intervened. He was a regular face at the Custer's and their social events in Kansas. But, when the 7th was assigned reconstruction duty, Company D was sent first to Chester, South Carolina, then on to Opelika, Alabama. After a brief reunion with the rest of the regiment, in Memphis earlier in the year, he and Keogh had been sent north to Fort Snelling with their men. Reno met them there and assumed command of the escort. Neither captain had served with Reno previously.

****

Weir returned his salute and said, "Good evening private. You're one of the new men that came in with Sgt. Morse aren't you."

"Yes Sir," Jake replied, "Private Rogers, Sir"

Weir nodded his head and asked, "Where do you hail from, Rogers?"

"Missouri, Sir! From down near Springfield."

"I spent some time in Missouri during the War. Down by New Madrid in the boot heel, lots of timber and hills, not like out here on the plains. What's your impression so far, Rogers."

"I like it, Sir. With few trees, it seems like you can see forever. Hard to sneak up on a body out here!"

"Don't be fooled Rogers, an Indian uses the land like a cloak. He can hide in every fold. This is has been their land for decades and they don't need maps to know where they're at. If they don't want you to see them, you probably won't."

"I'll keep that in mind, Sir."

"Very well, carry on Rogers"

Jake did an about face and as he stepped off towards the creek he saw Lt. Bell and two other lieutenants headed to the officers area. The length of the entire camp from creek to cook wagon was about 100 yards, as Jake paced it off. He settled on a routine carrying his carbine on his shoulder,

54

as he trudged back and forth. The buzz of cicadas and shrill croaking tree frogs filled the air, along with the smell of wood smoke and burning tobacco. A little after Retreat was sounded it was completely dark, except for the flickering lights from the fires and the soft glow of candle lanterns coming from the officer's mess tent. As Jake was approaching the rear of it, he stopped when he heard raised voices, recognizing Capt. Weir's and Lt. Bell's.

"I'm telling you Jimmy, this Reno is a pompous ass. The last thing he said before running off to the fort was "Have my tent made ready". Then he sends word to have his kit sent to the fort, and spends the night there. I'll warrant that we'll not be graced with his presence in this mess until we depart."

"Now Tom, you can't blame him for wanting to have a roof over his head." Bell replied condescendingly.

"Bullshit, he knew when he left that he would overnight at the fort. He's been pulling crap like that since we left Fort Abercrombie. Isn't that right, Porter? You're acting as his adjutant and have to be around him more than anyone."

A new voice responded, "You don't need to remind me, Weir. I get handed everything. 'Take care of this for me, Porter' is all he ever says. I'll warrant that he wears out his welcome with the post commander. Between bitching about Dr. Nash and not landing a staff position back at Headquarters in St. Paul, he's been very vocal about his talents being wasted playing babysitter to a bunch of surveyors. He let them know it too when we caught up with them at Turtle Mountain. When Commissioner Campbell arrived a week later they had quite a row about who was in charge. It will be interesting when we meet up with the Brits and Canadians at the new Depot on the Mouse River. Or should I say, 'Camp Terry' as Reno has decided to call it. A blatant attempt to toady up to the General if you ask me."

"What's his beef with Dr. Nash?" asked Bell.

"I think that Nash and he had words on the train from Ft. Snelling, and the good Doctor told him to go bugger himself." Weir stated, "A sentiment that I concur with." He added.

"He intends to get Nash kicked off the expedition." said Porter. "He tried to do it at Ft. Abercrombie and was overruled by St. Paul. I'll wager that Nash won't leave here with us. He strikes me as one to carry a grudge."

"Well, it looks like we're going to have to put up with this all summer, so you need to get with the sergeants and corporals to make sure they stay on top of the sections. You best be on your toes, Edgerly. As the junior officer you'll be a target of opportunity for him, once he doesn't have Nash to focus on. Best mind your Ps and Qs."

A voice that Jake assumed to be Lt. Edgerly answered, "I will Captain. I'll just pretend I'm back at West Point."

They all chuckled, and Weir said. "Once we get up to the depot we'll get out from underfoot and let him fuss with the Survey Party, the Brits, and Canadians."

Jake heard the clinking of glasses being filled and heard the captain announce.

"Gentlemen, I propose a toast to Major Marcus Reno. May he find fulfillment of his ambitions, Posthaste!"

****

1st. Lieutenant James Ezekiel Porter

Porter was born in Maine in February 1847 to a locally prominent family. After attending Norwich University he secured an appointment to West Point in 1865. He graduated in 1869 and was assigned as a 2nd Lieutnant, Company E, 7th Cavalry at Ft. Leavenworth. He was posted at Fort Harker and Fort Wallace before going on Reconstruction Duty in South Carolina. He was promoted to 1st Lt. in March 1872 and joined Company I in Kentucky. When Reno was assigned to command the Boundary Survey he chose Porter as his Adjutant.

****

2nd Lt. Winfield Scott Edgerly

Edgerly was born in New Hampshire in May 1846. Raised in Farmington, and attended the exclusive Phillips Exeter Academy before he was accepted to West Point in 1866. In June 1870 he was assigned as a 2nd Lt. in Company D, 7th Cavalry at Fort Leavenworth. He accompanied it went it was sent to the South on Reconstruction Duty. He was the junior officer of the Boundary Survey escort. At 6' 4" he was the tallest officer in the Regiment.

****

Jake figured he had probably better move on, and made his way as quietly as possible away from the area. He now had something to ponder on as he resumed his patrol. It made for an interesting train of thought to help wile away the rest of his guard detail time. It also gave him a little insight into the officer's world, and a new appreciation of the importance of rank.

For the rest of the week, Jake and the other new men, were introduced to the daily, and highly regimented, routine of serving in a cavalry company in the field. They became familiar with the various daily bugles calls. Mornings and afternoons were devoted to the care and feeding of their mounts. They seemed to catch a disproportionate share of fatigue and guard details, but Jake figured that it was all part of being welcomed into the outfit. They were finally allowed to spend an afternoon at the post traders, but most of the merchandise had been picked over, so they settled for a few beers and went back to camp. Jake had a new appreciation for the wisdom of Holden's advice back at Ft. Rice concerning their cache of goodies. The officers came and went frequently, leaving the sergeants to run things. A dozen wagons, pulled by six mule teams, showed up loaded with supplies, food stuffs, and forage for the horses. They were also accompanied by a small herd of cattle. The veteran troopers seemed to sense their impending departure and frequented the fort as much as they were allowed. Then, after evening roll call, Sgt. Martin announced to the company formation.

"Men, we're leaving in the morning. I hope you are all done with any business you might have at the fort. We will be staying in camp tonight and will break camp at first light. We're heading north to meet back up with Company I. We should link up with them and the survey party, in four or five days. Capt. Weir has informed me that we will be out until it turns cold, so make sure you get your greatcoats to Sgt. Rush and he will see that they're stored in one of the supply wagons. Our winter quarters will be at Fort Totten. I'm told that it's been renovated and is well built, with brick buildings. That's good, because we will probably be posted there for the next couple of years when we aren't in the field. Reveille will be at 4:30, and I intend for us to be on the trail by 6:30, so best you turn in and get a good nights sleep. Dismissed!"

As the formation broke up and the men wandered back to their tents, they talked among themselves speculating on the information they'd just received. Henry Holden and the section gathered round the fire where their coffee pot was put on to heat.

"Lads, we're away in the morning. I personally am looking forward to this expedition. We're about to see parts of this country that few white men have seen. So, embrace this as an opportunity of a life time. This will be something that you can tell your grandchildren about." Henry stated.

They all nodded their heads in general agreement.

"It beats hanging around here. I wonder if there will be any Indian lasses to be encountered?" offered Rooster.

Biscuit poked him in the ribs and said, 'Sure now, if there is you'd best be behaved or you might lose those lovely locks you're always fussing with."

They all laughed.

Big spoke up, "I heard Sgt. Flanagan telling Sgt. Morse that the Canadians don't even have any soldiers for an escort, and that they have wagons full of fancy food, wine and liquor."

"That sounds like the way to do it. Maybe we can learn something from them. I can just hear Cookie asking me if I'd like a glass of wine with my stew." Little chuckled.

"Well, I suspect they must have more money to spend then what our esteemed members of Congress authorized for the US effort. The British set great store in being professional." Charlie opined, "Isn't that right Sage?"

"Generally speaking I believe you're correct old chap, especially when it comes to any science related endeavors." Holden responded with an emphatic English accent. He reached for the coffee pot and asked. "Who's for a spot of coffee, mates? I persuaded Cookie to make us a dish of plum duff to top off our evening festivities. Hurry has gone to fetch it and smuggle it past the other sections. Let's enjoy our last evening before we cast off from civilization!"

The following morning Company D broke camp. Jake watched in amazement as the NCOs smoothly directed the troops and activities involved. Two hours after reveille was sounded the company formed up and was ready to move out. They stood waiting by their horses as the First Sergeant rode up and down the ranks. Capt. Weir stood talking with the other officers up in front.

"We ought to head on out and let Reno catch up with us." Remarked the First Sergeant Martin as he came even with Sgt. Morse.

"Aye Top, but he's our Battalion commander. Wouldn't bode well for us to leave him behind. He'd likely not take it too well." Pat replied. "He'll be along."

As if on cue, Reno and a group of riders appeared coming from the direction of the fort. One of them detached and headed towards the rear of the columns where the wagons were lined up.

"That's Dr. Coues! He doesn't look too happy." Martin said. "And, I don't see Dr. Nash. It appears that we'll be without the services of the good doctor. I'm supposing that it will fall on Dr. Coues to help us when we're ailing. He's made it very clear that he works for the Boundary Commission, primarily as a naturalist. I told you that he and Reno have already been at odds. The Doctor will be at dead run to the Commissioner when we get up there."

Reno rode to the front of the column and shortly thereafter the command was passed to move out.

"Pat, I want you to work with your new boys as advance party, flank and rear guard on our way north. Best you practice while we're in friendly territory. I want everyone up to speed before we head farther west. I'm not sure how we'll be operating once the Survey lads start up." The First Sgt. said before he turned towards the front of the column. "For sure I'll be wanting sharp eyes out front."

"No problem, Top! I'll have them up to speed."

The next several days were a blur to Jake as the unit settled into its daily march routine. They maintained a pace to travel 30 or so miles a day, alternating between walking and riding their mounts. He found himself enjoying being out on the advance party and seeing the countryside unfold in front of him, not to mention getting to be out of the dust stirred up from the ranks in front of him. He had always been blessed with good eye sight and was developing a knack for spotting movements out at distances. Several times he drew comments from the others when he pointed them out. Sergeant Morse, who was also known to have a keen eye, nodded his head several times when Jake beat him sighting. Late afternoons were spent settling into camp and tending to the horses. It was a daily routine that varied only with the weather. The countryside was mostly low rolling hills covered in prairie grass. The only trees to speak of bordered small creeks. There was an abundance of wild game, but with fresh supplies there was no reason to bother with shooting any. The sun beat down upon them but the evenings were pleasant. So far Jake was thankful to be on this expedition and not stuck at one of the forts. They were following the back trail that the company had used coming south. On the third day they came to a fairly steep escarpment that dropped down to the Mouse River, or Souris as it was called by the Canadians. It was a flat plain and they were to stay on the west bank and head north for the remainder of the trip.

In 1869 the Hudson Bay Company surrendered its Royal Charter to what was known as Rupert's Land. This consisted of the whole of central Canada ranging from Hudson's Bay to the 49th Parallel and from the Rocky Mountains east to Ontario. In July of 1870 the area was admitted to Canada by the British government. This event prompted the governments of the US and Britain, on behalf of Canada, to coordinate a survey effort to delineate a firm border between the two countries. The British Commission was led by Captain Donald Roderick Cameron, a 37 year old Scotsman and Royal Artillery officer, he had served in India, back in 1864-65 towards the end of the Mutiny. Posted to Halifax, Nova Scotia, in 1869, he married the daughter of a prominent Canadian politician who was also a member of the Prime Minister's cabinet. The American Commission was headed by Archibald Campbell, a 59 year old who was a 1835 graduate of West Point and had an extensive background as an engineer on various canal, river, and railroad survey projects. The diverse backgrounds and age discrepancy would prove to be a source of friction between the two on several occasions. The British Survey Party did have four Royal Engineer officers; Scottish-born Captain Samuel Andersen (Chief Astronomer), Captain Albany Featherstonhaugh (Assistant Astronomer), Lieutenant Arthur Clitheroe Ward (Secretary) and Irish-born Lieutenant William James Galway (Jr., Assistant Astronomer). All were highly qualified and had the advantage of being accompanied by four sergeants, 13 corporals, and 27 sappers of the Royal Engineers. They were all well trained and supplied with the latest equipment. The American contingent had Major William Johnson Twining (Chief Astronomer), Captain James F. Gregory (Assistant Astronomer), and Lieutenant Francis Vinton Greene (Junior Assistant Astronomer), and Civilian James E. Bangs (Secretary). Again all highly qualified, but dependent upon various civilian employees for support staff. They were also burdened by the initial parsimonious budget approved by Congress.

Beginning in July of 1872 near Pembina, Minnesota, preparations were begun for the survey to start immediately. Initially east to Lake of the Woods, then the following spring westward from the Red River. Progress would be measured by miles from that starting point. When they started west the first observations were done by both Commissions, at miles 20 & 35. When the calculation results were compared they were close enough that it was agreed by both parties that they would alternate observation stations going forward to expedite the work. The Americans set the next two stations at miles 47 & 77, while the British moved west and set up stations at miles 95 & 115. They were at east base of Turtle Mountain when the US Army escorts arrived on station. The British set up a supply depot there while the Americans moved on and set up station at mile 150 where Major Reno elected to set up a supply depot on the western base of Turtle Mountain on July 10. But, when Commissioner Campbell arrived there on July 18, he made the decision to relocate the depot to the station at mile

215, at the second Mouse/Souris River crossing. The Americans christened it Camp Terry in honor of the general commanding the Dept. of Dakota. Both survey parties camped there, briefly. At this point the American contingent consisted of 160 cavalry, 70 infantry, and approximately 120 survey staff, wagon drivers, livestock herders, and a few miscellaneous helpers. The British had 48 Royal Engineers, over 150 miscellaneous civilians, and the Métis contingent of 33 who provided security, in addition to herding livestock and guiding the parties.

CHAPTER 5

Camp Terry, 215 miles west of the Red River August 3, 1873

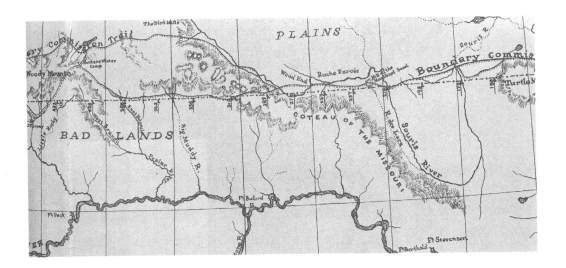

Boundary Survey Route- Summer 1873

Jake, Charlie, and the two Georges were detailed to the rear guard so they didn't get to enter the camp until the wagons were drawn in. Company I had been encamped for several days, along with Company K of the 20th Infantry on the west side of the Mouse. The river here was naturally sheltered in a 200' deep valley and was clear flowing over a gravely bottom and easily fordable. The Stars and Stripes waved above the camp. The troops had set up camp in the usual configuration with tents in neatly aligned rows. In the middle, next to the infantry company, were several large tents with a dozen or so wagons drawn up next to them. They belonged to the Boundary Commission. Across the river was the British Canadian camp with the Union Jack raised above it. The tall conical shaped tents nestled among the trees were a contrast to the lower pitched roof ones that the Americans used. They had dozens of wagons, and also a number of curious wooden carts with a large wheel on each side drawn by a single horse. Both camps had herds of livestock grazing around the perimeter. The British wagons were drawn by oxen, as apposed to the American mule drawn ones.

"Will you look at that!" Charlie exclaimed, pointing to some Indian tepees on the far side of the British encampment. "It looks like they have their own Indians."

Jake and the other two men nodded their heads. Many of the Brits were watching D Company as it began settling in. There was a group of thirty, or so, men lounging around a fire over by the tepees.

"Quit your gawkin' lads!" exclaimed Sgt. Flanagan, as he rode up. "Them there are Métis. Half-Injun, half-Frenchie,or Scot. This is their stomping grounds out here. They're hunters and traders and they have their own bands. Most of 'em speak English, so you boys can talk with them. The Brits have hired that bunch on as scouts and escort. They call themselves the 49th Rangers. From what I've seen they're handy to have around out here."

Jake looked to the north and asked, "How far you reckon we are from Canada, Sarge?"

"You're lookin at it, son. That side of the river is Canada. We're camped right on the line. You boys best go get your tents set up. I expect we'll get things sorted pretty quick. These Surveyors are anxious to keep rolling while the weather's nice."

That evening the ranking commission members and military officers gathered in a large tent near the center of camps. Commissioner Archibald Campbell, his secretary James Bangs, and the afore mentioned Dr. Elliot Coues were there. The Corps of Engineers Survey officers were Major William Twining, Captain James Gregory, and Lieutenant Francis Greene. They were all West Point graduates. In fact, Greene had been in the Class of 1870 with Lt. Edgerly. The military escort contingent was made up of Major Reno, Captains Thomas Weir, Myles Keogh, and Abram Harbach (20th Infantry), 1st Lieutenants James Porter, James Bell, and 2nd Lieutenants Winfield Edgerly and Andrew Nave. After a dinner of fresh beef and vegetables, Commissioner Campbell passed out brandy and cigars, then exclaimed. "A toast, Gentlemen! To good weather and fair progress for our survey!"

All glasses were raised and a general murmur of "Here, Here's" followed.

"I'm going to turn this over to Major Twining so he can explain the system he and our British compatriots have worked out. I think we'll all find that it's the most expeditious method for completing our mission."

Twining rose and turned to a map that was mounted on an easel so they could all see it.

"We are here." he said pointing at the map. "We are on the 49th Parallel, exactly 215 miles west of the Red River where the expedition began. Each observation station will be designated by the distance from the Red River start point. Our plan is to try and make it another 200 miles before winter comes. Our friends across the river have agreed that we will continue to alternate our survey and observation teams every twenty miles. We will erect mounds to permanently mark the border boundary as we go. The observatory teams will make their calculations while the tangent teams survey the terrain. We think that will give us plenty of time to compete our section and leapfrog to the next one. Captain Anderson, of the Royal Engineers, will blaze trail ahead of us so we shouldn't encounter any surprises."

"Why depend on the Brits to scout ahead?" queried Reno, "What are we here for?"

Twining looked at Reno and replied. "Capt. Anderson has thirty mounted Méti scouts. They know this land. Their people hunt buffalo out here every year. They know the local tribes from trading with them. The British are under strict orders not to get in a confrontation with any of the tribes. Our purpose here is to mark the border, not create any friction with the indigenous people. Your purpose is to provide a security escort if required"

"So you're saying we aren't needed?" asked Reno.

Commissioner Campbell spoke up at this point. "Major Twining has his orders Major Reno. You have yours. I suggest that General Terry has his reasons for your presence here. Perhaps he's concerned that Col. Custer's railroad surveying expedition might stir up the tribes as we get farther West."

Reno turned and looked at Campbell with a scowl.

"Well, I for one look forward to spending some time with the Brits. They always travel in style. Good wine and spirits, and they tend to set a good table." Keogh exclaimed. "They've been good company so far, eh Dr. Coues?"

"Yes, indeed, most of them are well traveled and have interesting tales. i find them to be very amenable hosts. Some, over here on are side, should take lessons." He smiled, while looking at Reno.

The rest of the 7th officers, who were standing behind the Major, had to struggle to suppress smiles.

"While the Major was gone to Fort Stevenson, we worked out a schedule with the survey teams to provide a section, supervised by a sergeant, for the tangent team. Capt. Harbach has done the same with a couple of his Infantry squads for the observation teams. We can rotate the men every two weeks. It's working out nicely." said Keogh.

"Well, I'm not so sure that is the correct way to utilize our troops. I don't like having our men out with no officer supervision, and I certainly don't have enough officers to send out with them." Reno stated.

"I would like to point out that myself, Capt. Gregory, and Lt. Greene will be with the men." Noted Major Twining.

Reno turned and regarded Twining cooly. "You are all Corps of Engineer officers, not cavalry officers."

"Hmm! I once knew a Corps officer that had some success commanding troops." Spoke up the Commissioner, "His name was Robert E. Lee, as I recall. I think your point is rendered moot, Major Reno."

"None the less! I'm the escort commander and I'll decide when and where my men will be deployed." Said Reno haughtily. He swallowed his remaining drink and set down his glass. "I bid you good night, gentlemen." He then turned and exited the tent.

There was a long pause as they all stood in silence. Finally Capt. Weir spoke. "I see no reason why we shouldn't finish enjoying these fine cigars, that the Commissioner has provided. Not to mention the excellent brandy. Myles, I suppose you've become quite chummy with your countryman Lt. Galway, the assistant astronomer, while I've been gone."

"Indeed Thomas, he's not a bad fellow even though he's from County Cork. He and I are close to the same age. We have been comparing the circuitous routes we both followed from Ireland, to arrive at this particular spot in the North American wilderness."

"I'll look forward to hearing the specifics. I noticed that there are some tepees over the river. Do you know anything about that?"

"That's a group of Métis families that are on their way to Fort Garry to trade buffalo meat and hides. They stopped for a couple of days to see if we would be interested in anything. They'll be moving on shortly. We've seen a few Indians off in the distance, but not encountered any up close."

Lt. Greene wandered over, followed by Edgerly, asked, "Captain Weir, good to see you back. Did you bring us any presents from civilization?"

"I can't say that Ft. Stevenson would be considered civilization. But I did manage to visit the sutler's and stocked up on some necessities. I'll be happy to share when you're in the vicinity. How goes the surveying?"

"Being the youngest and junior officer of the commission, I am tasked with supervising the tangent and topographical teams. Lot's of horseback riding and signal flag waving. I'd rather be doing that when the weather's nice. We'll see as we progress. I made sure to bring along a good hat and poncho, and we have several wagons to tote our supplies. I am thinking about trying to trade for one of those big wheeled carts. The Brits call them Red River carts. They seem to be pretty handy to maneuver."

"Well, good luck with that. I'm sure that it would be frowned on if we tried it. Our good Major likes to go by the book." Keogh replied. "Gentlemen what say we go across the river and see what my countrymen have for refreshments. I had my striker, Finnegan, procure a wagon for us to ride in. I'm still a British citizen you know. Let's poll the others. The night is still young and I think any objections just left."

****

Captain Myles Walter Keogh

Keogh was born in County Carlow, Ireland on May 25, 1840, the youngest of 13 children. After losing his father at an early age, Keogh was raised by his mother and maternal uncle who were from an old prominent Irish Catholic family of Clifton Castle, in County Kilkenny. Educated at St. Patricks's College in Carlow, he volunteered to be part of a battalion of Irish being raised in response to a call by Pope Pius IX to defend the Papal States. He served in the Papal Forces in the Battalion of St. Patrick at the defense of Ancona, and after it collapsed was recruited as a 2nd Lieutenant in the 46 member Company of St.Patrick, stationed in the Vatican State. By early 1862, he and several other officers had become disillusioned with the priestly officials who administered the temporal powers of the state. In March 1862, they resigned their commissions and returned to England where they booked passage to the United States. Once in Washington, they presented letters of recommendations to Secretaries Seward and Stanton that they had procured from pro-Union American Arch-Bishops in Rome. In April, Keogh was commissioned as captain and assigned to the staff of Irish born General James Shields, a politician and Mexican War veteran. After Shields defeat by Stonewall Jackson, in the Shenandoah Valley in June, Keogh was reassigned to a new cavalry brigade under General John Buford. After seeing action at the Second Battle of Bull Run, he was seconded from Buford's staff to General McClellan's where he met another staff officer, Captain George Armstrong Custer. After the Battles of Antietam, and Fredericksburg, Keogh reverted back to Buford's staff, and in the spring of 1863 he participated in the Chancellorsville Campaign, and when General Alfred Pleasanton took over as commander of the Cavalry Corps, was in the thick of the fighting at the cavalry Battle of Brandy Station. In June and July he participated in Buford's action delaying the Confederates on the first day of the Battle of Gettysburg for which he was brevetted as major in the Regular Army. After Buford's death from typhoid in Dec. 1863, Keogh joined General George Stoneman's staff in January. He served with Stoneman in the Army of the West, for the remainder of the war and participated in numerous cavalry skirmishes. He was with him when they were captured near Macon, Georgia, in August 1864. After being imprisoned, in Charleston, South Carolina for two months they were exchanged and returned to the Western Theater. Keogh finished the war with the silver oak leaves of a Brevet Lt. Colonel, having participated in over 30 engagements. He remained on Stoneman's staff in the Department of Tennessee until mid-1866. In July he was appointed as a captain in the new 7th Cavalry Regiment. Assigned to command Company I, he was stationed at Fort Wallace, Kansas during the Hancock Expedition of 1867. His comments about the pursuit of the Cheyenne and Sioux during this time were:

"I have concluded that without knowing exactly where to surprise their camp, or having a guide who can track then on the run, it is a complete waste of horse flesh and time to endeavor to come up with them!"

At the beginning of 1868 he was on leave back east, in Boston, when he slipped on ice and broke his right leg, rupturing the ligaments in his ankle also. He didn't return to duty until that summer. He was then assigned to General Alfred Sully's staff, on detached duty, so was not with the regiment for the winter campaign that resulted in the Washita Battle. He severely sprained his left knee during this time. After briefly resuming command of Company I in June of 1869, he was then appointed to serve on a court martial board. That August, he was granted a four and a half month leave to visit his home in Ireland. He was able to extend that leave to seek medical advice from a specialist in France about his knee, which was still not healed. He didn't rejoin his command until August 1870, first at Ft. Leavenworth, then at Fort Hays. This was the first time that he was stationed at the same post as the Custer's. That following February, he went on leave to New York, then reported for duty at Company I's new station in Baghdad, Ky. where it had been ordered for Reconstruction Duty and was posted at various stations around Kentucky for the next year and a half. Keogh also spent time on various court martial boards, in the Louisville area. In March 1873, he and Company I were ordered to Fort Snelling, Minnesota to join the US Boundary Commission escort, along with Capt. Weir and Company D.

****

Jake and the troopers in his section were lounging around their campfire, drinking coffee and jawing, when he heard the wagon load of boisterous officers roll out towards the river crossing.

"Sounds like they're all havin' a good time." commented Charlie Welch.

"Yep, I'll bet they got more in more in their cups than we do." said Smiley, "Probably some of that Scottish whiskey that I've heard the Brits are bragging about. Is that stuff worth drinking, Henry?"

"There's many types of Scotch whisky, Smiley. The few I've tasted were pretty smooth. I think it's all a matter of personal preference" Holden replied.

"Those Canadian boys seem to be quite proud of their Club whiskey, too." said Charlie.

"Well, I bet they can't hold a candle to genuine sour mash Kentucky bourbon." stated Jimmy Hurd, "Ain't that right Stiff?"

"Cain't see how. They ain't got our good water and charred American white oak barrels."

"Not to mention that sweet Kentucky corn for the mash." Billy Harris said in agreement.

"I heard those Company I boys brought along a good supply of bourbon when they left Louisville." George Scott added.

Golden jumped into the conversation, "Now if you Boyos want to talk about good whiskey, you need to talk to an Irish lad like myself. 'The Breath of Life' it is! I'm sure our Irish sergeants have some stashed in one of the supply wagons."

Elwyn Reid, not to be left out, said, "I was raised on rye whiskey back in New York. There's a man's drink."

"Well, now! Here's a thought! It seems that we have a whiskey competition, and chances are that we are in unique situation to be able to procure some of each." Henry said. "What say we pool our resources, nose around and see if we can buy or trade for these whiskeys. We have a couple of months out here and I'm sure that if everyone in the section helps, we can get this done."

This was met with general enthusiasm, and they all nodded their heads in agreement.

"I suggest that we designate a responsible individual to be in charge of the whiskey until the whole section will be able to share it. We'll need to find a secure place to store the whisky." Henry added.

By unanimous vote, Holden was nominated and the rest of the evening was dominated by discussions comparing the merits of the different spirits. Finally, they all decided to call it a quits and headed off to bed. It was a warm pleasant evening, so Jake grabbed his bedroll and lay down propping his head on his saddle.

"Charlie," Jake called softly, "I think I'll just sleep out here. See you in the morning."

He lay gazing up at the stars, and eventually drifted off listening to the camp sounds, and an occasional burst of laughter and singing, wafting faintly from across the river.

The following morning, after stable call, Major Reno and Lt. Porter walked over to the Boundary Commission camp. They returned an hour or so later and Porter put out the word for all of the officers and senior NCOs to report to the Headquarters tent. After everyone gathered Reno addressed the group.

"I've made my decision concerning our escort responsibilities. I spoke with the Commissioner, and I told him that since the British have sent their Capt. Anderson and his so called '49th Rangers' out to blaze a trail, I see no reason to assign an advance party to their teams. Major Twining and Capt. Gregory each have observation teams and we will attach four man details with them. They already have Capt. Harbach's infantrymen with them to provide security. We will rotate them out, when we escort the resupply wagons to the next sub-depots."

"What about Lt. Greene's topographical teams?" Keogh asked. "The current dispositions are good for keeping the men occupied. With two full companies we have plenty of troops to support the surveyors."

"I see no reason for us to use any of our men and horses to supplement the civilian surveyors. They are being well paid to do that job." Reno replied. "We can use the men to cut wood and improve the camp. Plus, we can insure that the mounts are cared for properly, and not overworked. We are cavalry after all. Our primary responsibility is to be prepared to act as such in the event of hostile actions." Reno said in a condescending manner.

This statement, in combination with the tone it was delivered in, caused Weir to quickly glance over at his fellow company commander. But Keogh just looked calmly at Reno and stated.

"I'm gratified that the Major has confirmed that I've not been operating under false pretenses for the last eleven years. If you'll pardon me, sir I will instruct my 1st Sgt. to coordinate the Major's plan with his counterpart 1st Sgt. Martin and report back to myself, Capt. Weir, and Lt. Porter. I'm sure the Commissioner will appreciate a prompt report showing our troop dispositions."

"Very well Captain, as my adjutant, Lt. Bell will act as liaison with the Commissioner and see that he's kept current. Capt. Weir, be sure to assign Lt. Bell a work detail for camp improvements. I intend to make this our base of operations. We may as well be comfortable while we're here. The Brits will be moving on tomorrow. Which is just as well. Having their camp in this close proximity could lead to discipline issues, if last night was any indication. Carry on gentlemen."

They all came to attention and saluted as Reno left the tent.

"Well, let's get to it." said Weir, "Sgt. Martin, make sure Lt. Bell get's what he needs. Work out an equitable rotation, but stay flexible. The situation may change as the survey gets farther west."

Sgt. Morse held a platoon call and informed the men about the escort arrangements.

"I don't particularly care who goes out and who stays here. You either want to stay around camp, or not. I'm asking for volunteers to go out with the surveyors. I have no idea what you'll do all day, but you'll be out for two weeks then probably back to camp here."

Jake looked at Charlie, and the Georges, raising his eyebrows in question. They all nodded.

He raised his hand and said, "Sgt. Morse, my set volunteers. We've been pulling more than our share of work details, and we need to get a little experience out in the field. This looks like a good opportunity."

Morse looked at Jake appraisingly, "Okay if you're sure? Get with me in the morning and we'll go see with Sgt. Ryan. You'll draw rations, extra ammunition, and forage. Then report to Lt. Bell and he will arrange for them to be hauled on one of survey supply wagons."

Later that day, at afternoon stable call, Jake was currying Ajax when Vincent Charlie walked up. Vincent, who was Swiss, had been with the company for a two and a half years and had recently been appointed as company farrier.

"Der Sarge vants me to look at look at da shoes on da horses going tomorrow." he said.

"That's good." replied Jake, "I think mine are okay, but I'd appreciate you checking them out anyway."

"Yah, yah, best be sure that dey are gutt to go"

While Vince was inspecting Ajax, Jake called to Charlie, and the two Georges. "I was thinking that after chow we might wander over and introduce ourselves to the survey party. What do you think?"

"Sounds good to me. A guy from I Company told me the civilians are pretty friendly, and they have whiskey." Big George replied grinning.

"I don't know about the rest of you, but I'm going to go take a bath in the river and wash out all my clothes. No telling when we'll have clean water like this again." Charlie announced, "And judging by my nose, all of you could stand too, also. Particularly if we're going over there tonight!"

The American survey team was headed up by Major William J. Twining, who graduated from West Point in 1863. A veteran of several major Civil War battles and an accomplished engineer, he had made an extensive reconnaissance of the northern Dakota Territory back in 1869. His civilian assistant aptly named, Lewis Boss, was in charge of the non-military members of the Boundary Commission survey party. There were two Astrological Observation teams, one headed by Twining, the other by Captain James F. Gregory, a 1865 graduate of West Point who had spent several years surveying the Great Lakes. The tangent team was led by Lt. Francis V. Greene, a great nephew of General Nathaniel Greene of Revolutionary War fame. He graduated from West Point at the head of his class in 1870. He was commissioned as a 2nd Lieutenant in the 4th Artillery, but transferred to the Corps of Engineers in 1872. This was his first engineering assignment. The tangent teams ran a line at right angles from the meridian, and continued in a straight line marking their progress at three mile intervals. He also organized two topographical parties under Charles L. Doolittle and Alfred Downing. They were responsible for mapping a six mile belt south of the parallel. Lt. Greene's teams contained the most manpower, and had a large supply train with mules, horses, and beef cattle. By the time they reached Camp Terry, the survey teams had become very proficient. They averaged about five miles a day, only pausing long enough to wait on an Observation team to determine the latitude. As they moved west they worked out a system of alternating stations with the British. This meant that the survey teams from both sides met up on the trail several times a month. The British teams being made up of armed Royal Engineers seemed unconcerned about encountering any tribes.

The next morning Jake and his men were saddling their mounts and securing their gear when Sgt. Morse came to get them.

"Good morning lads! I heard you went over to meet the survey team last night."

Jake replied. "Yeh, we did Sarge. They were friendly enough. I think that they are happy to see that we're going along with them, although I sensed that they were expecting more of us."

"Well, I expect that they will get their wish before too long. Rumor has it that the Commissioner is not pleased with our Major's decision to piecemeal out his men. I reckon that you'll be seeing me, and the rest of the platoon, out west, before the season is done." stated Morse. "Let's go get with Lt. Porter and he can officially take us over to the Survey team. Then we can see what we need to do about forage for your horses."

After finding Lt. Porter, he led them over to where the Survey team was assembling. There were over 100 men, including twelve soldiers from Company K, 20th Infantry, and 140 animals in the party. The two dozen wagons were drawn by mules. They had also acquired a couple of the 'Red River' two-wheel horse drawn carts from the Métis traders. Commissioner Campbell was talking to Major Twining and Capt. Gregory when the cavalrymen road up. Twining was a tall slender man with a narrow face, thin mustache and long chin beard. Gregory was also tall, but a bit heavier. He wore a light grey Stetson hat and had a prominent hooked nose above a full mustache and bushy beard. He, like everyone else in the Survey teams, was dressed in plain civilian clothes. Campbell looked at Lt. Porter and said.

"I see that Major Reno didn't come over to see our teams off. It's a shame, I wanted to thank him, in person, for the generous escort he has provided."

"I'll be sure to convey your gratitude to him, Sir." replied Porter with chagrined look.

"It's not your fault, Lieutenant. I'm sure Major Twining and his men will appreciate having these men along"

"Indeed, sir!" said Twining, "I'll have Mr. Boss find a wagon that they can put their supplies in. Which of these men is in charge of the detail, Lt. Porter?"

Porter looked over at Sgt. Morse, who nodded his head towards at Jake.

"Private Rogers is the No. 1 of his set of four, Sir."

Jake sat up straight and saluted. "Sir!"

Twining looked up at him. "Very well, Private. I intend for you men to be out front behind our guide. Capt. Gregory, here, will introduce you. Carry on." He said returning the salute.

Gregory, motioned for them to follow him. As he did he asked, "Tell me Rogers. How did you get picked for this detail?"

"We volunteered, Sir."

"Indeed, and why did you?"

"We were tired of work details, Sir, and wanted to see some new country."

"Well, you're in the right place. The country west of here has not been well mapped. It's just home to Indians and wildlife, I'm told that there are many different tribes. Our guide is half Irish and half Indian, his name is Val Wheeler. He speaks English and French, plus over half a dozen Indian languages. He's been pretty useful so far, and gets on well with the Brits' Métis scouts, who are out ahead of us blazing a trail along the Boundary line. My intent is to use your men to ride near him and to quickly notify us if anything comes up."

They worked their way along the forming wagon train until they got to the front. Several men were gathered around the back of the lead wagon watching as two others were looking at a map. One of them wore a wool hat with a crumpled crown, and narrow brim. He was tall, clean shaven, and much younger than the other, who was pointing at the map and making gestures towards the west.

"Dammit Lootenant! We need to get moving! We've got good weather and the trail looks to be good this week. But, when we get to the Great Coteau it'll change. That's when water and wood will become scarce. Capt. Anderson went ahead to cut wood supplies for us and set up a sub-depot about halfway across. Once we drop off the Major, we need to take all the water casks and a couple of extra wagons to haul wood."

The speaker was dressed in pants, cut off at the knees and tucked into Indian moccasin leggings. He had a breech cloth held up by a belt decorated with beads and brass around his waist, a gray flannel shirt, and an antelope hide vest adorned with beads and embossed designs. His black hair was in braids, wrapped with ribbons, and topped off by dark slouch hat with hawk feathers sticking out of an embroidered hatband. He looked to be in his early thirties, clean shaven, with pale grey eyes in contrast with his weathered complexion

The man with the map nodded his head in agreement, then looking over towards Jake and Capt. Gregory, he said, "It appears we can go now, Val. Our cavalry escort is here."

"Lt. Greene, Mr. Wheeler, this is Private Rogers and his men. Major Twining wants them up here with you." Gregory stated.

Wheeler looked at the troopers with a sardonic smile and said, "Well, I don't know what the hell for. These boys look greener than you,

Lootenant. They stumble around, I'll leave 'em for you to collect."

Greene grinned and said. "You men will find out that Val, here, likes to bark. But I figure that we'll do okay, glad to have you along, men. We're just about to get rolling. I'm in charge of running the tangent and the topographic teams. We'll be surveying out to six miles south of the parallel as we go. We're headed out to the next observation station, where the Major will set up shop, then Capt. Gregory will move on to pass the Brits. I'm sure we'll find something useful for you to do along the way."

As Wheeler walked away, Greene said quietly to Jake, " I'm told that Mr. Wheeler is quite knowledgeable about the area that where we're headed. He was raised out there, so he knows the route well. He came highly recommended by Mr. Hallet, who commands the 49th Rangers."

CHAPTER 6

Des Lacs River- 237 Miles West, Aug. 7, 1873

The entire American Boundary Survey Team was encamped along the river. Major Twining was setting his observation tents, while Captain Gregory and his men were preparing to move out in the morning to leapfrog the Brits, and go on to the next station point selected by British Capt. Anderson and his Métis troops, approximately 271 miles west of the Red River. It was decided that Jake and his men would stay with Gregory. Lt. Greene would keep moving west until he met up with the Brits, then bypass them and catch up with Gregory. The civilians had large tents and starting the first night out, they had invited the D Company troopers to share them. They also invited them to share their meals, which was a quite a bonus.

That evening, as they were caring for their mounts, Jake and the men were talking about the journey so far.

"I'm thinking that this ain't such a bad deal." Little George opined. "These guys are real nice to us."

"Yeh," Big George said, "Several of them are from our part of the country, New Yorkers, Rhode Islanders, and a few Boston lads."

"And we don't have any work details." Charlie added.

"I'm thinking that I'm going to talk to Capt. Gregory and see if there's anything we can help out with." said Jake. "It won't hurt to ask. Maybe we'll get to rotate back again?"

"I overheard Mr. Boss talking with some men that are going on with Capt. Gregory, too. He said that it would probably be the end of the month before we all were together again." Charlie stated. "It don't sound like we'll be headed back to the rest of the Company in two weeks, to me."

"Hey, we just take orders from Capt. Gregory now." said Jake. "I don't reckon that we can get in trouble for following orders. Besides, I like it out here."

The next morning, Jake approached Capt. Gregory about helping out. Gregory looked at Jake appraisingly and said. "I really would prefer to send you with Lt. Greene and his team. They could use the help with their topographic mission. He could use help in identifying terrain features. It's not really escort duty, though."

"What ever you think is best, Sir." Jake replied.

"Excellent, go give my compliments to the lieutenant, and let him know you're to accompany him."

"Yes, Sir! Thank You, Sir."

Greene and Val Wheeler were just getting ready to mount as Jake and the men rode over. Wheeler had a spirited pinto pony, with a simple padded saddle made from buffalo hide with no cantle, or pommel. It had open stirrups and bright, fringed beadwork for decorations. He was adjusting it and securing his kit. He carried a Henry lever action repeating rifle, lavishly adorned with brass tacks, in an equally decorated buffalo hide scabbard. On seeing them approach he exclaimed. "Oh Hell! Don't tell me I gotta put up with you soldier fellas, agin!"

Jake, who had warmed up to the guide over the past few days said. "We'll try not to slow you up, Val. Captain Gregory sent us over to help out with Lt. Greene's team. I'm sure the lieutenant will keep us busy so that we're not in your way. We can wave flags, or something."

"Hmmph, I reckon you'll still find a way to get underfoot. Say, I don't suppose any of you boys got some extra tobaccy?"

"No, sorry."

"Shit, I figured." Val said, then mounted and rode away.

Greene grinned as he watched Wheeler. Then asked, "So Gregory is giving you to me. That's good, we can use extra help. Any of you ever been around surveying before?" he asked.

They all shook their heads.

"Well, the first thing we need to teach you is how to read a compass. It's not hard and believe me it's useful to know out here. We'll start your lessons tonight. For right now, we'll just show you the spots where we need you to ride out to."

That night after supper, Greene gathered the troopers around him to explain rudiments of surveying to them.

He held up an instrument and stated. "This is called a transit. We mount it on this tripod and use it, and a compass, to determine an azimuth."

Noting the quizzical expressions on a their faces, he explained. "There are 360 degrees in a circle." He then held up a tin plate. "Pretend this plate is full of pie and you want to cut it into four equal size pieces. You cut top to bottom, and side to side. The top cut is North and the bottom is South. The line is called a meridian. The sides are East and West, this line is called a parallel. Each piece is 90 degrees. A compass is the same way, but each piece has 90 cuts." He held up a compass to show them then slowly rotated in place, then stopped. "Now it's pointing North. Private Welch come stand here." Charlie got up and did as directed. "You"re 0 degrees," Greene did an about face, and stepped off six paces, "Private Dann come stand here, you're at 180 degrees." Big stepped over and stood. Greene did another about face and stepped off three paces, then stopped, did a left face and paced off three more steps and stopped. "Private Rogers you come stand here, you're at 270 degrees." Jake did. Greene then stepped off six paces and motioned for Little George to come to him, "You're 90 degrees." Then he performed another about face and returned three paces to the middle. "Men, we are now a compass!" He placed the transit on a tripod where he'd been standing. Peering through the telescopic tube he sited on a tree a few yards away, between Jake and Charlie. Noting the markings on the transit, he said, "I've just shot an azimuth to that tree over there. It is at 315 degrees." He paced off to the tree and announced. "14 paces!" He drew his belt knife and cut a mark on the tree. Returning to the transit, he said he stuck his knife in the ground directly beneath it. "Each of you mark your spot, and then come back over here."

He took down the transit, then called over to where some of his surveyors were gathered. "Mr. Downing, could you come assist me for a few minutes?"

The man came walking over and asked, "What can you do for you, Lieutenant?"

Greene handed him a piece of paper, and a compass. "Stand right here above my knife. Would you please tell me what you make of these numbers?"

Downing looked at the paper then brought the compass up and peered through the aperture, then rotated slightly to his left. He then stepped off fourteen paces arriving at the marked tree. "I'd say you wanted me to find the blaze on this tree."

"Just so! Thank you, Al. That's all I needed." Turning to the soldiers he said. "That's a brief example of what you'll be doing. The observation team marks the spot on the Parallel, and we go directly west, marking the distance with a survey chain. The man running the transit makes sure we stay on a true 270 degree azimuth. Every three miles we will mark a spot by building a mound, or driving a metal post. Along the way we then use another transit to identify hills, streams, and other terrain features on our side of the border to the south. What the elevations are, and how far they are in relation to the parallel, can be measured and calculated. There's a lot of mathematics, and some magnetic adjustments to be considered to fine tune the process. But that's basically what this whole expedition is about."

"So, besides marking the border with Canada, you're making a map!" stated Jake.

"Yes!" Greene replied. "And the Brits are as well, over on their side."

The next day, Capt. Gregory and his team left, with Val Wheeler as guide. They were headed west another 40 or so miles, to set up another observation station. Greene and his teams were to work their way along the parallel until they came up on Capt. Featherstonhaugh at his station at 255 miles west. Then move on to link up again with Gregory. For the next two weeks, the daily routine didn't vary much. Rising early, Jake and the others cared for their horses, ate the hearty breakfasts the cook wagon served up, then mounted up and spent the day riding to and from the various terrain features that the topography team directed them to. They put in long days and were grateful when they made it back to camp, and only had to worry about taking care of their horses. The surveyors were glad to share their food, which was much better than typical Army rations. They saw a lot of wildlife as they moved across the plains. The weather remained pleasant for the most part, except for occasional rains. As they moved farther west they could see an escarpment rising off to the south, and angling towards them out front to the west.

"Looks like our easy days of flat prairie are about to run out, Lieutenant." remarked Charles Doolittle, who ran one of the topographic teams."

"Yes, that is the Missouri Plateau, or as our British friends call it, the Great Coteau. It rises abruptly 2-300 feet. We'll have to cross it eventually. Captain Anderson and his men told us about it when he was reviewing his last reconnaissance with us. He has set up a camp just ahead of us at 260 miles west, where the commissioners are going to meet again. He's also laid in wood supplies. He is also establishing a station, and a sub-depot, at 289 miles west just at the edge of it. We will catch up with Capt. Gregory before we get to it, at the 271 mile west station towards the end of the month."

"Well, it looks pretty rugged from here." Doolittle replied, "That's going to slow our pace a bit."

"It's supposed to be better going once you get on top. Short grass prairie, but very few trees, and water will be scarce. We'll have Val Wheeler to guide us across at that point."

They came up on the Brits at the camp they were calling 'Wood End' at 260 miles west. There was a creek there with good water, but west of the creek there was only prairie. Major Twining's party was also there. Twining decided to stay on at Wood End to await the arrival of the Commissioners, and had tasked Gregory with completing the rest of the observations. Capt. Gregory had already gone forward to the 271 mile west observation station. Twining assigned several of his party to help Lt. Greene, and also sent along the Company I troopers. They spent a couple days there while reorganizing the wagons to carry more forage, wood, and some water casks. Finally ready, they set out on the trail followed by Gregory's team and also the British team of Lt. Galway. The topographic teams benefitted from the extra manpower, and they pushed right along catching with Gregory towards the end of the month. The Mouse River looped back across the 49th Parallel once again. As they were working their way across a creek that flowed into it, they came across large seams of soft brown rock that Lt. Greene declared was lignite coal and had them collect some samples. They experimented with burning it in their campfires, and he was quite pleased at the result, noting it in his journal. They took along several bags of it in one of the wagons. Continuing on they came to the 289 mile station where the British had their sub-depot at the edge of the of the Plateau. They paused there to replenish their water and forage.

That afternoon a column of cavalry rode in from Camp Terry. At its head was Sgt. Morse, followed by Henry Holden and the rest of the section. Cpl. George Wylie and the rest of the platoon from Company D were also with them. Their arrival caused quite a stir, and most of the survey teams assembled to watch as the soldiers came to a halt and dismounted. Lt.Greene who had stood watching their ride up, strode over to them. Sgt. Morse saluted him and said.

"Reporting for Escort duty, Sir! Major Reno's compliments!"

"Sgt. Morse, I'm surprised. To what do we owe the pleasure of your company?" replied Greene.

"A courier from Fort Stevenson, arrived at Camp Terry several days ago. It seems Custer was attacked twice by the Sioux, early in August along the Yellowstone. He sent a couple of scouts to Fort Benton carrying dispatches. When General Terry was notified, he had orders dispatched to Major Reno to strengthen our escort parties. So here we are, Sir."

"Well, you're welcome, but probably unnecessary, Sergeant. We've not encountered any Indians, although the Brits have met a few. None have inclined to show any hostility that I'm aware of."

"That's good to hear. I heard that both Commissioners are meeting at the encampment at Wood End. I suspect he sent us ahead to make sure the trail was clear. At any rate, we were tired of sitting on our asses."

"Go ahead and set up camp. Sorry we don't have enough accommodations for all of you. We're headed out tomorrow. Come over to my tent when you're settled in and I'll brief you on where we're headed."

Jake and his troopers were standing over to the side watching. When Sgt. Morse spotted them he said. "I see you still have Private Rogers and his set. I trust that they have behaved, Sir."

"Indeed they have, Sergeant. I suppose you'll want them back, now?"

Morse grinned and replied. "Yes, Sir!"

"Very well, Sergeant. We'll see you in a while." Greene turned around and walked back towards the camp.

Morse waved over to Jake, "You lads bring along your kits. I suspect you've been spoiled by these kindly civilians."

Jake and his cohorts gathered up their gear and led their horses over to where Morse and the platoon were pitching their tents. Holden had saved them a spot. Big George gathered the leads of the horses, and took them over to the picket line, while the others began sorting out the A tents.

Welch, who had been bitching since he first saw Sgt. Morse and the troopers approaching continued. "God damn it! Just our luck, to have you boys show up and screw up our cozy arrangements, there goes our roomy tent and hot cooked meals."

"Sure now Charlie! Ya know you missed us." Goldie said grinning. "If it makes you feel any better, we brought along some of our cached goodies. Sgt. Morse made sure we had enough wagons to haul extra forage and rations. We may even have a bottle, or two, to share out."

"What did you do after we left?"

"Guard details and cut wood mostly. The officers spend most of their days out hunting, and then partying in the evenings. The Commissioner and his people stayed to themselves pretty much. Hurry and Biscuit found a good spot to catch enough fish to feed us a couple of times. We got Cookie to fry them up for us. They even traded some to the civilians for some whisky."

They finished getting settled in, and after chow, Jake and his cohorts, regaled the latecomers with their hard gained surveying expertise. Explaining in detail, their daily activities and how friendly the surveyors were.

"Henry, what do you make of this news about the Sioux and Custer?" Jake asked.

"Hard to say, Jake. I just was glad to get away and head west. Have you lads had any encounters?"

"Not many. and mostly from a distance. The guide for the surveyors is half Indian and Irish, his name is Val Wheeler and he was raised out here. He goes off to talk with them, and they move on."

Jake suddenly remembered something and called over to where the Kentuckians of Jimmy Hurd's set were sitting. "Hey, any of you boys got any tobacco that I can buy or trade you out of?"

Stivers answered, "Depends on what you got to swap. You're lucky the post trader from Stevenson sent a couple of wagons up to Camp Terry before we left. We got plenty."

Jake said, "How about some fresh pie? We stumbled upon a thicket of ripe chokeberries couple of days ago. We gathered up quite a few and took them to the cook wagon, over there. He's making pies out of them right now. I'm sure that I can go talk him out of a couple."

"Well, now, we just might be able to work something out." Stiff replied.

Sgt. Morse and Cpl. Wylie walked up and Morse said. "Rogers, I want you to go with us to meet with Lt. Greene, since you know everyone over there."

"Sure thing Sarge!" Jake said, the looked back at Stiff, grinning. "I'll be back with my trade goods. Make sure we got some fresh coffee."

Stiff grinned back and nodded his head in reply.

When they got to Greene's tent, Jake was surprised to see Val, who had been guiding Capt. Gregory's team. He grinned at Wheeler and said. "Good to see you back, Val."

"The Captain sent me back to nursemaid this lot across the Coteau." he groused, "Not much out there but grass, water is scarce, too. I see you found more soldiers."

"This is my Platoon Sergeant, Pat Morse. Sarge, this is Val Wheeler, the guide for the Surveyors, I've been told that his father was an Irishman."

"Was he now?" Morse queried, "Then I'm quite sure that Mr. Wheeler is going to point us in the right direction. This is Cpl. Wylie, another son of the Old Sod. Tis our pleasure to meet you, sir."

Wheeler looked up at Pat appraisingly, and said after a pause. "You carry you self well, Sergeant. I think you are not so green as these others."

"Yes, I've been a soldier for a dozen years, or better. Spent a lot of time in the saddle on the plains of the Cheyenne and Arapaho tribes. Met some Sioux also"

"The Arapaho and Cheyenne are our cousins." stated Val, "However, the Sioux are not well liked by my mother's people, or by me." stated Val.

"Can't say that I care much for them, either. Mean sons o' bitches. They killed a friend of mine and butchered his corpse. Not a memory that I like ta dwell on."

"They are a proud people. They revere the old ways. They haven't accepted that their way of life is ending. White men are coming from the east and west, pushing other tribes before them. They have no idea of the power that is causing that. The power that soldiers like you can summon. I have seen it, though!"

Lt. Greene, who was working at his field desk, finished up his writing and stood. "Sgt. Morse, thanks for coming. Would you care to share a bit of this fine whisky that I was able to procure from our British friends before we left the Wood End depot? I believe it's Scottish in origin, but still Gaelic."

"Indeed, Sir! It would be a pleasure. Good whiskey is a scarce commodity out this far. It would be foolish of me to decline your generous offer." replied Morse.

"Well spoken! Your corporal and Pvt. Rogers are included also, if they'd like."

Jake was quite surprised by the young officer's offer. He could tell Wylie was too. But Greene had shown a relaxed attitude about military etiquette. Perhaps because most of the people he was surrounded by were civilians. Greene had a couple of camp chairs, and several chests, in his tent.

'Gentlemen, please find a seat." said Greene. Then, after handing out small glasses from inside a small, polished wood case, he proceeded to serve each of them with a generous dollop.

"A toast!" He announced, "To continuing good weather and good fortune!"

A chorus of "Aye, Sir!"followed.

They all raised their glasses and Jake peaked over at Greene as he took a sip. His only experience with whiskey was confined to the cheap sutler's variety and some moonshine back home. He slipped it slowly, not wanting to cough, and let it seep down his throat. It was surprisingly smooth. Looking around he saw that the others reactions were similar.

"My, my!" exclaimed Morse. "You can indulge me with that any time you'd like, Lieutenant. That's as good as I've ever had, and believe me I've had many a taste."

"Splendid," replied Greene, "I'll make sure to see if I can lay hands on some more. Now, let me get the maps and sketches that Capt. Anderson left with me. We can go over the route and Val can let us know what to expect. But before I do, I need to know how you propose to utilize your men. Do you intend for them to be strictly escorts, or will you allow me to use some of them as flagmen, the way that Private Rogers and his men did. I want to say that they were extremely useful, and volunteered as well."

"You know what Major Reno's opinion on that is, sir."

"Oh, he made that perfectly clear, Sergeant."

"Of course, my understanding is that he will not leave the vicinity of Camp Terry unless hostiles threaten?" said Morse, "So, some of my troopers can escort the survey parties as they go about their work, and scout ahead and around them. I see no reason that they couldn't carry flags to communicate while they do. It would be most helpful if your cooks could assist us, though. That would free up all of my troopers for scouting duty. Myself, I intend to ride out front with Mr. Wheeler and the advance party."

"I believe that we could come to an accommodation on that, Sergeant. You could leave your rations in their charge. I'm sure that they can see to it that they are prepared along with our own. Particularly, once I assure them that they will be helping to expedite our mission. The equinoctial storm is due in three weeks, and we'll want to make a swift retreat. Now Mr. Wheeler, we'll be depending on you to make sure we find the few waterholes on the Coteau."

Greene rolled out a map and he, Morse and Wheeler leaned over it. Jake saw that he was not needed and carefully finished sipping his drink. After finishing his Jake stood up and said, "Begging your pardon, Sir. May I be excused? I left part of my kit in your camp. I'd like to go get it so I'll be ready to move out in the morning."

"By all means, Rogers. Go ahead."

"Thank you, Sir."

"Rogers, I'll be taking you and your lads with me out front tomorrow. You can fill me in on your activities over the last few weeks." said Morse.

Jake smiled and replied, "Yes, Sergeant."

Exiting the tent, Jake headed towards the cook wagon to see how many pies he could bargain for.

The next morning as they were preparing to move out. Jake walked over to where Wheeler was tightening his saddle.

"Here, I got some Kentucky boys in my section that are well fixed for this." He said, tossing a bag of tobacco to Val, who looked at him warily.

"What you want for it?"

"For you to give me answers when I ask you questions, and don't bullshit me."

Wheeler considered it for minute, then nodded at Jake. "Done, but that ain't much."

Jake grinned at him and said, "I didn't pay much."

They moved out following the trail. Up on the Coteau, there was an endless sea of short prairie grasses covering the low rolling hills with just a few specks of darker green vegetation. Wheeler and Sgt. Morse, with Jake and his set in tow, road out ahead. Morse motioned Jake to ride along side him.

"So what do you think, Jake? You missing Missouri, yet?" Morse asked.

"Not so much, Sarge! I'm just amazed out how big this country is."

"You can call me Pat when it's just us. And your Pa would be proud if he could see you now. You're turning into a good soldier. I reckon you'll be earning some stripes when you get some time in."

"I appreciate that, Pat, coming from you. I'm noticing that some men just seem to go through the motions. I don't quite understand that. I just want to a good job at whatever I'm doing. Seems easier to me."

"Good, that's all a man can do."

Wheeler dropped back to ride with them. "I smell smoke on the wind. Big grass fires out here this time of year, when its this dry. They can be a bitch."

"Yeh, I saw a few out in West Kansas. That can swarm you in a hurry. Had to set back fires with the wind a few times, and then follow them so close it singed your hair." stated Morse. "Jake, ride back and ask Lt. Greene to come up."

Jake turned Ajax and headed back to the main party.

"You seem to be pretty partial to young Rogers, Sergeant." Said Val.

Morse looked over at Wheeler. "I was in the War with his father. I've known Jake since he was a pup. He's a good lad. His Ma made me promise to look after him, when he left with me to join the Army."

"Yes, I think Jake will be fine. He likes it out here. Some men look at the land and see emptiness. Others see an unspoiled paradise."

"So what's your story, Wheeler?"

" My father had to flee Ireland over some troubles with his landlord and the law. He managed to dodge arrest and made it on to a ship headed to Quebec. Once he landed, he kept moving west towards Ontario. He fell in some Métis, at Ft. Garry, then spent a couple of years with them when they came west following the buffalo. He met my mother while buffalo hunting one year, out near the Milk River. She was of the Gross Ventre tribe and after he took her as a wife, he stayed there. He loved the land around there, but he always missed the green of Ireland. He always told me it was so green it hurt your eyes to look at it. He had no love for the British. My father was killed by some passing Sioux during a dispute over a horse. My mother saw to it that I was educated by a French Jesuit missionary. She stills lives near there, near Ft. Belknap with her people. I started trapping furs when I got older, and wandered down to Ft. Benton. I met a band Métis there while trading, and followed them back north. We gathered buffalo hides and meat, to trade, and eventually ended up in the Red River country near Ft. Pembina. A Métis friend told me that your government was looking for a guide. I wanted to come back out here anyway. Figured I'd make me some money while doing it. So my turn, how'd you end up a soldier?"

"I left Ireland as a boy. My Da had a brother that had left for the States and then settled out near St Louis. He wrote us to come follow him, and sent money. So, my family and another, made the journey. We landed in New York, then made it on out to my uncle's place. I worked on his farm until I joined up with the Army, early in the War. Afterwards, I didn't see myself as a farmer, so I enlisted in the 7th Cavalry. And here I still am."

Val just nodded his head. They both dismounted and waited for Greene to come up. After he did, they discussed the importance of quickly responding to a fire.

"I'd better set a rear party, and have them ready to touch off a back fire. I imagine that the wind gets up quickly out here." Greene said.

Wheeler stated, "We'll be eight or nine days on the Coteau. Best have your men try and go easy on water, and firewood. We'll get snow storms in a few weeks so better make sure your boys got coats, too. We get caught out here, we'll need to find a gully to hunker down in."

By the afternoon of the second day they found that a large fire had burnt over the prairie, and they were soon surrounded by a pitch black expanse, dotted here and there by bleached buffalo skeletons. Greene and Sgt. Morse, concerned about the lack of green fodder and water for the livestock, conferred with Wheeler who assured them that there were swampy areas up ahead where the grass was too wet to burn and that now they didn't have to worry about the threat of a prairie fire. Greene decided to keep moving straight ahead. On the fourth day, they passed the 289 mile station, observed by Galway, and marked by a large mound. The cavalrymen and the survey teams had worked out a smooth routine. Morse made sure to rotate the sets of four, to keep the mounts, and men, from getting worn down. The civilian teamsters and laborers kept everything moving, and the cooks churned out meals, and many gallons of coffee.

Four days later, now in Montana Territory, they dropped down off the Coteau and to find Gregory's Mid-Coteau, 312 mile station. Continuing on across an undulating countryside dotted with many alkaline lakes they descended into the Missouri River valley. The stream was almost dried up, and the only wood available was from stunted trees. The Brits, under Capt. Featherstonhaugh were camped there at the 338 mile station that they named 'Big Muddy', from where Lt.Rowe was running the tangent. This was their last station and they were preparing to make their way back to the east. Captain Anderson and his Rangers were returning from their fourth reconnaissance and siting the last stations. Gregory's team had moved on to the 363 mile station, while Lt. Galway headed for the Porcupine Creek station at 385 miles out. The final station would be Gregory's sited at 408 miles out at the West Polar River.

CHAPTER 7

Bully Springs - 363 Miles West, Sep. 21, 1873

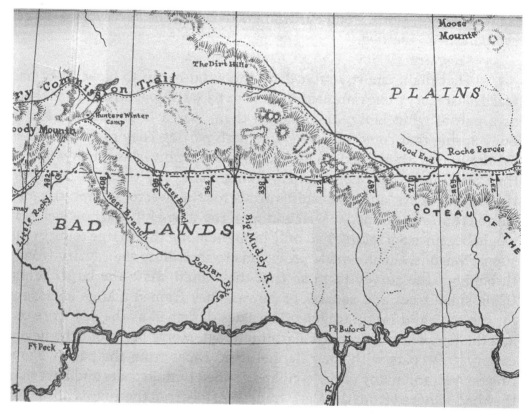

Boundary Survey - Late summer 1873

Two days earlier, they were still working their way west when they started seeing flocks of ducks and geese winging their way south in endless streams. Val Wheeler had stood gazing up at them, a look of concern on his weathered face. "That's not a good sign!" he stated.

Sgt. Morse and Lt. Greene looked over to him, and also looked up at the fleeing birds.

"Today is the 20th and last year's equinoctial storm hit on the 22nd, according to my records." said Greene."

"Out here, this time of year, winter can show up overnight. We need to be findin' us a place to hole up." said Val.

"When Captain Anderson passed us the other day, he told me that Capt. Gregory had a camp with good water, and timber, up ahead."

"Then I suggest that we head for it right away. We're close enough that we can send our people back out from there. You ain't ever tried to set up camp in a blizzard, have ya?"

"No, and I don't intend to now. I'll direct the wagons to start moving right away. Sgt. Morse, send out runners to call in the surveyors. Let's get everyone in and settled."

"Yes, Sir!"

That night, shortly after dark, the wind began to blow. They had reached Gregory's encampment in time to park the wagons and use them as a partial wind block. Fortunately, there was a large ravine next to Bully Spring that could accommodate both parties They ran picket lines for the horses, then piled up and covered with canvas as much wood as they could find. They continued working frantically the next day to to rig shelters, tents, and makeshift corrals for the livestock. Capt. Gregory elected to stay encamped to wait and see if the storm hit, and how severe it would be. Since Sgt. Morse had only brought along three large tents in his supply wagons, Greene made provisions to distribute the cavalry troops throughout the survey team so that they could share the larger tents. Using small trees and squares of canvas, they framed a large enclosure for the cook and ration wagons. The skies darkened as the day wore on, and the temperature dropped alarmingly. Sgt. Morse broke out the heavy cavalry greatcoats with their flannel lined capes from the pack wagon. Greene, Val, and many of the civilians donned buffalo coats and hats that they had acquired from the Métis traders. Aside from the guards posted to monitor the horses and livestock, everyone else huddled in the tents and shelters.They were hit initially by stinging sheets of sleet, which quickly coated any exposed surface, then heavy snow began to blanket everything. The officers and senior team members convened in one of the larger tents, huddled around a tent stove that Greene had stoked with some of his coal specimens, discussing their options. Meanwhile, Sgt. Morse, Cpl. Wylie, Holden and all of his section were settled in one tent where they had strategically secured a spot next to the cook tent. The cooks were pleased to have the soldiers as neighbors, and they were given ready access to what was the warmest place in the entire encampment. This was primarily due to Morse's timely procurement of a couple of bottles of whiskey from the head teamster, who had hidden reserves. Also, Jake had bagged a several braces of prairie chickens with a shotgun he borrowed. They were highly prized as a welcome change in diet from beef and salt pork, especially by the cooks. The few remaining chickens were protected as they were the only source of fresh eggs.

"How long you think this will last, Val?" asked Jake.

"Hard to say, it could be gone in the morning, or hang for days. We best be high tailing it back to Camp Terry, pretty damn soon, though!"

"Lt. Greene seems determined to reach farthest station on the line. I heard him and Gregory discussing it. They want to get to the West Poplar River yet, before they turn back."

"That's another 10 days, and that's after this blows over. It'll be slow going when this melts!" stated Wheeler, "You'd better caution him, Pat."

"He's a goer, I'll have to sneak up on him. I'm sure we'll be back out here again next summer. We just need to show him a stopping point. What's your take on how long we got?" asked Morse.

"Two weeks, on the outside! We get caught up on the Coteau, it would be very bad!"

"Okay, you and I will convince him. You'd best go with Gregory. He can go shoot his observation, then swing back before we can get halfway there. Then hook back up with us. They'll have all winter to make their maps and charts."

The storm lasted four days and nights, and it took several days for the trail to clear enough for them to move on. They hurried forward, as a sense of urgency was being felt by the whole party. The weather moderated a bit, but the nights were increasingly cool. As September came to an end, they were just short of the British station at 385 miles out, that they called Porcupine Creek. Lt. Galway was running the tangent line west to where Capt. Gregory had observed his last station at 408 miles out on West Poplar Creek. Gregory turned back on Sep. 30th and Galway immediately turned back upon finishing his line run to West Poplar. As they passed Greene's party, they held a quick conference. Both Gregory and Galway were low on firewood and feed for their livestock. They decided to leave immediately for the sub depot, 80 miles away, where there was a supply of oats. Greene felt he had enough supplies to push on to Porcupine Creek, then start back. He met with Wheeler and Sgt. Morse.

"Two more days and we will have completed over 400 miles from Pembina and the Red River. That's a good distance for the season. Val, since you just came back this way, if you'll accompany me, I feel you can help us move more quickly, and efficiently. I intend to travel light, no wagons, just the two wheel carts, with rations and water. We'll see if we can bag some game along the way."

Wheeler just nodded his head, in reply.

"Sgt. Morse, I'd like you to take charge of the train, and start moving east. It will be most important to protect what remains of our supplies. We'll be able to move at a quicker pace then we did crossing it on our way out. Optimistically we can make it to the sub-depot in 4 to 5 days, and gather up the last of the supplies there. At that point we will be through the worst section of the trail back. If the weather turns we have a better chance of shelter."

"I'm going to assign Cpl. Wylie, and Holden's section to go with you Lieutenant."

"Thank you Sergeant. I'll try and return them to you as soon as possible. Have them ready at first light."

"Yes, Sir!"

After Greene walked off, Morse looked over to Wheeler. "Keep him reigned in Val, two days and no more!"

The next morning Wheeler asked that Jake ride out with him. They made their way along the trail, staying just out far enough in front to pick out the easiest route. As they were cresting a low hill several deer broke from a thicket and bounded away.

"Think you can bag us some fresh meat for supper, Jake?" Challenged Wheeler. Jake quickly came to a stop and dismounted, bringing up his Spencer and cocking it with a fluid motion. He dropped to one knee and took aim at the deer as they ran away, already over hundred yards away. "Bam!" A large buck dropped in its tracks, and the rest kept running.

"Not bad, but you should have taken a smaller one. They're better eatin'."

Jake smoothly worked the lever action of his carbine, then cocked the hammer, and re-aimed. "Bam!", a smaller one fell in mid stride.

Jake stood and smiled at Val, "There you go, you can dress that one."

Lt. Greene came galloping up from the survey party.

"That was some good shooting, Rogers, I'm impressed. We'll eat well tonight." said Greene, as he pulled up.

"Not bad, for a soldier boy, I would've got them myself, but I wanted to see if he could hit anything. Won't be that easy if we run into some buffalo. You'll want something with a little more punch to drop one of them. A big Sharps rifle is the ticket for that." Val said.

"Indeed!" commented Greene. "I'll bear that in mind. Although we haven't come across any live ones so far."

"It's too late in the year, they come across the Coteau in the spring following the green grass. They're way west of here, right now, in the river valleys. The best time to hunt them is in the late fall. That's when the hides make the best robes. The buffalo have their fresh winter coats, and they aren't caked with mud and bleached out by the sun."

"You used to hunt them?"

"I did when I was younger, but not any more. The buffalo used to be everywhere. Now they come and go with the seasons. Sgt. Morse told me that down in Kansas they are being slaughtered by the thousands, and that he's seen whole train loads of hides and bones carried back to the East."

"Sounds kind of like our passenger pigeons back home." Jake said, "Just in the last few years we've seen fewer and fewer of them every season. I remember seeing people killing them by the hundreds and filling barrels as the birds came through in the fall."

"The deadliest killer in nature is man. When I was at West Point, they taught us that most wild animals only know one way to kill. While, as men we have invented innumerable ways." Greene said solemnly.

"That's what the roaming tribes out here don't understand. Traditions that have allowed them to survive out here for generations, will not protect them as your people keep pressing." said Val, "You are making a line across the land that you call a boundary, but they still think of that land as theirs. The Great White Father, and the Queen Mother are like spirits to them. But, the land is the land, it has always been there."

"But there's so much of it. It seems like there should be room for everyone," Jake said.

"You two are young! Too young to understand the power of greed. But you will learn. Now enough talk! Come let us go gather the food that the spirits, and Jake's good shooting, have allowed us."

After finally making it to the British 385 mile west station, Greene immediately reversed course and hurried east on Oct. 3rd. With only the two Red River carts they were able to overtake the rest of the survey party, before they reached the sub-depot. They took what little feed that remained there and pressed on. It was a desolate landscape, now covered by patches of snow in the low lying areas. Reduced to half rations for the livestock, they had to slow the pace. Finally on Oct. 13th, they rolled into Camp Terry where Greene was given a letter from Major Twining advising him that the rest of the Boundary Team members, and Capt. Harbach's infantry had departed for Ft. Totten two days earlier. Greene was also to head for Ft. Totten and join them. 1st. Sgt. Martin rode over to meet them and sought out Morse.

"Pat, good to see you back. Thought I'd come give you a heads up. Major Reno is in a tizzy. Seems his mother-in-law passed, but before he can head back east, he's been ordered to place us in winter quarters at Ft. Totten. But we have to return the wagon train and teamsters to Ft. Stevenson first. You'd best get your lads to sort out their kits if they're mixed up with the surveyors. We're leaving at first light."

"Well, aren't you full of good news. Why can't we stay with Lt. Greene, he's going to Totten? We really need to rest our horses for at least a day. I'm afraid we couldn't stay up with the command, if we don't"

Martin eyed the platoon's mounts and looked back at Morse. "I can see that. Okay, I'll let the captain know, but he's liable to catch hell from Reno. How are you fixed for rations?"

"No problem there, Top! These civilians have been very generous, and they eat better than we do. I see there's plenty of fodder left here so don't worry about us. I'll see you at Totten. Hell, I may even get there before you."

"Okay Pat, get your men settled, I have some mail for them, then come see me and we'll talk to Weir. I've got a bottle of that Club whiskey, that the Canadians are so proud of that needs drinking. I imagine it was a bit dry out there."

"Just a bit, but not totally, Lt. Greene is very resourceful for such a young officer," Morse said grinning.

"Well, except for escorting supply trains now and then, we've done diddly squat! The officers have had a relaxing camping and hunting trip. Their mess was the social hotspot and no lack for fresh game for the table. And the sutler out of Ft. Stevenson did quite well on his liquor sales, I'd warrant. You should have stayed put with us, instead of volunteering to babysit the Boundary Teams."

"Well now, then I wouldn't have learned so much about surveying. It might be a trade I could make a living at when I'm done soldiering."

"Hmm, well you'll have all winter to explain it to me. See you in a while, Pat. I'm off to let Weir know what we've decided. He won't be happy, but he'll back us. Reno would have left already, but he had to make sure Greene made it back."

When Morse passed out the mail, Jake received several letters from his mother. She wrote mostly about things and people back home. School was just starting up after the harvest, when she wrote them. His friend,

Colleen, was going to be helping out with the students. The men were all getting ready for the fall deer hunt. His friend Frank was talking about trying to get a job working for the railroad, over in Springfield. All in all, life back home seemed pretty much the same as when he left. She wanted Jake to try writing more often, worried about him, and prayed for him. She wondered if there was anything he needed, and she was knitting him a winter scarf and his father assured her that army blue would be suitable. He also told her that Jake was probably not near a place where it was easy to post mail. Jake had not been able to send a letter since he left Camp Terry, and he promised himself that as soon as they made it back to Fort Totten, he would write home more often.

The next morning, the main body of the 7th detachment headed out south in the direction of Fort Stevenson. Weir and 1st Sgt. Martin stopped by before they left.

"Sgt. Morse, I understand you had a bit of a rough time coming back. I was able to persuade the Major that it would be better to continue to leave you as escort for the surveyors all the way to Ft. Totten, just to insure nothing happens to them. I'll spare you his opinion, but suffice it to say that he wasn't pleased. I'm sure he'll have more to say at a later date. Fortunately he's in a big hurry."

"Sorry, Sir! Between the snow storm, the burnt-off prairie, and lack of fodder, it was fortunate we made it back without losing any horses."

"Well, make sure to rest them and join us at Totten as quick as you can."

Green's party spent the day resting the mules and horses, letting them fill their bellies with good water and forage. The cooks slaughtered one of their few remaining steers, and that evening they feasted on beef steaks along with fresh rations that were left for them by the departing cavalry. Morse and the Company D men were lounging by a large campfire, which they hadn't been able to enjoy for several weeks. The air was brisk, as the nights were cooling quickly. Most of them cradled tin cups of coffee and the smell of tobacco smoke mixed with the woodsmoke from the fire. Greene, accompanied by Val Wheeler, Downing and Doolittle wandered over to sit with the troopers. They brought several bottles of whisky with them.

"Gentlemen, I've been saving these, but seeing how we'll be back to civilization in a week or so, I thought this would be an appropriate occasion to share them." Greene announced, "Particularly since you had to remain here with us, instead of going with the rest of your command."

"That's very good of you, Sir! Although I'm pretty sure we're better off traveling with you." Morse stated.

"Oh yes, I heard Major Reno was quite upset about the condition of your mounts. I expect to see an official complaint of some sort before it's all over. Lt. Edgerly gave me a heads up last night."

As the liquor was being shared out, Greene and Val sat down near Morse.

"Val here wants to talk about our route back. He thinks we should take a different route than Major Twining"

Wheeler reached for stick with a glowing ember from the fire and used it to light up a stubby pipe. He puffed on it to get it going, then blew out a stream of smoke.

"Well, there's a better way to get to Fort Totten. Especially, to make it easier on the animals. Twining was out here several years ago, and knows a bit about the loop of the Mouse River. He's decided to cut across it and head directly to Devil's Lake and Fort Totten. But, we can follow the river valley south until we get to the bend, then strike straight east to Totten. I suspect the grass is all burned up either way. But, as long as we stay by the river, we'll have good water and wood. We'll load up what's left of the forage here, then we can make a run for it over the last leg. There are a few creeks, but I can't guarantee that they'll have water this time of year. The mules and horses should be up to it by then. Once we get on out the prairie, it'll be windy with a lot of dust, so it's no time to linger out there this time of year. You've already seen how fast a blizzard can brew up."

Morse nodded his head,"Makes sense to me. We know there's a good trail south."

"It will give me an opportunity to add to my maps, also." Greene noted.

"Once we turn east, there's not much of a trail. We'll want an advance party out front scouting the best way for the wagons." emphasized Wheeler. "Gimme young Rogers, and his boys. They did a fair job before. We need good eyes."

"Okay, I'll ride out with you, too." said Morse, "Let's start off easy tomorrow and make sure all the animals get plenty of water. How long you reckon it'll take to get to Totten?"

"I figure we can make it in six or seven days if the weather holds.

CHAPTER 8

Fort Totten, Dakota Territory, October 22, 1873

Greene and his party, accompanied by the Company D troopers, approached Fort Totten. Once they made it to the loop of the Mouse River where it started back to the north, their progress had been assailed by cold east winds carrying dust and ashes from the burnt prairie and occasional snow flurries. Covering their faces with bandannas and hunching down in their greatcoats, they had plodded on. They camped along the way by taking shelter behind the wagons lined up with canvas draped on the sides to block the wind. So, the fort and its cluster of buildings was a very encouraging sight as they neared it.

In 1867, General Terry founded the fort naming it after General Joseph Totten, the late Chief Engineer of the Army. The original construction was of logs, but construction crews found a good source of brick clay nearby, and built kilns. Now all of the newer buildings were made of them. The layout of the fort was typical, a parade ground faced by barracks, officers quarters, and stables. There was also a hospital, bakery, and sawmill. There were a couple of things unique about Ft. Totten though. The buildings were painted a pale grey with red trim and instead of a palisade it was surrounded by a picket fence. The fort sat on a treeless plain on a slight rise near the southeast shore of Devil's Lake. The Indians claimed that one of their spirits lived under its surface, and that the water was sacred. The salinity of the water, which varied according to water levels, was considered by the early fur trappers to taste bad, and led to the interpretation of "bad spirit". This led to the name 'Devil's Lake'. After the fort was built, an Indian Agent was assigned in 1871. The Indian agency was located in the old log structures, and was responsible for the Sisseton and Wahpeton bands of Dakota Sioux, that lived near the fort. The grounds outside the fort were usually dotted with their tepees. Companies of the 20th Infantry were stationed at the Totten, and occupied two of the four barracks buildings.

Fort Totten Dakota Territory - late 1870s

When they got to the gate, Major Twining and Capt. Gregory were waiting to greet them.

"Hello Greene! I'm surprised to see you already, you made good time. I trust you enjoyed a good journey." said Twining.

"I don't know about enjoying, but it has been very vigorous, Sir!"

"Well, let's get you settled in. The Quartermaster's Storehouse is at the far end on the right, the stables are behind it. You'll be staying with Capt. Gregory and I, in the officers quarters on the west side. Your men can take the bottom floor of the last barracks on the east side. Tell them not to get too comfortable, we're leaving in two days. You're headed up to Pembina, and we're going south to Fort Seward, then on to St. Paul."

Sgt. Morse spoke up, "Beg pardon, Sir. Has the squadron come in yet?"

"No, quite frankly, we expected to see them before you. A wire was sent to Fort Seward, from Bismarck, that they were on their way from Stevenson."

An Infantry captain walked over from the Adjutants Office just to the left of the gate. Gregory introduced him, "Lt. Greene this is Capt. Patterson, he commands Company A, 20th Infantry. He's taking his unit south to Fort Seward and will be assuming command there. The Major and I will travel with him. We can catch the railroad there."

Remembering his military etiquette, Greene saluted Patterson quickly, "Pleasure to meet you, Sir."

"I just wanted to see for myself, the resourceful young officer that these two have been regaling me with stories about."

"I"m sure they're good stories then, Sir, maybe they'll tell me one!" he replied with a smile.

Looking over at Morse, he asked. "How many men in your escort detail, Sergeant?"

"I've got two sections and a Corporal, Sir. We're part of Company D, Capt. Weir's men."

"Yes, well, you'll be staying here. The baggage and footlockers that were left at Fort Abercrombie were sent over several weeks ago. They are stored in the in the quartermaster's storeroom in the far corner, across the parade ground. You can take your men to the far barracks as well, the troop bays are on the second floor."

Morse saluted and said, "By your leave, Sirs. I'll be taking my men on in then." Turning towards the troopers behind him he shouted, "All right, now lads! We're back from the wild. I want a proper column of twos, while we head for our new home. Smartly now, smartly!"

The troopers were all looking at their new surroundings as they made their way along the street in front of the long row of brick barracks. A covered porch ran the length of each building. Three pairs of chimneys pierced the roofline of each barracks. The parade ground and the buildings were all covered with a dusting of light snow that swirled around them.

"Wiley, you take Hurd's set and see about finding some wood to get the fires going. I'm sure those survey fellows will help you. Turn your mounts over and we'll see to them. Holden, make sure we get the wagons unloaded. I'll go find someone to show me to the stables."

Jake, Charlie, and the Georges all hustled to help with the unloading. Morse came back with a civilian in tow. "This is the stable master, Mr. Smith, follow him and he'll show you where to put the horses. Help the teamsters with the mules and getting the wagons parked."

A couple of hours later, when they finished with their tasks, they were on the barracks porch getting ready to go inside, when they heard a commotion at the front of the fort. Looking that way, they saw Major Reno, and Capt. Weir riding in at the head of the cavalry column. Sgt. Morse saw them and said. "Well now, look who's shown up, boys. Let's be remembering that you'll not be hobnobbing with a bunch of civilians any longer. Top will have your asses if he catches you slacking, and not minding your manners. Lt. Greene is a nice young officer, but you'd best forget about his easy going ways, and snap to with our officers."

The cavalry column had had to put up with the same conditions that had tormented Greene's party on the way east to Fort Totten, and had endured it for the whole 124 miles from Fort Stevenson. Reno, Weir, and Keogh rode over to the Adjutants Building and dismounted. Reno struggled getting off and had to grab a saddle strap to stand.

"God dammit!" he cursed.

Weir came over and offered his arm. "Let me help you, Sir."

They made their way clumsily inside where they found a chair for Reno, and he collapsed into it, cursing the whole while.

"Major Reno I presume. It seems you're injured, Sir. Would you like me to send for our doctor?" Patterson asked.

"Yes, please." answered Reno wincing. "I stepped in a hole a couple of days ago and sprained my ankle badly. I've been miserable ever since."

Patterson turned to an orderly and instructed him to go fetch the post surgeon.

"The survey parties have all arrived. Lt. Greene and the detachment of your men with him just arrived an hour or so before you." He said. "Your Sgt. Morse is already over at the barracks, settling in."

"Hmm, well, Weir, Keogh, you'd best go see to getting your men settled in."

The door opened and the post commander, Lt. Col. Lewis Hunt walked in. Weir and Keogh came to attention, but Reno stayed sitting and said.

"Your pardon, Sir! I injured my ankle and find standing quite painful."

"That's quite all right, Major. Gentlemen, welcome to Ft. Totten. I'd wish you a warm welcome, but warmth is a relative concept here in winter. Major, I saw you struggling in as I made my way over. Nothing serious I assume."

"Your captain sent for your doctor That worthless excuse for a doctor that we had, Coues, deserted us two weeks ago."

"I see. That was unfortunate timing." Hunt replied.

"Well, he'll be hearing about it. I'm to repair to Headquarters in St. Paul and make my report." said Reno. "My wife's mother passed away last month and I'd like to get home as soon as I can,"

"Capt. Patterson is taking my Company A, to Fort Seward, near Jamestown, to assume command of the post. Major Twining and Capt. Gregory are going with them. They're leaving the day after tomorrow. Perhaps you can travel with them, if you feel up to it? You can catch a train east from Jamestown. The Northern Pacific finished the bridge across the Red River last summer, at Moorehead, and they have track on down to St. Cloud from there, that meets up with the Minnesota and Pacific Rail Road. You can ride on to St. Paul on it. You should be in St. Paul within a week."

"Yes, that will work out nicely. I'm sure your doctor will be able to help alleviate the pain somewhat. I'll leave Capt. Weir in command of my squadron." Reno said nodding in Weir's direction.

"Sir," Weir stated, "Captain Thomas Weir at your service, I command Company D, and this is Capt. Miles Keogh, commander of Company I. It's a pleasure to meet you, Sir."

"I'm sure we'll have plenty of time make acquaintances later. I'll let you see to getting your men settled in. We have two barracks waiting for your men. Your company laundresses, and their things, arrived from Fort Abercrombie, along with your storage items. The laundries are nice facilities here, just behind the barracks, and I'm sure your ladies are geared up to handle the influx."

"That's good to know. Two months in the field has us looking a little ragged." replied Keogh.

"Most of the buildings here are less than two years old, and we've got plenty of stoves for the quarters, and for the kitchens. I think you'll find your own quarters quite comfortable. They are just barely a year old. They're to the left as you leave, yours will be the fourth building, just the other side of mine. I saw some activity over at them on my way here, so you might want to have your strikers go supervise."

"Thank you, Sir. We'll see to it, right away."

Weir and Keogh walked out the door, mounted their horses and headed towards their quarters. The officers quarters were located along the west side of the parade ground with the post commander's in the middle, flanked by a larger one for Captains and 1st Lieutenant's, which was a large two story brick structure with three single story portico entrances. The 2nd lieutenant's quarters were separate and smaller at the ends. The ones assigned to the cavalry were north of the CO's. Each two story building had individual apartments for each officer, with shared attached kitchens, bathing facilities and outhouses.

"Well, Tom. What do you think? With no Reno to contend with for a while, this looks to be a snug place to huddle up for the winter." quipped Keogh. "Col. Hunt seems pleasant."

Weir smiled and said. "Indeed Myles! But it's still a bit isolated. We'll have to see that we keep the men busy, we'll have to consult with Col. Hunt on the surrounding area."

Sgt. Rush was supervising the off loading of the supply wagons that came in with the column. Noticing Henry, Jake and the rest of the section helping out, Rush called out to him. "Yo, Holden! I have your footlockers over here. They were sent up to Stevenson with the rest of our stuff, so I made sure they got up here."

"Thanks Sergeant! We were wondering about them."

"Well, the Army don't give you much, put it tends to keep track of what it does. I set 'em off to the side for you. Best come and get them right now, before the rest of the outfit comes looking for the stuff that got shipped over from Ft. Abercrombie."

They claimed their footlockers and lugged them up to the second floor. There were stairways at each end of the barracks. Sgt. Morse and Sgt. Flanagan were standing in the middle of a long, wooden floored barracks room when they got upstairs. The center of the room was open except for the building support columns. The walls, ceiling, and columns were painted white, while the floors were brown stained wood. There was a row of greenish blue iron framed beds, with wooden slats, along both sides of the room. Each bunk had rolled up mattress and pillow on the end closest to the wall. They were paired between large paned windows. Above the bunks were narrow blue painted wooden shelves with rows of hooks below them. A stone fireplace was blazing away at each end end, and there was a pot bellied stove standing on a brick platform towards the middle length. A long stove pipe ran from it to link into the fireplace chimney flu. A barrel on a stand served to hold drinking water, and there was a scattering of tables and benches between the columns.

"All right, listen up!" exclaimed Flanagan. "Holden, your section will take the first four bunks on each side. Hurd's section will take the next four . Get your boys settled in and then come back downstairs to help get the kitchen set up.
Let's be about helping out the cook, and don't dawdle, I'm hungry already!" he said, as he and Morse turned to go through the stairwell door.

Holden being in charge of the section, took the first bunk, and Hurry took the one next to him. They continued in bunkie order, with Goldie and Greene, then Jake and Charlie, and last with Big and Little. They slid the footlockers into position at the foot of the bunks, and quickly took the opportunity to inspect the lockers to see if the padlocks had been tampered with. They were all pleased to discover the contents intact, but jumbled.

"Okay, lads." Henry said, "Let's get our kits stowed. Watch me and follow along. I think I'm the only one who has experience with barracks life."Hang your belts, and holsters from the hooks under the shelves, along with your ammo pouches, carbine slings, and haversacks. The same with your canteens, mess gear, and tin cups.There's hooks on the end for your stable suits and coats also. Hats on the shelf, along with your dress helmets. Every thing else folded in the footlockers. Put everything in the same order as mine. I'm sure the 1st Sgt. will let us know how he wants it to look."

"Well, this sure beats a tent all to hell!" exclaimed Little George. The rest of them were looking around and a few nodded their heads in agreement.

"I think you'll find that barracks life has its advantages, but the routine can be tedious. Particularly, compared to the last several months, discipline will be much tighter. Every day is planned out, and when we aren't out on guard duty, or details, there will be training. You'll get used to having a solid roof over your head, and the food tends to be better. But it's also to a bit boring. However, I'm sure it beats winter field duty up here. One of the surveyors told me that after this month, it probably won't get above freezing until next spring. I warrant they'll be issuing us cold weather gear, before too long."

Enlisted Mens Barracks - Circa 1870s

The squadron spent the next several days getting sorted out. The sergeants set about establishing the daily routine and organizing fatigue details and guard duty schedules. Pistols, and sabers were turned in for storage in the arms room, and extra ammunition stocks were stored in the powder magazine building. The sergeants made sure to inventory everything and Sgt. Rush set about organizing the company supply room. The kitchen storage room was filled up and the stoves were fully equipped with cooking equipment and utensils. Fatigue details hauled and stockpiled wood supplies. Fortunately, there were some enterprising wood cutters set up in the hills surrounding Devils Lake, in addition there was a working sawmill to cut up logged trees. The stables were cleaned, and hay and fodder stored up. The wagons and field gear were thoroughly inspected, cleaned, repaired and stored away for the winter. The two story barracks had the large troop bays on the second floor. The Orderly Room and 1st Sergeant' quarters were on one end of the first floor, with separate cubicles for the other NCOs. The arms room, company storage rooms, the Day room and the mess area taking up the rest. The kitchens, bath houses, and the laundress quarters were single story structures attached behind, with underground brick cisterns. The fort also had several water wells, with the outhouses located well away downhill.

Company A, 20th Infantry assembled to depart, with Reno ensconced on a covered buckboard wagon along with Major Twining. Lt. Greene stood near, saying his goodbyes to the rest of the Survey Party. Greene was getting ready to head north to Fort Pembina, where he started from back in June. He had been tasked with resurveying the parallel back to the east from the Red River. The swampy terrain had been difficult for accurate observations and it was felt that it would be a good time to confirm the results on frozen ground

Gregory shook hands with him and said. "Make sure to procure some cold weather gear, Greene. You're likely to freeze your balls off up there."

"Don't worry, I solicited advise from the Canadians before we parted, and have compiled a list of clothing requirements for the coming months. Unfortunately, I'll have to buy most of it from the Hudson Bay Company when I get up there."

"Good, well you be careful, and I'll see you next spring."

Greene waved at Twining, as his wagon rolled by, who gave a wave back, but Reno chose to ignore him completely.

"Perhaps we'll get lucky and get a different escort commander next season." Greene stated. "I'm not a fan of his."

"Hmm, He and Twining seem to tolerate each other. He's going all the way to St. Cloud with us. Fortunately, we're headed to Detroit, and he's going on to St.Paul. But I'm with you, I'd prefer someone a bit less pompous"

As Gregory mounted his horse, Greene looked up at him grinning.

"I'll see you next spring. Make sure you bring plenty of whiskey and cigars with you."

Gregory gave him a thumbs up as he rode away.

Jake had drawn stable police for the day. He and Charlie were working at repairing some of the corrals that had been damaged by overcrowding when the cavalry and survey teams had come in. The last of the survey teams was assembling and they watched Mr. Doolittle and Mr. Downing get them sorted out. They were busy sawing some new rails, when Lt. Greene came over to talk with them.

"Private Rogers, Private Welch, I saw you working and just thought I'd come over and tell you goodbye. I'm taking my team back to Pembina to do some winter surveying."

"Sorry to see you go, Sir. We enjoyed working with you, and I now have a much better appreciation for maps." said Jake. "Will you be coming back? Our sergeants expect us to be going back out with you next year."

"Yes, I'm sure I will be. We intend to take up where we left off. We still have another 400 miles to complete."

"Is Val Wheeler going with you?"

"No, he's staying around here at an old trading post on a place called Graham's Island, although I'm told that the local Indians call it Big Foot's Island. He has some friends that live there. You'll probably see him from time to time when he comes in to trade at the post sutlers. He's contracted to guide us again next year."

"Well, I hope we get to work with you again next year, Sir. I'd like to learn more from you."

Greene held out his hand, "Here I have something for you, Rogers."

Jake took the object from him. It was a small round leather case with a clasp. When he opened it, a shiny, glass faced brass compass gleamed up at him.

"Gee, Lieutenant! Thanks." Jake said as he admired it

"Well, you keep practicing. I'm sure it'll come in handy during your wanderings. I hope to see you next summer out west. You fellows stay warm!" Greene exclaimed as they exchanged salutes.

It was announced that a traveling paymaster would be arriving in a couple of days. Jake and his set had missed the paymaster when he called on Camp Terry, since they had been out with the survey parties. They were looking forward to getting several months pay. They hadn't been to the Post Trader's store since they arrived, and they were anxious to visit it. Being first year men they received no clothing allowance and the last couple of months had been hard on clothing. Particularly socks, drawers and undershirts. What little washing they had been able to do was done hurriedly in creeks, and rivers, scrubbing on rocks. Most of their uniforms were ragged, the wool of their jackets and trousers thinning. Fortunately, what little money they had, was unspent and they were able to charge to their accounts with the quartermaster through Sgt. Rush. But their cache of canned food, spices and other items was sadly depleted, but they could use the money at the post traders. And now that the laundresses were working, they would need money to pay them. Payday arrived with a holiday like atmosphere. The whole fort bustled with activity as soon as the paymaster arrived with his escort. He set up at the adjutants office in the southwest corner of the parade ground. There the garrison was formed up by companies and the men stood inspection, then waited their turn to line up to receive their money, which was paid in greenbacks. Most settled their debts immediately to the laundress, then their fellow solders that moonlighted as company tailors, barbers, and cobblers, and also the inevitable usurious soldier/shylocks in the ranks. Most, however looked forward to a trip to the fort trading post.

The military post trader system was created to replace the Army sutler. Whereas previously the sutlers were appointed by the post commanders, starting in 1870 the Post Trader was appointed and licensed by the Secretary of War. They were virtual monopolies, that could not only sell to the troops but also civilians and Indians. They also were able to bid contracts to haul freight, supply wood, hay, and ice. All manners of goods, staples, hardware, clothing, firearms, and luxury items such as tobacco and spirits were available to buy. In the case Fort Totten, being on a military reservation, the trader was insured that there was no competition. Ernest Brenner ran the post tradership, at Totten. His partner was General Terry's brother, Robert, an attorney in Duluth. General Terry had appointed them in 1868, and insured that they were licensed after the transition. The trading post was located at the south end of the parade ground, next to the post bakery. It consisted of main room containing many well stocked shelves, a warehouse, offices, and a bar. Brenner was generally well regarded and made a point to make discounted deals with the officers, and sergeants. He extended $5 sutler's credits to the troops, and with his connections, he could obtain most anything by ordering it from his partner, Robert Terry, in Duluth via telegraph from Fort Seward. Then have it shipped to nearby Jamestown, down on the Northern Pacific

Railroad, 80 miles to the South. The whole Post Trader system was rife with patronage and was highly profitable. Particularly, when networked with the other surrounding forts.

When Company B, 20th Infantry, and its commander, Cap. J. C. Bates, arrived, the winter population of the fort was set. The various details were apportioned between the infantry and cavalry. With most of the post related details going to the infantry, while the stable guard and escort details fell to the cavalry. The rest were shared equally. The daily routine through the week was coordinated by bugle calls beginning with First Call at 5:00, and continued with Reveille and Roll Call, Guard Mount, Stable Call, Mess Call for breakfast, Sick Call, Drill Call, Fatigue Call, and Water Call. Mess Call for dinner at 12:00, then another round of Drill, Fatigue, and Stable Calls, before afternoon inspection and another Roll Call. The fatigue details varied from day to day, depending on the season, but, cleaning, wood, water, and kitchen details were all part of the daily routine. Mess Call for supper at 18:00. Tattoo and Roll Call came at 20:30 PM, with Taps and Lights Out at 21:00. Saturdays were largely reserved for cleaning, and getting ready for the weekly Sunday Dress Inspection. If everything went well during the inspection, the rest of the day they were on their own.

The daily post guard mount which rotated every four days between the companies on post. It was mounted every morning, and was usually interesting because of the competition to serve as the Commanding Officers Orderly. If picked for this, the soldier was not required to stand sentinel, and spent his time at the headquarters office. As the men stood inspection from the Officer of the Day, they were quizzed on general orders and military etiquette, then judged on the appearance of their uniforms and gear. The one judged best was selected. This was quite sought after by the men, with several of them becoming very proficient at it, becoming known as 'orderly buckers'. The rest of them had to stand guard at, or walk various posts around the fort. They were relieved every two hours, and had to return to the guard room, where there were cots to rest on, but they had to stay clothed. As it got colder, guard detail became very unpopular.

The temperatures continued to drop as the days got shorter. One day, The post quartermaster arranged with Lt. Bell to issue buffalo coats, leggings, muskrat caps with flaps, arctic overshoes, fur lined gloves for everyone. As they were standing in line for it to be issued, Sgt. Rush shouted out "Everyone needs to sign for this gear! This is post property and doesn't belong to the Regiment. Take care of it, you'll be turning it back in come spring."

"You think it'll really get cold enough that we'll need this stuff, Henry?" Golden asked.

"I think it's being given out for a reason. Remember the storm we were in, just think if it hadn't warmed up and thawed."

"Bejesus! I shudder to think." exclaimed Biscuit.

"Better get used to being cold, lads!"

Evenings were spent upstairs where it was warmer, the heat from the stoves below helped warm the floors. They were able to get some canvas to make heavy curtains for the windows, which helped keep the heat in during the night. The candles lanterns, along with a few lard oil lamps, cast vague shadows across the troop bay. Some sat at tables playing cards, or cribbage. A few scribbled letters. Groups gathered to tell stories and jokes, some more lively than others when a bottle of whisky was shared around. Once the sergeants conducted final roll call, the fires were banked and everyone settled into their bunks.

Jake was trying to write a reply to one of the letters that came regularly now that they were in garrison. His mother continued to let him know about the local news and anecdotes from home. Colleen was a great help with the school children, and had asked about him. Frank got on with the railroad, and moved to Springfield. His Father was fine and sent his regards. She was still a bit critical about his frequency of communication, and she wanted to know where he was and what he was doing. He couldn't find much inspiration to tell her about his daily routine, so he chose to write about the his experiences traveling and the expedition up on the boundary. He promised to do a better job now that they were at a regular post.

Winter settled in, and the main focus every day revolved around staying warm. They spent a lot of time caring for the horses at the stable. Fortunately their canvas stable suits provided an extra layer of clothing, and the physical labor helped generate a little body heat. They were also kept busy with guard duty and fatigue details, such as firewood, latrine, and kitchen duty. The latter being a preferred assignment now that it was cold. Weekly baths and clean uniforms were strictly adhered too. Payday was the only break in the routine.

As the Holidays approached, the women of the post made plans for decorations and elaborate meals and desserts. This
perked up the men and the whole fort in general.

CHAPTER 9

Fort Totten, Dakota Territory, Christmas Day, 1873

Snow had blanketed the entire fort for a week, and the temperature hovered below zero. Pathways had been carved between buildings and around the parade ground. Daily outdoor activity was restricted to wood, water, and stable details, and were conducted as quickly as possible. It was a Thursday and the holiday granted an extra day of leisure for those not chosen for guard. Roll calls, guard mount, and inspections were conducted inside the barracks. The mess hall had been decorated by the laundresses and a gaily decorated Christmas tree stood in the corner. Col. Hunt had been able to secure a shipment of smoked Virginia hams, and each company received a sufficient quantity to serve them for dinner. Several men had volunteered to help out the cooks, including Henry and George. Jake and the others were sitting around a table upstairs, where he was re-reading the last letter from his mother. She had sent it, along with a box full of jars of her homemade blackberry jam, carefully backed in straw and padded with multiple pairs of stockings . He had contributed several jars to the feast being prepared. The letter was several weeks old, written just after Thanksgiving. It sounded like everyone was doing well back home. Jake heard someone come up the stairs and saw Sgt. Morse, who called out.

"Come along Jake, my boy! Grab your coat. Let's be traipsing over to the store. Top took some money from the company fund, ordered a couple of kegs of beer and a bunch of goodies from the post trader. Bring Charlie and the Georges, 'Big' can push the wheelbarrow. We're to pick up our bread from the bakery on the way back. Maggie brought me a pile of fresh blankets to wrap it up in, and warned me to bring it straight back."

Maggie was the head laundress. She was married to Sgt. Thomas Harrison, from the other platoon. She held sway over the company when it came to the well being of "her boys", as she referred to them.

"Right Sarge! My Ma said to tell you hello, in her letter. She said that she's almost forgiven you for luring me away into the Army. " he replied grinning.

Morse laughed and said, "I'll not be truly forgiven 'til you get home, but it's good to know that Sarah thinks well enough of me to say hello. Now shake a leg, lads! We want to be out and about, and back quick as we can!"

The presence of the officers, Mrs. Martin, and the few married enlisted men's wives, most of whom were also laundresses, lent a more domestic air to the mess room during dinner. Capt. Weir led the company in a Christmas prayer, then said a few words praising everyone for their efforts over the course of the year, and expressed optimism that the coming year would be as successful. Ellen Martin encouraged a few of the better known vocalists to lead them in Christmas carols, and then to sing some more popular tunes. There was some surreptitious sharing of some Christmas cheer, and when the officers and women departed, the kegs were tapped and beer flowed briskly. Soon liquor bottles appeared and began making the rounds. Impromptu songs broke out, and a couple of harmonicas provided accompaniment. Cakes and various deserts had been left out for snacking. The cooks filled plates and stored them in the Kitchen for the unfortunate few men that still had duty. As the evening wore on, the festivities wound down, most of the men made their way upstairs, and gathered in quieter groups, some exchanging small gifts. Jake gave Charlie a watertight box of 'Lucifer" matches, and received a sealed vial of ink in return.

"Gentlemen, I bid you all best wishes for Christmas!' Henry raised his cup and toasted. "May we all live to see our love ones again."

"Well said, Sage! Here's to the families we left behind! toasted Jake.

As they made ready to retire, Jake asked Henry. "You still in touch with your family back in England?"

"Oh, I get a letter now and then."

"You never say much about it, I was just wondering. You ever think about going home?"

"Well, it wouldn't be easy. I left rather abruptly and there are some personal issues that would have to be resolved. Some, that I'm not sure I care to address."

"You seem to like the Army life, why didn't you join it in England?"

"Ah, you ask a good question young Jake! That would require a good answer that I don't have. Suffice it to say, that I took the easiest path, available. There is little to remind me of England out here."

"But you survived the War, didn't you want to return after that?"

"No, the Army is my home, for now. My only responsibilities are to obey orders and help out my fellow soldiers. I enjoy the camaraderie, living and seeing the different places."

"Well, I like that part too. But I can't imagine what combat would be like. I've barely seen any Indians."

"For your own sake, Jake, I hope you never get to experience it. Seeing the elephant changes you inside, and some can't deal with it."

"You seem to have dealt with it, okay."

"Have I now?" mused Henry, "Time will tell. Goodnight, sleep well, Jake. Tomorrow is on its way, with the next day close behind."

Jake made his way over to his bunk and laid down. He watched the shadows dance on the ceiling from the flickering logs in the fireplace, and heard Charlie snoring softly in the adjacent bunk. He dozed off pondering Holden's cryptic last comment.

The next day they fell back into the usual routine. Jake had drawn firewood detail for the barracks, and was just finishing up stacking wood supplies near the stoves and fireplaces. He was on his the last armload and had just stepped up on the porch when he saw a bundled figure headed towards the barracks from the direction of the front gate. Whoever it was, was bundled in a bulky buffalo robe and heavy wrapped leggings, wearing oversize moccasins, and long snowshoes. Jake saw that he carried rifle, cased in a beaded, fringed scabbard that he recognized.

"I'll be damned! That you Val Wheeler?" he called out. "Where'd you come from?"

"Jake! The guard told me that you boys were in the last barracks. Hope you got a good fire goin' in there. Where's Morse at? He owes me some whiskey!" Val exclaimed. "I come to collect a little Christmas cheer!"

"I reckon he's inside, Val. Come on in, we'll see where he's at."

Jake took Wheeler inside to the orderly room. Sgt. Martin was sitting at his desk and looked up when they stepped inside.

"Look who showed up, Top." said Jake.

"Wheeler, what in the blazes? I figured you being buried up in a wigwam somewhere, with a pretty little squaw keeping you warm. What the hell you doing out and about?

"Well, I ran out of tobaccy, and figured I'd come in and wish you soldier boys "Merry Christmas" while I was at the post traders."

"I never thought that you heathens would know about Christmas."

"Ahh, the benefits of good Father Vincent's years of preaching at me! But you know I missed it slightly. I've not much use for calendars. One of my Indian friends came back from buying supplies here at the post, and remarked about how everyone was so gay, so I came on in. It's only about seven miles now with the lake froze over."

Morse walked in exclaiming, "I was sitting over in the dayroom when I heard you caterwauling, Wheeler. What the hell you been up to?"

"Ahh, I ran into some of my Métis friends when we came in. They married into the Turtle Mountain Band of Chippewas. They're wintering over on Graham's Island and they invited me stay with them. Well, I damned sure wasn't going to hang around here all winter with you hard dick army boys, when I could cozy up with a little Chippewa gal."

"Can't say that I blame you there, Val. It's good to hear that your wintering well"

"Why don't you all come over to the trading post with me, and I'll treat us all to some drinks while I'm stocking up?"

Martin looked at a pile of papers on his desk and replied, looking at Pat, "You and Rogers go ahead. I'll be along once I get this knocked out."

"Say, Top, you reckon I can get a place where I can bed down here for the night? You wouldn't want me stumbling around in the cold dark?" Val asked.

"Only if you take a bath you smelly bastard!"

"Say, that's not a bad idea! I was gonna buy some new duds, anyway. Be good to go back to Shanaya all cleaned up. I get her a present to boot, she'll be right appreciative I expect."

"Off you go then, I'll see you in a while."

The following morning after breakfast, Jake saw Sgt. Morse and Val, a fresh flannel shirt under his hide vest, and new heavy whipcord pants with fresh leggings above his winter moccasins. They were standing by the orderly room talking. Val waved for him to come over.

"Here Jake, take this." Wheeler said, handing him a parcel wrapped in soft leather.

"What's this?" he asked.

"I ain't forgot you fixing me up with tobaccy when we was out in the boondocks. Just a little somethin' I stumbled onto, go ahead unwrap it."

When he unrolled it, he found a bone handled knife in a beautifully decorated sheath. The handle was carved with designs, and the sheath edged with intricate beadwork. He pulled the blade from the sheath, and light reflected off the polished sides. He hefted it as he admired the details.

"Noticed that cheap piece of crap you were sportin' when we were cleaning game last fall. Now that there's a knife! Those Métis buddies of mine claim that's genuine Sheffield steel. Same has those fancy swords the Brits are so proud of."

"Val, you don't owe me this. It's too much!"

"Not for you to decide, Jake. I'm fixin' to head out. I'll probably see you again before too long. Maybe I'll show you soldier boys how to ice fish."

CHAPTER 10

Fort Totten, Dakota Territory, February 1874

The temperatures had stayed well blow zero for weeks, dipping into double digit lows. The main struggle continued to be staying warm. Keeping the horses and livestock fed was the daily priority. Fatigue details were restricted to a minimum, and kept as brief as possible. Kitchen detail, normally disliked, became a welcome diversion with the kitchen area being the warmest place in the barracks. Most of the food was boiled in big pots into a stew called 'slumgullion'. Bacon, beans, coarse bead from the bakery were the mainstays of the menu, with an occasional appearance of fresh beef, when a steer was slaughtered. Coffee was brewed round the clock. And there was of course, guard detail.

"Say Show, you gonna for try for CO's orderly?" asked Tom Stivers.

"I'm gearing up for it, Stiff." answered Jake, as he was laying out his uniform on his bunk, "It's worth a shot to stay indoors warm and dry, instead of stomping around in the snow, freezing my ass off."

"You know 'ol Smiley prides himself as a top orderly bucker. You think you can beat him out?"

"Sage, here has been working with me, and I've been studying and working on my manual of arms. I came close the last guard mount I was on."

"Well, it'd tickle me to see you beat out that thick headed Dutchman. Hand me your boots, I'll whip a shine on 'em for you. Everyone wants you to show up the cocky bastard"

"You sure? It'll piss him off if he hears that you helped me."

"Tough titty! I won't take any shit off Smiley. I'll be rooting for you, Show. Make that sum bitch work for it!"

When a known "orderly bucker" was detailed to a guard mount many of the men chose not to compete. But when one of them was challenged, the guard mount was observed closely by the rest of the company. With snow and sub-zero conditions outside guard mount was held in the dayroom, by 1st Sgt. Martin and the sergeant of the guard, in this case Sgt. Flanagan. When they were satisfied the men were ready, they summoned the officer of the day, Lt. Bell. They were surprised to see Capt. Weir put in an appearance, also. He joined the 1st Sergeant, and Sgt. Morse off to the side. Bell made his way down the ranks, inspecting the men as they stood at attention with their carbines at order arms, He scrutinized the uniform of each trooper, and inspected each carbine as the men brought them up for inspection. He also asked them questions about their general and special orders. After the last man, he stepped back and moved to the center.

"Privates Sanders and Rogers front and center."

As Sanders and Jake stepped forward to comply, Bell announced, "The rest of you men report to Sgt. Flanagan for guard post assignments"

Some murmuring went on as the men filed out of the room. Bell looked at the two troopers in front of him.

"Pvt. Sanders you look very smart for guard mount, as always."

"Thank you, Sir."

Bell paused and looked Jake up and down.

"Pvt. Rogers, you have come a long way since I first laid eyes on you back in Sioux City."

"Yes, Sir!" Jake replied.

"I understand you accompanied Lt. Greene and his survey party last summer."

"Yes, Sir"

"Did you like being in the field?"

"Yes, Sir! Very much!"

"I imagine it took a while to get your gear looking this good after 3 months out there."

"It did, Sir. But I saw what it took at previous guard mounts, so I learned how to get it fixed up. Plus I had help from the other men in my section. I wanted see if I could be picked as CO's Orderly."

Looking back at Sanders, the Lieutenant asked, "Pvt. Sanders, I see you have a couple of service stripes. I assume you're a veteran of the War?"

"Yes, Sir!"

"And as an old hand, you probably have a special guard mount uniform?"

"Of sorts, Sir."

"I understand you've quite a reputation as a "orderly bucker"

"Well, I have been picked frequently, I try my best to look sharp, Sir."

"Hmm, well you both look sharp. Let me pose a question, the first one to answer it correctly will be the Orderly. Who is the new Sgt. Major of the Regiment back in St. Paul?"

Sanders wrinkled his eyebrows and gazed upwards in thought.

"Permission to answer the lieutenant's question, Sir." said Jake.

"Go ahead, Rogers."

"That would be Regimental Sgt. Major William Sharrow, Sir."

"That's correct. How is it you know that Rogers?"

"I believe it's posted in the orderly room, and Pvt. Holden of my section commented that the new Sergeant Major was an Englishman like him, so it stuck in my mind."

"Well, then that settles it. You're the CO's Orderly, congratulations! Pvt. Sanders you can report to the guard house with the others.

Sanders turned and glowered at Jake, before heading for the door.

"Don't get your uniform dirty, Smiley." Jake grinned and whispered, "And stay warm!"

Capt. Weir walked over to where Top Martin and Morse were standing.

"Your young Rogers did well, Morse."

"Indeed, Sir! I heard through the grapevine, what was afoot. I just popped out of my room to see if he could pull it off."

"I just received a report from Lt. Greene about you and your men. He was quite complimentary. He specifically noted that Pvt. Rogers displayed good initiative, even before you were present. He's requested your men to rejoin his party next season, if possible."

"Well, he's a nice young officer, and quite resourceful I might add. He's a goer that one, tis a pleasure to see such enthusiasm. But I suspect if our dear Major has a hand in it next year, we'll not be traipsing about with the Lieutenant again."

"I suspect you're right, Sergeant. But I don't anticipate Major Reno returning until spring. He's been busy pulling strings at Headquarters, in St. Paul. I received a dispatch informing me that his leave has been extended several times, and now he's not due back until the first of May."

Sgt. Morse nodded and said smiling, "I'll not complain about that, Sir."

"Let Rogers know that his hard work is duly noted, and also yours, Morse. Keep up the good work."

"Thank you, Sir. I appreciate it."

Val Wheeler made another visit, this time he hung around a couple of weeks. He showed Jake, and his friends how to dress for extended outdoor activities, by wearing layers of wool under their buffalo robes and leggings. Instead of boots they would wear layers of socks, then slippers, wrapped in strips of blanket, then stuffed inside oversize moccasins. The post trader had laid in a stock of colored spectacles with coquille shaped, smoke grey lenses and sold them quite reasonably. They helped offset the light reflecting from the snow and were very popular. He took them to see his Méti friends and they traded tobacco and whiskey for some snowshoes. Wheeler showed them how to track and hunt game over the snow and they were able to keep the cook well supplied with fresh venison and small game. As the weather slowly began to change, the days lengthened and the temperatures began to inch upwards. Outdoor activities were tolerable, particularly on sunny days. Wheeler took Jake, Hurry, and Big George ice fishing one Sunday after inspection. They got permission from Top to take their horses out. Val showed them a sheltered cove on the lake, where little wiki ups of tree branches had been setup over holes cut in the ice. They laid buffalo robes on the ice under the wiki ups and watched down the hole as they lured fish in using a string to suspend small pieces of bait, or carved bits of horn. A slender spear with a barbed head, was used to impale them. Horn broke out some of his hooks and rigged short poles for him and Big. But Jake enjoyed the challenge of using a spear, and stayed with it. They had a contest to see who could catch the most, and surprisingly Hurry won. They hauled in dozens of fat perch and large walleye, filling several flour sacks. After hauling them back to the barracks, they got the cook to fry them up along with piles of corn dodgers. They had enough to feed both Holden's and Hausen's sections, plus made sure to invite Top and the platoon sergeants. It was all washed them down with mugs of beer.

"Damn, that was right tasty!" pronounced Wheeler, "I usually roast 'em on a stick over a fire, with a little salt, for flavor. I'm gonna get me a big bag of cornmeal, at the traders, and take it back to Shanaya."

"Sounds to me like you're getting pretty domestic there, Val." Morse said. "you planning to make her full-time?"

"Naw, Chippewa women are too headstrong for me. I'm still planning on getting back out to the Milk River country. Winters here are too damn harsh. Come May, you'll be having to host me for the rest of the summer. Maybe earlier if she takes a shine to some other buck, that plans on living around here. Figured I'll take you boys out there and then stay put.

"What'll you do out there, when you get back?"

"The Gross Ventre still honor the treaty they signed almost twenty years ago. There is a trading post and warehouse, at Ft. Belknap, where the tribe receives its rations and annuity goods. Plus, they've always had the buffalo. But soon there won't be enough of them left on the lands to support the people. I have watched for years as the herds get smaller and smaller. A Métis named Johnny Grant started trading cattle down by Deer Lodge Valley several years ago, and some Texans have been driving herds north to Montana to sell to the Bozeman miners since '66. Some of them have started ranches, grazing cattle on the land where the buffalo used to be. They call the land open range, and turn cattle out to graze, gathering them before winter. The cattle are thriving. I think we can do that on the our lands, not only enough to feed our people, but to sell on the open market."

"So you're going to try to start a ranch?" Jake asked

"Not so much as a ranch, but to try and convince some of my people that the old ways are ending, and that there are new ways. The Chippewa and some the Métis are learning to survive without the buffalo, as are the people here on this reservation. As I have traveled, I watch to see how other tribes have learned to change their ways. I hope to share that when I return. You will see the land when we get out there this summer, tell me what you think then."

"I will, and I hope it works out for you, Val." Morse said. "It sounds like you've put some thought into it. But where are you going get stock from?"

"Well, you know your Army pays me very well, much more than you soldiers. I'm saving up as much as I can to buy some, and then of course there is the old fashioned way."

"What is that."Jake asked

Wheeler took a big swill of beer and said with a grin. "Why, we'll borrow some from the Texans, of course. I met some of them over by Bozeman a couple of years ago. They bragged on how they had borrowed cattle from across the border in Mexico, before coming north. So, we learn from them. They consider it open range, and we consider it our land!"

CHAPTER 11

Fort Totten Dakota Territory, Mid-May 1874

The coming of spring was welcomed by all. The last vestiges of snow finally disappeared, and the lake thawed. The garrison broke out of the winter's routine and drilling returned to the parade ground. The cavalry began mounted drills, and routine patrols resumed, most in the direction of Fort Stevenson which was a well worn trail, and passable. The route south to Fort Seward and the Northern Pacific Railroad was shorter, but involved crossing the Sheyenne and James Rivers which were usually swollen by the spring melt and unfordable. At the beginning of April, Capt. Keogh left to go home on leave to Ireland to settle some family estate matters and wouldn't return in time to accompany Company I in the field. Lt. Porter was left in command, assisted by 2nd Lt. Andrew Nave. Orders had not been received, but the two companies of the 7th anticipated another season up on the line of the 49th Parallel. Most of the supplies that they would need were being staged at Ft. Stevenson, where they had left the wagon train from the previous season. The post trader's store was very busy, not only with the soldiers who were stocking up for the field, but also fur traders, a few Métis, and the reservation Indians, who were getting ready to send out parties for the summer buffalo hunt. Limited credit was extended to the tribes pending the receipt of their government annuities and they used it to buy cooking utensils, clothing items, blankets, and staples, there were a few Winchester Model 1866 "Yellow Boy" rifles and .44 cartridges, 50-70 ammunition for the Government issued Indian rifles, files, chisels, and small kegs of scrap steel for making arrowheads and skinning knives.

Capt. Weir was standing under the portico in front of his quarters watching the guard mount across the parade field. He noticed Lt. Porter coming up the street from the direction of the Adjutants Office.

"I just got a message from Headquarters in St. Paul, Major Reno is still there on temporary duty awaiting orders." Porter said, as he came near. "He anticipates orders in the next couple of weeks, The government appropriation for this year's survey expedition is still awaiting final approval."

"So, he is conveniently staying there eh? Weir replied, "Let me guess, he wants us to have everything ready here to move out promptly, when it is."

"Yes."

"Well, I guess it's up to you and I, Jim. I sent Lt. Bell over to Ft. Stephenson to round up the wagons, and teamsters. As far as Company D is concerned, the men are faunching at the bit to leave. We've only four men that weren't out with us last year, so I think most everyone knows what to expect. I'm sure that's pretty much for your men, also."

"I've been pleased with what I've seen. Top Varden assures me that they are in good spirits. I'm a little concerned about Lt. Nave. He was coming back from escort duty over to Stillwater, when his horse threw him. He fell on his arm and shoulder, and is in great pain."

"What does the new surgeon, Dr. Ford, say?"

"He says it's badly strained, and put Andy in a sling. But, Nave is determined to come out with us."

"Well, Varden is a good 1st Sergeant. Keogh told me that he was quite capable for as young as he is. If Reno keeps you on as his adjutant, we'll have to depend on him to run Company I. Better find an easy mount for Nave, and get him a good man to be his orderly." said Weir

"I already have, Varden picked Pvt. O'Bryan. He was out with us last year."

"Good, keep me informed. Let's hope we get started soon. We're going twice as far as last year, and I like to be back here before October,"

Henry, Jake and the rest of the section were gathered around a table at their end of the squad bay, talking quietly about preparations for the coming expedition.

"I got permission from Top for us to buy a shotgun. We can use it to bag prairie chickens, and small game." Holden stated, "Based on last year, it will come in handy. Jake and I looked at one of those new Dangerfield & Lefever breechloaders, over at the trading post. It uses brass shells and we can buy enough reloading supplies to last the season. "

"I think we need to stock up on canned goods like fruit and vegetables, jams, and the like, maybe a few spices too. Like those little bottles of pepper sauce from Louisiana, the post store just got in." said Biscuit. "It's got a bite to it that can cover up a bad taste."

"Yeh, we never lacked much for regular chow." Little chimed in, "But that was with the surveyors. If we stay with the company, the food won't be near as good."

"I think extra soap and a good sewing kit would come in handy, too." added Charlie. "Maybe some cologne to sprinkle on Big, he's known to put off some mighty odors."

They all chuckled at Big, who flashed a middle finger at them.

"D'ya think that those Brits and Canadians will be well stocked with liquor again?" asked Rooster.

"Ah, I think so, those Scottish lads travel well stocked. But we ought to take what we can. We don't know how much dealings we'll have with them this time." opined Holden.

"One of the new men, Manning, was a shoemaker and I got him to resole my boots. But, I think a stock of extra shoe leather might come in handy. It would make good trading material, too" Jake said.

Holden nodded his head, "Good idea, Jake. Okay, let's see what all we can scrounge up, and then we'll pony up to buy the rest. I've heard through the grapevine that we'll be leaving at the end of the month."

Several days later, they were lounging on the front porch, after dinner, waiting for the sunset, when Val Wheeler rode up on his paint pony.

"Howdy Boys! I'm guessing that I missed supper, I meant to be here earlier but my little gal held me up a bit. The sweet thing made me a new vest, and some new moccasins and leggings. I'm gonna miss her. Hell, I already do, looking at the likes of you!"

"Now, don't be expecting us to feel sorry for you!" Rooster replied. "Ya spent your winter cuddled up somewhere, while we mucked about in the snow and cold!"

Val grinned. "You all signed up for it, me I'm just hired help. I expect you'll be wantin' to be a little more sociable once we get back up on the line and yor canteen's gettin' empty."

"Good to see you again, Val. We were wondering when you'd show up." said Jake.

"I thought I'd best be checking in. Didn't want you to leave without me."

Morse came out the door from the orderly room, followed by Top Martin. They watched as Wheeler dismounted and tied off his horse, "Bout time, we figured we'd have to come hunt you up and shanghai your sorry ass away from your sweet little blanket warmer."

"Naw, it was time for me to get gone from her. She's lookin' to start a family, and I'm headed west. You almost ready? We're into the good weather season now."

"Grab your kit and come inside. We got a spare bunk and I'll roust the cook to make you up a plate. We'll bring you up to speed on the plans for this season. These lads will see to your pony."

Jake stepped over to help Val, and Charlie grabbed the reins saying. "I got him Val, you want me to give him some oats?"

"Maybe a few, I don't want him to get spoiled."

"Rogers, you come with us." Martin said, surprising Jake. He turned and looked back at the others, shrugging his shoulders in surprise.

After stashing Val's gear in an empty NCO's room, they settled at a table in the mess. The setting sun coming through the window lit up the room. The cook heard the commotion and poked his head out of the kitchen. "I don't suppose you brought me any fish, Val?"

"No, Cookie, I was usin' my other pole this morning," Wheeler said grinning, "But, I'll see if I can catch you a mess in the next day or so."

"I'll rustle somethin' up for you. Bacon and beans okay? I got some fresh bread. too"

"Sounds just fine."

"Rogers, pay attention here." Martin said looking at Jake.

"Okay, Top!" he answered, wondering what was up.

"Lt. Porter got a dispatch from Major Reno today. We're to head over to Fort Stevenson, and pick up our supply train, then march overland to Fort Buford. They want us there by mid-June, so that means 15 days for us to get there. At Fort Buford, there are 5 companies of the 6th Infantry waiting. We're to rendezvous with them, and then the entire command, under Reno, will head northwest along the Big Muddy River towards the line, then swing west. They want us there by Mid-July. What do you think Wheeler?"

"I think that's a long damn ways, Mike. If we swing too far north along the Muddy, we'll run into the Badlands. Best to get across the Poplar River where the branches meet, then strike straight west to the Milk, and on to the Bear Paw Mountains. There's good water, grazing and lot's of wood along several creeks around there."

"I'll leave it up to you, Val. Pat, we'll be wanting the horses well fed, and shoed, before we leave. Make sure we're well supplied with spares."

"What about the Surveyor Teams? Where are they?" asked Wheeler.

"They're in St.Paul. They're expecting to leave about the same time we do. They'll board the train to Bismarck, then riverboat up to Buford. Hopefully, about the same time we get there. Once we leave Fort Buford, it'll be up to them, and Reno, to hash out where everyone goes."

"That'll be interesting." Morse commented.

"One last thing. Capt. Keogh is gone for the summer. Lt. Bell is on detached duty buying horses, in St. Paul, and with Porter gone with Reno, the two companies will only have 2nd Lieutenants Edgerly and Nave for officers, besides Capt. Weir. Lt. Nave is banged up pretty badly, and he may not see it through the summer. So Sgt. Varden and I, will be depending on all the other NCOs to keep things running smoothly. Rogers, effective immediately Capt. Weir and I agree to promote you to a Corporal. Get some chevrons sewn on before we leave. The paperwork and pay will have to catch up with you along the way."

Jake was stunned. He had just finished up his first year.

Pat was beaming. "Your folks will be proud, lad. Now close up your mouth before fly wanders in."

"Don't let them stripes go to your head, Pup. You're just the runt of the next litter now." Val cautioned him with a grin.

"Thanks for your confidence in me, Top. I'll do my best to justify it."

"I know you will, lad. Now go get your mates, and head over to the post traders. Tell them the first rounds on me!"

As Jake turned and walked out the door, the older men watched him leave.

"I wonder does he realize that every time there's a need for a junior NCO for a detail, that his name will be called?" Martin mused.

"Ah, he soon will, Top! It's the way if things. You and I were there once."

The cook brought out Val's food, and set it in front of him. "Let me know if you need more, Val."

"Many thanks. I'll see to getting you some fish in the next day or so. Keep some cane poles and tackle in your cook wagon. There's some nice trout where we're headed."

Morse had gone in his room and came back out with a bottle, and some cups. He sat down across from Wheeler. "How about a taste, Gents?"

He poured the whiskey in each cup, and slid them across the table. "A toast is in order I believe! Here's to good luck, and good weather in our travels!

They tapped cups together and Martin said. "Amen to that!"

Jake walked back outside to the porch where the rest of the section was still sitting and jawing. They looked up as he came over.

"What's up Jake?" Charlie asked

"Well, it seems you're going to have to start calling me Corporal Rogers, now. Top just told me."

"What, no shit! What's up with that?"

Jake shook his head, "Don't ask me. I'm dumbfounded. And, we're headed out pretty quick. We'll be 6-7 weeks on the march to Fort Buford, by way of Fort Stevenson."

Henry stood up and held out his hand. "Congratulations, Jake!"

"Henry, you're the one that should be the Corporal." he replied.

"No, lad! It's not something I'd care for. I've told Sgt. Martin that."

Jake looked at Henry quizzically and asked, "Why not?"

"Never mind that now. Let's go wet your stripes. Come on lads! Off to the post traders to toast Corporal Roger!"

They all cheered in agreement and started out across the parade ground.

The two cavalry companies continued vigorously preparing for the upcoming expedition. When the word got out about how far they were going, everyone scrambled to snap up the choice items at the post store, knowing that except for a brief stop at Fort Stevenson, that would be the last chance all summer to acquire anything. By the time they got to Fort Buford the infantry companies would probably have the post trader's shelves there, picked clean. The horses were carefully inspected along with their saddles and tack. The company wagons were overhauled and carefully packed. Extra water barrels were lashed to the sides, and fresh canvas spread over the bows. Sgt. Rush made sure that everyone had serviceable field gear, and that adequate supplies were in reserve.

Major Reno showed up on the 25th, with his escort and personal baggage. He came up through Fort Seward, pleased that the trail was in good shape and the rivers fordable. He sent for Lt. Porter first thing.

"Porter! Good to see you. I trust everything is in order."

"Yes, Sir! I believe we're ready to move out when you are."

"Yes, well my wife is in ill health, has been since her mother passed last year. I've been trying to get re-assigned, but without success so far. I've written several letters, and am still waiting for a reply. Col. Hunt is detached on court marshal duty and that puts me in temporary command of this post. I intend to stay here, until he returns."

"I see, Sir. But I understood that with the distances involved, we were to move out right away."

"I don't see that a week, or so, will impact that timeline. I may hear something by then."

"Very well, Sir. I'll inform Capt. Weir and Lt. Nave."

"Nave? Where's Capt. Keogh?"

"In Ireland I believe, Sir. He's to be gone several months. Family estate business he told me. It seems his Aunt left him some land."

"Hmm! Nave is quite junior to command a line Company."

"He's badly injured his shoulder, also. Any chance you can find someone else to act as your adjutant, Sir. That would free me to see to Company I."

"No, Porter! You know how I like things to be handled. Lt. Nave will have to muddle through."

Porter and Weir were sitting in the main room of Weir's quarters that evening, discussing Reno's stalling tactics. Weir poured them glasses, and then leaned back to light his pipe. Once he got it drawing, he looked over to Porter.

"We're ready leave, now. We need to take advantage of the weather. We've had our orders for a week, I can't believe that Reno is dragging his feet."

"None the less, here we are."

"Well, I sent a courier down to Fort Seward and had a telegram sent to the St. Paul Quartermaster requesting more tents, since it looks like we're going to be here long enough for them to arrive."

"But we have plenty of tents."

"Maybe, but that request will have to be approved and I'm banking on that it will be noticed."

Porter smiled, "I can't wait to see how that card plays at HQ. Sneaky, Tom, pretty sneaky!"

"What, just an ordinary request through channels." Weir replied, shrugging his shoulders and raising his glass. "Cheers, Jim!"

On the morning of the 28th, Reno stormed out of the Adjutants Office, heading for his quarters. Weir was standing nearby on the front porch with Porter. The Infantry duty officer came outside, and watched Reno, smiling as he did.

"It seems your Commander is upset."

"What's up with that, Lieutenant?" asked Porter.

He handed Porter a copy of a telegram. It said. "Let your cavalry move at once. You are expected to be in Bismarck, by the June 4, to coordinate with Major Twining about the supply logistics for the season." It was sent by the Assistant Adjutant General, O.D. Green, HQ, Department of Dakota.

Porter passed it to Weir, who read it and smiled. "Okay, it seems we're off at last!"

The next day, Reno informed Weir that he was to command the column on the march.. He had decided to go by rail out to Bismarck, and then riverboat up to Fort Stevenson. Ostensibly, to oversee the proper transportation of the supplies, but Porter privately informed Weir that it was in order to have access to a telegraph while continuing his efforts to get reassigned. Then Reno left to go back down to Fort Seward, taking Porter with him.

CHAPTER 12

Fort Buford, Dakota Territory Mid-June 1874

In 1828, John Jacob Astor's American Fur Company established a trading post at the confluence of the Missouri and Yellowstone Rivers. Originally called Fort Henry, the name was changed to Fort Union and for almost four decades it was the most important fur trading out on the Upper Missouri River. With the decline of the fur trade, it was sold to the U S Army, in 1867. and the Army demolished the existing fort. The 30 year old wood of the old fort was found to be superior to the green cottonwood available at the new site, and was hauled over to reuse the materials to build a new one which was located on the north side of the Missouri River in valley two miles away, to the east. The new installation was called Fort Buford after Major General John Buford, a Union cavalry commander, during the War. Originally manned by the 13th Infantry, it was attacked and harassed by the Lakota Sioux. After several expansions it was turned over to the 6th Infantry and by 1874, the six single story adobe barracks had been renovated with wood siding, tar and gravel roofs, and expanded to include attached kitchens and mess halls. The fort located about a quarter mile north of the Missouri River, was manned by six infantry companies and grew to encompass a square mile in area, including a hospital, warehouses, bakery, sawmill, and laundress housing. Due to its strategic location at the junction of the rivers and the traffic that resulted, the post trader, Alvin C. Leighton had one of the largest operations in the territory, just outside the fort to the West. He was also a partner in several other Post Traderships at other forts elsewhere along the Missouri River. A village of friendly Hidatsa and Mandan Indians lived permanently, two miles northwest of the fort. The two companies of the 7th Cavalry had made good time from Fort Totten. After a brief stop at Fort Stevenson to pick up the supply wagons waiting there, they settled into a daily routine, following the trail along the Missouri River. They maintained a steady pace of 30-35 miles per day. Val Wheeler had requested that Jake be assigned to assist him as a scout, which was fortunate for Jake as it got him out of camp guard duties and kept him out front. They roamed out ahead, picking out the best route for the wagons, and good bivouac areas with water, wood, and grazing. Val worked on teaching Jake sign language, tracking, and reading trail signs. Jake carried the shotgun with him and kept the cook supplied with prairie chickens, sharp tailed grouse, rabbits, and squirrels, along with an occasional antelope, or deer. He and Val made sure to save some for the officer's mess, too. Jake still spent his evenings camped with his section, and continued to share an A tent with Charlie. Val, stayed near the sergeants tents, but liked to drop by and visit with he, Holden, and the others. The weather cooperated and two weeks found them closing on Fort Buford. As they rounded a big bend in the river, they saw the sprawling fort come into view off in the distance, the bluffs behind it marking the course of the Missouri River

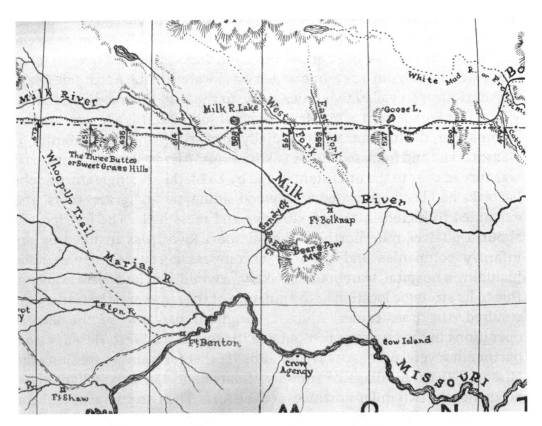

Northern Boundary Survey - Summer 1874

The entire expedition was staged on the plains surrounding Fort Buford.

Due to a mix of good planning and sheer luck, the 7th Cavalry troops had arrived on the 14th, one day before the river boat *Fontenelle*, carrying the Boundary Surveyors. The *Fontenelle* had been so overloaded and slow, that the mules had to be off loaded and herded along the river, but still arrived only two hours later. Major Reno who had been on the smaller riverboat *Eclipse* and had been the first to get there on June 11. He and Porter were busy arranging for a re-supply train to leave from Fort Benton and rendezvous with them up in the Milk River country the following month. His request was for an ox train of capacity to transport sufficient rations for 539 soldiers, half forage for 119 horse and 401 mules for 30 days. Also rations for 109 men, and half forage for the 142 animals of the Boundary Commission. Reno directed the 7th Cavalry and the ox trains move from Ft. Benton to the Milk River at the mouth of Box Elder Creek, just west of Bear Paw Mountain.

Val Wheeler would go out with Lt. Greene's party. A local guide, George Boyd would be responsible for guiding the re-supply trains to and from the survey line. 14 Indian scouts, from the village, were signed up and divided between Companies E & I, 6th Infantry, under the command of Capt. Edwin Ames. They would be accompanying the three teams of topographical surveyors, a tangent party and a mound building party.

Fort Buford Dakota Territory - Circa 1870s

The encampments were spread out northwest of the fort along

a creek. The Cavalry camp was closest to river, then the Boundary Commission camp. The Infantry consisted of Companies D, E, & I, 6th Infantry stationed at Buford, and Companies B & K had come up river from Fort Abraham Lincoln. They were all at the fort in barracks. The Post Trader's compound was located between the encampments and the fort, and was enjoying the bonanza of business being generated by the expedition. June 21 was set as the departure date, and last minute preparations were being made by all parties.

Jake and his section got settled in, setting up camp and caring for their horses. After a quick supper they headed over to the Boundary Commission camp for a visit. When they got there, Val was already in an animated conversation with Lt. Greene.

"You need to pay attention here, Lootenant! If you're gonna go start where you left off, as you work your way west we'll be in the Badlands. That's rough country, what little water there is will be alkaline, and we'll have to strain it to boot. We'll have to burn buffalo shit for fires. It won't get much better until you get to the grasslands. So you need to make the men ration their water, and fill those extra barrels whenever they can. I reckon it'll be at least 3 weeks for us to get back close enough to the supply depot at the Sweet Grass Hills."

"I understand Val, we'll need you to do your best to find us waterholes, while we work on the line."

"Hmm, you'll see when we get up there." Wheeler replied fuming.

"Lt. Greene, Sir, Good to see you again." Jake said.

Greene turned towards him and smiled, "Well Corporal Rogers! My congratulations! Val and I are just discussing the terrain we're to negotiate. I understand that I've been handed off to the Infantry this year. I was looking forward to working with you again, but it appears that's not to be."

"Yes, but I'm sure we'll meet up with you in a few weeks. Perhaps we'll get a chance then. Are Mr. Doolittle and Mr. Downing with you?"

"Mr. Doolittle is here, Mr. Downing declined to come out this season due to his health, but we have a new man, Dr. Valentine T. McGillicuddy. Capt. Gregory has Mr. Boss with him again, and Dr. Coues is traveling with him, also. You'll recognize most of the men though."

"I see you got promoted, Sir." Jake said, eyeing Greene's epaulets. "You're a 1st Lieutenant, now."

"Yes, I'm quite pleased. Unfortunately, I'm still outranked by my escort commander. Gets a bit awkward from time to time. We met up with Major Reno in Bismarck. He and Coues are still fussing. Bismarck was all abuzz with Custer's Black Hills Expedition. We were told that he has over

1,000 men and 100 supply wagons. They say the Sioux are very upset. I'm surprised that Custer didn't take your companies with him."

"I wouldn't know anything about that, Sir. We came up along the Missouri River, from Ft. Stevenson, with Capt. Weir. But I'm glad we're not with Custer, Val tells me we're sure to see huge herds of buffalo where we're headed."

"Well, we will if we get a move on! You're apt to see more Indians this year too. All the tribes will be out following the buffalo. Once we get on the Milk, we'll be in Indian Territory. Although it's supposed to belong to the Blackfeet, the Assiniboine, the Plains Cree, some Sioux bands will all be out and about." Val stated. "They'll shy away from you soldiers, but they'll be out there."

"What about the Brits, Sir?" Charlie asked.

"They're coming overland along the Boundary Trail. They should be getting close by now. I'm sure they will be on the line when we get up there. It's the same group of Real Engineers as last year." Greene answered.

Big George spoke up, "That's good, those Scots will be sure to have some whisky!"

"Yes, Indeed! Well, it's good to see you men, again. I propose we wander over to the post traders and enjoy a beer or two. First round's on me!" Greene exclaimed.

Leaving camp on June 21st, Reno and the entire command moved northwest in the direction of the Big Muddy. Going into camp there, he sent a courier to Fort Benton to establish a line communications for the rest of the season. Greene and his topographical surveyors split away on the 26th and headed up to the line along the Poplar River, to connect with last years final stations at 385 miles, and run tangents west to 408 miles. Captain Gregory and the astronomical party stayed with the main body until they got to the mouth of the Milk River, then diverged north, taking Capt. Montgomery Bryant's Company B, 6th infantry with them on July 2nd, towards Frenchman' s Creek where he would set up a station at 462 miles out. There, they made contact with members of Capt. Featherstonhough's astronomical party which was observing at 432 miles. This confirmed that the British were out ahead of the Americans. Meanwhile Reno and the rest of the command continued along the Milk River past Fort Belknap, to the west of the Bear Paw Mountains, and established a depot at the mouth of Box Elder Creek, on July 12th. They were expecting to meet up with the re-supply train that Reno had arranged for earlier out of Ft. Benton. When the supplies weren't there, Reno and Major Twining, who had stayed with the main column instead of going up to the line with his teams, decided to go to Fort Benton to check on them. The evening a courier arrived from Ft. Benton with a message for Major Reno. Capt. Weir and the other 7th officers were relaxing by the officers mess tent when Reno walked up.

"Captain Weir, may I speak to you in private, please?" Reno asked, as he approached.

Weir stood and said, "Of course , Sir." He walked over to where Reno was standing. Reno had a wooden expression on his face, and seemed quite solemn.

"I've just received notification from Pennsylvania. My wife died on the 10th."

'I'm so sorry to hear that, Major. May I offer my condolences?"

"I was afraid this would happen, that's why I tried so hard to keep from coming out this season. She'd been ill for some time."

They stood in silence for a moment. Weir vaguely remembered Mrs. Reno from his days around Ft. Hays. A pretty, vivacious young women, several years younger than Reno and always pleasant on the few occasions they met.

"I only met her a few times, and that was several years ago. I remember her as well liked. I'm sure you'll be wanting to head to Fort Benton immediately, Sir."

"Yes, well, you're the next ranking officer. I'm turning over command to you. I've written orders for you." Reno stated, as he handed some papers to Weir.

"Major Twining will be coming with me to Benton. He's going to look into the status of our re-supply column. We'll leave at first light."

"Yes, Sir! Let me know if I can be of any assistance."

Reno turned and made his way towards his tent, with shoulders sagging and head hanging.

When Weir went back to the officers tent, he informed the others about his conversation with Reno.

"That's a shame! I understand he has a young son, also. I feel sorry for him." said Porter. "Does this make me your Adjutant now, Tom?"

"If I need you I'll let you know. I suspect that your time is best spent with your company. Nave is not recovering well."

Weir moved over near a candle lantern, to read Reno's orders:

July 12, 1875

Attention: Captain Weir

Unforeseen circumstances imperatively demand my departure and it being impossible that I can return before completion of the seasons operation with the commission. I have the honor to transmit for your guidance instructions from the department commander regarding the return of the cavalry to Fort Totten, D. T. its designated winter quarters. You will consult with the Chief Astronomer and when in you opinion no trouble is anticipated from Indian depredations you will return with the cavalry at a sufficiently early date to secure the arrival of the battalion at its winter quarters on or before Oct.10th.

Marcus A. Reno, Major, 7th Cavalry

"Well, gentlemen, it seems the only thing I'm ordered to do is get us home before winter. I'm open for suggestions on how we spend the rest of the summer!" announced Weir.

The next morning shortly after Reno's departure, George Boyd rode into the camp. He had a message form Capt. Gregory and Lt. Greene and reported that they were making excellent progress. However the buffalo herds and dry conditions had caused them to be running low on forage. Furthermore, the available water sources were extremely poor. They requested some supply wagons to meet them at the East Fork of the Milk River where it crossed the parallel.

Capt. Weir, Lt. Porter, and both 1st Sergeants were sitting in front of the Headquarters tent talking with Boyd.

"Capt. Gregory sent me to guide the wagons to him. It's about 45 miles from here, to the East Fork. Once we get across the Milk we can make good time. He plans on setting up to observe on the 15th. Greene will just be starting to run the tangent. They'll still have about 80 miles until they get to the East Butte of the Sweetgrass Hills. The Brits are planning on a big camp at West Butte, there. We'll need about two weeks of supplies, mostly forage, and some good water and wood for cooking would be nice. We've been using dried buffalo shit for the last week or so."

Capt. Weir nodded, "What do you think, Porter?"

"Well, we may as well, the plan is to head up to the Sweetgrass Hills when the supply train with the forage and rations gets here. How many wagons are you thinking of sending up?"

"I think four will be enough. Sgt. Martin, have Sgt. Rush get them ready. Make sure to have fresh water in the barrels, and tie some firewood to the sides and backs. I'm thinking of sending Cpl. Rogers section along as escort. They got on well with the surveyors last season."

"Aye, Sir! I'll see to it."

"What's the country like from the East Fork to the Sweetgrass Hills like, Mr. Boyd? I'm think about having the wagons stay with Gregory until he gets there."

"It's fairly flat and easy going, it shouldn't be a problem. There're will be a lot of buffalo around, and Indians, also. Mostly bands of Assiniboine, a few Blackfeet, and Métis. They've been keeping their distance, though"

"Very good! That's the plan then! I expect them to roll out tomorrow morning."

Jake was summoned to the Company tent, where 1st Sgt. Martin and Sgt. Morse were waiting.

"Good morning Top! Sergeant Morse, You wanted to see me?"

"The Captain is sending four supply wagons up to the line to meet up with Gregory and Greene. He's picked your section to escort it. Once you rendezvous with them, you're to stay with them until the rest of the outfit gets up to the line. Probably two weeks all told. You good with that?"

"You bet, Top. We're tired of hanging around here. It's pretty boring here, compared to being out on the line. No offense to you!"

Martin chuckled, "None taken. Pat and I got our fill of that when we were chasing Mr. Lo across Kansas. We shot our share of buffalo back in those days, too."

Jake nodded his head, asking "When do we leave?"

"Be ready to roll at first light. Mr. Boyd will be guiding you up. Have you met him yet?"

"No, but I saw him with Capt. Gregory when they were headed out two weeks ago."

"He's been trapping furs and guiding out of Buford and Benton for years. Go look him up, and introduce yourself. Better let your men know so they can get ready, too."

"Will do Top, thanks."

"Rogers, be careful out there."

Jake alerted Henry and Charlie, then went to find Boyd. He found him by the cook wagons jawing with the cooks. As Jake approached Boyd watched him closely.

"You the Corporal there're sending out with me?"

Jake held out his hand. "Jake Rogers, pleased to meet you. I understand you just came down from the line."

"Yep, left day before yesterday. Those boys were fixin' to run some buffalo, when I hit the trail. Val was taking Lt. Greene and Capt. Ames out to show them how, so's they don't get killed, right off. Them big bulls can be skittish when you're a chasin' em on horseback."

"Sounds like it. I'm sure Val will watch out for them, cussing them the whole time."

"That's Val! You must be that soldier boy, Rogers, that he's so high on."

"Well, we spent some time up on the line with him last summer, and he wintered near us, at Ft. Totten. He can be a cantankerous old bastard, but he showed me a lot. You known him long?"

"Nigh on ten years, now! First met him at Fort Benton, when he came in with a load of furs, had a passel of Sioux scalps with him too. Word was they belonged to the ones that killed his father. He'd tracked them down and kilt 'em all. He still can't abide being around any Lakotas. They call him 'Pale Wolf" and steer well clear of him."

Charlie and Henry both raised their eyebrows and glanced over at Jake, who replied, "Hmm! Hadn't heard that"

"Yeh, well, he hasn't been around these parts for a while. He went east to the Red River with some Métis, but he told me he was fixin' to stay around for a bit."

"You see any problems getting the wagons up there?" Jake asked.

"Naw, but you never know, lot's of folks out chasin' the buffs. We get out on the prairie, best keep an eye out. It's a bad place to be if a big herd gets spooked. Be ready to stop, or head off at an angle and try to keep your distance. A big bull can turn on a dime and the cows will follow his lead. Keep the wagons faced away from them."

CHAPTER 13

Jake and the supply wagons had followed Boyd across the plains and crossed the West Fork of the Milk, which was just a shallow ribbon at that point, then continued until they came to the East Fork which was the same. They turned north and followed the riverbed through narrow valleys. It was hot, dusty, and they were plagued off and on by blackish brown grasshoppers. Boyd called them Mormon crickets, and said that the Indians would herd them into the river and collect them in baskets, then grind them up to make a flour. They covered the ground consuming what little vegetation there was. Fortunately, they were able to get past them before they stopped to camp. Finally, they came out of the valley and found the tents of the observation station pitched next to the riverbed which was practically dry, containing only a few muddied pools. As they rolled into the camp, they were greeted enthusiastically. Capt. Gregory, Lt. Greene, and Val Wheeler walked out to meet them.

"Well, now, look who decided to come calling!" Val exclaimed.

Jake looked at them, smiling as they halted. He and Boyd dismounted and Jake saluted the officers. "Corporal Rogers reporting , Sirs! We were told to get these wagons up to you as quick as we could. Capt. Weir sends his compliments."

"Weir? What happened to Major Reno?." Gregory asked.

"The Major left just before I got there." stated Boyd, " I heard he was sent word that his wife passed, and he was headed home back east."

"That's a shame! That's hard news for a man to have to find out way out here. Albeit he'll not be missed. Well, Rogers, did you volunteer again?"

Jake grinned and replied, "No, Sir. I believe that the Captain and 1st Sergeant did that for me, but we would have. I was told to stay with you until the outfit meets up with you at the Sweetgrass Hills. They're waiting on the supply train from Ft. Benton. It's late, and Major Twining is gone to check on it, so it might be a week or so, before they come up."

"Well, I'm going to send you out with Lt. Greene again. Major Reno ordered Capt. Ames and his infantry not to separate from the survey parties. Greene here, wants to cut loose and finish running the tangents out ahead. Your cavalry section can keep up with him. So we'll split up the supplies, and get him on his way. Wheeler assures me that the grazing and water will improve in a few days as we get farther west. I'll use Boyd to guide us. "

"What say you, Rogers? It'll be grand to be out ahead. We'll get to run some buffalo, eh Val?" Greene remarked.

"I can't see as how I can keep you from it Lootenant! Now that you've got a taste of it. But we don't want to get too carried away. People out depend on the buffs to live on."

"I'll certainly bear that in mind, Val. Come Rogers, bring your men over to my camp, you'll remember most of them. Capt. Ames and his men have their camp set up over by Capt. Bryant and Company B. I'll send over a couple of my light wagons to get our share of the supplies, and be sure to bring several barrels of good water. The coffee has been tasting like chalk around here for days. We're roasting some fresh buffalo meat tonight. Val's been giving the cook tips on the best cuts."

Later that evening they were sitting around a fire made with some wood from the wagons, drinking coffee.

"It's nice to enjoy a campfire again. Dried buffalo dung gets the job done cooking, but it's not much good to linger around. " said Greene.

Jake, who was leaning against his saddle, reached into a haversack and retrieved a bundle, then tossed it to Val. "Here you go. I got this from the Kentucky boys again. They always seem to have tobacco, figured you might be getting low."

Wheeler caught it deftly, smiling broadly. "Well, as my old priest Father Jacques used to say, "Bless you my son!"

Greene laughed saying, "It seems you've just been adopted, Rogers!"

Mr. Doolittle, accompanied by Dr. McGillycuddy, had just wandered up."Well, let's have christening then." Doolittle said, and produced a bottle. "We persuaded Capt. Featherstonhaugh to part with a couple of these when we were camped near them at Goose Lake, three days ago."

Greene spoke up. "This is our good doctor , Valentine McGillycuddy! He and Val have become friends, mostly based on their unique first names."

Jake looked up puzzled, then grinned,"Valentine?"

"I ain't no Valentine!" Wheeler barked, "I was christened 'Valentin', that's French! My father let the damn Jesuit priest and my mother pick it. I prefer just Val, or Wheeler, as you all know, and I'll caution you to remember."

They all smiled at his bluster.

"Hear, hear!" I'll second that!" stated McGillycuddy.

Doolittle made the circuit around, pouring a generous dollop for each. Greene raised his cup in toast. "Here's to fresh horizons and smooth terrain!" They all acknowledged and raised their cups in reply.

"For sure the way will be easier, as we go on." said Wheeler, "And your fresh horizon will be black with buffalo. We'll be seeing the big herds, soon.

"So Mr. Wheeler, do you anticipate that there will be more Indians about as we get to buffalo country?"

"They are already about, and they're keeping their distance. This is prime season for gathering meat for the winter. There aren't many Blackfeet as there used to be, but this is all their treaty land. The Assiniboines, Gross Ventres of the Prairie, Crow, and even a few bands of Sioux will be hunting. Then there's the Métis. You all have met the 49th Rangers as the travel through with Capt. Anderson, and last year we met a small band, early on. Out here there will be bands of up to 200 lodges, twice that number of carts, and over 500 horses. They'll kill several hundred buffalo each day, harvesting the best meat for drying and leaving the hides and forequarters lay. You'll smell the carcasses, before you see 'em, if the wind is right. When their carts get full they'll head down to Fort Benton to trade."

"Seems a waste." Doolittle said.

"It is, and the Indians aren't much better. The herds get smaller every year. But that's the way of things!"

"Do you expect any trouble?"

"Naw! The Rangers have told them that we're making a "Medicine Line" to protect the Great Queen Mother's land. Some of them may come sniffing around looking for gifts. Most are too busy. We may see a few scouts now and then, but I expect they'll stay out of our way."

"Well, I for one, am looking forward to seeing these great herds. I've heard stories from men who've had the experience. Sgt. Morse told me about seeing them down in Kansas." said Greene

Wheeler nodded his head, "It certainly is something to see. Best remember it, you'll probably not be able to in ten years. Sgt. Morse told me that with the railroad splitting the plains, the buffalo are being slaughtered by the thousands, the hides and meat loaded up and sent back east."

Capt. Gregory left to go to the next station at Milk River Lake, 588 miles out, and the topographical parties worked their way west. Greene and the tangent team scrambled to keep up. Not having the infantry and survey teams to slow them down they made good progress. As the plains leveled out, grass and water ceased to be issue, but wood was still scarce. This continued to be offset by large supply of dried buffalo manure. The teams all moved rapidly west along the parallel. Every morning the peaks of the Sweetgrass Hills beckoned in the distance. Wheeler, Jake and his section ranged out in front, accompanied by Lt. Greene most days. One morning just after breakfast, Greene was looking through a transit telescope, when he spotted a dark mass on the horizon.

"Mr. Wheeler!" he called out. "I believe that I am looking at one of the big buffalo herds you spoke of the other night!"

Val, and the cavalry troopers were in the process of saddling their horses. Jake and Val walked over to Greene where he motioned for them to look through the telescope.

They took turns peering through the scope, and Wheeler observed. "Yep! That's a fair size herd." Looking around at the campsite, which was located on tall bluff above a creek, he commented. "I think that they won't try cross here, but they're damn sure coming for the water. We best sit tight! Bunch the wagons together and block in the mules and livestock." Turning to Jake and Greene he said. "What say we mosey out there and get little closer? You boys game?"

Both of them grinned and replied "Let's go!"

They rode slowly out of camp and circled to the south along the creek, then crested a small hill. The herd had advanced and was loping along.

"How close can we get Val?" Jake asked.

"Depends on if you're set on killing one, or you just want to watch. The bulls will be outlying, while the dominant cows will be in the lead. I wouldn't try and get closer than fifty yards, or so. A buffalo, can outrun and out turn your horse if you get too close, so keep that in mind. The Indians normally ride up within good bow distance and start slinging arrows, retreating when the buffalo come at 'em. Once the herd gets up rolling, you want to be well off away from the direction they're running. They'll stay together, but don't think they can't change direction in a heartbeat."

"I think let's just stay up here and watch." Greene said, as he pulled out a set of binoculars.

"Okay by me." Wheeler replied.

The herd covered the horizon, stretching across the plains in a black undulating mass. It was impossible to estimate the number of animals. Suddenly the buffalo picked up speed and charged off to the north, just before the herd reached the creek. The ground seemed to tremble, and over the thunder of hooves shots rang out in the distance.

"That'll be Métis, they use rifles." Wheeler said. "Indians use arrows, they don't want to use up their supply of bullets."

As they watched, several dozen horsemen appeared, when the rear ranks of the buffalo came into view. Animals were dropping to the ground, as Greene was watching intently through his field glasses.

"By God! Those fellows are mowing them down. It looks like they all have Winchesters and Henrys."

"Oh! They'll have some Sharps, too. If you look behind them you'll see their carts coming on up. That'll be the women and kids. They'll finish off the downed animals, then start carving them up for the meat."

"That's quite a butchering operation they have organized."

"It is, they been doing that as long as I can remember. Guns have just made them more efficient. We'll sit here a bit, then go palaver with them if you want."

"Yes, I believe I'd like to do that." Greene replied. "I'd like to see their camp."

"Well, be careful around the damned Jesuit that's sure to be with them. The priests have a lot of clout, besides religion. It might be best to downplay the importance of marking the line. The Métis go where they want, when they want. Do you speak any French?"

"I studied French, but I can't say that I'm particularly fluent."

"Then you better let me do the talking. Most of them can get by in English a bit."

Wheeler went ahead alone, and several of the Métis rode up to meet him. They spent several minutes talking and gesturing, then rode off. Wheeler came back to where Greene was waiting.

"Okay, they'll let us visit. Be a good idea to come up with gifts, though."

"What do you suggest? We're pretty low on supplies."

"Coffee, sugar, maybe some flour."

"Okay, I'll see what we can scrounge up."

"You may as well bring a bottle or two along." Val said grinning, "Just in case."

The Métis summer hunting camp was formed by arranging their carts in a large circle parked closely together, where the pony herd was driven in at night. The tepees were pitched around the outside perimeter. Most were covered in buffalo hides, but there were some covered with canvas. Lt. Greene elected to set up camp within sight of the Métis, but at a distance. Val, Doolittle, and McGillycuddy loaded a cart with the gift supplies they had accumulated. Greene went over to Jake and the rest of the men and told them to remain behind and stand guard. They were disappointed that they couldn't go, but understood when Val pointed out that the Métis were very close knit and protective of their families.

"You've met the Rangers, these people are the same. They dress mostly like we do. The women wear dresses, and the children are schooled by the priest. They come south following the buffalo, hunt and trade with the local tribes, then head back north to their winter camps. They live by their own rules. I've spent time with them. It's not a bad way, but when the buffalo get scarce their ways will be changin'. Right now they just want to be left to their own devices." Wheeler told Jake.

After Greene and his party left, Jake settled down next to the fire with Holden and the other soldiers. They finished up supper, and had a pot of coffee warming, and Jake filled his cup.

"Well, Henry, here we are. I reckon that we're lucky to be out like this, instead of in camp."

"Indeed we are, Jake. We've come a long ways. But it seems to me that there's a lot more ahead of us. It's just now August and we are still a long way from Fort Totten, each day brings the chance for new vistas. And who knows what may have changed since we left the Company."

"You're right Henry, although Capt. Weir and the rest of the outfit are supposed to be up on the line soon. Sgt. Morse told me that they would probably be up in two weeks when we left, so we should running into them up ahead before too long."

"I find it interesting that the efforts and resources of two nations have been expended to mark a boundary that is really of no interest to the people that live here. They will follow the buffalo without any concern for what country they are in. The countryside is not suited to promote settlements, or farming. I suspect that aside from the buffalo, there are no resources really worth pursuing."

"Yes, but I'm glad we got the opportunity to see it anyway."

Major Twining had resourcefully managed to secure the missing 50 tons of forage supplies for the American contingent. It had been off-loaded at Cow Island, on the Missouri 120 miles short of Fort Benton, because of low water levels. He was able to put together a mule train, along with an infantry escort, and quickly retrieve the forage. He came north with what was on hand at Fort Benton, meeting up with Capt. Weir and his cavalry. The remaining infantry company remained at the Box Elder camp and would come up when the last of the forage supplies. On July 25th, the cavalry established an encampment at the bottom of the northern slope of the East Butte of the Sweetgrass Hills. There was a fine spring with pure cold water, good grazing on the prairie, and plenty of wood above them on the butte. Gregory would soon arrive there and set up his observation station at 635 miles out. Greene and the tangent team were busy running the line. They had left the other teams behind with the infantry escort. On the last day of the month, they were close to finishing up. Jake and Val were well out front as they approached the cavalry camp, when they saw a troop leave and head towards them.

"I see Sgt. Morse in the lead, I think that's Sgt. Flanagan and Jimmy Hurd's section with him." Jake observed.

They rode on to meet the troopers. When they came up. Jake waved at Sgt. Morse, who halted the troopers.

"You made good time, we've only been here a few days. Everything must have gone smooth." Morse stated.

"Yeh, no problems! The wagons are coming up with the infantry, should be here in a day or two. We're with Lt. Greene's tangent party. Glad to see you though, we're low on supplies."

"Well, we are well fixed here, and the Brits just got resupplied. They're west of here at the West Butte and their Commissioner, Anderson, rolled through here just as we were making camp. Major Twining intends to move over there just as soon as Commissioner Campbell arrives. He sent a courier to let us know that he's en route from Fort Buford, and should be here soon. Unfortunately, we also got word that Reno's on his way back. He got denied permission to return east, until the Boundary Escort is finished. He stayed at Fort Benton until he got confirmation from Major Twining that the missing forage was secured then headed back, he's due anytime."

"Bet he ain't happy." observed Val.

"I expect not. Capt. Weir and the other officers seem a little tense." said Flanagan.

"Well, Rogers, you'd best get those wagons rounded up and into camp." said Morse.

"Will do Sarge. Can we stay with Lt. Greene until he gets to the West Butte? Val tells us that you can see the Rockies from there."

"I guess so, but don't go any further. I imagine that they will be holding a big meeting over there, soon, and we can gather you up then. Best send those wagons in as quick as you can."

Major Reno arrived at the East Butte encampment and promptly summoned Capt. Weir to his tent. A bottle of whisky sat half empty on a table. He regarded Weir with bleary eyes.

"I see in your report from last week, that you don't expect the survey parties to receive any interference from the Indians." Reno stated.

"That's correct, Sir. We're well north and west of the areas frequented by the Sioux. The other tribes show no interest in the surveyors, other than asking for handouts."

"Good, I intend for us to be on the road back to Fort Totten by the 15th. I'll leave the three Infantry companies from Fort Buford here to stay on until the survey is done. We will conduct a sweep along the parallel within 50 miles of the end of the line in advance of the working parties, then start back. We'll leave the supply train here, and gather it up as we come back. See that everything is arranged."

"Yes, Sir! Might I add that you have my sympathy concerning your orders to stay in the field. Things were well in hand here, your presence was not needed."

"Hmmm, but here I am, none the less. I'm ordered to stay with the command until we reach Fort Totten. My in-laws are quite put out that I'm not there to comfort my son, not to mention that they had to handle all of the funeral arrangements. My patience is wearing thin, Weir. I'll not brook any delays. Make sure that you make that known!"

"I will, Sir. Will that be all?"

"I understand that one of your sections is out with Lt. Greene."

"Yes, Sir! We'll recover them when we catch up with the surveyors on our swing west."

"I'm disappointed that you saw fit to weaken the command by dispatching them to the line. Our mission is to be ready to react to hostiles, not nursemaid the survey party."

"Lt. Greene sent a messenger requesting supplies, I couldn't ignore that."

"He should have sent men to escort them, if he needed them so badly."

"I judged that we were under no threat from hostiles, Sir." replied Weir

"Well, I question your judgement. Perhaps you were too busy enjoying a summer picnic atmosphere, to maintain unit integrity and discipline?" Reno said with a condescending look. "I heard the officers mess was quite festive while I was away."

"What are you insinuating, Major?"

"We'll discuss this at a later date." said Reno, as he turned and reached for his glass. "Carry on, Captain."

The British had previously planned to establish a depot on the slopes of the West Butte, where a rendezvous with a forage train out of Fort Benton at the end of the month was scheduled. Commissioner Cameron arrived there, on July 25, just as Lt. Galway was setting up to observe at 651 miles out. Capt. Anderson, and the 49th Rangers had headed west that morning, but were recalled to the Depot. Capt. Featherstonhaugh arrived on July 30. The American Commissioner Campbell arrived at the East Butte cavalry camp on Aug. 2. After a brief and acrimonious meeting with Major Reno, he and Major Twining decided to move the Boundary Commission camp over to the West Butte to set up near the Brits. Lt. Greene and his tangent team were already working that way. Capt. Gregory would follow them, and they would all wait there for the topographical teams, including Captain Ames and his two infantry companies to catch up with them. Major Reno elected to keep the cavalry units at the East Butte encampment, with its good water and grazing, until he made his sweep.

CHAPTER 14

West Butte of the Sweetgrass Hills, Montana Territory - 651 Miles West, August 2, 1874

Both of the British and American Boundary Survey Commissions camped on the shoulder of the West Butte. It was the first time all season that they were all in one location. The British had been there for a week, and some of them, including Commissioner Cameron, had already moved west to the foothills when Commissioner Campbell arrived. He and Twining met with Capt. Anderson who had been left in charge while the British supply train from Fort Benton arrived that afternoon. Spread through the encampments were over 500 scientists, civilian workers, soldiers, scouts, and teamsters. In addition, there were over two hundred wagons, hundreds of horses, oxen, and mules. Anderson was preparing to leave with the final ox-train of supplies and pack-horses for the final Rocky Mountain leg. The Americans elected to spend a few days repairing their wagons, and resting horses and mules, before moving on. The ample supply of cold spring water was a luxury compared to unpalatable alkaline water they'd been forced to contend on the route previously. Baths and freshly washed clothes were enjoyed by all. The abundance of forage let the livestock fatten up a bit. They'd come across a few wild longhorn steers and managed to capture them, so the cooks had prepared fresh beef steaks accompanied by vegetables that came up with the supply train.

"Well, this is more like it." Val espoused as he reclined against a pack, puffing on his pipe. "A good feed like that helps make up for all the shitty ones a man's had to choke down."

They had all just enjoyed one of the best meals they'd had all season. There was a light breeze, and a bright moon. Jake and his fellow troopers were lounging around a campfire.

"I reckon you're right there, Val!" said Rooster, "Too bad we won't be able to stay here. Jake says Lt. Greene heard from Major Twining that Reno was quite put out when he found out that some of his men were sent up to the line."

"Is that right, Jake?" Holden asked.

"Unfortunately, yes! Apparently Reno complained to Commissioner Campbell about it when he got to camp. Major Twining took offense and abruptly pulled up stakes and relocated over here. "

"Well, aren't we glad we were here, already!" exclaimed Chas.

"Yes, but he sent strict orders for us to stay here. The whole outfit is coming this way and we're to join up with them as they head west along the parallel, checking for hostiles. It seems Major Reno intends to start back to Fort Totten in two weeks."

"I can't say that I'm in a hurry to get back there!" griped Big George. "The only thing waiting for us there is guard duty, fatigue details, and cold, shitty weather."

"How about you, Val? You make up your mind where you're going to winter?" Jake asked.

"Major Twining ordered some boats built at Fort Benton. He intends to load up in them and float back down the Missouri, all the way to Bismarck. My job is over when I get them back to Benton, so I suppose I'll head back over towards Fort Belknap, visit my mother, and some cousins, then find me a place to hole up for the winter near the Bearpaws. I can do a little trapping and gather some buffalo hides. Come next spring I'll take them down to Fort Benton to sell. While I'm there I propose to see what the market would be if I was gather up some of these wild cattle and drive them back down there."

"Don't sound as cozy a set up as you had last winter, Val." chided Rooster.

"Oh, I don't know about that. I might run into a woman friend that I might have dallied with in the past, this country being my old stomping grounds and all." he replied with a smile.

Jake made eye contact with him and said. "I wish you luck, Val. I hope our paths will cross again."

"Out here, you never know. Now somebody find us something to drink."

The next morning Greene came around after breakfast, while Jake was grooming Ajax.

"Corporal Rogers, Commissioner Campbell and I are going up to the top of the Butte. I thought you might like to go with us. Mr. Wheeler is going also."

"Yes, Sir!"

"Val says it's going to be a clear day, and we will have a grand view of the Rocky Mountains."

"I'm looking forward to seeing that!"

"Well, get sorted out and join us in front of the Commissioner's tent."

Wheeler led them on a winding ascent up the West Butte, which was the tallest of the Hills at just under 7,000 feet elevation. They passed through thick stands of fir trees, and spotted several Bighorn sheep. Just below the summit they tied up their horses and worked their way to the top on foot. Campbell, despite being 61 yrs. old, handled the steep grade pretty well. Once on top they had a magnificent view of the Rockies off in the distance, the prairie spreading like an ocean below.

"This is magnificent!" proclaimed Campbell.

"It's a sight not many white men have seen, Commissioner." Wheeler intoned, these hills are sacred to the Blackfeet."

"I count myself lucky then. Thank you for guiding us up here."

Greene produced a pair of binoculars and they took turns admiring the scenery.

Val retrieved a sack of Métis pemmican from his saddle bag. Sitting, they washed it down with spring water from their canteens. Campbell looked over at Jake.

"Lt. Greene tells me that you have been a great help to him during the time that you've been attached to him, Corporal Rogers."

"I've tried to be, Sir. Surveying is interesting work, and it was better than being stuck in camp."

"Well, it's too bad that your superiors don't all share that opinion."

Jake didn't reply, and tried to maintain a neutral expression.

"Be that as it may, I respect your silence on the matter. It speaks well of you, also. Thank you for your help."

"It was my pleasure, Sir."

Wheeler stood and motioned for Jake to follow him over to a spot overlooking the camp below.

"You'll be rejoining your company soon. I'll be going on to the Rockies with them."

Jake nodded his head, "I wish I was too. Thanks for all of your help, Val. You've taught me a lot."

"Well, it's easy to teach when someone wants to learn. Remember to pay attention to your surroundings. Here, take this." Val said holding out his hand, he opened it to reveal a· long white fang mounted in a silver setting threaded with a beaded buffalo thong.

"This is the fang of a great grey wolf. It's powerful medicine and will make you wary of danger."

"But you may need it worse than me."

Val reached in his shirt and pulled out another that dangled around his neck.

"I have the other one, I took them from the wolf." He said grinning. "My mother had them blessed by both a Jesuit priest and a powerful medicine man named Crow Necklace. Here take it, it will make you remember to use caution, instead of rushing headlong into trouble."

Jake put it around his neck under his scarf. "I have nothing to give you in return."

"You already have Jake. You give me hope that the future holds more young men like you. Willing to learn from your elders, but able to think for yourself, and not afraid to step forward when needed."

Wheeler held out his hand, and Jake took it.

"Don't look so somber, Jake. Odds are you'll see me again. I may come peddling beef to the forts. Now let's get back down to camp. You'll want to get your men sorted out. Reno will be coming, and when he does you best be looking like proper soldiers."

Reno and the 7th Cavalry companies showed up the next day. Jake had posted a lookout along the trail, and when he spotted them coming he hurried back to camp. Rogers quickly had the section mount up, and they formed a column of twos, moving towards the approaching column. He saw Sgt. Morse out front as usual. As they came together, Jake halted his detachment.

"Sgt. Morse, good to see you! We figured to meet you head on, out here, and maybe not make a scene in camp. There's a nice bivouac area all prepared."

Morse grinned, "Why that's a capital idea, Corporal. I don't suppose a wise ass half breed had anything to do with it?"

"He may have made a suggestion, or two. Should we wait here, or ride on to the company?"

"I'll take over, now. You just follow my lead. We'll go meet the Major and Captain."

They made their way back to the column, and halted just short. Morse rode up to Reno and saluted. "Corporal Rogers and his section are reporting back, Sir. They present

Commissioner Campbell's compliments, and are ready to guide us to a campsite that has been reserved for us."

Reno scowled over at the prodigal troopers, noting the condition of their horses and equipage. "Well, it appears that they weren't abused like last season. Corporal Rogers, report with your section to your 1st Sergeant.

I'll be the judge of where we elect to camp tonight. Sergeant Morse, take the advance party forward and survey the area."

Capt. Weir, who was riding next to Reno, looked at Morse wearing with an imperturbable expression and nodded his head slightly. Morse saluted in the direction of both officers, then wheeled his horse and rode off.

"Well, that went about as well as could be expected." he thought to himself smiling.

That evening Reno and his cavalry and infantry officers, were invited to dine with the Boundary Commissioner and his staff. After dinner, drinks and cigars were produced and they began to discuss the final approach towards the Rockies, and the wrap up of the parallel survey. Suddenly, Reno stood and addressed the group.

"Gentlemen, I propose to leave in the morning and spend the next week following the parallel trail west. I think a display of strength will be a sufficient demonstration to any Indians that you may encounter along the line, and discourage them from interfering with you. Then, I intend to start back towards Fort Buford with the two 6th Infantry companies from Fort Lincoln, where they can catch a boat. The three Infantry companies from Fort Buford, will remain with you until all parties start back. That way all units will be able to reach their home stations before cold weather sets in."

Capt. Gregory nodded his head. "I'm ready to roll. I'll follow you out of camp, later in the day, and head for my next observation station 672 miles out at Red Creek."

"I see no reason for me to be in a hurry. I'm going to stay here with Major Twining and Dr. Coues to explore these hills a bit. I'd like to observe some of the wild life and enjoy the scenery." Campbell spoke up. "I will keep the Infantry here with me to set up a depot for the return march. We will move to follow next week, and rendezvous with you along the line near the mountains, Capt. Gregory."

"We'll be looking forward to your company, Sir. Our scouts tell us there is a beautiful lake at the end of the line. Perhaps we'll have time to enjoy some fishing."

Reno's face began to darken, and he announced "I'm glad you gentlemen will be able to pursue such bucolic pastimes, while I and my soldiers, insure your safety. I've a dead wife, and a young boy waiting back in Pennsylvania for me. But I have responsibilities to fulfill before I can attend to them. Pardon me if I don't find your entertainments a priority. Good night, gentlemen, we'll be away at first light." He then turned on his heels and stalked away.

A pall of silence descended over the group.

"I suppose he has a point." Campbell stated.

"Yes, but he makes it difficult to sympathize." Dr. Coues said, "The man is such a pompous ass!"

"Be glad you'll be shed of him. We still have to endure him all the way back to Fort Totten." Lt. Porter said with chagrin.

Weir frowned over at Porter, "We'll let that rest, Jim. We have a mission to complete. He raised his glass. "Good luck and good weather, Gentlemen. May we all make it home safely!" After the toast was acknowledged, Weir gathered the 7th's officers and they took their leave.

"We'd best be ready for an early start, tomorrow. Make sure your sergeants have the men prepared for a brisk pace. I'll warrant we'll be covering a lot of ground."

`The two companies of the 7th Cavalry made it to the Belly River crossing at 716 miles out, in three days. They encountered few Indians along the way, and the ones that they saw, stayed at a distance. George Boyd was scouting, for them, while Val had stayed on with Lt. Greene's party. Sgt. Morse and Jake were out with the advance party as usual. They found the location clearly marked bay Capt. Anderson and his Rangers. Capt. Gregory was to set up for observation there, as soon as he finished up at the North Branch of the Milk River/ Red Creek crossing. Greene was already running the tangent in that direction.

"Gents, this is as good a place to camp as anywhere." Boyd announced to Sgt. Morse and Jake as they rode up. "I see that the Rangers left us some firewood. The water is good, and there's a little grass to be had by the river."

Morse nodded his head, "Looks good, George. I suspect that the Major has convinced himself that there are no threats around to the survey teams. I won't be surprised if we start back, soon, maybe tomorrow!"

"Yeh, I kind of got that impression this morning when he was asking me about the local tribes. I told him they were mostly small, poor bands of Blackfeet, that weren't big enough to threaten the surveyors."

Jake listened and then stated, "I reckon we can be back at the Sweetgrass Hills pretty quick, if this weather holds."

"Well, you boys know the way. I'm gonna hook up with Val when we run into him, and keep headin' west." said Boyd. "I figure to see it through with those engineer fellas. "Besides, I can squeeze out another months pay with them."

"You going to partner up with Val on his ranching idea?" asked Jake.

"Maybe! Val knows this here country. The local tribes think he's got big medicine. His mother, Shining Flower, is a powerful healer of the Gross Ventre, and he's respected by the Lakota. The agent at Ft. Belknap is a friend of his. Val saved his life one time. He's well known by the traders at the forts. If anyone can make a cattle ranch work around here, it will be Val."

That night, in the mess tent, Reno informed the rest of the officers that they had gone as far as he felt necessary to fulfill their mission.

"We will fall back along the line and collect the infantry at the Sweetgrass Hills Depot where we left Company B. I will send a courier to the Box Elder Depot and have Company K meet us near Fort Belknap. On reaching the Missouri, the two 6th Infantry companies will board a steamboat for their return to Forts Stevenson and Lincoln. The 7th will follow along the route we took coming out, via Forts Buford and Stevenson, then on to Fort Totten. Gentlemen, I intend that we will be there by mid-September."

Lt. Porter spoke up, "Since we'll be maintaining a brisk pace, I'd like to suggest that Lt. Nave be sent back with the supply train, to Ft. Benton. His shoulder has never fully healed from his fall back in the spring, and he's toughed it out all summer. Dr. Lord has recommended it, and is writing up a surgeon's disability certificate. I'll assume his duties with Company I."

Reno scowled a bit and remarked, "I'll still require you as my adjutant.."

"I shouldn't think that will entail too much, Sir. Everyone is already anxious to beat the weather. I don't expect there will be many issues to address."

"Very well. We'll be checking in with the survey teams as we pass them, but I don't intend to share campsites. We'll maintain strict march discipline. If we make good time, I'll authorize a day rest stop at Fort Buford. I intend to cover some ground tomorrow, so I'll see all of you at first light."

After Reno left, Weir lit his pipe and and looked thoughtfully at the others.

"Seems pretty straight forward to me. Have the sergeants keep a close eye on the condition of the mounts. The sooner we get there, the sooner he'll be gone. Let's make that happen!"

Jake, Boyd, and Sgt. Morse headed out with the advance party as soon as it was light enough to see. The column formed up quickly and followed. The men were in good spirits, and murmurs and low laughter was heard now and then. Since they had just been on this trail, there were no surprises. With only a couple of light wagons in the train, they fell into steady march pace. They paused for a quick lunch, and shortly afterwards they saw Val Wheeler and Lt. Greene's party coming towards them. The infantry and the wagons were keeping pace with the tangent teams as they paced off the distance with survey chains. Markers were being retrieved from the wagons and pounded into the ground.

"Well, gents! This is where we part ways." stated Boyd. "It's been a pleasure, but I think these lads are more my pace."

They stopped under a tree in the shade as Wheeler and Greene rode up. Dismounting, they gathered in a group. Morse and Jake saluted Greene, which he returned.

"Sorry to see you men go. It's too bad that you'll not get to see the end of the line and the Rockies up close. I'm looking forward to it."

"Well, you Engineer officers are a little more relaxed than ours. We've miles to go yet today, Sir." said Morse. "The command is coming up behind us. We're to keep moving."

Greene nodded his head and replied, "Very well. Perhaps we'll meet again some day. I'll ride up to meet them. Safe travels, men!"

As Greene mounted and moved off, Boyd called over to Wheeler, "I'll ride with the lieutenant, see you in a while Val."

Morse also mounted, then leaned over and held out his hand to Wheeler, "Good luck, cowboy!" he said with a grin. "Watch out for wild Indians!"

Val replied quickly, "You, more than me soldier boy. I know when they're around. You won't have me to spot them for you!"

"That's for damn sure. Take care." Pat said. "Jake, don't be too long. I'll wait up the trail a bit."

As Morse rode away, Jake looked down at his boots, then up at Wheeler. Before he could say anything, Val signed to him, "Until I see you again, watch around you. Try not to miss important things."

Jake signed back and patted the necklace at his throat. "I will. Thank you, Pale Wolf!"

Val raised his eyebrows, then nodded and smiled. He mounted his pony and rode away without looking back. Jake got on Ajax, and did the same.

CHAPTER 15

Fort Totten - Dakota Territory, March 30, 1875

The icy grip of winter was slowly loosening around the confines of Fort Totten. The days and nights were climbing back to double digit temperatures. The two 7th Cavalry companies had made it back on Sep. 14th the previous fall, just in time to get settled in for another Dakota winter. Major Reno, with little ceremony, handed over command to Captain Weir and left immediately the next day for Headquarters, in St.Paul.

Both units, with the experience of the previous year's frigid conditions, settled in as best they could. They were welcomed back by the families and laundresses. The Post Commander had insured that adequate supplies had been acquired and stored. So unlike the previous year, there was no frantic scrambling around and both companies were well provided for. The men re-occupied their barracks from the previous year, and the cycles of guard duty and fatigue details, resumed. After having spent two seasons in the field, having a roof over their heads and protection from the elements, was more appreciated. The Holidays were once again bright spots in the otherwise brutally monotonous routine of winter garrison duty. Captain Keogh had returned from his sojourn to Ireland in early November, and his garrulous personality was a source of amusement to the other officers. He regaled then with his tales of Ireland, and shared the Irish whisky he brought back. Unfortunately, in early February, he was incapacitated by acute diarrhea, and shortly afterwards summoned to St. Paul for detached service.

Jake was on duty as Corporal of the Guard again. Some of the senior NCOs, had been paying him to take their place, and he was glad to make a few extra dollars. It was a cool, cloudy day, and the wind was brisk out of the West as he was making his rounds of the different posts. He was walking by the Adjutants Office when Lt. Porter stuck his head out the door.

"Corporal Rogers, I need you to take some dispatches to Captain

Weir. I believe he's at his quarters."

"Yes, Sir! I'm just making my rounds and I can go right there,"

Porter handed Jake a thick envelope. "Tell him that I will be coming over as soon as I finish up some things."

Jake saluted and replied, "Yes, Sir!"

He hustled along the boardwalk to the North, watching for icy slick spots. The days were just warm enough to cause some thawing, but the nights were still below freezing. Capt. Weir's quarters were on officers row, in a house across the parade field from the barracks. He shared it with the now absent Capt. Keogh. Jake knocked on the front door, and was greeted by Weir's striker, Pvt. John Keller.

"Morning, Keller! Is the Captain in?"

"Yes, he's talking with Lt. Edgerly in his study."

"Lt. Porter sent me over with some dispatches for him."

"Well, come in, I'll tell him you're here. You want some coffee?"

"You bet! Guard duty today, and it's a mite chilly with the wind. Much appreciated."

Making sure to wipe his boots on a piece of rug by the door, Jake followed Keller. They entered a large room where Weir sat a wooden desk, and Edgerly lounged on a sofa, in front of a banked fire. As they entered the room, Keller announced, "Corporal Rogers is here with dispatches, Sir"

Looking up and seeing Jake, he smiled and said. "Ah, Rogers, I saw that you had the guards today. Is everything in order?"

"Yes, Sir!" Jake replied, "Lt. Porter flagged me down and sent me with these dispatches for you." He stepped forward and extended the papers. "He said to tell you that he'd be here before too long."

As Weir took them, he said. "At ease, help yourself to the fire, Rogers. I expect Keller is bringing you some coffee."

"Yes, he did offer me some." Jake answered and moved over to the hearth.

As Weir read the dispatches, Keller arrived with a steaming mug. "Here you go, Jake." He said quietly, "This'll warm you a bit."

"Thanks, Johnny."

"I've heard some good things about you, Rogers. The First Sergeant speaks well of you. The other sergeants do too." Weir commented.

Jake nodded his head as he sipped at his coffee. "Thank you, Sir."

Weir remained silent as he read, then looked up at Edgerly, "These are Change of Station orders, Win. We're being brought to Fort Lincoln and we're to be there by the end of April."

Edgerly smiled broadly, "That's wonderful news, Sir! I was

wondering where we might be spending the season. We haven't been with the Regiment since Fort Hayes"

"Yes, it will be nice to be back in the fold. It's been almost four years. I've heard Fort Lincoln is quite large, and has excellent cavalry facilities."

Weir looked over at Jake who had obviously heard the conversation, "Corporal Rogers, do you think you'll enjoy a change of scenery?" he asked.

"Well, Sir, I don't know what to think. I remember seeing the construction there as we passed by on the *Western* two years ago. But I can say that I'm sure it will be a change welcomed by the whole outfit, particularly after a second winter here."

Weir chuckled, "I couldn't have put it any better myself, Rogers. Feel free to spread the word as you make your rounds. I wager the news will help the men shake off the winter doldrums a bit quicker!"

"Indeed, Sir, and thank you for the coffee."

Sgt. Morse was stoking the orderly room stove when Jake came busting through door.

"Hey, Pat! Where's Top?" he asked

"He's in his room."

Jake opened the door to the hallway that lead to where Martin's and the other sergeants rooms were located. "Hey, Top!" he yelled. "I got big news."

Martin came down the hall, tugging on his uniform jacket. "What's up, Rogers?"

"I was just over at the Adjutant's Office, when dispatches came in for Captain Weir and Lt. Porter asked me to take it to him. When I got to his quarters, the Captain and Lt. Edgerly were having coffee. He invited me in to have a cup of and he read it while I was still there. They're change of station orders. We're being reassigned to Fort Lincoln. They want us there by the end of April. He told me that it was okay to tell you."

"Lincoln huh? Well, I can't say that I'll miss this place. I understand that it's just across the river from Bismarck, where the railroad construction stopped. At least there will be a town close by!"

"I haven't been to a town in almost two years," Jake mused.

"Well, you aren't the only one!" Morse stated. "This is great news."

Martin said, "That gives us just a few weeks to pack up. Pat, we'll meet after supper tonight, with the other NCOs, and get things sorted out.

"Aye, Top, it's a meeting I'll look forward to. I'll go run 'em down."

"Rogers, make sure you make your rounds in time to be there, too." said Martin.

"You bet, Top."

By the time Jake made it back to the barracks that evening, the whole post was buzzing with the news. Most of the men were lounging around the Dayroom, speculating on the news. The older troops were telling stories about Custer, and the Regiment, back in Kansas. First Sergeant Martin and the other NCOs were gathered in the orderly room.

"Okay, while we're getting organized, I want all of you to be aware that one of the downsides of where we're heading is, that we'll have to place more emphasis on strict military protocol. Those of us that have been around Custer will know what I'm getting at." Martin stated. "We need to start on the lads now, so they get used to it."

Everyone nodded their heads in acknowledgement.

Martin continued, "The Captain informed me that we'll be heading south to Fort Seward and Jamestown, to load up on a train. We'll offload at Bismarck and then ferry across the Missouri to Fort Lincoln.

Sgt. Rush spoke up. "We need to get everything inventoried, and ready to load up. Get with me and I'll let you know what we're taking. Most of the ammunition, except what we carry on us, will stay here. We'll only take enough rations to travel on. We'll have wagons for company property and arms, footlockers, and maybe some space left over for extras. Let me know what you have and I'll try to accommodate you. The officers property will be loaded on separate wagons."

"I want our part of the fort to be left in tip-top condition. I've already spoken with 1st Sgt. Varden, and he's going to be making sure Company I does the same. I'll not be pleased if the Captain gets a complaint from the fort commandant after we leave." Martin stated.

"Do you know the date we're leaving, Top?" Morse asked

"No, but plan on being ready in three weeks. That should be plenty of time. Make sure to spend extra time getting the horses in top shape, I want us to make a good impression when we get to Lincoln, so Custer will be sure to notice. And make sure the lads uniforms are respectable."

The next few weeks were a whirlwind of activity. The men went about their tasks with enthusiasm, even though the weather remained cool. The post trader made his usual appearance on payday, wanting to collect his credits before the cavalrymen left. However, he did mark down some items, anticipating reduced demand once they were gone. Jake picked up a couple of checked cotton shirts, and a new neckerchief. He had parlayed a couple of favors to Sgt. Rush in return for a new 1874 issue fatigue jacket and pants. His original uniforms were badly faded and patched, but he still saved them for the field, where dress requirements were pretty relaxed. Now that he was into his second year of enlistment he earned almost 10 cents a day clothing allowance, and he used some of it for new drawers. His mother had sent him several pairs of wool socks, and some gloves with her last letter. He'd paid Pvt. Dave Manning to replace the sole of his boots, again.

Even though he was a corporal, he still bunked with the rest of the men upstairs in the barracks. However he got to pick his bunk location, which was just inside the stairwell door, close to the fireplace. He was over both Holden's, and Hurd's section, while another Corporal, George Wylie, was over the other two sections of the 2nd Platoon. Sgt. Morse, and Sgt. Flanagan were over the Platoon. Jake liked to think his section was the considered one of the better in the company, particularly in light of the experience from the last two seasons.

Jake was in the process of laying out his uniforms, clothing, and gear deciding what he would pack away in his footlocker for the move to Lincoln. Charlie Welch, who had been paired up with Dave Manning when they'd reached Fort Totten, came over and looked at Jake's piles.

"I guess we won't need our dress uniforms until we get to Lincoln?" he asked.

"No, but we'd better keep our greatcoats handy. The weather's still not looking good. We'll be at least three days getting down to Jamestown. Top's warned us that the railcars we may get will be pretty chilly, even if they have stoves. Some of us may end up in the riding with the horses. We"ll be keeping our buffalo coats and arctic boots for the trip."

"Well, I can't say that I'll miss this place. I talked to a teamster over the post traders, and he was saying that there are six companies posted at Fort Lincoln, maybe there won't be so much guard duty."

"Yes, I hope so too. Although I've heard that the Sioux are known to raid right up to the fort from time to time, so guard duty will be a bit more serious." Jake commented. "So there's that to consider."

"Yeh, I wonder if we'll go after them?"

"I guess there is always that possibility. But, I think as long as they stay to themselves, not much chance. So, you ready to go, Charlie?"

"I'm pretty sure, Henry has been helping everyone. He's changed stations quite a few times, so he knows what to expect."

"Well, let's get the guys and go over to the post traders and have a couple of beers then. Last chance for a while, until we get settled in at Lincoln."

The two company column headed out on the trail to Fort Seward and Jamestown, 100 odd miles to the Southeast. A detachment from each company remained behind to escort wives and families of the married men, when the weather permitted. The companies maintained a brisk pace to the Cheyenne River on the first day. When the got there, the ford was found to be still sufficiently frozen for safe crossing with the wagons. They continued until they came to the banks of the James River and halted for the night and went into camp. Several wagons filled with wood accompanied the column, and large fires sprang up as they pitched camp. Parties were sent out to test the ice on the river to see if they could cross in the morning. Finding it solid, they broke camp at first light and got across. The two rivers could be a major obstacle during the spring when the thawing ice caused deep flowing currents. That was the main reason most supplies for Fort Totten still came by way of Fort Stevenson. Safely south of rivers, the trail ran all the way with no other impediments on the route. The next night's camp was on the banks of Pipestem Creek, a days march from Fort Seward. They arrived there without incident, and went into camp below the fort. The fort was built on a bluff along the James River and was located about 5 miles north of the fledgling railroad town of Jamestown. Capt. Weir and the officers, were invited to dinner by Capt. Patterson in his quarters. Meanwhile, 1st Sgt. Martin sent Sgt. Morse on into Jamestown, to find the local railroad dispatcher and coordinate the timing for the units to load and board the train that was going to take them on to Bismarck. He invited Jake to accompany him, and then report back in the morning with instructions from the dispatcher.

Jamestown sprang up along the tracks of the Northern Pacific Railroad starting in 1871. The construction crews had a campsite where near the railroad bridge that crossed the James River, and the town grew around it as settlers arrived off the trains. By 1875 there was a large NPRR repair yard, and thriving community to support it. Jake marveled at the number of new buildings and new construction, as they made their way into town along the road from the fort..

"Look at this Jake, we've not seen a town in almost two years, and I'd venture to say most of this place didn't even exist then." Morse exclaimed.

Jake just nodded his head as he took it in. "It's a wonder all right," he replied as he watched people bustling along the snowy streets. He admired the signs on the buildings, and the variety of the stores. They heard the horn of a locomotive up ahead and the chugging of its steam engine.

"I reckon that this street will lead us right to the Railroad station." Pat said.

Sure enough, the station appeared after several blocks. They dismounted out front and hitched their horses. There was a large covered platform and a big sign lettered,

JAMESTOWN, DAKOTA TERRITORY

They went through a door adjacent to the platform and entered a large room containing benches, a large wood stove, and a ticket counter. There were several offices also. Morse went to the one marked 'Dispatcher' and knocked.

"Come in! I'll be with you in a moment!" a voice shouted. Just inside a portly , balding man, with a bushy beard, was shuffling a stark of papers. When he looked up, he eyed their uniform greatcoats and stated. "I'm hoping you're with that detachment coming from Fort Totten, we've been expecting you. Are you all here?

Morse replied, "The rest of the outfit is camped at the fort. We were sent in to check on the transport arrangements."

"Well, you found the right man." he held out his hand, "I'm Murray Johnson, with the Northern Pacific. Pleased to meet you."

"Sergeant Pat Morse, 7th Cavalry, Company D. This is Corporal Rogers." he said, nodding towards Jake. "Likewise!"

Johnson pulled a large watch from his vest pocket, and looked at it. "Well, it's too late in the day to get anything done. Too damn cold too! How about you fellas come with me and we'll go get a bite to eat. We can talk over dinner, and a couple of beers. My treat!"

"We don't know where we're staying in town, tonight, and we have our horses out front, and need to see to them, also" Morse stated.

"No problem, there's a stable across the street from my hotel. We keep extra rooms at the hotel for customers. I reckon that's what you are."

Pat and Jake both grinned. "We'll just take you up on that offer Agent Johnson!"

"Aw, just call me Murray."

The Jamestown Hotel was a three story building of clap board construction, with an adjacent restaurant, located two blocks from the station. After seeing to their mounts, and putting them up in the stable, Morse and Jake carried their bedrolls and saddlebags with them as they entered the hotel lobby, where Murray was waiting for them. He'd already arranged a room for them.

"Hope you don't mind bunking together." said Murray

That caused some laughter all around, and Pat replied, "I think we'll manage."

"Well, you can put your things up, here's the key. You're on the second floor, 203. I'll go next door and get us a table. Take your time, I'll order some beer while I'm waiting."

When Pat and Jake found Murray, he had secured a table near a wood stove, several beer bottles were sitting on it. He motioned for them to sit down.

"Help yourself, these beers come all the way from Milwaukee. I get them shipped out to me."

Jake picked one up and saw the word Schlitz on the bottle. After undoing the wire bale, he pried the ceramic stopper loose and smelled the beer. He took a swig and said. "Seems pretty good, but then again I'm not real experienced with good beer, just mostly with what the post traders sell. No telling who made it."

Pat sampled his, "That is damned good, and I know something about beers!" he exclaimed.

Johnson beamed, "Glad you like it. That's a perk of being a railroad man out here. I can telegraph back and get good things shipped out for free."

Jake said, "I've got a friend back home that just went to work for a railroad."

"It's not a bad way to make a living." Murray stated, "Of course I grew up around railroads. My father, Edwin, was an engineer, I spent a lot of time with him. He worked under General McCallum, who ran the railroads for the Union Army during the War. I learned to run trains from both of them. Dad went to work for the Northern, and I followed him. Watched most of the track on this line being laid down."

Johnson went on describing his experiences working on the railroad for several minutes. Finally Morse asked him, "So what's the plan? I'm assuming you're ready for us."

Johnson sat his bottle down and eyed Pat. "Well, now. You just cut direct to the chase, don't you Sergeant. I like that to a degree, but hate to be pushed."

Morse smiled and replied, "There's over 120 men and horses camped out not 5 miles from here, after 3 days on the trail in cold, shitty weather. They are eating lukewarm food and freezing their asses off in tents. They are depending on you and me to get them loaded on a train, which is no small job, and then get them to Bismarck as quick as we can. Not being pushy, just staying on task."

"Well said, Sergeant! And yes we're ready. My men have been clearing snow and ice off the tracks for several weeks to get the trains running again. The train and railcars you'll be riding on are lined up on a spur not a 1/4 mile from here. They've been putting it together for two days now, working their asses off, in cold, shitty weather. Now that we've addressed that, I propose we get a good hot meal because you and I are going to be too busy for it tomorrow." Johnson countered, smiling back.

After their meal Murray summoned the waitress, and had her bring a bottle of brandy. He poured three glasses and offered a toast.

"Here's to a successful operation tomorrow!"

As they sipped their drinks, Johnson said. "Your General Custer came through here earlier in the month. He caught the first train of the season heading back east to New York. Had his wife with him, she's quite entertaining, although Custer seemed a bit stiff. They stopped here to eat, it seems the quality of the food in Bismarck is suffering from the long winter. The riverboats were still waiting on the ice to break, and we hadn't started running a regular schedule. Mr. Rosser, of the Northern Pacific, was at West Point with Custer before the War, and even though he fought for the South, they're still close friends. The General has been very helpful to the Northern and we make sure he travels comfortably. In fact, we're using the same Pullman car that they rode in, tomorrow."

"Yes, I'm well acquainted with Colonel Custer." Morse said. "I spent many an hour in the saddle riding behind him down in Kansas and Indian Territory. He does like to travel in style, when he can."

Johnson continued, "I had some Engineering officers and their surveyor teams through here last year. They were an interesting bunch. They were tasked with marking the border up North, with Canada."

Jake spoke up, "Hey! We were with them the last two seasons! Did you meet Lt. Greene?"

"Yes, quite a dynamic young man. He regaled me with some outrageous tales. His fellow officers seemed content to listen as he shared them."

"Ah, that would have been Major Twining, and Captain Gregory." Morse said, "We didn't spend much time with them. The Infantry companies escorted them."

"Well, they didn't have much to say about the 7th Cavalry, in general. Your commander, Major Reno made no friends there."

"Yeh, well he's not got many that I know of. The man is his own worst enemy." Pat replied.

"Yes, I had an encounter last fall with him. He was quite put out that I wouldn't put him in a Pullman car for his trip east. Pushy that one!"

Jake said, "We spent a lot of time with Lt. Greene. We got on well. I was hoping he made it back all right. He told me they were floating back down the Missouri to Bismarck in boats."

"They did indeed, it took them 18 days to float the 1,200 miles. Greene kept a journal. He let me read it and it was most interesting, as were descriptions of his travels up on the "Line" as he called it. In some of them he did make mention of an irascible mixed blood scout, and a young, resourceful cavalry corporal. He spoke highly of them." said Murray smiling.

Jake acknowledged that comment with a smile, and nod of his head. "Lt. Greene is not one to tarry! He and that scout, Val Wheeler, kept us on the move."

"Speaking of moving, let's finish talking about the plans for tomorrow." said Morse.

"Right, you get your men here as soon as you can. I put together a mix of rolling stock; 1 Pullman car, 3 Passenger cars, 20 boxcars, and 4 flatcars. I figured eight horses or mules per boxcar, and two wagons per flatcar. There will be ramps for the horses, mules and wagons. How you distribute the men is up to you. If all goes well, you'll ll be aboard by dark. The locomotive will be ready, with a full load of wood. Barring any problems, We'll cover the 102 miles, and you'll be in Bismarck the next morning. That work for you?"

Pat raised his glass in salute, "Mr. Johnson, I believe that will!"

The next morning, Jake got up early and left to go back to the fort. It was apparent that the agent was very experienced at moving troops, horses, and wagons. He had explained that due to the number of the forts up and down the Missouri, the volume of military related shipping going to Bismarck had increased significantly. Even though the Northern had been forced to halt construction due to bankruptcy, operations were still ongoing. Johnson had given him paperwork to give to Lt. Porter, and the two company First Sergeants. Upon reaching the camp below the fort, he sought out 1st Sgt. Martin and finding him standing near 1st Sgt. Varden, of Company I, near the cooks tent. They were sipping on their coffee, as the camp was being taken down.

They watched him ride up, and as he dismounted, Martin said, "You best not be telling us what you and Morse were up to last night. I'm trusting that he sent you back with a plan."

"We met with Mr. Johnson, yesterday and he sent this." said Jake, as he handed over the paperwork. "According to him, if we get loaded today, we'll be in Bismarck tomorrow morning."

Martin and Varden quickly scanned the documents, nodding their heads.

"Excellent, you'd best run these over to the officers mess and see that the Captain gets them. Then come back here and help get the boys ready to move out. Promptly now!"

"Okay Top!" Jake replied and mounted Ajax. As he made his way through camp, he marveled that this whole outfit would be over 100 miles away the following day.

CHAPTER 16

Bismarck/Fort Abraham Lincoln- Dakota Territory, April 25, 1875

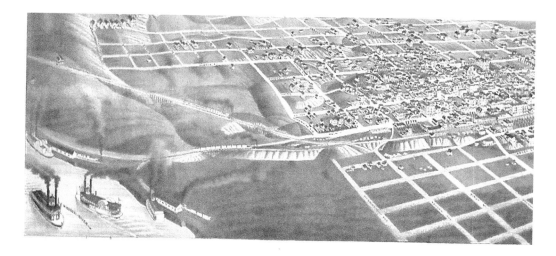

Bismarck, Dakota Territory - Circa late 1870s

Originally called Edwinton, it was a town that sprang up close to the Army's Camp Hancock, and along the incoming railroad tracks. The camp was established in 1872, by the 17th Infantry, to protect the NPRR construction crews. In 1873, with the railroad spurring its growth, the Northern Pacific renamed the town, Bismarck, in honor of Otto Van Bismarck, the German statesman, hoping to attract German immigrants. By 1875, the town was spreading out along the eastern banks of the river. With the NPRR in bankruptcy, the end of the line was at the Missouri River and there was no way to finance a bridge. A spur line was run to a steamboat warehouse district which was a collection of log and clapboard warehouses with storage yards, adjacent to the river landing. The riverboats that plied up and down the river would put into the local landing, to load out freight, goods, and livestock that were staged there before being sent onwards. This area was also home to cheap hotels, saloons, gambling halls, and brothels that catered to the rough crowd that worked the boats. The area had a well earned reputation for being an outlaw haven, with little or no laws. Meanwhile, the city center was growing in the area north of Camp Hancock, and east along the tracks, where the Depot was located. There were a few hotels, various merchants, restaurants, and a couple of churches Most of the settlers and immigrants stayed in this area when they de-trained. The merchants and businesses concentrated in this area were primarily focused on servicing the needs of the farmsteads being established on the surrounding cheap railroad, or homestead lands.

As the train slowed on the approach to the Bismarck depot early that morning, the men on it peeked out the windows and doors of the railcars. Most of the buildings within sight were made of wood logs, with several clapboard construction. Snow still blanketed the surrounding area. The train continued on past the regular station and came to a halt by the Camp Hancock just west of it, adjacent to the tracks. It was a small collection of ramshackle log structures surrounding a small parade ground. Behind the barracks there were several low warehouses that served as US Army quartermaster storage for the region supplying the forts along the Missouri River. Wisps of smoke drifted from numerous stovepipes protruding through the roofs of buildings, and a flag hung limply from the pole, highlighting the barren white plain beyond. The snow covered ground was a stark contrast to the brown, weathered logs buildings. Several men stood watching the train.

First Sgt. Martin stepped down from the first passenger car where he'd been riding, and hurried towards the Pullman car up in front, as Capt. Weir emerged at the rear of it and climbed down.

"Damn, Captain! We thought Totten was bleak post. I pity the poor sods that are assigned to this station."

"It brings to mind our times on the Kansas plains, eh, 1st Sergeant?"

"Aye, sir! At least there's a bit of a town here though."

"Well, I'll go over and check in with the Post Commandant. Perhaps he'll let us use the Mess Hall to get a hot breakfast in the men before we head to the river. Let's get them off the train and sorted out. There should be steamers to ferry us across the river, let me get me go see what's arranged."

"Yes, Sir!" Martin replied. "I'll get the cooks and some lads to help them unload first." He saluted and headed back down the train.

Lieutenant Porter had climbed down behind Weir, and came over to him.

"The end of the line, how appropriate." he stated.

"Not quite," Weir replied, gazing off to the West where the tracks curved slowly to the North towards a jumble of buildings, and tents. The superstructure of a steamboat was just visible behind them. "I hope that boat is here for us."

"I came through here with Reno last year. Fort Lincoln is just over there." Porter said, pointing off to the Southwest. "You can just make out the blockhouses of the Infantry Post there on the hills. The Cavalry Post is below it to the South on the river flats, not that I saw it in person. We were busy trying to round up rolling stock for our trip north with the Survey Teams, over here. Custer was preparing to head for the Black Hills, and had commandeered most all of the wagons available. He left with over 100, each pulled by 6 mules."

Weir nodded his head, "Custer likes his comforts."

"Hell, I heard he even took his black cook, Sarah, and the band."

"That sounds like him, all right. I want to get across the river, and get the men into quarters before dark. Come along, Jim, let's go pay our respect to the locals."

Later that morning both companies formed up and followed by their wagons, headed for the river landing. The sun poked in and out of the clouds, as the temperature climbed slowly above freezing. Following along the tracks, they maintained a walking pace to get the horses limbered up. When they got closer to the river, they got a better look at the buildings clustered around the waterfront area. They were roughly built, many with canvas roofs and tents attached to them, and were haphazardly scattered along both sides of the right of way. As they got closer to the river, they became more densely packed together with narrow alleyways running between them. At the end of the tracks there was a platform and series of wooden walkways, leading downhill to a large open area along river's edge. A sternwheeler was moored at the landing, with a ramp extending from its bow to the bank. Another smaller boat was in front of it. Smoke curled from the tall stacks of each. After halting the column, Capt. Weir and Lt. Porter rode down and dismounted next to the loading ramp where a man stood waiting.

"I assume that you're Captain Weir." he said.

"I am, and you, sir?"

"John Waddell, Captain of the *Denver No. 2!*" He replied, holding out his hand, "Pleased to meet you."

Weir shook the proffered hand, and asked "What happened to the original *Denver*?"

"Had a bit of a fire, back in '67 while tied up at St. Joseph. They rebuilt her as a sternwheeler to work the Upper Missouri. She's a good solid boat, but a bit worn and her engines are getting a bit weak. So, we do mostly ferry work here 'bouts, along with the *Union* over there. Captain Hart sends his compliments. We're here to pick you up and haul you over to Fort Lincoln."

Porter was gazing out at the river, where an occasional chunk of ice drifted swiftly by. He pointed towards them. "Looks like the river is flowing freely, but still some ice I see."

Waddell replied, "Yes, a bit. We just came upriver for the season last week, but we'll not have any issues. We'll be going downstream with the flow, and will just use the engines enough to maneuver. It's only about four miles to the Fort's landing. By the time we back out and get turned around, we'll almost be there."

"I'll count on you to get us safely loaded, Sir." said Weir, "I had some experience with riverboats during the War, down in Tennessee, but that's been awhile. I'll have a couple of my sergeants report to you, and they can assist you."

"We'll get the horses, mules, and then swing the wagons on board. We should be able to hold most of them, and the *Union* can get the rest. You and your officers are welcome to ride on the upper deck. We've got some cabins, but it's going to be a short trip."

"Thank you. Shall we get started? I'd like to get the horses stabled, and the men into barracks before dark." Weir said.

"I think we can oblige you, Captain. If you'll pardon me, we'll get cracking."

Since Sgt. Morse and Jake's section had previous experience traveling on the river, 1st Sgt. Martin assigned them to work with the mates and roustabouts of both steamers. They led their mounts on board. Joe Greene, and Big George were the # 4s of each set, the designated horse holders, and were left to tend them. Then the others went back to assist the rest of the company as they came down the ramp. Jake saw that Sgt. DeLacy, from Company I, had picked Pvts. Korn & O'Brien who had been with them on the *Western* to do the same, over on the *Union*. The loading progressed, and except for a few balky animals, went fairly smooth. When the entire outfit was on board, the ramps were raised and with shrill blasts, boat whistles were sounded and the *Union* let go it's mooring lines and slowly backed out into the current letting it take her bow around, as the paddle wheel bit into the water gaining steerage way. After waiting several minutes for the way to clear, the second steamer did the same. Within minutes they were mid-stream, drifting with the current. Jake found a spot on the bow where he had a clear view and was watching their progress. A deck mate was standing next to him.

"We'll just coast on down, and let the other boat get unloaded. The landing down there ain't much, only room for one at a time." He pointed at right bank. "Those are the blockhouses of the old Fort McKeen up on the hill there. The landing is just ahead on the right where the hill flattens out. The buildings above it are the Post Trader's. You'll see the Cavalry Post farther south with the stables closest to the river. The buildings around the parade ground are up the slope. It's all Fort Abraham Lincoln now, over a mile north to south since you boys in the 7th settled in."

"Damn, it's bigger than I expected." Jake said. The buildings appeared as dark splotches on a stark white canvas. There were no trees, except a few scattered along the river banks. To the east and south there were flat plains as far as he could see.

The mate pointed over to the East bank, "See that little cluster of shacks over there? It's called Whiskey Point, or just the Point. They cater to the boys that wants some cheap whiskey. Most say the post trader charges too much. When the river was froze, it weren't too hard to get over there. Now that it's spring and the river's thawed the "Union" will be running a regular schedule soon. You can get across on it, or go back up to Bismarck, if you've a mind. Either place, a man can get him a little pussy, iffin he ain't too picky. Ya want my advice, though, don't go by yourself."

Jake looked at the man and said, "I'll make sure to pass that on to the others."

Up ahead the *Union* had turned back into the current and eased over to the west bank. Lines were tied off and the loading ramp dropped. Shortly, a line of men and horses worked their way up through a cut in the bank onto the flat above. The *Denver*, still mid-stream slid past, then turned sharply and pointed back upstream. Jake could feel the vibrations under his feet, as Capt. Waddell increased revolutions to maintain position well south of the landing, while the other steamboat finished off-loading. Presently the *Union* raised its ramp and cast loose, easing back out as its paddlewheel churned faster trying maintain distance from the *Denver*, while gaining momentum against the river current.

"Okay, Corporal, now it's our turn. You may want to go back by your horse. Funny how quick everyone wants off when we get where we're going. Name's Cooper, Coop for short! I may see you again. We'll be working this part of the river all season."

"Thanks Coop, I hope I do. I'd like to learn more about things around here. Take it easy!"

Fort Abraham Lincoln - Dakota Territory late 1870s

The troopers and roustabouts, got the wagons unloaded, and manhandled them up the incline in the river bank. As the men led their horses up on the flat, the sergeants were quick to assemble them into sections and platoons. Weir, and the other officers were sitting astride their mounts off to the side watching the proceedings. A group of riders, approached from the direction of the fort.

Weir watched as they came closer. "There's Tom Custer, W.W. Cooke, and Jimmi Calhoun, I'm not sure about the other. Let's go say hello while the sergeants finish getting the men organized, Jim. Sgt. Morse told me that Mr. Johnson told him Custer and Libbie left for New York earlier this month. I'll warrant that Tom will have a welcoming party laid on."

When they got closer to the party from the fort, Tom Custer called out, "Weir! How in the hell have you been? I heard you were traipsing around up north, marking the border, and then holed up at Totten."

"Well, I suppose that's a fair description. We heard you three were out picnicking down in the Black Hills, along with the rest of the Regiment. We didn't make it in the newspapers like you did, though."

Tom laughed, exclaiming, "You didn't find any gold, either! It was a grand expedition, too bad you missed it!"

"Any idea if there's something planned for this season?" asked Porter, "I want to get Eliza and the boys settled in as soon as they get here in a couple of weeks."

"That depends on Mr. Lo." Custer answered, "Right now we've not heard any plans. Where's Keogh?"

"Ah, he's back at Headquarters, in St.Paul, sitting on court marshal boards, I believe he'll be along next month." Porter replied.

Tom motioned towards one of the others behind him, "Gentlemen, this is my little brother, Boston. Bos, this is Captain Tom Weir, Lieutenant Jim Porter, and Lieutenant Win Edgerly. Bos came out last year, and Armstrong found him a job doling out oats."

Boston, who resembled both of his older brothers, waved at them and said. "Well, someone has to see that the horses are fed! Pleased to make your acquaintance, Sirs."

"I suggest we escort you gents to your quarters, and catch up over dinner. Maggie and Annie Yates are putting together a welcome party." stated Calhoun.

"That sounds grand!" Weir declared, "We'll go tell 1st Sergeants Martin and Varden. I'll get Keller to see that our things get brought up. We'll not be long."

Morse had been overseeing the unloading of the *Denver,* and as the last wagons teams were being harnessed and hitched up, he rode over to where 1st Sgt. Martin was talking with another 1st Sergeant.

"Hey Pat, da ya remember Ed Bobo, from Company C? He's come to show us to our barracks."

"Sure, it's been a while Ed. How have you been?"

"I've been freezing my ass off! We got stuck here, while other companies went south to Louisiana."

"Now, wouldn't that be the way to spend the winter!"

Bobo nodded his head, "Yeh well, here we are. There's three barracks buildings that house two companies each. You're going in the one furtherest west, I suggest you send some men to get the fires going. I did see to having some wood stocked for you. There are stables just behind. I'll go along with you to help sort it out."

"Thanks Ed!" said Martin.

"There's a NCO Quarters on the east end of barracks row. There's plenty of rooms, and you've got your own cook and mess. I've got a place with the wife, over on Suds Row."

"I've got my Mrs. coming. Maybe you can help me get her situated?"

"I'll put my wife on it. She's sure to come up with something."

'We ready to roll, Pat?"

"You bet Top!"

"Lets get these boys put up, and then go find our rooms. Ed, I'm sure a little whiskey will knock the chill off if you've a mind to. We were able to lay in a good supply on the way."

"I've a mind, Michael! I already told the wife not to wait up." said Bobo with a grin.

Fort Abraham Lincoln was laid out around the large parade ground known as, Cavalry Square. Officers Row consisted of seven houses arrayed along a low bluff on the West side. Opposite to the East were the Adjutants Office, three double barracks buildings, the Band Quarters, and the NCO quarters. The commissary and quartermaster storehouses were to the south, and a pair of granaries, the dispensary, and guardhouse to the north. Behind the barracks and between the river bank, were seven large stables, the Laundress Quarters, a corral, and ice house. Scattered outside the perimeter, mostly to the north, were the officers club, hospital, and bake house. The post trader was located between the infantry and cavalry posts, not far from where the riverboat landing was.

The barracks were long, low single story buildings with a covered porch along the front, facing the parade ground. Behind them were separate kitchens, cisterns, and mess halls connected to the main structure by a wash area, for each company. Constructed from green cottonwood boards that warped as they dried, the walls were constantly being repaired and plugged by anything on hand, such as rags, wood scraps, and mud. Two fireplaces, and a wood stove were allotted to each wing.

As the men filed into the barracks, the usual bitching and moaning could be heard clearly. Jake stood with his back to the fireplace having already claimed a bunk along the back wall, close to the hearth.

"God damn, what a dump! Listen to the wind whistling through that wall!" exclaimed Sanders. "That window frame is about to fall out!"

"Yeh, Look at the damn cobwebs!"

"Hey! The shelves are falling off the walls!"

He let them vent a little longer, then stepped out into the middle. "Okay, that's enough! There's nothing we can't fix. Look, the layout is pretty much the same as back at Totten, and at least there ain't no stairs. Keep your bunks in the same order. Stack your gear, and let's get over to the quartermaster's warehouse and draw bedding. The wagons with the footlockers will be here before too long. A couple of days and we'll be settled in."

The grumbling toned down a bit, as the troopers sorted out their bunk dispositions.

Jake went over to Holden, and asked him to get his set to help out the cook, after they drew blankets and mattresses. Henry replied, "No problem Jake, we'll see that he gets help."

Rogers went towards the door and shouted, "Let's get a move on! At least we'll have a roof over us and hot chow. Better hurry, or we'll have to stand in line behind Company I!"

1st. Sgt. Bobo and all of the D and I sergeants were seated around tables in the mess area of the NCO quarters. They'd finished eating and several bottles were making the rounds.

"So Ed, bring us up to speed on the Regiment, since you returned from the Black Hills." Martin asked.

" In September, six companies were sent south to serve under Major Merrill, on Reconstruction duty. Companies B,E,H, &K are in Louisiana, A,E, & L are in Alabama. Company M is down at Fort Rice, where Major Joe Tilford is post commander."

"Fortunate timing, I'd say." Morse said, "I'm sure they hated to miss our Dakota winter."

"Well, we all know Custer and Merrill are not fond of each other, so Custer was not thrilled with the orders, but made sure that most all of the members of his 'Custer Clan' stayed here, except for Moylan in Company A. They had a grand time all winter. Lots of parties, sleigh rides, and other festivities along Officers Row."

"So, we heard Custer left on leave. Who's in command?" 1st Sgt. Varden, of Company I, asked.

"Well, Major Tilford is post commander down at Fort Rice, where Company M is stationed. My Captain, Verling Hart, is the ranking officer since Custer left. He's not too bad, but he's not a big Custer fan. He's senior on the captains list and its rumored that he's waiting for Majority to open up in another regiment. We've also got Lieutenants Henry Harrington, and Jimmi Calhoun, who's married to Custer's sister."

"So let's hear the other members of this 'Custer Clan' are so we don't run a foul of them."

"Right! You all know about Lt. Tom Custer, the younger brother, Boston, was with him today. He's our so-called forage master. He stays with his brothers up on Officers Row and we don't see much of him. Captain Yates of Company F was with Custer during the War, and has been with the Regiment since it was formed. His wife is good friends with the Custer women. He's well liked by his men and his 1st Sergeant, is a young buck and makes a point to keep his boys looking sharp. We like to call them the Band Box Troop. Lieutenant Calhoun is married to Custer's sister, Margaret, and Custer appointed him as his Acting Assistant Adjutant General so he could stay here. Captain Moylan of Company A, is married to Calhoun's sister. He was Custer's Regimental Sergeant Major back when the 7th was formed. He's a favorite of Custer's and he brought him up through the ranks. Then there's Lt. W.W. Cooke, the Regimental Adjutant, they call him "The Queens Own". He's a Canadian, but fought in War with the cavalry. He's been with Custer from the get go, too. Not a bad fellow, and he's one of the best marksmen in the outfit."

"Okay, I'm starting to get the lay of the land. But you know Captain Weir is from Michigan, and was part of the Clan back in Kansas, and Captain Keogh was known to spend time with them also." Martin stated. "Libbie Custer is quite partial to both of them."

"Keogh was close to them down in Kentucky, too." said De Lacy, looking over at Varden. "That may be why we've been stuck up north for the last two years, hey Top?"

"Michael, and I, have been with the regiment from the start. We've seen many an officer come and go. Custer keeps a close eye on his Libbie. He got court marshaled for it when he left his command out in Western Kansas and dashed back to Fort Hays. I recall rumors about Weir and Libbie going around back then," said Varden.

"Aye, I remember, though I can't speak to them for sure. Weir keeps a close hand."

"Well, then, it seems that life will be a little more interesting this summer if we stay here, fellas!" exclaimed Morse. "And with Bismarck so handy, a man can probably find a nice bar to wile away a few hours, from time to time!"

"You'll have to get away from the riverfront if you want to find one. Be sure to warn your men, particularly the younger ones, about that part of Bismarck, and Whisky Point, just across the river. They're rough places, run by scoundrels, pimps, and card cheats. They prey on our boys, and what they try to pass off as whiskey, can blind a man." Bobo said.

"Sounds just like Hays City, back in Kansas. Any local law they need to watch out for? They haven't tried to bring in someone like Bill Hickok, have they?"

"No, The last I heard about him was that he'd quit Bill Cody's traveling show, and was holed up over in Cheyenne gambling. Bismarck has a town Marshall, but he stays in the uptown area, around the Railroad

Depot, and stays well away from the riverfront." replied Bobo.

"How about the post trader? What's the story on him?" asked Martin.

"His name is Robert Seip. He showed up to replace our old trader last July, and immediately raised his prices on everything. All in all, he's okay. He carries the same goods as the other forts. We're pretty sure that he's in league with the Leighton brothers, up at Fort Buford. It's common knowledge they control many of the post traders and dictate the prices. It's rumored that his wife is one of their nieces. There's also a restaurant and small hotel for visitors. Seip runs the post office, and then of course, his store. He added on two billiard rooms, one for the officers, and one for the enlisted men, where he sells beer, wine, and whiskey. We've been able to negotiate with him on occasion, but he and Custer don't get along. Custer wanted some different colored hats for the troops, and bought some from St. Paul, at half the price. He intended to sell them to the men at a good price. When Seip saw them he complained that that violated the terms of his contract and that no one should be allowed to buy cheaper goods, elsewhere, and then bring them back to the fort and resell them. I think that the Leighton's complained to Secretary of War Belknap, because he sent out a letter taking their side, back in December. Custer wasn't happy to say the least, and has virtually ostracized poor Seip ever since, who is trapped between a rock and a hard spot. In the mean time, we run our own little smuggling operation with the help of the NCOs at Camp Hancock. They mix our special requisitions in with the regular supply wagons, and keep it way under wraps. Custer and the officers, turn a blind eye, as long as they get supplied."

"How's his operation, other than prices? We were used to the prices at Totten. The Post Trader there is in partnership with General Terry's brother, and we had no local town to go to. Is he fair with extending credit to the men?"

"Oh, he's the same. He does a pretty brisk trade with the local villages of Mandans and Arikaras. He also has the hay and wood contracts, and sees that we stay well supplied. He lets the men have chits, and collects from them on payday. The men know that they can drink cheaper across the river, in Bismarck and at Whiskey Point. But they have to get across. Most paydays, the boats do a brisk business. The brothels are what keeps the Point in business. Hell, the spring ice thaw last year wiped it out, and they were back in business within weeks. You know how it is, when it comes to whores, whiskey, and gambling. As long as they don't get too carried away, there ain't much we can do about it."

The next several weeks went by quickly as, and the weather continued to improve. The men settled in and they completed needed repairs to the barracks and stables. With the arrival of the laundresses and families, the companies quickly fell back to a normal routine. Fatigue details, guard duty, stable duty rotations got sorted out. With the warming weather, the troopers were able to explore the fort grounds and surrounding area. One of the biggest events appeared in the form of new weapons.

The Army Ordinance Department had conducted a series of tests and trials, back in 1873, conducted by a Breech Loading Small Arms Board. Both General Terry and Major Reno had been members of that board. The weapons selected were to replace the Spencer carbine and .44 Colt cap and ball revolvers carried by the cavalry troopers. These were the Springfield Carbine Model 1873, and the 1873 Colt Single Action Army revolver. The rest of the regiment had been issued these new firearms the previous summer, prior to taking the field for the Black Hills Expedition.

CHAPTER 17

Fort Abraham Lincoln - Dakota Territory May 17, 1875

Captain Otho Michaelis was the Regimental Ordinance Officer and showed up from Headquarters, in St.Paul. He contacted Capt. Weir, and Lt. Porter, to set up a schedule for trading out the weapons, and training sessions for the new ones. They both turned it over to their First Sergeants to co-ordinate.

1st Sgt. Martin summoned all of his NCOs and addressed them. "Well, I've been talking with Sergeants Bobo and Kenney about these new guns. They got them last July, and seem very pleased with them so far, particularly with the new Colt revolver. The cartridges being metallic are not prone to spoiling, and much faster to reload. They say the Springfields are simple and rugged, and have a better effective range, then the Spencers."

"Did they say what they thought about the carbines being single shot?" asked Morse.

"The biggest complaint was that it was difficult to reload while mounted. But since most fighting would be when deployed on skirmish lines, that it wasn't as much of a factor. They said the men liked not having to have the Blakeslee speed loader boxes hanging off their shoulders, also."

The group of NCOs nodded their heads in consideration, several of them with raised eyebrows.

"At any rate, we don't get a choice in the matter. Capt. Michaelis will meet us at the target range this afternoon, and walk us through the training procedures for the new guns." Martin stated.

****

Captain Otho Ernest Michaelis

Michaelis, who was born in Germany in Aug. 1843 and emigrated to the United States as child. After graduating as class valedictorian from the City College of New York, he joined the Army in 1862, and served in the ordinance corps, where he became the first non-West Pointer to enter the Ordinance Corps. He participated in the Gettysburg Campaign and also served as Gen. George Thomas' chief of ordinance. He served as Chief Ordinance Officer for General Terry, and was generally well regarded as one of the best ordinance men in the Army. A slight dark haired man in his early thirties, aside from being a weapons expert, he was known as one of the best amateur chess players in the country.

****

The firing range at Fort Lincoln was located behind a bluff, southwest of the cavalry post, facing west towards a low hill. A large canopy was set up with several tables, benches and chairs underneath it. There were several wagons, loaded with crates parked near it. A series of target panels were staked at intervals out towards the hill. The NCOs from both Companies D & I, gathered around.

"Good morning, men! My name is Captain Michaelis and I'm here to bring you new weapons. Your units are almost the last ones in the Regiment to be issued the new carbines and pistols." he announced, "I think you'll be pleased. Both of these weapons have been through extensive testing and were chosen, both for their accuracy, and reliability." Holding up one of the new carbines for them to see he continued. "This is the Springfield Model 1873 Carbine, it weighs 7 pounds and is 41" long. It shoots a .45 caliber bullet weighing 405 grains, using 55 grains of powder in copper cartridge with a center fire primer, and is highly accurate out to 300 yards. With practice, an experienced man can consistently hit targets farther away, using the graduated ladder rear sight."

"So what would you say is the best range for the average trooper, then?" asked Sgt. Varden.

"Well, that depends on the situation." answered Michaelis.

"Shooting at Mr. Lo, while he's on his horse coming at you!"

The captain considered this for a second, then answered, "Well, given that I've not personally been in that situation, I would venture that 200 yards would be a good range to have a fair chance of hitting him."

"Okay, let's say you missed with your shot. How fast can you reload, and can you do it without taking your eyes off Mr. Lo?"

"Hmm! That would have to be practiced. Maybe 4-5 seconds, providing you have another cartridge handy."

"Fair enough, Sir! My point is that Mr. Lo has probably closed half the distance, if he kept on coming, so it would seem to me that our Spencers would be better in that situation."

"I see your point, Sergeant!" said Michaelis, "However, I'm an ordinance officer, and you're venturing off into tactics. But, since you won't have a Spencer any more, and if you don't hit him the second time, then I'd recommend you use this." He bent to the table and held up a pistol. This produced a round of laughter among the non-coms.

"This is a Colt Single Action Army, Model 1873 Revolver. It weighs 2.3 pounds and has a 7 & 1/2" barrel, It shoots a .45 caliber bullet weighing 230 grains, using 28 grains of powder in a copper cartridge with a center primer. It's accurate at 25 yards if you can hold it steady. You have six shots and if you can hit your Mr. Lo with this, he will notice!"

This brought on more chuckles, and Varden nodded approvingly. "I'll bear that in mind, Sir!"

Michaelis continued, "The Army has decided, based on their trial results, to issue these weapons as the most reliable, accurate, easiest to use and maintain. I'm here to help train you and answer your questions about them, so you can train your men. You will have to find the best methods to use them. They are both more powerful than what you are carrying now, so I'd start there. One word of caution though, concerning the pistols. They are highly sought after on the civilian market, I recommend that you take steps to control access to them while you're here at Fort Lincoln. The other companies have already discovered this. Now, let's get these guns passed out, and we can start shooting!"

Capt. Michaelis had requested that each of the companies assign a NCO to liaison with the Ordinance team. They would be given advanced training on trouble shooting and maintaining the new firearms. In addition, they were to help verify weapons serial numbers, and the men that they were issued. Sgt. Martin, discussed it with Sgt.Morse and decided that Rogers was to stay at the range and help train the sections. For the better part of the following week the air was filled with the sounds gunshots echoing off the surrounding hills. Jake found that he liked the new carbine. It was solidly built, and well balanced. The rear sight was indexed for longer ranges, and with a little practice he could hit out to 500 yards, but needed to find a good rest. The pistols shot well, and the long barrel aided the accuracy. 1st Sgt. Martin and Sgt. Morse rode out one afternoon to observe.

"So, Rogers, how are the men progressing?"

"Well, Top. They're only being given 20 rounds to shoot in each gun. It's hard to get proficient with that little. The guns are simple enough to load and clean, so I'd say for now, we're okay. If we go out in the field, we'd better scrounge up some more ammo for practice."

Martin looked over at Morse, who asked. "What do you think, Rogers? Are they more accurate than the Spencers?"

"Yes, they are at longer range. Most of the men are okay at 100 yards, though they still tend to shoot high. They are still getting used to the heavier bullet and recoil. We need to make sure that we practice ranging with the sights. We're still working on speeding up the reloading procedure. I talked with some of Capt. Michaelis's ordinance men. They said that the Army is looking into having some canvas bandoliers made for the bullets, that can be worn around the waist. That's the best level for reloading, and it facilitates grabbing another round. Some of the other units have experimented with sewing cartridge loops on their pistol belts."

"Okay, makes sense to me, particularly with the new pistol rounds. Let's see what we can come up with."

"I already have Pvt. Manning working on one, for me." Jake said with a grin.

Jake continued to spend his days at the range, working with the men. Corporal Michael Caddle had been chosen by 1st Sgt. Varden to train the Company I troopers. Jake had met him a few times, and knew that he was well liked by the men in his company. He and DeLacy were good friends. Caddle was a light haired Irishman, from Dublin, about Jake's age, in his early twenties, and had an easy, outgoing personality. He was also a very good shot with a carbine, or pistol. They were taking a break, waiting on more men to show up.

"So, Rogers, where'd you learn to shoot so well?" Caddle asked.

"I grew up in the woods down in Missouri. My Pa taught me, and I started hunting when I was a boy. When you just have an old cap and ball rifle to shoot, you learn to make your shots count, or go hungry." Jake replied with a grin. "How about you?"

"Oh, back home I worked on a farm belonging to a wealthy man named Arthur Leech. He was the head of the Irish Rifle Association. One of my jobs was tending his target range. The members would let me shoot now and then, and taught me the basics. I just took to it."

"Well, I can tell that. How'd you end up out here?"

"After I came over, I was working as a conductor on a local train line in Brooklyn. The National Rifle Association built the Creedmoor shooting range out, on Long Island, and many people started going there. One of them, an Army recruiting officer, was a frequent passenger and we got to talking about shooting. Well, I'll be damned, the next thing I knew, he had me joined up! I can tell you, it's a far cry different from what he was selling!" Caddle said, laughing.

Capt. Michaelis walked up just then and asked, "I have a couple of rifles that I'd like to show you, if you're interested.?"

They both responded, "Sure Captain!" then followed him as he turned and led them over to where two rifles were laying on a blanket covered table.

"These were sent to me by the Sharps Rifle Company. They lost out on winning the Army contract, but are still building these special long-range rifles for buffalo hunters, and other big game shooting. They sent these two for me to evaluate. They're chambered for the 45/70 cartridge that the Infantry uses. Go ahead, look them over."

Jake picked one of them up, it was a heavy rifle around four foot in length. A long tube with brass capped ends, extended the length go the barrel. The stock and forearm were checkered walnut, and it had double triggers.

"These are 1874 Sporting Models with double set triggers, and 6X Malcolm Scopes. I'm told that they can reliably reach out to 1,000 yards. Would you two like to try?"

Both Jake and Caddle who were still admiring the workmanship, looked up smiling at Michaelis, and nodded their heads in unison.

"Well, let's give a go, shall we?" he stated.

The ordnance men had already set up 6' tall steel targets down range at 100, 200, 400, 500, & 1000 yards. Michaelis produced a small, flat rectangular brass device with V-shape cut out and a sliding aperture. There was a length of string attached to it.

"This is a range estimating stadia and it's quite simple to operate. The string is calibrated for me, but it can be adjusted to anyone."

Jake asked, "How does it work?"

The officer held it out at arms length. "The reason that we have 6' tall targets is that more or less the height of the average soldier. I've calibrated this one at 100 yards. I will put the knot at the end of this string between my teeth, then pull it taut. Then when I sight through the aperture I'll slide it until the target fills it and that verifies that range."

"Kind of like the old rule of thumb method my Pa taught me." Jake stated.

"Exactly! But this one is adjustable and good out to seven hundred yards, which is close to the maximum effective range of the average rifle."

"But you said we were going to shoot out to 1,000 yards." Caddle remarked.

"Yes, but for practical use in the field these stadia can be useful.

They were manufactured at the Frankford Arsenal, near Philadelphia, during the War, and are becoming scarce. I have one for whoever hits the most targets. Just a little incentive for you both to give your best effort." Michaelis said, smiling.

"Hah! Well, no doubt I'll be sporting that when we're done, sir!" Caddle said grinning over at Jake.

"Yes, well, we'll have to shoot first won't we?" Jake queried.

Michaelis interjected, "Before we begin let's discuss ballistics. Do you know what I'm referring to?"

"Bullet drop." Caddle offered.

"Precisely! The velocity of the bullet is determined by its weight, the amount of powder, and the length of the barrel, which in turn is effected by gravity and distance to the target. The sights on your carbines have markings for 100 yard intervals, in between them is pretty much a guess based on the shooters ability. The Malcolm Scope with its magnification power, has more graduation marks on its range adjusting bracket, so a finer sight picture is possible. Of course it helps that we have known ranges to the targets, so you can dial in the elevation corrections. The six foot targets will help you develop range estimating skills, with practice. Then of course there have to be windage adjustments."

"I've used vernier tang sights before, they take some practice." said Caddle.

"Yes, they do, and you still have to allow for windage with a scope, also. Let's try some shots. I have several boxes of the 45/70 cartridges that I borrowed from over at the Infantry Post."

The two men settled down on the firing line, and experimented with sighting the rifles from a comfortable position. Michaelis gave them each a box of shells, then he said. "Let's shoot at the 200 yard targets first, and check to see that the rifles are zeroed. I've seen you both hit them with your carbines, so you shouldn't have any issues. It'll give you a chance to get the feel of the weapons"

They both chambered rounds and peered through the scopes. After several seconds they fired, almost simultaneously. Two resounding clangs sounded downrange.

"Excellent! Now, we've a bit of a wind coming from the South. As we move farther out, you both know that you need to apply windage, and you'll have to adjust the calibrated index marks on the rear scope mount to compensate for bullet drop. Just to give you an idea of the drop, the scope will have you holding almost 40 yards high at 500 yards, and at 1,000 yards you"ll be double that."

Jake and Caddle looked at each other with raised eyebrows, then adjusted the scopes to shoot at the 500 yard targets, as the Ordinance officer used a telescope to spot the targets. After a few trial shots, they were hitting consistently. They continued, matching each other shot for shot, while alternating turns, when Michaelis had them stop.

"This would be a good time to clean the bores, before we try the longer ranges. I'm going to show you a trick on how to keep your rifles from fouling so quickly." He reached in his pocket and held what appeared to be a small candle. "We will use this to lubricate your cartridges before you shoot. It's 2 to 1 mixture of beeswax and a petroleum jelly that I found on my last trip back to New York. It's being sold under the trade name, Vaseline. I've experimented with the mixture and found this to be most practical, for actual use out in the field. Just give your bullets a light coat, and you'll be surprised how well it works."

Jake noticed three riders coming from the fort, and pointed it out to Michaelis. As they got closer, they saw that it was Capt. Weir, Lt. Edgerly, and also Capt. Keogh who had just arrived from St. Paul earlier in the week. Jake and Bustard scrambled to their feet and saluted as they rode up.

"As you were, men." Weir said, turning towards Michaelis, "Otho, we were sitting on our porch, when we heard the shooting and wondered at what you were playing with, its bit loud for a carbine. Thought we'd come and watch."

"Ah! Thomas! Just playing with a couple of Sharps sporting rifles that I acquired. I borrowed a couple of your men to check them out."

Keogh looked at Caddle, who had a big grin on his face. "Having fun, Corporal?"

"Indeed I am, Sir! You need to come shoot one of these beauties. Why a man could bag supper without having to leave camp."

"I will, but continue on and we'll just watch for a while."

"Yes, Sir!" Caddle exclaimed, the looked over at Jake, "Rogers, shall we have a wee bet, on who does best?"

"Loser buys the beers!" Jake replied.

While the two soldiers finished up up cleaning the rifles, the officers dismounted and tethered their mounts away from the firing line.

"Well, my money is on Caddle." Keogh announced, as they walked back. "What do ya say, Thomas? You back your lad?"

"I've seen Rogers shoot, and it wasn't targets. I'm game. How about you Edgerly?"

The junior officer replied, "Oh, I think I'll just be a bystander."

The officers found some seats on nearby ammo crates and the two soldiers settled back behind their rifles.

"There's a bit more pressure on ya, lad." Caddle wisecracked, "I'm tasting that free beer already!"

Jake looked over at him and replied, "You can pick your turn, Mike. Makes me no difference."

"Okay men," announced Michaelis. "The 1,000 yard targets are in play. Now you'll each have three shots each, the best out of three wins. If no one hits the target, we will alternate shots until someone does, and the other misses." The captain said as he handed them the bullets.

Caddle got into position and fiddled with the adjustments on his scope, and then took careful aim. "Boom!"

"Just short and a bit to the right!" Michaelis announced.

Mike nodded his head and reloaded, "Boom!"

"Right in front of it, online though!" came the call from the officer.

Caddle reloaded and made a slight adjustment to the scope, then settled in behind the big rifle. "Boom!" Seconds later, a dull clap sounded down range confirming a hit, and he looked over at Jake grinning and exclaimed, "There ya go! I'm on the board!"

Jake smiled back at him and replied, "Good shot, Mike!"

He loaded his first round and took a couple of deep breaths to clear his mind. Then he hefted his rifle into position, peering through his scope, and focused on the target while he slowed his breathing. The double set triggers were smooth as silk. "Boom!", it surprised him when the rifle fired.

"Over! To the left" Michaelis called out.

Jake went through the motions of reloading, and then slowly got back in firing position. He willed the crosshairs onto the target, envisioning the shot and caressed the trigger. "Boom!" From downrange, the sound of the bullet striking sounded clearly.

"Hit!" came the call.

Trying not to hurry, he ejected the casing and calmly grasped the third bullet, and seated it in the breach. Bringing the stock up to his shoulder as he chambered the round, he reacquired the target, focusing on the crosshairs, then took an extra breath before stroking the trigger again, sending the third shot on its way, "Boom!"

"Another hit!" Michaelis exclaimed, "That's good shooting, Rogers!"

"Just like shooting squirrels back home!" said Jake, grinning over at Bustard.

"That is some fine shooting, Corporal!" called out Weir.

Jake stood up slowly and looked down range, replaying the shots in his head. He looked over at Weir, who nodded his head in approval and then said to Keogh. "I told you that I'd seen him shoot, Myles."

Keogh stood and looked at Weir, "Sure now, you won that one! I think it only appropriate that you give me a chance to win it back. I fancy that we should take a crack at these fancy rifles ourselves."

"I'll be part of that action!" exclaimed Edgerly.

"Okay, let's agree on a format." replied Weir, "Otho, will you stay and call the shots?"

Keogh said, "Corporal Caddle, why don't you and Corporal Rogers take the rest of the day off. I've heard the post trader got a fresh load of beer in this morning. Tell him the tab is on my account!"

"Yes, Sir! Very good, Sir" said Caddle, grinning "And thank you, Sir!"

He and Jake hustled to gather their things, and then retrieved their mounts that were hitched just beyond the Ordinance tents. As they mounted up, Caddle leaned over to Jake and said, "Ah now, lad! Let's see if you ride as well as ya shoot!" Then wheeled spurring his mount toward the fort. Jake followed, urging Ajax to a quick gallop.

As they rode off, Michaelis commented to the other officers, "I'd love to have those two on my Ordinance team. I don't suppose you would consider letting me recruit them?"

Keogh laughed, "No, I think you'd find Caddle a hand full. He was on his best behavior today! Besides, my First Sergeant and I have plans to promote him before too long. He's one of our most promising young NCOs."

Weir chimed in. "Corporal Rogers, has proven himself to be quite enterprising. Not to mention that my First Sergeant and another senior NCO, would be very upset if he was to be out from under their wings. I'm flattered that he made such a good impression on you though, Otho."

"Well, Thomas, I have a Sergeant's slot available, it would mean a promotion for the lad."

"That's already in the works, Michaelis! You'll see another stripe on him, soon. Now, Gentlemen! Let's see if we can hold a candle to those two marksmen. Though I'm glad Myles sent them away. I fear that we will have a hard time matching their shots, and it's just as well they don't know it!"

As Jake and Caddle made their way across the fort, they stopped at their barracks to report to their respective First Sergeants. When Caddle came back out he was followed by Sgt. DeLacy.

"Hey Jake, do ya mind if Milt comes with us? He's at the end of his enlistment. Keogh is after him to sign on for another 5 years and he's trying to decide if he will. Milt has until Friday."

"Sure Jim, I know DeLacy. He and Morse brought me out from

Jefferson Barracks two years ago." Jake said, waving at Milt. "I wouldn't mind hearing your thoughts about re-enlisting if you don't mind? Not that I have to worry about it any time soon!"

"Sure, Rogers! Just call me Milt. You've come a long way since I first set eyes on you back in Sioux City, although I'm not surprised. Pat said you'd be a quick study when it came to soldiering."

"Well, I'm glad that I didn't let him down, he'd probably write my Ma and then I'd have to deal with that!" replied Jake, laughing. "Come on, your Captain is buying! We don't want him to think that we're ungrateful!

The three of them had settled at a table on the long shaded porch out front of the traders, and were working through a round of beers.

Caddle finished his, and signaled the waitress for another round. He looked at DeLacy and asked. "So Milt, have ya made up your mind?"

"I'm thinking I will, Mike. I can't see going back home to New York and working at the waterworks in Kingston. I want to stay out west. I've thought a bit about signing on with a riverboat, but I don't know what I'd do in the off season. So, maybe I'll just do another 5 years and see then. The officers let Top Varden run the show, and he likes me. So, there you go."

The round of beers came, and the waitress, a young, petite, dark haired brunette with bright, blue eyes, smiled at them and said, "Here you go boys! I brought you a bowl of pork cracklins, and some peanuts. Let me know if you want more."

"Why thank you, lassie, you're a dear!" exclaimed Caddle.

"My name is Holly Walker, and you're welcome!""Just let me know when you're ready for another round." She replied, smiling as she walked away.

Caddle nudged Jake's arm and whispered, "I think she's taken a shine to you, Jake."

"Yeh me, and a few hundred other troopers!" He replied sarcastically.

"Mark my words, lad, I saw her watching you when we came in!"

"Sure, sure! So what about you, Mike? What's your plans?"

"I'm like you, I've a ways to go. But all in all, I'm liking it here. Keogh and Varden both treat me well, and I suspect they'll give me another stripe soon. I don't have a clue what I'd do as a civilian."

They sat discussing the merits of Army life, and decided to stay and have one more round, when Holly brought it over, she brushed up against Jake's shoulder as she set her tray on the table.

"So, you fellows must be with the new cavalry companies that moved in."

"Indeed, Miss Holly!" Mike replied, "I'm Mike Caddle, and this is Milt DeLacy. We're with Company I, and Jake Rogers here, is from Company D."

"So why is it that Capt. Keogh is picking up the tab for you? We don't get many officers buying rounds for their men without them being here."

"Jake here, won it for us. We were showing our officers how to shoot a new rifle, and Keogh lost a bet to Capt. Weir, Jake's company commander. This lad can shoot!"

Holly looked down at Jake, "Really! Well, I'd think that comes in handy in your line of work, Jake."

He smiled at her and replied, "Occasionally!"

"So how is it that you work here? Seems an odd place, in the middle of nowhere, for a pretty girl like yourself ?" DeLacy asked.

"My Uncle Bob, is the Post Trader." She answered, as her smile faded, "I was raised in Ottumwa, Iowa and came to live with him after my parents died."

"Oh! Sorry to have brought it up." DeLacy said quickly.

"It's quite all right. He's taken me in, and this fall is sending me down to Leavenworth, Kansas to attend St. Mary's Academy there. He knows the post trader there, a Mr. Goodfellow, and I'm to live with him and his daughters."

"What will you study there?" asked Jake.

"Oh, I suppose that I'll be a teacher someday."

"My mother is a school teacher!" He replied brightly. "Although when I was younger, I wasn't too thrilled about it. But, she made me learn in spite of myself."

Holly looked at Jake and smiled, "So, you weren't a good student?"

"Well, reluctantly!"

She gathered up the empty glasses, "Anything else? I can see what we're serving tonight?"

"No, we must be heading back, now. Our cooks would be upset if we missed dinner and they found out that we were hanging out over here!" Caddle said, jokingly.

"Perhaps you'll come visit again? Jake, you could tell me how to be a proper school teacher." She said and laughed.

"I look forward to it Miss Holly!"

As they headed towards the fort, the two Company I men ribbed Jake about his new girl friend, and offered him advice. He didn't really listen, he was busy picturing her smiling face and bright blue eyes.

The two Companies from Ft. Totten soon discovered that the routines followed at Lincoln called for a little more spit and polish than they were accustomed to. They spent more time addressing their appearance and correct military etiquette. As the weather continued to improve the Sunday Dress Inspection turned into a weekly spectacle attended by all the dependents, and a fair amount of local visitors. Jake spotted Holly, sitting in a carriage with a couple, who he assumed were her uncle and his wife.The Regimental Band in particular enjoyed putting on a show as the Companies of the 7th turned out in their finest. Afterwards if it was good weather, afternoons became quite festive on both sides of the parade ground, although the socializing along officers row was more formal. The areas surrounding the barracks were used for baseball games, foot races, horseshoes, and other activities. There were many spectators, and they were enjoyed by all, excepting of course those on guard duty, even they got to watch the proceedings.

Weir, Keogh, and Edgerly, were standing on the porch of the Bachelor Officer's house when they saw Jimmi Calhoun's wife Maggie, who was Custer's sister waving at them from next door.

"I wonder what she's so excited about?" Weir said.

"No telling," Keogh replied. "She and her bother Tom, are always up to something."

Edgerly, who was engaged to be married that fall, said, "They're probably scheming on a way to embarrass Boston. I swear that I've not ever seen the likes of how they are always tormenting each other."

"She's still waving at us, I suppose we should go see what's up." stated Weir.

They got up and strolled over to where Maggie stood waiting.

"Wonderful news, Gentlemen! A courier just brought Tom a telegram. Armstrong is on his way back. He plans on being here by mid-week. I thought we'd plan a welcome back party. I know you haven't seen he and Libbie in two years. It will be fun, and a good way for everyone to catch up on what they've been doing."

Fort Lincoln Post Traders Bar - circa 1875

CHAPTER 18

Fort Abraham Lincoln - Dakota Territory June 2, 1875

The usual mid-week routine of the fort was disrupted, as the officers of the 7th scrambled to put together a welcome for Custer and his traveling party. Capt. Hart delegated the task to Lt. Cooke, as Regimental Adjutant, and he in turn, recruited Tom Custer and Jimi Calhoun to help. A lookout was posted upriver, to watch for the *Denver*, when it backed away from the Bismarck landing. Carriages were harnessed and staged along Officers Row, to transport the wives and children down to the river landing area. The Band shined and tuned their instruments, and was prepared to assemble when notified. Pvt. Burkman, Custer's striker, had groomed and saddled Custer's favorite horse, Dandy, and had him hitched in front of the Custer residence, where many of the officers were gathered waiting on the porch. Tables were being stacked with various foods and dishes, inside. A rider was seen galloping from the direction of the river landing, and a boat whistle sounded upriver. Tom Custer, led his sister Margaret, followed by Jimi Calhoun and Boston down the front steps, along with George Yates and his wife, Annie. After handing the women into the carriages, the men mounted their horses, and the whole procession left to head for the river landing.

The *Denver* pivoted in the current, and began nudging towards the Fort Lincoln boat landing. As preparations were made to lower the boarding ramp into position, a small crowd assembled. The steamer sounded its shrill whistle. The 7th's Bandmaster, Felix Vinatiera, stepped forward, did an about face and as he raised his arms, the band launched into a rousing rendition of "Garry Owen". Custer appeared on the deck, with his arm wrapped around Libbie, and small knot of people standing behind him. When the ramp was in place, Custer led the way up. Tom Custer, Cooke, and Calhoun all stepped forward and saluted when he stepped off. Custer, who was obviously pleased, returned their salute.

Libbie waved gaily to the women from the fort that had come down to greet them. A youth with a pasty complexion, and three pretty, dark haired young women, two of them obviously sisters, followed in behind them, along with the black Adams sisters, Maria, the maid, and the cook, Mary. They moved into the welcoming throng, and after a few minutes the women were handed up into the carriages, Pvt. Burkman led Dandy over to Custer for him to mount, and soon they all moved out along the road headed towards Officer's Row. The band followed in their wake.

"Well, here they come, Gentlemen. The General and his entourage, returning from what I'm sure was a successful campaign, in New York." exclaimed Capt. Hart, with a touch of sarcasm.

Weir, Keogh, and the other officers that had not ventured down to the river landing, were standing on the front steps of Custer's house, watching as the cavalcade approached.

"Custer has always enjoyed parades, hey Keogh?" ad-libbed Weir.

"That he has, Thomas! I recall that the last time we saw him down in Memphis. It was after he assembled the Regiment, prior to our heading north for the Boundary Survey. It was a much larger affair, though."

That drew a round of chuckles from among the other officers.

"Oh, you'll see much bigger ones every now and then. Custer likes to put on for the locals, Sunday Dress Inspections will be grander from now on. We've just been practicing, this last month." said Lt. Harrington, who was the junior lieutenant of Company C. "It's the only show in town, so to speak!"

"Yes, with five companies to play with, you can be sure that Custer will come up with some new flourishes!" said Hart.

Custer rode up and came to a halt just below the steps. While he waited for Burkman to come grab Dandy's halter, he looked over at the waiting crowd.

"Captain Keogh, it's been a while. I hope you are well!" he called. "Captain Weir! The same to you! I'm glad we were able to bring you back into the fold, so to speak."

"Thank you, Sir" they both answered.

"Captain Hart, I trust all is well, with the rest of the troops."

Hart replied stiffly, "All is as it should be, Sir! We've been shaking off the winter rust."

The carriage carrying Libbie and the others in Custer's party pulled up. Custer dismounted handing his reins to Burkman, and walked over to help them down.

"Libbie dear, would you like to introduce our guests"

As the girls made ready to step down, Custer sprang to assist them. He held out his hand to help them, grasping theirs as they descended, one at a time.

"May I introduce Nellie and Emma Wadsworth, and Emily Watson, from Monroe, Michigan. They are the daughters of some of our dear friends back home, who have come to spend time with us during the summer months."

The pale lad climbed dawn on his own, and stepped to the side.

"And this young man is, Bertie Swett, his father was the late Mr. Lincoln's law partner. He came out from Chicago, to be invigorated by our fresh Dakota summer air. I'm sure that you all will become accustomed to seeing him around the post!"

Bertie managed a brief wave.

"Let's all move inside. I'm told Sister Margaret has arranged a marvelous homecoming party for us all!" announced Libbie.

As she turned and led the way up the steps, Custer had a Wadsworth girl on each arm, and was introducing them the younger officers. Libbie paused briefly near Keogh and Weir. She nodded her head, smiled brightly at them, and then said quietly, "Hello you, two. I'll want to hear about everything you've been up to since we said goodbye in Memphis. I've dearly missed both of you."

Later in the afternoon, across the parade ground, many of the men were sitting on the barracks porches watching the sun go down. As dusk descended, the houses along Officer's Row, particularly Custer's, blossomed with lights.

"Man, that's some kind of party they got goin' on over there!" Pat Golden exclaimed.

"Yes, indeed, do ya suppose they forgot to send you an invitation, Rooster?" asked Big George.

The sounds of laughter, singing, and a piano wafted with the evening breeze. The glow of cigars twinkled in clusters, designated groups gathered outside.

"Well, it just don't seem right! We're stuck over here with a bunch of ugly hard dicks, while they have pretty girls to flirt with. I saw several riding in the carriages as they passed by us."

"Careful there, Laddie!" admonished Joe Greene, "One of them was sure to be Mrs. Custer. Don't be lusting after any women, over there. Best save your romancin' for the Bismarck dollies, lest you want to end up on permanent privy duty."

"Ah, I was just sayin! Speakin' of Bismarck, when da ya suppose we'll get to go over there?"

Holden leaned forward in his chair, tapping on his pipe. "You may as well wait until next payday. You'll find nothing free across the river, that will have anything to do with the likes of you, Patrick!"

"He's got you there, Rooster!" laughed Hurry, along with others.

"Ah, Henry! Tis a mean thing for you to say. You know that it's the stimulating conversation with the fair sex, that I crave!"

Jake was sitting quietly, listening to the banter. Their comments about the girls had got him thinking about Holly. She'd let dangle that invitation to come back. It had been a while since he received a letter from Colleen, and the prospect of writing her one, paled in comparison to the lure of visiting the post trader's again. He speculated on how to approach Holly, if he did.

"Hey, Jake!, You up for a game of cribbage?" asked Charlie Welch, breaking into his reverie.

"Huh? Yeh, why not?" he answered.

Later in the week Capt. Michaelis finished up his weapons exchange and training programs. He summoned Jake and Caddle.

"I'm done with you men. I want to thank you for your help. I spoke with your Captains and let them know that you both did a great job. In fact, I told them that I'd like to have you come work for me."

Both men looked at him without saying anything for a minute.

"Why, thanks Captain!" said Caddle. "But I expect that I'm a better fit for a line company. Besides, I've several good friends, and they'd be furious if I left them!"

Michaelis nodded his head, "I understand. How about you Rogers? I've a sergeant's slot to fill. I'm headed down to Louisiana to equip and train Company K. After that, you'd be stationed at Fort Snelling, near St. Paul. It's a nice post. Lots for a young man to do!"

Jake looked Michaelis in the eyes and answered, "Well, I did join up to see the country, so it's a tempting offer. I appreciate it, but I think I'll stay put."

The Ordinance officer laughed, "Well, Keogh and Weir were right. They said that you two were both Company men. But let me know if you ever change your minds. Ordinance sergeants are paid more. I will be sending a letter of appreciation to both of your captains."

Both men's eyebrows raised for a second, then they came to attention and saluted. "Thank you, Sir!"

"Very well! Dismissed!"

They did an about face, and as they walked towards their horses,

Caddle slapped Jake on the back. "What da think about that, me Bucko? We just turned down a hefty pay raise!"

Jake just grinned, and said. "I think that's because Ordinance Sergeants stand a fair chance of being blown to bits, and I think that you still owe me a beer!"

Several days later, after roll call, 1st. Sgt. Martin called out. "Corporal Rogers, report to the orderly room after formation!"

When the platoon broke ranks, Jake headed towards the barracks building. As he passed Sgt. Morse, he received a wink. Rogers stepped up onto the porch, and walked over to the orderly room door, where Martin was waiting. Martin turned and opened the door.

" Captain Weir, I have Corporal Rogers as you requested." Martin called out.

"Come in, both of you."

They entered and stood at attention. Weir was standing and looking at the various mementoes and souvenirs that Martin had hanging on the walls. He turned around and said, "At Ease! Top, you were already with the company when I took over?"

"Yes, Sir! Myself, Sergeants Morse, Flanagan, and Harrison were all prior service and have been with the Company since the Fort Riley days. There's others in the ranks, too. There's always old hands to show the new lads the ropes. Soldierin' ain't for everyone!"

"Hmm, so loyalty to the Company is very important to you."

"Why yes, Sir! Very important!"

Weir stepped forward, producing a piece of paper. He stopped in front Rogers. "Good Morning, Corporal Rogers!" he said quietly.

"Good morning, Sir!"

"I received a letter from Capt. Michaelis. He gave it to me at the officer's club two nights ago. He praised your efforts in helping him to distribute and train our men on the new weapons."

Jake nodded his head. "To tell the truth, Sir, I just like to shoot. Seemed like a good way to get more practice."

Weir smiled, "He also told me that he offered you a position as an Ordinance Sergeant and that you declined, is that correct?"

"Yes, Sir!"

"You turned down a pretty good pay raise."

"Yes, Sir! I'm aware of that."

"The Company and I both appreciate your loyalty."

"Thank you, Sir!"

"First Sergeant Martin and I have been discussing this for a while.

You seem to do well with accepting responsibility."

"Just try to do my best, Sir!"

Weir looked over at Martin, an asked, "Do you have the items we discussed, Top."

"Most certainly , Sir!"

"Very Good, then! I have here orders promoting you to Sergeant, Rogers. We need young men, like yourself. It's important to the Army, and the Company, to identify good soldiers, and encourage them to assume responsibility. As Sgt. Martin said, it's not a life that many choose."

Jake was surprised. He'd been expecting a pat on the back, and maybe a day off.

"Ah, I'm not quite sure what to say, Sir. But, thank you! I'll always try to do my best."

"That's all that anyone can ask of you Sergeant Rogers! First Sergeant, I'll leave you to get him sorted out." said Weir, "I'll see you both at evening roll call."

Martin produced a packet and handed it to Jake. It contained several sets of chevrons.

"Congratulations, Rogers! We'll be wetting these tomorrow night at the NCO quarters. You can wait until tomorrow to move. I expect your mates will want to celebrate with you tonight. I suggest that you go see the Quartermaster about new trousers. If you'll give me your extra fatigue blouse, and dress jacket, my wife, Ella, told me to tell you that she'll see to getting the stripes sewn on properly for you. Now go see, Pat. He's waiting to congratulate you!"

That evening after roll call, Weir stood in front of the formation and made a formal announcement to the Company.

"It's always a pleasure for me, when I receive praise from another officer about one of our men. I was told by Captain Michaelis, that Corporal Rogers, was extremely helpful to the Ordinance Team, during the weapons exchange. In fact, they tried to get him to stay with them. He declined a promotion, and pay raise, to stay with us! Fortunately, he was already being considered for promotion, here. Unfortunately, Cavalry Sergeants don't get paid as well!" That got a few chuckles, and cat calls. Weir continued, "So, as commanding officer of Company D, U.S.7th Cavalry, I am promoting Corporal Rogers to Sergeant, effective today. Aside from his 1st Platoon duties, he will also be in charge of weapons training and developing marksmanship for the whole outfit. Please join me in congratulating him!"

That evening, Henry, and the other troopers of his section, arranged for the cook to bake a large cake. They invited Jimmy Hurd's section to celebrate with them. Stivers, and the other Kentuckians, produced a couple bottles of whiskey, and several toasts were offered.

Holden produced a package and offered it to Jake.

"Just a little token from us, Sergeant!" he grandly announced.

Opening it up, Jake was surprised to see new saber belt with a brass US marked buckle, and with rows of cartridge loops sewn on.

Dave Manning spoke up. "I tried to make sure that both the new carbine, and pistol bullets, would fit. Let me know if I need to change anything, Jake."

"No, this looks fine. Let me experiment with it. I'll show it to Top and maybe he'll have you make one for everybody. Let me know what you would charge."

'Smiley' Sanders came over and said to Jake good naturedly. "I figured you'd make sergeant, Rogers. You're too damnt smart!"

Jake eyed the service stripes on Smiley's sleeves. "Why don't you have any stripes above them? You not a dumb ol' Dutchmen like you make out to be."

"Ach, I been der! Life is more better for me in da ranks. I went over the hill, back in Kansas one time, and Top, he remembers. It's okay though. Life is simpler in the barracks for me."

Chas Welch, and Manning, came over and offered to help him move his things to the NCO quarters.

"Thanks!" said Jake, "I thought that I'd see if I could come up with a wheelbarrow to tote my footlocker."

Jake excused himself and went out back to the privy. When he came back he made his way out to the front porch. He stood looking out at the parade ground and the lights of Officer's Row across it, lost in thought.

Henry came out and fired his pipe. He said quietly, "Your last view from here, Jake, it all changes tomorrow. I wouldn't worry about it, though, you'll do well."

"Henry, you should be a sergeant. You've helped me and the others, and who knows how many more during your time in the Army. I guess you have your reasons."

"I do. You'll find that some people are comfortable with the lack of responsibilities, and favor relative anonymity. There will come a time, when you may have to make a decision that may cause someone to die. I've chosen to limit that decision to myself alone. But, let's not dwell on matters maudlin, let's go back in and celebrate with your mates. They enjoy seeing one of their own being promoted. Particularly, when it's someone they know who has an appreciation for their circumstances."

"See, you always know how to sum up situations, Henry. Thank you, and I'll depend on you to always feel free to do that with me."

"Why thank you, Jake! I'll strive not to over burden with my observations." Holden smiled and patted Jake on the back.

The following morning, after formation and roll call, Jake was able to scrounge up a wheel barrow. Assisted by Charlie and Dan, he piled his entire kit on it, and they took turns pushing it down the street in front of the barracks buildings, to the NCO quarters, at the north end just beyond the Band quarters. It was a building about half the size of a barracks wing, and a similar in layout for the kitchen and mess hall. There were two floors with wrap around, covered porches. There were eight rooms on each floor, with a window and a door that opened to the outside. An exterior staircase was located on each end. Three four way fireplaces had openings in the center corner of each room.

As they approached the building Jake saw Pat and Sgt. Tom Russell, the junior sergeant from the 2nd Platoon, waiting for them. Jake knew that Russell was from Indiana, and had been with Company D about a year before Jake was assigned. He was in his late twenties. Short, with a dark complexion and hair, Jake had talked with him occasionally back at Ft. Totten, when they met during various fatigue and work details. Russell was energetic and well liked by the 2nd Platoon. He knew that Sgt. Harrison thought highly of him, and like Jake, he had been promoted fairly quickly through the ranks.

Pat came over as they rolled up with the wheelbarrow, "Isn't it ironic that all of your possessions can fit in such a small space?"

Jake answered, "You know, I was just thinking the same thing, earlier this morning, Pat."

"Well, at least you can call me that, now. Welcome to the club!"

Russell called out, "Hey Rogers! You're my new roommate. I hope you don't snore!" He walked over and held out his hand. "Congratulations on your promotion! Now I'm no longer the junior sergeant of the Company. Though that doesn't, mean anything in particular, I suppose."

Jake shook his hand and replied, "I don't think I snore!"

Charlie, and Manning, chortled with laughter, "Sure! Just ask anyone in the 1st Platoon!"

"Well, that's okay, I'm pretty sure I do to." Russell said. "Let me help you carry your things. We're upstairs, we've the young knees, don't you know." Turning to grin at Jake, "The senior men like Pat Morse claim the lower rooms

"We'll get your footlocker, Jake." Charlie said, "I mean Sergeant Rogers!"

Jake replied with a grin, "I have to get used to that. Thanks Welch!

When they got up to the twelve foot square room, Russell ushered them in. It was located on the northwest corner, The beds were the same as the ones in the barracks, along with the shelves. There was a small table with two chairs, and a cabinet with a wash basin and water pitcher. There were stands with oil lamps next to each bunk. Yellow curtains hung at the window. A small hearth, drew off of the centrally located fireplace that heated both floors, and was located in the interior corner.

"Welcome to you new luxury accommodations, Rogers!" Russell announced.

"Looks good to me, Sergeant Russell."Jake said. "and it sure beats what I'm used to!"

"Jake, just call me, Tom."

"Oh! Right, I'll have to get used to it."

"Hey, I remember." Tom said, "It was just last year for me."

Jake went out the door and walked to the corner of the porch. The view of the parade ground was mostly blocked by the guardhouse and dispensary, and he could see the rooftops along Officer's Row, beyond. The hospital was just across the road to the west. Looking north, just over the roof of the band quarters, he could see the Post Trader's residence and other buildings all in a cluster, with the Infantry Post on the hill rising behind them. To the east, the Missouri River flowed down from the direction of Bismarck, and he could just make out one of the riverboats, moored at the landing, with smoke drifting up from its stacks.

Jake spent most of the day organizing his clothes and gear. That evening Jake went downstairs to the NCO mess hall. Mrs. Martin had come by earlier, and had given him his fatigue jacket, freshly laundered, and sporting his new chevrons. She'd also sewn a one inch stripe on a pair of his trousers. He was a bit nervous about meeting all of the NCOs, from the other Companies of the Regiment. Fortunately, Top Martin came to his rescue. When he entered the room, Martin called out.

"And here, lads, is the 7th Cavalry's newest sergeant. For those of you who haven't met him, I present Sergeant Rogers, 1st Platoon, Company D!" As everyone stood and applauded, Martin continued, "Best make your way around the room and shake hands, Jake. Don't worry too much about names, you'll have plenty of time to learn them."

Jake circuited the tables, shaking hands. When he got to where

DeLacy was standing, Mike patted him on the back. "Good on you Jake! Keogh told me that you were getting your third stripe. He was a bit miffed that Capt. Michaelis tried to steal Caddle away."

"Yes, I sensed that Capt.Weir was also, but I was still surprised."

Jake saw that DeLacy was sporting a service stripe on his sleeve, "Well, it looks like we have something else to celebrate!"

Pat had saved him room at a table with the other Company D sergeants. Motioning Jake, to sit down, Morse waved to the kitchen door where Flanagan was waiting. He moved out of the way, as the men on kitchen detail started toting in cases of bottled beer. "I went to Bismarck, today, and ran into Mr. Johnson, from the Northern Pacific. He's been transferred there. When I told him of your promotion, he sent his regards, and several cases of his Schlitz beer! So Cheers, all!"

As the beers were passed out, Pat leaned over and said to Jake, "Best eat hardy, my boy! We've got fresh beef steaks for supper, and I brought some potatoes back from Bismarck. I've reserved us a table in the billiard room at the Post Traders this evening. We'll wet your stripes down proper, then, eh?"

Jake smiled at the thought, more in anticipation of the chance that he might see Holly, then the party. "Thanks, Pat. Though I don't know how to play billiards."

"Ah, don't you worry! It's all aiming at the balls, and figuring angles. With your sharp eyes, you'll catch on quickly!"

Just north, along the road that led to the Infantry Post, there was a cluster of small buildings consisting of the Post Trader's residence, the boarding house, then the main building and post office. The restaurant was located to the west, along the road coming from Officer's Row. Morse and Top Martin had arranged to borrow an ambulance to haul the NCOs back and forth. First Sergeant James Butler, from Company L, along with Bobo, Martin, First Sergeant Micheal Kinney of Company F, Morse, and Harrison went on the first load. They were all senior, both in age and rank, and were all veterans of the Kansas campaigns and the Washita fight.

"We'll get you a proper introduction to Mr. Bob Seip, the Post Trader. He kowtows to the officers, but knows that we sergeants run things. He's been pretty friendly with us since he and Custer had their argument about importing goods from Bismarck. And he knows we're the ones that control the men's off duty time, so he's good about doing us wee favor now and then." Bobo stated.

"That's good to know!" Martin replied. "We had the same

arrangement at Totten. Our trader there was hooked in with the Leighton brothers, also."

"Yes, the Leighton's have quite the empire. They have interests in most of the trading on the Upper Missouri, not only the trade and supply contracts with the forts, but also with the Indian tribes. They also do a brisk business selling guns and ammunition, particularly when the Tribes get their treaty monies."

"That doesn't set well with me." Morse stated emphatically, "Old single shot rifles are one thing, but when they're Winchester repeaters, it's another!"

"Aye, I agree." Butler said, "But that's the way of it!"

When they arrived at the Post Traders main building, a short, balding civilian was waiting to greet them.

"First Sergeant Butler, First Sergeant Bobo, First Sergeant Kenney, good to see you. A pleasure as always!" he said.

"Likewise, Mr. Seip!" replied Butler. "Allow me to introduce First Sergeant Martin of Company D, First Sergeant Varden of Company I, Sergeants Morse and Harrison of Company D. They recently arrived from Fort Totten. But, we all go back a ways to the early days of the Regiment."

"Gentlemen, nice to make your acquaintance! I understand that you've a small celebration, tonight."

"That's correct, Mr. Seip. We're celebrating one of our young lad's promotion to sergeant. Plus we've another sergeant that's seen fit to sign over for another tour"

"Please call me, Bob. I think you'll all be pleased with what I've arranged."

"Right, Bob! There's to be a dozen, or so of us. Keep a tab, and I'll see to it that you're paid." Martin replied.

"Of course, and I'll be sure to extend a special rate, and as a further show of my appreciation, I'm be putting you in the officer's billiard room. You'll have it all to yourselves for the evening." Bob stated, proudly.

"Well, now! That's a fine thing! Won't they be upset if they show up with a mind to play a few rounds?"

"No! To tell you the truth, they don't come down much any more. Custer contracted to rent a couple of billiard tables from a merchant over in Bismarck. He has one in his house, and the other is set up in the Officers Club. Even the Infantry officers go there." Seip said with a frown. "So, I'm thinking of reserving it for NCOs."

"Okay, we'll be the first to try it then, eh Bob?" Bobo said.

"Yes, I've got you set up with a bartender, and a couple of waitresses.

I've put out some snacks, fresh beer, and the good whisky. Come on in, and I'll introduce you."

Jake, Caddle, DeLacy, Flanagan, and Russell rode down together on the next load. The others were ruminating on the daily lot of junior sergeants, and telling Jake what he could expect as the most junior. He already had a good idea, but he enjoyed listening to their beer enhanced embellishments realizing that this was their way of accepting him into their circle, coming from the ranks. The ambulance driver, a hospital steward, who was equivalent to a NCO, had been recruited by the First Sergeants to convey them back and forth. The steward was a teetotaler and had a nice side business going acting as a taxi to and from the Trading Post and river landing, after hours. When they rolled up out front Morse was waiting to escort them inside to the festivities.

"Come inside lads! The bar is open!"

They clambered down and Pat guided them to the billiard room where the collective group of First Sergeants already had a game of fifteen ball in progress. Jake remembered watching his father play on one of their Springfield excursions, and knew enough about the game to know it would be going on for some time. The billiard table was located at one end of the large rectangular room, while the bar was opposite at the other end. He was surprised to see a large round Schlitz beer sign on the wall over the bar. He and the others made their way over to one of several round tables that were arrayed in the middle of the room. They settled on one where they could watch and listen to the gamesmanship. No sooner had they taken their chairs, when a female voice behind Jake asked.

"What can I get you fellows to drink?"

Pat answered, "Two of these lads are our guests of honor. I propose you serve them first! Go ahead, Jake take the lead!"

Turning to look, Jake saw that it was Holly. Before he could say anything, a man came up behind her, and said, "Gentlemen, welcome! I'm Robert Seip, the Post Trader. Looking at Jake he continued, "I understand that this is a party to celebrate promotions, and reenlistments. I want you all to know that I think Sergeants are the wheels that keep everything in motion around here. If I can ever help, just come and see me."

"Why, thank you, Robert!" Jake replied. "That's good to know."

"And this is my niece, Holly Walker. She's staying with me for the summer and helping me out while she's here."

Pat stood up, "Well missy! We're pleased ta meet you also." He said gallantly.

"Oh, I've met a couple of these Sergeants already, excepting Sergeant

Rogers, here." Holly said, winking at Jake. "What would you care for, Sergeant?"

"I think I'll just have a beer, Holly, thanks"

"Sure thing! How about the rest of you?"

The others placed their orders, and as Holly turned to leave, she leaned down and whispered in Jake"s ear. "Congratulations, Sergeant Rogers!"

Jake grinned up at her. "Thanks!"

After the first round of billiards was finished, Pat dragged Jake over to the table, and explained the scoring for the game of Fifteen Ball.

"Just shoot to make the higher numbered balls, if you can. The first team to reach 61 wins the frame. There are 21 frames, by the time we get there, you'll have it figured out!"

They were matched against Varden and Caddle, and it soon became clear that they and Pat, were accomplished players. The frames went quickly, as Bustard bombarded Jake with continuous banter. Jake was able to make some long straight shots, and slowly got the hang of some of the angle shots. However, he could see that the use of english, or side spin, and banking off the rails was something that had to be acquired by practice. He was pleased that he and Pat actually won a few frames, but was slightly relieved when Caddle sank his last ball to win 11 frames.

"Come see me when you want spanked again, Rogers!" crowed Caddle.

"Oh, I will, Jimmie!" replied Jake laughing.

Jake made his way through the surrounding tables, back to where Russell and DeLacy were still sitting.

"Well, that was interesting." He stated.

"Yes, it's easy to tell the veteran players, they are quick to take advantage." DeLacy said. "We'll have to come back, and get you some more practice, You showed some potential."

"Thanks."

Russell looked past Jake, and said quietly, "Ah, here comes Miss Holly, I think you have at least one fan!"

"Sergeant Rogers! I brought you another beer, figured you'd need something to drown your sorrows!" she said.

"Why thank you Miss Walker!"

She gave him a petulant look and said, "Oh! You know that you can call me, Holly!"

"Only if you call me, Jake." he countered, with a grin.

Russell and DeLacy rose to their feet. "I think we'll put up our challenge to the table. Excuse us Miss Holly!" said DeLacy, as they headed away.

"So, Jake, now that you're a sergeant, perhaps it won't take two weeks for you to come back. Maybe, we'll see more of you here."

"Well, the NCO Quarters are just down the road, so it could be."

"I know. We pass by them on our way to to watch the Sunday Dress Inspection. My Aunt and Uncle always attend it. Custer doesn't like him, but Uncle Bob's determined to try and socialize with the locals, and doesn't work on the Sabbath though he doesn't mind having his clerks working."

"Yes, I can just see his house from the porch outside my new room, which is on the northeast corner. My door and window face the hospital"

She looked at him curiously. "I'm glad to know that, if the Indians cause trouble, you're one of the closest soldiers."

"I suppose so, except for the Commissary Sergeant's Quarters. But, I'm usually only there in the evenings.

She smiled, "Oh! Just think, you're only a short walk away. Well, I suppose that I'd better get busy."

Jake watched her work her way back to the bar, pausing to laugh and chat along the way. He wondered at the conversation they'd just had. Just then he heard his name being called from the middle of the room.

"Sergeant Rogers, Front and Center! Top Martin called out.

Jake made his way over to where all of the First Sergeants were gathered.

"It's time for a toast!" Sergeant Morse, I think it only right that you do the honors, since you're the one that signed him in the first place."

"Aye, Top! I can do that." Morse said. He grabbed a bottle, poured a shot, and passed it on. "I propose a toast to Sergeant Jacob Rogers, I served in the War with his Da, and I've known the lad since before he could shave. He can be a little chuckleheaded, but you'll not find a steadier mate to have at your side should you ever find yourself in a bind! Cheers me boy!"

They all raised their glasses and tossed back their shots. Jake was proffered a shot, and gamely downed it. His eyes watered, and he winced as the liquor burned its way down his throat. He was pounded on the back and treated to a hearty round of Here, Heres! Then DeLacy, was brought forward and toasted for his reenlistment. After downing the last shot, Jake quietly made his way away through the crowd seeking some fresh air to clear his head a bit. He stepped out the front door and walked a few steps, taking deep breath. It was fully dark, and the stars were brilliant overhead. From the direction of the fort he heard the call for tattoo sound, and a few lights shown through windows. As he turned to go back inside he saw

Holly watching him from dim light of the doorway.

"Are you okay, Jake?" she asked.

"Oh, yes! Just needed a bit fresh air. I'm just not much for drinking shots of whiskey like that, and some of those cigars are just rank. I don't know how you stand it."

"The same as you, I take fresh air breaks. Besides, I don't usually work nights, unless we're short handed."

"Well, I'm glad you did tonight."

"My uncle asked me to, and I'm glad I did, too. By the way, I don't work Sundays, either. I like to get out and take walks or go riding." Holly said, then turned to go back inside. "Just thought you'd like to know, Sergeant Rogers."

It took a second for Jake to fully comprehend that last statement, and before he could say something she was out of sight. He smiled, to himself, and headed back inside.

The next day was Thursday, and when First Call sounded, it took Jake a bit to get moving. He was glad that the festivities were ended shortly after the toasts were proffered. During roll call, Top Martin, had made a point of looking directly at him with a critical gaze. Jake had done his best to act normal, but was grateful when he got breakfast and some coffee down his stomach. After drill call, he was summoned to the orderly room, where Top and Morse were waiting.

"Have a seat, Rogers." Martin said.

Taking a chair, Jake replied, "Thanks, Top."

"How's the head this morning?"

"Okay, I was a bit fuzzy when I woke up, but I'm fine now."

"That's good! I depend on my sergeants to set a good example. Too many of the lads seek comfort in a bottle. Are you all settled in over at quarters?"

"Yes, Tom Russell helped me."

"Good, Tom's a fine lad! He was fast tracked up to Sergeant, same as you. Now you two are more closely tuned into the men in the ranks, then are us old hats. I'm counting on you to help me gauge their moods. I'll brook no deserters! Captain Weir and I have placed a lot of confidence in you."

"I won't let you, down First Sergeant!"

Martin nodded his head and smiled, "Very well! Just remember that you're not a ranker anymore. I'm sure Pat here will help guide you through the transition. Now go see to your duties, Sergeant."

Jake stood, and Morse did also. They walked outside, and headed over to the stables, where the men were seeing to the horses.

"I noticed that you, and that cute little lass that was flirting with you last night."

Jake looked over at Pat, smiling, and said, "She is cute, isn't she?"

"Well, it's better that you stay on this side of the river, instead of pining after one of those painted dollies across the way. Mind you, I've seen many a lad ruin himself over the years."

"She invited me to visit her, on Sunday."

"You'd best be clearin' that with her Uncle, first!"

"Hmm! I suspect you're right, Pat."

"Oh, I know I am. There's a pecking order on this post, and Mr. Seip is higher on it, then a freshly made sergeant. He's not popular with Custer, but he still has some clout."

"I guess that I'll just have to go ask him, then."

Morse looked at Jake thoughtfully, "You best have a plan, then."

"I think I do!"

The next day as soon as the afternoon Water Call was completed, Jake went back to his room, and put on a clean uniform, and buffed his boots. He headed up the road towards the post office with a letter for his mother. After he dropped it off, he strolled over to the store. Being in the middle of the week, and the middle of the month, there were not many customers. He wandered over to the where the guns were racked along the wall, and looked at them. There were numerous Winchesters, 1866 Yellow Boys and several of the newer 1873 Model that was chambered for the 44 Winchester brass centerfire cartridge. There was also a shiny new Springfield Sporting rifle, chambered in 45/70. As Jake was admiring it, Mr. Seip came up behind him.

"Hello, Sergeant Rogers! How are you this afternoon?"

"Just fine, Mr. Seip, how about yourself?"

"Good, but business is a little slow right now, it being well between paydays and all. I see you're looking at that Springfield. It's a brand new, a Model 1875, Officer's Model that they introduced this year."

"It is a nice looking rifle."

"Here, pick it up and look it over." Seip offered.

Jake hefted the weapon and examined it. It was a beautiful piece, with sporting style, checkered walnut grips on the stock and forearm. Scrolled engraving on all the metal parts, with silver accents. A folding vernier tang sight with windage adjustments and a single set trigger identified it as a serious long range gun. It had a 26" barrel and a hickory cleaning rod with nickel plated ferrules underneath.

"Are you interested in a hunting rifle?" asked Seip.

"Well, sort of. I was working with Capt. Michaelis, earlier this month, and we were target shooting a Sharps 45-70 Sporting rifle. I was wondering how the Springfield version compares."

"Ah, Capt. Michaelis! Quite an interesting fellow, Regimental staff as I recall. How did you come to be working for him? I seem to remember that you're with Company D."

"I was assigned to help train our men on the new carbines and pistols. Of course our carbines are just a plainer, shorter version of this"

"Oh! You must be a fair hand with a gun then, although you seem a bit young if you don't mind me saying it. No offense!"

"None taken, sir! Do you shoot?"

"Not very well, I wish I was a better shot!"

"I could help you with that." Jake offered.

"Well, I'd like to, but finding time away from the store is always an issue."

"How about Sunday? I'm free after the Dress Inspection. I bet I can have you on target with a few lessons. Plus, you'd be more comfortable discussing guns with your customers."

Seip considered it for a second, "You have a point, Sergeant and I'd like to practice more shooting, but I hate to impose. I know most Sundays are free afternoons for you boys."

"Nonsense, Mr. Seip! I like to shoot, and we could try out different rifles. It would help me decide what I might want to buy!"

Seip nodded his head, "All right! If the weather is nice, I could come get you, and we could go to the range. I think I'll see if the Mrs. and my niece would like to come along in the carriage. I will bring several different guns. We can make a picnic of it. I'll have them bring some refreshments."

"I'll look forward to it Mr. Seip. I'll find you after the parade."

"Excellent, and call me, Bob!"

"Right, and I'm Jake!"

That night Jake told Pat about his arrangement with Bob.

"Well, I've got to hand it to you, Jake. You wrangled an invitation from her uncle. How'd you know he couldn't shoot well?"

"I didn't, but Holly told me that Bob has been trying to make friends, and because of his friction with Custer, hasn't had much success. Besides, I figured a storekeeper would be keen to know his wares."

"I'll let Top know what you're about, just so he doesn't get surprised. She's a pretty thing, can't say as I blame you."

"Don't worry, Pat, she's leaving this fall for school. I'm not planning on anything serious. She's just nice to be around!"

"Aye, lad, you don't have ta tell me. I've been there!"

Saturday, Jake spent extra time inspecting his dress uniform. He had cajoled Sgt. Rush into issuing him some new trousers, and he carefully brushed his jacket with its yellow piping, shoulder epaulets, and bright new chevrons. A shiny brass numeral 7 was pinned on the collar. He took his dress helmet off the shelf and removed the cotton sack cover it was stored in. The black felt dress helmet with its long front and back visors, was topped by a yellow horse hair plume dangling from a brass spike affixed to its peak. It was decorated with intricate yellow braid, brass buttons on the side, and a large brass US eagle emblem on the front. He took the long yellow helmet cord that attached to the left side, it was over five feet long, and hung from a nail below the shelf. Once dressed it would be looped round his neck, and across his chest where it would be attached to the left epaulet button, where ornate braided discs with knotted tassels hung below it. Although Jake knew the helmet was liked for its appearance, it was hated by the men. Besides being heavy, it weighed over a pound, it was uncomfortable and gave most of the men headaches. The length of the visor obstructed vision, and it was too hot in warm weather, and too cold in the winter. In addition, it was very hard to keep the cheap brass from tarnishing, and the yellow cords and braid from getting soiled. He laid out his saber belt, and saber to clean and polish, along with his boots. He had freshly laundered underwear and socks, for the morning. He'd already visited the company barber, and was heading down for a bath later.

Tom Russell came in and saw what Jake was doing. "My, it looks like you're really trying to make an impression tomorrow!'

Jake grinned sheepishly, "Well it is my first Dress Inspection as a Sergeant."

"Oh, I'm sure that's it." Tom replied, "I'm sure you won't be looking over at a certain carriage to see who's in it. Don't think we all haven't noticed the last couple of Sundays. Pat and I, in particular."

"I was that obvious?"

"Oh, yes!"

"I'll have to practice being more discreet."

"Yes, you'll not be in a file tomorrow. So, you'll need to be looking straight ahead. I'd hate for you to stumble."

"I suppose Pat told you about my plans for after the inspection."

Tom grinned and nodded, "He may have mentioned it. Now, let's get us both ready, then we can go downstairs. There are still some of those beers left from the other night, and the cook has them stashed by the icebox where they'll stay cooler. I'm on Guard Duty tomorrow night, and I don't think they'll last until after."

CHAPTER 19

Fort Abraham Lincoln-Dakota Territory June 6, 1875

The following morning broke bright and clear, with just a few clouds. A light breeze stirred the folds in the large garrison standard that was hoisted for the Inspection. With Custer in residence now, the ceremony began as he stepped down off the porch of his house, resplendent in his gold braided dress uniform, white gloves, glistening boots. Light sparkled off his helmet emblem and the golden hilt of his saber as he marched towards the flagpole in the center of the parade ground, and came to a halt underneath it. The companies, which had assembled in front of the barracks across the way, quickly assumed formations, and with guidons fluttering began their march towards the flag, each man carefully maintaining correct intervals and pace. The entire contingent came to a halt in front of Custer. The Regimental Band, assembled on the north side, marched forwards, then halted to the right of the companies, and struck up the National Anthem. As soon as it ended, the ritual of salutes and inspections began. All companies opened ranks and prepared for inspection, with all but the one undergoing inspection put 'At Ease'. Custer casually progressed through all five Troops, pausing here and there to converse with a NCO, or trooper. As soon as he was done and had returned to his position in front of the flag, the companies closed ranks and marched past him, as the Band launched a rousing rendition of "Garry Owen", followed by "The Army Song", and "The Girl I left Behind Me", then ending with "The Yellow Ribbon". On return to the barracks side of the parade ground the troops were dismissed from formation, where they quickly dispersed to change out of their dress uniforms. The band moved over and set up in front of Officer's Row and began playing popular tunes for the spectators that had congregated along the street.

Jake made his way over by the commissary building, where Bob Seip had parked his carriage on the street next to it. They stepped down and watched him as he strode up. Bob was waving at him, but Jake was focused on Holly. She was dressed in a blue, checkered dress, with layered skirts, and a straw bonnet adorned with a band of flowers. Her aunt was dressed in similar fashion, but with red. When he got closer he looked at Seip and said.

"Hello, Bob. I hope you enjoyed watching, it was a great morning for it."

His wife, held out her hand to Jake, "Sergeant Rogers, I don't believe we've been introduced, my name is Kathleen, and it seems you've already met our niece, Holly!"

"Pleased to make you acquaintance, Madam! And yes, I've met Holly at the store. Might I say you ladies look quite patriotic this morning?"

"Why thank you, Sergeant!" replied Kathleen, "But, I must admit it was Holly's idea. You, yourself look very dashing. There's something about a fancy uniform I suppose. Don't you think, Holly?"

Holly's blue eyes sparkled in the sunlight, and she laughed, "Oh, Aunt Kate! You say that about all of the soldiers!"

"Then it must be true." Jake said.

"Are we still on for our shooting lessons?" Bob asked.

"Of course! I just need to go to my quarters, and change into something more comfortable. I'll return quickly."

"Hop in, offered Bob, "We'll give you a lift over and we can leave from there."

"Thank you, that's the best offer I've had all morning."

Bob drove the carriage along the front of the Quartermasters Warehouse and then turned left along the company street. As they rolled along past the barracks row, some of the men from D Troop were lounging on the front porch.

"Hey, Sarge! Top of the morning to you!" yelled Rooster. That got the attention of some others, which produced some waving, finger pointing, and whistles.

Jake tried to appear nonchalant, but doubted that he was succeeding.

"I take it those were some of your men." Bob said. "They seem to be in a good mood today."

Jake nodded his head. "Yes, they seem to be." He said with a slight grimace.

"I think it's a sign that you're popular with them." Kathleen said. "I've overheard some of the men that come in to the store, they seem to have a very low opinion of their sergeants."

"Oh, there's always some that feel that way, Ma'am. The Army gets men from all walks of life. Some are just here until they can find a chance to desert."

"Yes, I've heard that."

"Our company is fortunate, our Captain and 1st Sergeant have been together since the Regiment was down in Kansas, almost eight years. They're firm, but fair."

"So, how long have you been in, Jake?" asked Bob.

"Just over two years, it's gone quickly for me."

"That's pretty soon to make sergeant, isn't it?" asked Holly.

"Not really! My roommate, Sgt. Russell, did it also. It really depends on the what you make of Army life. Personally I enjoy most days, but there are some that I'd rather forget."

"So what made you join up?" asked Kathleen.

"Mostly, I just wanted to see some of the country."

"And have you?"

"Yes, Ma'am, I've seen a fair bit! We spent the last two seasons up on the border with Canada, escorting the survey team, not to mention traveling back and forth to Fort Totten."

" I'm impressed, and would like to hear more about that and please, call me, Kate!"

Bob pulled up in front of the NCO quarters, "Here you go, Jake."

"Thanks, Bob! I won't be long." Jake said as he got down, and headed upstairs.

Jake hung up his saber and belt, then shrugged out of his dress uniform and carefully put it away. He elected to don his only civilian clothes, which consisted of brown corduroy trousers and a brown broadcloth jacket that his mother had sent him for Christmas last year. He pulled on a faded blue flannel issue shirt, and tied on a red neckerchief. His plain black leather belt with a brass buckle had been made for him by Dave Manning from surplus tack. He opened his footlocker and retrieved the knife and scabbard, that Val had given him, and slipped it on the belt. He tucked his pants into the tops of some Wellington boots that Manning had rescued from a teamster, who had discarded them, then grabbed his black slouch hat. He'd never had much occasion to wear the clothes anywhere, but Pat had assured him that it would be good to have them if he planned on visiting Bismarck.

"Well, here I go!" he thought to himself and pounded back down the stairs.

He rounded the corner and walked over to where Bob had parked the carriage out of the way, and climbed in. Holly and Kate both did a double take.

"And who might you be?" Kate exclaimed, "We're waiting on Sergeant Rogers!"

Jake turned around and smiled at them. "Will Mr. Rogers do?"

They both started giggling, and Bob laughed, "That's quite a transformation, Jake!"

Jake looked at them and said, "It's been a while. I haven't had much use for civilian clothes for a long while. The other sergeants recommended that I have some."

"Oh, you look fine, Jake. You just caught us off guard. We'll get used to it." Kate said, while Holly just smiled at Jake, and winked.

"Tell me where we're headed, Jake, and we'll get going." Bob said.

Jake had Bob circle around between the barracks and the stables, then turn right just past the Adjutants Office, then head out to the west behind the warehouses. The tall buffalo grass whisked along the side of the carriage as they left the fort's perimeter and rolled towards the Ordinance range. He had Bob pull up along side the small lean to shed that was built by the firing line.

"We should probably unload here, then move the carriage back. I'm not sure how your horse will react to the gunshots" he cautioned. "So, it might be better to unharness him and I'll picket him back aways."

"Good thinking Jake!"

There was a heavy blanket roll, was strapped to the rear of the carriage seat, with several guns wrapped in it, A wood box containing ammunition was underneath it. While Jake took care of the horse, Bob carried them over by the shed. Kate and Holly remained seated in the carriage.

When Jake returned, Bob had unrolled the blanket, displaying several rifles. There was the Winchester, and Springfield that they'd talked about. He'd also brought several pistols.

"I brought a couple of Colt New Line Pocket Pistols chambered in .22 and .32 caliber. They're both seven shot revolvers that the girls want to learn to shoot. And I want to try that Smith and Wesson Model 3 .45 caliber Schofield."

"Okay, I'll go set up some rifle targets, first. There's not much wind right now. We can shoot at some close in pistol targets, later."

Jake went to the shed and found some of the targets and stands. Stakes were already in place at 25, 50, 100, and 200 yards. He set up the targets and walked back to the firing line. Kate and Holly stayed seated in the carriage, and had produced a pair of binoculars.

"Hey, that's a good idea!" Jake said.

"Yes, we use these to watch the riverboats coming down from Bismarck."

Jake walked over to where Bob was waiting looking at him expectedly.

"Well, Bob, what do you want to shoot first?"

"I think the Winchester. It seems to be becoming the most popular."

"Okay, but I have to admit that I've not shot one yet, although a friend of mine favors a 1866 'Yellow Boy' .44 Henry and I've shot it a few times."

"Here, take a look at it." Bob said, handing the rifle to Jake

The Winchester was surprisingly heavy, weighing a bit more than the carbines Jake was used to. It balanced easily, and was just a few inches shorter than the other rifle. He worked the lever underneath, and looked in the open chamber. The octagonal barrel had a tubular magazine beneath it that was fed by inserting bullets through a gate in the side of the receiver.

"Nice!" Jake said, "How many rounds will it hold?"

"I'm told, fourteen!"

"Okay, let's load it up."

While he was loading the rifle, Jake asked Bob, "What do you know about shooting?"

"Very little!" Bob replied, "Basically, just point and pull the trigger."

"Well, that works if you're not too far away. Let me just show you a few basics."

Jake spent the next few minutes showing Bob the basics, in gun handling and safety. He got a stick and drew pictures in the dirt, and explained the sight and distance relationship. The talked a bit about breathing and trigger control.

"Anyhow, I think that's enough for now. Let's shoot! That's what we came for."

He had Bob lay down on the blanket to shoot, using a carriage blanket for a rest. Jake just wanted him to get accustomed to the recoil, so they started with the 25 yard target. After a few shots, Bob was hitting consistently. Then they moved on to the 50 yard target, and repeated the process. Jake could see that Bob was gaining confidence, particularly as Kate and Holly applauded his hits.

"Okay, now let's move out to 100 yards. This is where it gets a little tougher. Your breathing is more important, so is squeezing the trigger, both of them can effect your accuracy, take your time!"

Bob managed to hit the target five times out of fourteen, and Jake could see that he was getting frustrated.

"Okay, why don't you take a break!" Jake offered.

Bob nodded his head, "You try it."

Jake loaded up and started with the 50 yard target, to get used to the rifle. He was impressed with how natural it was to point. After multiple hits, he moved out to 100 yards, and rapidly levered the rifle, emptying the magazine. He hit the target every time. He paused to reload then laid down, and using a barrel rest, proceeded to shoot at the 200 yard target. He found that the rifle was even easy to cycle in that position. Jake was confident that he'd hit the target most every shot. He laid the rifle down, stood, and turned around. Bob and the women were clapping their hands.

"Wow!" Bob exclaimed, "That was impressive!"

"Yes, it was." Jake replied, "But I'm talking about the rifle! I thought my old Spencer was fun to shoot, this new Winchester is twice as good!"

Holly was staring at him in amazement. Jake smiled at her and waved.

"C'mon Bob, Let's go look at your targets and see how you're grouping."

They walked out to check the targets, and discussed Bob's progress along the way.

"The more you shoot, the better you'll get, Bob. You're already as good as half my men. I'd wager they'd be hard pressed to hit it more than once."

"Really? I'd have thought they would be more proficient."

'No, the Army only lets us have 10 rounds a month, per man, for training. You've already fired several months worth."

They headed back towards the carriage and saw the women waving at them. They had gotten down and were sitting on the blanket. It appeared that they had opened a basket and were setting out some food.

"Well, I'll be! A regular picnic." Jake exclaimed, "I can't remember when."

"Yes, they were quite excited planning for this today. It's good to see them happy! It's been a transition for Holly, her parents were killed, last year."

"She said that they had died, but didn't elaborate"

"Kate's sister and her husband were killed in a railroad accident. He was going to be the Post Trader, here. They'd left Holly with us, while they were setting up the partnership with her uncle. After the funeral, he offered us the opportunity and we accepted and brought Holly with us."

"She seems to be coping well."

"Yes, but we're a little concerned that this is no place for a young woman and dealing with the isolation of winter. We're sending her off to a school this fall."

Jake nodded his head, not letting on that he already knew that. "My only experience with being in garrison was over at Fort Totten. There wasn't much of a social life there, particularly for a soldier in the ranks. It's pretty isolated."

"Well, aside from several hundred soldiers, there's few people to socialize with here. While most of the officers are polite, they are very reserved when they're around. I sense that they consider us a necessary evil. I will say most of the sergeants treat us well, though."

"Take that as a good sign, Bob."

Jake thoroughly enjoyed the snacks that the women laid out. They'd brought fried chicken, pickles, cheese, rolls with butter and jelly. He hadn't eaten such treats since leaving home, and tried to make sure he didn't take too large of portions."

"It's good to see you that have a hearty appetite, Jake. I wondered that I'd brought too much." Kate said, as he handed her his empty plate.

Jake wiped his mouth and replied, "You don't know how much that I enjoyed that, Kate. Our army cooks strive for quantity, and don't worry a lot about quality. Not to mention that only so much can be done with bacon, beans, and bread!"

"I hope you saved room for dessert, Jake." Holly said, "I made pound cake and we have canned peaches and fresh cream."

"Oh, my! I'll sure find room!"

While Katie and Holly packed the basket, Jake and Bob went over to where the guns were laid out.

"Do you want to try the Springfield, Bob?"

"Okay, but I really brought it for you to try."

They set up a shooting stick and Bob settled in behind the big rifle. He had Bob fire a few rounds at the 50 yard target. He hit it a couple of times, But Jake could tell the recoil was bothering, Bob.

"Try and relax, hold it tight against your shoulder and don't fight the recoil. Now let's try out to 100 yards. Aim low, I think you're shooting high, but that's not unusual."

Bob didn't have much success, finally he looked over at Jake, rubbing his shoulder, and said.

"That's enough for me! I think the Winchester is the one for me. It's easier to shoot. The Springfield is more powerful, but I don't see that I'll be doing much buffalo hunting. Why don't you go ahead and try?"

Jake picked up the Springfield, which wasn't much heavier than the repeater. He

settled in behind it using the shooting stick, and tried a couple of shots at 100 yards."

"Yep," he thought to himself, "These sights are off a bit at the lowest setting, which made sense, since this was a longer range weapon." He adjusted them for 200 yards, and fired a couple of more times, hitting the target easily. Satisfied that he could hit consistently, there was no point in shooting any more at these close in distances, he got up and turned around. Bob was standing by the carriage, and they were all applauding, once again.

"There's no sense using up all your ammunition, Bob. These are both fine rifles!"

"And we can see you're a fine shot, Jake!"

He grinned back at them, "Thanks, I appreciate you letting me shoot. Perhaps the ladies would like to try the pistols."

"I would!" exclaimed Holly, "But, you'll have to show me how."

Kate looked over at Bob, who shrugged his shoulders and nodded his approval.

Jake picked up the .22 revolver, as Holly got down from the carriage. She walked over and he showed her how to hold it, and walked her through how to aim it.

"Now this pistol, might jump a little, but it won't hurt your hands, Holly. It's a little bitty bullet meant for shooting varmints."

Holly nodded her head, "I can do this."

Jake walked out to get the 25 yard target and moved it in to around 10 yards. Retracing his steps, he took the gun from Holly and showed her how to insert the small bullets into the cylinder. Stepping to her left side, he pointed it down range and demonstrated how to stand, then handed it to her.

"Always point it away from you and others, with the barrel lowered, or raised to the sky. It may be a little bullet, but it can still kill!"

Holly practiced aiming at the target. "Okay, I'm ready."

"Just pull back the hammer with your thumb, then aim at the target and pull the trigger."

The pistol discharged with a "Bang!" Dirt jumped up in front of the target.

"Good, that was good! Shoot a few more times and get a feel for it!"

She emptied the pistol with slow steady shooting, hitting all around the target.

"Okay, let's reload."

"Let me do it!" she insisted.

When the gun was reloaded, Jake said, "Take your time! You need to slow your breathing, and just before you pull on the trigger, hold your breath. It should be a surprise when it goes off."

Holly looked over at him with a determined expression, and nodded her head, leveled the pistol to take aim.

"Bang!" The bullet tinged off the target. She slowly cocked the pistol and aimed again.

"Bang!", another ting!

She continued to shoot and was able to hit the target all seven shots. She jumped with excitement.

"That was so much fun! Can we do it again?"

Jake looked over at Bob and Kate, who were watching and smiling. Bob shrugged and nodded his approval.

As the day wore on, they all took turns firing the pistols and shooting at various targets.The women liked both of the small Colts, but declined to shoot the .45. He and Bob were both pleased with the Schofield. The top break design and auto ejector, made it much faster, and easier, to reload than the Colt Army version. They were so absorbed, and their hearing ability partially compromised by the shooting, that they were surprised to find that they had acquired an audience. Kate was the first to notice, and quickly tapped Bob on the shoulder. He turned around and saw Capt.Weir, Lt. Cooke, and Tom Custer, sitting on their horses, watching. Bob quickly went over and got Jake's attention by pointing. Jake saw the three officers, and hustled over to them, came to attention, and saluted.

"As you were, Sergeant Rogers! We just came to see what all the shooting was about." Weir said.

"We were just target practicing, Sir! I was showing the ladies how to shoot pistols, and Mr. Seip and I were trying out a couple of rifles."

"Yes, I saw."

Bob stepped over and said, "Perhaps you gentlemen would care to try shooting. I have plenty of ammunition. These rifles are of the latest design, I just received them."

****

1st Lieutenant Thomas Ward Custer

Tom, the younger brother of George, by six years, was a highly decorated veteran of the War and was the only soldier to be awarded two

Medals of Honor. Enlisting at sixteen, he had served as an enlisted man in the Western Theater until 1864. He fought in most of the major battles in Kentucky and Tennessee, with the 21st Ohio Volunteer Infantry. Upon re-enlistment, he was promoted to corporal and assigned to escort duty for several general officers, including Generals Thomas and Grant. He served in this capacity all the way to the capture of Atlanta. In early November, George then arranged for his transfer and promotion to the 6th Michigan Cavalry as a 2nd Lieutenant and Aide-de-Camp. He served with George the rest of the War, winning his medals in April, 1865 near Namozine Church, and Sayler's Creek, Virginia, for charging and capturing Confederate battle flags, for which he'd be breveted as a Lt. Colonel. He was appointed a 1st Lieutenant in the Seventh Cavalry, in July 1866, and had served as company commander for several different troops. Tom participated in every Indian campaign, including the Washita, Yellowstone and Black Hills expeditions. He'd spent Reconstruction Duty with Company M, under Cap. French, in Spartanburg, NC, as part of a battalion commanded by Major Reno. Away from his bother's influence, he turned to gambling and alcohol. They were reunited in the spring of 1873 for the move north to the Dakota Territory.

Like his brother George, he was an avid hunter, and outdoorsman. He loved playing practical jokes on his brothers. Currently, in command of Company L, Tom was popular and well liked by both the men, and women of the Regiment, and was a frequent visitor to most of the houses along Officer's Row. He and Boston both lived upstairs in George's house, when he was there, but moved to Batchelor Quarters when he wasn't. He was pleased when W.W. Cooke showed up at Lincoln. He and Cooke were good friends, and they were in the inner circle of the Custer Clan. Tom had a wild streak, and was prone to gamble and go on drinking binges occasionally. His fiancée, back in New Jersey, Lulie Burgess, had died earlier in the year, and Tom, Boston, and Cooke had been making frequent trips to Bismarck. Now that George and Libbie were back, they had to be on better behavior.

****

1st Lieutenant William Winer Cooke

Cooke was born to a wealthy family near Mount Pleasant, Ontario, Canada, in 1846. He moved to Buffalo, NY at the age of fourteen to live with relatives. A year younger than Tom, in the summer of 1863 he had also enlisted as a teenager with the 24th New York Cavalry, then was commissioned as a 2nd Lieutenant, in January 1864. He was wounded in the leg at Petersburg and after recovering was promoted to 1st Lt. He participated in the Richmond campaign, where he fought in the cavalry battle at Sayler's Creek and was breveted Lt. Colonel for his actions.He returned to Canada after the War, but accepted a commission as a 2nd Lieutenant in the 7th Cavalry, in November 1866. He quickly gained the favor of both George, and Tom Custer. He served in several different troops, and acted as aide-de-camp, regimental adjutant, regimental quartermaster. He commanded a detachment of sharpshooters at the Washita fight. Cooke was well liked by the two Custer's. So much so that he'd been invited to go on leave with them, in late 1869, to Chicago, New York, and Michigan for several months, while Libbie remained at Fort Leavenworth. He spent his Reconstruction Duty at Louisville, KY, and was a frequent guest of George and Libbie, down in Elizabethtown, KY. He'd missed the Yellowstone expedition in 1873, while gone on leave over to Europe. After his return, he'd missed the Black Hills expedition while on detached duty to Headquarters in St.Paul. Cooke reported to Fort Lincoln, in October 1874, and had been appointed Regimental Adjutant, in November. He'd gone on leave the week after the two Fort Totten companies arrived, and had just returned. He had a reputation as one of the best shots, and fastest runners in the Regiment. Cooke was inordinately proud of his huge pair of Dundreary whiskers, that hung to his chest.

****

Cooke, who was known as crack shot, quickly dismounted and exclaimed, "I believe I will. That Springfield looks to be interesting."

"Yes, I have the new 1873 Winchester, also."

Tom Custer spoke up, "I've heard that it's more accurate than the 1866, more powerful also."

"Well, here's your chance to see for yourself." Bob replied.

Jake said, "Here, let me take your horses, Sirs. I'll move them back to where Mr. Seip's is tied." He moved to take the horse's reins, and Weir climbed down also.

Weir said, "Sgt. Martin told me that you were coming out here, Rogers. We were just sitting around, and when they heard the shooting, they were curious." Looking over at Kate and Holly, Weir smiled. "You have attractive students!" then walked over towards them.

When Jake returned, the officers were examining the rifles. Kate and Holly were standing by the carriage, while Bob conversed with them. Jake offered to set up more targets.

Cooke suggested, "Perhaps you could put some out a bit farther, Sergeant. Let's say 500 yards." He hefted the Springfield.

Jake went over to the shed, retrieved another target and started walking down range.

Custer laughed, "Do I sense a challenge, Cooke?"

"No, I just want to get a sense of how this shoots. I may want to buy one. This is the new Officer's Model. I saw the old 1873 version, when I was in St. Paul. 500 yards is more of a test, anyone can shoot 200yards with this gun."

"Sgt. Rogers is an excellent marksman. I had him with me up on the border. I suspect his main interest in being here, is not to shoot rifles." Weir said, nodding in the direction of Holly.

Custer looked over appraisingly, "Yes, I see that. You know that Armstrong is not fond of our Post Trader, don't you Weir? But I must admit, his women are comely!"

"Post Traders are a necessary evil. I met his boss at Fort Buford, last year. Alvin C. Leighton is who your brother needs to combat, I suspect Mr. Seip is just a pawn in the game."

Jake returned from setting up the targets, and approached the officers. Cooke looked at him. "Weir tells me you're a good shot, and Captain Michaelis is quite complimentary, also. "

"They're too generous with their praise, Sir. But, my Father was very parsimonious with bullets when I was young. It was learn to be accurate, or be hungry"

"Ah, a well phrased answer, Sergeant!" Cooke replied, with raised eyebrow. "How does this rifle shoot?"

"It's bit high close in, I haven't shot it at longer ranges."

"Well, let's try it then, shall we?"

Bob came over with a new boxes of cartridges, and set them down.

"Be my guests, gentlemen, I look forward to your evaluations."

Cooke laid down and chambered a bullet, then settled in behind the rifle bracing it on the bipod shooting stick. Using the barrel mounted sights he fired at the 200 yard target, hitting it solidly. After taking several more shots, hitting the target each time, he flipped up the tang vernier sight, mounted on the stock, loosened the eye cup and adjusted it for 500 yards. He plucked a piece of grass and held it up, gauging the wind, then looked up at Jake.

"Back in New York last fall, they had a shooting match between the Irish and American shooting teams. They shot at 800, 900, and 1,000 yards. We used Remington and Sharps breechloaders and the Irish used Rigby muzzleloaders, all custom built match rifles with no telescopic sights. The American team won by 3 points, but the Irish scored higher at the 1000 yard targets"

Jake looked down at Cooke and replied. "That's very impressive, Sir! I'd of liked to have seen that."

"Yes, well those gentlemen spend countless hours practicing. We, however, don't get that opportunity and I suspect the winds out here vary a bit more. We seldom have need of shooting at that distance, let alone at a stationary target. Being able to hit something at 500 yards is a commendable skill. This rifle should be able to do it, easily."

"Yes, Sir!"

Turning back towards the targets, Cooke aimed carefully and fired. Dust flew up just to the right of the target.

"Not enough windage!" he said as he reloaded, then made an adjustment.

He took aim again and fired. A distant clang rang out after a slight delay.

"There, that's more like it," Cooke declared, and fired several more times, striking consistently.

"Ah! The Queen's Own strikes again!" declared Lt. Custer, who was standing over by Kate and Holly, with Weir.

"At any rate, Sergeant, our Indian foes are not prone to standing around waiting for us to range in on them. We seldom even get to see them, so bear that in mind." Cooke looked over at Weir and Custer, then asked, "Care to shoot, either of you?"

Both officers declined. Cooke handed the rifle to Jake, who took it, folding the vernier sight.

"Not going to shoot, Sergeant?"

"No, Sir! I'm afraid that I'll get spoiled shooting a fine gun like this. I'm still getting used to my new carbine."

"Yes well, I try and keep note of the better marksmen in the command, I will add your name to my list."

Jake nodded his head, "Thank you, sir!"

"Hey! Let's try out that Winchester!" Tom Custer exclaimed, "That is if you don't mind, Bob?"

"No, Lieutenant, please be my guest."

Custer quickly loaded the repeater, and fired it rapidly at the 200 yard target, hitting it several times, then flipped up the sight and moved out to the 500 yard target raising dust all around it and hitting it once.

When it was empty, he examined it closely and nodded his head.

"I like it! It packs a little more punch than a .44 Henry."

Bob quickly replied, "I can make you very good deal one that on if you'd like."

Custer handed the Winchester to Cooke, who started inspecting it, then asked Seip. "How good of deal?"

While Custer and Bob began dickering, Jake carried the Springfield rifle back over to the carriage, where Kate and Holly were still sitting and talking with Weir, who turned to him and said.

"I'm pretty sure that you could out shoot Lt. Cooke, Sergeant."

"Well, it seems to me that it wouldn't be too smart on my part to out do the Regimental Adjutant at something that he obviously prides himself in being very good at. Especially, since I just met him for the first time."

"That's probably a wise choice, Rogers! I've known those two gentlemen for a many years. They are both very competitive."

"Besides, I'm sure Mrs. Seip, and Miss Walker don't want to waste the rest of this beautiful afternoon watching us shoot."

"It has been most interesting, Jake." Kate said, "I now appreciate how difficult it is to actually hit a target, let alone something alive and moving."

Holly nodded her head in agreement. "Yes, and I thought it was fun shooting the pistols!"

"Let me gather up my comrades, and we'll leave you to enjoy the rest of your day." Weir said, tipping his hat and nodding his head, "Ladies!" Then walked past Jake, giving him a slight wink.

While Bob was engaged with the officers, Jake started cleaning up all of the fired cartridges, and secured the targets. After the officers left, Bob wrapped up the guns, and put them on the back of the carriage. They got the horse hitched up, and headed back to the fort.

"That was a good outing!" Bob declared. "It was a stroke of luck that Cooke, and Tom Custer, showed up. I think that they might buy something. I certainly offered them attractive terms."

"Yes, and thank you, Jake." Kate said, "Our relations with Custer and his staff have been pretty chilly. We've not had the opportunity to deal much with them. Perhaps, this will help break the ice."

"Well, I think Jake deserves a nice supper!" announced Holly.

Kate looked at Bob, "Yes, I think he does too. When was the last time you had a home cooked meal, Jake?""

"The night before I left home to join the Army, but I don't want to impose, Kate."

"Nonsense!" Kate said, "We insist!"

When they got to the house, Kate and Holly went inside, while Jake helped Bob tend to the horse and carriage. Jake offered to clean the guns and while he did, Bob watched him closely. They carried them inside and set them in the living room by the fireplace. After two years of tents and barracks living, Jake was struck by the comparative luxury of his surroundings. There was a sofa and a couple of over stuffed chairs, tables with lamps, rugs on the floor, large bookshelf, and a clock on the mantle. A wonderful smell was wafting in from the kitchen.

"Let me take your hat. Thanks for spending your day off with us, Jake." Bob said. "I'll get us a beer, while we wait on supper. There's a wash room at the end of the hall with a pitcher of water and soap."

"Thanks, Bob."

Jake went to wash up and marveled at the cleanliness of the simple furnishings, and bathtub. He looked in the mirror and ran his hand through his hair, which fortunately he'd had cut reasonably short. He was a little apprehensive about being in these surroundings, and hoped he'd remember his etiquette. When he went back to the living room, Bob handed him a beer.

"Here you go, the girls are whipping up a feast."

"I'm sure it will be wonderful, if lunch was any indication."

"I think both Cooke and Custer, are going to order the Officer's Model Springfields. I made them good deals!"

"I don't really know either of them, I've just heard a few stories. I've met Lt. Cooke while on guard duty, but just in passing."

"Well, they're both close to Colonel Custer, and he's been difficult. Maybe this will get me some points with him."

The women finally summoned them to the dining room, and Jake was astounded by the meal they laid out. Fried steaks and onions, potatoes and gravy, canned green beans, fresh bread, butter, and pitcher of milk were all laid out on the table. Holly led them in saying grace. Jake struggled to mind his manners as Holly took his plate and heaped servings on it, then laid it in front of him.

"Here you go Jake! I hope you like it, Kate let me cook most of it."

"Miss Holly, if you knew what I was used to, you wouldn't worry about that!"

They watched him in amazement, as Jake ate every bite. When his plate was empty, Holly took it away and returned with a slice of apple pie.

"Oh my, I've died and gone to heaven!" Jake announced.

Finally done, he wiped his face with a napkin and declared, "That will be a meal that I'll always remember!"

Kate said, "It's always a pleasure to see someone enjoy our cooking. Some people take it for granted." She smiled sweetly over at Bob, who raised his eyebrows.

"Not me, dear! I always appreciate your cooking. But you need admit we don't eat this well every night."

"Well, I suppose that is true. But we don't get to entertain, often."

Come, Jake! Let's grab some coffee and sit out on the porch. I have a couple of cigars, if you'd care for one?"

"I enjoy one now and then."

They moved outside smoking and chatting about the day's shooting, and what Jake thought would help Bob improve. The porch faced east, and some of the rooftops of Bismarck could be seen to the North across the Missouri. When the women were done cleaning up, they joined them.

"So, Jake, your Captain was quite complimentary of you today." Kate said. "He said that you are very enterprising."

"Really? Well, I don't know about that. Being in the Army is not very difficult. It's mostly routine and just doing what you're told to do, when you're told to do it."

"So, do you intend to stay in the Army?" Bob asked.

"I really haven't given it much thought. I still have three years to go."

"What spurred you to join in the first place?" Holly asked.

" You've met Sgt. Morse. He served with my father during the War, and would come and visit us. He's kind of the reason that I joined up. I was fascinated by his stories about the West, chasing Indians, and cattle towns with cowboys. Heck, he even knows Wild Bill Hickok! But, he also described the country that he saw, endless plains covered with buffalo, mountains on the far horizon, and river valleys full of game. It was like books that I'd read."

"But, he's a senior sergeant, and a lifer, isn't he?" Bob said.

"Oh, I think Pat just hasn't figured out what he wants to do. But, I sense that he's ready to move on. We both enjoyed working with the Boundary Survey Teams, and we have a friend that's starting a cattle ranch, up in Montana. I'd be surprised if he signs over again."

"It sounds to me that you're not interested in the Army as a career." Kate commented.

"Probably not, it's pretty boring on a daily basis. I like being out in the field, but garrison duty, not so much."

They sat chatting about the day to day life at Fort Lincoln, and it was interesting for Jake to hear their perspective of the Regiment, particularly the Custer's and their entourage. Jake heard the clock in the living room strike Seven.

"Well, I guess that I should be heading back, soon." Jake stated. "Thank you for a most enjoyable day, and the magnificent supper!"

"Thank you for the shooting lessons." Bob replied. "Perhaps we can try again some time."

Kate said to Bob, "You should go over to the store, and help them close up. Bring back the day's receipts and I'll help you go over them."

"Okay, I'll see you around, Jake." Bob said, as he stepped off the porch and walked towards the nearby trading post.

"I'll get your hat, Jake." Holly said, as she and Kate went inside. Jake stood waiting until she returned.

"Here you go. We should really see about getting you a nicer hat. This one is pretty beat up." she said smiling.

"Yes, it is. It's got a few miles on it."

Holly's eyes met his, and Jake was amazed how blue they were.

"I think my aunt and uncle like you. That was pretty clever, how you arranged things today."

Jake felt himself blushing, "It worked though, I got to see you. Even though we didn't get much of a chance to talk."

"Well, we'll have to work on that, won't we?"

"Yes, we will!"

Holly grabbed Jake's hand. "I'm sure that Aunt Kate is peeking through the curtains, so you'll have to settle for this." She leaned into him, and gave him a kiss on the cheek. "Have a good night, Jake! Come see me when you can." Then she turned and went quickly into the house.

Jake stood there, stunned for a moment, savoring the lavender scent of her Florida Water. He turned, went down the steps, and headed toward his quarters. He scarcely remembered the walk back when he thought about it later. When he got there, 'Tattoo' was just sounding. He was glad that Tom Russell was Sergeant of the Guard that night, as he removed his clothes he lingered over his shirt collar he fancied that it still smelled vaguely of the lavender fragrance. He laid down and while the notes of 'To Quarters' sounded and was still awake, reviewing the days events for quite a while after 'Taps', before he finally drifted off to sleep.

The next couple of days flew by as Jake adapted to his new NCO duties. He had just come back up from morning stable call, on Wednesday, when he was summoned to the Orderly Room. When he got there, Capt. Weir, 1st Sgt. Martin, and Sgt. Morse were waiting.

"Good morning, Rogers!" Weir said, returning Jake's salute, "At ease!"

"Yes, Sir!"

"It seems that you've made a good impression on Lt. Cooke. I just came from the Adjutants Office. Captain Michaelis has submitted a request for Corporal Caddle and yourself to accompany his Ordinance team down to Louisiana as additional security escort. There's still a lot of civil unrest down there. Companies B, G, & K are all down there."

"I'm surprised, Sir. I told the Captain that I was content where I was at."

"This will be temporary detached duty. You'd be back in a couple of months."

Jake looked over at 1st Sgt. Martin and Pat, who were both smiling, then said, "Well, if you're okay with it, Sir?"

"We think you'll do well, Rogers. It reflects well on the Company, also. You'll probably find time to visit your folks sometime along the way."

Jake smiled at the thought. "When will I leave,Sir?"

"This Friday by train from Bismarck. You'll travel to Fort Snelling to pick up weapons from the Armory, then head south."

Martin spoke up, "You'd best be seeing to your kit, you'll want to look sharp at Headquarters in St. Paul. You're relieved from duty until then."

"What about Ajax?"

"Oh, you'll be taking him along with you. You're still a cavalry trooper." Morse stated.

After leaving the Orderly Room, Jake headed for his room, his mind swirling with the preparations he would have to make. When he got to the building, he looked up the road to the Post Traders, and thought of Holly. If he was going to be gone for two months, he would have to ask her if it would be okay to write. Since he was free for the rest of the day, he decided to go see her. When he walked into the store, she was standing behind the counter, with Katie.

"Jake, I'm surprised to see you, here, in the middle of the morning!" Katie exclaimed.

"Ah, I have the rest of the day off, and all day tomorrow."

"How did you manage that?" Holly asked, smiling.

"Well, I'm being sent down to Louisiana. I leave Friday and I've been given time off until then. I need to get my kit ready."

Holly's smile faded quickly, "Oh! Why are they sending you?"

"Captain Michaelis requested me, and Corporal Caddle. We're to help provide extra security for the Ordinance Team when they take the new guns down to Company K.
I may be able to go see my folks while I'm down there."

"How long will you be gone?" Holly asked

"Well, I'm not sure. I haven't talked with Captain Michaelis yet, but I suppose at least a month or so. Plus, I hope to get to spend a few weeks at home."

"But I'll be leaving in two months!" Holly exclaimed.

Jake hadn't thought that through, and suddenly realized the ramifications.

"Yes, well, darn!"

Seeing the disappointment on Holly's face, Kate said quickly, "There's no reason that you two can't write to each other, and you wouldn't want Jake to miss a chance to see his family."

"Yes, you're right, Aunt Kate!"

"I tell you what. We'll have a going away dinner for him tomorrow if he can come? How about it Jake?"

Jake nodded his head, "I don't know why not, Kate."

"Good, we'll plan on seeing you at 6:00. Now, why don't you two exchange addresses and I'll go tell Bob."

After Kate left, Holly looked at Jake with a downcast expression and said, "Oh, I wish you weren't leaving!"

"Well, I don't have a choice, Holly." He said, reaching for her hands, and looking into her eyes. "The orders have already been cut. I know we haven't known each other long, but I'll miss you and I'll write you as often as I can. I'll try to make it back before you leave for school!"

"Okay, Jake. I'll miss you, too. We'll just have to see. Now, promise me you won't let yourself be charmed by some cute Southern Belle!" she said smiling.

"Oh, you probably don't have to worry about that, from what I hear, they aren't too friendly to us Boys in Blue down there."

CHAPTER 20

Shreveport, Louisiana - Headquarters, District of the Upper Red River, June 28, 1875

Shreveport, Louisiana - Circa 1870s

Shreveport was chartered in 1839, after Captain Henry Shreve finally cleared the Red River Raft logjam and steamship navigation was made viable on the Red River. It became the commercial shipping center for the region, with cotton being the main crop. A stronghold for the Confederacy during the War and their temporary State Capitol, Shreveport was ably defended by General Kirby Smith. He repulsed the efforts of the Union General Banks and Admiral Porter's Naval Brigade during the Red River Campaign until he finally surrendered on June 2, 1865, almost two months after Lee's surrender at Appomattox. The region continued to be a hotbed of ex-confederate veterans, pro-white militias, and gun clubs that were virulently opposed to the free black Republicans and carpetbaggers of the Reconstruction government.

When Jake and Caddle had been assigned to Captain Michaelis they had no idea what they were getting into, other then a chance to travel down to Louisiana. They boarded a train, at Bismarck, and arrived at a station in St. Paul two days later. Michaelis's orderly came and found them, then took them to claim their horses. They joined Charles Brown, the Ordinance Sergeant in charge of the rest of the team, as it unloaded the wagons of old weapons and left for Fort Snelling. The fort was located several miles to the southwest where it sat on a bluff overlooking the confluence of the Mississippi and Minnesota Rivers. At the Armory building, they unloaded the wagons, then re-loaded with the new weapons that were to be issued in Louisiana. Two days later they were back on a train, heading south, and eventually worked their way down to Shreveport, Louisiana, via St. Louis, Little Rock, Texarkana and Marshall, Texas.

The three companies of the 7th Cavalry assigned there were B, G, & K, they had all been sent in the fall of 1874, after returning from the Black Hills Expedition with Custer. The squadron was under the command of Major Lewis Merrill. Company B, under the command of 1st Lt. Bell, with 2nd Lt. Benjamin Hodgson, Company G, under 1st Lt. Donald McIntosh, with 2nd Lt. George Wallace, who was assigned to Merrill's staff, and Company K under 1st Lt. Godfrey, with 2nd Lt. Luther Hare. There were also several companies of the 3rd & 16th Infantry Regiments stationed in Shreveport and Monroe. They were tasked with assisting the local authorities in controlling the various militant factions.

The civil unrest in Northern and Central Louisiana had been exacerbated by the continuing political turmoil surrounding Republican Governor William Kellogg's legitimacy versus his Democratic rival John McEnery. Militant members of the White League, mostly white ex-Confederates, had perpetrated a series of raids, murders, and other crimes against the Republican faction of carpetbaggers and freed blacks. There had been several confrontations back in late 1874. Company B and Lt. Hodgson were involved in one at the small-town of Vienna, which resulted in Hodgson's arrest by Democratic authorities. He was court marshaled and reprimanded, then sent on six months leave in April. A compromise had been reached in January, and a fragile truce was in effect and Governor Kellogg was allowed to serve out his term. Companies B and G were posted in Shreveport. The officers rented houses from sympathetic locals, and the men were camped along the banks of the Red River outside of town. Company K established a post at Colfax, which was about 120 miles south of Shreveport. Colfax had been the site of a massacre two years prior, where over 100 freed blacks had been executed, and the court house burned down. The area was still a hotbed, so Company K, and a company of the 3rd Infantry were there to keep the militias in check.

As the train rolled into the station at Shreveport the breeze through the window died. Jake had forgotten how stifling the fierce combination of heat and humidity could be after two years up north. Ever since leaving Little Rock, the troopers had suffered through the torrid days, drenched in sweat. He and Mike were fortunate that they were able to ride in one of the passenger cars, instead being in one of the boxcars assigned to the wagons carrying the crates of guns, ammunition, other gear, and horses. As soon as they came to a stop, they grabbed their bags and stepped off the train.

"B' Jesus it's sweltering!" exclaimed Mike, "Let's find some shade!"

"We'd best go see to our horses. They'll need watering. Captain Michaelis said that we'll probably only stay here a day or so, then go on to Company K. I'm sure he'll arrange for billets." Jake said.

They made their way back along the train, where they found the rest of the Ordinance team unloading. After securing the horses, they made their way towards the North Louisiana and Texas Railroad Station to find a horse trough. They lingered there while the horses drank, surveying the town. The station was on the southern edge of the city just west of the Red River. It was bordered by rows of long squat warehouses, and tufts of dingy cotton littered the area. Presently, they saw Captain Michaelis and another officer striding towards them. Jake recognized Lt. Bell and came to attention, saluting.

"Well, Rogers! I see that you've prospered over the last couple of years." Bell said. "Good to see you."

"Yes, Sir! It's been a while, we heard that you were with Company B, down here."

"I trust all is well with Capt. Weir, and the rest of the Company?"

"Yes, Sir! We're at Fort Lincoln now."

"Yes, Capt. Michaelis has so informed me. He said that you were just there."

"Well, it's quite a contrast, let me tell you. Up there I'd almost forgotten what trees look like!"

"Well, we do have plenty here, particularly when you get away from the river bottoms."

"Lt. Bell has offered to set us up with a bivouac area next to Company B, just south along the river. Perhaps you, and Cpl. Caddle, could ride ahead and let them know."

"Yes, if you'll just find 1st Sgt. Hill, he will get you settled." Bell said. "He's a gruff old Scot who just took over, don't mind his bark!"

"And let them know our Ordinance team will have their own provisions. I believe there's a cook stove in one of the wagons." Michaelis said. "But we'll appreciate any help with buying from local sources. Speaking of that, have Sgt. Brown buy a good supply of beer and put it in the wagons. The men have been on the move for a while, they deserve a break."

"Yes, Sir! I'll make sure of that!" grinned Caddle.

"There's a general store and saloon two blocks over to the North, where you can get beer, and some fresh produce. Look for a sign advertising Pelican Beer out front." Bell suggested.

They found the Company B area later that afternoon, and set up camp next to them. First Sergeant Hill, a tall grizzled Scot, was a veteran of the War, with four service stripes on his sleeve. He invited Jake and the other NCOs to pitch their tents close to his, and picket their horses nearby, where they could be surveilled by the guards. He also offered them supper, which turned out to be freshly caught catfish and hush puppies. After supper Hill sat down with them and they handed out beers.

"So Top! Give us the lay of the land down here." said Caddle.

"Well, Laddies, we mostly ride around and try and look like fierce Indian fighters. We seem to have our bluff in on the local militias. I just signed over after a stint in the 19th Infantry, back in March. I've been a soldier my whole life, starting with the Brits. I came over to Canada, and bought my discharge. Then I got caught up in the War. I was an Artilleryman when but I fought against the Johnnies at Shiloh. There was right fook up! Say boys, might you be have'n a bit of whiskey to share? This piss water they call beer around here, lacks a proper bite."

"How'd you get to be First Sergeant already?" Jake asked. "Ours has been with the troop for years."

"Ach! There's been a bit of round robin with that. It seems that old Captain Thompson, ran a slipshod company. When he didn't come south with it, there was only Lt. Hodgson in charge at first. He's a wee bit of a pisscutter, that fancies himself a ladies man. He got himself in bit of trouble. Lt. Bell stepped in and began sorting things out. When Capt. Benteen signed me down in New Orleans, he sent me straight up to Bell. I was a First Sergeant in the 19th, so after I got here, Bell found that out. 1st

Sgt. Criswell's term expired, and he elected not to sign over. Sgt. Gannon preceded him, but Bell wanted an old hand, so he picked me."

Jake went over to the wagons and secured a bottle, then returned to where he'been sitting. "Here you are, Top!"

"Aye, Laddie! That's more like it!" Hill said, taking a drink. "Now, keep that away! I've a weakness, that's seen me up and down the ranks over the years. I'm determined to keep my stripes this go round."

"So, we're tasked with fitting out Company K with their new guns. How far away are they?" asked Brown.

"They're a fair bit down the river in Colfax, just over 100 miles. You'll have to cross over to the East side of the Red on the bridge downtown, then work your way south. I'd say four to five days with the wagons. There's plenty of places to bivouac along the way. You'll find the blacks friendly, and they'll bring food to your camps to barter. That's where we got the catfish we had tonight."

"So, do you have any trouble with these militias?"asked Jake.

"Not so much now, I'm told that last year they murdered and lynched six White Republicans, and executed a dozen black freed men offhand, over in Coushatta. Several weeks later Lt. Hodgson got in a confrontation with them, over in Vienna and ended up arrested. Lt. Bell went and had him released. Hodgson ended up being court marshaled, and is on leave. Things are relatively calm right now. It's rumored that we'll be pulled out next year, when a new Governor takes office, so the White Leaguers are content to stay in the shadows."

"So you don't expect us to run into any confrontations?" Brown asked.

"Well, now, I don't! But I don't fancy having a couple of wagon loads of guns and ammunition being seized by the Johnnies. Lt. Bell has directed me to send a section with you. I'll put Sergeant Pete Gannon, and Corporal Jimmie Dougherty in charge of them. They know the area."

They left the wagons loaded, so the next morning after breakfast they quickly assembled and headed up to Shreveport and the bridge. Capt. Michaelis and Lt. Bell met them en route with Jake, Gammon, and Caddle in the advance.

"Ah, Sergeant Rogers, I trust you had a good evening?" Michaelis asked

"Yes, Sir! 1st Sgt. Hill was very accommodating. He shared his supper, and we shared our beer. He sent Sgt. Gannon and his section to escort us."

"Excellent! Thank you for the loan of your men, Jim."

"Just return them when you can, Otho. I'm sending the latest mail along with you." Bell said, handing a bulging saddlebag across to Jake.

"Yes, I'll be back as quickly as we can get Lt. Godfrey and his men equipped."

"Tell Ed, Hello for me!" said Bell, and then turned his mount back towards town.

After crossing the bridge over the Red River, they turned south and followed a well worn road along the East bank. They maintained a steady pace, and took every advantage to water the horses. Large cotton fields filled the bottom land on both sides of the road. The prevailing wind, when they had any, was out of the Southwest, and was just slightly cooler when it blew across the river. Most of the time it was just stifling hot and the high humidity just sapped energy. Michaelis seemed to be in no hurry, and allowed them to break often and bivouac early. On the third day, they rode into Coushatta, the county seat of Red River Parish, where the White League had murdered the hite Republican carpetbaggers the previous fall. There were a few people on the street, the whites seemed sullen, while the blacks waved to them, and their children ran along next to the column laughing and begging for treats. Jake had a sack of hard candies in his saddle bag and tossed them some. The Ordinance men did like wise, but the B troopers ignored them and shooed them away. When they camped that evening, some of the blacks made their way to the camp bringing fresh vegetables and yams, offering to trade for flour, beef, and coffee. The cool evenings brought out swarms of mosquitos, and the men smothered their fires to produce smoke and ultimately had to seek the shelter of their blankets to fend them off. After two more days they finally reached Colfax, where they found Company K encamped just north of town in a wooded area along the river. Large awnings and tents, were strewn through the timber, in addition to the neat rows of A tents. A patrol came out to meet them, one of the riders broke from the rest, racing his horse towards them, reining in just short of Jake, who saw that the rider was an officer. The spirited horse pranced around, and as the rider got him under control, Jake saluted.

"Good afternoon, Sir!"

"Ah, I'll bet you'll be bringing us our new guns, Sergeant!"

"Yes, Sir! We're here with Capt. Michaelis, the Regimental Ordinance officer."

Michaelis had ridden up behind Jake, and spurred his horse forward. "I assume this is Company K, and you, Sir, are?"

The officer who was youthful looking and clean shaven, offered a snappy salute to the brim of his forage hat, said. "Second Lieutenant Luther Hare, Sir! Welcome to Colfax, Captain Michaelis! Please allow me to show you to the area we have reserved for you. I think you'll find it pleasant enough, as opposed to being on the road in this heat anyway. We saved you some nice shade trees."

Michaelis took out a kerchief and mopped his face, "That will do for a start, Lieutenant! Lead the way!"

The Ordinance detachment aligned their wagons in an open box with the opening towards the river. They strung a picket line between some trees for the horses, and erected several large tents. Jake, Caddle, and the two Company B NCOs were invited to camp with the other NCOs. Company K's 1st Sgt. Louis Rott, was a Bavarian with a dark complexion and brown hair.

"You can stay mit us, over der. We been feedin' pretty gut. Der schwartzers been bringin' us fresh corn and green beans."

"Sounds good, Top. We appreciate it. You boys eat a lot better down here, then we do back at Fort Lincoln."

Sgt. DeWitt Winney, a short stocky man, and a bit older replied, "Well, Lt. Godfrey gives us a free hand to barter with the locals. Most of them are freed darkies, and they like having us around, so they treat us well. We hire them to bring us firewood, and hay. We give them flour and they bake our bread for us. We even get fresh butter and milk. To tell the truth them helping us out like they do, gives the men a lot of time to get up to no good. We got a few problems with the White Leaguers, riverboat gamblers and local thugs, getting our men liquored up, and taking their money."

"Sounds like back in Bismarck, across the river from Fort Lincoln. Though we don't have White Leaguers." Caddle said.

"Well, come on, I'll help you get set up. How'd you get picked for this detail, from Fort Lincoln, anyway?" asked Winney.

"Believe it or not, it's because we're fair shots with the new Springfields." Caddle said, "Capt. Michaelis seems to think we can help train your men, so he got us detailed to him. Although, we're really not sure what he's planning on having us do."

"My boys could use some training, some of da new men, dey don't shoot very gut." Gott said.

Winney said, "Sounds to me like you two got lucky. I spent a year at Fort Rice. Compared to up there, this place ain't bad, 'ceptin the heat and skeeters! And a man can get him a little now and then, iffin you like your meat a little dark, you get my drift?" he said winking.

Gannon replied, "Bet they ain't as fine as some of those Creole whores we got up in Shreveport!"

"Well, I can't say as I know to compare. Maybe next time I get up that way, maybe I'll look you up and you can show me."

Jake looked over at Caddle, who raised an eyebrow.

"Hey, we've got some beer in the wagons, we'll go grab some." He said, to change the subject.

"That's good! We're planning us a little 4th of July celebration for tomorrow. We got some of the local corn liquor, that we confiscated. It'll put a knot in your tail!"

Capt. Michaelis had directed his men to erect several large awnings, and set up tables underneath them. He was studying some papers when Lt. Hare and another officer approached, and saluted.

"Ah, Captain Michaelis, may I introduce Lt. Godfrey." Hare said. "He's in command of Company K."

"1st Lieutenant Godfrey, at your service, Sir! Welcome."

Godfrey was a tall slender man, with an erect posture, and sported a huge mustache under a rather prominent nose. He wore an officer's black slouch hat.

"Thank you, Godfrey. Are you ready for some new weapons? You're the last company in the regiment to receive them."

"Yes, Sir! Though I'll be sad to see the Spencers go, but the new Colts will be welcome."

"Yes, Yes, that seems to be the common sentiment." replied Michaelis, "We can discuss the merits of each, but the decision has been made by the Army, and we must comply."

****

1st Lieutenant Edwin Settle Godfrey

Born in Kalida, Ohio, in 1843, Godfrey originally enlisted as a 90 day volunteer private in 21st Ohio Infantry, in early 1861. Shortly after participating in the brief Battle of Scary Creek, Virginia, he was discharged. He applied for, and was admitted to the military academy at West Point, in July 1873. Upon graduating on June 17, 1867, 53rd in a class of 63, he was assigned to the Company G, 7th Cavalry, under Capt. Albert Barnitz, at Fort Harker, Kansas. The following August he was transferred to Company K, under Capt. Robert West. He commanded Company K that November at the Washita battle, and was responsible for engaging and delaying the nearby Arapaho and Southern Cheyenne warriors from closing on Custer while he was in Black Kettles village. He conducted a fighting retreat back to Custer, and warned him of the huge villages further down the Washita. Back in Kansas, he married the following year, and continued with the Regiment during all of its remaining time there. He was considered by some a bit of a lax officer who enjoyed his comforts, and was almost sent before the Hancock Officer Evaluation Boards, in 1870. He and Company K, under Capt. Owen Hale were posted to Yorkville, South Carolina, a relatively calm posting, during Reconstruction duty, beginning in March of 1871 for two years. Posted to Fort Rice, they participated in both the 1873 Yellowstone Expedition where they where they were engaged in the Bighorn fight against the Sioux on Aug. 11. Company K, along with H and M were posted to Fort Rice on returning and spent the next year there. In June 1874, they went along on the Black Hills Expedition and upon their return, Hale was detached to St. Louis on recruiting duty, so Godfrey assumed command of K when it was assigned Reconstruction duty that fall. They were assigned to establish a garrison in Colfax, Louisiana, the county seat of Grant County, an area prone to violence towards black freedmen.

****

2nd Lieutenant Luther Rector Hare

Born in Noblesville, Indiana on Aug. 24, 1851, Hare was raised in Mesilla, New Mexico and Sherman, Texas, following the War. He entered West Point in Sept. 1870, and graduated 25th in a class of 45. Assigned as a 2nd Lieutenant to Company K, 7th Cavalry, Fort Rice, in Sept.1874, on its return from the Black Hills. He arrived just in time to travel with K, down to Louisiana. He was eager, energetic, and still getting adjusted to life in a regular company.

****

"So, Captain, I'm glad to see you. You're a welcome diversion. It's hard to keep the men from getting bored. Aside from the regular routine of caring for the horses, and the daily drills and details, there's less and less for them to do. They tend to find ways to wander around, getting up to no good, even my sergeants. The political situation, here locally, seems to be shifting. The Democrats are gaining power, and they have no use for us. They've just about run off all of the Carpetbaggers and Republicans. We're not called out to help the sheriff at all, and the US Marshalls have little power over the local elected officials. While most locals aren't outright hostile, the men sense that they aren't wanted here."

"Well, Godfrey, it has been ten years since the end of the War.

Personally, I think it's time that we let the South rule themselves, but, that's just my opinion. Many of the men are Southerners, it's only natural for them to sympathize. After all, we are all Americans!"

"Indeed, Sir! So, what do you require from us? I've got my sergeants working on getting all of our weapons cleaned up."

"Good, good! We will do it by sections. I'll need a target range set up, out to 400 yards. We'll do an exchange, and get the paperwork over with, then conduct training on field maintenance. I've brought a good supply of ammunition, and a couple of marksmen to give your men some tips on shooting,"

"I'll see to it, Sir. Just let me know if you require anything else."

"There is one thing. Since tomorrow is Independence Day, and a Sunday, why don't we have a celebration. I took the liberty to bring some old signal rockets, and some Italian aerial displays, and several boxes of Chinese fireworks. I thought that maybe tomorrow night we might put on a little display."

Godfrey grinned, "That would be capital, Sir! I'll let the men know, and we'll send out word to the locals. You won't believe the taste of the barbecue meats they cook up. I'll see if I can procure a couple of kegs of beer, also."

Michaelis smiled and nodded his head.

The next morning, Jake and Caddle went over to the Ordinance team area, looking for Capt. Michaelis. He was in his tent, with the flaps opened wide, writing intently. Jake coughed to get his attention.

"Ah, good morning, Sergeant Rogers! What can I do for you?"

"Well, Corporal Caddle and I, we're wondering what you want us to do today."

"Lt. Godfrey and I have decided to have a 4th of July celebration, tonight. You can ask Sgt. Brown if he needs help with anything. Other than that, enjoy the festivities."

"Thank you, Sir, we'll do that."

They found Sgt. Brown, and he gave them a couple of signs inviting the locals to watch, and asked them to go post them in Colfax. After saddling the horses, they headed down the road that ran along the river in that direction. When they came to the town the road was lined with small, narrow shacks, with raised floors, and small porches. Black face peered from the doors and windows, while a few children ventured out into the dirt yards to wave at them. Eventually, they came to a few buildings facing the riverfront. where they found a general store and post office. Jake figured that it was a likely spot for the sign. It was built up off the ground, and had a wide porch across the front, it was pierced by a central breezeway with doors and tall windows in the rooms along either side. A faded sign hung out front, lettered with 'CALHOUN GENERAL STORE'. Several locals were sitting in chairs, on the covered porch of the store, watching as they rode up. One of them, a one-legged veteran in a faded grey coat and kepi eyed them as they reigned in near a hitching rail and dismounted.

"That's a fine looking horse you got there, Yank."

Jake looked up the man and said, "Thank you, sir. He and I have done many a mile together."

"I ain't seen you boys before! You must be with that bunch that came in yesterday."

"We are, just came down from Fort Lincoln, up in the Dakotas."

"Injun fighters, huh? I see that fancy sheath that you're a sportin'."

"No, we're just soldiers. The knife was a gift from a friend."

"Well, them Blue boys that's been here for a while, they talk like they done whupped every Injun out west."

"I don't know about that, there's a hell of a lot of them. I wouldn't care to tangle with them all at once." replied Jake, as he wrapped Ajax's reins to the rail.

"Hah! Listen to you! What's your name, Sarge?"

"Jake Rogers, from Springfield, Missouri! How 'bout you?"

"Bob Taylor from Calhoun's Landing, Louisiana!"

"Where's that?" asked Jake.

"Why, it's right here damn you! Least wise, it used to be, afore they changed the name. 'Twas my uncles place, Meredith Calhoun. Biggest planter in these here parts, o'course that was before. Now they call it Colfax, after that damn Yankee Vice President!"

"What happened to your uncle?"

"He got disgusted with the Republicans and Carpetbaggers! He sold everything and moved to Paris, France, where he died a couple of years ago. His boy, Willie, my cousin, has done turned Democrat and nigger lover. He helped split up the parish, and they named this part round here after that damn General Grant. My Ol' Unc, he's over there a spinnin' in his grave!"

"I don't know anything about that, Bob. I'm just here to invite folks to watch the fireworks tonight."

"We had us some fireworks here big time, year before last!" Bob said, nodding in the direction of the charred Grant Parish courthouse ruins. Some of the boys got a bit carried away. Most of them weren't even from around here. It was a bad thing happened, I'll tell you!"

"I heard tell about a little of it." Jake said, "Lot's of old wounds around here that haven't healed."

Bob stared down at Jake, "Yes, indeed! You gonna be here for a while, Sergeant Jake?"

"Nope, just a week or two! I hope to get home for a few weeks after that. Then back to Fort Lincoln."

"Ain't that Custer and his bunch?"

"Yes."

"The stories true about that gold in the Black Hills that he found?"

Jake smiled up at Bob, "I wouldn't know. My company was up at the Canadian Boundary, escorting some surveyors. But, the soldiers garrisoned here were with him, why don't you ask them?"

"I ain't had much call to mix with them fellas!"

Jake climbed the steps and stuck the paper on the wall with tacks. He walked over to Bob, and said. "There are men in my outfit from the South, there's even one from New Orleans. I grew up in Missouri, and some of my neighbor folk were Confederates. My Pa fought for the Union. They've all put the War behind them. Looks like it might take a little longer in these parts, but I reckon we're all Americans. You might want to think about that, it'd be a shame to miss a good time and some fireworks, tonight."

Taylor reached for his crutches and struggled to stand up, he locked eyes with Jake, and after a few seconds, said, "You're right Sergeant Jake! Some things take longer to heal, and then some don't heal at all. You enjoy yourself tonight!" He turned and clumped his way to the breezeway, then disappeared through a doorway.

Jake and Mike decided to ride around the town and made their way away from the river. Most of the town consisted of more wooden shacks of various designs, all on raised floors, many with dirt garden patches being tilled and tended by more blacks. As they got further away from the river, closer to the edge of town, there were several bayous that meandered through the landscape. They saw some larger two story homes, with wide verandas, scattered along them. They were cordoned off by fences, and had long tree lined driveways. Fields of cotton, sugarcane, and corn, surrounded them.

"This must be what they're all fighting over." Jake said.

"Indeed, my friend! It brings Ireland to mind, for me. The rich English estates, lush with crops, while the poor Irish peasants scratch out potatoes from a tiny plot of ground. I can't say that I have much sympathy for old Bob and his sort." Caddle replied.

"Well, let's go back to camp. I think we've seen all we need to see around here."

The Independence Day Celebration was a big success. The weather co-operated with a bright cloudless day. An area adjacent to the encampment was set up and cordoned off. Trestle tables were set up, under awnings, and were loaded with barbecued meats, fresh corn on the cob, beans, corn bread, and pies. Kegs of beer were tapped, and by dusk, everyone was looking forward to the fireworks show. Many of the locals, mostly freedmen and their families, brought blankets and pieces of canvas and spread them out between the camp and the riverbank, where Sgt. Brown and the Ordinance detachment had spent the day setting up. Out on the road, some wagons were pulled off to the side, and even a few boats were tied up on the riverbank. These latter spectators were mostly the local poor whites that didn't want to be seen fraternizing with the Yankee soldiers, but didn't mind watching the fireworks. Jake wasn't sure, but he thought he spied a gray clad figure, with one leg, perched on one of the wagon seats. Capt. Michaelis and Sgt. Brown had planned the sequence and it went off without a hitch, lasting over thirty minutes. The aerial explosions reverberated down the river valley, while the multi-colored displays reflected off the water. The grand finale was augmented by dozens of signal rockets. Afterwards, the celebration continued after the civilians left, and the soldiers broke up into smaller groups. Here and there, shrill female laughter and sounds of gaiety pierced the darkness, some from just outside the compound.

The next morning, things quickly reverted to the cavalry routine, albeit more slowly for some. After stable call, Jake and Mike, reported to Capt. Michaelis tent.

"Good Morning Sgt. Rogers! Did you enjoy yesterday?"

"Very much, Sir! It was quite the show!"

"Yes, Yes! I was very pleased, but now we must get down to work. I plan to do this by sections, just like we did back at Fort Lincoln. The shooting range that they had here has been expanded out to 400 yards. Mind you, we'll only take a few shots out that far, but I want to demonstrate to the men the advantage of the Springfield's power and range, over the Spencer. We'll take two days with each section, I see no reason to hurry. Two weeks should see us finished and ready to head home."

"Yes, Sir! What do you want us to do?"

"You, and Cpl. Caddle will be helping to instruct shooting the carbine. I want you to perform a practical shooting demonstration, then be available to answer questions, and give out shooting tips and advice, as the men familiarize. That shouldn't be too difficult, eh?"

"No, Sir!" Jake answered, "I think that we can handle that."

Towards the end of the first week, Capt. Owen Hale, the actual commanding Officer of Company K, arrived from St. Louis on the weekly Mail Packet with a couple of recruits in tow. After being welcomed, by Godfrey, he announced that he was staying for a week.

****

Captain Owen Hale

Hale was a descendent of Nathan Hale, the Revolutionary War hero, and had fought with the 7th New York Cavalry during the War. Initially, he was a Sergeant Major and then was promoted as a Lieutenant and breveted as a Captain. He was one of the original officers of the 7th. Known as "Holy Owen" he was considered the personification of the ideal cavalry officer, which was a contrast to the sometimes rumpled Godfrey. However, they had served together several years back in Kansas, and were good friends. Hale was one of the original officers of the Regiment, and had been at the Washita fight. During Reconstruction Duty, he and Company K, had been garrisoned at Yorkville, South Carolina. He had been involved in the fighting during the 1873 Yellowstone Expedition, and wintered at Fort Rice. After the Black Hills Expedition, he was assigned to recruiting duty at Jefferson Barracks. Hale was popular with both the officers and men, and was a confirmed bachelor, and was known for his colorful profanity. He had a reputation for being the life of the party, and was fancied a ladies man, though he was impeccable in his treatment of the wives of his fellow officers.

****

"So what do you think of this place, God?" asked Hale.

"I think you should trade me places and give up your cushy billet in St. Louis." replied Godfrey.

"Oh, I think not. This place is a bit isolated for my sophisticated New York tastes."

"Well, aside from the warm winter, I'd much rather be in the field out west. The men are getting stale, and desertion rates are up. The men whose terms are up, aren't re-enlisting, except for 1st Sgt. Rott, and I may bust him down if he doesn't straighten up!"

"What's his problem?"

"He's in hock to some of the local gamblers, and spends too much time in town with one of the mulatto women. He thinks that I don't know, but I overheard Sgt. Hughes, and Sgt. Winney discussing it. They're suspicious about some missing money from the company mess fund."

"See there, God, I don't miss that shit at all, but it's good to know that you've got your finger on the pulse. But hang in there, I hear rumors that Grant is growing frustrated with the whole Indian and Black Hills situation. It's said that he's leaning towards a military solution. Benteen was sent to Fort Randall at the beginning of June. He has Companies A, and E assigned to him also, and they should be arriving about now. He's supposed to intercept miners on their way to the Black Hills, and evict any he finds already there. General Crook is also supporting the effort from the Department of the Platte. A Sioux delegation was in Washington, back in May, and left without agreeing to any new terms. You'd better enjoy the weather down here, until next season. Best try and keep an edge on these boys with that in mind."

The time passed swiftly for Jake and Mike as they spent their days on the range demonstrating the new weapons. They enjoyed not having any responsibilities, other than caring for their horses, and spent time catching fish along the river. Some of the local freedmen showed them how to set bank lines, and they wandered the banks checking them. The fish were welcomed by the mess cooks, who became very adept at frying it up in corn meal and the local spices. A couple days a week a steamboat out of Alexandria pulled into the boat landing and delivered supplies to the outfit, including beer. Finally at the end of the second week, Captain Hale, who had visited the range a couple of times, came to see Capt. Michaelis again. Michaelis sent his orderly to summon them.

"Sergeant Rogers, I believe you've met Capt. Hale." Michaelis said.

"Yes, Sir! We met at the range, a couple of days ago." Jake replied, looking at Hale, and nodding his head.

"Well, he has a proposition for you."

Hale spoke up, "Otho, here, has explained that he is finished with the weapons exchange. He also told me that you were promised furloughs when he was done."

"Yes, Sir! That was our understanding."

"I'm going back to St. Louis, and he's suggested that I take you with me. If you travel with me as my escort, I can voucher your rail passes and lodging, along the way. That would be a quicker way to get you out of here. Then, I'm going over to Springfield, where I'm told you want to get to, I assume Corporal Caddle is going to accompany you?"

Jake smiled, and looked at Mike, who said, "Well, Dublin is a bit too far, but I'm looking forward to seeing Missouri. So, that would be excellent, Sir!"

"Well, then. I see no reason that you two can't start your furloughs once we reach Springfield. I can still voucher your return to Jefferson Barracks from there. Then we'll see about getting you back to Fort Lincoln. I may have some men to send up with you by then."

Michaelis spoke up, "You men have done a very good job for me. It seems only right that I should speed you on your way. If you ever decide that you're done following the guidons, just contact me and I'll make a place for you."

"Thank You, Sir!"

"I'm planning on leaving tomorrow. I'm catching the Mail Packet back up to Shreveport. Have your kits together, and we'll go aboard in the morning, when it pulls in." Hale said.

Jake and Caddle both saluted. "Thank you, Sirs!"

They spent the evening sorting out their kits, and saying their goodbyes to the other NCOs. Gannon and Dougherty were a bit jealous that they were stuck escorting the Ordinance Detachment back, via road. The next morning they mounted up after breakfast and rode over to the Company K Headquarters tent to find Capt. Hale. He came out with Lt Godfrey.

"Well, God! Remember what we discussed the other day. I'll keep you up to date as much as I can."

"I will, Owen. Don't get too fat and lazy up there in St. Louis!"

Hale mounted his horse, "I won't! Take care!" He waved, turned his mount and they all headed for the river landing

CHAPTER 21

Springfield, Missouri - July 29, 1875

Captain Hale proved to be a remarkable traveling companion. Bluff and outgoing, he was always talking to the people around him. Hale regaled Jake and Mike with stories about the campaigns of the 7th during its years on the Kansas plains, and the recent expeditions into Sioux territory. He being one of the first officers in the Regiment, knew everyone and had an endless supply of anecdotes about them, both officers and the senior sergeants. Hale enjoyed telling bawdy jokes, and was prone to rattling off colorful strings of profanity. He insisted that Jake and Mike were extended the same courtesies in travel and lodging accommodations as he enjoyed as they made their way back up to St. Louis saying, "This is my treat, men, I know what you're used to. I was a Sergeant once." When they arrived at Jefferson Barracks, Hale took them to the headquarters of the General Mounted Recruiting Service where he was assigned. They were standing outside the door when a middle aged officer, wearing eagles on his epaulettes came through it. Jake and Caddle came to attention while Hale introduced them to Col. Sturgis, who was the Superintendent of the GMRS, in addition to being the actual regimental commander of the 7th Cavalry.

"Good afternoon, Sir! These men are Sgt. Rogers, and Cpl. Caddle, they're the two men that Capt. Michaelis borrowed from Fort Lincoln to assist him with the new carbine training down in Louisiana." Hale said. "I brought them back with me, and am taking them to Springfield on my recruiting trip, young Rogers here was raised near there."

Sturgis was middle aged, with a plump face topped by a full head of curly, dark hair streaked with gray, and a sported a neatly trimmed mustache and goatee. He looked them up and down.

"Louisiana, hmm! Didn't care for it when I was down there after the War. I'd dare say it hasn't gotten much better. Though it's probably better than being stranded up at Fort Lincoln, eh Sergeant?"

"I wouldn't know, Sir. We'd only been at Fort Lincoln for a few weeks before Captain Michaelis asked for us. We were up north with the Border Survey, and at Fort Totten, until then. But yes, it was warmer, and at least there are towns in Louisiana."

"Ah, you were part of Reno's battalion then."

Jake started to say something about not seeing much of Reno, then just said. "Yes, Sir! Although, Captain Weir was in command most of the time."

"Hmm! Well, enjoy your detached service duties. We need more recruits, and I'm sure Captain Hale will appreciate your assistance. It's too bad we've no extra money to spend on training the new men how to shoot, or I'd be tempted to keep you both here. Carry on." He turned and went back through the door.

"Come with me, let's get you two some place to stay, we'll be here a couple of days." Hale stated.

****

Colonel Samuel D. Sturgis

Sturgis was born in Shippensburg, Pennsylvania in 1822. He graduated from West Point, in 1846, where he was a classmate of George McClellan and Ambrose Burnside. He served as a 2nd Lieutenant in the 1st Dragoons during the War with Mexico, and then on frontier duty in Kansas and Missouri, where he was promoted to 1st Lieutenant in 1853, and Captain in 1855 when the unit was re-designated as the 1st U.S. Cavalry. Prior to the War, he was involved in skirmishes with the Apaches, Kiowas, Comanches, and Southern Cheyenne. He was serving as the post commander at Ft. Smith, Arkansas, when the War broke out, and his rescue of the government stores located there, which he transported to Fort Leavenworth, Kansas, gained him a promotion to Major. He was given command of the 4th Cavalry just before the Battle of Wilson's Creek, where he received a brevet as a Lt. Colonel, for gallantry after assuming command after General Lyons was killed. He was transferred to the Eastern Theater and fought in most of the major campaigns with the 4th Cavalry, then was breveted as a major general after Fredericksburg. He returned to the Western Theater where he served briefly in commands in Tennessee and Mississippi. His forces suffered a bad defeat at Brice's Crossroad, at the hands of Nathan Bedford Forrest, effectively ending his war career. He was given command of the 6th Cavalry, at his regular Army rank of Lt. Colonel and sent to Austin, Texas in November 1865, where Custer still held the rank of Major General of Volunteers, and was in command. The two clashed immediately, the 43 year old Sturgis resented the younger Custer being in command while technically ranked a regular Army captain. Custer was reverted to his regular rank at the end of January 1866, and turned over the command to Sturgis, then left to go on leave back to Monroe, Michigan. Sturgis served at various posts in Texas for the next 2 years, then was posted to Washington DC, until being given command of the 7th Cavalry, in May 1869, when Col. A. J. Smith retired to become the postmaster of St. Louis. Custer who had been the field commander of the 7th since 1866, resented that he had been passed over for the vacancy, and the two men resumed their contentious relationship. Sturgis was aware that Custer was a favorite of Gen. Sheridan, and generally preferred to keep Custer stationed elsewhere. When the 7th was sent up to the Dakotas, in May 1873, Sheridan solved their bickering by first assigning Sturgis to regimental HQ, in St. Paul with Gen. Terry, and in October 1874 making him the Superintendent of the Mounted Recruiting Service, in St. Louis.

****

The training center brought back memories for Jake and Mike. They watched the recruits being harried and hurried around the parade ground from the transient NCO quarters Hale had arranged for them. They marveled that little had changed, and now had some appreciation for the process that tried to winnow the recruits somewhat, before sending them on to line units. Hale had them check their carbines at the armory, but they retained their sidearms, when they left for Springfield. They were booked on the morning train, and Hale had arranged for them to travel in a chair car. He encouraged Jake and Mike to relax and enjoy its comforts and its plush seats, then took them to the dining car for dinner on their way down from St. Louis.

"One of the owners of the A&P is Clinton Fisk, in St. Louis. He was a general on Custer's staff during the War. He and I are friends, and he makes sure to arrange for my comfort when I ride his trains." Hale commented. "He is also a good friend of Col. Sturgis."

The eight hour journey to Springfield went smoothly and they arrived around four in the afternoon. Hale sent them to unload the horses, and instructed them to meet him at Delmonico's Restaurant a couple blocks away from the passenger station on Commercial Street. Jake was amazed at the changes to North Springfield over the last two years. Where the Ozark House Hotel had stood, there was only a blackened stone foundation, while next door a three story brick building was under construction. A sign advertised it as the new Lyon House Hotel. The corner of Jefferson and Commercial was occupied by Jackson Grocery, the Southwest Cigar Factory, and the Railroad Land office. Further to the west along Commercial were numerous buildings and businesses; lumber yards, warehouses, livery stables and stockyards, printing companies, barber shops and jewelers. Wagons and carriages traveled the street, while the sidewalks were full of pedestrians.

When they arrived at the restaurant, they hitched the horses out front and went in. Captain Hale was sitting at a large table engaged in conversation with several men. He noted their arrival, and as they approached he waved to them to sit down.

"Gentlemen, let me introduce Sgt. Rogers, and Cpl. Caddle! Rogers is one of your own lads, raised in theses parts, while Caddle is an Irishman. They've been with the 7th out west, and recently were down in Shreveport, where they were training our boys to shoot their new carbines. Both are deadeye marksmen!"

"So, where about does your family live, Rogers?" asked one of the men at the table.

"Over at Henderson, Sir! I'm headed there as soon as I can. I've been gone two years, and my friend Mike here, is coming with me."

"Well, now! I daresay it's a bit late to start, today. Come, sit down and eat with us. I'd like to hear first hand what one of Custer's lads has to say about things out west. Particularly a local lad! Captain Hale has already arranged rooms for you men at my hotel for the night. You can get a fresh start in the morning." He held out his hand to Jake, "I'm J. M. Doling, and this is James Stoughton." he nodded towards one of the others.

"Well, thank you sir! But, I need to see if the Captain needs us first."

Hale spoke up, "Oh, these gentlemen will see that I receive any assistance that I might require. Mr. Doling and Mr. Stoughton are both friends of Mr. Fisk, and are prominent citizens here. They are also very supportive of the Army. Besides, I need to get with you in the morning to arrange your vouchers before I head back to St. Louis, so no sense hurrying away."

"Yes, Sir!"

Stoughton said, "You fellows have a seat. I'll have them rustle up some steaks. I think a round of beers is in order also."

For the next two hours, they were barraged with questions about Indians, buffalo, and life on the plains. Finally, when they were stuffed, Stoughton proposed that he would have their mounts boarded at his livery stable, and they would all catch the trolley down to the Metropolitan Hotel in South Springfield, where Doling would put them up for the night. The hotel was located on College Street just west of the square. Advertised as the finest hotel in the city, it was a four story brick building with metal balconies on the upper floors, and contained only the second elevator in Springfield. A large awning covered the entrance to the lobby where a grand staircase led to a ballroom on the mezzanine, that also served as a dining room during the day. The Post Office and Western Union office were located on the ground floor, along with a saloon.

Doling dismounted from the trolley and led them in. "Let's get you men some rooms, then we'll all meet at the saloon. The bellboys will see to your bags. Don't worry about paying, it's all on the house!"

Jake and Caddle were in awe of the ornate furnishings of the lobby. They followed the bellboys up to their rooms, which were next to each other. After freshening up, Jake met Mike and they returned downstairs. Jake saw Hale talking with a couple of well, dressed attractive women who were sitting in chairs across the lobby. One had blonde hair and was smiling at Hale, obviously having an animated conversation with him, while the other, a bit more slender with a mass of brunette hair cascading to her shoulders, looked directly at Jake. Her dark eyes seemed to lock onto his, and she looked a bit startled for a second. She turned and made a comment at Hale, who looked back at Jake, then waved. A few minutes later, Hale came over to where Jake and Mike were standing.

"Nice digs, eh men? Just relax and enjoy the evening. The A & P Railroad is footing the bill, and has arranged everything. You'll be treated well." He said with a wink.

"Thank you, Sir. But I'm not sure we'll know how to act!" Jake said hesitantly.

"Ah, now, laddie, I watched the wealthy lords at the shooting club back home." Caddle said. "Just follow my lead!"

"Yes, Rogers, just be yourself, and try not to drink too much." said Hale, smiling.

The saloon had a high decorated ceiling over a long shiny polished wood bar, backed by a huge mirror with myriads of liquor bottles arrayed in front of it. Gaslights provided the illumination. A dense cloud of cigar smoke lingered overhead.

"Come lads! We've a private room in the back!" called Hale.

They negotiated a short hallway that led to a large room filled with comfortable chairs and several tables. There were several other civilians already there, and a card game was in progress.

"Gentlemen, I'd like to introduce these gallant troopers from the 7th Cavalry! Captain Hale, from Troy New York. Sergeant Rogers, who hails from these parts. And Corporal Caddle, an Irishman helping them to vanquish the heathen Indians!" Doling announced.

There was a polite round of applause, and several "Hear, hears!" as a round of whiskey was passed around.

"A toast! To the Army that helps to protect the Railroad, that makes us all money!"

Jake sipped at his whiskey, watching the men playing cards, and catching snippets of conversations that all seemed to evolve around various businesses. A new railroad was being proposed from Springfield to Kansas City and was to be called the Springfield and Western Missouri, with a terminal a few blocks away. The new Gaslight company that provided the lights in the hotel would soon have 50 street lamps working in the downtown area, and over 80 customers. The Springfield Manufacturing Company was almost recovered from the Wilson Creek flood last month, and was beginning to produce wagons again. However, the grain mills were still not operational. A grasshopper plague was devastating crops in the western part of the state. He fielded a few polite questions about the time he'd spent so far in the 7th Cavalry, but then was largely ignored. Hale was in the midst of a group, and Mike was engrossed in a conversation with Stoughton. Jake decided to go find the facilities, and afterwards went across the lobby to stand on the steps admiring the gaslit view of Springfield. He took in a deep breath of the cool night air, relishing the fragrant smell of the Ozarks. He detected a whiff of perfume and became aware of someone standing behind him, and turned his head to look. Standing just outside the doorway he saw the long haired brunette, who he'd made eye contact with earlier. She had an amused expression on her face, and her dark eyes seemed to grow as she came closer.

"Well, you don't seem to be interested in the scintillating conversations going on around you!" Her voice was low and silky, with what he suspected was an English accent.

"I'm afraid that I don't have much to contribute to them. My life is not very complicated right now, at least for a couple more years."

That drew a low chuckle from her. "I'll bet not! The military tends to simplify things." She held out her hand, "Tell me your name, Sergeant, mine is Julia."

"Jacob Rogers!" he replied as took her hand. "What do you know about being in the military, Julia?"

"Oh, my Father was a soldier. He served in the British Army, in India.

He was a sergeant, also."

"Well, then, you may appreciate my current state of affairs, Julia."

"Indeed I do, Jacob! Pardon my forwardness, but you look remarkably like someone I used to know."

"Well, I was raised not far from here."

"No, this was back in England. He was a soldier also. I'm sorry, am I keeping you from your festivities inside?"

"No, Ma'am!" Jake replied smiling, "I'd much rather be right here talking with a pretty woman like yourself!"

She laughed softly, and Jake noticed that her dark eyes grew larger, seeming to draw him in.

"Perhaps we can go somewhere more comfortable to continue our conversation then?" Julia offered. "I assume that you have a room upstairs, you can escort me to it."

Jake was stunned and looked back at her incredulously.

"The long and the short of it is that I'd like some companionship this evening and it might as well be you." She said with a beguiling smile.

Jake was momentarily at a loss for words. Julia sensed it and continued. "Certain parties have arranged that some of us ladies have been retained as companions for the night. You mustn't fret about being obligated."

Jake felt his face redden, and struggled to maintain his composure. "Well, I ah, don't, ah, I mean I haven't much experience."

Julia chuckled again, "Oh dear! Well, we must rectify this. Lucky for you, Jacob, I'm very good at it. Let us adjourn upstairs and we'll begin your lessons." She grabbed his arm, turned back to the lobby, gestured grandly and asked, "Shall we!"

The rest of the night became a jumble of frenetic activity and leisurely recovery. Julia patiently introduced him to experiences he had only imagined through the tales of others. After she explained what a condom was, she smoothly applied it, and proceeded to mount him. She taught him where to place his hands, and how to position his body to respond to hers. During one period of recovery, as her head lay on his chest, she sighed.

"Dear boy! I must admit that you're a pleasant surprise. I'd anticipated having to couple with one of those fat, sweaty railroad men. You're quite a bonus!"

Jake didn't reply, but couldn't help but wonder how Julia had come to this way of life.

"Jacob?"

"Yes, Julia!"

"You're wondering why I live this way, aren't you?"

"Maybe a bit, but I'm just trying to enjoy the moment. Thank you for making it so enjoyable."

"It was my pleasure. It's not often that I'm attracted to a customer, particularly one so innocent."

It was Jake's turn to chuckle, "It's not like I've had many opportunities where I've been."

They laid in silence for a few minutes, then Julia spoke quietly.

"My mother was Indian. She married my father and they had me. When he was sent back to England, we accompanied him. We lived near London, and after my father died in a training exercise, his commander saw that my mother and I were taken care of. I was trained to be a governess, but when my mother passed away, I was left alone. A wealthy man hired me to care for his children, and I accompanied him to America. When I resisted his advances, he fired me, and abandoned me in St. Louis. One of his American friends was a railroad man who courted me and persuaded me to be his mistress, not that I had much of a choice. Eventually his wife found out, and he discarded me. However he was kind enough to provide me with some money, a house, and a referral to some of his railroad cronies. I still travel to various destinations like here in Springfield, where I and my fellow hired companions as we like to refer to ourselves, are occasionally retained to entertain select customers."

Jake remained silent for a moment, then said, "Thanks for telling me that, Julia. You didn't have to."

"Well, I want be sure that you understand. I wanted you to enjoy your first time, and always remember it fondly. But don't confuse it with love, this was just sex. But I will tell you that it was quite pleasurable for me. Thank you, Jacob."

She kissed him on the cheek and laid her head on his chest. Jake fell asleep and slumbered soundly the rest of the night. He was surprised when he awoke, and Julia was gone. He got up and looked around spotting a note on the stand near the wash basin. It read;

"Jacob, you're a dear! Stay that way. You'll make some girl a wonderful husband."

Julia

Jake dressed and exited his room on the third floor, and took the stairs down to the dining room. As he entered, he spotted Capt. Hale sitting at a table with Caddle, drinking coffee. Hale motioned for Jake to join them.

"Good morning, Rogers! We were wondering if you were going to join us. We're just getting ready to order breakfast."

"That sounds wonderful, Sir!"

Hale looked at him grinning, "Did you sleep well? I looked up last night and saw you being captured by some young exotic thing."

Caddle chortled, "And ya didn't look like you were putting up much of a fight, boyo!"

Fortunately for Jake, the waitress came to take their order, and poured him a cup of coffee. When she left, he said, "I suspect you arranged the whole thing, Sir. I saw you talking to those women in the lobby. "

"Well, I may have made some inquiries." grinned Hale. "Her companions dragged us away shortly after."

"Aye, we struggled mightily, but succumbed to superior forces." Caddle replied. "The Captain advised me to surrender, just before he was captured."

"Well, sometimes you have to know when resistance is futile." Hale stated. "I trust you two enjoyed your captivity."

Caddle nodded his head and Jake smiled sheepishly, which Hale noted.

"Do I sense that was your first time being incarcerated, Rogers?"

"Well, ah, yes, I guess it was, Sir."

Hale pounded the table, "Capital, just capital! You were very lucky, I've heard Julia is quite enjoyable."

"You know her, Sir?"

"Not well, but I know her friend, Angela, who I've met quite regularly. They travel together sometimes. I do know some of their other clients, and they hold Julia in high regard."

Jake struggled to comprehend what Hale was saying.

"She left while I was sleeping and I didn't get to talk to her this morning."

"That's their way, son! They like to keep a low profile during their travels. Being discreet is part of their allure, and adds to the value of their services, which is very expensive! Fortunately, the railroads have a lot of money, of which the Army pays them a large amount."

"I'd still have liked to tell her goodbye."

"Well, Rogers, I wouldn't dwell on it. Now, let's discuss your leave time here, and travel and meal vouchers. I was only able to authorize two weeks. You're technically on recruiting duty, so it wouldn't hurt if you brought back one or two candidates. Capt. Michaelis vouched for you with Col. Sturgis, who is still in nominal command of the Regiment. I'll be here for a couple if more days if you need to get in touch with me."

"Yes, Sir! We'll do our best."

"Good, now I'll expect you both back by Sunday the 15th. We need to get you back to Fort Lincoln by the beginning of September."

The waitress brought their breakfast and Jake attacked it with gusto. When they were finished, he and Mike went up to get their bags. Caddle ribbed him a little about their liaisons of the night, and bragged that his seemed very accomplished based on his previous experience. Jake ignored him and went to his room to gather his things. He carefully folded Julia's note, then picked the pillow off the bed and held it to his nose, inhaling her fragrance. He looked around wistfully, then left the room. Hale met them out front where they were going to catch the trolley back up to Stoughton's Livery Stable, and get their horses.

Jake and Caddle made sure to thank Capt. Hale for arranging their furlough, and the festivities of the previous night. Hale called Jake over, and said to him quietly

"Rogers, don't think harshly of Julia. You were fortunate to have someone like her as your first lover. Find yourself a good woman when you can. I personally haven't yet, and don't expect to while I'm still in the Army. It can be rough life for a wife, following the guidon, as I'm sure you've seen."

"Yes, Sir! Thank you, Sir! I'll bear that in mind."

"Now, go enjoy your family!"

The day was already warm, and promised to get hotter. When Jake and Caddle left Stoughton's, they headed east on Commercial Street to Jefferson Street. Mike wanted to buy some cigars at the Cigar Factory, and Jake went into Jackson's Grocery and browsed while he did. He marveled at the abundance, and selection, of foodstuffs and canned goods. He made a mental note to himself to stock up when they came back to catch the train on their return journey. They rode south along Jefferson, which Jake recalled ran all of the way through Springfield. Just to the East, stood Fairbanks Hall, where Drury College first held classes, and there were several new buildings, some still under construction. A few blocks farther south they crossed Jordan Creek, not far from where Jake used to pitch camp with his father. It was still mostly woods, but Jake remembered one of the railroad men talking about a cotton mill being built in that area. Then, they came to what Jake considered the church district, first a couple of colored churches, then several white churches just two blocks past them. The town square was just two blocks to the West, and Jake briefly considered going there, then decided he would take Mike there upon their return. They continued on south and crossed South Creek and followed the road as it turned east. When they got to the edge of town, they saw the road in front of them ran straight away towards low rolling hills and stands of trees.

"This is the mail road that goes towards Henderson. We'll follow it to the James River ford, then it keeps going pretty much east." Jake stated.

"'Tis beautiful country, Jake, reminds me a bit of Ireland, though I'm finding it a bit warm for my tastes." Mike said fanning his hat.

"We'll be in the trees after we cross the river, and it'll be cooler. We've only about ten miles left. Funny, I used to think it was a long way, back when we went in to Springfield. Now, after my travels of the last two years, it's just a morning's easy ride. It would be nice if a breeze came up, though. You'll find that it cools off nicely most evenings."

"Are your folks expecting me, also, Jake?"

"Well, I wrote them that you might be coming, so they won't be totally surprised, but I'm sure they will be a little."

They rode at a leisurely pace and as the sun rose higher, it shined in their faces, causing them to lower the brims of their hats. They stopped to water their horses when they reached the James River, then crossed over a wooden bridge into the woods on the other side. The road meandered through the countryside, making jogs here and there to go around low hills, and they eventually came to a stretch of cultivated fields.

Jake pointed, "There's a valley just on the other side of that wooded ridge ahead of us, that's where my home is. Sayers Creek runs through it all the way back up to the James River. The water is crystal clear and cool. I caught a lot of fish out of it when I was growing up."

"I could do with a bit o' fishing." Caddle remarked.

"Oh, we will! I'll show you some of my best fishing holes. We'll catch goggle eye and brown bass. Good eating, I tell ya! Look at the corn in these fields, we're just in time to have fresh roasting ears!"

"Stop Jake, me breakfast wore off, and it won't be seemly for me to meet your folks with a growling stomach."

"Oh, you needn't worry, if I know my mother, she'll be fussing about feeding us before we can get off our horses."

They continued following the road until they reached the woods again and wound around the northern edge of the ridge. They came to a drive leading off to the left and turned to follow it. It had split rail fences and rich stands of corn on either side. Blackberry bushes grew along the fence rows, loaded with ripening fruit.

"This is my father's farm land on both sides. I helped build these fences, when I was a boy. We own all the way to Sayers Creek, over to the right and all along it to the North and the next ridge line, 200 acres of rich bottom land." Jake said proudly.

Presently the drive ended, and they came to a large field with rows of fruit trees, grape vines, and some stacks of bee hives. Beyond it stood a single story wooden house, nestled among a stand of tall oaks. It was painted white and had a large covered porch, with a shimmering covering over the windows out front. A barn, several out buildings, and a corral were scattered around further on. They were all tucked up close in the shelter of tall ridges to the North and west..

"Those windows on the porch are new." Jake commented, "I wonder what's up with that?"

Two hounds came running towards them barking, as they approached the house. Jake called out to them, "Yo, Romulus! Yo, Remus! Hey boys!"

The dogs quieted and began wagging their tails and whining. Jake leaned down and talked to them. "Hey boys! How ya been? Are glad to see me?"

He looked up and saw his parents standing on the steps, watching him with smiles on their faces. He reined in and dismounted, petting the dogs and scratching their ears.

"They've missed you and so have I, Jacob!" his mother called out. She was smiling, but he could see tears in her eyes. His father helped her down off the steps, while Jake wrapped his reins around the hitching post, then walked to them.

"Hey you two! I've missed you, also!" He said as he wrapped his arms around both of them.

"Best introduce your friend, Jake." His mother said, "Mind your manners."

Jake turned to Mike, where he stood holding his horse. "This is Mike Caddle, he's the one I wrote you about. We've been helping out a captain, named Michaelis, with some training down in Louisiana. He arranged for us to get a furlough while we were in St. Louis, before heading back up to the Dakotas."

"Well, welcome Michael! It's a pleasure to meet you!"

"Likewise, Ma'am, Mr. Rogers!" Mike said nodding his head, "Your place is just as lovely as Jake here has been telling me. It reminds me a bit of back home in Ireland!"

"Oh, you're too kind, Mike. Please make yourself at home." She replied. "You two will want to freshen up and get out of those uniforms after you see to your horses. Leave them in the washroom when you're done and I'll wash them for you. Jacob you can put your things in your old room. I kept some of your clothes though I doubt that your shirts will fit you any more. You've grown a bit!"

"Well, it's not from eating too much!" Jake said with a grin.

"I can fix them for you though, or make some new ones. You can probably find some for Mike, too. I've made up pallets for you out on the porch."

"I saw the new windows, and was wondering." Jake said.

Zeb spoke up, "Yes, we decided to close in the porch, and put them up, when Frank brought us some of those new painted wire screens. The railroads have been using them to keep out soot and sparks from the passenger car windows, and he was able to get us a bargain on some. We can sit and open all the windows to enjoy the evenings, while not being eaten up by mosquitos, and pestered with flies."

"Mother wrote me that Frank was working for the railroad."

"Yes, he has a good job at the railroad yards, over in North Springfield. He's done quite well."

"You'll see him tomorrow, he comes home every weekend. He and Colleen are engaged to be married this fall." His mother said, offhand.

"Oh, really?" Jake replied, a bit stunned. "She didn't let me know that in her last letter."

"Well, Jacob, you have been a bit recalcitrant in your correspondence with us. We just have to speculate about your whereabouts most of the time."

"Now, Sarah," Zeb said, "Let's leave these lads to get settled in. They can tell us all about their travels over supper."

"I've some fresh baked bread and sliced ham for lunch. Milk and a pitcher of tea to wash it down with. For supper I'll make some of your favorites, Jacob. Fried chicken, fresh corn on the cob, sliced tomatoes, and fresh rolls with butter and honey. I can even whip up a blackberry cobbler for desert!"

"Ah, Mrs. Rogers! It's quite remarkable, that you've managed to name me most favorite dishes, also." Caddle said grinning.

"Pay him no mind, Mother. His favorite food is what ever he's eating."

Sarah laughed, "He reminds me a bit of Pat, just a smaller version."

"That's Sgt. Morse she's comparing you to, Mike. I'm not sure you should take that as a complement." Jake said.

"Oh, I do. Morse is a fine Irishman, and model soldier, don't ya know?"

"See! There you go!" Sarah chortled as she headed towards the kitchen.

"I put some beers in a gunny sack and lowered them down in the cistern. I'll go hoist them up, and meet you out under the shade tree." Zeb said.

Later on, after the two soldiers gorged themselves during supper, they all adjourned to the porch, to sit in rockers and watch the sunlight fade.The whippoorwills and hoot owls began to serenade them, while cicadas and tree frogs kept a constant refrain in the background. Lightening bugs flickered all around the grounds, and along the creek, where bullfrogs chimed in at intervals. Zeb fetched a bottle and popped the cork out.

"This is some of John Campbell's corn liquor. He fancies himself a master whiskey distiller. This is from one of his better batches that he aged in a charred oak barrel, like they use over in Kentucky. I can't vouch for the aging time, but I'll admit it's pretty smooth, and it's also a might strong. I'd go easy on it."

The men passed the bottle around and took sips. Sarah stood and announced, "That's it for me! I'll leave you men to visit." She came over to Jake and bent to kiss his cheek. "I'm so glad to see you again." She ruffled his hair, then went to Zeb and kissed him goodnight. "Don't get too carried away, we've a bunch of folks coming over tomorrow night, and I'll have breakfast and coffee going early. Good night!"

After she went in the house, Mike passed out some of his cigars. After they got them lit, they sat in silence for a while puffing on them. Eventually Zeb asked, "So how's Pat?"

"Pat is well." Jake replied, "He's back at Fort Lincoln. There's no expedition planned for this season, so I imagine he's busy finding ways to keep the men occupied."

"I just wonder how long he's going to keep soldiering? He's been at it while."

"I think that maybe he'll be done when this hitch is up. He's met a lot of people, and made some friends that might be interested in hiring him. We've spoken a little about it. His enlistment is up at the end of next year."

"How about you, Mike, are you a career man?"

"Lord no, sir. I just needed to get away from New York, and the Army was my way out. Now that I've seen more of the country, I think I'll stay out in the West somewhere. I've still got three years left to decide where."

Jake spoke up, "I'm thinking the same way, Pa. I'm almost halfway done, and I can see that there's lot's of opportunity to be had. It's just a matter of finding the right one, and going after it."

"Good, Son! Soldiering is a hard life, and it's only a matter of time before the Indians get tired of being abused. They're bound to fight back at some point. Custer's Black Hill Expedition was illegal and broke the terms of the Treaty of Laramie, from what I understand."

"Well, that may be, Pa. But you know that's not for me to decide. The Army just does what it's ordered."

"Oh, I know, the government is responsible, and I'm having doubts about the Grant Administration. What with the Panic of '73 and the railroads, Secretary Delano and the corruption in the Dept. of the Interior, and now this Whiskey Ring scandal are coming out. It doesn't play well in the newspapers, even The Springfield Patriot-Advertiser which is staunchly Republican, has been critical of the goings on!"

"We don't hear too much about that. The news is slow to reach us, and we're usually several weeks behind the times." Jake replied.

They paused to pass the bottle around and puff on their cigars, again.

"So, have you lads met General Custer?"

"Well, technically he's just a Lt. Colonel now, and we've just seen him from a distance. We did get to meet his brother Tom, who's a 1st Lieutenant, and generally well liked. They have another brother, Boston, who is some sort of contractor for the Army staying with them. We haven't been out in the field with them, but we're told they're fond of hunting and playing practical jokes on one another. Both of our companies were detached from the rest of the regiment until this April. Custer was gone on leave when we arrived at Fort Lincoln, and didn't arrive back until a few weeks before we left. We just saw him during inspections and on parades." Caddle spoke up.

"Custer's got a big house across the parade ground from the barracks. He and his wife like to throw lots of parties there for the other officers, and visitors. Seems like they had something going on constantly before we left. We got asked for fatigue details to work for Mrs. Custer quite often." Jake added. "I suppose we'll see more of him when we get back."

"Pat and I have discussed him over the years. He's of the opinion that Custer can be reckless and that he got lucky at the Washita fight." Zeb stated.

"Yes, I've heard Pat talk about that with the other senior sergeants that were there. I know that there are a few officers that don't like Custer and his style, but he keeps most of them at the other forts. We weren't exposed to regimental politics when we were at Fort Totten, but we've been having to learn about them now." Jake said. "But, like I said earlier, the campaigning season will be close to being over when we get back, so we'll probably stay at the fort. Winter comes in fast up there and I'm not looking forward to it. At least we'll have a town nearby this year."

Zeb corked the bottle and tamped out his cigar. "All right, I'm for bed. We'll need to get around early. Your Mother will be up and around early I expect. You two have a good night."

"Good night!" They both replied.

The next morning, the smells of coffee and bacon cooking wafting onto the porch roused Jake and Mike. Sarah had the table set by the time they got dressed in their civvies and sorted out. She told them to sit down when they came in the door. A basket was piled high with biscuits, a bowl of butter and a jar of preserves placed next to it in the center of the table, and also a pitcher of milk. She sat steaming mugs of coffee in front of them.

"Good Morning! Your Father has already eaten and has gone to see to the livestock, and also your horses. He said for you two to enjoy your breakfast and he'll see you in a while. I'll have eggs and bacon for you shortly. Over easy for you, Jake, how about you, Mike?"

"Over easy would be just grand, Mrs. Rogers! Thank you, you're way to kind!"

'Nonsense, and call me Sarah."

"You'll have to let out our pants if you feed us like the entire time that we're here, Mother."

"I can do that!" She replied, "And you both could use some mending on your uniforms. Some of the stitching is terrible! You both could use new shirts, that flannel is way too hot for the summer heat."

"Well, our laundresses and seamstresses, have over 60 men to accommodate, so they're pushed to patch things quickly on occasion. And, the Army deems flannel to be a fine year round fabric."

"Hmm, I'll be sure to check all of your things while you're here. Mike, yours too!"

"Aye, Sarah, I can see that you'll brook no argument. But, I'll be obliged to bother you for some tasks that I can help with, by way of repaying you."

"Well, we'll see. I may come up with something."

She carried full plates to the table, and sat them down with a flourish. "Now enjoy your breakfast!"

Jake and Mike wandered down to the barn where they found

Zeb feeding the horses in the corral. When Jake approached, the horses nickered and whinnied.

"Hey, Hector! Hey, Ulysses! You still remember me, don't you?"

He offered them a couple of sugar cubes that he'd slipped in his pocket during breakfast. Ajax reared his head and stomped his foreleg, in protest until Jake went over to give him one, also.

"Now don't be jealous, Ajax!"

"That's a good looking horse, Son." Zeb said, "Your bay is also, Mike. They mount you boys a mite better these days, then when I was trooper."

"That's because the Regiment was headquartered in Kentucky a couple of years ago. Custer traveled the area looking at horses and procuring them. He's an avid horseman and likes to have his men well mounted. Each company is mounted on different colored horses. My Company D rides Blacks and Mike's Company I rides light Bays."

They walked over to where their saddles were and retrieved brushes and curry combs, then started grooming the horses.

Zeb said, "When you get done, let's go for ride in the buggy and I'll show you around. I put the north forty in wheat this year and it promises to be a good crop, though I was worried when we had that big rain come through last month."

"Yeh, we heard a little bit about that, in Springfield. They said Wilson's Creek was out of its banks and flooded out several businesses."

"Fortunately, Sayers Creek comes up from south of here and we didn't get as much rain as they did north of Springfield. And, we've not had the grasshoppers reach us, either. I've been reading about how devastating they've been out to the west of here, and out on the Plains."

As they made their way around the farm, Jake pointed out his old swimming and fishing holes along the creek to Mike. They circled back around to the south and got back on the mail road, following it to where the schoolhouse and local church stood. Just past them was the general store which also served as a post office. Sarah was waiting there on the front steps.

"Good, you're just in time to help me with a few things" She said.

"Why didn't you just ride with us, Mother?" Jake asked.

"I walk here all the time, son. Now come help me."

They went inside where Zeb checked on his mail. Sarah had several bags of food had also bought some more of the beer that Zeb had given them yesterday. The bottles had large capital *A* pierced by an eagle with spread wings, and the wooden crate they were in was labeled, *E. Anheuser & Co., St. Louis, Missouri.* They carried them outside and were putting it all in the buggy when a rider came down the road towards them. He waved at them as he stopped.

"Hey! Jake is that you?"

Jake looked up and recognized Frank Armstrong. "Yeh, it's me Frank."

"When did you get in?"

"We got into Springfield on Thursday afternoon and rode over yesterday. This my friend and fellow trooper Mike Caddle! Mike, this is my old friend Frank Armstrong, we met when I first moved to Henderson."

Frank dismounted, hitched his horse and came over to shake hands.

"Pleased to meet you, Mike." Frank said, "Gee, I wish I'd known, I'd have shown you guys around. Where'd you stay?"

"We stayed at The Metropolitan Hotel." Jake replied.

Frank's eyebrows rose, "Whoa! That's the best hotel in town! The Army must be paying better, these days."

"Well, the officer we were with had connections with the railroad and he got them for us."

Sarah came over to the buggy, and seeing Frank she said, "Frank, you come over to the farm later on. We're roasting a pig tonight and having a little get together for Jake."

Frank hesitated a bit then replied, "Ah, well, sure. I had something else going, but I can probably change it."

"Don't worry, I saw Colleen a few minutes ago and she's coming. I already told Jake about you two." Sarah commented.

Frank looked over at Jake, who said. "Yeh, she told me. I'm happy for you both! I'm off to who knows where for the next couple of years. You two will probably have kids by the next time I come back around."

Frank gave Jake a relieved smile. "Well, then we'll see you later."

He got back on his horse and trotted off.

"You did well, Son." His mother said, patting his arm. "Those two both worry about you."

Mike, who had been standing there observing, said with a laugh, "Now ya needn't worry about mentioning your friend Miss Holly, back at Ft. Lincoln, Jake m'boy!"

Sarah raised her eyebrows and exclaimed, "Indeed! Well, you must tell me about this young woman, Jacob!"

Jake looked at Mike with chagrin and said, "Thanks, Mike!"

Zeb came out of the store with a newspaper and a few letters, and said, "All aboard, let's go home and have some lunch, Mother!"

The spent the rest of the afternoon, getting the fire pit ready for cooking. One of the neighbors brought over two whole rib roasts that Sarah had arranged for. They got a good bed of coals going and then put the roasts on spits, which they hung over the pit. Jake and Mike took turns to keep the spits rotating every few minutes while Zeb tended the fire and kept the meat mopped with Sarah's secret basting sauce. Jake and Mike set up some board tables under the big shade oak and then took the beer to the creek where they submerged it in the cool flowing water, taking the opportunity to go for a swim. When they got back Sarah put them to work setting up stools and chairs. The sun began sinking below the ridge line to the West, and a slight breeze continued to swirl. A few neighbors showed up, and Jake was introduced to them by Zeb.

"This is Thurlo Watts, and Jefferson Williams, they've got land to the west and south of here. We've just gone into partnership and have purchased one of those new fangled combination reaper/binders, and a horse drawn threshing machine we bought from H. O. Dow & Company in Springfield. We'll get to try them out before long, and if they work as well as we think, we're going to hire out once we get our harvests in."

Jake shook hands with them and nodded politely.

"So Zeb here tells us you're a cavalry trooper with Custer." Thurlo said.

"Yes, I'm in the 7th Cavalry." Jake answered.

"Seen any wild Indians?" Williams asked. "That's a fancy knife sheath on your belt!"

"Oh, most Indians aren't wild, they just live different, than us. Most aren't too keen on farming. The knife was a gift from a friend, who's part Gros Ventre"

"What the heck is a Gross Venetray?"

"They're an Indian tribe up in Montana Territory, he was a scout for us." Jake answered.

"What's it like up there, Jake?" asked Thurlo.

Jake spent several minutes talking to them, and telling them about the Boundary Survey. Neither man had even heard about it. He spotted Frank and Colleen coming down the driveway in a buckboard, and took the opportunity to excuse himself, then went over to where they were parking the wagon. Colleen was dressed in a light blue, flowery dress, and had a matching bonnet covering her long brown tresses. She saw Jake and smiled.

"Hello, Jake!"

He reached up to help her down, taking her hand, and said, "Hey Colleen, good to see you."

Frank got down and tied the horse up, then said, "We brought a couple of watermelons. I'll go see where Sarah wants them." He then headed towards the house.

"So, I hear that you know about me and Frank." Colleen stated.

Jake looked at her and nodded his head.

"Are you mad at me?" She asked.

Jake smiled, "Oh, I was a bit surprised. But, you know, I can't fault you. I'm the one that wanted to go see other things. You and Frank both fit here, and make a fine couple. I do hope that you'll still write to me from time to time."

Colleen stepped towards him and put her hand on his cheek. "Of course I will! And you have to promise to do the same, and a little more often than what you have been."

"I'll try! It's difficult to find time when we're out in the field, and finding a way to post a letter is spotty at best."

"Well, please try, we want to hear from you."

Frank came back from the house, "Sarah wants us to go put them in the creek. I'll drive the buckboard over and wrap them in gunnysacks and tie them to a tree."

"I'll go with you," Jake said, "and we can bring back some beers."

Colleen said, "I'll see you two later. I'm going to go help Sarah."

On the way over to the creek, Jake asked, "So, what's your job on the railroad, Frank?"

"Right now, I'm an assistant to Mr. C. O. Ingraham, he's the foreman over the Western Division of the A & P. which is the tracks from Springfield to Vinita, over in the Indian Territory. He's going to be in charge of the new Bridge Shop that's being planned for next year. All of the materials used for bridges and buildings will be assembled and framed there."

"So, do you get to ride on the trains, like you always wanted?"

"Oh, yes! I go over to a new town in Indian Territory called, Vinita, several times a month and occasionally up to St. Louis for meetings. I'm also learning Morse code and how to operate a telegraph, wherever the railroads go, the telegraph lines follow. That's how we coordinate our schedules so it's very important in railroading. They say in the next ten years we'll be all the way to California!"

"It sounds to me like you've found your calling."

"Yep, I think so. I'm staying at a boarding house right now, but I'm looking to buy a house in North Springfield."

"So is Colleen fine with that?"

"Yes, she's been offered a job at Drury College as a teaching assistant."

Jake nodded his head, but didn't say anything.

"So how about you, Jake? What are your plans?"

"Well, for couple more years, the Army. I did learn quite a bit about surveying when I was helping out on the Northern Boundary Survey over the last couple of years. I enjoyed doing that."

"There you go! Let me tell you, the land is where the real money is at for the railroads. The government grants the land to the railroad and they get to sell it. It has to be surveyed before they can. Surveyors are going to be in great demand, as the railroads expand. Plus, they get to see all of the prime parcels before anyone else."

"I can see the benefits of that. During my travels, I'm learning a little about the way railroads operate, also. The Army is one of their best customers. They need us to protect them as they keep laying tracks west."

Frank replied, "Yes they do, so it might be a good way to make some contacts."

They reached the creek, and got busy swapping out the watermelon for beer, then headed back. While they were gone, a game of horseshoes had been started and the players were enthusiastic about the arrival of some refreshments. Caddle was being targeted as a rookie, but Jake knew that he was anything but, having seen him win many contests down in Louisiana. Jake watched for a bit, then went to take Zeb a beer.

"Looks like it's goin to be a nice evening, Pa!"

Zeb took the proffered beer and replied, "Yes it does! I saw you and Frank together. Everything all right between you two?"

"Oh sure! I've got no hard feelings, I'm the one that left."

"I'm glad to hear you say that. Good friends are hard to find, and I know they both are. Frank is a fine young man and he and Colleen make a good couple. They come over and help me and your mother out when they can. Now go tell your mother that the meat is almost ready, and she can start sending the rest of the food out."

The following week, Jake and Mike spent their days helping Zeb on the farm, and when they weren't, they roamed the countryside fishing and hunting small game. Jake dug out his old .32 caliber cap and ball squirrel rifle, and they took turns bagging squirrels and rabbits. Jake showed Mike how to find and catch small crawdads under rocks and backwater pools, in the creek. Then they used them to catch brown bass, and goggle eye perch. Sarah cooked it all for them, and was constantly spoiling them with her baking skills.

CHAPTER 22

Springfield and North Springfield, Missouri - Week of Mid August 1875

Frank had talked them into coming back over to Springfield on Friday, to tour the railroad yards. They decided to take Sarah's buggy along so they could bring back the items on the shopping list she was putting together for them. They left Friday morning, planning to get there by noon. Denton's Livery Stable, was across the street from the Metropolitan Hotel where they used one of the vouchers provided by Capt. Hale to book a room. Jake took Mike over to the St. Louis Street House for lunch on the square, and while they ate lunch, Jake told him the story of the Hickock gunfight.

"I'll be damned! You're telling me Sgt. Morse saw the whole thing?" Mike asked Jake, "I'll have to razz him when we get back, I knew he'd been around for a while, but not that long!"

"Pat's an old hand all right, he's seen a lot. Capt. Hale knows him from the old days in Kansas. I'll bet those two both have stories on each other. Let's go to work on Mother's shopping list, most of the stores are handy from here. Then we can catch the trolley up to North Springfield to meet Frank."

They went over to College Street to drop off a list at Cass & Co. Grocery and told them that they would be back to pick the goods up on their way out of town the next day. They walked back over to the square and went into Peck and Clark to buy some Butterick dress patterns for Sarah and Colleen. Dropping down South Street, they came to Lee & Co. Merchant Tailors where they looked at some civilian clothes and some other items that were not usually available at the Post Traders. Jake picked out a new wide brimmed grey Stetson hat. While Mike was trying on a pair of whipcord trousers, Jake went across the street to J. H. Koch Jewelry, and picked out a small oval shaped, silver locket and chain. The jeweler agreed to engrave it with a stylized *H* and have it ready for Jake to pick up in the morning. Capt. Hale had seen to it that they'd been paid before they left St.

Louis, so they were fairly flush, especially with the vouchers he had given them to take care of their food and lodging. They made their way back to the hotel to put away their purchases. Mike went up to his room, and Jake went down to the post office and mailed a letter to Holly that he'd written. Stephen's Bookstore was next door, and on an impulse he went in. He found a book on Surveying and one on Telegraph procedures, deciding to buy both. He went up to the room and found Mike standing on the balcony looking out over Springfield.

"This isn't a bad place, Jake! You know I've lived in Dublin and New York, but never a small city like this. It's easy to get around and everyone is so friendly. Not to mention that you're only a few minutes away from being out in the countryside."

"Well, the biggest places that I've been to are St. Louis and St. Paul. I didn't see much of them except for barracks, train stations, looking out from a train car window, but I can see your point."

"Aye! Da'ya think you'll come back here after the Army?"

"You know, Mike, I don't know. I've seen and done more in the last two years, then Frank, and other people around here have ever dreamed of. I'm still thrilled with seeing new horizons and what lies beyond them. I'm waiting for something that will cause that to go away. You must feel the same way."

"Indeed, my friend! Come on, let's go look up, Frank."

They met Frank at the A&P Railroad shops which were located at the east end of Commercial Street on a 40 acre tract in North Springfield. Frank was very enthusiastic as he showed them the roundhouse that could accommodate twelve locomotives, and the repair shops where five could be worked on at once. Jake could tell that his friend was still bitten by the railroad bug. He bragged that the machine and blacksmith shops were equipped with the latest in support tooling. Frank told them that the complex employed over 100 men and construction was underway for additional facilities. They had toured most of the complex when the end of day whistle blew and the workers began filing out. Just west along Commercial, several taverns and cafes were located that catered to the workers, and they began filling with the Friday after work crowd. Jake, Frank, and Mike strolled down the street in the direction of the passenger terminal where they'd arrived the week before. Frank waved them across the street to one of the taverns, which sported a large sign that proclaimed it as *The Caboose.* They followed Frank, who led them around to the east side of the building where a covered area was filled with tables. There was a crowd gathered round, most with mugs of beer and plates of food.

"It's Friday Night Fish fry!" Frank yelled over the hubbub, "They serve beer, and all the fish and chips that you can eat for only 6 bits cents, until 7 o'clock!"

Mike smiled broadly, "Well, now, I could do with a good batch of fish and chips. But tis hard to find them made like back in the auld Sod!"

"I don't know about that but Mickey, the owner, is Irish and a Catholic as are many of these fellows. He started doing it last year, on Fridays, and it became quite popular."

Frank led them inside where the queue was formed up and they waited to be served up. The tavern was packed and after they got their beers and fish platters they made their way back outside and found a spot at one of the tables that some of Frank's friends had held for them. He introduced everyone and they sat down.

"So, you fellows are soldiers, eh?" asked one of them.

"Yes, we're with the 7th Cavalry." Jake answered.

"Frank says you've been out west with General Custer. Have you fought any Indians?"

"No, but we've seen a few. Most of them are pretty peaceful right now, except for a few Sioux. They've raiding a few gold miners that are trespassing in the reservation on their way to the Black Hills."

"Really, I've been thinking of havin' a go at that m'self." said one of the others, a bright haired red head.

Mike looked over at him, "Ya might want to reconsider, laddie, if you're partial to the flaming hair of yours!"

"Hear that Red?" laughed another, "You'd be an easy target, they'd see ya coming for miles!"

That brought a round of laughter from the group.

"Ah, youse, can kiss my flaming red arse! All of you!" and hoisted his mug to them.

"So what's the Army paying these days?" asked one of the others.

Caddle answered, "Not nearly enough! $13.00 to start."

"That's not too bad, that's about what we make for a 50 hour week. How many hours do you have to work?"

Jake almost choked on his beer, then said, "You misunderstood Mike, that's $13.00 a month. I only make $2.00 more as a sergeant."

The railroad workers, all looked aghast, "Shit, man, you boys work cheap!' one of them exclaimed.

"But the room and board is free ain't it, Jake?" Mike laughed, "Cheers lads!"

After they left the tavern, Frank took to them some of the

residential areas located just south of the railroad tracks where houses were going up. He was thinking about putting a down payment on one of the lots, so he and Colleen could build a house after they were married. They took State Street west just north of the railroad tracks until they were opposite from the freight depot. As they started cutting across the rail yards, Jake saw some men, off to the side in a grove of small trees, camped in rough shelters, and gathered around a fire cooking.

"What's up with those men, Frank?"

"Oh, they're vagrants. They hop the freight trains and travel around. They seem to have little camps outside every rail town. They're mostly harmless and just looking for work. From time to time, the sheriff tries to clean them out but they come back."

Mike looked over at Jake and said. "There may be some lads we can recruit."

Jake nodded, "Good idea! We'll go see them before we leave for St. Louis."

They ended up back on Commercial Street and Frank pointed out some of the businesses, that had sprung up as a result of their proximity to the A&P.

"That building and yard, over there, belongs to Mr. J. M. Doling. He's our largest shipper west of St. Louis! He also has a hardware and dry goods store, and Delmonico's Restaurant."

"Yes, we met Mr. Doling, and had dinner with him there the day we arrived." Jake said, nonchalantly.

Frank's eyebrows rose and he looked at Jake appraisingly, "Really?"

"Yes, our Captain was meeting with him, and Mr. Doling invited us to eat with them. He seemed like a nice gent."

"Well, he's probably the wealthiest man in this area. He sells a lot of grain to the Army and we ship it up to Quartermaster Department in St. Louis, for him."

Jake told Frank about how Mr. Fisk was an ex-Custer staff officer, and they speculated about the close connections that the railroads and the Army appeared to have.

"I suppose that having the Army as a steady customer is good way to make money." Frank conceded. "I'm starting to appreciate how important having connections is. I've been watching my boss, Mr. Ingraham, also. He's always saying to me, "There are wheels within wheels, young Mr. Armstrong.""

Jake nodded his head in agreement. "So what now, young Mr. Armstrong?"

"Well, there's some saloons out on the edge of town, but I'm told they're pretty rough joints. Other than that, most everything else there is to do is in downtown Springfield. We can go there for a while, but I have to work in the morning so I can't stay out too late. My room is just over there on the second floor, if you want to come look at it?"

"That's okay, Frank, it'd probably just remind me of my room back at Fort Lincoln, just four walls and a bed. We want to get an early start back to Henderson. Mother was wanting some of the things on her list, and we told Pa that we'd be back to help him tomorrow afternoon. Let's call it a night and we'll see you later, over in Henderson."

"Sounds good to me. I'll see you then." Frank replied, looking at his watch. "The trolley should be along shortly."

The rest of their time in Henderson had flown by, after they returned from the day in Springfield. He and Mike had pushed Zeb to let them help out with whatever jobs he had to get done on the farm. There had been a going away party on the last weekend, and it seemed like half of the community showed up. He had been showered with presents: shirts, neck scarves, socks, and gloves. Sarah had mended both he and Mike's uniforms and made them new flannel shirts. She'd also knitted them both wool caps, apparently horrified by some of their tales about the frigid Dakota winters. When Wednesday rolled around, Jake had exchanged a tearful goodbye with his mother. She gave him one last desperate hug and brushing back tears she said, "You be careful up there! I expect that I'll not see you again for a couple more years. So, you promise me to write more often, Jacob!" She stood on the porch waving goodbye, as Zeb mounted up and rode out with them. When they got to the James River, they got off to water the horses. Zeb went over to shake hands with Mike and they exchanged goodbyes. He turned and walked over to Jake.

"Your Mother will be quite vexed if something should happen to you, I will too! Give my best regards to Pat!" He put on a big smile and said, "I want you to remember me smiling, and not with tears in my eye. Now go on!" He got on his horse and rode back in the direction of Henderson.

They rode on into Springfield and opted to go on up to North Springfield where they would be close to the Railroad Depot, and Frank. They made their way to Stoughton's livery stable and checked the horses, then went to the North Springfield House and found that they had a room available for their use for two nights. Their plan was to spend the next day roaming around the rail yards and try to find some recruits. Then do some last minute shopping at the grocery and dry goods stores looking for items to take back up to Ft. Lincoln. Frank came by and took them to Brunaugh's

Restaurant for supper. The next day after breakfast at the boarding house, they dressed in their uniforms, and went to the stables for their horses. They rode over in the direction of the vagrant campground.

"So, how do ya think we should approach these men?" Caddle asked.

"Let's see if they're hungry. We can buy them supper. A man is always more amiable when his stomach's full."

"Aye, that's true!"

As the neared the camp, several men took off running into the brush. Jake waved his arms in an all clear motion, but they ignored it. Several others just stood watching as they rode up.

"You fellas, lost? They're no Injuns here 'bouts, that I know of." One of the group said smiling.

"No, we're looking to see if any of you would like to join up." Jake stated.

"Well, I hear tell, that soldierin' ain't much fun."

"Well, I don't expect that hopping freight trains, and scrounging for food and shelter every day is much fun, either." Jake replied.

"That is a good point."

"We're with the 7th Cavalry and headed back to St. Louis tomorrow. I'll pay for supper tonight for any man that wants to consider joining up. There's a paid trip to St. Louis on a passenger car, three meals a day and a roof over your head waiting at the other end. The 7th is up in the Dakota Territory, that's where you'd end up. Lots of opportunities up there that man can turn to after his hitch is up. Farming and cattle, land is cheap, there's still buffalo hunting, and the railroads are pushing farther west."

"I'll bet there's Injuns, too. I'm pretty partial to my hair."

"I'll not deny it. They're the reason we're there. Tell your friends that ran off about our offer."

"They thought you was railroad bulls, come to bust up our camp. I'll tell them, but some don't speak English too good."

Caddle grinned, "Ya know, we don't really care. Many of our lads are from across the water, m'self included. Tis a good way to see the country, besides scrounging around next to a rail siding. Pass the word, we'll be over outside *The Caboose*, enjoying a beer or two!"

They'd returned to Jefferson Barracks with three recruits in tow, a skinny young Irishman and two Germans with limited English vocabularies. But Captain Hale was quite pleased when they reported to him.

"I hoped you two would come back with some bodies. That really helps me justify using you two."

"So what now, Sir? Do we wait around here for a while, or head back up to our outfits?" Jake asked.

"Let me check on getting you back up to Fort Lincoln. We're planning on shipping the men being trained right now up to the Regiment in early October, so there's no sense for you two to stay here. Besides, the situation is getting worse in the Black Hills. They estimate hundreds of miners are already up there and that number is growing. Captain Benteen just hauled in several hundred of them and escorted them back to Fort Randall. He sent out a telegram as he was leaving for Fort Rice and that the miners were probably headed back to the Black Hills as soon as he was gone. There are a lot of rumors floating around that there will probably be some kind of campaign next season. General Terry is headed out to Omaha to join a Commission headed by Senator Allison, of Ohio. They're going up to the Red Cloud Reservation next month to meet with the Lakota Sioux tribes about buying the Black Hills, or at least the mining rights, but I doubt that they'll have much success. I hear that Sioux are asking for way more than the government is willing to pay!"

"It doesn't sound good. From what little I know, both the Lakota and Northern Cheyenne consider the Black Hills to be sacred ground."

"Well, I guess we'll see. I'm going in to St. Louis for the weekend, and I'll see if I can come up with some train tickets for you. In the mean time, you two can do what you want for a couple of days"

"Thank you, Sir." Jake said. "We'd like to get back while it's still good weather up there."

When they got back to the NCO quarters where they'd stored their gear, Jake had several letters from Holly waiting for him. He noted the postmarks and saw that first was dated shortly after he left Lincoln, and the others followed at weekly intervals. He felt a slight twinge of guilt that he'd only written to her a few times. He waited until Mike left on an errand to open them, and read them in order. They began with brief descriptions of her daily activities, the weather, and were full of news and gossip relating to Fort Lincoln. It seems that the Custer's female houseguests from back in Monroe, had been given the run of the fort and that they were quite scandalous in their treatment of all the bachelor officers, and even some of the married ones if certain rumors were to be believed. They'd visited the store and were not very friendly, even though Holly had took pains to be extra courteous. A large camping and picnic excursion to the Little Heart River had been put together for them and Holly mentioned some of the items that had been purchased from the store. Her Uncle Bob got upset because he suspected that many of the supplies were smuggled in from merchants over in Bismarck, particularly alcoholic beverages. She said that Capt. Weir and Sgt. Morse had stopped by several times and were always sure to visit for a while. Her uncle was still taking her and Kate to practice shooting pistols and she was starting to fancy herself a decent shot. She wondered what he was doing a lot, and after she got his first letter in reply, wanted to know all about Louisiana. Her letters always closed with declarations of her fondness for him, and how much she missed him and hoped to see him before she had to leave for school. Evidently, she'd put a dab of her Florida Water on each one, and a faint fragrance of lavender wafted from each envelope as Jake opened them. When Caddle returned he got a whiff.

"What's that I'm smelling, Jake? It wouldn't be coming from those letters, now would it?"

Jake nodded, "Holly has been writing me every week, and I'm just now getting them."

"Well, lad, we've been out and about a wee bit, now haven't we? What did she write about?"

Jake proceeded to tell him the high points of the letters and skipped over the more personal ones.

"I'd say she's taken a liking to you. Too bad she's off to school when we get back."

"Yes, it is!"

The following Wednesday, Jake stood just outside the lobby of the St. Louis railroad depot on the passenger platform waiting for their train to start boarding passengers. Mike had taken the horses back to the livestock cars to load them, and Jake was watching their bags. He watched the people around him juggling their luggage and as they hustled to catch their connections. The Union Depot had just opened in June, and it was already proving to be unable to handle the 52 departures and arrivals of rail traffic that tried to flow through it on a daily basis. This was Jakes third trip leaving from this station and he still marveled at the hustle and bustle. Frank had given him a Railroad watch, with bold black numerals and hands, as a present. He took it out of his pocket and checked the time, it was almost time to board.

His thoughts drifted back to his visit home and a conversation he'd had with Zeb. They'd been sitting out under the big shade oak sharpening reaper blades, while Mike tending the horses.

"Well, Son, You're almost halfway through your tour now. Have you given any thought to what you are gonna do when it's up? You're not thinking of staying in are you?"

"No, I don't think so. I set out to travel and see the West. It's a little early but I'm considering trying my hand at surveying. I learned a lot helping Lt. Greene up on the border and liked it."

"You've certainly seen a large part of the country."

Jake looked up from his filing, "Yes, that's true, but it looks like I'll probably be at Fort Lincoln for the rest of my time. Of course that depends on what the Sioux do."

"Have you had any dealings with them?"

"Some, there are many different bands, some live on reservations, the rest continue to roam father west, for the most part in what they call the unceded lands that are reserved for the use of all the Indians in the region. They're the ones everyone is concerned about. They think that as long as they stay out there things won't change."

"So, you think that there's gonna be trouble?" Zeb asked.

"The Indians, and I'm talking about all of the different tribes, have been living on the lands up there for generations. A good friend of mine, named Val, is half Indian. He explained to me that all of the tribes are being pressured by the continued expansion of the railroads, and the settlers that follow. Their way of life is being threatened and they are being faced with change. Some have excepted that it is inevitable, and are trying to adapt. The biggest problem is that treaties are being ignored, promised annuities and supplies are not being delivered. Crooked, inept Indian Agents and Traders appointed by politicians from back east are causing the biggest problems. This aggravates the situation on the reservations, driving some of the tribes to abandon them and to go join back up with the roaming tribes and revert to the old ways."

"So what you're saying is that they are slowly being backed into a corner." Zeb said thoughtfully.

"Exactly! And to make matters worse, the buffalo herds that they depend on for food, are getting over hunted. I personally have seen hundreds killed in just a few days."

"Sounds to me like a keg of gunpowder waiting on a fuse."

"I'm afraid you're right, Pa."

"Well, I hope you don't get caught up in the explosion."

Jake's thoughts were interrupted by Mike who finally showed up, and they stood waiting to board.

"It's a good thing that we that we didn't find anything else to tote back, or we'd need a pack horse!" Caddle said eyeing their bags.

"Yeh, we keep it up, we may have to hire a wagon when we get to Bismarck."

Jake heard light footsteps behind him and turned to see a woman carrying a parasol. She was wearing a blue and white sailors bonnet with an upturned brim, trimmed with flowers and broad blue ribbon tied in a bow under her chin. Her dress was light blue, with a narrow waist and flowing bustle, Her dark hair trailed down her back from under the bonnet. She looked at Jake and asked.

"I say, Sergeant, do you know if this is where one would board the train to St. Paul?"

Detecting the slight English accent, Jake did a double take as she focused her large dark eyes on his and smiled.

"Yes, Ma'am, it would be." He replied, "That is where I am bound, also."

"I thought you might be, a friend told me that many soldiers are traveling there." She said brightly.

"Your friend, wouldn't happen to be in the Army, also?"

"Why yes, he does! He is an officer in the cavalry, I believe."

Out of the corner of his eye, Jake noticed Mike turn and move away.

He said quietly, "And how are you, Julia?"

"Well, I have been called that on occasion. Let us use that name, Jacob. I'm quite well. I suppose you are wondering how I come to be here?"

Jake nodded his head, "Ah, yes I am."

"I've business in St. Paul and our mutual friend informed me of your schedule when I saw him a few nights ago. I thought it would make my trip less tedious if I had a companion, and you might also. So, I arranged my schedule to coincide."

Jake smiled and replied, "I like you're thinking, it would be my pleasure to accompany you."

"Oh, I was thinking a bit more than that. You see, my current employer arranged for a private suite in a Pullman Hotel Car for my use. I think we can avail ourselves of the privacy, and find clever ways to pass the time." She replied with a twinkle in her eyes.

"Your employer must be quite wealthy."

"Yes, one might say that he is extremely well connected in the railroad business. My car is near the end of the train, just forward of the caboose. I'll notify the porter that you'll be coming." Julia said, as she turned and strolled away, twirling the parasol.

Mike came back over smiling, and said, "Isn't that your lady friend from our little Springfield frolic?"

Jake looked at him, still a little taken aback, and replied, "Indeed it is."

After he filled Mike in on Julia's invitation, they agreed that Mike would look after their gear, and mounts. He patted Jake on the back.

"You'll owe me a major favor m' bucko! Now, were I you, I'd be making a beeline to follow that lass. I'll see you in St. Paul!"

Julia hadn't exaggerated when she had said that she was in a suite. There was sitting area, a separate bedroom, and a private washroom. The white jacketed porter, a middle aged black man, attended to providing meals and refreshments, and had already furnished a bottle of champagne before Jake arrived. Shortly after the train left the station, Julia introduced Jake to the intricacies of disrobing a fully dressed woman, and proceeded to educate him further on satisfying one. During a lull, they laid in bed rocking to and fro slightly with the motion of the railcar.

"So, my dear! Are you heading straight out west to your unit at Fort Lincoln immediately, or will you be in St. Paul for a while?" Julia asked.

"As far as I know, I'll be going straight on to Lincoln. How about you, will this be a short trip?"

"I'm not sure. I've been retained to provide companionship to a German investor who is looking to acquire railroad lands to market over seas. It depends on his schedule, and whether he elects to go look at the properties. I just came to an arrangement with the Northern Railroad and will reside in St.Paul from time to time."

Jake nodded his head, "I see. You seem to be well informed about your clients."

"Yes, I stand to benefit if he buys, it's part of my job. Do you disapprove, Jacob?"

"No, I was just wondering why you chose me to accompany you on the way up."

"Let's just say that you're a work in progress and I wanted to help you along. And, you remind me of someone that was dear to me years ago."

"Well, you've altered my whole perception on women. I won't ever forget you. Thank you, Julia."

She leaned over and whispered in his ear, "Good, and my real name is Vanessa, and here's your next lesson." She began to kiss his chest, and then began to work lower.

They spent the rest of the trip in the bedroom, only dressing to take meals in the sitting room. They talked and Jake found himself telling Vanessa about his adventures on the Boundary Survey, about Pat, Val, and

Lt. Greene. He described the magnificent vistas, herds of buffalo, desert stretches, and also the harshness of the weather, terrible rations and lack of water. He told her of the drudgery of Army garrison life, and how he came to be on the Louisiana mission. She listened patiently the whole while, occasionally becoming caught up in his enthusiasm. He even told her about Colleen, and Holly. She even suggested that he try being a bit more romantic with Holly, and gave him some examples. From time to time, George the porter, discretely checked in on them. Jake noted that he clearly doted on Vanessa and commented on it.

"George is a dear. His real name is Moses, but people tend to call all Pullman porters, George, so he just goes by it. We've traveled several times together." Vanessa told him.

"Well, this is some way to travel, I can see why you like it."

"Yes, and it's more fun when I get to pick my traveling companion!"

"Lucky Me!" replied Jake.

George knocked quietly on the bedroom door.

"Miz Vanessa, we'll be gettin' to da station in St. Paul in about an hour. Let me know if you be needin' anything."

Vanessa who was dressing, called out, "Okay, Moses. Thank you!"

Jake was laying on the bed, propped up on the pillows admiring the show.

"I'm ruined, you know. I'll never be able to look at a woman again without wondering what she has on underneath."

Vanessa grinned, "And you'll be comparing them to me!"

"Most probably!"

"Good, then I know you won't forget me."

"Not likely that is going to happen." replied Jake, pointing a finger at his head, "You're etched in my memory."

Vanessa went over and sat on the bed near Jake. She reached for her handbag on the night stand, look out a piece of paper and handed it to him. He read it.

V. Blake
1500 Northern Pacific Road
Brainerd, Minnesota

"The Northern will forward letters to me. Please write me on occasion, Jacob. I'd like to know that you're safe. In my travels I overhear some rather privileged information on occasion. There is much afoot out in your west and the railroads will not be stopped. There are forces at work at the highest levels of power that drive everything. The Indian tribes will be moved aside one way or the other. I lost a dear friend back in 1868 due to similar events."

"Oh, sorry to hear about that, where was he killed?"

Vanessa stared off at the window and said, "Down in New Zealand, fighting the Maori tribes. They are a primitive people, similar to your Indians. They fought modern progress and lost, but they fought very hard. Jamie was a young officer in the 14th Regiment of Foot, and was killed in an ambush." She turned and looked at Jake, "You remind me very much of him."

Jake was silent for a while, then put his hand on Vanessa's shoulder. "He was very special to you, wasn't he?"

"Yes, we were to be engaged upon his return."

Vanessa was quiet and then turned and smiled brightly at Jake, "There now, enough of that, dear boy. Let us adjourn to the sitting room. Where you can enjoy more of Moses' good food, before you have to go back to your Army rations."

When the time came to get off at the station, Vanessa hugged him fiercely and whispered in his ear. "Do try and be careful, Jacob. Please try and jot me a few lines from time to time."

Jake hugged her back and saw Mike leading the horses towards them.

"I have to go Vanessa, and you do too. Take care, and thank you!"

CHAPTER 23

Bismarck, Dakota Territory - September 1, 1875

After their travels and spending time in the middle of the country, Jake watched out the windows and was struck by the contrast of the treeless, barren landscape as they approached Bismarck. When their train finally pulled into the Depot building there, Jake saw Murray Johnson, his acquaintance from the Northern Pacific, standing on the platform looking at his watch. He and Caddle dismounted from the train and walked over towards him.

"Excuse me, but can you tell me the time, sir?"

Murray looked up in irritation, them recognizing Jake, he grinned and replied, "Well look here! Where in the hell have you been, Rogers?"

"I've been on detached service since June. I heard that you working here in Bismarck now."

"Yep, I got transferred during the summer. There's lots of things going on around here these days. I assume you're bound for the fort?"

"Yes, we have to go get our horses off first, then we'll head that way."

"Well, go do it and then we'll go grab a beer. You can tell me what you've been up to, and I'll bring you up to speed on things around here."

Jake nodded his head and replied, "Sounds good, where do you want to meet?"

"Meet me at Forster's, it's across the street from here on Main. The food is decent, plus they've got cold beer and I'm buying!" Murray said.

After rounding up their mounts Jake and Mike went to Camp Hancock and checked to see if there was a supply wagon going to Fort Lincoln. Jake found the commissary sergeant, one of Pat Morse's and Top Martin's smuggling network and bribed him with a good bottle of Kentucky whiskey that they'd bought for just that purpose. Jake arranged for him to see that extra bags, and a footlocker that they'd acquired at Jefferson Barracks, would be delivered across the river to the NCO Quarters at the fort. They checked with him to see when the next ferry ran, which was at 5:00, then headed back down Main Street to meet Murray. Jake noted that there were several new brick buildings going up, in contrast with the older wood framed ones. When they reigned in front Forster's, Murray was sitting out front on the porch, sipping a beer.

"You fellas look pretty fresh compared to the soldiers I see around here. Fresh uniforms, shiny boots, I'm guessing that where ever you were, it was better than around here."

"I suppose it was. We were moving around a lot, mostly on trains. We were in St. Louis last."

"Ah, they have good beer there! Well, come sit and I'll fill you in on the local goings on."

Jake and Mike dismounted and tethered their horses. They grabbed a couple of chairs and sat down. Murray signaled the waitress to bring a round of beers, and they ordered food.

"Well, the biggest news today is that Secretary of War Belknap just arrived from upriver on the *Key West*. He has been on a tour of the Montana Territory. General Terry has been here all week over at the Capitol Hotel waiting for him. Belknap's staying there tonight, and is going over to Fort Lincoln tomorrow to call on Custer, then he and Terry are headed out on a special train on Friday that I've arranged."

"I'm glad that we're not over there right now. Custer will have everyone jumping around polishing doorknobs and spittoons." Caddle said.

"Word has it that Custer ain't too thrilled about this visit. He's still suspicious of Belknap for forcing that new post trader on him last year. Particularly, about how much prices went up on everything."

"I know Bob Seip, he's just running the operation for the Leighton Brothers up at Fort Buford. They set the prices." Jake said.

"Ah, I've dealt with Alvin Leighton, he's a crafty one. He ships a lot of his merchandise in with us. He's got quite a little empire going." Murray stated.

"So what else is going on? We heard rumors at Jefferson Barracks about some big powwow with the Sioux that's being set up."

"Yes, it's down near the Red Cloud Agency down on the White River. It was supposed to start last month, but I've heard word that the Sioux are feuding with each other over participating. General Terry is to be part of the commission and it seems interesting to me that he is here waiting on Belknap. Custer has been over several times meeting with him. Terry is headed east on the train Friday, but is scheduled to rendezvous with the other Commissioners, in Cheyenne in a couple of weeks. He hasn't had much to say about it. This weeks edition of the Bismarck Tribune front page news headlines are mostly about how easy it is to find gold in the Black Hills, and nothing about the upcoming treaty discussions. And, to top it off my boss, C. W. Mead, the General Manager of the Northern Pacific came in earlier this week, and is staying in the same hotel as General Terry. Do you believe in coincidence, Jake? I don't. I think plans are being made to move against the Sioux, if they don't agree to sell the Black Hills."

Jake considered what he'd just been told, and recalled Vanessa's cryptic warning. Looking over at Murray, he asked. "Do you think they'll get anywhere with the Sioux?"

"I doubt it, the tribes are very upset about the Black Hills being invaded by miners. I hear that the Commissioners are going to threaten them with cutting off their annual subsidies of food, which is ironic because according to some people, much of it is being stolen before it gets to them, and what does get through to them is poor quality."

Jake considered that statement. "When we were stationed at Fort Totten, that didn't seem to be the case."

"It's different here along the Missouri, there are too many opportunities along the river for thieves to get at them. Both Capt. James Emmons, a local business man and former steam boat operator, and Ben Ash, a Deputy US Marshall, claim to have seen dumps, containing empty boxes and bags marked USID scattered along the eastern banks upstream. Jim said he's even received a payment by the captain of the *Silver Lake*, of 7seven bags of flour so marked that way. The story was published in the Bismarck Tribune a couple of weeks ago."

"What's USID stand for?" Mike asked.

"United States Indian Department." Johnson replied. "That's kind of a smoking gun don't you think?"

Jake and Mike nodded their heads in agreement.

Murray continued, "Linda Slaughter, the postmaster here, is friends with Clement Lounsberry, the publisher of the Bismarck Tribune. She brings the mail to the depot every other day, and keeps me informed on the latest gossip. And, there's a fellow named Mark Kellogg who used to work for me as a dispatcher from time to time. He's been writing articles for the Tribune and has been hinting around about some kind of investigation into the Post Traders and their activities."

"Well, it sounds like you have your ear to the ground. I don't imagine there's much that gos on around here that you don't know about."

"I pride myself on staying informed. By the way, let me know if you run into a man named Thompson. He struck me as a curious fellow when he showed up in town earlier this summer asking questions. Linda helped him get a job over at Fort Lincoln."

The waitress came out, signaling that their food was ready, and they went inside to eat. The rest of their conversation consisted of Jake and Mike telling of their travels down to Louisiana and Missouri. The time came for them to leave and catch the last transfer of the *Union* over to Fort Lincoln.

"Murray, I'll try and come back over a couple of times a month if I can, and look you up."

"Good, we'll meet and compare notes. If the Sioux don't make a deal with the Commission, I expect that come next spring we'll both be kept hopping! Say hello to Pat Morse for me."

As soon as the *Union* tied up, Jake led Ajax up the gangway. Mike had decided to go on to the Company I orderly room and report in, but Jake decided to go over to the Seip house to see Holly, before checking in. As he was riding up. Holly came rushing out onto the front porch.

"Sergeant Jacob Rogers! Is that really you? I'd almost despaired of seeing you before I had to leave!"

Jake grinned as he dismounted, "Well, I tried to hurry, but the Army keeps its own schedule."

Jake led Ajax over to a hitching post and bent to loop his reigns around it. He went up the steps and she came towards him, smiling, and then gave him a big hug. "I'm so glad you made it back. I'm set to leave in two weeks."

"Me too! I hope we can spend some time together."

"Well, we'll just have to make time, won't we?" She exclaimed. "Come inside, Uncle Bob and Aunt Kate are at the store, making sure it's ready if Secretary Belknap wants to see it. I'm making supper."

"Yes, I heard over in Bismarck, that he was supposed to be here tomorrow. I have to go report in and get Ajax put up, so I can't stay long. Maybe I can come over Sunday afternoon."

Jake removed his new grey Stetson hat when they got inside, Holly turned and took it from his hand and put it down on a table. Then she reached for him and drew him towards her. She looked up at him, and he couldn't resist pulling her into an embrace and giving her a kiss, which she returned.

"I was wondering if you missed me?" she sighed. "I've read stories about those southern girls."

"They don't hold a candle to you, Holly. Most of them wanted nothing to do with a damn Yankee soldier." Jake said.

"Well, you'll have tell me all about your experiences, this weekend. Kiss me again!"

Jake thought to himself, as their lips touched, "Not all of them!"

They held their embrace for a minute then hearing footfalls on the steps, they quickly separated, just as Kate and Bob walked through the door.

"I thought that was you that I saw riding up from the landing." Kate remarked, eyeing the two of them, "Welcome back, Jake."

"Thank you ma'm, it's good to be back. I was just telling Holly that we weren't to popular down in Louisiana."

Bob was visibly agitated and glared at Jake. "Your Colonel Custer is a pompous ass!"

Jake considered that statement and replied, "I don't know that I can argue with that, Bob. I've scarcely met him, but I can see that about him." That seemed to mollify Bob a bit.

"Well, I sent him some wine and cigars for Secretary Belknap's visit tomorrow, and he sent them back!"

"I'd say that that's more a reflection of his opinion on Mr. Belknap, than you. He saved you money."

"I guess one could look at it that way." Bob conceded, "But, it still rankles!"

Holly spoke up, "Why don't get you ready for supper, Uncle Bob? It's almost ready. I've invited Jake to stay, if it's okay with you? He can tell us about his travels."

"Well, all right! I suppose it's not fair to judge Jake because of his commander."

As soon as they finished supper Jake excused himself, saying that he needed to report in. Holly escorted him outside, and kissed him discreetly on the cheek. As he headed towards the fort, Jake decided to drop off his kit at his room in the NCO Quarters on his way by. He waved at some of the other sergeants that were lounging in the mess, or outside their rooms, as he hurried up the stairs. Tom Russell wasn't in, so Jake dropped his things on his bunk, and then went down to take Ajax over to the stables. Once he got him cared for, he walked up to the Company barracks, and went to the orderly room, where he found Tom Russell playing a game of chess with Henry Holden.

"Hello, Tom. I'm guessing that you are Charge of Quarters tonight?"

"Well, I'll be! The prodigal son returns!" Russell replied.

"Yep, I just came in on the train, today."

"I'm glad to see you. Now you can be in the duty schedule too."

"I must say that I've enjoyed missing out on that fun." Jake replied, "Hello, Henry! How are the rest of the guys?"

"Oh, they're well, though they won't likely admit it to you."

"I hear there's a big wig visiting tomorrow."

"Yes, we've been getting ready all week. Dress parade tomorrow morning, better get your uniform ready." Tom said.

"Thanks, I'll go check on it. I just wanted to report in first."

"I'll note it, and make sure Top logs it in the Morning Report." Russell said.

"Right! Well, I'll see you in the morning."

Jake made it back to his room before tattoo was sounded, and proceeded to unpack and sort out his uniform for the next day. He went downstairs and drew some bedding, then settled in for the night, after listening to Taps. He was back, and actually looking forward to settling into the routine again. He laid down and was thinking about Holly as he slowly drifted off to sleep.

Secretary Belknap's visit proved to be anti-climactic. The next morning, Custer declined to meet Belknap and his entourage when they arrived at the steamboat landing, pleading an illness. A quick cursory inspection of the troops and a short tour of the post was conducted, then the visitors adjourned to Custer's residence where there was a brief visit in the parlor. They left and returned to Bismarck where the special train was waiting, boarded, and were gone.

After the departure of the VIPs, the officers and NCOs were relieved that all had gone well. The troops at the fort were stood down and the companies returned to their barracks to exchange their dress uniforms for their regular ones. Except for stable call, and guard duty, there were no details scheduled for the remainder of the day. and the men were in almost a holiday mood. The Company D, NCOs were gathered in the orderly room.

"Well, that was all for naught!" exclaimed Pat Morse.

"Oh, I don't know, Pat." replied 1st Sgt. Martin, "The lads looked extra sharp, and the whole fort is in tip top shape. I've heard that Sunday's parade is to be canceled and that we're to have the whole day off."

"I guess that makes it all worth while then." Sgt. Harrison remarked. "Hey, Rogers, glad to see that you could make it back. We all look forward to your presence in the duty rotation."

"Oh, I hurried back as quickly as I could Tom, I knew you'd be missing me." Jake replied sardonically.

That drew a round of chuckles.

"So, Rogers, do ya have any news for us? Particularly seein' as how you've been rubbing elbows with the regimental types, and all." Martin asked.

"I just heard rumors, Top. The word is that the Allison Commission meeting with the Sioux later this month will determine what happens. It doesn't appear that the miners can be stopped from going into the Black Hills."

Martin nodded his head and replied, "Yeh, it doesn't help that the newspaper prints front page articles about it how much gold there is. Desertion rates at all the forts in the territory have gone way up. Fortunately, we've only had a couple, but it's bound to get worse."

Jake reviewed his conversation with Murray Johnson, and his suspicions regarding the higher level meetings taking place, in Bismarck. The sergeants all listened intently.

"Well, it's damn sure that we'll not be goin' out this year at any rate. But, m'thinks you're on to somethin', Rogers. Let's bear it in mind over the winter. Rush, see if you can scrounge up some extra ammunition so that we can get some target practice in when the weather's good. Rogers, you're to conduct weapons training company wide, with the lads. I'll talk with the Captain about what we're up to."

"I think we need to stay in touch with Murray Johnson." Morse said. "He can keep us informed."

'I agree!" Martin said, "You and Rogers stay in contact with him. Oh, by the way, Rogers!

"What's that, Top?"

"You need to go see that lass, Holly, over at the Traders. She's been asking after you all summer."

A general round of laughter ensued, and Jake felt his face reddening. "I've already seen to that, Top."

Jake spent the rest of the day settling in and making sure that he picked up his share of details on the duty roster, but also finagling to keep the next two weekends open. Pat Morse and he slipped up to the Post Store that evening, and discussed his visit back home to Springfield, bringing Pat up to speed about Zeb and Sarah. Holly came over and waited on their table, stopping by as much as she could with a busy crowd on premise.

"She's a sweet lass, Jacob, but ya know she's off to school, soon." Pat said, "Don't be letting your little head tell the bigger one what to do!"

Jake laughed, "I know, Pat. We're just friends, we wrote letters back and forth while I was gone. Besides, I see how tough it is for wives out here. I wouldn't dream of contemplating getting married while I'm still in the

Army."

"Good lad! Be careful though, Bob Seip has some powerful partners, and it wouldn't pay to make him an enemy."

"I will, but he and I get on well enough and like you say, she's leaving soon."

Holly came back by and said, "I spoke with Aunt Kate and she said it was okay to ask you to dinner on Sunday, Jake. Please say you'll come."

"I will, I've already made sure that I won't have duty."

Holly smiled and said, "That's good! Now I won't have to go ask Sgt. Martin to let you off." Then she walked off.

Pat grinned at Jake's raised eyebrows and said, "Yes, that girl is a pistol, she is!"

Jake spent the next couple of days getting back in the routine of garrison life. The footlocker that he'd had shipped from across the river, arrived and he unpacked it. He got his new civilian clothes out and made sure they were presentable. He decided to take some of his mother's blackberry jam with him as a present to the Seips. He was hoping for an opportunity to get Holly alone with him, so that he could give her the locket in private. When Sunday finally arrived, Jake prowled around the river banks after stable call, and Henry helped him find some purple wild flowers which he picked and carefully carried them back to his quarters wrapped in a damp horse cloth. He got dressed and asked Tom Russell to give him a once over, which he did along with a little ribbing at Jake's expense. When he went down the stairs, Jake quickly headed out in the direction of the Seip residence before anyone could note his attire, but he hadn't gone but a few steps when he heard a few whistles and catcalls behind him. Without turning around, he just waved back. He mounted the steps when he got to the house, and Holly came out to greet him. They went inside where Bob and Kate were waiting, and they greeted him.

"Jake, I must say, you look very nice. Civilian attire becomes you!" Kate said, smiling.

"Well, I was able to spend some time back home, and my Mother insisted on helping me improve my wardrobe." He replied, "Here are some wildflowers that I found down by river this morning," He held them out, " I hope you like them."

"Yes, these are called Dotted Gayfeather, I often gather them. Thank you." She replied. "Let me put them a vase." and went into the kitchen along with Holly

Bob asked Jake, "So, you're back for a while?"

"Yes, sir! I don't expect I'll be going anywhere else until next spring, if we take the field."

"Do you think that will happen?"

"I think it will depend upon the Indians, the miners, and the government." Jake answered. "And, who knows how that will play out."

"So, Jake, you seem like a nice young man, and I can see that you are fond of my niece. But you know that she is leaving for school?"

"Yes, sir! She and I are going to write to each other, just like when I was away. I figure that she will be busy with school and I still have over two years left on my enlistment. It's nice to have someone that I can write to, besides my folks."

Bob nodded his head, "I see. It's unusual to see a young fellow like yourself to look at the long view. Most of the soldiers I deal with on a daily basis tend to live from day to day."

"That's true, Bob. But when I was up on the boundary the last two years, the guide that was with us taught me to not only try to always look ahead, but also to be aware of my surroundings. Being a soldier, out here on the frontier is not a place that is friendly to supporting a wife, even for officers. Now, I do like Holly, and when I'm finished with the Army, and if we're still so inclined, we may get more serious."

"Hmm! I can see why you're already a sergeant, Jake. I hope that your plans work out. It doesn't look like Kate and I will have children, so Holly is very dear to us. Please remember that."

"I will, sir!"

Kate came back in and summoned them. "Come on you two. I've cooked Jake fried chicken and all the trimmings. Let's eat it while it's hot."

After they ate they adjourned to sit out on the front porch. The early September evenings were beginning to cool, and the women covered up with shawls. Bob seemed to relax a bit, and went out of his way to be polite to Jake, filling him in on recent events effecting Fort Lincoln and Bismarck, and asking his opinions. He talked about how well things were going at the store, and was bragging about a recently hired worker by the name of J.D.Thompson.

Jake recalled his conversation with Murray Johnson, and said, "I'll have to make a point to meet him. Thompson, you say his name is?"

"Yes, he's been a tremendous help. He's traveled extensively around the Plains, and was down in Colorado until recently. He is very personable, and gets on well with the soldiers. I've put him in charge of dealing with the company First Sergeants. He's even convinced me to do some advertising in the newspaper."

"I wonder what brought him up here?"

"I asked him that. He said that he was interested in seeing the Black Hills, but wants to see what happens with the Sioux."

As dusk settled in, Jake checked his watch, and then thanked Kate and Bob for the supper. When he stood and made ready to leave, they went inside, allowing he and Holly a bit of privacy.

"You look very respectable, Jake, but I kind of like you better in your uniform."

"Well, I just wanted them see me in a different light. I think it worked."

"Me too! Aunt Kate approves of you, and I think Uncle Bob is coming around."

"I'll try to come see you as much as I can, before you go." Jake said, then held out his hand, offering her the box with the locket inside. "Here I found this back home, and thought you might like it. It's a little something for you to remember me by."

Holly opened the box and held up the locket in the fading light. "It's beautiful, Jake. She spun around, and held up her hair. "Here, help me put it on!"

Jake fumbled with the clasp, as he admired the line of her neck and the fineness of her hair. He focused and he got it fastened, then she turned back to him, and stood on her toes and quickly kissed him on the lips.

"Thank you, Jacob. Now I know that you were thinking of me, while you were gone. I'm trying to figure out how to get us some more time alone, so I can kiss you properly."

Jake grinned and said, "Well, I'll be looking forward to that! Have a good evening!" then headed off to his quarters.

CHAPTER 24

Fort Abraham Lincoln, Dakota Territory - Monday Sep. 6, 1875

On Monday, Jake took his turn as Sergeant of the Guard and was making his rounds after checking on the granaries. He turned south along the road in front of Officers Row when he noticed a civilian leaving the Custer residence. As the man approached Jake, he pulled his bowler hat lower and nodded his head, mumbling a "Good evening Sergeant." In the dim light coming from the houses, Jake noted that the man had a distinctive gray beard which contrasted with the darker hair peaking out from under his hat. Jake turned his head and watched as the man appeared to be following the road in the direction of the boarding house near north of the fort, which was near the trading post. The next afternoon Jake was able to go over to the trading post while Holly was still working. When Jake arrived at the store, he noticed that the Seips seemed a little pre-occupied, and were poring over several ledgers with another man. When the man looked up, Jake saw that it was the same man that he'd seen last night, coming from the Custer house. He took a seat at a table and Holly came over bringing him a beer.

"Who's that guy with Bob and Kate?" Jake asked.

"Oh, that's J.D.! He's the guy that Bob was telling you about the other night."

"Hmm, I saw him at the fort last night, when I was on guard duty."

"Yes, he goes there quite a bit. He was probably delivering something."

"Funny, he was walking, and it was getting pretty dark."

Holly shrugged her shoulders, "Who knows," Then she moved to stand in front of Jake. "You're supposed to be looking at me."

"Okay, I will, and I must say that you look nice."

"Oh Pshaw! I've been working all day, helping with them take inventory."

"What's up with that?"

"Bob's partner, Alvin Leighton, is coming down from Fort Buford.

They're going to meet over in Bismarck, on Friday."

Kate looked over at them, and waved for him to come over.

"I think Kate wants you." Holly said, "I'll come back later."

Jake got up and walked over to where Kate standing.

"Jake, I'd like you to meet J. D. Thompson. J D this is Sergeant Rogers."

Jake held out his hand and Thompson shook it.

"So you must be the young man that Miss Holly is so enamored with!"

"Well, I hope so, unless I have competition."

"Not that I've seen. Although she's very popular with the your fellow soldiers, she just seems partial to you. You're the lucky fellow. So, what Company are you with?"

"D."

"That's Capt. Weir's Troop isn't it? I've heard some stories about you boys. You spent some time up on the border, working with the Boundary Survey Team."

"Yes, we did. I'm surprised that you heard about it, most of the publicity went to the Regiment's expedition to the Black Hills."

"From what I hear that was more like a big picnic, than an expedition."

"Well, we weren't picnicking, at least most of us."

"I've never been up that way, what's it like?"

"There's not much up there, besides a few Indians, and a lot of buffalo." Jake answered.

"That sounds like the plains down south of here used to be, though that changed with the arrival of the railroads."

"I'm sure it did. I've heard that the buffalo are getting harder to find down there. Many of our senior NCOs spent time there, and I've heard their tales of the huge herds."

"They're not so huge anymore. I was in Dodge City, last year, and saw a hide yard that had over 40,000 hides waiting to be shipped. The market for them is tremendous right now. I've heard there is a new curing process that makes them tougher, for use as machine drive belts."

Jake thought back to the Métis hunt that he'd seen and he remembered thinking that that was a slaughter. He couldn't imagine the huge quantity J D was talking about

"That's just incredible, I've seen buffalo killed but not on that scale. No wonder that they are getting scarce. Say, I thought I saw you at over at the fort yesterday, up on officer's row."

J D looked at him curiously, "Ah, you may have, I go there frequently.

I was delivering a package to Mrs. Yates."

"Oh, I see, she's a nice lady."

"Well, I'd better get busy, Bob wants to have everything ready for Mr. Leighton's visit. Nice to meet you, Jake."

Jake went back over to his table, Holly returned shortly and sat down.

"So what did you think of J D?"

"I can't say for sure. He seems to be pretty well traveled, I can't see him wanting to stay here long."

"Me either! I know Uncle Bob isn't paying him much."

"When I was making my rounds last night, as Sergeant of the Guard, I saw him coming from Custer's house, but when I mentioned that I'd seen him at the Fort, he said he was making a delivery to Capt. Yates wife."

"So?"

"I watched him walk down Custer's steps, the Yates' house is next door to it, and I was standing in front of it when I saw him. And, I wonder why would he be making a delivery that late. It was after Taps."

"Who knows? Now, let's talk about this weekend, it's my last one before I leave, and I want it to be special."

"Okay, I'm sure we can come up with something. You think about it, and let me know."

The following night, Jake had Charge of Quarters duty and ate supper at the barracks mess. Afterwards, he was sitting in the orderly room when Mike Caddle stopped by to visit.

"So, Jake, I hear your lass is headed south to Leavenworth for school next week."

"Yes, and I'm trying to think of something to do with her, this weekend."

"Well, I heard Capt. Keogh telling Top Varden that he and some other officers went to the Fort Lincoln Restaurant the other night. There's a new owner, W.S. Ressegieu, who used to work for the Bismarck Tribune as a reporter. He's supposably hired a trained chef who can prepare wonderful meals. Anyway, Capt. Keogh said it was pretty good food, and I'd say he's been to many a fine restaurant in his travels."

Jake considered that and replied, "That sure would be easy. Maybe I'll go see this Mr. Ressegieu, and talk to him about it. You can see that restaurant from the Seip's house, they should be okay with me taking her there. Thanks for telling me about it!"

"I'd say that it's a good thing she's away to school soon, you'd end up married if she stayed." Caddle stated.

"Oh, I don't know about that, she's quite adamant about becoming a teacher, or something similar like a governess. She wants to live somewhere with trees, and there's sure none around here. We'll see what happens then."

"Good, it's just as well, you know there's a heavy rumor going round that Custer has some kind of agenda against the Post Traders here along the Missouri. I think you'll be better off not consorting with the Seips as much."

"I knew that Custer isn't happy about some of their prices, but I hadn't realized that it was more serious."

"Oh it is, it's just that you've been busy mooning over Holly and haven't been paying attention."

"Hmm! I guess I'd better start."

Jake went over to the Ft. Lincoln Restaurant, Thursday after supper. When he walked in he spotted JD Thompson, sitting at a table talking with two men. One of them was dressed in a dapper suit, had his dark hair slicked back and sported a thin mustache. The other, in a slightly rumpled suit, was slightly older with greying hair and long Napoleonic sideburns and wore spectacles. He was writing in a notebook, while the other two were talking. JD quickly gathered some papers from the table when he saw Jake, and he detected a quick nervous twinge on his face. Jake waved at him and walked over to the table.

"Hello JD, how are you today?"

"Good, Sergeant Rogers, how about yourself?"

"I'm fine. I just came over to talk with the new owner about booking a table for Saturday night."

"That would be me!" announced the other man, "And I'm sure that we can accommodate you." Standing, he extended his hand, saying, "I'm Winfield Ressegieu, pleased to meet you Sergeant."

"They are saying good things about your restaurant over at the cavalry post. I have a friend that's leaving, and I wanted to treat her to a nice supper. I just wanted to see about making some arrangements."

"Yes, of course, have a seat and we'll see what we can do. Let me introduce you to my friend Mark Kellogg, we used to work together over in Bismarck"

"Hello, Mr. Kellogg, Murray Johnson has mentioned you a couple of times."

"Oh, How do you know Murray?"

"I worked with him when we moved over from Fort Totten. I see him from time to time."

JD rose up and said, "Well, I need to get back to the store, I'll see you later, Win, you too, Mark."

Jake followed JD for a few steps and said to him quietly, "Please don't mention this to anyone over there, I haven't exactly got this all cleared with Bob and Kate."

"Hey, no problem, Jake! I'm sure it will be all right, they speak highly of you, and I'm sure Win will arrange a nice evening for you and Miss Holly."

As Jake returned to the table, Kellogg stood up saying, "I need to get going if I'm to catch the *Union.* It's nice to have met you, Sergeant, if I see Murray, I'll let him know."

After Kellogg left, Ressegieu asked Jake, "So, your friend is Miss Walker, Bob Seip's niece? I've met her, she's a delightful young woman!"

"Yes, she's leaving for school, down at Leavenworth Ks, next week."

"So, what did you have in mind, Sergeant? Are you proposing to her?"

"No, no, and please call me, Jake. I just want to give her a pleasant evening. I thought maybe something besides the usual fare could be found. Perhaps flowers on the table and a bottle of champagne might be possible, also."

"Well, Jake, we can do that. I purchased some several dozen quail this morning, how about that a couple of them for a main course? Then my chef can come up with suitable side dishes to accompany them. We have several different champagnes to choose from. It depends on how much you want to spend."

Jake replied, "I have a few dollars saved up."

Win looked at Jake's chevrons and said, "Well, I know what sergeants make, let me see what I can put together for you."

"I'd appreciate it, Mr. Ressegieu. I'll be hunting quite a bit as the weather cools. Perhaps I can provide you with some fresh venison in return?"

"I believe we can work something out. What time were you wanting to dine, on Saturday?"

"I was thinking maybe 6 o'clock, or so, if that would work?"

"I'll look forward to seeing you and Holly, then. You must know the Seips well, for them to trust you with their niece."

"I've spent some time with them, they're nice people."

"I hear that Bob has several partners in his enterprise."

"I don't know about that, I do know that he has at least one though,

Mr. Alvin Leighton, who is the post trader at Fort Buford." said Jake.

'Yes, Mr. Leighton and his brothers are quite well known up and down the river. I hear that Kate is his niece, it's nice that she's well connected. I hear they make lots of money."

It struck Jake that Win seemed to be more than casually interested in the Seips, and their business.

"I wouldn't know about that, but I appreciate your help, Mr Ressegieu, I'll plan on seeing you this weekend."

Jake went straight over to the trading post store and found the Seips working at the counter. He waved at them as he walked towards them.

"Looks like you two are still at it."

"Yes, but we're about to wrap it up. What brings you around? Holly just left to go start supper."

"Well, I wanted to ask for your permission to take Holly to the Lincoln Restaurant, Saturday evening, as a going away present. I'll have her home by dark."

Kate, who was standing slightly behind Bob, smiled at Jake and put a hand on Bob's shoulder.

"Well, that's nice Jake. Is there something special about the occasion? You aren't planning to ask her anything are you?"

"No Ma'am! I just want her last memories of this place to be pleasant. I expect that she and I won't be seeing each other for some time."

Bob looked at Jake and asked, "So what are your intentions regarding Holly?"

"We're just good friends! She's got plans that she's committed to, and in my case, the Army has claim to me for another two and a half years. Who knows what will happen during that time."

Kate nudged Bob's arm and he turned to look at her. She nodded her head.

Turning back to Jake, he said, "I suppose it will be okay. I can speak to Win Ressgieu about making arrangements for you."

"I already have, sir. It's all set up for 6:30 that evening, I just came from there."

"That figures!"

"Well, I'd better go ask Holly. She may have other plans."

Kate laughed, "Oh, I think she will find a way to change them if she does. We're going over to Bismarck tomorrow for a meeting, so JD and Holly are going to mind the store while we're there. We'll make sure she's got plenty of time to get ready on Saturday."

Jake left the store and headed over to the Seip's residence. When he got there, Holly was waiting at the front door.

"I thought that was you a while ago, when I looked out the kitchen window. What were you doing over at the restaurant?"

Jake grinned. "Making reservations for us Saturday night!"

Holly's mouth dropped open. "What! You're kidding me!"

"Nope, I just cleared it with your Aunt and Uncle. You want to go with me?"

"Of course I do, don't be silly!" she replied, grabbing his hand and pulling him inside, then hugging him. She tilted her head up and looked him in the eyes. "I can't believe Uncle Bob agreed to letting you take me."

"Well, I think it was Kate's call."

"Probably, I know she likes you."

"So, I'll be by to pick you up at 6 O'clock."

Holly reached up and pulled his head down, until their lips merged and pressed together. After several moments, she pulled back and they locked eyes.

"I'll look forward to seeing you then, Sergeant Rogers."

Suddenly she winkled her nose and exclaimed, "Oh my gosh! I'm burning supper! I gotta go." And dashed towards the kitchen.

Jake called after her. "I'll probably come by the store tomorrow. See you later!"

The next morning, during Stable Call, Jake was checking his section's saddles and tack when Pat came over to him.

"Jake, I was thinking about going over to Bismarck, tomorrow and looking in on Murray. Do you want go along?"

"Ah, no thanks Pat, I've got plans with Holly."

"Do ya now?"

"She's leaving on Wednesday, and I'm taking her out to dinner."

"Well, now! You'll be needing something else to keep you occupied then. Perhaps we can start hunting?"

"That's what I was thinking. I talked with the new owner of the restaurant about selling him some venison." Jake replied.

"Ressegieu? You'd best be careful dealing with that one. Top and I were discussing him the other day. He showed up around Bismarck and quickly earned a reputation for being a bit of a character."

"You know, I saw him huddled up with a fellow named Mark Kellogg, yesterday, and JD, who's working at the trading post. They were looking at some papers and put them away quickly when they saw me coming."

"Funny, both of them showed up here at the fort about the same time. Could be that they're in cahoots. I'll ask Murray what he knows about them. And, it seems like I've heard of that fellow Kellogg, he's known to be involved in local politics over in Bismarck."

"Yeh, say hello to Murray for me, and let me know what he has to say."

"I will. Tell Miss Holly that I'll come round to tell her goodbye, before she's away."

"I will."

The bar at the trading post was doing a brisk Friday night business when Jake showed up there. Holly was waiting tables, and waved to him, while JD was running the counter in the store. He went to a table and sat down as Holly made her way over carrying a beer for him.

"Good evening, Sergeant, would you like a beer?"

"You bet! How's it going?"

"We've been busy, but it's starting to slow down. Let me go tell JD that I'm taking a break, and I'll come sit with you."

Jake smiled and replied, "That's great, I was able to work a deal with 1st Sgt. Martin and I have tomorrow free."

Holly's face lit up as she said, "Good, now don't move, I'll be right back."

She went over to the store, and came back in a few minutes. She sat down, across from Jake.

"I just found out that Bob and Kate aren't coming back tonight. They just sent a telegram that they're having a late dinner with Mr. Leighton, and are staying over at the hotel. JD and I are supposed to close up tonight and they'll see us tomorrow."

"Well, I'll just stick around and help out, then I can walk you home. It looks like it will be a beautiful evening."

She reached over and put her hand on his, "JD told me that he could handle it on his own, that I could go ahead and leave when I want."

"All right! Let me finish my beer and we can go for a walk."

The stars began appearing, vivid against the darkening sky, as Jake and Holly strolled towards the Seip residence. Just before they reached the porch steps, Holly remembered that she'd left her clutch bag back at the store, so they made their way back. Holly went inside, while Jake waited by the door. He watched Holly walk towards the small room behind the counter that Bob used for his office. He saw her pause when she got there, and heard her talking, but couldn't make out any words. She went in the office and emerged after a minute or two, talking over her shoulder. She hurried towards Jake, with a puzzled look on her face.

"What's up?" he asked.

"When I got to Uncle Bob's office, I found JD going through some papers, and looking at the company check book. It looked like he was writing down dates and amounts. I asked him about it, and he said that Bob was having him check to see that the balances were correct."

"So?"

"Bob is very particular when it comes to his banking affairs, he doesn't even let Kate do any of it. I don't believe he would ask JD to be involved in them."

"Hmm, maybe you should tell him about it when they get back, tomorrow."

"I will." Holly said, "Now let's go back to the house, and I'll fix us a snack."

They held hands as they walked, and marveled at how brilliant the stars were. They stopped along the way to embrace and exchange some kisses. When they reached the house they went inside, where Holly lit a lamp. Jake became acutely aware that he'd never been this alone with Holly. He nervously looked around the living room, while Holly went down the hallway towards the kitchen.

"I'll go back out on the porch, while you're doing that." He called out to Holly.

He went out and set down in a rocking chair, and contemplating the situation. He wasn't sure how to act. He supposed that he would just stay for the snacks, and a few more kisses, then head back to his quarters."

"Jake!" Holly called softly, after several minutes went by, "Come inside, please."

Jake went in, and by the dim lamp light saw that she'd donned a house robe and let down her hair.

"Oh, I thought that you were in the kitchen."

"I will be later. Right now, I've a better treat for you." She said, letting her robe fall open, revealing that she was naked underneath.

Jake was taken aback for a second, and asked, "Ah, okay, if you're sure about this?"

"Jacob Rogers, I'm going away in a few days and may never see you again. I want us to have something to remember each other by on lonely nights. I'm sure!" She grasped his hand and pulled him to her. "Let's go back to my room, and get you out of that uniform, soldier!"

When they reached her bedroom, Jake quickly disrobed and sat down on the bed. Holly lit a candle, then came to stand in front of him and slowly dropped her robe.

"I'm hoping that you know how to do this, cause I've just heard stories from the laundresses, and Aunt Kate has explained some of it."

"Well, I think between us, that we can figure it out." Jake said softly as he looked at her, admiring her full breasts and curvaceous figure. He took her hands and drew her down to him, and they melted into a passionate embrace.

As things heated up, Holly raised her head and looked Jake in the eye. "We have to be careful, I have some protection. I have it on the nightstand. It's called a condom, and is made of sheep membrane."

"I'm surprised that you were able get them out here."

"Oh, we order quite a few. Mostly for the laundresses, but some women come over from Bismarck and buy them, so no one will know, Kate handles them. She gave them to me. I had them in my purse that we went back for."

"Kate, really, she gave them to you? She knows about this?" Jake said incredulously.

"Of course, silly! How do you think we are able to finally be alone together? She made sure that her uncle invited them to dinner, and they'd have to stay overnight. Now, let's keep figuring this out! We can talk about it later."

Jake woke later on and laid there reflecting upon their lovemaking while Holly cuddled next to him sleeping. After some initial reticence, she'd become quite enthusiastic about their coupling. Fortunately, Jake remembered the guidance that he'd received from Vanessa. He replayed it in his mind and was glad that he'd been able to control himself, pleasuring Holly. He wondered what to make of it all particularly Kate's complicity. He supposed that some kind of commitment had been incurred as a result, although the prospect of it was not altogether displeasing. It was something for him to mull over and discuss with Holly. He felt her stirring next to him. She rose and kissed him, then whispered in his ear.

"Can we do that again?"

Jake smiled and said, "I believe so. How would you like to try being on top this time?"

Holly's eyes got big, and she said, "Okay, you show me what to do."

"I can do that!"

He woke again near morning and wondered about heading back to the fort before daylight. He decided that he would head to his room at the NCO Quarters and try and slip up the stairs just after Reveille Call, when the other sergeants would be busy with Roll Call. He slipped his arm from around Holly and eased out of bed. As his feet touched the floor, he felt her grab his shoulder, and pull him backwards.

"Oh, no, Jake, we have to do it one more time. Three's my lucky number!" she said as she put one of her hands down between his legs.

He turned back to her and said, "We'll have to hurry, unless you want me to be seen leaving your house. The whole fort would know about it by lunchtime."

Holly chuckled and replied, "Well, I'm leaving on Wednesday anyway, let them talk." She pulled him towards her, using his stiffening penis for a handle.

Afterwards, Jake scrambled to pull on his uniform while Holly lay watching him dress. He retrieved his watch, noting that it was almost 5 o'clock. If he timed it just right his plan would still work.

"Tell me about that animal tooth you've got hanging around your neck." Holly said.

"It was given to me by a friend, who is half Indian. It's a wolf's fang, and it's supposed to protect me from danger."

"Does it work."

He leaned over Holly and kissed her. "Maybe, it's kind a tingling right now." He chuckled, "I gotta get going, Darlin', I'll see you this evening and we can talk about it then. You have a real nice day!"

"I will. But it won't be as nice as last night!"

Jake made it back to his room without an incident. He'd managed to time his return to just after the other NCOs left for their various units. He put on some civilian clothes and went downstairs to the mess room, where he was sat drinking coffee until the others returned. He grabbed a plate and got in line, then grabbed his usual chair. His room mate, Tom Russell, came and set across from him.

"Well, I guess you decided to wander back from wherever you spent the night." Tom said quietly. "I have my suspicions, but I'll keep them to myself. Top was asking about you,"

"What did you say?"

"I told him that you were sleeping in this morning and spending the day getting ready for your big date tonight. I'm glad you made it back."

"Thanks. I owe you one."

"Yes, you do."

Pat Morse came in also dressed in civilian clothes and sat down next to Tom. He looked over at Jake, and said, "What're you up to today, Jake?"

"Not much, I thought that you were going over to Bismarck to see Murray?"

"I am crossing over on the *Union* at 10 o'clock, and meeting him for lunch, if you've a mind, you can tag along. You can catch the 2:30 crossing and be back for your date with Holly."

"What the hell! Does everyone know about it?" Jake exclaimed.

"Well, it's gone about a bit. Holly is a popular lass and the fact that you seem to be the only one she's interested in has not gone unnoticed around here. You yourself jockeyed the duty schedule with Top to get the today off. What do ya say? Come along and Murray will buy lunch."

Jake thought about it, and decided that he would talk with Johnson about J.D..

"All right, Pat, I believe I will."

When they got across the river, they went to meet Murray at Forster's again. When they got there a waitress showed them to a table.

"You're a bit early, Mr. Johnson always show's up promptly at 11:30."

"Yes, we know, lass. He's a man on a schedule. We'll have a couple of beers while we wait." Pat replied. Presently, Murray came strolling through the door and waved at them.

"Ah, I see that the cavalry has already arrived! And, I see you brought Jake along."

"Hey Murray! Good to see you again." Jake said.

"You too, what have you been up to?"

"Just settling back into the garrison routine, and getting reacquainted with Army cooking."

Murray sat down and said, "Well, I recommend the Saturday special here, steak with potatoes and fresh green beans."

After the waitress took their orders, Murray proceeded to fill them in on the local events over the last week. He shared a few anecdotes with them about Secretary Belknap and his party. It turned out that they had left town in a hurry, mostly to dodge questions from local authorities about irregularities in the distribution of Indian annuities and also the sale of modern breechloading rifles and ammunition to the tribes. In the mean time, the Allison Commission was having issues with the Sioux tribes on where to hold their meetings. It seemed that Red Cloud and Spotted Tail, the two most prominent chiefs, couldn't agree on the location. And, to compound the problems it was estimated that there were over 1,500 miners already in the Black Hills. After the waitress brought their food, they dug in and were busily cutting up their steaks.

"I hear tell that your Post Trader, and his wife, stayed over in

Bismarck, last night. I'll bet he was nervous about leaving his business and wares untended overnight."Johnson said offhand. "My sources tell me that Custer is breathing down his neck, and has information detailing corruption and payoffs."

Jake remembered Holly's comments from last night about J.D. and the check register.

"Last week you mentioned a fellow named J.D. Thompson and asked me to let me know if I ran across him. Well, he's working for Bob Seip over at the trading post."

"Now that's interesting, because just about the time that he showed up is when articles about corruption and payoffs in the War and Interior Departments began appearing in the newspapers back east under the byline of a Ralph Meeker. I've read some of them and whoever this Ralph Meeker is, he seems to have some inside source for information about it."

"Are you suggesting that this Thompson fellow is feeding him information?"

"No, the articles suggest first hand knowledge, he may actually be Meeker."

Jake mulled that over then proceeded to tell Pat and Murray about his observations of Thompson, coming from Custer's house and how he stumbled onto JD and Ressengieu conferring.

"I'm familiar with Winfield Ressengieu. He showed up this spring, flashing a lot money around. He worked for the Bismarck Tribune for a while, and was always nosing around town. If he's involved, he's in it for gain. He's an opportunist, always looking for a fast buck. He went out of his way to ingratiate himself with Libbie Custer, and is on excellent terms with Col. Custer, also. His restaurant venture at the fort is a good example."

"It sounds to me like it's a good thing your lass is leaving, Jake. You'll not be getting caught up in this intrigue that way. I know Custer well enough to know that he'll pursue his suspicions. Best for you to focus on staying out of the way and just soldiering." Pat said.

"I agree." said Murray, "It's all about money and politicians, and I've heard Custer is quite popular with the Democrats. Besides, if the accusations prove to be true there will be repercussions."

"I suppose you're both right, although I think Bob Seip is a pawn in this. Once Holly is gone to school I'll try and stay neutral."

"Well, if the Allison Commission doesn't get a treaty done with the Sioux, you two will have more to worry about than prices at the post traders." Johnson stated.

"I've got to get going." Jake said rising from the table, "I want to make sure to catch the 4 o'clock crossing, and I want to shop for a going away present for Holly."

"Okay, Jake, keep watching your side of the river and we'll see what happens." Murray said.

"I will, watch out for Pat! I think he's set on getting you both drunk tonight, don't let him drag you down to the Point."

"No way!" Murray exclaimed, "I know of a few higher class establishments here in town."

"Aye now! That's what I like to hear." Pat said grinning, "You enjoy your dinner with Miss Holly tonight and tell her that I said Hello!"

Jake made it back to his quarters at the fort just as Tom Russell was finishing up for the day. Jake changed into his best civilian clothes, then joined Tom out on the porch. They sat there for a while watching the comings and goings on the road below them, occasionally bantering with men they knew.

"Well, I guess that I'd best be on my way." said Jake.

"So, I assume that you're gonna be back tonight." Tom stated, "What with her Aunt and Uncle getting back from Bismarck, this afternoon."

"Yes, I expect that I'll be sleeping here. I'd appreciate it if you not advertise my absence last night. Time just got away from us."

"Oh, I covered for you, and you don't have to worry. You're a lucky man to get to have a girl like her."

"Yes, but I'm kind of glad that she's getting out of here. There's not much for her here, and the way it sounds we may be out in the field a while next year. "

"Sounds like you're serious about her."

"Yes, I'll miss her, but I also want what's best for her. We'll see what happens. I'll see you later."

Jake had gathered a handful of Black Eyed Susans on the way up from the boat landing earlier. He clutched them nervously as he mounted the steps at the Seip's. He went to the door and knocked. Bob answered the door and came out. He immediately sensed that Bob's demeanor seemed off a little and Jake braced himself.

"How are you this evening, Bob?"

"Ah, I'm okay. I'm just getting ready to go back over to the store. A couple of things came up yesterday, and I have to look into them. I might see you later, when you bring Holly back after supper. Go on in, the girls are waiting for you." He said, then turned to leave.

Jake breathed a sigh of relief and went in. He saw Kate coming from the hallway towards him.

"Hello Jake, you look very respectable, I trust that you are?" she said smiling.

Jake felt his face reddening, as he saw that she was teasing him.

"I like to think that I am."

"Then you probably are." Kate replied. "Holly is just about ready. Would you like something to drink?"

"No Ma'am, I believe that I'm fine."

Holly appeared behind Kate, and Jake was stunned when he saw her. Her dark hair was done up in the back, and she wore a pale grey dress with blue ribbons that matched her eyes. It had a v-shaped neckline where the locket that he'd given her hung.

"Doesn't she look nice, Jake?" Kate asked.

Jake realized that he was staring, and quickly recovered. "Holly, you look beautiful!"

Both women giggled, as Holly replied, "Well, I'm glad that you think so. We spent all afternoon getting ready."

Jake remembered the flowers that he was holding and held them out.

"I picked this for you!"

Holly took them. "Why thank you, that was thoughtful. I'll have to get a vase."

Kate said quickly, "You two go on, I'll tend to them. You have a good time, and try to be back at a respectable hour, please."

The dinner turned out to be excellent. Whatever faults that Win Ressengieu may have had, his restaurant was well run. Win met them at the door and personally escorted them to a corner table. Jake noticed that there were several officers and their ladies already seated. He saw Capt. Keogh with one of the Wadsworth sisters, and Jake tipped his head in acknowledgement as they passed.

"Thanks for setting this up, Win, it looks like you're busy."

"Oh, we have a nice crowd most Saturday nights. How are you this evening, Miss Walker? You look lovely!" He said as he pulled out a chair for Holly.

"Why thank you, Mr. Ressengieu!" she replied, taking her seat.

He proceeded to light a candle for them, and motioned to a waiter, who brought over a bottle of champagne, and glasses.

"Charles will be your waiter, tonight. I'll stop by later to check on you."

After filling their glasses, Charles said, "I assume that you'll be having the quail, as arranged, Sir. Our chef has a special recipe with some wonderful side dishes?"

Jake cocked an eye towards Holly, who nodded.

"Yes, that will be fine." He said.

Charles left, and Jake raised his glass for a toast. "To the prettiest woman, here at Fort Lincoln!"

Holly touched her glass to his, and replied, "I didn't realize that you were so gallant, Sergeant Rogers."

"My mother made me read a lot of books. Some of what was in them must have sunk in."

Holly's blue eyes bore into his and she said, "Last night was amazing, and you're not doing too poorly tonight! To us!" and she took a sip.

Jake did also, then said quietly, "I wanted this night to be special for us. I have a present for you." He reached in his pocket and pulled out a small box, opened it and reached across the table, placing it in front of Holly.

"I'm not asking you to marry me, but if you agree to take this, I'm promising to come to you as soon as I'm done with the Army. Then we'll see what happens."

Holly saw that it was a simple silver ring, engraved with roses. She took it from the box and put it on the ring finger of her right hand. She looked up at Jake smiling, then held out her hand for him to take and simply said, "Okay."

The spent the rest of the evening enjoying the food and each others company. When they were done eating, Charles produced coffee, and some kind of chocolate desert topped with whipped cream, which they shared. Jake saw through the window that it was getting dark.

"I suppose that we should be getting back to the house, your aunt will be wondering where we are." He said.

"Kate told me that she and Bob would probably be working late at the store, tonight, so we can walk for a while. I don't think she's too concerned."

Jake laughed, "I guess it's a bit late for that."

He summoned Charles for the bill.

"Mr. Ressengieu instructed me to tell you that everything is taken care of, and that he'll be in touch with you."

"Tell him thank you for me, Charles." Jake reached for his wallet, intending to leave a tip.

"Don't bother, sir. It was a pleasure to serve you and this beautiful young lady." Charles said as he pulled back Holly's chair. "Have a wonderful evening!"

When they got outside, Holly pulled Jake close and gave him a passionate kiss, then whispered in his ear. "I'm thoroughly impressed and will never forget these last two nights."

"That was the idea. I feel lucky to have been with you." Jake said softly, kissing her again.

They finally broke their embrace and began to walk arm in arm towards the house. Lights from the Restaurant behind them and the Trading Post store and bar, provided just enough illumination for them to make out the pathway that led in that direction. It had cooled off a bit and they leaned into each other as they slowly picked their way, pausing to kiss occasionally. When they reached the house, they mounted the steps to the porch where a candle lamp shown through the windows. Jake took Holly in his arms and they exchanged one last passionate kiss. Holly pressed her body against him, and he felt himself straining against the fabric of his trousers.

"You'd best go in Holly, I have to go. It's Sunday dress parade in the morning, and I have to be up early."

She hugged him tightly around the neck, kissed his cheek, then placed her hand there as she released him.

"Okay, but I'm going be there watching, I want to see you one last time in your fancy soldier suit. Good night, my dear!"

CHAPTER 25

Fort Abraham Lincoln- Dakota Territory, September 18, 1875

Saturday afternoon, Jake was sitting in the orderly room of the barracks, visiting with Pat Morse and First Sgt. Martin. He had agreed to pull extra duties in return for his days off the previous weekend, and also Wednesday morning to see Holly off. He had already pulled CQ Duty Wednesday night, and Guard Duty on Friday, and was scheduled to pull Tom Russell's CQ again the next week.

"Well, Rogers," said Martin, "I'm glad to see that you're not moping about all love sick and the like."

"Nah, Top!" Jake answered, "Not me, besides, I've been too busy. I think you've been making me work double for the time off that I had."

"Ah, now, I wouldn't do that. Eh, Pat?"

"No, Mike, I think young Jake here, is feeling a mite sorry for himself, is all." Morse said with a grin.

"Tell you what, I'll spring for the first round of beers up at the trading post." Martin said. "You two up for it?"

"Sure!" they replied.

Jake had not seen the Seips since Wednesday, when Holly left. They had arranged for her to travel by steamboat all the way down to Sioux Falls. From there she would travel by rail to Kansas City and then on to Leavenworth. Jake had gone over to the Post Trader's, Tuesday evening, where they had a going away party for Holly in the bar. Afterwards, he and Holly had gone to sit on the porch at the house where Holly had given him a couple of presents. Jake opened the first one and found a pair of binoculars in a leather carrying case.

"You're always telling me that you like to be out in front scouting, when you're in the field. I figured those will come in handy." She said. The second was an envelope containing a small photograph of Holly to put inside his watch lid, and a chain for it made of woven hair and silver beads.

"So, I figure that every time you look at your watch, you'll think of me." Holly whispered to him softly, with a tear in her eye. "I got one of the laundresses to have an Arikara woman from the fort, to weave it from some of my hair. I was told that one of their holy men blessed it and it would protect you."

Jake had promptly got out his watch and installed them. "You're right," he said showing her, then gathered her in an embrace.

The next morning, he went to see her off at the boat landing, where they said their good byes, and shared a last kiss, before she went on board. He'd stood with Bob and Kate and waved to her as the boat drifted out into the current and got underway, and watched it as it quickly faded into the distance.

When they got to the bar, Kate was waiting tables and greeted them warmly.

"Why if it isn't my favorite sergeants! Come sit down, and I'll bring a round of beers." She said.

When she returned, she asked Jake, "Have you heard that JD quit us? He told Bob that he decided to go back east." She said as she served the beers.

"No, I hadn't heard that. Seems kind of sudden."

"Yes, Bob is not happy, and on top of it, Col. Custer wants a meeting with Bob on Monday. He wants to discuss our prices." She said as she served them

Jake watched her turn and leave, then said to the others, "Excuse me a minute." Then got up and followed her. When he caught up with her, he said, "Kate, let me ask you something."

"What's that?"

"Well, I know that you know what was going on last week when you spent the night in Bismarck."

She looked at him and smiled slightly, not commenting, so he proceeded to tell Kate what Holly had seen when they'd doubled back to the store that night, although he omitted the actual purpose. That drew a frown from her and she said. "I'm sure Bob never authorized him to be looking at that register."

He went on to tell her about seeing JD coming from the Custer house, and catching him meeting with Win Ressengieu.

"Yes, Win is quite friendly with the Custer's and his circle." she commented.

Jake continued to explain about Murray and his suspicions about JD and the possible newspaper connections.

"Sorry, I never had a chance to talk with you about it until now."

Kate considered what she'd heard then exclaimed, "Shit! I knew that there was something about JD that was too good to be true, Damn it to hell!"

Jake said, "I'm sorry, but I thought you should know."

Kate looked at Jake with chagrin and said. "Well, what's done is done. I'll have to find a way to tell Bob."

"Surely it can't be that bad."

"Jake, there are things about our business that you aren't aware of. We are beholden to several other partners, and they have powerful connections. They control the trade at the forts up and down the Missouri River, and even beyond. There's huge amounts of money involved. You do yourself a favor and stay away from us for a while, until we see what happens."

"You're serious?" He asked.

Kate looked him in the eye and said. "Absolutely! Now thanks for telling me. I'll reach out to you if I need to. And please, don't mention anything about this to Holly in your letters."

When Jake returned to the table, he related his conversation with Kate. 1st. Sgt. Martin nodded his head and looked at Jake.

"Ye'd best do as she says for now, lad, and see what comes of the meeting come Monday. But, I wouldn't worry about it too much, Sgt. Major Sharrow told me that the Custer's, and all their guests are leaving for the East at the end of next week. Tom Custer and Lt. Cooke left Tuesday for St. Paul, and our own Lt. Edgerly who is on his way to be married is going along as well."

"So who will be in command of the fort?" Jake asked.

"Capt. Hart, and he's rumored to be leaving soon. A Majority is coming open in the 5th Cavalry soon, and he's senior on the list according to Ed Bobo, so I don't see him worrying much about the prices at the Post Traders." Martin stated.

"There you go Jake, just let things play out, and keep a low profile. Capt. Weir is in Custer's good graces and will be sure to deflect any negative repercussions from your dalliance with Holly." Pat interjected, "So let's have another beer and you can tell us more about your travels down to Louisiana and back home to Springfield. Cpl. Caddle, over in Company I, has been telling Frank Varden some interesting stories about train travel."

Jake grinned, "Oh, I wouldn't put too much into his tales. You two should know better than anyone how an Irishman can tend to exaggerate!"

On Monday, Jake began concentrating on reconnecting with his section, and the rest of the 2nd Platoon. There had been few changes made while he was away. He and Jim Flanagan still served under Pat and the daily routines went smoothly. The temperatures during the day were pleasant, and the nights became cooler as the days began to shorten. All around the fort, preparations for the coming winter began in earnest. The hay and wood contractors wagon trains were steady streams coming and going. The grain and forage warehouses were packed full, and cords of firewood were staged around the roadways and buildings. Having endured winters at Fort Totten over the last two years, D and I Companies were well versed in the what to expect, with the exception of having a town nearby to help break the monotony. Jake hadn't had the time, or inclination, to go to the Post Traders and spent most of his off hours catching up on his letter writing. He wrote to the folks back home, a first letter to Holly, and just as an experiment, he even wrote Vanessa. The NCOs had arranged a steady supply of beer through their pipeline with Camp Hancock, and most evenings those so inclined enjoyed sitting around the mess area talking and playing cards. There was also usually a copy of the weekly Bismarck Tribune laying around for those that wanted to keep up with local and national goings on. Jake was just getting ready to turn in when Pat came in sat down next to him.

"Top just told me that we're to go along with the paymaster detail at the end of next week when they leave for Fort Rice. They're sending us along as an extra escort due to the number of Sioux coming back to the reservation for the winter after they've been out with the roaming bands."

Jake asked, "How many men are we taking?"

"The whole platoon, so we'd best start having the men check their field gear. We'll take a wagon with us, to haul the A tents and a stove. I'm figuring two days down, maybe two days at Rice, then two days back. It'll do us good to get out before the weather turns. Make sure they take their great coats, we could get some snow while we're out."

Jake nodded his head. "I'll start getting the men ready. It'll be interesting to see Fort Rice again. It's been over two years since we came through there."

"I'll warrant it's not changed much." Pat stated, "And, it wasn't much to start with. There may be some barracks space available. Capt. French, and his Company M, and Company D of the 17th Infantry, have been there all summer. Company K, is still in Louisiana, but Capt. Benteen and Company H are just returning from there. So, we'll see when we get there."

"I heard a little about Capt. Benteen when I was down in Louisiana, but he was down in New Orleans and I never met him."

"He's a good officer, but not popular at all with Custer and his crowd. That probably accounts for him always being assigned elsewhere. Say, have you ever played baseball?"

"No, but I've watched a few games"

"Well, you'll probably get a chance if the weather holds. Benteen is an avid baseball enthusiast, he likes to play and always has a handpicked team."

"Okay, that will be interesting."

Wednesday morning during stable call there was more activity than usual. Custer and his entourage were leaving. Several wagons and carriages were made ready, and fatigue details were assigned to handle the loading of the luggage and other baggage that was going with them. They were lined up out on the street in front of Custer's house and after everyone was loaded up, they made their way down to the boat landing. Jake was conducting mounted drills with his section, in the field north and behind the hospital, and had a good view of the procession. He noticed that both Capt. Yates, and Capt. Weir rode along side.

Jake had the men practice forming skirmish order, where the #1s, #2s, and #3s dismounted and took 5 yard intervals, while the #4s held back to the rear holding the mounts. The section in this order extended 30 yards total.

"Damn, with nothing to hide behind it makes a body feel like a target out in the open like this!" exclaimed Rooster.

"The idea is to take advantage of accurate longer range gunfire while kneeling or prone, without having to worry about your horse." Jake called out. "Besides, we're not likely to be in a stand up fight, we're more likely to be chasing them. But if they do turn to fight, a line of firepower should discourage them."

Henry Holden looked over a Golden and said, "If you'd like, I'll exchange you with Greene, and you can hold the horses"

"Aw, Sage, I was just jawing."

"It's best to practice this now, when there's no one shooting at you. Trust me when I tell you that you'll be glad that you did if our Mr. Lo comes calling."

Jake's old set, with Welch #1, Little George as his #2, and Dave Manning #3, were checking their intervals, while Big George held the horses. He circled around behind them, watching.

"Right, that was okay, but we need to be quicker. Let's mount up and do it again."

They remounted and practiced deploying a couple of more times while Jake timed them. When he was satisfied, he had them take a break.

"Well done, Sgt. Rogers!" Jake heard from behind him. He turned to see Capt. Weir sitting on his horse watching.

Jake quickly turned and saluted. "Thank you, Sir. Just getting the horses and men a little exercise while the weather is still good. We'll be seeing plenty of stable time before too long."

"I see. Come ride with me for a few minutes, I haven't had a chance to visit with you since your trip down south."

"Private Holden, take the men back to the stables and have them see to their horses. I'll catch up to you."

"Yes, Sergeant! All right lads, you heard the man, let's be on our way!"

As the section moved away, Weir pointed to the north and said, "Let's ride up the hill, towards the Infantry Post, have you ever seen the fort from up there?"

"Can't say as I have, Sir. I've noticed the blockhouses though, it must be a grand view from there." Jake answered.

When they reached the high ground, they stopped to rest the horses. Off to the east, Jake could see where the Heart River flowed into the Missouri, and beyond that he could make out some of the taller buildings of Bismarck. Looking back, the whole of the Cavalry Post lay spread out along the Missouri riverbank as it flowed to the south.

"Quite a view, eh Rogers?"

"It is that, sir."

"So, how was your journey with Capt. Michaelis, Rogers?"

"It was quite an experience, sir. I have a whole new appreciation for how big and well organized the Army is."

"Well, in most cases, there are areas that could be improved."

"I also learned something about the importance of the railroads and how they are driving the westward expansion. It's all about the land out here, isn't it, sir?"

"That's very astute observation, Rogers! I'm impressed. The Indians claim it, and we want it." Weir looked off to the south and continued. "The Allison Commission is meeting with the Sioux only 50 miles that way. I'm told through the grapevine that the negotiations are not going well."

"All I know is what I've read in the Tribune, sir."

"It's only a matter of time, before Grant runs out of patience. The lure of gold in the Black Hills will force his hand."

"I suppose it will, sir. The flow of miners is getting more everyday, and that's just the ones heading out from this direction."

They sat in silence for a while, and Jake wished he had the binoculars Holly had given him. As if reading his mind, Weir said.

"So, I hear that you and Miss Walker are close. Keogh told me that he saw you with her at the restaurant a few days back."

"Yes, but last Wednesday she left for school down in Leavenworth. We promised to write each other."

"She seemed a sweet girl, a pretty one at that."

Jake nodded his head smiling, "Yes, sir"

"There might be some trouble brewing for her uncle."

Jake looked over at Weir, and said, "I think that maybe he is anticipating some from what I've seen."

"Well, Custer has been presented with some information. It involves alleged payoffs to certain parties, and they are influential acquaintances of Secretary Belknap. It may expose corruption at the high levels, and several prominent officials profiting from the current Post Trader system. He is taking it back to New York with him, and proposes to make it public."

"Well, sir, I suppose if it's true, it could shake things up a bit. Where did this information come from, and why are you telling me this sir?"

"I imagine that given your familiarity with the Post Trader's niece, that you met Mr. J D Thompson.

"Yes, I met him."

"His real name is Ralph Meeker, and he is a reporter for the New York Herald sent here to dig into this matter. Custer and the Heralds's publisher, Gordon Bennett, schemed to provide him a cover. He's headed back east on the train with Custer."

Jake said nothing in reply, and was thinking about the implications.

Weir continued, "I'm telling you this, because I suspect that the repercussions will be felt most out here, where each Post Trader operation will be scrutinized. I personally have nothing against Mr. Seip, but he has raised Custer's ire, and I suspect that will be enough to insure that he loses his contract. I'm not sure how that will have an effect on your Miss Walker, but it gives you some advance notice. I sense that you've already realized that you're not going to make a career of the Army, and that you are weighing your options."

"Yes, sir, I set out to see the country. I've seen quite a bit of it already and suspect that I will see more. I have a much better understanding of how things are changing, and what other opportunities are available. I intend to be the best soldier that I can for the rest of my enlistment, but then I'll be done. So thank you for trusting me with this, sir. I won't let you down."

"Good, now I suspect that there will be no treaty with the Sioux this year. When spring arrives things will begin in earnest. Right now I'm trying to think of ways that will help the men cope with the winter. I'd appreciate any suggestions."

"Yes, sir, I'll think on it."

Jake led the advance party along the trail towards Fort Rice at a walking pace, while Sgt. Morse and the rest of the Platoon escorted the Paymaster wagon and company wagon. Since the weather was good, Morse had decided to overnight en route instead of pushing straight through. The trail south generally stayed close to the Missouri while cutting across several bends in the river. The halfway point was a campsite at the base of some hills near the second bend, in a stand of timber along the mouth of a creek. Aside from the availability of wood and water, the adjacent hills were a good area to hunt game and the men could fish also along the riverbanks. They reached the area around noon, and while Morse and the others stopped to make camp, Jake led Holden's set on a sweep past the camp, and west along the flat ground below the base of the hills where several ravines led up into them.

"We'll circle back and get settled in with the rest of the Platoon. After lunch we'll bring the shotgun and see if we can scare up some prairie chickens. We may even come across some white tailed deer up these draws."

"If it's all the same to you Jake, me and Hurry would just as soon see if we can pull in a few catfish?" Big George asked."

"Yeh, okay, you may have more luck and between us maybe we can come up with something besides salt pork and beans for supper." Jake replied.

When they got back to the camp, the cook was brewing up some coffee and starting lunch, while the Platoon was watering horses, pitching tents, and gathering wood. Morse had detailed guards. The previous fall had been the last time that they'd way laid a trail, but most of the men were veterans and they fell back into the routine quickly. Jake went over to where Morse, Jim Flanagan and Cpl. Wylie were sitting on a log, watching the activity around them.

"I'm not really expecting any trouble, but make sure the men stay armed and alert. Most of the Sioux coming back to Standing Rock should be traveling well south and west of here, and supposedly the rest are gathered up for the Treaty meeting. But it wouldn't do to lose horses to any that might have a mind to sneak up on us." Morse stated, "Jake, lad! Scout those ravines up there this afternoon and while you're at it, I'd sure be partial for some fresh meat!"

"That's what I had in mind, Pat."

"Right, so let's have a bit of a picnic this afternoon, and we'll be about early tomorrow. I'd like to be at the fort by noon. Wylie, you're in charge of posting the guards."

As they approached Fort Rice the next day, Jake realized that he had never seen much of it from the outside, except from the river. They had continued along the west bank of the river staying below the line of wooded bluffs on the flats. The bluffs gradually sloped down and merged onto a wide open plain. Several miles to the south he could make out the stockade walls of the fort, capped by the two blockhouses. As they drew closer, he saw that the northern wall had been removed, revealing the buildings and parade ground. Jake recalled that the main gate had been on the south side of the fort, and also the stables and corrals. The sentries up on top of the block houses waved to them as they skirted the west wall and turned back towards the river. Jake, halted his section and waited for the rest of the platoon to close up, then reported to Morse.

"Looks pretty much the same, Pat. I did notice that there's a few more houses between the stockade and the river, now."

"Well, let me get the paymaster and his boys settled in, and I'll see where they want us." Morse said. "Flanagan, it looks like there's plenty of room in the corral, so go ahead and have the men see to the horses. Keep the wagon handy in case we have to tent. I'll get back to you as quick as I can."

It turned out that with Company K still down in Louisiana on Reconstruction Duty, there was a vacant barracks available. The platoon wagon was parked adjacent to it and the men went inside and sorted out some bunks, then Pat sent a detail to the commissary building to draw some rations while their cook cleaned up the kitchen and fired up the stove. Ironically, it turned out the barracks was the same one that Jake's section had stayed in 2 years previously.

"Ain't that curious!" commented Rooster. "Wish we were getting back on a boat like we did back then."

"Not me, boyo!" replied Biscuit, who was pushing a wheelbarrow that they'd found. "I'd just as soon be hauling wood here, as on a damn boat. Come on, Pat let's go find some firewood for the kitchen. Maybe Sgt. Morse will let us go to the post traders's for a beer after supper?"

"Come on you two, let's be getting busy." said Jake, seeing Sgt. Morse returning with a 1st Sgt. that he didn't recognize, headed in their direction.

"Jake, this is 1st Sgt. John Ryan, Company M. He's another old timer from the Regiment's time down in Kansas. He and I were both corporals back in '67 at Fort Riley."

"Good to meet you, Sergeant. We're just getting settled in and trying to scrounge up some wood for the stove."

"There's plenty over at my barracks next door, there's a big stack back by the kitchen, help yourself." Ryan said.

"You heard the man, you and Greene go get it." Jake directed Golden.

"We were just headed out to the stables to check on things, you want to come along?" Pat asked Jake.

"Sure, I've got Holden and Hurd in charge of getting the barracks squared away."

When they got to the stables, Jake checked to see that the platoon's mounts and equipment were all secured. As he looked over towards the post traders, he noticed a large net stretched between two tall poles, and the field west of it mown down smooth, with pathways that merged into a diamond shape. Ryan noticing him looking at it

"That's Capt. Benteen's new baseball field, there. Company H, just got here Monday, and he had them set that up the second day they were here. He has his own Baseball Club."

"Pat was telling me about that. I know the basics, but we never had enough boys at school for a full team. I'd like to see them play."

"Well, after chow, we'll come down for a few beers and we can watch them. They'll be at it until it get's too dark."

Jake nodded his head in agreement.

The post trader at Fort Rice was a man named J. G. Pitt, he'd only been there since last fall and was happy to have an influx of new customers. To encourage spectators he'd reduced beer prices while the team was practicing. Jake, Pat, and Sgt. Ryan grabbed beers and found a bench where they could watch. Ryan filled them in on the make up of the baseball team.

"They're called the Fort Rice Athletes and their two best players are Joe McCurry, who's not only their best pitcher but was promoted to be their First Sergeant earlier this week, and 'Fatty' Williams the second baseman, who supposedly has been offered a contract to play professionally. Rumor has it Benteen recruited a pair of brothers, Alex and Charlie Bishop, down in Louisiana, just to play on his team. I heard that they trashed the 1st Infantry team down at Fort Randall. I know for a fact that the players get excused from the worst of the fatigue details and get preferential guard duty while the weather is nice enough for them to play."

"Hmm! Seems like a lot of fuss for just a game." Pat observed.

"Benteen himself played in St. Louis before the war, and still bats and plays a little first base during practices. He claims that it's good for morale and discipline."

"I was never around him much. He was sent to Fort Harker down in Kansas that fall, along with Capt. Hale and your company. I only saw him a couple of times over the years after that."

"Here he comes now with his boys." Ryan said inclining his head.

As the ballplayers approached, Jake saw that they were dressed in tight fitting short sleeve shirts, short pants over blue stockings, and light soled shoes. They also sported short billed caps on their heads, most wore fingerless leather gloves and several were toting ball bats over their shoulders. They were led by a tall, broad shouldered man with very light hair, who was busy gesturing with his hands as he spoke with some of them.

"I see that they brought back some new uniforms from Louisiana. Benteen likes to keep up appearances." Ryan said.

Presently, they broke up and ran out onto the field while Benteen took a bat and stood over the white stone plate. The players got busy tossing baseballs around and presently Benteen started hitting them grounders.

****

Captain Frederick W. Benteen

Benteen was born in 1834 and raised in Petersburg, Virginia. His mother died when he was seven and eventually his widowed father moved he and his younger brother to St.Louis in 1849. The young Fred worked in the family business as a painting contractor and was a promising baseball player for the St. Louis Cyclones Baseball Club. In 1861, to the chagrin of his Virginian father, the 27 year old Benteen joined the 1st Battalion, Missouri Cavalry and was elected a 1st Lieutenant. He was quite possibly influenced by his staunchly Pro-Union fiancee, Kate, who he would marry in 1862. He fought in most of the early battles across Missouri and Arkansas as a captain in the 9th Missouri Cavalry, and later in the Vicksburg campaign as a major in the 10th Missouri. He continued to serve in the 10th Missouri, eventually becoming its commander and was eventually promoted to colonel, commanding the 4th Brigade of Gen. Pleasonton's Cavalry Division. His brigade was heavily involved in the pursuit and defeat of Gen. Sterling Price's invasion of Missouri. Benteen finished the war down in the Georgia and Alabama theaters, and was recommended for brevet brigadier general for his actions, though it was never accepted before he mustered out in 1866.

In July of that year he received a Regular Army commission in the new 7th Cavalry Regiment being formed at Fort Riley, where he was assigned command of Company H. He and Custer were complete opposites. Benteen, ever the gentleman, had a quiet soft spoken manner and was popular with his fellow officers and men. While with his nervous energy and personality, Custer tended to be sarcastic, absolutely dominated conversations, and preferred to surround himself with his wife, Libbie, and a close circle of his favorite officers. Benteen quickly grew to dislike this, and was quite vocal about it, particularly when drinking. By the end of the year Custer arranged for he and Company H to be reassigned to Fort Harker commanded by Major Elliot, approximately 100 miles to the southwest. Company M under Owen Hale was also posted there, and the three of them became good friends. Benteen was able to bring his wife and young son in Feb. 1868 and move them into quarters there. The rest of that year was spent roaming across Kansas in pursuit of marauding Cheyenne and he was awarded a brevet to full colonel for his actions at Elk Horn Creek during the War. Benteen then joined the rest of the regiment for the winter campaign that resulted in the fight on the Washita in November. Most notedly for Benteen, he had his horse shot out from under him and got in a pistol fight with a young Cheyenne brave, and then proceeded to kill him. During the fighting his Battalion commander and friend, Major Elliot, took off in pursuit of some warriors, then became surrounded and was killed along with 16 enlisted men. Benteen blamed Custer for not attempting to go to Elliot's aid and eventually that led to a confrontation over a letter that Benteen had authored, which was very critical of Custer's actions. After spending the winter around the Wichita Mountains and Fort Cobb, the regiment helped construct the new Fort Sill, before heading back up to Kansas in April. Custer reassigned Benteen to Fort Dodge, while the rest of the regiment went on to Fort Hays, but by June 1869 they were also at Fort Hays where his Company H, along with Company G and several Infantry companies were posted for the winter. The following spring, he went on leave back to St. Louis. On his return, Benteen found that his Company H along with B, L, & C, was in Eastern Colorado under the command of the regiment's new Major, Marcus Reno. They were deployed to protect the Kansas Pacific Railroad construction crews. They spent the rest of the summer along the Republican River chasing bands of hostiles, then returned to Fort Hays for the winter where Reno assumed command of the post. In May 1871, Benteen and Company H were assigned to Reconstruction Duty in Nashville, Tennessee. While in route, at Louisville, Benteen met with both of the Custer's and his ex-Lieutenant W W Cooke, refusing their request to exchange his assignment to Nashville for one in South Carolina, so that Tom would be closer to his brother. Benteen went so far as to have Col. Sturgis, the 7th's actual commander, support his refusal.

Most of the next two years were relatively peaceful, and Benteen enjoyed the company of his family. The Headquarters of the Department of the South was in Nashville, and it was commanded by Gen. Alfred Terry. Benteen spent his off duty time socializing with the other officers and organizing baseball games, rarely leaving the confines of Nashville. In early 1873, Gen. Terry was reassigned to the Department of Dakota and asked for the 7th Cavalry to be reassigned with him. Terry tasked Col. Stanley and his 22nd Infantry, accompanied by 7th, with escorting the Northern Pacific surveyors. Benteen and Company H participated in this Yellowstone Expedition, where Custer assigned him to stay behind at supply stockade, erected near Glendive Creek, Montana. On the return march he ordered Benteen to slog across the Badlands on the return to Fort Rice. While Custer and 6 companies moved to the new Fort Abraham Lincoln he left the other four, including Benteen and Company D, at the older and more isolated Fort Rice. The following year after the controversial Black Hills Expedition, Benteen and Company D along with two other Fort Rice units were reassigned on Reconstruction Duty in Louisiana. After spending an enjoyable winter in New Orleans much the same as he had in Nashville, Benteen was recalled in May 1875, to Fort Randall, Dakota Territory. He commanded a battalion that included Companies A and E, on an extended patrol into the Black Hills to evict miners. After escorting a large group of them back to Fort Randall, he left and took Company H back to Fort Rice for the winter.

****

Jake enjoyed watching the baseball practice and marveled at the athleticism of the players. Benteen was quite vocal throughout, cajoling his men and offering a few ribald comments when errors were made. Finally, Benteen called the men in together, declared practice over and led them to the post trader's bar.

"First round is on me, Sgt. McCurry!" Benteen announced when they arrived and they all gave out a cheer as they filed inside to get beers.

"Well, that's a jolly bunch." Pat observed, "What I remember of Benteen is that he was always one to watch after his men."

Ryan looked over at Morse, "You've not been around him much since the Washita, he may be jolly now but Benteen has turned into a mean drunk. I've been stationed with him many times over the years and once he's had one too many, it's best to stay well clear of him. We usually get word to his orderly, who can usually coax him back to his wife."

"Aye, tis a pity that drunkenness when it comes to officers tends to get overlooked, when the rest of us have to toe the line." Pat said.

Jake thought about that and was trying to recall any incidents with officers as Pat continued.

"We're fortunate, our Capt. Weir tends to get mellow when he's in his cups, and young Edgerly always seems to be able to pace himself.

" Our Major Tilford likes to tip a cup, and then there's Capt. French, he likes to chase a skirt when he's got load on. There's several of the laundresses that he favors. I have to go retrieve him on occasion." Ryan laughed, "The rest of our lieutenants are all married."

"Up at Lincoln, we're fortunate that we've got Bismarck handy for the single gentlemen. Tom Custer and his friend Cooke, are quite well known among certain circles there." Morse said.

"We've the booze here, but alas few women."

"Next time you're up to Lincoln, I'll show you the sights across the river"

"Right, I'll take you up on that!"

The following day was Saturday in addition to being a payday, so there was almost a festive attitude among the troops. Jake and Pat were invited to go hunting with Ryan that afternoon.

"John's almost an Irishman, his Ma was pregnant when she left to come over, so he's got that goin' for him!" Pat told Jake, as they were going out to the stables to meet Ryan."

"It's a wonder that you tolerate a poor American lad like me."

"Now! I know for a fact that your mother was a Byrne, from Sligo, so you 're half Irish."

"I'm glad you can overlook the wild Welsh blood in me from my Pa."

"Yeh well, Sarah tamed him a bit, didn't she, now?" Pat chuckled.

"I suppose she did. Too bad some of it didn't rub off on you!"

As they were saddling their mounts, Pat stated "You'll find that John Ryan is a fine shot, maybe as good as you. He fought at Gettysburg, and was wounded at Petersburg. He was in the thick of the fighting at the Washita and fought the Sioux on the Yellowstone under Tom Custer, who was with

Company M for several years. He's a steady man in a fight."

When they left the fort, Ryan took them west from the fort and they came to a line of buttes with timbered draws along a creek. They stopped to water the hoses, and Ryan unlimbered a long rifle that he had strapped to his saddle. As he pulled it from its case Jake let out a low whistle.

"That's sure a nice Sharps rifle, John. You don't see many like that out here."

"I got it from a gunsmith up in Bismarck, last month. It's chambered for a 45/70 bullet and has a double set trigger, the scope is a 6 power Malcolm scope and it will let you reach out a ways."

"What'd that set you back?" Pat asked.

"A smooth $100 dollars! I had to wait darned near 4 months for it."

"Damn, how'd you come up with that much money for a rifle?"

"Here and there, but most of it came from buying up some of the old style uniforms. When the Commissary had to quit issuing them they auctioned them off, but it's still okay for the men to wear them. So, I hired one of the tailors to help me sort and alter them, then sold them. I did the same with some damaged gear. It pays to stay on good terms with your post commissary sergeant."

Jake and Pat looked at each other, nodding their heads.

"I'll be doing that, as soon as we get back to Lincoln." Pat said.

They moved on up several of the draws until Jake spotted a large white tailed deer through his binoculars in a clearing several hundred yards out.

"John, do ya see him? He's just up there." He said pointing.

"Yes, I've got him spotted." Ryan answered, then dismounted. "Here hand me those binoculars, and you can take the shot."

"You sure?"

"Well, I reckon it's about 700 yards. Pat here has been bragging on you. Let's see you shoot."

Jake took the proffered rifle, and went down on one knee. While he was adjusting the scope, Ryan passed him a shooting stick. Jake worked on his breathing as he aligned the sights on the front shoulder of the deer, then set the trigger.

"Boom" The sound echoed in the draw and the deer reared then dropped straight down.

"See, I wasn't joshing you, John!" Pat exclaimed. "You owe me five dollars!"

"That was good shooting, Rogers. You handled that rifle well for the first time shooting it." Ryan stated.

'Oh, I fired one of these quite a bit, a few months back." Jake replied.

Ryan looked up at Pat and said wryly, "I should've known, Morse, you neglected to share that with me."

Pat grinned, "What with you having all that money, I figured you might want to share some of it!"

On the return to the fort, in addition to the deer, Jake bagged several brace of prairie chickens with his shotgun, and Ryan took down an antelope. When they got there they dropped them off with the cook, and went to put away their horses. As they were leaving the stables, Pat offered to buy a round of beers at the post traders before they went back to the barracks.

"That's mighty generous of you, Pat!" Ryan observed, dryly.

"Hey, I think it's only fair ta share my good fortune, eh, Jake?"

Jake grinned and answered. "Indeed, Pat, indeed!"

Major Tilford, the post commander, had them fall out for the Sunday dress parade, even though they only had their regular uniforms, and he gave them a cursory inspection. Morse made sure that they looked as good as possible, and Tilford even remarked on it. They relaxed the rest of the day, and left for Fort Lincoln on Monday morning. Sgt. Ryan rode out with them and they had only gone about 5 miles when the sky began to darken, the temperature dropped and it started snowing. Jake rode back to where Pat was riding with Ryan as it got heavier.

"What do you think, John? You've been out here a while."

"Well, you'd just as soon not get caught out on the trail, so I'd push on through." Ryan advised.

Morse nodded his head in agreement, "Okay, I'll inform the Paymaster, that we're going to pick up the pace so we can make it home before dark. I'm sure he won't mind. Stay within sight, Jake."

"Will do. Good to have met you, John." Jake said.

"Likewise, I'll probably make my way up towards you guys once in a while, depending on the weather."

"We'll look forward to it!" Pat said.

By the time they made it back to Fort Lincoln, snow had begun to accumulate and the fields around them turned white. Fortunately the flurries let up a bit, but they'd been served notice that winter was coming.

CHAPTER 26

Fort Abraham Lincoln - Dakota Territory, Late October 1875

As the weather began changing, preparations for winter began in earnest. Most riverboats hurried south carrying miners and traders fleeing the winter. Meanwhile, others came upriver to Bismarck and Fort Lincoln, then scrambled to unload their last cargos of the season before heading back to their winter refuges at Sioux City and farther south. Contractors continued to bring hay and firewood, stacking it where ever they could find a spot. Jake was sent on a patrol up to Mandan, just across the river from Bismarck. While making a loop along the Heart River, he came across a large seam of brown lignite coal. Remembering his experience with Lt. Green during the Boundary Survey, he filled several haversacks with it. When he returned to Lincoln, he conferred with Capt. Weir, and 1st Sgt. Martin about it. Although the existing stoves were meant to burn wood, they experimented with mixing the coal and firewood. Weir checked into it and discovered that the troops at Fort Stevenson had been doing that for years. He sent Jake and a detachment back to the seam with several wagons, where they were able to fill them, and then store the coal strategically near the barracks, for emergency use during heavy snows.

Even though the riverboats had all departed for Yankton and Sioux City for the winter, the trains were still running regular schedules. The NPRR was busy trying to fill Bismarck warehouses before the snow halted them for the winter. Mid-month, a bevy of new replacements arrived from Jefferson Barracks. Top Martin was pleased that he was able to pick up a saddler, aptly named William Sadler, and a blacksmith, John Quinn, along with eight others replacements. Most of them went to the 1st Platoon which had suffered the most losses due to enlistment terms expiring. The lure of the goldfields, and their proximity was negatively impacting re-enlistments through out the regiment. Jake, Pat, and Tom Russell, along with Milt DeLacy, James Bustard, and Mike Caddle, who had been appointed an acting Sergeant pending regimental approval, frequently spent their evenings together playing cards or shooting billiards at the post traders's bar, when they didn't have any duties. They occasionally journeyed over to Bismarck for a change of pace, and to flirt with some of the saloon girls. Pat and Jake continued to keep in touch with Murray Johnson whenever they could, comparing local news from both sides of the river.

The Allison Commission had been unable to negotiate any sort of new treaty with the Sioux and their allies. The general consensus seemed to be that the following spring Grant would put troops in the field to put some pressure on the tribes. One evening Jake was reading the latest copy of the Bismarck Tribune, when he ran across a notice announcing an auction by the Post Commissary of a Lot, consisting of uniforms and various equipment. He and Pat related to the others on how Sgt. Ryan, from Company H, had profited off a commissary auction down at Fort Rice. They all went together, pooling their resources, and prepared to make a bid on an upcoming Lot by Nov. 2nd. Milt had been the battalion quartermaster during the first year of Border survey, and was well acquainted with the current regimental, QM-Sgt.Thomas Causby. Jake suspected that Milt was getting some inside information from Causby,.

The regular duty rotation meant that each sergeant in the company had to serve as Charge of Quarters, or Sergeant of the Guard, at least once a week. Jake used these hours of boredom to write letters. He had started receiving regular letters from Holly. She wrote that she enjoyed school, but missed him. She found Mr. Goodfellow and his daughters a bit stuffy, and had to endure long Sunday sermons with them. Fort Leavenworth was much different from Fort Lincoln, the area was very hilly and had lots of trees. The cavalry troops were mostly units of the 9th and 10th Regiments which were made up of negroes commanded by white officers. There was also an Army prison and she described the prison work gangs that were detailed around the fort, accompanied by grim visaged, armed guards. Holly found the social makeup of Fort Leavenworth to be stifling but enjoyed going to the nearby town, which was bustling with the railroads and people. She described the many stores and shops, along with theaters and parks. To Jake it sounded much like Springfield. He made it a point to respond to each letter, mostly just keeping her apprised of local news. He also wrote to his folks, and occasionally Frank and Colleen. His latest CQ duty was on Halloween night, and that morning when 1st Sgt. Martin came into the orderly room.

"Morning Rogers! How'd it go last night?"

"All good Top! It was a fairly quiet night." Jake answered. "A few of the boys got up to some pranks and mischief, nothing serious. I told them to keep it civil, or I'd see to it that they'd draw privy detail."

"Well, here's a trick for us, Major Reno is back! He got into Bismarck yesterday and just sent word to Capt. Hart to see that his quarters are cleaned up and ready for him. There's a big shuffle going on over at Officer's Row today, as the junior officers have to shift to accommodate him. Fortunately, Capt. Weir is not effected, but Lt. Edgerly is being bumped and I have to detail some men to move his things to a storeroom. He can figure it out when he comes back with his bride."

"Reno, huh? I was hoping he would find another posting and we wouldn't see him again."

"You aren't the only one, Jake m'boy. Go get some sleep."

"Thanks, Top! I'll see you later."

Tuesday afternoon, just before supper, DeLacy came hurrying into the NCO mess, where Jake and the others were lounging.

"We got the bid!" he said excitedly. "We got it!"

The other partners gathered round as Milt flourished some paperwork.

"Here's the inventory list!" he continued. "I persuaded Lt. Nowlan to give us until the weekend to pick it up. Where can we take it?"

Pat said. "I've already asked Murray about that. He can arrange for us to use a space in one of the NPRR warehouses down by the river. He said that he can also help us sell it and that we need to get him copy of the bid inventory. Of course we'll have to pay him a fee."

"Gee, if we get many more involved, we'll be lucky to break even." Bustard groused.

"If you're worried Jim, I'll buy your share back." Caddle offered.

"Naw, I'll see it through."

"Right then! Let's get our hands on a couple of wagons and meet Saturday afternoon."

Once they got everything in the wagons, they went down to the landing and loaded them on the *Denver*. When they reached Bismarck they found Murray waiting for them at one of the piers. As they were unloading, he motioned for Pat and Jake to come over.

"I've been approached by the owners of the Peoples Supply store, a Mr. McLean, and a Mr. Macnider, they are prepared to buy the whole Lot from you pending inspection. You boys won't have to repair, or mend anything."

"How much they are they willing to pay?" Jake asked.

"One thousand dollars!" Murray replied. "Cash."

"What do you think, Murray? Is it worth more?"

"I think you'll make a tidy profit for a days work. They tried to bid on it, but somehow their bid was misplaced. Funny how that happened!"

Jake looked over at Milt, who suddenly had taken an interest his boots.

Pat smiled and said, "Yes, it is. Let us talk over with the others, and I'll get you an answer."

They huddled together and Jake did some quick calculations. They were surprised that the amount offered was that high. After all was said and done, they stood to make a quick profit of almost $150 each, which amounted to almost a years pay. They all elected to take the deal. Within an hour they had the money in hand and were headed downtown to cerebrate. Murray invited Pat and Jake to Forster's for dinner, and after they ordered he looked at them smiling, and raised his beer glass.

"A toast to your intrepid endeavors! You know that you won't be able to pull that off again. I guarantee that McLean and Macnider will see to that." Johnson stated. "Word will get around to the other bidders, too."

"Why is it so important to them? It seems a lot to pay for surplus and used goods." Jake asked.

"It gives them a legitimate cover for having government issue goods. That way when they sell something marked U S, they have a convenient alibi."

"So what are you saying, that they're crooked?" Pat asked.

"I suspect that they re-market many such items and not all are surplus. They are also networked with several Indian Agents. Read their ads in the paper and you can draw your own conclusions."

"Well, now, that doesn't sit so well with me." Jake stated.

"Be that as it may. You've just learned that entrepreneurs out here on the edge of civilization, where the lines are blurred, seize opportunity where it lies and the ramifications be damned. But, I think it's going to blow up on some of them before too long. With the Indian troubles brewing out here, these greedy activities may undo them. I've heard that the Democrats back in Washington are seeking to expose the rampant corruption in the current system."

"I think that I'll stick with being a soldier, where the lines are plainly marked" Jake replied.

"I'll drink to that!" Pat exclaimed.

After they toasted Murray announced that he was heading to St. Louis for the winter the following week. The last scheduled train had gone earlier so Murray was taking most of the rolling stock, and the last locomotive, back to Fargo for the season.

"I hate to leave you fellows out here in the cold, but there's nothing for me to do until probably mid-April. That's when we started this year if you two will recall? We are supposed to be getting some big snow plows to mount on the front of our trains next spring."

"Well, keep in touch and send us some St. Louis newspapers once in a while." Jake said.

"I'll do it!" Murray replied.

Jake reached into his pocket and extracted several letters that he written, including one for Vanessa, and handed them to him. "Here, post these for me when you get there, would you? "

After looking at the addresses, Murray said. "I'll see that they get mailed. Now let's you two and I go celebrate! You can spend some of your new found cash on the first round!"

The following Tuesday Nov. 9th, Capt. Weir informed the Company D NCOs that orders had been handed down from Headquarters that the Army would no longer interfere with miners headed to the Black Hills. They all found this ironic because since Benteen's return to Fort Rice, the regiment hadn't done anything of the sort. Besides, with the arrival of the Dakota winter, no one in their right mind would be moving about. That evening at the NCO mess there was more discussion about it.

"Sounds to me like the government has made up its mind to ignore the treaty." said Bustard.

"Yep, it sure sounds like it, and that's bound to get the Sioux riled up." Tom Russell commented, "I sure hope that they stay in their camps until spring."

"Aye, those of us that were at the Washita fight remember traipsing around in the snow. I'll warrant that the winter snows up here are much deeper!" Pat said.

"Yes, and have you noticed the drift ice beginning to come down the river, I'd bet that it will be frozen solid in a couple of weeks!" Caddle exclaimed. "The temperature has been falling steadily."

"Well, you can bet Reno will not be keen to run after them. He's not spent a winter out here, yet. I'm surprised that he hasn't found an excuse to leave and head back east." DeLacy said.

"Oh he likes being in command, he's got Lt. Porter again as his acting Adjutant until Lt. Cooke returns. Reno actually does very little but strut around Officer's Row, socializing." Bustard declared. "Our Capt. Keogh has no other officers to help him, with Lt. Nave still off recovering, fortunately we've been used to that, eh acting 1st Sgt. DeLacy?"

"Yes, but I'll be glad when Top Varden gets back from leave in a couple of weeks. I don't enjoy dealing with the paperwork."

"The last train ran on the 3rd. They quit running when the tracks got covered with snow and ice. He'll have a rough time getting back." Caddle said.

Sgt. Daniel Kanipe from Company C who had been listening, spoke up. "There's an express stage that runs between Bismarck and Fargo along the telegraph road once a week during the winter. It carries the mail and a few passengers, though I've heard it's a cold ass journey. It takes at least four days depending on weather."

"Were you here last winter?" Jake asked.

"Yep, and the one before that, too! That was right after the fort was built and the unseasoned cottonwood boards used for the building walls all warped. Snow would drift up inside the barracks, we like to froze our buts off! They're better now though, most of the holes got plugged up."

"At least the buildings at Fort Totten were all made of brick. It was still damn cold though!" Mike said.

"So, I reckon you fellas already know how cold it gets, but the snow here can drift up so bad, it's almost on the roofs and the wind can be so fierce that a body can get blown over walking, Them's the days to just hunker down!"

"Yeh, we had those days at Totten also. But I reckon that here, at least a man can get over to Bismarck once in while, particularly after the river freezes over." Bustard commented.

"Yes, that's true, there's an omnibus line that runs back and forth when weather permits. Plus, we've gotten pretty good at converting some of the wagons to sleighs. We have a couple of covered ambulances rigged out to maintain the telegraph. That's a volunteer duty for a hardy soul, by God!" Kanipe stated.

Nothing much of consequence happened over the rest of November. It was growing steadily colder and the daily formations were curtailed during snow storms and most inspections were held indoors. The sergeants made sure that the men had all of their winter clothing and cold weather gear ready. The buffalo coats, leggings, muskrat fur caps were re-issued, along with arctic gloves. Jake was grateful for the woolen neck scarf his mother had made him, and was envied by his friends. He went to the Post Trader's on occasion to visit with the Seip's, where he and Kate visited a little about Holly. She told him that Bob was still fussing about the dirty trick that had been perpetrated on him by Custer and Ralph Meeker and was worried about repercussions from it. The Missouri River was frozen solid by the last week of the month, and several parties were sent out from both Bismarck and the fort, to test the thickness and mark a trail across. A regular scheduled omnibus began daily service between the two. The saloon and brothel entrepreneurs over at The Point did the same. The companies were careful to rotate their men assigned to the dreaded water details, which entailed keeping a hole in the ice broken and filling water barrels to distribute to the stables, barracks, and other quarters. Stable call was limited to feeding and caring for the horses and other livestock.

On the 27th, Lt. Tom Custer and Lt. WW Cooke made a return to the fort after having taken a special stage from Fargo to Bismarck. They were 14 days overdue and after their arrival, Major Reno required that they write letters explaining their delay. The Bismarck Tribune ran an article announcing that General Crook was preparing for an expedition at Fort Laramie, against Sitting Bull and the bands wintering with him, which caused quite a stir among the officers.

The first Sunday in December, Jake and Pat took advantage of a break in the weather to go over to Bismarck for the day. They had a shopping list for the NCO mess, and after filling it, went to Camp Hancock to arrange for its covert delivery on the next commissary run . While they were talking with the NCO over the warehouse, he told them the latest rumors. Supposedly, the Bureau of Indian Affairs was getting ready to issue an ultimatum to the tribes. All of the roaming bands were to report to the various Indian Agencies by Jan. 31st, or they would be classified as hostile and military force would used to return them to the reservations.

"You can tell that whoever decided that has never been out here in the dead of winter. Hell, nothin' moves out here at that time of the year, not even the Sioux! Sounds to me like they're just cookin' up an excuse to start a fight!" The Infantry sergeant exclaimed.

"Yes, it seems so," answered Pat, "But, I'll worry about that when it happens. In the mean time, let's worry about making it through the winter. Here, I want you keep a copy of this list and we'll send you a telegraph when we want another special requisition. We'll pay you when it's delivered."

"Sure thing, you tell Ol' Ed Bobo that Billy Jackson said hello. We served together down at Leavenworth, years back."

"I'll do it!"

In early December the shuffling continued along Officer's Row, as Capt. Hart left to accept a Major's slot in the 5th Cavalry, and Capt. Thompson, the nominal C.O. of Company B who had remained at Fort Lincoln when it was posted to Louisiana, retired from the service. Tom

Custer was promoted to Captain, and assumed command of Company C. Lt. Cooke reassumed his position as Post Adjutant, much to the satisfaction of Capt. Keogh and Lt. Porter of Company I. A telegram arrived from New York on the 13th, notifying Major Reno that he would continue as Post Commander. It seems that Custer had been able to get his leave extended for another two months. Word had it that Reno had been very pleased when he received it.

The temperature continued to drop and stayed below zero, even during the day. As Christmas drew near, the companies took turns planning parties and balls. The men cleaned and cleared space inside the barracks, helping the laundresses in decorating with whatever they could. The cooks prepared special menus and the regimental band provided the music. The few officer's wives, and the laundresses showed up in their fanciest gowns and danced with some of the single men. Strict social protocols were followed by the officer wives, but the rest of the women didn't lack for dance partners. The ambulances had been converted with bobsled runners and served as sleighs to deliver the party goers from their various quarters. When it became Company D's turn, since Capt. Weir was a bachelor, 1st Sergeant Martin's wife, Ellen served as hostess of the Company D gala. She and the other enlisted mens wives and laundresses oversaw all of the preparations. Jake and Tom Russell were assigned as ushers, and saw to it that the guests were escorted to their tables. Since Col. Custer was on leave, Jake had checked with Top Martin to see if it was okay to extend an invitation to the Seips. It was customary for all of the regiment's officers to be invited to each party. He took note that Capt. Keogh, Capt. Weir, Capt. Custer, and Lt. Cooke were in all great demand as dance partners among the officer wives, while Major Reno received a token dance from each of them. Jake found himself taking a couple of reluctant turns on the dance floor and managed to not totally embarrass himself. One of the highlights of the evening was when Pat Golden, Joe Greene, and Dave Manning put on a dazzling display of footwork of Irish dancing. Once the band finished playing, Jake and Tom resumed their roles as ushers, and co-ordinated with the Ambulance drivers to get the partygoers delivered back to their various quarters. When the last of them left, Jake sat down with his section to share a drink and visit with the members of his old 'set of four'.

They were talking about the holidays back when they were at Fort Totten, when Jake asked, "You boys still have your dark glasses?"   .

"Sure, except Dave here?" Welch asked, "They still come in handy with all of the snow. Why are you asking, and why do I think you've got something in mind?"

"Well, how would you all like to get out of the regular company details?" Jake queried.

They all looked at him expectantly and Big George replied, "And how would we go about that, Jake?"

"I'm thinking of volunteering for the telegraph line repair and mail route. I'd like to have some men that I can depend on with me."

"That sounds like a good way to freeze to death to me!" Charlie exclaimed.

"No, we'll have a couple of the covered ambulance wagons, converted to bobs just like the guests rode in tonight. They'll have small sheet iron stoves in them for warm at night, if needed. We'll go out following the telegraph lines along the railroad and then meet the Fargo crew at the halfway point, in Jamestown. There are stage stations to stay at along the way. We'll be out for two weeks at a time."

"Ah, still sounds iffy to me!"

"Hey, we'll be better prepared then when we got caught in that blizzard up on the boundary couple of years ago. We have our arctic gear now and know how to dress, remember when Val Wheeler took us ice fishing? Plus, we can hunt some game along the way."

"I'm in!" Little George stated. "I hate that damn water detail!"

Charlie looked over at Big, who nodded his head in affirmative.

Dave Manning stared at the others for a few seconds, then said. "Ah hell! I hope that you boys know what you're up to."

Jake grinned, "Trust me, it'll be okay! I propose a toast! Here's to a short winter!"

The following Monday after morning formation Jake asked Top Martin and Pat about his plan. They looked at him quizzically at first, but then saw that he was serious.

"I think you'll have to clear this with Capt. Weir." Martin said. "Let me tell him what you're up to."

That afternoon Jake was summoned to the Orderly Room to report to Weir.

"So, 1st Sgt. Martin tells me you want to volunteer for the telegraph line and mail detail."

"Yes, Sir!"

"You realize that you'll be on your own if things get bad?"

"Yes, Sir! But I learned a lot over the last two years. Val Wheeler showed us how to hunt and move around during the winter back at Fort Totten. I feel confident that we can handle ourselves out there. Besides, it'll be a break from the day to day monotony around here."

"I can't say as that I can blame you for that, Sgt. Rogers. Very well, you have my permission to go see Lt. Cooke at the Adjutant's Office. He makes those assignments."

When he went, Lt. Cooke quizzed Jake about his experience and winter survival skills. Jake related their activities back at Fort Totten, and up on the Boundary. He made sure to note that he was well versed in land navigation from his two years up there assisting Lt. Greene, and then mentioned that he had been studying telegraphy and the Morse Code.

"I seem to recall that you're very proficient with a rifle, also. I believe that I can put you to work, Sgt. Rogers. How soon can you have your team ready?" Cooke asked.

"Give me a few days, to gather our gear, and work things out with Sgt. Martin, and we'll be ready to roll."

"Good, I'm going to schedule you for the next run. Sgt. McDermott and his men from Company A are out right now, and will be back at the end of the week just in time for Christmas. I don't intend to send anyone out until January the 3rd, unless we have a break in the line."

"We'll be ready, Sir."

Cooke wrote at length on a piece of paper, then handed it to Jake.

"Give this to Sgt. Major Sharrow, he's in charge of equipping the teams. He'll see that you and your men are excused from regular duty at the end of the month so you can get prepared. I suggest that you go to the telegraph office and spend some time practicing, when you can. See that you learn how to make a good telegraph wire splice while you're there."

"Yes, Sir! Thank you sir." Jake said, saluting.

"Carry on Rogers, and be careful out there."

On Christmas Eve, the newly promoted Capt. Custer, his brother-in law Lt. Calhoun, and his sister Maggie went to great lengths to put on an elaborate ball in the Company C barracks. Aided by Capt. Moylan, Lt. Cooke, and Lt. Smith, the commissary officer, they were able to arrange quite a holiday extravaganza. They borrowed Win Ressengieu's head chef to put on the banquet. Many prominent people from Bismarck were invited and the Regimental Band played the whole evening. Mean while, over at the NCO mess, a tree had been decorated and a special menu had been arranged for the other sergeants, along with a variety of beverages to sample. Jake and Pat had each received packages from back in Springfield, and proudly compared the heavy wool socks that they had each been sent. Jake also got a package from Holly containing a new razor, and whet stone.

Later on, they bundled up and went out on the porch to listen to the fort minstrel group that billed themselves as the 'Sable Warblers'. The troupe made their way along Officer's Row and back along the various barracks singing Christmas carols. As the evening progressed and they imbibed the Christmas cheer handed out by their audiences their singing began to deteriorate, but not their enthusiasm.

New Year's Day was on a Saturday and most of the troops were grateful for the lighter schedule and duty rosters, especially those that had overdone their celebrations the night before. Jake and his men were sorting through their gear, and getting fitted for their moccasin overshoes that Dave Manning was making. He had heard that the Arikara scouts had some moose hides and talked Jake into going to see if he could go barter with them for some. Dave swore that it wore better and was less apt to get saturated than buffalo hide. Jake had gone to see them and bartered for a couple of the hides, and several sets of their snowshoes. Lt. Cooke sent over a couple of civilian teamsters who would be in charge of the mule teams and driving the ambulance wagons. The older one, Jack Ward, was an ex-soldier familiar with the trails, and the other one, Joe Martin, looked to be part Indian. They had been out with the regiment during the Black Hills Expedition.

"You boys, know what you're fixin' to get yourselves into?" Martin drawled, "It gets colder than a witch's tit out there on the trail."

Jake eyed him, and replied. "While you were picnicking your way down to the Black Hills and back, we were up north surveying the Boundary. Then we spent the last couple of winters over at Fort Totten. We know what cold is."

Martin nodded his head, "Okay, don't get riled up, I reckon you do. Me and Jack here just want ta make sure we ain't puttin' our butts on the line with some tenderfeet."

"So you fellas have been running this route for a while?" asked Welch. "You know the trail well?"

"Yeh, I reckon we know it as well as anyone. It pretty much follows the railroad tracks. The stage line from Fargo to Bismarck and some freight haulers use it too." Ward replied. "It's pretty well marked, ceptin' during a blizzard. Then it's best to find a place to hunker down for a spell when the snow starts pilin' up. There's a few places along the way to shelter and get out of the wind. They're stocked with firewood and feed."

"So, it sounds like we won't be all by ourselves out there." Jake said.

"Oh, most likely we'll run into some other fools too dumb to stay home." Martin stated. "How you boys fixed for grub?"

"We'll get by, and I'm sure we'll come across some game. You and Jack are welcome to mess with us."

"Good to hear. I think we ought a get goin' at first light tomorrow, if that's okay with you, Sarge?"

Jake nodded his head, and said, "We'll meet you at the Adjutant's Office at 7:00 to pick up what ever Sgt. Major Sharrow has, then head over across the river."

Jake was surprised when they made it over to Bismarck the next morning and were met by several local businessmen. Jack Ward went over and met with them, then came back over to Jake. He showed him lists of items that they had ordered by telegraph, and that were being shipped to Jamestown via the telegraph crew, out of Fort Seward, on their return leg from Fargo.

"They pay us to back haul this stuff for them, Sergeant Rogers, cause we can haul more than the stage line, and we don't charge as much. Me and Joe, will split it with you boys."

"Well, I suppose there's no harm in us helping them out, seeing as how we'll be coming back this way."

Ward grinned, "Hey, we're the ones taking the risks out on the trail. We may as well make a little bit extra. Based on these lists, we stand to make some good money this trip."

Jake's eyebrows rose and he said. "Jack, you and I are gonna get along just fine!"

They made the trip to Jamestown and back with little trouble. Once they left Bismarck, the landscape became a vast white expanse from horizon to horizon. Fortunately, the trail was marked by the telegraph poles sticking up through the snow drifts and they just followed the them. Most nights they sheltered the mules under canvas tarps stretched as a lean-to from the wagons sleds. They slept on stretchers inside the wagons, taking turns to keep the small, sheet iron stoves banked. The Seims Express Company operated a bi-weekly stagecoach/sleigh service between Fargo and Bismarck, and had built depots along the way. They met several of the stages coming and going, and shared shelter and firewood when they could. Snow fell frequently adding to the accumulation already on the ground and several days they were limited by blowing snow and poor visibility. The wind blew incessantly out of the north and snow frequently drifted over the trail. They had no option but to plunge through them, staying at all times in sight of the telegraph poles that marked the way. As they plodded east, they only found one broken wire and repaired it using the Western Union splice method they had learned. Jake picked Charlie and Little George to climb the poles. The galvanized wire was difficult to work with in the cold, and while wearing gloves. They had to take turns rotating every fifteen minutes or so. While the wires were being repaired Jake roamed the area seeking small game and was able to bag some prairie chickens and rabbits, being careful to not range too far from the team. They found that their winter gear allowed them to move about comfortably as the temperature hovered just above zero during the days, dropping below after dark. After five days on the trail they made it to Jamestown, where they spent a couple of days resting at Fort Seward. Companies E and L of the 7th were assigned there and welcomed them with indoor accommodations. They loaded up the Army mail and the goods that the Fort Seward team had just hauled back from Fargo on their return leg, then left for Bismarck. The return journey proved to be uneventful and they made it back to Bismarck on Friday the 14th. As soon as they reached the downtown, a crowd quickly gathered.

"Damn, these folks are like vultures hovering about!" Charlie commented as the locals gathered about the wagons.

"Well, there ain't much excitement goes on around here during the winter." Ward stated, "I'd guess we're the closest thing to it today. I'll start going over the lists of goods with our local merchants and collect our money as they claim their goods. You boys see to gettin' the mail sorted out that stays here at Camp Hancock. I'd say we can still make the fort by dark."

Ward proved to be a shrewd negotiator as he bargained with the locals and collected the fees. When they headed out he divvied up the money and they were all quite pleased. As they crossed the river on the trail to Fort Lincoln, Jack spoke up.

"Now lookee, here fellas, I know that you're cold and tired, but when we get to the fort it won't hurt to ham it up a bit. We want them to think that we're about all in so folks feel sorry for us and we can goldbrick for a few days. We'll go out again in a couple of weeks and will probably get a least one other run in before spring. We don't want to jeopardize our little freight business, so don't go tellin'everybody."

Jake looked over at Welch and said. "Charlie, you see to it that the others keep a low profile. I'll check in with Top and let you know about the duty roster."

When he got to the orderly room, he found 1st Sgt. Martin and Pat Morse waiting for him. They had a pot of coffee sitting on the wood stove.

"Well, Rogers you look like a mountain man in that get up." Martin said, "Would you care for a cup of coffee?"

"Thanks, Top, I believe I would." Jake answered, shedding his gloves, he produced a bottle of whisky from his coat pocket, "And, perhaps a bit of this to go in it. We backhauled several cases of this for Robert Wilson's store over in Bismarck. He gave me this bottle and a bundle of cigars as bonus for bringing them back safely."

Morse replied, "Sure now! And you're always one to share your good fortune!"

Jake told them about his trip along the line, the conditions that he'd encountered, and also about the freight backhauling enterprise. The two older men nodded their heads in appreciation.

"Good on you lad!" Martin exclaimed, "Let me think on that. We may have to take advantage of that on your next outing. Now go see to your lads, and come see me tomorrow. We'll see about easing you back into the duty schedule until you go out again."

CHAPTER 27

Fort Abraham Lincoln - Dakota Territory March 1, 1876

Jake and his trail team had gone out again in early February. The weather was better than their first trip although the temperature never rose much above 20 degrees. They had learned from the first trip and developed a daily routine, striving to maximize the daylight hours and not overtax the mule teams. They took along some buckets of lignite coal with them, to augment their wood supply. Jake developed a firm liking for Jack Ward, and enjoyed his gruff banter. Ward knew the route like the back of his hand and Jake deferred to him on setting their daily progress, traveling as the weather dictated. Joe was more taciturn, but was a whiz at caring for the mules. Jake came to realize that all of the men that worked the trail on the stage coaches and freight wagons, had a loose camaraderie and took pride in braving the elements. This trip, Top Martin sent along some money from the Company D food fund, and Jake and his men were able to procure some goods for the mess. When they returned with them to Fort Lincoln, they discretely off-loaded them at the barracks and NCO quarters, where they were greatly enjoyed as a pleasant change in the monotonous fare of winter rations. Their turn in the rotation came around again and they were making preparations to go back out. Sgt. McDermott and his team brought back word that the Northern Pacific had sent out a work train from Fargo the week before to attempt to open the road west. Work crews accompanied the train, clearing snow and repairing the tracks. It hadn't reached Bismarck, but was expected before the end of the week, so this would probably be their last trip of the season.

When Jake and the team made ready to leave Bismarck, the local merchants, anticipating the renewal of rail services, had only a few small lists of goods for them to back haul as they headed out towards Jamestown. The weather was moderate, but still below freezing during the day.

"Everyone is getting too worked up about the winter being over." Jack commented, "I've seen some damn big snow storms out here in March! The snow can drift up somethin' fierce. We'd best keep an eye out for places to hole up."

The following afternoon, they were approaching a cut along the rail line called '16th Siding' which was a collection of boxcars with their wheels removed. The whole cut was mounded over by snow and only the top few feet of the telegraph poles protruded. The teams used the boxcars as a stopping point and regularly over nighted there. They saw smoke on the horizon and were soon treated to the sight of an enormous snow plow mounted on the lead locomotive as the Northern Pacific work train approached. There was a crew of men out front walking the tracks, checking for debris and prodding the snow where it drifted over the right of way. Another crew was attacking the drifts of snow and ice with picks and shovel until they were reduced enough for the snow plow to bull through. They saw the two Army sled/wagons and waved over at them to stop. Jake got down and met them as they walked towards them.

"You fellas must be from Fort Lincoln. How'd the tracks look from here back to Bismarck?" one of the men asked.

"Not bad! At least not as bad as it is around here." Jake answered, "We heard you left Fargo last week, and you're just now getting here. It must be slow going for you!"

"Hell yes! We've been busting our asses the whole way!" one of the rail workers exclaimed.

"Seems like a waste of effort to me, if you boys would just wait a few weeks the thaws will be starting." Jack called out.

"I agree, but everyone is clamoring to get the road open. There's a shit load of miners all aiming to head for the Black Hills and boxcars full of goods for the businesses of Bismarck to sell to them. Hell, the mayor and newspaper publisher from Bismarck are in Fargo lobbying my bosses to get the trains rolling."

"Well, good luck!" Jack replied. "I hope you don't get shit on by Ol' Man Winter! He may not be done yet."

The team made it to Jamestown without difficulty on Tuesday, the 7th. Just before they got there, the work train traveling at regular speed passed them on its return leg back to Fargo. As they got up to Fort Seward to settle in for the night, snow began to fall. Sgt. Fred Hohmeyer, the acting 1st Sergeant, invited them to bunk in the Company E barracks. They were in the mess hall when he came in and sat down with them.

"It's snowing outside and it seems to be gettin' heavier, you might wait bit and see before you head out in the morning, Rogers."

"I thought it was looking a might blizzardy!" stated Ward, "I was telling these boys that winter wasn't done."

"Yeh, and we just got word that a special train is being put together, over in Fargo, to head for Bismarck tomorrow. It seems that General Custer has persuaded the Northern Pacific to get him back to Fort Lincoln right away. So, there's no need for you to be in a hurry. The train may be here before you can get back on the trail."

"Well, we'll see what it looks like in the morning." Jake said, "We may wait a day and before we head back out."

The following morning they woke to find the wind howling out of the north and a total white out. The snow was drifting rapidly wherever it found a vertical barrier in its path.

Jack Ward and Joe Martin went to see to the mules, and when they returned they voiced their displeasure.

"Ain't fit for man or beast, out there. We damned near got lost between here and the stables. I'd say we ain't goin' anywhere soon!" Jack exclaimed, as he shook the snow off his buffalo coat. "Old Hawkins is out today I tell ya!"

Jake came over offering Ward a cup of coffee. "Here, I think you're right. We'll just wait and see when this breaks."

The storm raged on for two more days before abating. Word reached the fort that the special train had been unable to get through to Bismarck, and its whereabouts were a subject of speculation. Jake consulted with Jack Ward and they decided to venture forth on Friday morning. After stopping in Jamestown briefly to pick up their loads, they broke trail through the drifts, and headed west using the line of telegraph poles as guides. The weather cleared but was cold and brisk and they set as fast a pace as the mules could maintain without overtiring them. By Sunday they were past the halfway mark and Monday morning as they set out their goal was to make it to the parked boxcars, at 16th Siding. By afternoon they were still several miles out when they spotted the train sitting motionless on the tracks. Jake pulled out his binoculars to get a better look. Small tendrils of smoke wafted from stove stacks in the railcars and he could see men moving around outside the train. It appeared that the engines had been disconnected. He could just make them out farther along the tracks off in the distance and handed the glasses to Jack.

"What do you make of that." he asked.

Railroad Snow Crew - Circa 1870s

"I'd say they got stuck, and tried to buck the snow drifts with the plow and engines. Looks like they got a pretty good running start but I guess they got stuck." Ward replied, as he handed the binoculars back.

"Well, I guess we ought to go see what's up and see if we can help." Jake said.

As they approached the train several men dismounted from the last car, and stood waiting for them. Jake saw that they were officers and recognized Lt. James Bell, but none of the others. When they were close enough Bell called out.

"Where are you men from, and are you headed for Bismarck?"

Jake climbed down and turned to salute.

"Sgt. Rogers, Sir! It's good to see you again. We're the mail and telegraph team out of Fort Lincoln and we're our way back there, now."

Bell peered at him closely, "Sgt. Rogers, you always surprise me when you show up. It's a mite bit colder here though then down in Louisiana isn't it?"

Jake grinned and replied, "It is indeed, Sir!"

"Luckily, I'm due 6 months leave as soon as I report back to Lincoln. I'll be headed back this direction in a week or so, hopefully the trains will be running regularly." Bell turned to introduce the other two officers, and a civilian "These gentlemen are Lt. William Low, and Lt. Frank Kinzie, of the 20th Infantry. They are in charge of the battery of Gatling Guns aboard the train. They're on their way to join the 7th at Fort Lincoln. The other man is Mr. Mark Kellogg, a newspaper man, sometime Northern Pacific train dispatcher, and erstwhile telegraph operator. Gentlemen, let me introduce you to Sgt. Jake Rogers, don't let his youthful looks deceive you, he's extremely well traveled."

Jake saluted them, "Welcome to Dakota in the winter, Sirs."

Bell continued by informing Jake, "You just missed General and Mrs. Custer. Tom Custer came out with a sleigh and hauled them back to Lincoln. Mark here found a pocket relay and battery to connect to the lines, and was able to contact Bismarck and the fort. His boss, Mr. Lounsberry, and Mayor McClean, were also picked up. They rest of us are waiting for manpower to arrive to dig out the locomotives and reconnect them to the rest of the train."

"Well, Sir, being as we're Company D troops on this team, we'd be glad to escort you, if you want to ride with us. We can be in Bismarck by dark if we hustle."

"I think that's a capital idea, Sgt. Rogers!" He turned to the others and said, "I feel sure that Low and Kinzie must stay with their detachment, but you're welcome to hitch a ride, Mark, if you'd like. I'm sure Sgt. Rogers can find a spot in one of the sleigh wagons."

Kellogg looked at Jake and said, "Hello, Sgt. Rogers, we meet again. I'd like to join you but I believe that I'd better sit tight and monitor the pocket key relay until we get moving. I'll need to climb up and repair the splice where we tapped in, but thanks for the offer."

Jake noticed that Kellogg had his brown corduroy pants tucked into tops of tall linesman boots, with leather straps encircling them to secure pole climbing spikes.

"Suit yourself, but that was pretty damn resourceful idea to climb up and hook onto the line. You're a man of hidden talents, Mr. Kellogg." Jake observed.

"Yes, you can bet that Custer won't forget that. He'll find a way to reward you, Kellogg." Bell stated. "Let me grab my valise and I'll be ready to roll, Rogers."

When they got to Bismarck, Lt. Bell left them to catch Deitrech's Omnibus wagon sleigh across the river trail over to Fort Lincoln, while Jake, Ward, and the other men offloaded the few crates and packages that they'd hauled. Most of the merchants crowded around them wanting information from them about the status of the train. There were several with large shipments of mining goods inside the stranded boxcars that had been ordered to outfit the anticipated serge of Black Hills bound gold seekers. Once they settled up, the team went on to the fort. Dusk was settling in when they pulled up in front of the Adjutants Office. Jake went up the steps, and found the regimental Sergeant Major, William Sharrow getting ready to walk out the door.

"Excuse me Sergeant Major. I just brought in the mail and dispatches from Jamestown."

Sharrow pointed over his shoulder, "Just set it in there on my desk, Rogers. I'll see to it in the morning. I'm just headed over to see General Custer, he's just made it back."

Jake looked over across the parade ground to Officer's Row, which was all aglow with lights, and replied. "That's what I heard too, Sergeant Major."

"Well, good job Rogers! I think you're done for the winter. Best be getting your lads ready for the field, there's plans afoot and with the Custer back, they'll be pushed ahead. He's not much for patience. I'll tell Captain Weir, that you're back."

"Oh, he'll probably know it, we brought Lt. Bell back with us from the train."

It turned out that Custer's return was brief. While on leave, Custer had gotten himself embroiled in the Post Tradership Scandal that his friend James Gordon Bennett, of the New York Herald and his Democrat cronies had stirred up. Custer was summoned back to Washington to testify before a Congressional Committee chaired by the powerful Democrat Hiester Clymer, investigating allegations of corruption and kickbacks in the post tradership/sutlers along the Missouri River forts. Custer left to head back east to Fargo on the Seim's stage line on the 20th, the same day that the stranded train finally rolled into Bismarck. He had decided to travel by himself, leaving Libbie at Fort Lincoln. Both Bob Seip and Wilson, the former Post Trader at Fort Lincoln, had also been summoned and were traveling to Washington to give their testimonies.

Spring was slow to arrive and the continued winter weather resulted in the slowing the ongoing preparations for the coming campaign. The roaming bands of Sioux and Cheyenne had not come in to report to the reservations. General Sheridan had directed the plans and intended to have three converging Columns in the field. The Montana Column consisting of five companies of the 7th Infantry and four companies of the 2nd Cavalry was assembled at Fort Ellis and would be under the command of Colonel John Gibbon. It was already moving east on March 17 along the Yellowstone River. At the same time, the Wyoming column with five companies each from the 2nd & 3rd Cavalr and two companies of the 4th Infantry, was under the command of General George Crook. It had left Fort Fetterman on March 1 and battled blizzards and frigid weather as it made its way North. On March the 17th a strike force under the command of Col. John Reynolds led a disorganized attack on a village of winter roamers along the Powder River. After capturing the village and pony herd, then burning most of the lodges, Reynolds turned back towards Crook and the main Column abandoning some of his dead. The Indians followed him that night and recaptured most of the pony herd then scampered away. Crook was furious when he found Reynolds, and was forced to turn back to Fort Fetterman due to lack of rations and forage. The Column straggled back into Fort Fetterman, hungry and disgruntled, on the March 26.

In the mean time, General Terry was tasked with organizing the Dakota Column which was to consist of the 7th Cavalry, and several Infantry companies. Terry planned to assemble it at Fort Lincoln and originally planned for it to depart in mid-April. On his way back to Washington, Custer spent several days in St. Paul with Terry and the two discussed plans for the coming campaign, which included requesting the return of the 3 companies of the 7th still down South on Reconstruction Duty. But with Custer's absence, and the continuing inclement weather, preparations were delayed. Major Reno who was in command at Fort Lincoln, went about preparing the companies assigned to the Dakota forts for the field. Reno began lobbying for command of the expedition and in mid-April, when informed that Custer was delayed again, he even bypassed Gen. Terry by appealing directly to Gen. Sheridan via telegram. Sheridan replied the following day and firmly stated that Gen. Terry had entire charge of the expedition. Reno continued his preparations and increased the daily drills with the troops on hand.

"That damn Reno! Does he think Mr. Lo is going to stand still while we run around doing fancy maneuvers?" stated Pat Morse. "You can tell he hasn't spent much time chasing the Sioux. We need to be concentrating on skirmishing tactics and getting in some carbine practice. Some of these new lads, haven't ever fired their weapons."

They were down at the stables tending to their mounts after a long afternoon of mounted drill ending in a dress parade. Reno seemed to be more concerned about formations and uniforms than readying the men for the coming field campaign. He was adamant that they were needed and concentrated on them daily.

"Top Martin told me that Captain Weir and Capt. Keogh have been trying to convince Reno to let the individual companies conduct training on the skills that they'll need out in the field." Jake said.

"I noticed that Weir didn't even come out for the dress parade this afternoon. I saw him over on Officer's Row sitting on a porch watching."

"Yeh, I did too. I also saw Major Reno looking at him and you could tell that he was not pleased about it. I think there's still bad blood between those two from when they butted heads up on the Boundary Survey the year before last."

"Well, hopefully, Custer will make it back before we head out. We don't need our most senior officers feuding amongst themselves." Morse said. "By the way, I got word that Murray is back in Bismarck. What do you say we go over tomorrow night and see him? I'll get Top to give us a pass for Saturday and we'll make a night of it."

"Yeh, I'd like to hear what Murray thinks about things. We can go by the trading post on the way by, and look in on Kate, Bob Seip isn't back yet and I want to see if she's doing okay. Plus, I can ask her what she's heard from Holly."

When they reached the trading post the next afternoon, they were welcomed by Kate, who brought over a couple of beers and sat down with them.

"Good to see you two. Things appear to be picking up around here and I'll be glad when Bob gets back."

"Have you heard anything from him?" Jake asked

"Yes, he sent a telegram today. He is leaving Washington tomorrow, and should be back here by the end of next week."

"It will be interesting to hear what he has to say about the hearings. I read in the Tribune that Belknap has already resigned and the new Secretary of War, Alphonso Taft, is going to let the post commanders out here select their own post traders."

Kate looked over at Jake with a worried expression, "Yes, I'm afraid that we'll end up losing the store and the other contracts here. General Terry has already awarded the field sutler contract for the spring campaign to John Smith, another partner of my Uncle Alvin's. My uncle is not at all happy that Bob got dragged into all of this. We did everything that he wanted us to do, while paying him, and his cronies, $3 for very $1 we made. It was that reporter posing as JD Thompson that stirred everything up. He spied on us for Custer and the newspapers."

"What will you do?" Jake asked.

"Oh, I suppose we can move across the river to Bismarck and open a store. With the railroad and the influx of miners there should be plenty of business. Bob has a lot of business contacts over there. We'll probably make it until the end of the year here at the fort, although with all of the troops out in the field we'll be pretty slow."

"That's too bad!" Jake said, "But, maybe you'll be better off over in town. At least the women over there will probably be friendlier to you. What about Holly, will she stay down at school?"

"Probably, my uncle is still very influential with all of his connections. I think he'll help out if needs be, I'm still his niece after all."

"I haven't mentioned any of this in my letters to her." Jake said.

"Thanks, she doesn't need to be worrying about any of this. Well, I see we're getting busy and guess I'd better go and help out. You two let me know if you need to get anything special to take with you when the regiment takes the field."

"Thanks, Kate, we will."

When she was gone, Pat said, "Tis a shame that a nice woman like Kate got caught up in all this. There's a lesson here to be had. You want to be higher up on the hill when the shite starts rolling down!"

Murray Johnson had moved back in to his accommodations at Forster's. When Pat and Jake walked in, he was sitting at his usual table and waved for them to come over.

"Well, I was wondering when you two would show up. I trust you made it through the winter okay."

"We did at that." Pat answered, "And I see you managed to survive St. Louis."

"Yes, I managed quite nicely, thank you! Have a seat and let's catch up."

They drank several rounds of beer and ate while discussing their winter activities. Murray was duly impressed when he heard about Jake's exploits along the telegraph road.

"I heard all about that special train fiasco back in March. I'm glad I wasn't on board. My winter was much less demanding and I spent the last few weeks in meetings discussing preparations for supplying the Army this season. I met your commanding officer, Colonel Sturgis and Capt. Hale, at Jefferson Barracks. They're busy trying to round up recruits and horses."

"We could do with the horses, but new recruits will just be dead weight when we get out in the field." Morse stated. "Although, they would be handy to have them for pioneer details."

"What else have you heard, Murray?" Pat asked.

"Grant means to have the Black Hills and the Sioux be damned. There will be no more negotiations. The Sioux on the reservations on other hand, are still under the illusion that the Treaty of 1868 will still be honored. The Indian Agencies are reporting that many of the reservation bands are fed up with the poor quality and quantity of the rations that the government is supposed to be providing. Many of them are preparing to head out to the unceded lands along the Powder and Tongue Rivers to join up with the roaming bands."

"Any idea how many?" Jake asked.

"There could be several thousand." Murray answered, "The newspaper has been running stories that the Sioux chief, Sitting Bull, has declared that he is prepared to fight and die rather than move to the reservation."

"Hmm!" Pat murmured, then quaffed his beer.

Murray looked over at Jake, "I was at a railroad banquet and met a delightful woman named, Vanessa. During our conversation, when it came up that I had been in Bismarck near Fort Lincoln, she mentioned that she had met some young cavalryman, from Fort Lincoln while on a train to St. Paul last fall and remarked how nice a young man he was."

Jake looked back at Murray, and replied calmly, "Well, it's a small world, isn't it."

"Yes, it is! At any rate she sent her regards and I also have a package for you up in my room. I'll see that I get it to you before you go back across the river."

They got rooms at Forster's, then joined Murray as he made the rounds of several saloons. Murray sought out several individuals and the conversations all tended to be about the gold fields in the Black Hills, the coming Expedition against the Sioux out of Fort Lincoln, and when Custer would return. The next morning Pat and Jake met Murray for breakfast.

"So tell me, when do you think you'll move against the Sioux?" Murray asked.

"I think Gen. Terry is waiting for Custer to get untangled back in Washington. He's not really a field commander." Pat answered.

"Well, I can tell you that many of the supplies are still on their way from Chicago, and I can't see them all being ready to load out until the first, or second week in May." Murray said.

Pat nodded his head, "That's good to know, I'll pass that along."

After breakfast, Pat and Jake were going to visit several stores and shop for some supplies. As they prepared to leave Murray handed Jake a parcel.

"Here's the package your friend Vanessa sent." Murray said with a big smile.

Jake hefted it, and smiled back at Murray, "Thanks!"

It turned out that Major Reno was more than a little aggravated with Capt. Weir. He formally charged Weir with insubordination the following week. When the charges reached Gen. Terry, he being fully aware of Reno's behind the scenes attempts to assume command of the expedition, didn't feel that they were warranted and dismissed the charges. Preparations continued as reports from the various Agencies began to filter in stating that large numbers of Sioux were leaving to join the roving bands in the Unceded Territories along the Big Horn and Powder Rivers. As the supplies for the expedition flowed into Fort Lincoln, the delayed departure date enabled Gen. Terry to adapt his plans to incorporate two steamboats and a supply depot location on the Yellowstone. He chartered the *Josephine* and her captain Mart Coulson, along with the *Far West* and Capt. Grant Marsh. Both the boats were built specifically to navigate the upper Missouri, the Yellowstone River, and their tributaries. The men crewing them were highly experienced. Orders were prepared and sent up to Fort Buford for Major Orlando Moore to take Companies C, D, & I of the 6th Infantry and prepare to move up the Yellowstone via steamboat, to the mouth of Glendive Creek and establish a supply depot. A stockade had been located there, back in 1873, during Stanley's Surveying Expedition and it was on the overland route that Terry had selected for the march of the Dakota Column. At Fort Lincoln, Companies E & L arrived from Fort Totten towards the end of April, followed by arrival of B,G, & K from the South, picking up 62 new recruits as they passed through St. Paul. Several days later, Capt. Benteen brought Companies H and M up from Fort Rice. Lacking quarters for all the companies, Reno had a camp was established south of fort. For the first time in the 10 years of its existence, the entire regiment of the 7th Cavalry was stationed together. Reno decided to reorganize the regiment into three battalions under the command of the ranking captains: Benteen with Companies A, D, H, & K, Keogh with Companies B, G, I, & M, and Yates with Companies C, E, F, & L. Reno was also tasked with finding mounts, of which there was a shortage. The supply train being assembled consisted of over 200 packers, teamsters and herders,150 wagons (114 six-mule government wagons and the balance two-horse contractor wagons), and a drove of cattle. In addition to the cavalry there were also three companies of infantry, Companies C & G from the 17th Infantry, Company B, 6th Infantry, and the battery of Gatling

Guns from the 20th Infantry that had been on the snowbound train back in March. 2nd Lt. Charles Varnum was detached from Company A, and assigned command of the scout detachment which consisted of approximately 40 Ree (Arikara) scouts hired for the campaign, and Bloody Knife, a favorite of Custer's who had been with the 7th in the Black Hills two years earlier. There were also 4 Dakota Sioux scouts, the half-blood Blackfeet Jackson brothers, the interpreters Fred Girard and Isaiah Dorman, and the well known scout "Lonesome Charlie" Reynolds.

Capt. Weir called a special meeting with his NCOs to discuss the coming campaign. They reviewed the roster and platoon assignments, particularly the recruits that they'd received back in late October.

"We're pretty close to a full roster, but still have no mounts for the new men, Sir." 1st Sgt. Martin reported. "I've put in several requests to Lt. Nowlan and QM Sgt. Causby, but they tell me that we've been short over 70 mounts all winter, not counting the newly arrived companies. They even canceled the sale of some condemned horses, and assigned them to pulling the Gatling guns."

"Well, those men without mounts will just have to march with Company wagon and help out there. They'll be back with the infantry and the supply train." Weir said.

"Right, Sir. I'm leaving Pvt. Hall and Pvt. Mueller here to tend the garden while we're gone, and Pvt. Day is due for discharge on the 19th. He's told me that he's not going to reenlist, so I see no point in dragging him along. Sgt. Rush is still in the hospital with the flu, and it doesn't look like he'll be able to go. Lt. Cooke requested some dependable men for mounted messengers duty at the Regimental HQ, so I'm sending over Pvt. Harlfinger, he's an old hand and steady, I also sent Pvt. Cowley to help out with the horses over there."

"So, what's our full mounted strength?" Weir asked.

"That leaves us with 53 enlisted, Sir, countin' m'self" Martin answered.

Weir nodded his head in acknowledgement, "Very good, First Sergeant. See that everyone has their gear in top shape, it may be a long summer. Come walk with me."

When they were out of earshot Weir stopped, and said. "I think that we're in for a hard campaign, Top. The Army intends to run these roaming bands to ground. Do everything that you can to keep discipline up."

"Aye, Sir, I will, don't be a worryin'. We've got a good bunch and I pride m'self that they're the best Company in the Regiment."

"I'd like to think so." Weir agreed.

"Yes, Sir! Will the lads be getting paid before we go out? Some have been asking."

"I'll look into it."

"Right, Sir! Any word on Custer?"

"I've heard rumors that he'll be back to go out with us, maybe as soon as next week."

Martin grinned and replied, "I'll pass that along. The lads will be pleased, I know I am. I remember Major Reno up at the Boundary. Let's just say he's not really one to inspire confidence."

Weir looked at Martin and gave a slight nod. "That will be all First Sergeant."

CHAPTER 28

Fort Abraham Lincoln, Dakota Territory - Wednesday, May 17, 1876

4 AM - Jake woke to the sound of reveille and rolled out of his blanket and pulled on his boots. He took a moment to admire the plain german silver spurs that Vanessa had sent to him, recalling the note that came with them, "To my favorite rider!". He, Tom Russell, and Jim Flanagan were sharing an A tent for the present. The other two stirred as Jake stepped out and wandered towards the river to take a leak. There were a few lanterns lit and cook fires were popping up all over the large camp. Jake could see that there was a heavy fog covering the area. He heard the men stirring behind him in the Company D bivouac. The entire Dakota Column had assembled south of Fort Lincoln along the river on Saturday, and Monday morning was originally set as the departure date. However Sunday brought drenching rainfall and the ground was saturated, prohibiting the mass movement of the heavily laden wagons of the supply train. Gen. Terry had decided to stay put and allow the ground to dry out, postponing the move until this morning. As Jake turned back towards the tents he passed several other men intent on a similar mission.

"Damn fog!" Flanagan barked "It better burn off quick if they're gonna get all those wagons sorted out and on their way"

"Yep," Jake said, "But at least there's no rain. We'll be heading out."

"Damn silly if you ask me. We could have been high and dry back at the fort for the last 4 days, but Custer and Terry wanted to have their grand send off parade."

****

General Alfred Howe Terry

Terry was born in Hartford, Connecticut in November of 1827 to a prosperous family. After the family moved to New Haven, he attended the Hopkins School and then Yale Law School. He traveled through Europe on an inheritance, becoming fluent in French and German. On his return to the States he became a lawyer and clerk of New Haven County Superior Court. When the Civil War began he raised two infantry regiments, the first being the 2nd Connecticut Infantry, a 90 day militia unit which fought at Bull Run, and the second was the 7th Connecticut Volunteer Infantry, a three year regiment. In early 1862 he was promoted to Brigadier General in command of a division of the X Corps which fought along the coastal areas of South Carolina and Georgia. Recalled to Virginia, X Corps participated in operations around Richmond and Petersburg. General Grant sent Terry and his X Corps to North Carolina in late 1864, where they became the Fort Fisher Expeditionary Corps tasked with capturing the fort that guarded the port of Wilmington. Terry demonstrated personal bravery and led the storming and capture of the fort, for which he was rewarded with a promotion to major general of volunteers and a brigadier general in the regular Army. The Corps was renamed X after the fall of Wilmington and Terry commanded it during the final stages of the Carolinas Campaign, under General Sherman, until the war was over. He was well regarded as a capable general, even though he had no formal military training. After the war he stayed in the Army and was given command of the Dept. of Dakota which included Minnesota, along with parts of the Dakota and Wyoming territories. He became involved in negotiations with various Indian tribes, participating in the peace commission that drew up the Medicine Lodge Treaty of 1867. He was transferred to the Department. of the South in1869, to oversee Reconstruction efforts, where he first encountered Custer and the 7th Cavalry. When he was recalled to Dakota in 1872, the 7th Cavalry was reassigned under him. He made his headquarters in St. Paul and was strong advocate of Indian rights. None the less, he oversaw the various expeditions that were sent into the reservation lands, including the Black Hills. He was assigned as a member of the Allison Commission of 1875, which failed to negotiate the sale of the Black Hills by the Sioux tribes. When Custer became entangled in the Belknap scandal, Terry assumed command of the Dakota Column. It was due to his intervention and requests that Custer was allowed to return and accompany the 7th as its commander. Terry, mild mannered and well spoken, was very solicitous in dealing with his subordinate officers which tended to be the opposite of the impulsive and mercurial Custer. He was also well regarded by the rank and file. In addition to the Dakota Column, he was also responsible for overseeing and coordinating Col. Gibbons Montana Column.

Custer had arrived back at Fort Lincoln with Gen. Terry and his staff, the previous Wednesday. He wasted no time no time in making his presence known, quickly reviewing the preparations that Reno had made. He was very dissatisfied with the failure to acquire more horses. When he found out about the battalion assignments, he immediately re-shuffled the companies into 4 battalions split into Left and Right wings, commanded by Benteen and Reno respectively. Weir was in command of a Left Wing battalion containing Companies A,D, & H. Custer's plans included an elaborate departure parade with the band playing as the regiment made its way through the fort, while the wagon trains and infantry units assembled on the plains near the fort. At 7 o'clock Custer, accompanied by his wife Libbie and sister, Maggie Calhoun, led the procession of the 7th out of camp. He was dressed in a pale buckskins, with a blue shirt, flowing red scarf, and a wide brimmed light grey hat. They rode towards the fort passing first through the scout's village and then laundress row, before pausing at the parade ground to allow the officer's with wives and families to say their good byes. The fog was beginning to burn off as the regiment began to ascend the hill onto the plain above the fort. Some of the local prominent citizens and merchants, including Murray Johnson and Mark Kellogg, were watching. Kellogg had been invited to accompany the Column by Gen. Terry and would join him later in the day. The scout detachment had ridden out in advance and were fanned out along the planned route. The supply train moved out and the cavalry battalions assumed station on both sides and behind, while Custer and Terry rode at the head with their entourages. When everything was in motion the column was almost two miles long. Weir's battalion was assigned out on the left flank for the first day. The plans were to rotate the battalions on a daily basis, with the lead companies to act as pioneers for bridging and overcoming obstacles where they would be supervised by 1st Lt. Edward Maguire, Terry's Engineering Officer. Maguire and a his squad of enlisted engineers had been given a four mule drawn ambulance to which the official odometers for the expedition were mounted. They traveled just to the rear of the advance party. Gen. Terry's headquarters staff was escorted by Capt. Baker's Company B 6th Infantry followed by the two Companies of the 17th Infantry, and the Gatling Battery of the 20th infantry. The dismounted detachment and the company wagons of the 7th Cavalry were commanded by 1st. Lt. Mathey, from Company M, and were just ahead of the supply train. The cavalry maintained pace with the wagons, which spent a lot of time standing still, waiting their turn to be dragged through the mud bogs that rapidly developed on the route as the heavily weighted wagons churned up the prairie. Custer and Terry led the column into a bivouac area on the Heart River about 13 miles from Fort Lincoln. The campsite was located on a low plateau with a stand of cottonwood trees and with the river on three sides. It had been used on several previous occasions by the 7th. The lead elements went into camp about 1:30 in the afternoon. The troopers spent some time beating the tall grass and sage brush for rattlesnakes before pitching tents. Terry had brought along a paymaster who set up and started doling out 2 months back pay for the troops. Bob Seip, back from his travels, had brought along several wagonloads of merchandise and setup near the paymaster to redeem his sutlers checks and ply his wares. The regimental band set up and entertained everyone as the camp filled out, and by late afternoon all but a few stragglers were in. It was a pleasant evening and a few sounds of revelry rose around the camp as the soldiers and civilians enjoyed sampling some of the post trader's more potent wares.

Sometime during the night a grassfire broke out and the command was called out to contain it. The next morning, after breakfast, Lt. Charles Varnum led the scouts out of camp across the river.

****

2nd Lt. Charles Albert Varnum

Varnum was born in Troy, New York, in June of 1849, and raised in Maine until 1866. His father was an infantry officer during the Civil War and was posted to Pensacola Florida afterward. He moved the family down after mustering out and going to work for the Quartermaster Department. Young Charles worked several jobs clerking for several various military auxiliary operations and was able to secure an appointment to West Point. He graduated in June 1872, 17th out of a class of 57, and was posted for duty to the 7th Cavalry as a 2nd Lieutenant in Company A, assigned on Reconstruction duty at Elizabethtown, Ky, where Col. Custer was in command of the garrison of Post #198. Company A was commanded by Capt. Myles Moylan who was a brother-in-law to Lt. James Calhoun, who had married Custer's sister, Maggie, and was part of the Custer Clique. Varnum and his fellow officers participated in many hunting and horse racing excursions with Custer, as he scoured the countryside buying and trading blooded horses. Many of the officers also acquired a taste for thoroughbreds and when the 7th was sent up to the Dakota Territory,

Varnum took several fast horses with him. He participated in the 1873 Yellowstone expedition and was present at both of the fights with the Sioux. Custer took note of his coolness under fire and mentioned Varnum in his official report of the action. He went out again on the Black Hills expedition in 1874, and on returning to Fort Lincoln, Company A was sent down to Livingston, Alabama for Reconstruction duty. They were recalled to the Dakota Territory the following spring and posted with Benteen's detachment, where they patrolled the routes to the Black Hills out of Fort Randall. In September they marched up the Missouri, back to Fort Lincoln. He was approved for leave in late October and went on the last train east. He was down in Florida visiting his family when he was notified that the 7th was preparing to go out and promptly left to report to Gen. Terry in St. Paul. He was ordered back to Fort Lincoln where Custer had arranged for him to be assigned as commander of the scouts for the coming campaign against the Sioux.

****

While Lt. Maguire and the pioneer battalion for the day proceeded to clear the river banks and cut trees to "corduroy' the steep riverbanks on both sides to facilitate the wagons as they descended into the 3' deep river, then climbed out the other side. At 8 o'clock the signal to move out was given and the wagon train began fording the river. It proved to be a laborious process, entailing lots of manpower and ropes. It took 3 hours to get all the wagons across, and as the column formed up to move out, Custer lagged behind with Libbie and the party returning to Fort Lincoln. After saying his goodbyes, he galloped to the head of the column. Ominous clouds appeared on the horizon, and the wind picked up sharply. Custer, with the advance party, hurried ahead almost 11 miles to find a suitable bivouac area near Sweetbriar Creek. Stopping at 2 o'clock, it took almost 4 hours to get the last of wagons across the low hills and boulder strewn route into camp, particularly after a violent lightning and thunder storm struck around 3 o'clock.

Weir's battalion had been assigned rear guard for the day, and it got caught out in the storm. Even with their slickers on they go soaked. The men wearing the issue campaign hats with the fold up brims, found out that they quickly that the shape quickly collapsed providing no protection. Jake had elected to wear the wide brimmed Stetson hat he'd picked up back in Springfield in the field and was glad he had. The companies had to assist in dragging the wagons through the mire. Jake found that one of them was crewed by his old telegraph trail companions, Jack Ward and Joe Martin. He had never heard so many different cuss words as Jack, Joe, and the cavalry troopers struggled to extract the heavy wagon from one of the bogs. All of them were muddy, cold, and soaked to the bone when they finally got to their bivouac area. Fortunately, 1st Sgt. Martin had ridden on ahead to find the company wagon and the unmounted recruits. He'd had them pitch tents and get some cook stoves going. When the weary troopers straggled in they scrambled to finish getting their tents up and tend to the horses before dark. Fortunately, the storm subsided and they were spared from more rain.

"Shit, fire, and damnation! At the rate that these wagons are movin' the only thing we're goin to catch is a cold!" cursed Flanagan, as he scraped thick mud off his boots, "There's no fookin' way we'll catch up with the Sioux like this!"

Jake was sitting on his saddle by a small campfire where a pot of coffee was brewing. "Oh, just wait! In a couple of days it'll be hot and dusty and you'll be wishing for it to cool off. I heard from Lt. Edgerly that the plan is to reach the Yellowstone River where there's a supply depot waiting for us, then strike out after Mr. Lo."

"Then why the fook didn't we just take a boat?"

"Well, I suppose that they aren't sure where the Sioux are. It was rumored that Sitting Bull wintered along the Little Missouri and they need to make sure that he went west. Besides, we haven't been out in the field for a while and we all need to get used to being on the march."

Tom Russell walked up carrying a sack of fresh biscuits and offered them. "Here take some of these. I got them from Cookie, he made extras."

The three of them sat enjoying the biscuits and coffee, listening to the sounds of the camp. Russell spoke up. "Top says that we're back out on the flank tomorrow. Hopefully, we'll have better weather."

Friday the 19th turned out to be worse. Movement commenced about 6:30, and no suitable ford could be found across the Sweetbriar which had risen to a torrent. The column turned south in an attempt to skirt the creek valley and ventured out onto a marshy prairie. The wagons became so mired that multiple mule teams were required to pull them through the worst places. About noon another thunderstorm struck bringing hail the size of hickory nuts. Men and beast were pelted as the infantrymen and troopers moved to seek shelter with the wagons. After over an hour the storm subsided, and the sun broke through accompanied by a drying wind. Camp was made on a butte, which the men soon nicknamed 'Turkey Buzzard Camp'. The last wagons didn't make it in until almost 6 o'clock, having traveled 12 1/2 miles through the mire, arriving to find little water, wood, or grazing. After a cold, wet, windy night, the column woke to find rain falling. While the men had cold rations for breakfast, Terry sent a scout party with Charlie Reynolds and ten Ree scouts to the next water course, Muddy Creek, nine miles ahead to find a suitable crossing. The ground was a bit better, the two horse, contractor wagons experienced less difficulty, but the mule drawn heavier wagons continued to struggle. After crossing at two slippery fords along the creek, Terry decided to go into camp after only 9 1/2 miles when they came to the next one, and allow the men and animals to rest. Sunday morning Reveille was sounded at 3 AM, but the decision was made to cross over to the west bank so the column didn't move until a bridge was constructed. Weir's battalion had been assigned as pioneers for the day. Around 6 o'clock the first wagons made it across and again encountered more marshy ground. The morning overcast began to slowly burn off and by noon bright sunshine broke through. About the same time the route transitioned into firm grassland. The column made over 13 miles as the sun warmed everything and went into camp after another crossing. The Dakota Column had logged 60.5 miles since leaving Fort Lincoln.

Most of the following week the weather was moderate and the terrain more suitable to wagons, however the route required crossing creeks and ravines and the troopers tasked as pioneers to Lt. Maguire grew to hate it when their turn came up in the rotation. Wednesday was an exceptionally nice day and the column logged 19 miles by 2 o'clock. They reached Stanley's Crossing at the Big Heart River and Terry called a halt. The water was crystal clear and swift flowing over a gravel bottom. After bivouacking the men quickly took the opportunity to bathe and wash their clothes, hanging them out to dry in the sun. Some went upstream and fished, while Custer and some of the scouts roamed the area hunting for elk and antelopes that had been spotted. The next two days found the column crossing tributaries of the Heart as they followed it to the southwest seeking the old trail that Stanley had used three years earlier. Friday, the frequent bridging slowed progress and the terrain changed to an ascending arid plain. The temperature rose to 79 degrees and they began encountering swarms of grasshoppers, then were plagued by hordes of tiny black mosquitos that hovered over the pools of alkaline water. Gen. Terry, who had taken to riding with the advance party, called a halt after only 12 miles when they came to grassy area. Ominous cloud formations were forming on the horizon as the wagons filed into the campsite and extra care was taken pitching the tents and drainage ditches were dug around them in preparation for the storm. Jake and Tom Russell were just finishing up when Pat Morse came over to them.

"We're to be in the advance in the morning. Make sure the lads know that we'll have Custer riding with us."

"Well, at least we'll not be having to shovel and swing axes." Russell said.

"You know, I've only been around Custer a few times during a few dress parades last summer. I've seen him from a distance on the march so far, but it will be interesting to see him up close." Jake said.

"Well, he's better out in the field, not so much a stickler. You'll find that he's a very good horseman and excellent shot. If I know him, he'll be way out front with Bloody Knife and his Ree scouts." Morse stated. "You'll find out why they call him 'Hard Ass'. The man logs more miles in the saddle than anyone else."

The storm hit around midnight. It was a typical violent high plains thunderstorm with vivid displays of lightning and rolling thunder. Torrents of driving rain drenched the bivouac area. Fortunately, it didn't last long but when Company D formed up for the advance at 4:30, fog set in. Lt. Varnum and the scouts were already riding out when Custer and his brother Tom, along with Lt. Cook, rode up to Weir.

"Weir, I'm hoping to pick up the trail we used when I was out with Stanley back in '73. We've the badlands out in front of us and I don't fancy trying to pick a new route through them. We'll be looking for old wagon tracks."

"Yes, Sir! I'll have my best men with sharp eyes looking out."

"Good, I'll be out front with the Rees. Try and stay within eye sight." Custer said, then turned his horse to ride away.

Weir called out, " Sgt. Morse, Sgt. Rogers, pick some men and fan out on both sides. Have them keep an eye out for anything that looks like old wagon tracks"

Jake picked Welch's set and they set out following Custer, fanning out and picking their way along the west side of his trail. They got their first sight of the Badlands of the Little Missouri River off in the distance. After about 7 miles, Jake came across narrow draw with what looked to be a game trail heading into the hills. Using his binoculars, he saw what looked like old wagon tracks farther up the draw. He took Charlie with him, sending the others on, then they followed it for a ways, picking their way along before finally cresting a ridge. They could see a prominent pair of buttes off in the distance and a valley at the bottom of the slope. He and Welch made their way back down the trail, and by the time they got down, the column had already passed by moving on to the south, so they hurried to catch up. Custer had halted the column and went back to confer with Terry. As he went past Weir, he called out that we must have missed the trail. Presently, Capt. Michaelis and about a dozen men left the column to go on further to south just in case. The scouts began riding back north along the trail, while Custer and his group trotted over to Weir and his men.

"We must have missed it! I sense that we're too far south." Custer stated. "Gen. Terry is none too pleased about it. The tracks must have been washed away over the last three years. We need to find some high ground and look for the Sentinel Buttes. We're going back to see if we can spot them."

Jake and Charlie had ridden hard to overtake the column and rejoin the company. Jake went over to report to Weir, and said quietly. "I think I might have seen them, Sir. About 3 miles back I followed a rough track up to a ridge where I spotted some big buttes off to the west."

Custer overheard Jake and spoke up, quickly, "What's that you said, Sergeant?"

"I think I might of seen them, Sir!" Jake answered.

"What's your name?"

"Jacob Rogers, Sir!"

"Well, come on, Rogers, lead us back to where you saw them. Ride with us."

Custer who was mounted on his dark bay Morgan horse, Dandy, took off riding north at a fast gait, accompanied by Tom Custer and the rest of his other staff. Jake followed, urging Ajax on to stay up with them.

When they got near the draw, Jake waved over at Custer and pointed towards it.

"Over there, sir" Jake shouted as he guided Ajax to it.

"Show me where you saw the buttes, Rogers!" Custer exclaimed.

When the got up to the ridge line with the buttes in view, they halted and dismounted.

"That's them all right, eh Tom?" Custer stated.

"Yes, and I think I see some of the trail over there. We need to get down to that valley over there. That should be Davis Creek."

Lt. Cooke nodded his head, "I'll send a man back to notify Gen.Terry."

Tom Custer looked over at Jake and said, "Sgt. Rogers, that was good work."

"Thank you, Sir. I thought it was just a game trail at first, but I've always found that most of the trails out here were originally hunting trails made by following game, and tend to be the easiest way across country."

"Well, it looks like you were right." Col. Custer said, "Now, let's see if we can find a way to get the wagons down there. "

They went into bivouac as soon as all the wagons made it into the valley. It was long and narrow so the camp was stretched out along the creek. While they were making camp Custer had the regimental band play and the notes echoed down the valley. Custer scouted on ahead for a ways, and when he returned he reported to Terry that multiple bridges would be needed along the route the next day. Shortly after Reveille the following morning, Lt. Maguire and two pioneer companies, headed out along the colorful, rugged valley followed by the column about 4:30 AM. The valley narrowed to a deep ravine after a few miles. Maguire ran low on bridging materials and had to improvise using available materials including spare wagon tongues. As the day wore on the clear blue skies caused the temperatures to soar to over 80 degrees within the confines of the canyon and the column labored to keep moving forward. The heat and fatigue caused by having to construct eight bridges took its toll. One wagon slid off into a deep, narrow gully and attempts to retrieve it were deemed futile, so its cargo was transferred, and it was abandoned. Terry finally called a halt when a good campsite was found after seven torturous hours. Most of the men were allowed to rest for the rest of the day in preparation for another round the following day. However, three companies were detailed to pre-construct a pair of bridges for the next morning, Monday, May 29. The wagons began rolling again at 4:45 and after the first two bridges were crossed the valley began to open up. Terry, Custer and the advance party rode out ahead and reached the Little Missouri River about 6:30, and the first wagons arrived about 9:30. The total distance traveled since their departure from For Lincoln was 166 miles. The area proved ideal for a bivouac with plenty of timber, abundant grass, and several clear springs. Since the intelligence reports that Terry had indicated that Sitting Bull and the other roamers were somewhere in the area, the decision was made to establish a strong defense around the camp. Mounted guard details were posted on the surrounding hills and along the river. Terry decided that before the column crossed the Little Missouri and continued on in the direction of the Sentinel Buttes, Custer was to scout the area seeking signs of their presence while the rest of the column rested for a day. Custer selected one company from each battalion to accompany him. At 5:00 A.M., Companies C, D, F, & M, along with Varnum and the Ree scouts, left camp to scour the upper river valley ahead looking for Indian sign. They proceeded with caution initially finding no indications that there had been any kind of presence in the vicinity for months. Custer had them ranging back and forth, crossing and recrossing the river several dozen times, before stopping to enjoy a leisurely lunch with his officers along a riverbank.

"Seems like Custer is having a grand time today, don't you think, Pat?" Jake asked as they were sitting in the shade under a large cottonwood, watching the group of officers as they laughed and joked. Jake had delved into his saddlebags for some hoarded treats and was enjoying them. Pat was chewing on some pemican while sipping on fresh crystal clear water that he'd filled his canteen with earlier.

"Yeh!" Pat replied, "He's just like he was down in Kansas years back. He and his brother love to range out hunting, They treat it all like a lark, playing jokes on each other and riding about. They can certainly stay in the saddle for hours and not to seem to get tired."

"Well, it is good to be out away, instead of playing shepherd for the wagon train, or pioneer duty. Plus, we haven't seen any signs of the thousands of Indians that Murray said were out here. It seems that I remember that his sources seemed to think that Sitting Bull and the other roamers would be farther west, along the Powder or Tongue River."

"Capt. Weir told Top that we're to head out for the Yellowstone tomorrow and will be resupplied at a depot there. Then, we're to try to link up with Col. Gibbon's Montana Column somewhere upriver."

"How many men is Gibbon supposed to have with him?" Jake asked.

"Six companies of the 7th Infantry and four companies from the 2nd Cavalry."

Jake nodded his head thoughtfully, "Well, that should give us plenty of firepower if it comes to a fight, anyway."

"We'll see. The infantry can never catch the Sioux. I think the plan is for us to drive Mr. Lo towards them and force him to surrender."

"You think it will work?"

"I think Custer's intent is to chase them down where ever he can find them. M'thinks we're in for a lot of hard riding ahead."

Jake smiled and replied, "I suspect that you're right, Pat, but at least the weather is getting better."

Morse peered up at the sky saying, "Aye, tis today, lad, but we'll wait and see what tomorrow brings."

Custer and the detachment made it back to the camp by about 6 o'clock, where he reported to Terry that they had found few signs and what there was were several months old. Terry decided to push on to the west towards the Powder River country in the morning. A heavy thunderstorm brewed up near midnight, dumping heavy rain on the camp and leaving it soaked. The columns departure was delayed until 8:00, and the weather was a heavy gray overcast as it began crossing the river. The trail ahead wound through narrow canyons flanked by sizable buttes. The track was just wide enough to accommodate one wagon at a time and had several steep grades. The winding route proved tortuous and the column paused at one point, sending out Varnum and the scouts to find a passage through. Custer had ridden out of camp with his brothers and escort, and was nowhere in sight, much to the displeasure of Gen. Terry. They were assumed to be somewhere out ahead. Charlie Reynolds and Mark Kellogg left the train to pursue some mountain sheep and were able to bag three of them. The wagons began reaching the bivouac area along Andrews Creek near the base of the easterly Sentinel Butte, where Custer was waiting, about 2:00. Terry rebuked Custer for abandoning the train and Custer apologized, saying he would remain closer to the column in the future. Later that afternoon clouds began forming and a blustery cold breeze began blowing. Rainfall soon followed, turning to sleet near dark. When Reveille sounded it was discovered that several inches of snow had blanketed the camp and it was still coming down. Terry made the decision to stay put until the storm passed, so the men wrapped themselves in their blankets and overcoats, huddling around fires or laying in their two-man dog tents. Terry, Custer, and the officers had wall tents and congregated in them writing letters and playing cards. Snow continued to fall and high winds buffeted the camp. The next morning the weather eased a bit and by noon the snow finally stopped. Terry sent Charlie Reynolds, and the Wagon Master, Charles Brown, to scout the route ahead. They reported that except for one rough stretch about two and a half miles out, the route was good. Terry dispatched Lt. Maguire to look at the rough stretch, then ordered the teamsters and wagons across the stream to a hill on the other side. He hoped to get a quicker start in the morning and sent along a company of the 17th Infantry to stand guard. He elected to keep the rest of the soldiers in camp so the cooks could serve up some hot food before they had to spend another chilly night.

"Hard to believe that just two days ago we were sitting on a riverbank enjoying sunshine." Jake said. He was sitting in the cook tent, sipping coffee with several others, including Pat Morse and Tom Russell. "This reminds me of our first year up on the boundary."

"Indeed it does, Jake, but that was in late September, this is June. Who would have thought?" Tom remarked.

The tent flaps opened and 1st Sgt. Martin pushed through. He'd gone out to check on the men and moved quickly to the stove, backing up against it.

"Tis cold out there! The lads are settling in as best they can, at least they got a hot meal. They've got wood gathered for the night and have stoked the fires."

Morse produced a bottle, pouring some in a coffee cup before offering it Martin. "Here you, Mike, a wee dram to warm you."

"Thanks Pat! You're a saint."

"Any idea about tomorrow, Top?" Russell asked.

"Oh, we'll be moving on! Charlie Russell reported that there's a wide valley ahead and it's slightly downhill. Terry is determined to make up some ground tomorrow, and with the wagons already across, we should be able to depending on how the trail holds up."

"Well, as long as it ain't snowin! And it'd be damn nice to see the sun again!" Morse stated, "I for one, am ready to get on with it."

The others nodded their heads in agreement.

"We're to be out on the flank tomorrow. Rogers, you range out and see if you can bag us some game."

Jake grinned and replied, "You bet!"

The temperature hovered at 35 degrees and a bitter wind blew out of the northwest as the column moved out. The trail ahead began a slow descent and the temperature warmed as the sun rose higher in the sky and the wind died down. The valley they were in opened up into low rolling grasslands and antelope were spotted along the ridges. The column rolled along maintaining a steady pace and by late afternoon with the sun beating down, a halt was called on the banks of Beaver Creek. The 25 miles that they'd traveled was the most recorded in a single day since leaving Fort Lincoln. The creek water was cold and clear, and the bivouac area had good grazing with plenty of wood to burn. As the men made camp, rumors flew about that some couriers that arrived earlier in the day, bringing messages from the Montana column.

Jake had been successful in bagging three antelope. He and Charlie Welch were helping the cook hang them, when Tom Russell came up.

"Capt. Weir was just summoned to an Officer's Call, something's up."

"What do you reckon it is, Tom?" Jake asked.

"Some men came in from Major Gibbon. It's rumored that his scouts may have spotted a big village."

"Where at?"

"Supposedly, somewhere along one of the rivers further west."

"Hmm! It'll be interesting to see what happens now." Jake said.

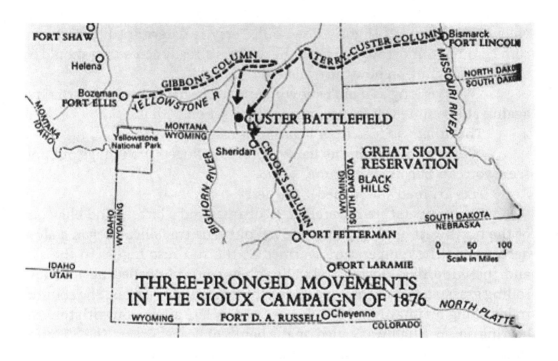

FORT SHAW

Helena

Bozeman
FORT ELLIS

MONTANA
IDAHO

GIBBON'S COLUMN

YELLOWSTONE R.

TERRY-CUSTER COLUMN

Bismarck
FORT LINCOLN

NORTH DAKO
SOUTH DAK

MISSOURI RIVER

Yellowstone
National Park

MONTANA
WYOMING

CUSTER BATTLEFIELD

Sheridan

CROOK'S COLUMN

BIGHORN RIVER

GREAT SIOUX
RESERVATION

WYOMING
SOUTH DAKOTA

BLACK
HILLS

IDAHO
WYOMING

FORT FETTERMAN

SOUTH DAKOTA
NEBRASKA

0   50   100
Scale in Miles

FORT LARAMIE

IDAHO
UTAH

THREE-PRONGED MOVEMENTS
IN THE SIOUX CAMPAIGN OF 1876

WYOMING   FORT D. A. RUSSELL   Cheyenne

NORTH PLATTE

COLORADO

CHAPTER 29

Along Beaver Creek, Eastern Montana Territory - June 3, 1876

General Terry read the dispatches to the assembled officers, then said. "Gentlemen, since it's obvious that the hostiles are much farther to our west, I can see no benefit in continuing to follow this trail on to Stanley's Stockade on Glendive Creek. Therefore, I propose to follow this creek south for a day or two, then turn west and march towards the Powder River. I'm told by Mr. Reynolds that he and the other scouts have no direct knowledge of the area, so we'll be blazing our own trail. I anticipate that it will be rough country similar to what we crossed last week, so be prepared to encounter obstacles. Once we strike the Powder, we'll follow it up to the Yellowstone. I've sent orders to Major Moore to bring up the steamer *Far West* with a load of supplies and meet us there. I've sent instructions to Col. Gibbon to halt his command where he's at on the Yellowstone, until I can get a better feel for where the hostiles are located. We must reach the mouth of the Powder at as fast of a pace as is possible."

The following morning, June 4, the march was resumed and they followed Beaver Creek, staying on the east bank. After bridging another creek feeding into it, they encountered a series of ridges and were again surrounded by grasslands teeming with antelope and rabbits. As they crossed over it, a couple of the infantry officers lost their horses while hunting and were stranded on foot. Fortunately for them they were spotted by a couple of cavalry troopers, who were able to recover their horses after being offered a $5 reward. Custer had four staghounds with him and they roamed around pursuing rabbits, keeping many bystanders entertained. Some scouts returned reporting recent Indian sign, which consisted of a small hunting camp. After an advance of 18 miles they went into a camp along the Beaver once again, after having crossed into Montana Territory. The two days of easy going came to an end on Monday as Terry made a decision to cross the Beaver and head off to the southwest.

The column made about 20 hard miles before going in to a poor camp on a prairie along the headwaters of Cabin Creek. There was little wood in the area and thin grass for the livestock. The men were forced to gather sage brush for fuel and search for pools of melted snow for water. Several hunting parties had been successful during the day, bringing in deer and antelope, however two men from Benteen's Company H failed to make it into camp and it was speculated that they may have been taken by a Sioux hunting party. Tuesday morning they continued southwest until they struck a branch of O'Fallon's Creek. The two missing troopers re-joined the column mid-morning after they admitting that they'd became lost and had been forced to endure a night alone in the badlands. After crossing the creek, Charlie Reynolds led them along them along it for several miles before he realized that it was not the main branch and the column had to turn around and backtrack. The trail began to break down and the wagons started getting stuck, so a site was found to bridge the creek and after crossing the decision was made to establish camp. Wood was found, but snow water was again the only available and there was again no grazing for the hungry cattle herd. That evening a fierce thunder storm struck which turned the creek into a raging river. As the men were huddling in their tents, Terry held a meeting at his with Custer and Reno. A decision was reached to march at once in the direction of the Powder River. Custer would be in the advance with the scouts, along with Weir's Company D which was deemed more qualified due to the time it had spent in the field surveying, plus its roster had the most experienced veteran troopers in the regiment. Their job would be to help find a route that the column could follow to the Powder River.

Weir called a meeting with Lt. Edgerly and the NCO's to inform them of the decision.

"Have the men pack extra rations and make sure that they carry as much forage as they can. Col. Custer has promised that we'll make it to the Powder by late afternoon so it will be hard riding. I doubt that we'll see the wagons until tomorrow. There be no hunting, the sound of rifle shots could alert any Sioux that may be in the vicinity. Sgt. Morse, I want you and Sgt. Rogers out front. The scouts will be in the lead but, they don't know what's ahead. You two have the best eyes and feel for terrain."

"Yes, Sir!" Morse spoke up, eyeing Jake.

The next morning was damp and overcast with dark clouds threatening more rain. As they got ready to mount up, Pat came over to Jake and said, "Now lad, you're going to get a full dose of Custer today. He's going to have us moving at quick pace. Be sure to keep within sight and don't be wandering too far ahead. I've heard that signs of buffalo are starting to show, and you know as well as I that Mr. Lo will be about chasing them if we come up on some."

"Right, I'll keep an eye out."

They moved out with Custer, Lt. Varnum and his Rees fanning out to the front. Jake and Pat rode out ahead of Capt. Weir and the rest of the company. They picked their way along small creek that led west, while Custer and the scouts roamed both sides of it. As the morning wore on the clouds lifted just enough for them to see wooded buttes appear on the horizon. Jake took out his binoculars and studied them, noting a shallow notch in them that led upwards. Just to the south, a valley skirted the buttes and looked to be an easier route for wagons. He saw Custer and the scouts riding in that direction.

"What do you think, Jake?" Pat asked.

"Well, it depends on how far that butte stretches to the west. If that's as high as it gets, that could be the shortest way across."

Capt. Weir came up even with them and said, "It looks like Custer is going to check out that valley to the left."

"Yes, but that high ground is close to the creek that we've been following. I'll bet it cuts right through and I can't make out any higher points beyond." Jake said.

"Why don't you take a couple of men and go up there and check it out. If it's as you think, send a messenger back and let me know. I'll hold here to see which way Custer wants to try."

Thirty minutes later they reached the notch, and found that it was indeed the divide. The slope leading up was steep and would need some rocks and trees removed, but all in all it wasn't any worse than others that they'd traversed. And the wagons were much lighter now after three weeks on the trail. The way down looked to be similar, and off in the distance they could make out a pine fringed ridge line that must be the Powder River. Pat sent a messenger back to report to Weir, and while they waited, Jake scouted down the slope for a ways. He had just made it back to where Pat was sitting as Custer, Lt. Cooke, Weir, and Lt. Varnum rode up. Custer got down off Dandy, and peered through his binoculars.

"Yes, yes!" He exclaimed, "This will work. Well done, men!" Turning to Varnum he said, "Have the trail marked and let's get down there, Varnum."

Weir said, "Sgt. Morse. You, Rogers and the men can re-join the company now."

Custer spoke up, "If you don't mind, Weir, I'd like Morse and Rogers to ride with me. I've not seen Sgt. Morse for a long while. And, I don't know that I've met your Sgt. Rogers. Lt. Cooke and my brother Tom speak well of him and this is twice now that he's shown that he's got a good eye for terrain."

"Very well, Sir." Weir nodded, then looked at his sergeants, "I'll see you when we get to camp."

The descent proved to be difficult in a spot or two, particularly along a couple of ridges with steep drop offs on either side, but Custer felt that the wagons should be able to negotiate them safely. Jake watched Custer and was impressed by his seemingly boundless energy as they progressed. Green hued stands of cedar, spruce, and pine trees grew on the buttes around them, with low rolling, grass covered hills stretching off to the north. Custer proclaimed that off in the distance the bluffs they could see marked the course of the Yellowstone River. Finally, they dropped down into the Powder River valley which looked to be a mile wide with scattered stands of timber and plentiful grass for grazing. They rode to the river and began watering their horses.

Custer pulled out his watch noting, "Well, I said we'd be here by 3:00, and it's 3:30. If I hadn't taken that little detour to the south back there, we would have! Eh, Cooke?"

"Indeed, Sir!" Lt. Cooke replied, "Though I think no one will fault you the 30 minutes."

"Well, send a message to Gen. Terry and advise him that we've found the Powder and that it is well timbered with good grass. We will bivouac here and rest the horses. Let him know the route will require some work and that he should follow our trail tomorrow."

Just then Lt. Varnum rode up announcing, "Sir, the Rees have found fresh signs of four Sioux, tracks made since the rain. Also, those of a few buffalo."

"Better put that in the message, Cooke." Custer said, then turned to Varnum, "Show me where these tracks are."

Nearby, Weir and Company D had dismounted and were seeing to their horses. Jake led Ajax to the river and looked at the flowing water. It was only 2-3 feet deep and had a muddy yellowish cast to it. He could see sandy particles stirred up by the horses hooves mixed in it.

"Well, it ain't the worst water we've come across, but close to it." He thought to himself. "I'd better let it settle a bit before I fill my canteen."

As if reading his mind, Tom Russell said as much out loud. "Damn dirty looking water."

"Yeh well, at least it's a good camp site. Let's get a wood detail out, and get some fires going." Jake replied, "Once we make coffee you won't notice it."

Gen. Terry and his staff rode in around three hours later having decided to push on through. The wagons followed, the last straggling in around 9 o'clock. Both the men and stock were exhausted and trail weary from the ascent and descent of the rugged track across the divide. A courier arrived from the Stanley's Crossing depot on the Endive bearing a dispatch from Major Moore. It notified Terry that the *Far West* had been dispatched as ordered and should be awaiting him on the Yellowstone. Terry immediately sent Ree messengers off in that direction to verify that the steamboat was there. The column settled into camp to rest and wait for their return. The next morning the Rees returned with a dispatch from Capt. Powell the commander of Company C, 6 Infantry. He was on board the *Far West,* which was loaded with forage, rations, and ammunition. The riverboat had arrived at the mouth of the Powder River late the day before and was waiting for the column. More importantly, Terry was informed that the scouts that he'd sent to the Montana column had failed to reach it, and had encountered a band of hostiles near the Tongue River. Terry, who was anxious to establish communications with Gibbon, decided to leave immediately for the Yellowstone where he could use the steamer to go upriver to find him. He held a council with Custer and Reno, informing them that they should prepare the 7th for scout to the upper reaches of the Powder, when he returned. Since wagons would not be practicable, a train of pack mules was to be used. They would be drawn from the teams hauling the heavy wagons, that were near empty after three weeks on the trail. The wagons would be escorted by the infantry and sent on to the Yellowstone. While Terry was gone, the command would work on re-training the wagon mules to haul pack saddles, which had been brought along in anticipation. Terry left camp just after noon with Companies A & I, heading north where he would attempt to find a suitable wagon route down the valley of the Powder for the wagons and infantry to follow.

"No, not that way you knuckle headed dip shit!" shouted Joe Martin, "You won't get a hundred yards before those packs fall off!"

Jack Ward and Joe were attempting to show the men of Company D how to rig a pack saddle on one of the mules, and tie a diamond hitch to secure the load. The mules were not cooperating and balked at efforts to hold them in place while the attempt was made. Plunging and lashing out with flying hooves, the animals resisted the efforts of the wary troopers. Jake would have found the spectacle more amusing if it weren't the drizzling rains that fell intermittently all day, turning the ground into gumbo. Each company was being given eleven of the animals and this scene was being repeated across the entire encampment. He and Pat were standing nearby, encouraging and cajoling their men as they wrestled with the beasts.

Jack came over and said to them, "We need to try and come up with some blindfolds. Joe thinks that may help settle them down a bit."

"We've got some canvas in the company wagon, will that work?" Jake asked.

"Yeh, I suppose we could cut some strips."

Nearby, a mule ripped its halter out of the hands of the man holding it, and began bucking, running around the field trying to dislodge its unfamiliar burden, as men frantically pursued them.

"Ya'll, best be ready to spend a lot of time pickin' up your shit, if'n you don't get them boys to learn to throw a better hitch on them packs!" Ward stated dryly.

Gen.Terry finally made it up to the Yellowstone at 8:00 that evening to find the *Far West* waiting. He had been unsuccessful in finding a wagon route and had to ford the Powder several times, which precluded wagons following his trail. In addition to the riverboat he found that Maj. Brisbin and several men including a scout, George Herendeen, from Gibbon's column had just arrived from upstream on several small skiffs bearing dispatches. As Terry was greeted by Capt. Powell, he learned that the band of hostiles that had caused the scouts dispatched to the Montana column to turn back five days earlier, were actually Crow Indians, not hostiles. Brisbin informed him that Gibbon was but a days march away on the other bank of the Yellowstone. Terry immediately dispatched Herendeen to carry orders back to Gibbon that evening, to halt and await Terry's arrival on the *Far West* the next day.

Meanwhile, Custer, and the rest of the Dakota column stayed encamped, working with the mules between bouts of drizzle and rain which evolved into a raging thunderstorm late in the afternoon. Huddled in tents and the wagons as best they could, some of the men passed the time playing cards or other games. Jake took the opportunity to write a few letters, anticipating that mail would be sent up to the river depot and sent back downstream on the riverboat. That evening he and Pat were drinking coffee in the cook tent when 1st Sgt. Martin came in bringing word that Gen. Terry had just returned.

"I just heard Lt. Varnum talking to Capt. Weir. There's to be a big meeting in the morning. Terry made contact with Col. Gibbon and received news on the location of the Sioux. It seems that some big villages were seen in the vicinity of the Tongue River and Rosebud Creek back a couple of weeks ago." Martin stated.

"How far away is that?" Jake asked.

"Off to the west a good distance. I suspect we'll find out in the morning. Terry brought a new scout back with him, a mixed blood named Mitch Boyer, he's supposed to know the country around here."

Terry held his meeting the next morning and afterwards the camp burst into activity. The plans called for Major Reno and the Right Wing companies, along with one of the Gatling guns, to scout up the Powder River, then on further west to the Tongue River then descend along it back to the Yellowstone. Custer was piqued that he, and the remainder of the 7th were to accompany the wagons and infantry north along the Powder to establish a depot where it flowed into the Yellowstone. Terry was able to placate Custer, who wanted to take entire regiment in pursuit, by pointing out that supplies were not adequate to do that. Most of the rations and the best mules were turned over to Reno's detachment and they departed camp late in he afternoon riding upriver. Terry had assigned Weir and his Company D to find a wagon route along the right bank of the Powder and they also left camp riding north.

Jake and Pat Morse led the advance party and hadn't gone very far when it become obvious that staying along the river was not going to be a practical route. The ground that was level enough for the wagons had turned into a thick mud, and the badlands that lined it were impassable. Jake had run into Mike Caddle before they left camp. Caddle's horse had come up lame on the way back from the Yellowstone and he was not able to ride out with Keogh and the rest of Company I. 1st Sgt. Varden had assigned him to take charge of the Company I wagon and unmounted troopers. Mike had described the route along both sides of the river to Jake that they'd taken, confirming that what was ahead of them wasn't going to improve.

Jake dismounted and peered through his binoculas."That escarpment up ahead runs all the way to the river. We'll have to go look for a route up to higher ground, so we can see what's on the other side of these river bluffs." Jake said.

"I think you're right." replied Morse, "I'll ride back to Capt. Weir and let him know what we're doing. Don't get too far ahead, we'll be running out of light soon."

Jake was able to pick his way east and followed a sloping rise until he came to it's crest. The sun was beginning to set as he looked at what appeared to be relatively flat bench land that veered off to the north, it reminded him of the terrain that he'd traversed going down to Fort Rice last year. He turned to ride back down towards the rest of the company when he met Pat coming back.

"It looks better up there, I think we should try that way." Jake said.

"Okay, let's go back and tell the captain. He's decided that we're going to bivouac down by the river instead of trying to make it back to camp. It'd be completely dark by the time we got to those tricky parts of the trail we went through earlier."

Terry and Custer had met to discuss the concerns about getting the wagons through to the new Powder River Depot without being forced to abandon them. A decision was made to lighten and redistribute as much of the wagon cargo loads as they could onto the pack mules. Terry was sightly concerned that Weir and his company had not returned to camp, but Custer assured him that Weir had probably decided to waylay the trail and would be waiting for them. At 5:00 the next morning the column moved out with Lt. Godfrey and Company K in charge of the pack mules bringing up the rear. Custer and the Ree Scouts went in the advance following the Company D tracks and by 10:00 they made contact with them. Weir had Jake and Morse ride out with him to greet Custer.

"Good morning, Sir!" Weir said saluting, "We've been waiting for you. We think we've found a better route to advance the wagons."

"Excellent, let's go get a look at it."

"Sgt. Morse, take Sgt. Rogers and show Col. Custer the route you found."

"Yes, Sir!" Morse replied.

Custer looked over at them and remarked, "So, you two have been pathfinding again! Let's go see what you've found this time."

Jake and Pat had gone back up earlier that morning and scouted ahead a ways, so they were confident as they led the advance party up the draw to where the flat benchland could be seen. When they got up to the vantage point, Custer paused to look through his binoculars, then turned to Lt. Varnum.

"I can see bluffs way off to the north that must be the Yellowstone. Send a scout back to Terry with a message. Tell him I have discovered a way that the wagons can negotiate, and that I'll be waiting there for the column to close up."

"Yes, Sir!"

"Sgt. Morse, you and Rogers can report back to Capt. Weir. I'll take it from here. That was a good move on your part, if this plays out we'll be bivouacking at the new depot tonight."

CHAPTER 30

Powder River Depot, Montana Territory - Monday, June 12, 1876

The Far West - Circa 1876

The Dakota column campsite was about a mile upstream from the actual mouth of the Powder River. Having marched 294 miles in 26 days, the column had welcomed the halt, although the site selected for the supply depot was not particularly a good one for the troops. It stretched across an open plain with few trees, except along the riverbank of the Yellowstone where the *Far West* was tied up. The soil was a yellow, powdery fine sand and a heavy rain during the night had turned it into muck. The paths beaten through the dense sagebrush that covered the area were slick with it. The morning dawned clear and the men hoped for better weather. As they went about their morning routines, rumors spread quickly that a sutler had set up shop.

"Did ya hear that they've whiskey ta sell?" Pat Golden exclaimed to Biscuit Greene, as he finished currying his horse.

"Yes, and it's supposed to be a dollar a pint." Greene replied, "So you'll be broke before ya know it, Goldie!"

When Jake walked over to inspect their work, Golden asked him, "When are we to be allowed to go to the sutler's?"

"Well, we'll be breaking in some more pack mules today, so I expect that you can probably go after that. Top will let us know."

"Good, I fancy a drink or two. It's been near on a month since I've savored a drop."

"Best not be overdoing it, Goldie. Better to use your money to buy some canned goods. We'll not have wagons where we're headed."

"Ah, I will Jake. What's the rumors?"

"Just the usual, we'll be here a day or two, so stay out of trouble. There'll be lots of officers milling around, so be sure to watch for them."

After breakfast, Top Martin called the NCOs together.

"Listen up, lads! I'm told that we'll be here for several days. Let's take the opportunity to rest the horses. Get with the farrier and make sure all of the horseshoes are good. We'll not be taking sabers along when we leave. Custer feels that they're a nuisance and make too much noise. We'll leave them boxed up here, along with the company wagon. Cpl. Wylie will be staying here with the new men to watch out for them. Let the men know that if they have mail to send out, that they need to get it to me this morning. The *Far West* is heading back downstream this afternoon to the Stanley Stockade depot to bring up the rest of the infantry and supplies. Mail and dispatches will be forwarded on to Ft. Buford from there. Now, I'm sure you've all heard that the sutler has whiskey, and I know that most of the men still have money left, so I want the men held to one pint, per day."

They all looked at Martin with chagrin, and Morse spoke up, "We'll pass that on Top. Most of the lads will be okay, but you know there's a few that will overdo it."

"Aye! I know. But let them know that Custer has threatened that drunkards will be turned out of camp until they sober up."

The sutler had erected a large tent to accommodate his merchandise. He'd set up a bar by placing long planks on top of kegs, and put up a wall of canned goods and boxes across the middle that served as a partition between the officers and enlisted. When Jake and Tom Russell arrived that evening there was a line of men waiting with their canteens in hand. Jake elected to go around to another part of the tent that served as a store, while Tom took a place in line. Jake was surprised to find when he walked in that there weren't many others, compared to the lines at the bar. He began looking at the piles of goods that were stacked on crates; wide brimmed straw hats, shirts, underwear, socks. Boxes of canned goods and various bottles lined the canvas walls. Jake noticed a label on one of the boxes and bent over to read the print, it read "Leighton and Jordan Company, Fort Buford, Dakota".

"Can I help you, Sergeant?" asked a voice from behind him.

Jake straightened up and turned around, "Yes, I'm looking to stock up on some canned goods and was just looked to see what you have. I noticed that some of your merchandise comes from the post trader at Fort Buford."

"Indeed, Alvin Leighton and his brother Joseph are my business partners. They helped me accumulate all this. Without their backing I wouldn't have been able to offer such a variety."

"Yes, he's a partner with Bob Seip, back at Fort Lincoln, also." Jake said.

"Well, that's true, although that's not common knowledge. You must know Bob well." The man replied, holding out his hand. "My name is John Smith, I'm the sutler."

Jake shook his hand and said, "Jake Rogers, and yes I know Bob. He, Kate, and his niece Holly are friends."

"Ah, I see." Smith said, "I met them once in Bismarck, last summer, while traveling with Alvin and Joseph. Holly is quite pretty as I recall."

Jake smiled, "Yes, she is."

"You must be that young soldier that Kate was telling her uncle about. The one Holly was so enamored with."

"Yes, well, Holly's down in Kansas at school now, but we write to each other."

A commotion broke out not he other side of the tent and Smith peered over at it. "My bartender, Jim Coleman, seems to be getting overwhelmed. I need to go see if I can help. I tell you what, if you don't mind, look around for a bit while I'm gone and keep an eye on things. I'll make you a deal when I get back."

"Sure, I don't mind, it's not like I have anywhere else to be."

Later that evening, Jake, Tom, Pat, and Jim Flanagan were sitting around a fire sipping on dark green bottles of ale that Smith had sold to Jake.

"Ah, it's a wondrous thing that you found good Burke Ale, from

Ireland, all the way out here, Jake." Flanagan proclaimed.

"Well, there's not much of it, and what there is, is purchased by the officers. But the sutler, Smith, made me a deal. He knows Bob and Kate Seip, so he let me have some."

Morse nodded his head, "Good on you, Jake. We'd better make sure Mike Martin gets a bottle, else he hears about."

"Oh, I have a couple for Top."

"I'll wander over there tomorrow and make my acquaintance with Mr. Smith." Pat replied. "He might have some good whiskey stashed away, also."

The following day, the companies of the 7th's Left Wing continued to prepare for a march and the process of breaking in the pack mules continued. The entire wagon train including the regimental baggage would remain in camp. Custer had expected more mounts to be available, but when he found none, decided to leave the regimental band at the depot and their pale gray horses were reassigned to Company E and the trumpeters. The newest soldiers who had walked or rode on wagons, were still without mounts, and each company was to leave them behind at the depot, also. Major Moore along with three companies of the 6th Infantry and two from the 17th Infantry would remain to guard the base, while Capt. Baker and Company B, 6th Infantry would be stationed on the *Far West,* where Terry had established his headquarters. By early afternoon, preparations were complete and the men were given time to go visit the sutler. The rest of the day and evening was spent indulging in alcohol, gambling, and games, while the band provided music. The *Far West* returned about 8:00 with the rest of the stores, supplies, and infantry from the Stanley's Stockade.

In the morning, Terry and Custer formed plans for the Left Wing to follow the Yellowstone along the south bank, to the Tongue River confluence approximately 40 miles away and wait there for the Right Wing under Reno to return from its scouting mission. Terry would follow on the *Far West* with additional supplies and the remaining Gatling guns. They would make further plans pending the reports that Reno brought back. The infantry soldiers, along with the 7th's rear detachment and band members, went about improving their camps, erecting shelters, building bread ovens, and digging latrines, while the Left Wing cavalry troopers inspected mounts and tack. Each man was responsible for making sure his shelter half, rubber ground cloth, and blanket was in good shape. Many took advantage of the commissary stores aboard the steamer, and exchanged them for new ones. Those that hadn't squandered their money on whisky and gambling packed their haversacks with extra goods from the sutlers tent.

"Sutler Smith is damn proud of his goods, too proud if you ask me." groused Jim Flanagan, "Hell, his prices are twice as high as back at Lincoln, and they were too damn high there."

"Well, what're ya gonna do?" asked Russell, "Go without?"

"No, but I ain't gotta be happy about it."

Jake and the others were busy sorting out their kits in preparation for leaving camp in the morning. Gen. Terry ordered Custer to march upstream along the Yellowstone towards the Tongue River, where Reno was supposed to report after completing his scout.

"Well, I've got a few dollars left, and I don't suppose we'll have many chances left to get a drink if the last month is any indication. Let's go check on the men, and then I'll stand for the first round over at the bar." Tom stated.

"And, I'll get the second one." Jake said.

The Left Wing didn't depart until 7:00 the next morning. Custer had been summoned for a final conference with Terry on board the *Far West*. The riverboat would haul extra rations and forage, in addition to the Gatling guns and extra pack mules. They crossed the shallow waters of the Powder and then proceeded to detour up to higher ground to avoid rougher terrain. The day was clear and warm and the pace was not hurried, as the distance was only 40 miles to the Tongue River. Custer anticipated that Reno and the Right Wing would not be arriving there for a couple of days. As usual, he was out in the lead and bagged an antelope that ventured too near. Occasionally, the men were able to catch glimpses of the riverboat's smoke stacks as is churned its way upstream. They went into camp after making 28 miles and enjoyed a calm night. They resumed the march the next morning and as they descended back to the river plain they came upon an old Sioux camp. It was just across the river from the site where Custer had engaged the Sioux back in '73, while with Stanley. Knowing that the Tongue confluence was just ahead, Custer elected to stop and examine it then issued orders to make camp there. As the men rummaged for firewood they came upon a human skull in a fire pit and nearby it the remains of a cavalry overcoat. It was speculated that the skull belonged to a captured soldier who had been beaten and burned to death by the Sioux. They also found several burial scaffolds containing dead Sioux. They were scrapped for use in fires and the bodies were stripped of blankets and trinkets, then thrown in the nearby river. Custer secured a bundle from one of them that contained a pair of beaded moccasins and a bow with six arrows, giving them to his nephew, Autie Reid. The *Far West,* which had been broken down the previous day, caught up with the column and pulled into the bank near the camp. Some of the men explored the area while many of them spent their time fishing. The morning brought a slight mist but after breaking camp, Custer led them out of camp at 6:00, moving at a trot. They reached the heavily wooded area of the Tongue River by 8:30, and the *Far West* working against the current, arrived around noon. The entire command settled in awaiting contact from Major Reno and the Right Wing. Other than the normal daily details, the men spent their time hunting, fishing, and wandering the immediate area. Most took advantage of having a plentiful supply of water to bath and wash their clothes. Many of the officers congregated on board the *Far West,* playing card games and enjoying the relative luxury of her simple accommodations. Jake and Tom took shotguns and explored the timber upstream. They found a good place to ford the river and were able to bag some sage grouse on the bench land on the other side, before returning to camp.

"Those birds were tasty, lads." 1st Sgt. Martin said, "Between them and the fish that we've been catching, it's been pleasant change in diet."

"It has that. Especially with the advantage of having extra rations on that riverboat, not to mention Sutler Smith and his wares." Morse added.

"Any word on when we'll be leaving here, Top?" Jake asked.

"The captain says maybe tomorrow or the next day. We're waiting on Reno to show up. It's speculated that the Sioux are located to the south and west along the headwaters of one of the Big Horn tributaries."

Later that afternoon two Crow scouts rode in with a dispatch from Maj. Reno. Not much later, Capt. Hughes one of Terry's aides, was seen departing camp with the same scouts. Rumors quickly began circulating to the effect that Reno and the Right Wing had struck the trail of a large band of Indians along Rosebud Creek. Most of the officers went on board the *Far West,* where Terry and Custer were looking at a map. Capt. Weir sent Lt. Edgerly back to the company area with a message to 1st Sgt. Martin.

"First Sergeant! The captain sent me to tell you that we'll be moving in the morning. Reno's eight miles up along the Yellowstone. We'll move to meet up with him in the morning."

"Can you tell me what's up, Sir?"

"Well, it seems Reno found a big trail and followed it well beyond the area he was to scout. Terry and Custer are furious about whether he's spooked the Sioux. We'll know more when Capt. Hughes gets back, Just be sure to have the men ready. We'll be in the advance with Custer and you can bet he'll be in a hurry to reach Reno."

At 8:00, on Tuesday, June 20, Custer led the six companies of the 7th out of camp. Terry and his staff, along with the Gatling guns and extra mules, stayed on the steamer which was heading up the Yellowstone to Reno's bivouac. The Tongue was too deep to ford close to camp, so Custer turned south following the east bank to look for a place to ford the river. Jake had visited with Lt. Varnum and Charlie Reynolds earlier about the crossing he had used the day before. The two Crow scouts confirmed it and Varnum had been appreciative, noting that Custer was going to set a quick pace and was is no mood to stray far from the Yellowstone once they were across. The first few miles were relatively easy and the column maintained a brisk pace. Then they encountered some badlands where they had to negotiate narrow, twisting defiles and then ascend steep buttes. As the sun rose the temperatures climbed baking the troopers as they struggled through narrow canyons. The twin columns of smoke that marked the progress of the *Far West* along the Yellowstone were spotted from some of the high points, as it seemed to pace them. Three hours passed before the terrain gradually transitioned to a plateau and Custer raced out ahead with the scouts towards the creek where Reno had bivouacked the previous day. The *Far West* could be seen making its way to the riverbank nearby as the main body of the column rode in. Lt. Cooke sent messengers to the company commanders, informing them that they should stand by before making any moves to encamp. As they dismounted to care for the horse's some of the men from Reno's detachment came over.

Milt DeLacy walked over to where Jake while he was leading Ajax towards the riverbank for water.

"Damn glad to see you boys! That Reno like to run us ragged chasing up and down creek and river valleys."

"There's all kinds of rumors going around, did you find the Sioux?" Jake asked.

"No, but we came pretty close. We came across several abandoned camps, and the scouts returned from following the trail to tell Reno we were within a days ride of closing with them."

"I can tell you that Custer is upset with Reno. I over heard him talking with Capt. Weir. It seems that he disobeyed orders."

"Well, maybe so, but at least we got on their trail. That scout we got from Gibbon, Mitch Boyer, he counted the number of lodges and fire circles at each campsite. There were over 400 and growing at each campsite. He also found signs that there are some Cheyenne bands with them. Some of the travois trails were fresher than the campsites and Boyer thinks that Sioux from the reservations are arriving. He told Reno there could be over a 1,000 warriors. I'm telling you that some of us were getting right nervous until he persuaded Reno to turn around and come back north."

"I'll bet! We were sitting over on the Tongue River waiting on you boys to show up. We've seen little to no sign of Mr. Lo."

"Boyer says it's as big a village as he's ever known of and because of the size of the pony herd, the Indians have to move on every few days to find adequate grazing."

1st Sgt. Varden came over to DeLacy, "Keogh just sent word. We're heading back up towards the Rosebud this afternoon. Get the men cleaned up and draw some forage from the boat."

DeLacy cocked an eyebrow at Varden and said. "That's some rough ass country to be starting out this late. I don't know if some of the mules and those Gatling gun horses will make it."

"Ah, there's one bit of good news, the guns are to be loaded aboard the boat and we'll sort out the pack train up at the Rosebud."

After Varden walked away DeLacy said, "Those Gatling guns are a pain in the ass out in this terrain. Those poor bastards crewing them wore themselves ragged just trying to keep the damn thing from tipping over. They had a hell of a time staying up with the column and Reno even left them behind at one point."

"All of the wagons are back at the Powder River Depot. We have everything on pack mules just like you boys, now." Jake said. "They loaded some extra mules on the riverboat so I suppose Custer will have us all out on the trail, soon."

"Well, he'd better let the Right Wing companies rest up for a day or two. We just rode 240 miles over the last 10 days. We ran out of forage two days ago and the grazing was poor. The horses need a break."

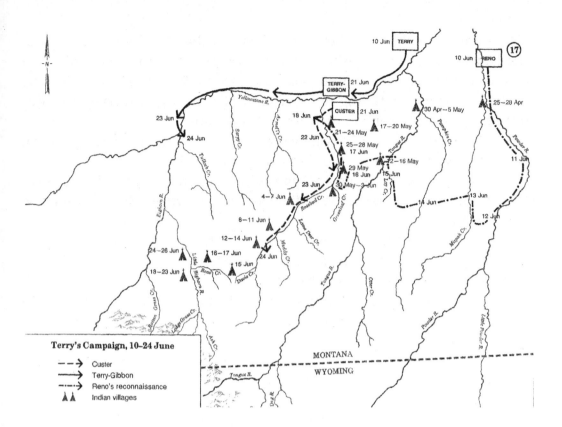

Terry's Campaign, 10–24 June

- - - →   Custer
——→   Terry-Gibbon
—·—→   Reno's reconnaissance
🛖🛖   Indian villages

MONTANA
WYOMING

CHAPTER 31

Yellowstone River, 2 miles east of Rosebud Creek - June 21, 1876

Custer had marched the reunited 7th about halfway up to the Rosebud before stopping to bivouac and then had the whole outfit back in the saddle at 6:00 that morning. The *Far West* passed them as they went up river, it was on its way to meet up with Col. Gibbon and the Montana Column. When the regiment dropped down on the tableland along the Yellowstone they could see Gibbon's command marching over on the other side. Custer rode on ahead to find a good spot to bivouac, selecting a spot just short of the mouth of the Rosebud right along the riverbank. Soon after, the *Far West* moored to the south bank and began unloading rations and forage. Sutler Smith was onboard with his wares and the Right Wing companies swarmed aboard to pick over them. Gen. Terry held a conference in his cabin with Gibbon, Custer, and Maj. Brisbin, who was the commander of the four 2nd Cavalry companies attached to the Montana Column. They pored over a large map of the Missouri and Yellowstone Rivers. The map was originally based on a 1860 survey, but had been updated and enlarged by the Terry's chief engineer officers prior to taking the field. As the distances from the two main rivers increased, the water courses and streams showed on the map were projected and probable routes that had not been surveyed. They speculated that the big village they were seeking would be found somewhere in the vicinity of the upper Little Big Horn River, if it continued along the trail that Reno's scout had found. George Herendeen, a civilian scout with Gibbon's column was summoned and they questioned him extensively about the area south and west of the upper Rosebud. Herendeen was familiar with that area and speculated that the Sioux were following the buffalo and would continue in that direction. Gibbon asked Herendeen to accompany Custer to act as a guide and courier. Terry then ordered Custer to take the entire regiment of the 7th Cavalry and go up the Rosebud following the trail of the Sioux bands. Custer was to constantly dispatch scouts to insure that the Sioux had not turned back to the east. Gibbon's column would march up right bank of the Yellowstone to the Big Horn River, where the *Far* West would ferry it across to continue up the Big Horn River to the Little Big Horn. Based on the map and projected march times, Terry hoped to have both commands in position by Monday, the 26th. Herendeen was to carry a message back to Terry when Custer reached the area near the headwaters of Tullock's Fork. Terry offered to send the Gatling gun battery with Custer, but he declined noting that that it would cripple his mobility and slow his march. He did accept the loan of Mitch Boyer and six additional Crow scouts from the Montana Column. The conference broke up and Custer returned to his camp to brief his officers. The *Far West* cast off and ferried Gibbon, Brisbin, and the Gatling battery, along with 13 mules that were in poor shape after Reno's scout over to the north river bank. The steamer returned promptly with the Crow detachment.

1st Sgt. Martin summoned the NCOs of Company D to meet and pass on the orders he'd been given by Capt. Weir.

"Right! Now listen up! We'll be leaving in the morning. Custer is taking the entire regiment in pursuit of the Sioux. We're to take rations for 15 days. Each man will be issued 50 carbine rounds and 24 pistol rounds to carry with them. The pack train will carry extra ammunition and forage."

"Damn, it sounds like he's expecting a fight if we catch them." Flanagan stated. "Which is a big if, hell, we ain't even seen a Sioux since we left Lincoln!"

"Well, supposedly Major Reno and the Right Wing followed the trail and came on some big campsites, maybe better than 400 lodges, which could mean several thousand Sioux." Martin said.

Jake said, "I talked to Sgt.DeLacy over in Keogh's company and he said the same thing, maybe 1,000 to 1,500 warriors."

Pat Morse spoke up, "So what's the plan if we catch them."

"Knowing Custer, like as not try we'll try and catch them unawares like we did down on the Washita, then attack." Martin answered. "By the by, Custer has decided to dispense with the wing and battalion assignments. He's to call the shots himself."

Morse nodded his head, "Well if Custer's been given his head by Gen. Terry, we're in for some hard riding, Lads. We'd best see that the men take some spare horse shoes and pack what extra forage they can."

Martin said, "Aye, I'm sending Farrier Charlie around to inspect the mounts to be sure. There'll be precious little room on the mules for any extras, and make sure the lads don't try to pack too much on their horses. Stragglers will be sent back to the pack train. The captain says that Custer intends to chase the Sioux wherever the trail leads and we may be eating horse meat before we get through, so pack what salt you can."

The sutler stayed open for business and the men filed on board the *Far West* late into the evening. Lanterns glowed brightly on board the riverboat and many of the officers gathered to play cards and write letters. Captain Marsh hosted a poker game in his cabin that included Custer, his brother Tom, his brother-in-law Lt. Calhoun, and several others. Jake and Tom Russell wandered around the main deck sipping on beers and looking out at the river flowing by.

"So what do you think, Jake?" Tom asked "You worried about what happens if we catch Mr. Lo?"

"Well, I reckon that we'll find out if they'll cut and run. From what I know about the Sioux they may not, particularly if there's as many as they're rumored to be. I overheard Lt. Varnum talking to Lt. Wallace. He was telling him about the fights they had with the Sioux back in '73. It wasn't too far from here and they gave Custer all that he could handle."

A voice came from behind Jake, "Ah Sgt. Rogers! I see that you've managed to find your way to a beer."

They turned around to find Capt. Michealis, standing with Capt. Weir, and saluted, "Good evening, Sirs."

Weir said, "At ease, sergeants. Are you ready to march in the morning?"

"Yes, Sir!" Jake answered.

Michaelis asked, "And where's Corporal Caddle?"

"He's a sergeant now, sir. I believe he's back at the Powder River depot. His horse went lame and he was put in charge of the Company I detachment left behind there. I'm sure that he's not too happy about it."

"That's too bad! Good marksmen may come in handy very shortly."

Jake looked over at Capt. Weir, then replied, "Well, probably so, sir"

"I say Weir, I still have those Sharps sporting rifles that we were shooting back at Fort Lincoln last year. Perhaps you'd like me to send one of them with Sgt. Rogers?"

"That would be fine, Otho. I'm sure Rogers would find a way to put it to some use." Weir replied.

Jake smiled and nodded his head, "Oh you can be sure that I would, sir."

"Very well. Come and see me in the morning, Rogers and I'll have one ready for you, along with some ammunition."

"Thank you, sir, I'll do that."

"I guess we'd best be on our way, Weir. I promised Godfrey that we'd thrash he and Edgerly once again at a game of Whist."

When the officers were gone, Russell said, "So, I expect you to bag us some game with that fancy rifle."

"Yeh, that should be fun. I've only shot at targets and it'll be interesting to see how it shoots in the field." Jake said. "Let's go get another beer, then call it a night."

When they got to the sutlers, Jake saw Mark Kellogg sitting on a barrel, wearing spectacles and writing in his notebook by lantern light.

"Good evenin' Mr. Kellogg!"

Kellogg looked up over the rim of his glasses, "Oh, hello, Sgt. Rogers. I'm just trying to finish up a dispatch so it can go out with the mail in the morning."

"So are you going out with the 7th, or staying with General Terry?" Jake asked.

"Well, I was going to stay with Terry, but I'm afraid that the bigger story will be with Custer. I want to be at the death."

"That's a curious way of putting it."

"Keogh told me that it's a fox hunting term for the end of the hunt." Kellogg said.

"Hmm, you'd do well to remember that the fox that we're hunting has a lot of friends, Mr. Kellogg." Jake stated, "And no one is sure just how many there are."

"I have confidence in Custer, I'm sure he will prevail."

"Let's hope you're right."

The following morning was cool and damp when Reveille sounded so the men welcomed a hot breakfast and coffee. Company quartermasters issued ammunition and the boxes were lashed to the padded aparejo saddles on the larger mules, one per company. The other supplies were taken to where the other dozen or so mules assigned to each company were being staged. The boxes of hardtack and supply bundles were lashed to sawbuck packs, which were difficult to load without causing discomfort to the animals. Meanwhile the men sorted out their kits and stuffed their saddle bags and haversacks. Jake went onboard the steamer in search of Capt. Michaelis. He found him standing off to the side watching the supplies being handed out from the *Far West's* hold.

Jake saluted him, "Good morning, Sir!"

"Ah, Sgt. Rogers, I've been expecting you. Let's go to my cabin and I'll get you that rifle."

They picked their way across the deck and climbed a ladder up to the cabin deck and went along the covered walkway to the one Michaelis was in. The room was a narrow cubicle with a small bunk and a shelf above it. There was a wooden case laying on the bunk, which Michaelis opened revealing a brown leather rifle scabbard with a flap and several straps. He picked it up, hefted it, and passed it to Jake.

"I had this scabbard made specially for this gun. It has a wood frame and padding to protect the riflescope, go ahead and check it out."

Jake unbuckled the flap covering the rifle butt and folded it back. He tilted the scabbard and was surprised how easily the rifle slid out.

"You see, the inside is lined with polished leather at all of the contact points. I'm quite proud of the design." Michaelis said.

"Yes, it's very impressive. Are you sure that you want me to take it, Sir? We'll probably be traveling through some rough country."

"Quite sure, Rogers! The straps are positioned to facilitate attaching it to a McClellan saddle. I've done it several times. You'll be surprised how well it rides. Not to mention that you won't be encumbered with a carbine sling over your shoulder."

When Jake fingered the rubber caps covering both ends of the scope, Michaelis stated, "Dustcaps, and the pouch on the inside of the flap holds a silk cloth for wiping the lenses. Theres a shooting stick in a pocket along the back. And, I've reached out to one of the infantry companies to fill this 45-70 cartridge belt to go with it." he added pointing at a belt hanging from the shelf.

Jake slid the Sharps back into the scabbard and secured the flap.

"I'll take real good care of this, Sir."

"Of course you will, Rogers. I trust that you'll find it a bit more useful than your carbine. Let me know how it works out."

"I'll do that, sir. Thank you"

When Jake got back to where Company D was, he saddled Ajax and attached the rifle scabbard to his saddle. He was adjusting it when Pat Morse came over to look.

"That's quite a rig, Jake!"

"It is that. Any word on when we're moving out?"

"Well, Custer is still in his tent, writing. But Sgt. Major Sharrow has passed on that there's to be a parade review as we leave camp. Top wants us to make sure the men sit tall, and keep their intervals."

At noon, the assembled regiment filed past a slight rise along the river where Custer and his color bearers sat on their mounts along with Gen. Terry, Col. Gibbon, and Major Brisbin. The column of nearly 650 men was to follow the Yellowstone towards the Rosebud with Varnum and the scout contingent ranged out front, and as each company passed, the officers rode up and exchanged salutes with the reviewing party. The pack train of 175 mules brought up the rear, and was struggling to remain closed up. Custer, shook hands with Terry and exchanged a few goodbyes with the other officers, then wheeled Dandy to gallup along the entire length of the regiment column, followed by his orderlies. He took his place at the head of the column and upon reaching the mouth of the Rosebud, called a halt to repack the mules. They crossed the narrow creek and turned south following a trail up to the bench land that overlooked valley. After several miles the bluffs closed in and the command was forced to cross over to the flats on the eastern side. The pack mules became unruly when they were forced to negotiate the gullies and rocky terrain of the creek bottom, and the lashings on the packs had to be constantly retightened. The Rosebud Valley narrowed considerably as the column pressed on. Bends and ravines blocked by cactus and rocks necessitated crossing the stream back and forth several times. Each crossing causing difficulties for the pack train. Finally, at 4 o'clock, after making only 12 miles, Custer called a halt at a good site along the high ground of the timbered creek that had adequate grazing. Mounted pickets were sent out and sited strategically up and down the valley..

Jake had been sent to check on the company pack mules as they straggled into the camp. He saw Jack Ward, yanking on the leads of one, cussing a blue streak.

"Jack, you need some help?" he called out.

"God damn mules, and these fooking idiots that can't learn to hitch a load properly. I don't likely reckon that one's smarter than the other! They'd best send me somebody else tomorrow, or I may have to take my whip to these dumb sum bitches!"

Jake saw that Pvt. Hurd and his set of four, were wearily leading their mules behind Ward. Both men and animals were covered with dust, while their pants and boots were layered with mud.

"You boys look like you've had a time of it, Peaches." Jake said.

"That ain't no shit!" Hurd replied, "These mules just don't like crossing that damn creek. They balk at going in, and then start bucking until the packs come loose, especially the boxes of hardtack and ammunition. Then we got to re-tie everything after we get over."

"Well, I expect it'll get better as they get used to it."

"Please tell me that we ain't gonna have to do this again tomorrow, Jake." Pvt. Stiver protested.

"That's up to Top. But I think he plans on rotating the sections."

"Gawd, I hope so. I'd rather pull guard duty as have ta do this every day!"

"Come on follow me. I'll take you to the company bivouac area. Jack, you and Joe are welcome to eat at our mess if you'd like."

Ward looked back at Jake with bleary eyes, "We'd be obliged. Me and Joe was kinda drunk when we agreed to tag along on this here jaunt. Most of our victuals are back down at the Powder with the wagon, where we was plannin' to go back to it when Lt. Nowlan upped the ante on us."

Jake grinned, "Well, be sure to take care of the packs, then. That's all we got until we get back."

"Back to where?" Jack asked.

"That's entirely up to Custer, and the Sioux."

Near dusk, Officer's call was sounded and they all reported to Custer's tent on a rise overlooking the creek. After a lengthy meeting, they returned to their commands to relay the orders that they received. Capt.Weir and Lt. Edgerly met with the Company D NCOs. Effective immediately, Trumpet calls were to be suspended. The men assigned horse picket duty were to make sure to rouse the camp at 3 AM, and the command would ready to begin the march at 5:00. Lt. Mathey was designated to command the pack train and would inspect each company's mules daily. The ones that were found to be packed poorly would dictate which of the companies would be assigned to the rear detachment that day, and would then be responsible for herding the pack train and keeping it closed up. The first few days were to be short easy marches to try and acclimate the mules. Each company was to maintain its interval on the march so as always to be within supporting distance. The men were to keep their weapons at the ready and close to their bedrolls at night. There were a few eyebrows raised when Weir reported the number of hostiles that might be encountered. The estimates were based on the village sites that Reno had come across, 1,000-1,500 warriors depending on how many reservation Sioux had come out for the summer. Weir ended the meeting and they wandered back to the campfires that flickered around the company area. Jake was in charge of the horse pickets that night and went to make his rounds. He was working his way around when he came upon another man. Light from several campfires revealed him to be Lt. Godfrey, from Company K.

"Good evening, sir! I'm just checking on my horse pickets."

Godfrey leaned close peering at Jake. "Ah, Sgt. Rogers isn't it?"

"Yes, sir!"

"Yes, I remember you from Louisiana last year. You were one of Capt.

Michaelis' marksmen as I recall."

"That seems like a long time ago, now." Jake said.

"Is this your first time out in the field, Rogers?"

"No, sir! I spent quite a bit of time out with the Boundary Survey when we were on escort duty."

A campfire flared up momentarily as more wood was thrown on it, revealing a group of the scouts. They were using sign language and Jake could make out a little of the conversation.

"They seem to be a little concerned about how many Sioux we are chasing." Jake said.

"You can make out what they're saying?" Godfrey asked.

"Well, some of it. I'm a little rusty." Jake answered.

Godfrey walked over to the campfire and Jake followed. He saw that Bloody Knife and some of the Ree scouts were there, along with the new Crow scouts that had just been added. One of them turned towards them. He was wearing a calfskin vest and whipcord britches tucked into tall brown boots. He reminded Jake of Val and he saw that it was the scout Mitch Boyer.

"You fellas lost?" he demanded, as he removed a stubby clay pipe

Jake answered, "No just making the rounds of my pickets. I saw you signing, and was just watching to see what it was about."

"So can you sign?" Boyer asked.

Jake signed back, "I made out most of it."

Boyer laughed, "Well, well! We don't meet many bluecoat soldiers that can. Where'd you learn?"

Jake answered saying. "I worked with a guide named Val Wheeler for couple of seasons up north of here, he taught me." He reached up and pulled out the wolf tooth necklace.

Boyer gave him a long appraising look, "I know of this man, the Sioux call him Pale Wolf. He's a man to be respected."

Godfrey spoke up, "So, Rogers said that you were discussing the number of Sioux ahead of us."

"Have you ever fought the Sioux, Lieutenant" Boyer asked.

"I have." Godfrey replied, "Three years ago, just across the Yellowstone. I was with Custer on the Railroad Survey."

"So how many do you expect to find?"

"It is said that there may be as many as 1,000-1,500."

Boyer stared intently at the officer, puffing on his pipe, then asked, "Do you think that you can whip that many."

"Yes, I guess so."

The scout turned back to the others and began signing to them. They all had solemn expressions as they looked over at Jake and Godfrey.

Boyer turned back around and then said emphatically. "Well, I can tell you, we are gonna have a damn big fight!"

Godfrey stood silently for a moment, then replied. "I guess we'll see. See you on the march, Rogers." Then turned and walked away.

As Jake turned to go, Boyer came closer. Jake nervously fingered the wolf's tooth at his neck. Boyer saw it and raised an eyebrow. "Hey boy, you hold that close. It's powerful medicine and may protect you. Pale Wolf must hold you in high regard to give you that. You'll need to remember what else he taught you. Custer thinks that the Sioux are running, but he's wrong. They're gonna fight!"

Jake stared back at Boyer, nodded his head, then left to check the rest of his pickets.

When they moved out of camp the next day the Crow scouts with Mitch Boyer went out ahead, while the Rees ranged along both flanks. Company H had the misfortune to be judged the worst packed and therefore Capt. Benteen was put in command of the rear battalion along with two other companies. The column crossed over to the east bank and with in the first 3 miles was forced to ford the creek five times. This rugged stretch was heavily wooded and had dense undergrowth, with many thickets of thorny rosebushes. Eventually the ground leveled out and Custer, who was anxious to see the site of the first abandoned village, advanced rapidly towards it, leaving Benteen's battalion and the pack train far behind. Pausing briefly to examine it, the main body crossed over to the west banks and followed along the Sioux lodgepole trails, encountering three more campsites along the way. Each site littered with the remnants of the buffalo taken by the Sioux hunters while the surrounding grazing areas were stripped down to the soil. By 3:00 the main column reached the location where Reno had turned back towards the Yellowstone the previous week. Custer decided to push on along the trail until about 4:30 when the valley began to narrow. He decided to bivouac there along the east side of the Rosebud on a sage covered plain. Benteen's battalion, now several miles behind, resorted to herding the pack train along by encircling it and herding the mules forward, which helped increase the pace, but it was still near sunset when Lt. Cooke rode out to meet Benteen and lead him to his section of the camp.

Jake and most of the Company D sergeants were lounging near a campfire discussing the campsites they'd come across during the day.

"I'm thinkin' that we're followin' a shitpot full of Sioux. Did the rest of you notice that this trail seems to be gettin' bigger?" Flanagan exclaimed. "What do you think Morse?"

"I'll not dispute that." He replied, "I've spotted some signs of Cheyenne, too."

1st Sgt. Martin said, "We need to keep the men from wandering too far. There's to be no lallygagging. Did you notice that the Rees were staying well within sight of the column all day. They're acting a little spooked if you ask me."

Jake spoke up and related his encounter with the scouts the previous evening. When he told them of Boyer's final statement there was silence.

"Well, Jake m' boy, what do you make of the Mitch Boyer fella?" asked Morse.

"He seems pretty solid to me, Pat. He reminds me of Val Wheeler. I'm inclined to think he's right."

"Well, we can count on Custer to go pell-mell after them." Martin stated, "All we can do is make sure the lads keep their guns handy and don't let them get in a panic if it comes to a fight."

The column broke bivouac and was on the march at 5:00 the following morning. As they followed the east bank the tracks of the travois poles widened and a few smaller campsites were encountered. Custer set a brisk pace and as the day grew warmer swarms of flies and ants swarmed the troopers. The pace was slowed to a walk and Capt. Yates, who was in charge of the rear detachment, sent word to close up. The column halted when the Crow scouts returned reporting fresh sign ahead about ten miles. After calling a brief conference with his officers, Custer rode out ahead with the scouts and two companies. Before they'd gone too far, they came to the site of the largest campsite encountered yet. A large lodgepole structure stood in the middle and Custer halted near it. Custer's Dakota scouts explained that this was a Sioux Sun Dance lodge and that it was used to make powerful medicine. While he and the scouts were walking around inspecting the area, the orderly carrying Custer's personal flag had planted it in the ground. The area surrounding the abandoned lodge bore the marks of innumerable moccasin prints, indicating that it had been well attended by the village occupants. A fresh scalp was found hanging in it, and Herendeen professed to recognize it as having belonged to a trooper from the 2nd Cavalry who had gone missing. The Dakota scouts pointed out many markings in the sand and to an arrangement of a bull buffalo skull and a pile of stones they said indicated that Sioux medicine was strong, and that they were not afraid to fight. A sudden breeze came up and blew Custer's standard over. Lt. Godfrey, who's Company K had been on the advance with Custer, picked it up and replanted it only to have another gust blow it down again. Godfrey forced it into a nearby clump of sage brush where it finally stayed up. The scouts took notice of this and made some warding signs with their hands, then scurried away.

The march was resumed and as the day became warmer, the dust stirred up by the advance party hung in the air choking the following troops. Custer sent word for the companies to spread out a bit and seek less trampled ground. The pace was much slower than earlier and several halts were called to keep from overtaking the scouts as they carefully examined the trail. Another large trail, coming from the left, intersected the one that they were following, which was close to a mile wide where it crossed the Rosebud. Custer summoned Lt. Varnum and sent him with some of the Rees to investigate a trail that led off to the right, then sent the Crow scouts on ahead, calling a halt for the rest of the column in the mean time. The men were allowed to start small fires for coffee and eat lunch.

"What did you make of that last camp site, Jake" asked Tom Russell, as he poured coffee.

"I think that there was a big powwow of some kind. It's got our scouts a bit spooked, particularly those Dakotas. The Rees are getting jumpy, too."

"Yeh, am I the only one noticing that the trail is getting a lot bigger?" Flanagan asked, "The ground is so stirred up with travois pole tracks that it almost looks like it's been plowed."

"I'm starting to wonder about the spacing of these camps and maybe that it's not one big band of Sioux, but several of them moving together." Morse spoke up. The others looked over at him quizzically as he continued, "These new trails we've come across could be made by others joining up with them. I think Custer shouldn't be in such an all fired hurry to catch up with them until we find out."

Russell said, "I think that's why we're stopped right now. I saw Lt. Varnum and some scouts ride off."

The regiment remained halted strung out along the Rosebud, watering the horses and mules. By 4:00, Varnum and his scouts had all returned, and after meeting with then, Custer had the column move out. They continued on up the valley passing several more large campsites. About 6:30, they came to a break in the line of bluffs off to the north, and the scout, Herendeen, rode to inform Custer that this gap led to the Tullock's Fork. Herenden asked Custer if he wanted him to carry a dispatch to Gen. Terry, but Custer felt that it was unnecessary due to the fact that the trail led west in the direction of the Little Big Horn River. Terry, along with Gibbon's Montana column, would be coming up that valley according to the plans made on the *Far West*. The regiment continued the march until 7:30, then crossed the Rosebud to bivouac in a wooded area below a steep bluff. The troopers were allowed to make fires for cooking, but to extinguish them afterwards. Benteen, who once again was in charge of the pack train, straggled in to find that Capt. Keogh had reserved an area for him. Keogh and his Company I would take over the pack train and the mules were to remain packed in anticipation of a quick start in the morning. Around 9 o'clock the Crow scouts came back and Mitch Boyer informed Custer that the trail ahead indicated that the Sioux were across the divide and in the Little Big Horn Valley. Custer immediately had Varnum, accompanied by Charlie Reynolds, Mitch Boyer, the Crow scouts, and a few Rees to act as couriers, leave camp to ride to a vantage point up on the divide. The Crows said that it provided a good view into the valley of the Little Big Horn. They also informed Custer that there was a good place below it on the Rosebud side, where he could hide the regiment. After the scouts left camp, Custer summoned his officers to inform them that a night march was to be made. They picked their way across the bivouac where many of the men had laid down to rest. On their return they tasked the sergeants to go about rousing them. The moon was hidden by clouds and the troopers stumbled about in the darkness, cursing and fumbling to get their gear secured on their horses. The companies were formed up as best they could when Custer, led by one of the Crow Scouts and accompanied by Bloody Knife and Fred Gerard, crossed over the Rosebud around 11:30 and proceeded to follow the lodgepole trail. The night was still and as the column strung out they stirred up clouds of dust, further reducing what little visibility there was. Keogh who was encountering much difficulty getting the mules of the pack train to enter the water and cross the river, was already well behind.

Weir assigned Jake and Pat Morse to lead the advance for Company D, and keep the interval with the company ahead of them. Their mounts plodded along in the darkness and they listened closely for the sounds of equipment rattling, and the horses of the troops in front.

"I've no fookin' idea how we're expected to keep up!" Pat cursed, "Sod it all!"

Jake adjusted the neckerchief that he'd tied across his face to keep from breathing in the dust. "I'll ride out ahead, and when I close up, I'll bang my tin cup. You can relay it on back."

"Right, don't stray too far, best to stay in the dust, at least you'll know we're still on the track."

Time dragged on, as the regiment plodded along, sometimes at a trot, then coming to an abrupt halt. The column followed Custer's advance like an accordion as they began encountering broken ground and ravines. Jake fell into a trance like state, banging his cup on his saddle pommel and peering off into the cloying dust filled gloom. Fortunately, Ajax seemed to sense the presence of the horses in front and kept them within earshot. An interminable amount of time passed before the column halted just as light began seeping through the dust around 2:30. The regiment was strewn out along a narrow creek, along a wooded ravine. The men, weary and slightly disorientated by the night march, slid from their saddles. Permission to start small cooking fires for coffee and breakfast was passed along. What little water found along the creek, proved to be so alkaline that the horses and mules wouldn't drink it and the men boiled it for their coffee in an attempt to improve the taste. Except for those posted as sentries, the men were allowed to sleep, with their mounts still saddled nearby. Word was sent down that they would not be moving out at 5:00 as usual, but should be prepared for movement by 8:00. Keogh's Company I, struggling with the balky pack train arrived a full hour after the other companies.

Custer was waiting for word from Lt. Varnum and the scouts. Around 7:30, as the sun was rising, one of the Ree scouts rode in and went to where Custer was eating breakfast with his brothers Tom and Boston. Bloody Knife and Charlie Reynolds were there also and had been cautioning Custer about the number of Sioux and Cheyenne that were probably in the camp they were stalking. While Bloody Knife and Gerard questioned the courier, Custer read the note that he'd brought back from Varnum. Then Custer leapt on his horse, Vic, and rode bareback along the bivouac, stopping to visit with his officers, giving them instructions. He went back to his campsite and had his striker, Burkman, saddle Vic, then gathered Reynolds, Gerard, and Bloody Knife, and several other of the Ree scouts, and immediately rode off in the direction of the divide.

Jake had been able to grab a couple hours of sleep and upon waking had joined some of the other sergeants where they were gathered around a small fire, drinking coffee.

"Here you go, Rogers, try some of this." offered Flanagan. "We all added some good water out of our canteens to cut the alkaline taste a bit."

"Thanks, Jim." Jake said. "Any word on what's going on?"

"Well, we saw Custer come by and speak with Capt. Weir earlier, then he rode out with group of scouts heading up hill. Word has it that Lt.

Varnum and those Crow scouts have got eyes on a big village in the next valley over."

"So are we waiting here?"

"No, we're going to move out at 8:00." 1st Sgt. Martin said. "You'd better eat something, then go get the lads ready to ride. I think the plan is for us to move closer to the divide and find a place to hide until tomorrow morning, then we'll hit the village early."

"Well, let's hope that works out, but I've a sneaky suspicion that Custer may lose patience." Pat Morse spoke up. "Best get the horses fed with what's at hand and let's hope to find better water, soon."

Martin added, "I want all of the guns inspected and make sure that the men have their ammunition handy."

The regiment didn't move until 8:45 and was led by Lt. Hare, from Company K. He had been temporarily re-assigned and put in command of what remained of the scout detachment. Tom Custer and Adjutant Cooke headed up the column, and once it was on the move, Cooke rode back along the command admonishing the companies and the pack train, to ride adjacent to the hostile trail to help reduce the dust cloud that was being thrown in the air. Major Reno, without a battalion to command, rode along with Capt. McDougall and Lt. Hodgson of Company B. Lt. Mathey and the pack train continued to struggle as packs loosened and fell off. Around 10:00 the column came to a halt in a wooded ravine a mile below the divide. A Company F mule was found to have lost a box of hardtack and when it was discovered, Sgt. Curtiss and a detail from that company went back along the trail to find it, only to discover two Indians in the process of trying to break it open. The Indians quickly mounted then rode away and the hardtack was retrieved. Upon his return Sgt. Curtis reported the incident to his company commander, Capt. Yates, who then relayed it to Lt. Cooke and Tom Custer. They immediately left to find and report this to Custer, who met them as he making his way back down. When Custer discovered that the command had moved up closer to the divide he was displeased, although he hadn't canceled his 8:00 movement order before he left. Upon his arrival at the bivouac he sent out a summons for an Officer's Call.

1st Sgt. Martin roamed the Company D area speaking with the men and looking at their horses. He paid special attention to the ammunition carried by each man, then checked their weapons. When he got to Morse's platoon he waved for Pat and Jake to come over to him.

"I'm not sure what's up, but Capt. Weir sent word with Charlie

Sanders, his orderly today, to have me get the men ready to move out within the hour."

"I thought we were gonna wait a day?" Morse asked, "What happened?"

"It seems that we've been spotted and that Custer is afraid the Sioux are going to scatter. So, my guess is that he's decided to go after them right away."

Hearing horses coming up behind them they turned to see Mitch Boyer and Charlie Reynolds riding by as they headed back in from their scout.

"What have you seen, Mitch?" Jake called out.

Boyer stopped his horse and looked at them. "A big village, the biggest one that I've seen in all my years." They stood silently as he added. "You're gonna find more Sioux down there than you can count. You will have yourselves a fight, that's for damn sure!"

Reynolds looked at them solemnly nodding his head in agreement, then prodded his mount on.

"You'd better hope that the medicine in that wolf fang of yours is powerful," Boyer said grimly, looking at Jake, "You'll be needin' it before the day is over!" Then he followed after Charlie Reynolds.

As the scouts rode away, Morse looked at Martin and said, "I'm inclined to take that man seriously, Top. He doesn't strike me as a fellow prone to panic."

Martin replied, "You're right, all the more the reason to make sure the lads pack extra ammunition. The pack train may not be handy. You remember the Washita fight, eh Pat?"

"What happened?" asked Jake.

"Well, 'twas a wee bit hectic, and we fired off most of what ammunition we had with us in attacking the Cheyenne camp. We discovered that there were several larger camps farther downstream, and a large group of warriors from them were headed towards us. Fortunately, Lt. Bell made a mad dash to us with the wagon that held our reserves."

"That Washita village only had about 50 lodges and they put up a good fight. If there's as many as the scouts claim up ahead, it'll be warm work." Morse said. "You got plenty of bullets for that fancy rifle of yours, Jake?"

"I have a cartridge belt, two bandoliers and my pouch is full. In a pinch I can shoot the carbine rounds."

"Hmm, let's hope it doesn't come to that."

CHAPTER 32

The Upper Little Big Horn River Valley, Montana Territory - June 25, 1876

Custer led the troops of his command across the divide just before noon, following the lodgepole scored trail that descended towards a broad ravine. After a short distance a halt was called and Custer gathered with his officers again. He'd decided to form several battalions and assigned Benteen to take his Company H, along with D & K totaling 125 men, and instructed him to move off in a left oblique towards a line of bluffs to the southwest. He was to check to see if there were any Sioux present. He sent Lt. Cooke to find Major Reno, who was riding further back along the column with Capt. McDougall and Lt. Hodgson. Cooke issued him orders to assume command of Companies A, M, and G with approximately 112 men, and be prepared to maneuver as Custer would direct. Reno appointed Hodgson to be his acting adjutant and they signaled the three companies fall in behind them, then moved out to the left. McDougall's Company B with 40 men would escort the pack train, still commanded by Lt. Mathey with 130 men counting the company detachments and civilian packers. Custer, with his brother Tom acting as aid de camp, kept the other five companies, consisting of 225 officers and men under his direct command. Once the battalions were formed the advance resumed.

Before Benteen led his battalion away, he asked for two experienced men from each company to be in the advance under 1st Lt. Gibson. They were to ride to the high ground where they could look to see what was ahead, allowing the rest to remain below the ridge, preserving the horses.

"Rogers, d'ya have those looking glasses of yours handy?" Martin called out.

"I do, Top."

"Good, take someone with you and report to Lt. Gibson up ahead. You'll be acting as the advance."

"Right, I'll take Pvt. Welch."

Jake called to Welch, "Come on Charlie, let's go."

They rode to the head of the column where Capt. Benteen was talking with Lt. Gibson.

****

1st Lt. Francis Marion Gibson

Born in Philadelphia, in Dec.1847, Gibson served in the Paymaster's Department in Washington D.C. at the end of the Civil War, and parlaying some connections, applied for a commission. After passing an examination before an Army board, he was appointed as a 2nd Lt. in the cavalry service and was sent to join Company A of new 7th Cavalry at Fort Leavenworth. He was a veteran of the Kansas campaigns and fought with the regiment at the Washita with Company F. Gibson's wife, Kate, had a sister who was married to Lt. MacIntosh, the officer commanding Company G. Gibson was popular, light hearted, and became a favorite of the Custer Clan. When he was promoted to 1st Lt., in July of 1872, he was assigned to Benteen's Company H, where he served during Reconstruction duty, and on the Yellowstone and Black Hills Expeditions. He'd recently served as post adjutant at Fort Rice when the company returned from New Orleans and had considered a transfer to one of the Fort Lincoln companies, before declining it. Being subordinate to a dominant commander like Benteen, who mildly disliked him, he maintained a very low key presence.

****

Jake rode up, and saluted, "Captain Benteen, Sgt. Rogers from Company D."

Benteen looked at him and said, "Weir says that you're pretty experienced at following a trail. We're supposed to see if we can find any signs of any Sioux off to our left. I want you to go with Lt. Gibson here, and see what you can find."

"Yes, sir!"

"Well, go on Frank!" Benteen called to Gibson, "Stay within eyesight and send me word if you find something."

The detachment departed, galloping on ahead towards the first line of bluffs. As they got to higher ground, Jake looked to his right and could see the grey horses of Company E leading Custer's main column. They were heading north along the east bank of the creek, with Reno's battalion in close proximity on the west side. When Jake and the others reached the top of the bluff, the valley on the other side was empty. Lt. Gibson scanned the distance using binoculars, as did Jake.

"I don't see anything moving, sir.", Jake said, "And no signs of a trail."

"Yes, well, I guess we'll go back and report." Gibson stated.

When they turned to go back, Jake noticed a rider coming towards them, at a gallop.

"Looks like Capt. Benteen is sending us some new orders."

The messenger, who Jake recognized as one of Benteen's baseball players, rode up and halted.

"Lt. Gibson, Sir! Capt. Benteen's compliments, Col. Custer sent him word with Trumpeter Voss to have us ride on to the next line of bluffs, and look into the next valley."

Gibson looking a bit perturbed, replied, "Very well, tell the captain that we've seen nothing so far. When we get to the next bluff, I will wave my hat if there's nothing to be seen."

The same scenario played out multiple times over the next two hours. The rugged defiles of the broken terrain they were encountering, began to effect the horses. As the sun bore down on them they removed their blouses, rolling them up and tying them to their cantles. Finally, Benteen, who had been riding out well in advance of the rest of the battalion waved for them to come back. The battalion turned to the north and started down the valley they were in. When Gibson and his detail made it back, Benteen was waiting with Capt. Weir as they rode up.

"That's enough of this valley hunting and damnable terrain, the Sioux would have more sense than to come this way!" Benteen stated, "Let's get back to the regiment. We haven't seen any signs for 5 or 6 miles, and the horses need water. Thomas, you take the advance."

Weir nodded, and acknowledged Benteen, "I agree Fred." Turning to Jake, he said, "Sgt. Rogers, take Pvt. Welch and join Sgt. Morse out front."

"Yes, Sir!"

They trotted up past the rest of the battalion, which was moving at a walking pace. They caught up with Morse, who had the rest of Welch's set of four, and was out ahead by 100 yards.

Reining up to ride along side Pat, Jake said, "Well, that was a hell of a waste of time!"

"Nothing, huh?" Morse asked, "We thought we heard some random shots and cheers coming from Custer's boys the last we saw of them. They were moving at a good trot."

"I saw no signs at all, not even buffalo tracks. Do you think Custer has found the village?"

"I'd be surprised if he hasn't. I guess we'll find out before too long."

They reached Custer's trail around 2:00, just as the pack train was coming up. Jake saw Boston Custer ride out from it and call out a greeting to Lt. Edgerly, then he hurried along the trail without stopping. The broad trail was full of travois pole drag marks, over ridden with hundreds of hoof marks from the shod cavalry mounts and fresh horse droppings.

"Where d'ya suppose he's off to in such a hurry." Welch commented.

"Off to catch up with his brother I suppose." Jake speculated. "I'd say that's where we should head."

They had followed the trail for about 30 minutes when they came to a swamp-like morass with several pools of water. Morse sent one of the Georges back to report it to Capt. Weir while they let their horses drink. Weir sent his orderly back to Benteen, halting Company D. Shortly afterwards the entire battalion began to dismount to water the horses and fill canteens, taking turns to get access to the pools of water. Back along the trail, the dust cloud from the pack train rose into the sky. Suddenly, the faint but unmistakable gunfire sounded from the trail ahead, and the volume indicated that contact had been made with the Sioux.

"D'ya hear that Jake?" Morse called out, "They've started the ball without us!"

Jake who had just finishing filling his canteen, turned to make room for the men of Company K, which was the trailing company. Their commander, Lt. Godfrey, was watering his horse nearby. Jake overheard Capt. Weir, who had sought out Lt. Godfrey, say uneasily, "We need to get the men mounted and move out."

Godfrey looked down the trail towards Benteen, where he and his orderly had already ridden some distance ahead. Benteen was looking through his field glasses.

"We'd better wait to see what he wants to do."

Heavy gunfire sounded again in the distance.

Weir looked at Godfrey and stated, "Well, I am going anyhow!" and quickly called for his men to mount up, and started Company D down the trail.

"Sgt. Morse, you and Rogers take some men and get out front. Keep a sharp look out!" Weir said urgently, "Watch for couriers, Custer is bound to have sent one looking for us."

"Yes, sir!" Morse replied, then called out, "Holden, you and your set with me!" then spurred his horse Gus forward while Jake and the others followed him, keeping pace.

As they drew near Benteen, he lowered his binoculars and looked over at them, then turned his horse to come back towards them, and as he reined in to ride alongside Weir, his orderly continued towards Companies H and K. Shortly after his arrival they formed up and soon exited the morass just as the first of the pack train mules came bolting down the trail scenting the water. The rest were strung out for several hundred yards, as Company B attempted to help the struggling civilian packers and the frustrated troopers assigned to assist them. They pulled and wrestled with the animals to keep them from pitching off their loads.

Jake and Morse led the advance party following the regiment's trail of hoof prints. They scanned ahead and could see smoke rising in the distance, still hearing scattered firing from that direction, although it seemed less intense than what it had been previously.

"What do you think, Pat?" Jake asked. The wolf fang at his neck seemed to tingle and he fingered it nervously as he rode. He and Morse had both unfastened their pistol holster flaps, and the troopers behind them had their carbines handy across their saddle pommels.

"Hard to say, but what ever is going up ahead, it don't sound like a stand up fight. I'm not hearing any volley firing. It sounds more like the skirmishes we had back in Missouri during the war."

As they rounded a bend in the creek they saw a large teepee ahead. The trail led to it and as they cautiously made their way, they saw signs where maybe a dozen other lodges had stood. Hundreds of shod hood prints, indicated that the regiment had been there, and they led off to the northwest still following the creek bed. When Benteen and Weir came up, they waved at Morse to keep going as Benteen dismounted to inspect the teepee.

"That doesn't look like a much of a village for as much sign as we're seeing." Jake said to Morse.

"Aye, but let's keep a sharp lookout around us. Boyer said it was the biggest one he'd ever seen. That's bound to be where the gunfire was coming from."

A lone rider came appeared on the trail ahead of them, coming towards them and waving. When he got closer Jake saw that it was Sgt. Kanipe, from Company C.

"Hey boys! We've got 'em on the run!"

"Where at?" Morse asked.

"A couple of miles up the river, we've struck a big camp. Capt. Custer sent me with word to hurry the pack train forward."

"Well, you'd better ride on back and report to Capt. Benteen then. The pack train is well back behind us." Morse replied, turning in his saddle to point.

Kanipe trotted off towards the column.

"Well, it sounds like Custer is going at them." Jake said.

"Yes, but it sounds like he's worried about the pack train. Let's keep moving and see where the trail leads."

As they picked up the pace, Jake was riding past Holden who said quietly, "Best be patient, Jake! We'll be in it soon enough, one way or the other. These things have a way of going at their own pace."

Jake looked over at Henry and realized that the veteran trooper was right. They knew very little of what was transpiring ahead.

"Thanks, Henry, I appreciate your advice. Keep an eye on me and try to not let me do anything stupid."

"You'll be fine Jake, trust your instincts. The worst part of a battle is just before, and afterwards if we're both still alive, we can reflect on our stupidity."

A bunch of horses appeared from the timber ahead, with several of the Ree scouts herding them along, heading back towards the pack train.

"It looks like they've been raiding the Sioux pony herd." Morse called to Jake, "That's a good sign."

Shortly after the Rees passed them, they arrived at the timber where the Rees had emerged, finding it to be a fork of the creek that they'd been following. The trail appeared to split, some hoof prints going left towards the river, and some leading to the right heading up a rise towards a ridge. They spotted a trooper on a grey horse working his way down that ridge. Jake recognized him as the Company H trumpeter, John Martini. The horse was favoring its right hindquarter as the rider spurred him on. When he got nearer he waved at them but continued back along the trail until he reached Benteen, where he reined in then handed something to the captain.

Morse had the advance halt, "Something's up!" he exclaimed.

Jake saw Benteen read the piece of paper and then handed it to Weir. They talked briefly, then headed towards the advance party at a gallop.

"Well, here we go." Morse said excitely.

Just as the officers reached them, the sound of gunfire crackled again from up ahead, becoming louder, more intense and seeming to get nearer. Weir cocked his head, listening, "What do you think? Should we march to the sounds of the guns, Benteen?" he asked, then rode out a ways in the direction of the river.

"It seems we have the two horns of a dilemma here." Benteen stated. "Sgt. Morse, where'd you first see Trumpeter Martini?"

"He came down that ridge, Sir," Morse answered, pointing.

"Well, Martini said he followed Custer's back trail, and passed Boston Custer along the way. He said the Sioux were skedaddling, or some such, his English is pathetic."

Some more Rees came from the left driving captured ponies, and one of them pointed up towards the ridge to the right, calling out, "Otoe Sioux! Otoe Sioux!" and signing.

"What's he saying Jake?" Morse asked.

"Many Sioux, many Sioux!"

"All right! That decides it" Benteen exclaimed, then waved at Weir, "We go to the right! Let's go, Weir!"

Benteen led the advance party with all three companies following and increased the pace. As they made their way up the slope the trail followed along the edge of the bluffs, and they could begin to see down into the valley to the left. Through the swirling dust and smoke glimpses of the fighting below began to appear. Jake could see a skirmish line, with a dozen or so men in the process of being overrun by mounted Sioux warriors. Behind them small knots of mounted troopers were frantically spurring their horses in the direction of the river followed by swarms of warriors firing into the fleeing cavalrymen and at some who had already plunged into the river. Others soldiers were already across and scrambling up the steep bank, then making their way up several ravines and draws that led to the top of the bluffs ahead where some figures could be seen bunching together. Benteen issued orders for the entire battalion to charge forward, with pistols drawn. When they arrived, he ordered skirmish lines over to the edge of the bluff.

Jake dismounted, drawing the big Sharps out of its scabbard, then quickly handing off his reins to Big George, who was the #4 of Welch's set, and hurried the others forward.

"Form a skirmish line, keep your intervals, now!" he called out. "Set your sights for 200 yards."

As he strode forward he craned his neck to look down the edge of the bluff and was greeted by a panoramic view of the river valley below. There was heavy timber just below, and just beyond it wide prairie. He could see hundreds of mounted warriors milling around in the swirling dust and smoke.

Awestruck he gasped, "Oh my God!"

Morse came up next to him. "Jesus, Mary, and Joseph! We're in for it now Jake, if they all come at us."

Some of Reno's men were still struggling up the steep defiles. They were being fired upon by the Sioux below them and by others milling about across the river. To the north from some bluffs across a wide ravine, there were several warriors taking long range pot shots in their direction.

"Okay lads!" shouted Morse. "Let's give our boys some cover fire. Take your time and aim. Jake, do ya think you can hit some of those braves over there"

"I'll give them a hello for you Pat." Jake said, as he hefted his Sharps.

Nearby, a hatless and frantic Major Reno was gesturing wildly as Capt. Benteen approached him. "For God's sake, Benteen, halt your command and help me! I've lost half my men!"

Benteen held up his hand, "Where is, Custer?" he asked.

"He rode off that way with the other companies!" Reno exclaimed, pointing to the north. "Cooke assured me that they would support me with the whole outfit!" Reno strode towards the bluffs edge and began firing his pistol in the direction of the Sioux hundreds of yards away. After it was empty he turned back to Benteen. "Benny Hodgson is down there, he may be badly wounded."

Benteen handed Reno the note that Martini had brought from Custer. Reno read it and looked up. "Yes, we need to secure the pack train. We'll wait here for it. I'm going to take some men and go down to look for Hodgson."

While Reno went about gathering some men, Benteen met with the other officers and instructed them to post their men in a skirmish line facing along the river. That would allow the companies that had been in the valley fight time to regroup. While the men were so engaged, the sound of heavy firing began to reverberate from the north.

When Jake succeeded in hitting a couple of Indians, the rest disappeared below the bluffs. As he continued to scan for more targets, Tom Russell came over and sat down beside him.

"They've pretty much quit shooting Jake, I wonder why?"

As the fighting lulled, the sounds of gunfire from the north became apparent. Most of the Indians wheeled around and began galloping off in that direction. Jake used the rifle scope to watch them as they were now well out of range.

"Something's got their attention, they're leaving in a hurry, it must be Custer." Jake said. "What do you think we'll do now?"

Russell answered, "Well, I can tell you Capt. Weir is getting impatient. He and Lt. Edgerly have been watching the clouds of dust building up down river ever since the Sioux began pulling back. He's pacing up and down."

Weir stood peering through some binoculars several yards back from the bluff on a small rise. He motioned for Edgerly to come over.

"We need to be on the move. Are you with me if I decide to go on ahead?

Edgerly answered, "Of course,Sir!"

"Okay, I'm going to talk with Reno and Benteen. Be ready to move." Weir stated and strode away.

It had taken Reno over 20 minutes to find Hodgson, and he was dead. Reno secured some personal items including Hodgson's West Point ring and gold lieutenant's bar. After hiding the body in a clump of bushes, he and the detail made their way back up by a shallower defile, where they came across Dr. DeWolf's scalped body. When they made it back to the top Benteen hurried over to Reno.

"We should probably work on speeding up the pack train." Benteen stated. "They're taking too long!"

Lt. Hare who had been standing talking with Lt. Godfrey, his commander from Company K. Most of the officers were gathered watching the Sioux down below and speculating on the crashing volleys of gunfire that they were hearing. They edged closer, listening to the two senior officers. Hare had been in the valley fight along with Lt. Varnum and the scouts. He had attempted to rally the men and establish a rear guard during the retreat to the river, and was still very worked up.

Reno summoned Hare, "I'm appointing you as my adjutant. I want you to ride back to Lt. Mathey and have him cut out a couple of mules with ammunition, then send them ahead to us. Tell McDougall to push the train, tell them to move as fast as they can. Come straight back!"

"Yes, sir!" Hare acknowledged, then looked at Godfrey, "God, let me use your horse, mine is winded."

Godfrey nodded his assent and Hare quickly mounted Godfrey's horse then spurred away.

Reno looked over at the group of officers and said, "Lt. Varnum, take a detail down to bury Hodgson."

"We have no spades, but there are some with the pack train. I'll take care of it when they get here, Sir."

"Very well."

At this point, Weir came up to Reno.

"We should be moving in the direction of the firing, Sir." he stated

Reno looked back at Weir, "We're waiting for the pack train to come up, Captain. We need more ammunition."

"My company still has plenty! Let me advance."

"We will wait for the pack train, Captain."

Sounds of gunfire erupted again from the north.

"Custer is engaged, we need to be over there, Sir!" exclaimed Weir, pointing in that direction.

"And I'm telling you that we'll not move until we secure the pack train." Reno stated heatedly. "I'm senior officer here!"

"That you are, Sir. But I fail to see why we shouldn't be sending part of the command forward to see what is going on over there."

"That will be all, Captain. You're bordering on insubordination and I'll not discuss it further with you."

"Very well, Sir. I'll take my orderly and ride out a ways. If I see anything, I'll send him back." Weir said and walked away.

"Weir, I'll remember this." Reno said loudly, "Tread carefully!"

Jake was tending to Ajax, when he saw Capt. Weir walk purposely to his horse and mount up, followed by Trumpeter Bohner, who did likewise. They spurred their mounts, and headed off to the north at a canter.

"Where da ya suppose the captain is going?" asked Goldie.

"I don't know, I guess to have a look see." Jake said.

Lt. Edgerly had been talking with 1st Sgt. Martin, watched as Weir rode out then suddenly gave the command for the entire company to mount. The company formed up in a column of fours along the trail following their captain. Martin called out to Sgt. Morse.

"Pat, take Rogers and a section to catch up with the Captain. We'll be right behind you."

"Right, Top! Come on, Jake, bring your boys. We'll not be wantin' to let the captain get lonely now will we?"

Weir and his command followed the trail made by Custer's battalions for a little over a mile, coming to a saddle shaped hill with two peaks. Weir called for a halt and climbed to the top of one of the peaks followed by Bohner, while the rest of the company stayed below the hill. Presently, Bohner came back down and told Lt. Edgerly to come up along with the guidon bearer, and bring any of the sergeants with binoculars. Jake and Jim Flanagan joined Edgerly as he complied. When they got up near Weir they were stunned to see the size of the village that lay along the other side of the river, stretching several miles in length off to the left. Weir was pointing at large dust clouds off to the north.

"I think that's Custer over there. Start waving the guidon, maybe he'll be able to spot us."

Jake dismounted and got out his binoculars, peering intently through them. He was able to make out mounted figures riding around in random circles on a distant ridge. They appeared to be shooting at dark objects on the ground, the crackling sound of their gunshots sounded in the distance. Jake scanned quickly towards the huge village where he could see many woman and small children scattered in bunches through the stands of teepees. A huge herd of ponies was farther west, out on the bench land beyond the village.

"Edgerly! Have the men get ready, we're going to go over there." Weir called out.

Flanagan spoke up quickly, "I don't know about that, sir. I think that those are Indians. Here take a look!" he said, offering up his binoculars.

Weir took them and looked through them for several minutes, then said. "You have a point, Sergeant. Edgerly! I want you take a couple of sections and ride out in that direction. Be sure to stay within sight of me and I'll signal to you."

Jake responded, "I'll go, Sir!" looking over at the lieutenant.

"Very well, I want to see how those people react." Weir said. He turned and looked back down the trail, "Well, here comes Benteen and at least two other companies. I think I see Godfrey. Don't go too far. We'll want to move with them if we go."

As Jake was gathering his men, Morse came over to him and said, "I'm going with you. All of those Sioux warriors that whipped Reno are out there and who knows how many others. You just saw that village, there's a hell of a lot more than 400 lodges, probably three times that. There has to be at least couple of thousand warriors. I suspect they whipped Custer and now they'll be coming for us."

"Do you think they beat Custer?"

"Look at their numbers Jake, and they appear to have a lot of guns and bullets from what I've heard them firing so far. Custer most likely is hightailing north to find Terry, if he's still alive?" Pat relied grimly.

Jake stared back with raised eyebrows, then looked over at Edgerly, who was nervously checking his pistol. Morse looked over at him also.

"He'll bear watching Jake, he's never been in a fight to my knowledge."

"Well, neither have I!"

"That's why I'm going along. There's no point in losing more men. Capt. Weir has to be able to say that he tried, but I'm afraid that it's already too late. Edgerly will follow my lead and you keep an eye out with those field glasses. When, I think it's time, we'll be coming back here in a hurry.

So, keep the lads together!"

Edgerly led them out, swinging around the hilltop and following the high ground for several hundred yards, which led down to a shallow ravine. When they reached it he had them halt and turned to look back at Weir on the high point. Jake used his binoculars to look ahead, panning the defile ahead of them, and then towards the village. The number of Indians heading in their direction was growing steadily. The sound of multiple shots started coming from the left, but none were reaching anywhere near them, yet.

"Sgt. Rogers, what can you see?" Edgerly asked nervously.

Jake answered, "Warriors moving this way from the village, and I see some coming down from that distant ridge ahead. There's a lot of them, sir, and they're coming quick!"

"Well, look back towards Capt. Weir, see what he's doing."

"It looks like he's waving at us to come back, sir."

Morse called out to Edgerly, "Right, Sir! Let's circle back and rejoin the company on the higher ground. We're sitting ducks out here."

The young officer peered back to the north, "I think that's a good idea, Sergeant!"

When the scout detachment made it back they saw that Weir had been joined by Capt. Benteen and Lt. Hare. They were standing on the tall peak looking at the ridges to the north. The rest of Company D and the troops of H, K, and M were deployed in a skirmish lines on each side hill facing towards the oncoming Sioux. Edgerly had them take up a position to the right, then went up to join Weir.

1st Sgt. Martin came over towards them and asked Morse, "Well Pat, we're in for a fight it seems. What da ya think happened to Custer and the others?"

Morse replied grimly, "I think they ran into more than they could handle and are either retreating towards Terry, or cornered somewhere over there. Based on the numbers coming at us, we'd best better be finding a better position than this, Mike." Looking up in the direction of where the officers were gathered, he asked, "Where's Major Reno?"

"He hasn't come up yet. He's still back with the pack train, supposedly getting the wounded sorted out. He wants us to try and get through to make contact with Custer. At least that's what Lt. Hare told Capt. Weir just a few minutes ago when he got here."

"Well, obviously that's not happening! Someone better take command, and be damn quick about it." Morse stated.

Suddenly, Benteen and Weir left the other officers and descended from the hilltop. Weir rode off to the south, while Benteen went to his company, ordered them to mount, and followed in the direction of the pack train.

"What do you suppose is going on?" wondered Jake out loud, watching as Company H trotted off.

Shortly, Lt. Godfrey, Lt. Hare and Company K mounted and following in Benteen's tracks.

Edgerly came down and said, "We're to maintain our skirmish lines along with Company M to hold back the hostiles until Godfrey gets his company positioned, then fall back through him. We're all going back to the bluffs and the pack train. Benteen and Capt. Weir feel that this is no place to fight them."

Martin nodded his head, "Yes sir, there's too many ways that those bucks can sneak behind us. They may already be down by the river!"

Morse began walking along the company skirmish line yelling for the men to set their carbine sights for 300 yards. "Take your time! Remember aim low, and don't get in a rush, We'll be wanting want to slow Mr. Lo down a little, and most of their guns can't reach us."

Jake found a good position on the rise to get set up with the Sharps. Morse looked up at him, "Ok, Jake, give them something to think about! Drop some of their ponies!"

Jake peered through the scope and ranged about for targets. He began firing and was pleased to see that he was hitting. The clamor of carbines firing assaulted his ear drums and he could hear Martin and Morse cajoling the men. It seemed like the Indians slowed their pace and disappeared into lower ground.

"That's it boys give 'em hell!" Morse yelled.

After a few minutes, the Sioux began popping up from cover as they crawled closer and shooting at the troopers. Jake caught one of them in his sights, and sent him reeling backwards.

The command rang out to mount up, and Jake scrambled down. He went over to Big George, who handed him Ajax's reins. "Did you get any of them Jake? he asked.

"Yes, but there's too many of them. I don't think we have enough bullets and men to hold them long."

Lt. Edgerly's horse had gotten spooked by the gunfire, and the young officer was having difficulty mounting. The rest of Company D followed French and Company M moving off at a gallop. Jake's old guard mount adversary, Charlie Sanders, who was acting as the young officer's orderly, stayed to help him. Charlie was smiling broadly at the closest warriors who were shooting at them. Jake and Tom Harrison went to help and snapped off several shots at the hostiles. Once Edgerly got his horse reined in, they all spurred their mounts to catch up.

Jake yelled over at Sanders, "What the hell are you smiling about?"

"Yoost marveling at vat terrible shooters dos heathens be!" Sanders called back, still smiling.

The company rode in a loose column of fours covering the ground as fast as they could. Off to the right, several warriors appeared after making their way up the slope from the river, and began firing at the soldiers. A trooper ahead of them tumbled from his saddle, and when they got up to him Jake saw that it was the farrier, Vincent Charley, he was shot in his right hip and couldn't stand.

"Ach! I'm shot bad, sir." Charley called out to Edgerly, whose horse began to rear again.

"I see you Charley! Lay low and hide! I'll go get some more men and we'll come back for you!"

"Ya, okay! Please hurry, Sir!" the farrier groaned, as he dragged himself towards some sagebrush.

Up ahead, Lt. Godfrey had dismounted his company and formed a skirmish line, sending the mounts back to the area of the pack train a few hundred yards behind them. He paced up and down the line, and as the retreating troopers dashed past he had his men begin firing volleys at the pursuing Indians. As Edgerly's detachment crested a ridge, the rest of the regiment came into view. It was spreading out near the top of the bluffs around a shallow bowl shaped depression. Jake spotted the hatless Major Reno, who was now wearing a white kerchief on his head, watching as the troops with the pack train were frantically unloading the mules. Ration boxes and other bundles were being used to hastily erect some makeshift breast works around the wounded men. The mules were milling about, while horses were being picketed by the horse holders of the various companies. Benteen appeared to be directing the other companies towards defensive positions facing out in all directions around the animals. Captain Weir stood near the rest of Company D where a defensive line was being spread out on the crest of a slight rise. The sergeants were placing the men at 20-25 foot intervals facing to the north and east. The troopers lay down among the sparse clumps of grass and sagebrush seeking what little concealment was available.They rode over to rejoin the company and Edgerly went to ask Capt. Weir for some men to go after Farrier Charley. Jake saw the crestfallen look on the young lieutenants face when Weir shook his head no. Jake got down off Ajax, making sure to secure his rifle and a bandolier of bullets before handing him off to Big George. He ran back to a spot where he could see the Company K line, and began looking for targets. He admired how Godfrey strode among his troopers, keeping them from bunching up and panicking as they continued to fire volleys at the approaching hostiles. Jake saw Lt. Varnum run up to Godfrey and the two of them began directing an ordered withdrawal. Taking a knee, Jake scanned past the retreating skirmish line and saw large numbers of mounted warriors on the horizon just out of range, while other dismounted and crept forward individually, utilizing shallow depressions, small gullies, and vegetation to conceal their approach. They popped up randomly to fire their guns in the direction of the troopers. Jake fired several rounds at some of them then dropped flat and began to crawl back towards the company, as bullets zipped overhead. After several yards he leapt to his feet and ran.

"What do ya think, Jake?" queried Charlie Welch as Jake dove to the ground near him.

"I think that we've kicked over a hornets nest." he answered, then rolled over, raising his head to peek off to the east. "There's more over there!" he said pointing.

He looked to his left and saw Golden furiously clawing the ground with his knife, pushing the loose soil trying to make a pile.

"Goldie, what in the hell you're doing?"

"I'm trying to dig a hole to get in."

"Well, quit!" Jake yelled, "They'll see you moving and you'll draw fire. You're better off staying still. Besides, we'll probably move."

Goldie stared back at Jake, his eyes wild with fear, "I don't wanna die, Jake!" he cried.

"Yeh! Me neither, so settle down. You lie still, and I'll watch out."

The rest of the section was spread out on both sides of him and Jake low crawled along the line to Henry Holden, who was calmly looking to his front. He turned his head when he heard Jake.

"Ah, it seems our quarry has suddenly gained the upper hand." Holden said with a grim smile.

"It looks that way."

"They'll be testing us soon, I'd suppose." He looked over to where Golden lay, "I'll see to Pat and keep him in hand."

"Thanks. How are you fixed for ammunition?"

"Not too good, the lads have used most of the rounds on their belts, and several forgot their pouches when we dismounted."

Pat Morse came crawling towards them and from several yards away called out, "Jake, don't let them shoot unless they have a good target, and be prepared to volley if they try to rush us. It's more likely that they'll try and sneak in on us. Be sure not to poke your head up in the same place, twice."

Jake nodded then looked back at Henry, admiring the calm demeanor of the Englishman.

Jake changed positions several times and crept forward looking for targets. After loosing off one or two shots, he pulled back down the slope, when bullets began impacting near him.

 Jake paused to rest near Holden again, who commented,"Well, Jake, it seems that our Mr. Lo resents your attempts to keep him at bay."

"Yes, it does it does seem that way." Jake replied. Peeking quickly through his field glasses, he said, "Although I can see that many of them staying out of range, and appear to be just watching. They may be just waiting for an opportunity to rush us."

"We're getting a bit low on carbine rounds. Perhaps it would be prudent for some to be brought forward. I'll take Horn and go fetch some if you'll stay here with the lads."

Jake looked at Holden, admiring his calmness, "Okay, find Big George and the other horse holders and have them help you. See if you can find some 45-70 shells for me, there were some on one the company ammo mules." Jake said.

"Right O! I'll be back, keep my spot warm." Holden quipped, then dashed away in a crouch towards the pack train, as bullets struck the ground causing clumps of dirt to erupt around him.

Jake settled in to wait as the heat of the late afternoon sun bore down. He wished that he'd thought to grab his canteen before he handed off Ajax. Pulling out his watch he noted that the time was 6:15.

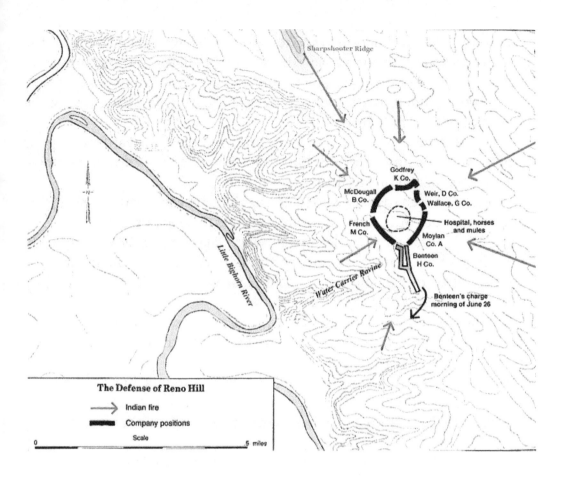

Sharpshooter Ridge

Godfrey
K Co.

McDougall
B Co.

Weir, D Co.
Wallace, G Co.

French
M Co.

Hospital, horses
and mules

Moylan
Co. A

Benteen
H Co.

Benteen's charge
morning of June 26

Little Bighorn River

Water Carrier Ravine

The Defense of Reno Hill

Indian fire

Company positions

Scale

0   5 miles

CHAPTER 33

Along the Little Bighorn River, Montana Territory - June 25, 1876, Late Afternoon

The remnants of the regiment were spread out like a horseshoe, with the open end facing the river bluffs. McDougall's Company B and Benteen's H secured those flanks, while the other five companies: M, K, D, G, and A respectively, were arrayed around the perimeter from north to south. A shallow swale in the center was open to the south where a hastily erected barricade offered some protection for the pack mules and horses, along with the wounded. The Sioux and Cheyenne warriors on the high ground surrounding the enclave maintained a steady rain of bullets towards it with many striking the hapless picketed animals. Others struck around the exposed rear of the troops from Company H where they lay on a knoll, defending the bluffs to the south. Small groups and individual warriors dodged along concealed ravines and depressions, trying to draw fire from the soldiers, so their fellow braves could shoot at the telltale smoke from the carbines when they fired. This back and forth firefight went on for several hours, waining and waxing at different points along the defensive perimeter.

Company D's quadrant was between Godfrey's Company K on the left and facing north and the remnants of Company G on the right and facing east. The latter was now commanded by Lt. Wallace, as Lt. McIntosh had been killed during the retreat from the valley fight. They were positioned on a low ridge that sloped gently on both sides. The officers and sergeants took turns crouching behind the men, directing the firing and watching for any attempts by the hostiles to rush the line. When they spotted a group that was creeping in, they would call the men to rise up and deliver a volley, then lay back down. As the afternoon wore on, several men in the other platoon were wounded, but none severely. However, 1st Sgt. Winney from Company K, who Jake had known down in Louisiana, was killed near Lt. Godfrey who was walking the line, trying to control the ammunition being expended by his troops. His trumpeter, Pvt. Helmer, was hit in stomach and began screaming, begging to be put out of his misery, before finally succumbing. Godfrey was eventually persuaded by his orderly, to lay down and quit drawing fire.

As twilight arrived, the Indian fire began to slacken and eventually ceased. The troopers cautiously began to stir from where they had lain all day, and the officers of the various companies sought out each other. Weir, Edgerly, Godfrey and Wallace, whose companies were defending the north and east of the perimeter, met briefly, then directed their NCOs to have the men begin digging entrenchments and rifle pits. With only a few spades available, most of the men attacked the soil with tin cups, knives, and boards from the wooden ammo crates. Details were sent to the pack train area to retrieve the ammunition crates, hardtack boxes, and saddles to build makeshift breastworks. Major Reno appeared and made a cursory inspection of the positions, then left. 1st Sgt. Martin and Capt. Weir made the rounds and sorted the men out from where they had been intermixed with Company K. After taking roll, they were pleased to find that the only man missing was the farrier Charley. Weir issued orders to Martin, who then summoned his NCOs.

"It's a damn shame about Charley!" Martin exclaimed, "I heard that Lt. Edgerly wanted to go back for him. I wonder if he found a place to hide?"

Jake spoke up glumly, "I doubt it, he was on the other side of that ridge to the north. They've been shooting at us from there for the last couple of hours. There wasn't much cover, and he couldn't walk."

There was silence for a minute, then Flanagan said quietly, "Damn, I hope they killed him quickly."

"Well, we've only had a couple of flesh wounds so far. We're in good shape compared to some of the other companies, like G on our right. Lt. Wallace had only had 3 men on the line and most of his NCOs were killed down in the valley. He's getting back Sgt. Brown, two corporals, and eight men who were with the pack train. Morse, I want your platoon on the right next to them, your lads can help steady them."

"Will do, Top!"

"Let's get busy, we can't move the seriously wounded, so I expect we'll be sitting ducks again tomorrow if we don't dig in. Have your boys scavenge from the packs for food and we'll sort it out later." Martin said.

As the men began to dig, strange lights refracted off low hanging clouds and flickered from what had to be massive campfires in the village beyond the hill to the north. The pounding of tom toms and discharging firearms sounded in the distance, accompanied by occasional shrill screams and shrieks.

"Will you listen to that? It sounds like those red devils are whooping it up!" Pvt. Stivers, from Hurd's set, exclaimed.

Goldie who was digging in another pit next to him, was on his hands and knees scooping dirt with a tin cup. He was uncharacteristically morose and muttered loudly, "They'll be the death of me tomorrow, I feel it in me bones."

"Ah now, perk up Goldie! We'll dig us a nice hole. Then we can pop up and blast the beggars if they get too close." Biscuit Greene remarked. "Ain't that right, Jake?"

Jake was standing nearby, where Holden and Horn were digging a rifle pit using a piece of board from an ammo crate. He replied. "Henry here knows about digging in. He was at the siege of Petersburg during the War, weren't you Henry?"

Holden answered, "Indeed I was, though we had a bit more sophisticated tools at hand back then. But having a nice hole to lay in as bullets buzz overhead does have certain benefits."

Golden was silent as he continued his excavation efforts, piling dirt into a mound at the front of the rifle pit.

"I'm going to go see if I can find a couple of our company packs, and find us something to eat." Jake announced. "Biscuit, you come with me and help me find where you picketed the horses. We'll try and bring something back."

As they made their way over to the area of the pack train, they dodged the dim figures of other troopers moving about in the dark. Teams of men were dragging dead mules and horses over to the barricade across the open end of the swale, that helped shelter the other animals. Dr. Porter had set up a hospital for the wounded, surrounded by piles of saddles and packs in the middle of the them. Biscuit had had the presence of mind to picket their horses near the company packs, where Jack Ward and Joe Martin had gathered them back closer to the bluffs. As they picked their way through the milling animals, Jake heard Jack's gravelly voice emitting a long string of elaborate cuss words, and used the sound to navigate in that direction.

"Jack!" he called out, "It's Jake! I'm coming in."

Ward and Joe had made a small barricade out of packs and boxes and were leaned up against it.

"Ah, glad you're still with us, Jake. I was afeared that the damn Injuns might have done for some of you boys. Shit fire! They sure rained plenty of lead down on us!" Jack exclaimed.

"We got lucky, we just lost one man, the farrier Charley."

"Too bad, I kinda liked that red headed Swiss boy, he was pretty handy! Where you boys set up?"

"We're digging in across from here on the east side, right in the middle of the line. I need something for the men to eat cold, we can't risk a fire."

"Well, I reckon we can scrounge up somethin'. I got some hardtack and a sack of potatoes, here." Ward said, "Let me gather some up."

"That'll have to do. We'll go check on our mounts, and I'll come back and get it."

He followed Biscuit to where the horses were picketed, then directed him to to check the picket ropes and gather any water canteens he could find. Jake went to Ajax and the horse snuffled nervously as he approached. He reached out to stroke his muzzle whispering quietly. "Easy boy, easy! We'll be okay." He loosened the saddle girth and retrieved some sugar cubes from one of his saddle bags and fed them to him. He also grabbed his canteen, and poured a little water into his tin cup for the horse to lap up. Jake slung a saddle bag over his shoulder that contained several cans of fruit and some jerky that he'd gotten from the sutler on board the *Far West*. He saw Pat's horse, Gus, and went over to check on him, and loosened his cinch also, repeating the sugar and water routine. Then he headed back to the packer's enclave, where he was surprised to find Sgt. DeLacy, from Company I.

"Milt, I never expected to see you, here. I figured you were out with Keogh and Custer."

"No, it was my damn turn for the Pack Train detail. I was wrestling with those fuckin' mules all day."

"So what're you doing here?" Jake asked.

"Well, Lt. Mathey isn't giving us any orders and I have seven men with me. Including Pvt. Korn who had his horse bolt on him. He was with the rest of the company but some how made it back here. I thought I'd see about throwing in with your lot." DeLacy replied.

Jake nodded his head, "All right, we'll go see Capt. Weir. I'm sure he'll welcome the reinforcements. He has us digging in next to Company G under Lt. Wallace. He's down to only 15 men."

"Sounds good to me, I'd rather be up where I can shoot back at someone, then to be laying around back here wondering if a bullet is going to drop in on me. Let me round up my men."

When DeLacy returned, he said, "Okay let's go. I left Korn to watch our packs. He's good with horses and is still shook up about his ride back."

Jake guided the group back towards the Company D positions, the reflected light from the Indian village helped to keep his bearings as they made their way through the gloom. They encountered a few others looming up out of the eerie darkness, stumbling in the dim light carrying boxes and bags, as they made their way back to the line. When Jake judged that they were close, he called out softly.

"Pat, Pat Morse, it's Jake, you there?"

"Over here!" came a hushed reply from off to the right.

Jake moved cautiously in that direction, until he could make out the form of Morse standing a few feet away.

"Hey, Pat! I found some rations, and I've got Milt DeLacy with me. He's got seven Company I troopers with him. They were on Pack train duty and he wants to join up with us."

"Good, we can help them dig in next to us. Leave them with me while you and DeLacy go find Top Martin, and get him to clear it with Capt. Weir."

When Jake and DeLacy picked their way along the line until they were able to find the First Sergeant. He quickly led them to where Capt. Weir and his orderly were sitting near a small entrenchment below a small, improvised breastworks of boxes and dirt.

"Sir, I have Sgt. DeLacy from Company I, here. He's come from the pack train and wants to join us on the line."

Weir quizzed DeLacy on what was going on around the pack train area, and asked about the whereabouts of Major Reno. He didn't seem too surprised when the Company I sergeant replied that he hadn't seen him. Weir told 1st Sgt. Martin to have DeLacy and his men stay with Morse's platoon on the right of the line.

As they headed back, DeLacy asked, "So what do think happened to Custer, Jake?"

"It's hard to say, Milt. There's a lot of damn Sioux and Cheyenne out there. I'm afraid that he got whupped. Hopefully, he was able to get away towards Gen. Terry's column coming up the river."

"You sound pretty sure, Jake."

"I spoke with that Mitch Boyer fella this morning. He told that it was the biggest village that he'd ever seen. Well, now we know he was right! We saw it this afternoon and you can hear it over there right now. Custer only had five companies with him, and judging by how many of them came after us, that doesn't seem like near enough right now."

Jake couldn't see Milt's face, but detected the concern in his voice as he said, "I'm afraid you're right. I just hope that Capt. Keogh led the rest of the company to safety somewhere."

"Me, too!" murmured Jake quietly.

They walked the rest of the way in silence until they got back to the platoon positions where Milt gathered his troopers and began directing them to begin digging entrenchments. After Jake passed out the rations that he'd gotten from Ward, he sat down near Pat, handing him a canteen, a can of fruit and some of the jerky from his saddle bag, along with several pieces of hardtack.

Morse hefted the canteen and asked, "Thanks Jake, I'm parched. You didn't happen to see how Gus was faring while you were back there?"

"He's fine. Jack Ward is watching out for our horses and mules."

"Good, that cantankerous, old sum bitch is handy to have around sometimes."

"Yes, he is." Jake said, as he used his knife to pry the lid off his can. "He and Joe are both steady when things get tough."

"I reckon that tomorrow may get that way. We need to make sure the lads don't waste ammunition. I doubt that the Indians will charge us, more likely that they'll try and sneak in close enough to pick us off a few at a time. You'll not want to give them much of a target, best be quick and stay low when you have to move around."

After midnight the temperature dropped and a few scattered showers passed through. Most of the command attempted to get some sleep, while pickets kept watch.

About 2:45, just as the first of dawn began to peek over the hills to the east, two shots rang out. As if in defiance, the notes of Reveille sounded from Benteen's position, and rifle fire began coming in from all directions. Some of the troopers began shooting back until their officers and NCOs halted all firing to wait until targets could be better identified accurately. The Indian fire was primarily directed at the center of the defense where the hapless mules and horses were picketed.

"Wait a bit lads! We'll wait for better light and then we'll pick off some of these goddamn sons a bitches!" cussed Morse, "Just keep your heads down!"

Jake had been laying in one of the rifle pits trying to get some sleep when the shooting started up. He rolled over and peered through a small opening next to a hardtack box, watching the muzzle flashes on the high ground.

"Well, they appear to have plenty of bullets judging by what I can see, but they don't seem to have the range. I suspect that they'll be trying to creep in closer." he commented.

Holden, who was also in the pit, replied, "It seems that our Mr. Lo is making an early start of it today."

As it got lighter, the intensity of the firing increased as more warriors arrived from the village. After one particularly intense barrage, a group of mounted warriors gathered on a ridge several hundred yards away and then charged towards the line from the east.

Weir rose up and called down the line, "Set your sights at 200 yards, men. Volley fire at my command!" He paced calmly along the Company D position carrying his Spencer sporting rifle, watching the hostiles approach. As the men rose in their entrenchments and took aim, Weir dropped to one knee near Jake.

"Sgt. Rogers! Give me the high sign when they're in range."

"Yes, sir!' Jake acknowledged, watching the Indians through his scope. He raised his hand, paused for several seconds, then dropped it.

"Fire!" shouted Weir.

A crashing volley from over 50 carbines rippled down the line.

"Reload and fire at will"

Ponies and warriors tumbled to the ground along the front ranks of the warrior, as the troopers fire began taking toll. The charge wilted and became a rout as the torrent of lead decimated it.

"Cease fire, and take cover!" Weir commanded, then calmly walked back to his command pit. Minutes later the volume of inbound rifle fire increased again and resumed whizzing over head.

Jake marveled at his captain's composure and heard shouts from up and down the line.

"Take that Mr. Lo, and stick it where the sun don't shine!" Yelled Stivers.

"Yeh! Kiss my ass, you red fuckers!" His cousin Billy Harris chimed in.

"That'll teach 'em to mess with Ol' Dog Comp'ny. We'll bite 'em in the ass!"For the next several hours the Indians sniped from the surrounding ridges and ravines, then launched probing attacks looking for a weak spot. Eventually they resorted to trying to decoy the soldiers into firing at them so that they could mark the locations of the various rifle pits and firing positions. Jake scrambled along the line, using his big Sharps to good effect. The daring warriors that popped up and down in front of the Company D defensive line seeking to draw the trooper's fire, were soon disabused of that game. But as the sun rose higher and the temperature began to rise, the troopers lying exposed to it began to feel the effects. On the knoll overlooking the south side of the perimeter Benteen's Company H was taking fire from three directions. They had not dug in like the other companies and were taking casualties as a result. Benteen had placed his second in command, Lt. Gibson, in charge of the knoll's southern spur where his men commanded a good field of fire on the ravine that Indians were using to try and infiltrate the perimeter. Benteen got word that the spur was in danger of being over run. He went to the vicinity of the pack train and gathered up some men and materials for a barricade, to reinforce the position. Commanding Lt. Gibson to hold fast at all costs, he then left to find Maj. Reno who had moved up to Company D's entrenchment line. Benteen found him in Weir's rifle pit and demanded some reinforcements. After some discussion, Reno allowed Benteen to move Capt. French and his Company M to the south, leap frogging McDougall's Company B, and use it to bolster his defense. As Benteen made his way back to Gibson, he gathered up some skulkers and volunteers from the pack train again. When he arrived back at the line he found the hostiles were so close that they were throwing rocks and shooting arrows at the position. Sensing the desperation of his men, he jumped up and walked along the line, cussing and telling his men that he'd had enough, and that they were going to charge. He led them screaming and yelling in a headlong charge that surprised the Indians, who broke and scattered back down the ravine. After going about 100 yards, Benteen halted his troops and led them quickly back to the defensive positions, where they immediately set about digging in and building breastworks on the downslope. However, incoming rounds from the high ground to the north and east continued to impact around the knoll. In particular, there was a ridge to the north, several hundred yards, where an Indian sharpshooter with a long range rifle had been wreaking havoc.

Benteen hurried back down to where Major Reno was still laying in Weir's pit. Jake who was on the right with Lt. Edgerly, saw Benteen walk calmly and stand at the edge of the pit, where he appeared to be having a discussion. Finally, Benteen nodded his head and went to the highest position on the line, rallying the men along the way.

"What the hell, is Benteen up to? He's asking to be shot!" declared Biscuit.

Holden who had been watching also, said calmly, "It appears to me that he's going to lead us in a charge."

Goldie, who had been cowering in his hole all morning, moaned, "Please no dear God! I just know I'll be killed."

Jake declared, "Well I for one, am damn fed up of getting used for target practice! I'm for it!"

Word quickly passed along the line, and when Benteen waved his arm all four companies bounded up and charged the Indians who had been creeping closer. Screaming like banshees, they rushed forward firing their weapons rapidly. The encroaching warriors leapt to their feet and made a hasty retreat. After advancing twenty yards or so Major Reno who had also gone forward, called a halt and had the men retire back to the entrenchments. The jubilant troops made their way quickly back without losing a man. Jake and his section were milling around celebrating the successful charge. Jake, Holden, Hurry, and Biscuit were elated, pausing to watch the retreating hostiles before reoccupying their respective entrenchments. He noted that Golden was missing from the set of four, and looked along the row of rifle pits and saw that he was still laying in his hole. Suddenly, the Indians began to resume their firing and the troopers quickly dropped down seeking the nearest cover. Lt. Edgerly and Pvt. Stivers had been standing near Golden's rifle pit quickly joined him. Jake and the others had piled into the nearest entrenchment and from behind its breastworks Jake saw a sudden barrage of bullets impact around the mounds of dirt and ammo boxes in front of the position where Lt. Edgerly and Stivers had joined Golden. Shortly afterwards, Jake heard Stivers cry out.

"They've done for Goldie!"

"Aw, no!" Biscuit yelled, "Are ya sure, Stiff?"

"He's shot right through the head! He's dead!"

Biscuit started to get up to go over to see, when Jake stopped him.

"It's no good, Biscuit! You'll get yourself killed to boot! Goldie wouldn't want that."

"Aw, Jesus! No, no!" Biscuit wailed and began to blubber, "Pat can't be gone! I need to see to em m'self!"

Holden reached over and grabbed his arm, "We'll see to him later, Joe. Hurry and I will help you. Now, just stay here with us. We've still a fight going on."

As the morning wore on, the sun continued to beat down relentlessly on the soldiers. The only water to be had in the whole command was what the men had in their individual canteens from the previous day. The animals and the wounded men were suffering the most from the lack of it. About 11:00, Lt. Godfrey attempted to send a water detail down to the river, but there were too many warriors lurking in the trees and brush along the river below his positions and the effort was driven back. On his way back to his company, Capt. Benteen had stopped to check in at the hospital area where Dr. Porter pleaded for water to give to the wounded. When he returned to the southern perimeter, Benteen considered a plan to send a party down the wooded ravine where they'd driven the Indians off, earlier. He called for volunteers and had Sgt. George Geiger pick three of his most accurate sharpshooters to provide cover fire from the edge of the bluffs. Meanwhile, buckets, canteens, and kettles were collected for the rest of the men to carry water. The marksmen began to concentrate their fire on the brush on the other side of the river, while the water party slid down the ravine to its mouth. Once down, they had to dash 30 yards to the river bank to fill their containers, then scramble quickly back up the slope. The first water carriers made it back up without suffering any casualties and delivered most of the water to Dr. Porter to give to the wounded. Word quickly went out to the other companies about the success and several more water parties were sent down. When the call for volunteers went out, Charlie Welch, Tom Stivers, George Scott, Billy Harris, along with Frank Nolan and Adam Brandt from the other platoon held their hands up and were pulled off the line. Jake elected to follow them and they took turns making their way to the Company H positions near the area at the top of the ravine, carrying as many canteens as could be gathered, along with various kettles and coffee pots. When the Company D men arrived, Jake ran into Sgt. Ryan from Company M and several other men who were carrying extra ammo bandoliers.

"What's the plan here, John?" Jake asked.

"Shit, there ain't been a plan since we attacked the village yesterday Jake, and we were damn lucky to get up here, then. So far, what seems to be working is that some of the better shooters try to keep the Indians down there nervous, while the rest sneak down for water." Ryan replied, hefting his Sharps sporting rifle, "Care to join me, Rogers? I reckon that you and I can make some of them pretty uncomfortable.

"Okay, you find us a spot with a good view and I'll join you. Let me get my men sorted out and we'll give 'em hell."

Jake motioned for Charlie Welch and the others who were next to go down for water. He told them, "Try and stay behind cover on the way down. When we see you start your run to the river, we'll blast hell out of the Sioux."

Charlie looked back at Jake "Well, that's a pretty simple plan. I'll see you if it works out," he said, holding put his hand for Jake to take, "And if it don't, hell I guess we'll just see what happens then. You take care Jake, and don't miss."

"Yeh, Sarge!" Stivers exclaimed grimly, "We'll be hauling are asses back up here in no time! Billy, George, Let"s get this done!'

Jake nodded his head in reply and said, "Good luck! All of you, let's get going."

They made their way down the ravine to a point where it began to narrow about halfway to the river, where some bushes and small trees began to provide some concealment. Bluffs on each side overlooked the ravine providing good fields of fire for the rest of the way down to the river and across to the other side. Jake, Ryan, and the other men designated as sharpshooters, took positions on them and began sighting their weapons looking for any hostiles alone the riverbank. They watched closely as their fellow troopers cautiously worked their way lower.

Jake was gazing intently through his rifle scope when Ryan called out, "I see several warriors sneaking up in the timber across the river, just at the bend. Do ya see 'em?"

Jake saw movement and then spotted several figures flitting from tree to tree. Several more lay down in the brush and then began pointing rifles in the direction of the mouth of the ravine, where the troopers would begin their dash towards the river.

"I see them!"

"Let's see if we can make them uncomfortable, shall we?"

Ryan's big Sharps sounded and Jake saw one of the hostiles drop his rifle and spin to the ground, then crawl behind a tree. Jake picked out one of them in the brush and fired at him. The other marksmen started banging away, and soon the Indians retreated out of sight. The troopers below sprinted to the water's edge, and plunged into the water, immersing canteens and whatever they had that could hold water. In the meantime several rounds impacted around the men on the bluffs. Jake heard a thud near him and looked over to see a trooper near him fall to the ground.

"Shite, the bastards hit me leg!" he cried out.

Jake recognized the wounded man as Pvt. Mike Madden, from Company K. He remembered him from down in Louisiana and recalled that the Madden was a grizzled Irish veteran with a penchant for drunkenness, but was also one of the better shots in Godfrey's unit.

"Can you walk on it?" Jake asked.

"Naw, m'thinks it's broke! But I can still shoot, we'll worry about that when the lads get back up here."

They kept up a deadly covering fire for several minutes until they saw that the water party had returned to the relative safety of the ravine below them. The hostile fire continued to diminish and the marksmen could see some groups of mounted warriors retiring in the distance, beyond the timbered bend to the northwest. Jake watched them through his field glasses.

Ryan moved towards Jake crouching as he came. "It looks to me like they're clearing out along the river. What can you see?"

"I'm just seeing a few braves and they're staying well out of range. I'm also seeing a lot of smoke off to the north. It looks like the grass is on fire. Something appears be going on over there."

"Capt. French told me that Terry and Gibbon were expected to come up the river valley. But what ever it is, they appear to be easing up on us. Let's see if we can get Madden back up top and get that leg of his looked at."

They were able to get the wounded Madden to the hospital area, and were dropping off some water there, when Jake noticed Korn toting at least a dozen canteens in. His uniform was torn and muddy, and he was hatless.

"Hey Korn, you been down to the river?" He asked.

"Ja Sarge!"

Dr. Porter looked up from the wounded man he was working on, and said. "I think that's at least his third trip."

"You okay, Yankee? I don't see any blood on you, but you might take a break."

"No, is okay! I take break while the canteens are filling. I stay in da vater mit only my nose out." Korn said with a grin, then dropped the canteens, grabbed some empties and trudged away.

Jake, Ryan, and the water detail troopers began making their way back along the defensive positions. The slain animals that helped comprise the barricades had bloated and swollen during the heat of the day. They were beginning to putrefy, with noxious odors and swarming flies blanketing the area. They hurried away, reaching the Company M line, just as firing broke out and the Indians suddenly resumed their attacks. They quickly took cover among the few rifle pits and waited to see what developed. Captain French, came along shortly, seeking Sgt. Ryan.

****

Captain Thomas H. French

French was born in Baltimore, MD, in March 1843, His father died when he was 15, and he was adopted by his uncle Colonel Martin Burke, an old line officer in the Regular Army since 1820. After French completed his early education, Burke tried several times to get his nephew appointed to West Point without success. In the meantime French worked as a low grade clerk for the State Department. When he turned 21 in 1864, Burke interceded with Secretary of War Stanton, seeking a commission for him in the Army. French enlisted in the 10th Infantry, at Fort Lafayette in New

York Harbor, where Burke was in command. He was commissioned as a 2nd Lt. in early June, and a 1st Lt. by the end of the month. That August he participated in the battles around the Weldon Railroad, near Petersburg, where he was breveted as a Captain and also received a leg wound. After convalescing, he was re-assigned to Fort Lafayette with Burke, where he served out the War. In March 1868, he was promoted to Captain and transferred to Fort Ripley, Minnesota, still with the 10th Infantry. The following May, he was assigned as a Judge Advocate down in Austin, TX. His uncle continued to lobby for him, finally procuring an assignment in the 7th Cavalry, at Fort Hays in January 1871, where he would command Company M. After only 2 months at Hays, he and his company were transferred to South Carolina near Unionville, for Reconstruction Duty until 1873. When the regiment was sent to the Dakotas, Company M participated in the Yellowstone Expedition of 1873 where they fought against the Sioux. French, himself, was noted several times in Custer's official report, praising his actions under fire from the Sioux. His company was assigned to Fort Rice on their return, along with Companies C, H, & K. They accompanied Custer the next year on the Black Hills Expedition of 1874, and then returned to Rice, but were not sent back on Reconstruction Duty that fall. They remained there until the entire regiment was reunited at Fort Lincoln in May 1876. French was generally well liked by both his fellow officers and enlisted men. Unfortunately he, like many of the other officers had an acute alcohol problem, which in his case rendered him quite enigmatic and caused severe health issues. However, when sober he was well spoken and good humored. He had a reputation as a crack shot and carried a 1873 Springfield Officer's Model Rifle. He had personally conducted what little rear guard actions had been present during the Reno battalion's retreat from the valley fight the previous day, had been a visible presence along the Company M defensive perimeter since then.

****

"Glad to see you back, Ryan. The damn sharpshooter up on that ridge to the north is back again. We need to take him out." French declared, "He's wounded several of the men."

Ryan replied, "Right, let's find a spot where we can get a clear bead on him. Jake you game?"

"You bet!"

The three of them ran at a crouch to the north, until they came to a rifle pit protected by some saddles and wooden boxes where they took up positions. Jake and Ryan had the advantage of their telescopic sights, whereas Capt. French had only vernier sights on his rifle. Ryan ranged on the ridge line where he saw a puff of smoke erupt and, shortly after, heard the boom of a large rifle, then the crack of a bullet passing overhead, and then the impact behind them.

"Yep, that sum bitch is up there all right, that sounds like a big buffalo rifle. Do you see the pile of rocks just below the high point?"

"I do." Jake answered. "I think he's moving from one side to the other, after he shoots. What are you guessin' for range?"

"Near on 500 yards, maybe a skosh more." Ryan stated.

French rolled over and worked on adjusting the elevation of his rear sight, saying, "Let's wait until he fires again, then I'll shoot back. I'm setting my sight for 500 yards. You two watch and see if you can see were my bullet hits."

"Right, Sir! Ready when you are."

A minute or so went by and they saw another plume of gun smoke rise from the ridge. French fired immediately and Jake saw his round strike just short of the rocks.   "Just short, Sir, maybe 5 yards, or so."

"Okay. You two take a couple of ranging shots, but try not to get too close. We want him to think we're not sure of where he is."

Jake and Ryan both fired several times, while French spotted with field glasses.

"Okay, you seem to have the distance. Next time he fires I want you each to take a side, and I'll aim for the opposite from where he shoots. Let's give the bastard a taste of his own medicine!"

"I'm on the east, Jake." Ryan called out

"Right, I'm west. Let's take him out."

Shortly, they saw smoke blossom again, and were almost simultaneous in pulling the triggers of their rifles. Jake saw one bullet strike near the base of the rock, and another in the dirt near it.

"That should give him pause!" Ryan cried, "Lets give him another couple of rounds!"

After they quit firing, they watched the rocks for any signs of movement. Fifteen minutes went by and French said. "I think maybe we scared him off. He seems to be done for a while, anyway, but we'll keep an eye out. Good shooting, men!"

As suddenly as the renewed firing had broken out, it ceased. Jake made his way back to his rifle pit and found Pat Morse and Tom Russell sitting in it."

"Ah, glad to see ya, lad! Twas a wee bit worried, when you went galavanting off."

"Well, someone had to do it. When some of my section volunteered, I felt obligated to tag along."

"I suspected as much. Your Da would be proud, but your Mother would be in a tizzy. Probably best that she doesn't hear of it."

Tom got up and motioned for Jake to take a seat, handing Jake a can of peaches and some hardtack. "I'm going check the line, I'll let you know if anything happens."

"Hey, thanks, where'd you find these?"

"Jack Ward came up with them, he said something about finding them laying around. He mumbled something about Major Reno's pack mule getting shot, also." Russell said with a grin, then walked away.

Jake sat and leaned up against the breastworks, opening the can. "So Pat, you think that the Indians are going to attack again?"

Morse pointed off in the direction of the village where smoke was rising. "It looks like they're setting the grass on fire. They usually do that when they are being pursued. My guess is that the rest of the column is coming towards them."

"Why wouldn't they stay and keep attacking? Hell, they'd probably still outnumber us, there's a lot of em!"

"The Sioux don't like to fight the Infantry, they know that the long rifles out range them. Plus, I suspect they may be running low on ammunition as much as they've wasted on us. I hear we are, too"

They heard a commotion over by Company B's perimeter, and saw the troops there, standing and pointing down towards the river.

Pvt. Davern, Major Reno's orderly, came running up.

"Where's Capt. Weir?" he asked Morse.

"Up along the line somewhere. Why what's going on?" Pat asked.

"The Sioux! They've packed up and are heading south across the river. You should go look, there's thousands of them. It's a wonder we ain't all dead! Major Reno wants an Officers Call."

"All right, Davern, go on, I'll round up the captain and let him know."

"Thanks Sarge!"

The cavalcade formed by the Sioux and Cheyenne villages was immense, stretching several miles in length and over half of a mile wide. A large contingent of warriors formed a flank guard watching the soldiers up on the bluffs. The men stood watching in awe, as the spectacle played out below. The pony herd was a huge moving mass out beyond the procession. It took most of the remainder of the afternoon for it to disappear over the horizon in the direction of the mountains, and the remaining flank guards to ride after them. Unsure of the Indians intentions, Reno decided to wait and see what developed. The way down to the river appeared to be entirely open, and troopers began leading the parched surviving horses and pack mules down to water them. Meanwhile, the stench from the carcasses of the slain ones was becoming overpowering. The bodies of the dead soldiers were hastily gathered and buried in a couple of the larger entrenchments. Reno had finally been able to secure Benny Hodgson's body and see to its burial, while he tasked Capt. McDougall to supervise a move by the entire command to the south of Company H's positions, nearer to the river. The rest of the hours before total darkness were utilized to do this. New rifle pits and breastworks were established along the perimeter of the new position. As the companies got reorganized, rations were gathered and the cooks threw together some meals for the famished troops. After dark, The scouts Fred Girard and Billy Jackson, who had been hiding in the timber along the river, hailed the pickets and came in, followed closely by Lt. DeRudio and Pvt. Tom O'Neill from Company G who had been with them.

Jake and Pat had joined Holden, Hurd the rest of the platoon, to see to the burial of Goldie and Ed Hausen. Henry showed the others how to smear horse liniment under their noses to combat the smell as they placed their bodies in the rifle pit near where they'd been slain. Biscuit was distraught and teary eyed as he bent to wrap his bunkie in a blanket. The others used some broken boards and a shovel that they'd scrounged, to cover them with dirt from the breastwork. After they were done, Morse spoke quietly.

"Lord, please take these young men into your embrace. They were good lads and died way too young and far from home."

The others intoned a solemn "Amen!" then turned and trudged away.

Later on Jake, Morse, DeLacy, Tom Russell, and Jim Flanagan were sitting around a tiny fire pit near the edge of one of the new entrenchments drinking coffee. They heard someone approaching out of the darkness and a voice that Jake recognized, called out softly.

"Hello the fire! You boys mind some company?"

"That you, Jack?"

"Indeed it is!" he said as he sat down. "Ain't it a lot more peaceful tonight without those damn Injuns caterwauling? And it smells a whole lot better down here, don't it? Do ya think the Sioux will be back come mornin'?"

"I think that they're moving away to protect the women and kids. Chances are that they won't bother us unless we go after them. Which I don't see Reno doing, but I guess we'll find out for sure come daylight."

Morse answered.

Ward fumbled inside the pocket of his jacket and produced a bottle. "Anyone care for a taste?"

"Where in the blazes did ya find that?" Morse exclaimed.

Ward grinned and said, "Well, as we were picking through the saddles and packs of the dead animals, I stumbled on to it. Thought I'd just commandeer it, seeing how it was just laying there."

The bottle was passed around and they each put some in their tin cups.

"Here's to still being alive!" Ward toasted.

They all raised their cups in silent acknowledgment.

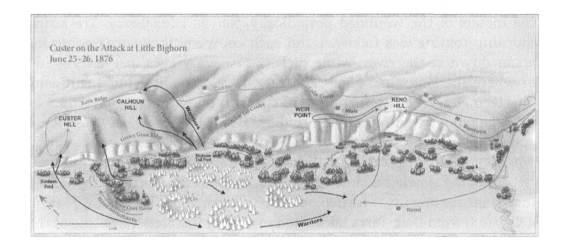

Custer on the Attack at Little Bighorn
June 25–26, 1876

CHAPTER 34

Along the Little Big Horn River, Montana Territory - Morning June 27, 1876

The weary troopers of Reno's command had a relatively peaceful night, with the exception of those nearest Dr. Porter's hospital area where the moans of the wounded periodically pierced the silence. The usual morning routine was followed and each company took turns going for water down at the river, while pickets cast wary eyes in the direction of where the Sioux had gone. The packers and the individual company quartermasters began sorting out the surviving mules and supplies taking a quick inventory hoping to find rations for breakfast. Later, Reno summoned the officers and was discussing a possible reconnaissance, when a large dust cloud materialized to the north around 9:00. It appeared to be moving slowly towards them. Shortly thereafter, pickets reported a lone rider coming up. It turned out to be a scout, Muggins Taylor, bearing a dispatch from Gen. Terry addressed to Custer. It stated that some of the Crow scouts had reached Terry with news that the Sioux had killed many soldiers and that while he didn't give it much credence, he was coming up with medical assistance as quickly as he could. Reno quickly dispatched Lt. Hare and Lt. Wallace to ride out and try to make contact with Terry's command. A detail was posted on a high point along the bluff to keep watch. Meanwhile, rumors spread like wildfire through the survivors of the seven companies and pack train.

1st Sgt. Martin summoned his NCOs to inform them of what he knew.

"Well, it seems that Gen. Terry and Col. Gibson are approaching from the north, up near where we saw the large village. Major Reno sent some scouts and a couple of officers to contact them."

"Any word on Custer's whereabouts?" asked Morse.

"Capt. Weir told me that Terry's dispatch mentioned that some of the Crow scouts that had been with Custer, came back and reported that there was a big fight where many soldiers got killed." Martin said solemnly.

"I wonder was that Boyer fella with them?"

"Can't tell you that, but supposedly all of the Crows up and left Terry to go home."

"That don't sound good! So, what now?"

"The captain wants us to get the men ready. It seems that us and Company B are in better shape than the other companies with only a few killed and wounded. Plus, most of our horses survived. So, let's see what ammunition and rations we can rustle up for the men. Then we'll just have to wait and see what happens."

Jake went around checking on the men in his section. They were all in decent spirits, except for Biscuit, who was glumly sitting nearby digging in the dirt with a stick.
Jake went to him and sat down.

"You okay, Joe?"

"It's just not the same, I'm missin' Goldie. Me an' 'im met on the ship comin' over, he was like a brother to me."

"Well, you have Henry and Hurry left that you can depend on. We'll find someone to take Goldie's spot and you'll have to show him the ropes."

"Don't you be gettin' in a hurry on that, Jake!" Biscuit declared, with tears in his eyes.

About 10:00, Varnum and Hare recrossed the river leading General Terry, Col. Gibbon, and his chief of scouts, Lt. James Bradley, up to the bluffs where Reno and most of his officers stood waiting. When they drew close the men began cheering, but when they saw that the arrivals were all grim faced and several in tears, they soon lapsed into silence. The men all craned their necks watching as the officers shook hands and spoke. Several of them turned their heads and began wiping tears, and others shook their heads in disbelief. Presently, Weir and Benteen left the meeting and marched resolutely over to where their units were standing. Weir stopped and took a minute to compose himself, running a hand across his face. Straightening, he said in a strained voice.

"I've just been informed by Gen. Terry, that Col. Custer, and his entire command have been found dead."

A collective gasp arose from the men.

"It seems that they were surrounded and killed about 4 miles north of here. Their bodies were found earlier this morning by Lt. Bradley and his scouts. Gen. Terry is sending Capt. Benteen with a detail to go and look at the scene and I am going, also. In the meantime, Gen. Terry and Col. Gibbon are establishing a bivouac across the river. The wounded are to be carried over first, then the rest of the regiment will cross over make camp. I will have more to tell you when I return. 1st Sgt. Martin, pick out a couple of sergeants to accompany me. We will be leaving shortly." Then Weir turned away, as tears began streaming down his face.

"All right men, you heard the captain! Take a few minutes, then let's get ready to move!" Martin called out, "Sgt. Harrison, take a section over to help with the wounded. Morse, Rogers, report to the captain, and take Sgt. DeLacy with you."

The detail was also accompanied by several of Terry's staff officers, including Capt. Michaelis and Lt. Nowlan, who had been serving as assistant quartermaster for Gen. Terry, and was one of the original officers of the regiment.

****

1st Lt. Henry J. Nowlan

Henry Nowlan was born on the island of Corfu in 1837 to Irish parents. His father was a quartermaster in the British Army. Raised in a military family on a series of posts around England and Ireland, he applied and was eventually admitted to the Sandhurst Military College where he secured a commission as an ensign after graduating, in July 1854. Nowlan served with the 41st Regiment of Foot during the Crimean War, and was at the siege of Sevastipol. After having been passed over for promotion several times and not having the means to purchase another commission, he sold his lieutenancy. He came to the US where he secured an appointment as a 1st Lt. in the 14th New York Cavalry, in Jan. 1863. He was captured that June at Port Hudson, Louisiana, and was a prisoner of war until he escaped in February 1865, returning to his regiment and serving out the remainder of the war. His unit was sent down to Texas in 1866, during the beginning of post war reconstruction, where he was mustered out. Nowlan received a commission as a 2nd Lt. in Company F of the newly formed 7th Cavalry, and reported to Fort Harker, Kansas that December. He was promoted 1st. Lt. in Aug. 1867 and assigned as regimental commissary officer in November. Highly efficient and organized, he served in this, or quartermaster capacity until he was transferred to Company L in 1870. He commanded it until being appointed regimental quartermaster on Gen. Terry's staff in March 1872. The gentlemanly, well spoken Nowlan was very popular within the regiment and became good friends with his fellow Irishman, Myles Keogh. Just before Keogh left the Rosebud bivouac with Custer, he left a copy of his will with Nowlan.

****

Lt. Bradley and Benteen led them, following the trail of shod hoof prints along the bluffs above the river. When they came to the twin hills where they'd reached two days previously, they stopped to determine what route Custer had taken. Large numbers of unshod hoof prints from the Indian's ponies were now co-mingled along the trail. Those with field glasses looked to the north and could see several white objects dotting the distant ridge top. They continued following the trail until they came to where a long ravine descended to the river. There, the trail split with some tracks entering the ravine, while others continued along the ridges to the northwest. Benteen elected to follow the trail down into the ravine and when they came to the end of it they could see the abandoned Indian village across the river. There, Lt. Bradley had them turn north, they ascended another ravine towards the high ground. The trail they followed didn't show that many shod horses had passed that way, and most of the tracks were made by Indian ponies. They could now see that the ridge, dotted with the dark and white objects ,was probably a half of a mile long and ended at small peak on the northern end. They hadn't gone very far from the river when they first started noticing a heavy odor of decay, and soon came upon a body, it was laying near a dead horse. The man's boots and shirt were missing, along with his belts and weapons. Morse dismounted, then went over to it and turned it over. They could all see that the body had been mutilated and scalped.

"Ah, Jeez!" Morse gagged, as he was shooing buzzing flies away, "Tis Jimmy Butler, the 1st Sgt. of Company L! I recognize his mustache and side whiskers!"

"Well, it looks like he put up a hell of a fight before he went down." Benteen said quietly, "Look at all of the empty cartridge casings lying about. Come on Sergeant, he's just the first of many I'd hazard. We'll see to him later."

"Aye, Sir!" Morse replied, and got back on his horse.

They continued up the coulee and about halfway up to the nearer end of the ridge where they could see what appeared to be dark and white stones scattered around, were actually dead horses and bodies. As they got closer the stench became over powering, and most of them wrapped bandannas over their faces. Jake also applied a liberal dab of horse liniment under his nose to try and block some of the smell.

Jake was riding next to DeLacy, who had gone noticeably pale.

"You okay, Milt?" he asked

"I'm dreading what we're liable to find up there. I thought it smelled bad back on the hill."

As they drew nearer, they had to pick their way up to the south end of the ridge dodging the bloated bodies and the bloated carcasses of slain horses. The majority of the dead had been stripped of clothing. Most were scalped, mutilated, and had arrows protruding from them, some were dismembered and disemboweled. Benteen made his way slowly around the small knoll then dismounted near a pair of bodies laying behind a line of others.

"This must be Company L. I'm pretty sure that this is Lt. Crittenden, that's his glass eye shattered by that arrow and it looks like that's probably Lt. Calhoun over there." He stated as he walked along, leading his horse."

The rest of the party dismounted also, as they worked their way along the spine of the ridge. Scattered corpses were strewn here and there, some in bunches, others alone. About halfway along the ridge they noticed a large cluster of bodies laying off to the right down below the crest. DeLacy turned in that direction.

"Most of the dead horses down there look like they might have been Bays. That may be Company I. I'm going to look."

"We'll go with ya, Milt." Morse said quietly.

They slowly walked down and were drawn to a pile bodies grouped right in the middle. DeLacy approached them, and bent closer, peering intently.

"Oh my Lord! That's Capt. Keogh all right, and there's Jimmy Bustard, and Top Varden!" sobbed DeLacy, "It looks like that's Trumpeter Patton laying across the captain, and I think that's Corp. Wild over there!"

"Aye, and I'm pretty sure that's poor Ed Bobo from Company C, laying there with them." Morse stated, "I wonder how he came to be here, and where his men are?"

A voice came from behind them, and bore an English accent, "I think most of Company C are laying scattered down the other side. I was able to recognize Sgt. Finley, he and I both served in the British Army during the Crimea War. Sgt. Finkle is lying there also, judging by his height, he was one of the tallest men in the company."

The speaker, Lt. Nowlan, was coming down towards them accompanied by Weir, who was silent and wore a look of abject dejection.

"It appears they were in skirmish formation when they were killed." Declared Lt. Nowlan. "Have you found my friend, Capt. Keogh, Sgt. DeLacy?"

"Sorry to say that I have, Sir! I think this is where most of my company lies. It looks like they went down fighting, judging by the amount of empty cartridges laying around."

"Well, then, let's have a look, shall we? I'd like to see him." Nowlan said, as he wiped tears from his eyes.

They rolled the bodies and uncovered Keogh. He'd been stripped naked except for his socks, and had a massive wound in his leg, which appeared to be broken. A medallion on a chain still hung from his neck. Nowlan bent to retrieve it, then stood.

"He always wore this, and was quite proud of the fact that he'd been given it by the Pope. It's a wonder that the savages didn't take it! I'll save it to send to his family."

Weir nodded his head at Jake and Morse indicating that they should move on. Jake reached over to Milt and patted him on the shoulder, "We'll leave you and Lt. Nowlan to take a few minutes. Capt. Weir wants to move on."

They moved back up to the ridge, following it just behind Benteen, Bradley, and the staff officers. As they moved towards the small hill at the northern end, Capt. Michaelis dropped back to ride along side Weir. He looked over at Jake, with a grim smile and pointed at the Sharps scabbard strapped to his saddle, nodding his head slightly.

"I'm very pleased to see that you're still alive, Rogers."

"Well, so am I, sir. This helped." Jake replied patting the Sharps.

Michaelis gave him a tight smile, and nodded in reply.

There were many corpses strewn randomly on both sides along the ridge and just before they reached the high ground, they dismounted and handed their horses off to a couple of Benteen's privates. They could see 40-50 bodies spread out down the slope along with many dead cavalry horses. Up near the crest was a cluster of dead mounts that might have been used as makeshift breastworks. There appeared to be 8-9 bodies sprawled on the ground behind them. One of Benteen's men, Pvt. Jacob Adams, climbed the upper slope, and when he got there he called out.

"It's Custer, Sir! I think I've found him!"

Benteen looked at Weir and shook his head in disbelief. The officers stepped gingerly around bodies and waved their hats to ward off the clouds of flies that swarmed everywhere as they made their way up. Jake, Morse and several of the enlisted troopers followed at a distance. When they got up there, they looked down at the bodies. Custer lay on his back, stripped, with his head uphill. His right leg lay across the body of trooper with the heel on a dead horse. He had a bullet wound near his left breast, and another in his left temple. He hadn't been scalped, but the trigger finger was missing on his right hand, his thighs were slashed, and had an arrow stuck up his penis.

"There he is, God damn him! He will never fight any more!" Benteen declared.

Some of the other bodies that lay near Custer, had been brutally mutilated. Jake recognized Lt. Cooke because of his distinctive long mustaches, one side of which had been torn from his face. Another body lay face down, the head having been scalped, then pounded almost flat, with an arrow shot into it, and several others were sticking out of the back. One of the men pointed to a tattoo on one of the right arm with the initials *TWC*, Lady Liberty and the flag

"That must be Tom! I recognize that tattoo." Weir stated grimly.

They turned to make their way farther down the slope, looking for any signs of recognition among the other dead soldiers. Weir stood, looking around at the bodies.

"Oh! How white they are!" he remarked quietly, almost to himself.

The bodies of some of the other officers were found a little ways down. Capt. Yates, Lt. Reilly and Lt. Smith were identified, but several others were not.

Benteen asked Weir, "Why do you suppose that except for Keogh , Calhoun, and Crittenden, the rest of the officers were all gathered on this hill, with Custer? I see no evidence of company deployments or lines, they're all mixed together here."

"It is puzzling." Weir replied, "It doesn't look like they may have had time."

They counted 39 dead horses scattered on the hill, some were used as obvious breastworks, while others lay with their legs sticking up from swollen carcasses. They found Boston Custer, laying near his nephew, Harry Reid, lower down.

Jake spotted several corpses scattered along the edge of a ravine that led down to the river. As they approached them, Jake noted the absence of dead horses, so it appeared that the men may have been on foot making an effort to reach the timber along the river. They followed the trail of bodies until it ended, then turned around and headed back up the hill. Jake spied a body laying face down that had been shot in the back. Laying near it was a ripped piece of a calfskin vest. He went over to it, noting that the head had been caved in with a club and a broken clay pipe lay in the dust next to it.

"I think that this is probably Mitch Boyer!" he called to Morse.

Pat came over and looked, "Aye, could be. He'd probably have been trying to get to some cover. Poor Bastard! He was trying to warn Custer and look where it got him."

When they got back up to where Benteen was, they found that Lt. Nowlan and Sgt. DeLacy had come up and were viewing the hilltop. Jake saw Capt. Weir riding slowly back along the ridge by himself. Jake and Pat mounted their horses and followed him. Shortly after, Benteen and the others mounted up also and the rest of detail headed back in the direction they'd come from. Jake and Pat rode back along the ridge in silence and when they reached the end of it, they found Weir had halted near where Calhoun's body lay. He was sitting on his horse, Old Jake, smoking his pipe and staring off in the distance at the twin peak hill to the south. They rode up slowly beside him and stopped. Weir looked over at them with a solemn expression.

"We saw this from over there, didn't we?" he asked.

"Aye, Sir!" Morse replied, "But I feel it was already too late, by that point."

"Perhaps, you're right, Sergeant. Somehow, that doesn't make me feel better right now."

"I don't suppose it ever will, Sir."

When they got back they found that in the two hours of their absence, Gen. Terry had the wounded and remains of the Regiment, moved across the river where they went into camp. The officers went to find Gen. Terry and while the rest of them sought out their companies. Jake and Pat spotted the black horses of Company D and rode over to them. The men were busy watering the horses and collecting wood for cooking fires. They saw 1st Sgt. Martin, sitting on a hardtack case with a tin cup in his hand, he watched them as they rode up.

"So?" he asked.

Morse shook his head, "Terrible! I've no words to describe it to you, Mike. Do ya remember what the bodies of Sgt. Major Kennedy and the men that were with Major Elliott looked like when we found them after the Washita fight?"

"Aye, 'twas a gruesome sight, that!" Martin replied. "One that I'd just as soon never lay eyes on again!"

"Yes, but they were frozen when we found them two weeks later. The bodies up on that ridge were treated as poorly and they have been lying in the sun for two days!" Morse stated. "It'll be worse tomorrow I'd warrant!"

Martin grimaced and then said, "Ah well, then I'll be seeing them. Gen. Terry has ordered Major Reno to have us go bury 'em in the morning. Go see to your horses and we'll talk later."

The camp was in the area that Reno had retreated from on his way across the river to the bluffs and burial parties had been at work that afternoon. The bodies of Lt. McIntosh, Charlie Reynolds, Isiah Dorman, and Bloody Knife, along with the other troops killed in the valley fight had been found, and their mutilated remains buried. However, many horse carcasses were still scattered around and details were assigned to drag them a distance away, but the odor and swarms of flies still prevailed and the soldiers endured it all night. The next morning after Reveille, the men that still had mounts tended to them. At least 50 horses had been killed or seriously wounded up on the bluffs. Company D had been fortunate and had only 6 horses killed. A detail of troopers without mounts was assigned to finish off any horses too badly hurt to be saved, and then bury them.

Reno gathered the remaining companies and led them back up to the bluffs where they followed the route taken by Benteen's detail the day before. After going to the ford at the bottom of what was being called Medicine Tail Coulee by the scouts, the command watered their horses, then Reno assigned sectors for each company and had them deployed up across the field. The area assigned to Company D was up along the long ridge. When they got up on the high ground, the men were deployed in skirmish formation and began walking towards the ridge searching for bodies. DeLacy and the remaining troops of Company I accompanied them. 1st Sgt. Martin had procured a couple of shovels and a pick axe, and when they stumbled upon a body, the men took turns hacking a shallow trench next to it, then rolled the body into it. Most of the bodies had arrows sticking out of them, and they had to be broken off. They piled what dirt and brush was near to cover the bodies, before pounding a wooden stake near the head. As they got closer to the high ground the pace slowed considerably, with the discovery of multiple bodies. As the temperatures rose, the conditions of the remains were rapidly deteriorating and many of the men were weakened by vomiting and retching. Flies swarmed each corpse, the open cuts and exposed body cavities teemed with maggots, many had limbs cut off and a few had been decapitated. All the while the stench was pervasive and overpowering. The burials became rushed and shallow as the troopers hurried to cover them. The officers went ahead in a group seeking out the bodies of their fallen comrades, and some pains were taken to identify each officer grave by writing the name on a piece of paper, then inserting it in an empty cartridge casing and pounding it into the top of a wooden stake. When Company D reached the area where Keogh had been found, Sgt. DeLacy and his men took over. As they were burying their comrades, a horse whinnying could be heard faintly from some bushes and small trees lower down on the slope. While the men were digging, DeLacy headed down towards the clump, drawing his pistol as he went. A horse suddenly sat up on its haunches, and slowly shook its head. DeLacy went over to it, intending to put it down, when he saw that it was Keogh's clayback horse, Comanche. The horse struggled to stand up, bloody and wounded in several places, its saddle hanging upside down underneath. Milt heard someone running down behind him, shouting.

"Nein! Nein! No shoot, Sarge!" cried Pvt. Gustav Korn as he staggered to a halt, placing himself between DeLacy and the horse. "Leave me have a look!"

"Okay, Korn. But, he ain't lookin' too good!"

Korn turned and went to Comanche talking softly, "Mein shatzi, is okay, is okay."

"Well, if you can help him fine! I'll leave it to you if he has to be put down."

"Sure, sure, I'll see to him, Sarge."

DeLacy turned and walked back up to the burial detail, where he saw that Lt. Nowlan and Capt. Weir standing nearby watching.

"Isn't that Keogh's horse? Nowlan asked, as DeLacy got nearer.

"It is, Sir. Looks like the shot that hit the captain's leg got him too. I don't know if he'll make it."

"Well, it looks like he might." The officer replied, nodding his head down the slope.

DeLacy turned and looked back, seeing Korn gently lead the animal back up towards them. "Well, I'll be damned!"

Nowlan said quietly, "See that you do everything possible, I'd really like to save him."

"Yes, Sir! Me too!" DeLacy exclaimed.

They continued working their way along the ridge, finally coming to the hill where Custer and his men had made their last stand. A grave site was selected near Custer and while several men began digging, 1st Sgt. Martin had Jake take a couple of men down to the abandoned village site where he was able scrounge up a piece of canvas, a travois frame, and as many rocks as they could carry. After laying the canvas in the hole, Custer and his brother Tom were lowered on to it and wrapped up. They scooped dirt over them, then placed the woven frame over them, weighting it down with rocks to try and prevent the scavengers from getting at it. When it was done, they all stepped back.

Most of the officers were there, including Major Reno. Everyone stood at attention, saluted, then walked away. Jake saw that there were some burials still going on near the ravine down slope towards the river.

Little Big Horn Battlefield - Graves of the unknown, 1879

"Do you want to go check on Mitch Boyer's body?" Jake asked Morse.

"No, I've had my belly full for the day." Pat sighed. "Let's gather the lads and get down off this ridge. We'll get them washed up in the river while we water the horses. I think we'll feel better getting rid of some of the stench."

Upon their return from the burial details, Reno had the regiment move north and make camp below Gibbon's column to get away from the worst of the smells from the dead animals. The men were exhausted and morose that evening. Most of the officers of the 7th were gathered over around Gen. Terry's encampment, where various scenarios of how Custer was overcome were played out. The same thing was happening around the campfires of the individual companies. Jake and Tom Russell sat listening to 1st Sgt. Martin and the other senior NCOs who had campaigned with

Custer down in Kansas.

"It's plain to see he went galavanting off without knowing the ground and let the companies get spread out. They were strung out along that ridge for good half mile, with no cover." Harrison postulated.

"Yeh! Just like at the Washita fight. We got lucky there when the warriors from the big villages downstream wouldn't attack us because of the hostages we'd taken." Martin stated.

Morse frowned, and nodded his head in agreement. "I think maybe Custer was trying to get to some of the women and children, and use them to do it again. Once he got a good look at the size of the village, he'd have figured that was the quickest way to over come the numbers advantage."

"Why do you suppose he didn't keep all of his companies together, then?"

"Probably because he was waiting for Benteen and us. Remember his brother Boston passed us on his way up from the pack train and he was dead up on that hill. I'm sure he'd have told Custer about where he last saw us. I think that Calhoun and Company L were posted at the end of the ridge to guide us to him."

No one said anything for several minutes, then Martin spoke up. "So, you're thinking that when Benteen stopped to help Reno, that Custer and the others were still alive."

"Yeh, that's what I'm thinking. I'm also thinking that it would have been a near run thing, if we'd gone on to him."

Martin sat up, looking over to where the area of Terry's tent was lit by several lanterns, "They'll be over there, figuring out a way to lay this all on Custer. If Reno hadn't run for the bluffs, Custer's plan may have worked. When we stopped to help him that freed all the Sioux and Cheyenne warriors to go towards Custer's command and surround them. Our boys didn't have a chance strung out in the open like that."

Morse nodded his head, and looked over at Jake who had been listening intently.

Jake said slowly, "I heard the Captain talking to Benteen. They were both wondering why so many officers were around Custer, and maybe that he'd had an Officer's Call on the hill when they were attacked."

"That seems unlike Custer! Once he was in motion he was unlikely to halt for something like that. I think maybe the reason might have been that Custer was wounded, and they were trying to get sorted out. I noticed that Dr. Lord, the head surgeon, was laying up near him. Capt. Yates would have been senior officer." Martin said.

"It seems to me like the Indians would have worked their way up the ravines and gullies surrounding them, then popped up to shoot at them from cover like they did us, over on the bluffs. It looked to me like the Sioux rolled them up the length of the ridge line from the south towards the hill, then overwhelmed them from all directions. It looked like some of them tried to make a run for the river where Jake and I saw Mitch Boyer's body."

"Well, lads! What's done is done! It's our lot to keep the men busy and be ready if the hostiles return. Let's turn in and we'll see what the General decides in the morning."

Capt. Ball of the 2nd cavalry had led his Company H south along the hostile's trail seeking to gain some intelligence on their activities. He followed the wide trail made by the travois and ponies across the burned benchland. He encountered the same difficult terrain and ravines that Benteen's battalion had struggled across three days earlier. As he navigated the ravines and gullies, he stumbled across numbers of dead warriors abandoned by the fleeing Indians, and many items had been thrown away, scattered along the route. About 12 miles out he found a campsite where they'd halted for the night, and there the trail split, with many of the travois heading southeast while others led to the southwest. Confident that Indians were not gathering to return, and without any scouts, Ball opted to return to inform Terry.

Gen. Terry decided against remaining another night in the area, and was anxiously wanting to get away from the flies and pestilence. He'd had the men of Gibbon's column busy all day preparing to move the wounded downstream to the Big Horn River, where the *Far West* was moored waiting. The Infantry companies had scoured the village, searching for poles to construct litters to carry the 21 wounded who weren't capable of walking or riding. Hides were removed from dead horses and secured to the poles. Buffalo robes, blankets and grass were used to pad them. The movement was to be delayed until the afternoon heat subsided. In the meantime Terry ordered the 7th Cavalry to conduct a sweep of the entire village and destroy anything that could be of use to the Indians. Piles of lodge poles, robes, skins, and anything that could burn were put to the torch. The same thing was done with surplus ration boxes, saddles and pack saddles, weapons, and miscellaneous items left up on the bluffs. Company D was up towards the northern portion of the village conducting searches for Indian possessions when Lt. Varnum and his remaining Ree scouts rode up. The scouts had been given permission to pick and choose from the spoils. Varnum sat watching them and Lt, Edgerly went over to talk with him. The Rees picked through the various items finding new pans, kettles and tin cups and crockery, many of them trade goods fresh from Agency traders. Edgerly rode back to where Jake and his section were piling lodge poles, hides, robes and blankets.

"Sgt. Rogers, let your men have a free hand to pick out anything that we can use, but they'll have to carry it with them. We're short pack mules."

"Yes, sir! We've found several bundles of new government issue blankets that we're glad to exchange for our trail weary ones. It's a damn shame that we have to destroy all of this, there's probably several wagonloads of it."

"Lt. Varnum told me that this was a Cheyenne camp circle according to his Ree scouts. We can't leave it for them to reclaim if they come back, better to burn everything."

Once they got the bonfires going, Jake led the men to the river to wash up near a shallow ford. He looked back up to the south, noting dozens of smoke columns rising. He was getting ready to take off his shirt to wash it, when he saw several soldiers across the river coming down to the ford. One of them, an officer by his uniform, called out.

"Over here! We need some of you men."

Jake saw that the officer was Lt. Bradley, Gibbon's chief of scouts. He called out, "Okay, sir!" then said to Charlie Welch and Henry, "Get your men, and let's go see what he wants."

When they got across, Bradley said grimly. "I'm over here with Col. Gibbon. He wanted to have a look at the field. We've found a couple of more bodies. Follow me, Sergeant."

They rode up a gully, then came out onto a slight rise. Gibbon and several of his staff were sitting on their horses looking at a body on the ground. When Jake reigned up, he saw that the corpse appeared to be fully clothed and in civilian dress. It had been scalped and one ear was missing.

Bradley said, "We haven't found anything to tell us who he might have been."

Jake dismounted and went closer to the body, "It's Mr. Kellogg, the newspaper man. I recognize his boots, with those leather straps. He was with Custer when I last saw him." A leather pouch, lay near by, with papers scattered near it. Jake bent to gather them. "This is his journal, I remember seeing him writing in it."

Col. Gibbon spoke, "Please bring those to me, Sergeant. I'd like to go over them."

Jake walked over and handed them up to Gibbon. "I'm Sgt. Rogers, with Company D, sir. We buried Custer and the men near him but never identified Mr. Kellogg. I wonder how he came to be down here?"

"Do you suppose he was fleeing the fight?" Bradley asked.

"Could be, but I don't see his mule." Jake noted a fairly heavy trail of shod hoof prints leading up towards the hill about a mile away, where Custer lay, "Have you been up there, yet, Sir?" He asked pointing.

"No, we crossed the ford earlier and went up the river a ways when we found a body. It was scalped and stuck full of arrows. It appeared that he may have been a trumpeter, judging by what was left of his uniform."

"It could be Trumpeter Voss, he was with Custer also, and was used as a messenger that day. I recall him coming with orders for Capt. Benteen once."

Bradley looked back and pointed, "Well, he's over there, and he'll need to be buried, too."

"I'll send for some shovels and we'll see to it, sir."

"Sgt. Rogers, since you're familiar with what's up there, I'd like you to accompany us." Gibbon said.

"Of course, Sir! Holden, I'll leave you in charge of getting Mr. Kellogg and the other body buried."

Gibbon's party started up the slope. Lt. Bradley and Jake rode out ahead following a trail of shod hoof prints.

"Well, there appears to be sign that at least one company came down this way, then turned around and went back up." Jake stated. "I see a lot of empty cartridges scattered along here, and I see pony tracks. There must have been some fighting going on."

Lt. Bradley frowned and replied, "That really doesn't fit with any of the scenarios that have been speculated upon by Gen. Terry and his staff."

Jake continued to peer down at the trail, and said, "Well, I'm just telling you what I see."

"I wish our Crow scouts hadn't gone home. It would have been helpful to have them look at this and confirm it."

"No disrespect to you, Sir, but I learned from a very experienced guide, and the signs I'm looking at are quite obvious."

"Well, see where it leads."

Jake followed it for a few hundred yards and came to a relatively flat area where he could see that the trail showed signs that the shod horses had halted.

"It looks like they stopped here, then fanned out along that ridge below the hill."

Bradley nodded his head, then rode over to Col. Gibbon, where he had a brief conversation, then came back.

"Thanks for your help, but I think we can find our way now,

Sergeant." Bradley said curtly, "Why don't you go back down and see to your men."

Jake looked up in surprise and said, "Very well, Sir! Glad that I could help out." Then he turned Ajax around and headed downhill.

He saluted Col. Gibbon and his staff as he rode past, noting the puzzled looks on their faces as he left.

The two combined Columns set out in the late afternoon, with the wounded being borne on hand litters and carried by two of the Infantry units. By the time darkness settled in it became apparent that the litters were both inefficient and tortuous for the wounded troops. The eight men assigned to carry each of them were quickly exhausted. After several hours, they had only reached a mile past the end of the village. Terry called a halt, and after a discussion with his officers, Lt. Doane, 2nd Cavalry, asked to be given time the next morning to assemble some litters that could be carried by mules. Camp was made and the men settled in gratefully, relieved to be well away from the decaying remains on the battlefield and the odorous, smoldering bonfires of the Indian village.

The following morning Lt. Doane sent details back to find a quantity of lodge poles and more hides to construct his litters, which were to be carried by two mules each, led by one man in front, one to steady the litter, and one leading the rear mule. Gen. Terry dispatched his engineering officer, Lt. Maguire, escorted by Benteen and Company H to make a map of the battlefield. The rest of the regiment fell back into the discipline of daily routine and spent most of the day checking out the men, horses and equipment.

Word was passed down that the column would make another attempt to move downstream transporting the wounded at 6 o'clock, and that the men should take the opportunity to rest. Jake found a nice shady spot under a big cottonwood and was leaned up against his saddle when Pat and Tom Russell came over to join him.

"So, I heard that Mark Kellogg's body turned up, yesterday." Pat said.

"Yes, we buried him and another, who may have been Trumpeter Voss, just across the river from the Cheyenne camp." Jake said. He then related what he'd come across with Bradley and Gibbon.

Morse nodded his head thoughtfully, "So, you're thinking some of Custer's men made it all the way down to the river that day, then made a fighting withdrawal?"

"Yeh, but it's a puzzle why. And there were no bodies left."

"I think they were after hostages and ran into trouble. Custer would have been leading. You remember that wound in his chest? Maybe he got shot? That would have caused a panic, now!"

Russell spoke up, "If it was Voss, maybe he and Kellogg were trying to head north to find Terry and Gibbon with a message. That would account for them being found where they were. Hell, it sounds like they almost made it."

"Well, unless we find someone that may have survived, we'll probably never know." Pat stated, "After every fight that I've ever been in there's back patting and finger pointing going on a plenty. The higher ranking officers will be not wanting any blame to be cast upon them. I'm hearing that it's to all be laid on Custer for disobeying orders."

"So what now, Pat?" Jake asked, "Will we go after them once we get the wounded sent off?"

"Oh, I think not. I believe the Indians are moving away from us, just like we are from them. They didn't come out without losses, I heard they counted 25 bodies in the village, and Capt. Ball found many more on his scout. We just saw what they left behind in their hurry to break camp. No, they need time to lick their wounds the same as us. Gen. Terry will want to get back to where the riverboats can get to us with supplies, plus we've only enough mounts for half the regiment. We'll need replacements. And, don't forget all of the men we left back at the supply camp on the Powder, we'll need them and more. I for one, will be glad to sit on my arse while it all gets sorted out."

The column set off at 6:00 PM, with two infantry companies guiding the litters carrying the wounded. The first several miles went smoothly, and the two scouts that Terry had dispatched to find the *Far West* two days earlier, found them just as darkness closed in. They assured Terry that the riverboat was moored waiting on them at the confluence with the Bighorn River and was being prepared to receive the wounded. Terry decided to press on and at first they were aided by moonlight, but as the ascended to a plateau clouds moved in and rain began falling. The column got strung out and at one point the advance party resorted to bugle calls to get closed up. When they finally arrived at the bluffs above the river, no route could be found down. After several attempts, lights were seen and a party stumbled towards them. A detachment from Capt. Baker's 6th Infantry serving as escort on the *Far West* lighted fires along a ravine, and then helped convey the wounded down to be carried aboard where doctors and their medical orderlies were waiting on them. The rest of the rainy morning was spent getting supplies from the steamers hold and loading the Gatling gun battery. That afternoon, the riverboat cast off to head downstream to the base camp near the junction with the Yellowstone River. Where a trading post called Fort Pease, had been built on the north bank just below the mouth of the Big Horn the previous year. Terry and Gibbon had left their wagons there prior to marching south to the proposed rendezvous with Custer. Gibbon who was now in command of the column, ordered it across a ford to the north bank of the Little Horn and it went into bivouac among a grove of large cottonwoods. Reno had a muster taken of the remainder of the 7th Cavalry. Of the 5 companies that had been with Custer's two battalions, there were only 6 sergeants, and 39 other ranks remaining and present for duty. On that solemn note, the regiment was allowed to rest in preparation for the march down the Big Horn, along with the soldiers of Gibbon's Column, to the banks of the Yellowstone 50 miles away.

CHAPTER 35

Near Fort Pease, Montana Territory, 7th Cavalry Bivouac - July 4, 1876

Fort Pease was named after Fellows David Pease, the expedition leader of a group of Bozeman traders trying to establish a trading post and riverboat landing on the Yellowstone in 1875. Unfortunately, it was in the heart of some the prime Sioux hunting grounds and it was virtually under siege after it was built the preceding year. The 2nd Cavalry out of Fort Ellis had been sent to evacuate it in March and it was abandoned. Col. Gibbon found it still standing when he led the Montana Column east back in April, and he reoccupied it establishing a supply depot there.

The 7th Cavalry went into camp 2 miles upriver from the log buildings and stockade of Fort Pease where Terry established his headquarters, ironically very near the site of Custer's fight with the Sioux back in 1873. The *Far West* had departed the previous day for Bismarck and Fort Lincoln carrying the wounded, mail, and dispatches. Gen. Terry had sent his adjutant Capt. Smith along and had tasked him with presenting Terry's reports and requisitions, particularly for horses, uniforms, and supplies. The exertions of two months in the field had taken a toll on all, and some of the men were virtually dressed in rags. Terry had very quietly signaled his intent to his officers that they would stay in place for at least a week. Fortunately, before the boat left, all remaining supplies were off loaded so there were plenty of rations. Sutler Smith and James Coleman had set up shop with what merchandise they had remaining, so there was limited supply of goods and alcohol available. The *Josephine* was rumored to be on its way upriver and was expected any day.

The day was pleasant, but the mood of the men was still pretty solemn, and no elaborate plans were made to cerebrate the holiday. Some of the men had gone to the river to fish, and the rest lounged around under shade trees. Jake was writing a letter to Holly while listening to the other NCOs who were playing cards around an improvised table of stacked hardtack boxes, He looked up to see a group of men, led by 1st Sgt. McCurry from Company H, approaching. He was the youngest first sergeant in the regiment and popular with his men. McCurry had received a shoulder wound in the fighting up on the bluffs, but had elected to stay in the field.

"Afternoon, gents! I'd like to show you this petition that's going round."

Martin looked up from his cards and asked gruffly,"What petition might that be?"

" It's one asking that the officers that led us in the fight on the bluffs be the ones that get promoted to any of the positions that have become vacant within the Regiment."

Sgt. Harrison put down his cards and guffawed, "Hah! I can think of one or two that we could be doin' without, m'self."

McCurry frowned, "Well, why don't you read it first, then make up your mind about signing it?"

Jake reached out his hand, "Here, I'll take look at it."

He read the petition noting the flowery descriptions and respectful tone.

"That's a fair piece of writing, I'd say that someone put some thought into it. However, I don't know if I'd go so far as to say that the decisions made over those two days saved that many lives. A fair amount of luck was involved."

"What else does it say, Jake?" asked Pat, "Give me the highlights."

"Basically it credits Major Reno and Capt. Benteen for bravely saving our hides, and asks that they be promoted."

"Well, that's a crock of shit!" barked Morse, "Although, I'll not dispute that Benteen was braver than many."

McCurry said hotly, "Yes, and if it wasn't for him we'd all be dead!"

Martin stood up, "Here now, Joe! Some of us have been in this man's Army a long time and with this regiment since it was formed. There's not much that we haven't seen from our officers over that time. We've a fair idea which ones are worth their salt and which ones ain't. Now, I'll not dispute your intentions, but I'm not inclined to see them all rewarded because a few of them showed some grit and acted their part."

McCurry stood glaring at them silently, then said, "Okay, but this is going forward, whether everyone signs it, or not!" then stalked away trailed by his companions.

Martin looked over at Morse, "I don't know the lad all that well m'self. I've heard tell that he's one of Benteen's favorite baseball players, and the captain of the team. I know he went from private to first sergeant of Company H in just over two and a half years. I suspect that he's just trying to make Benteen look good, but he can't do it without including Reno, too."

Pat looked over at Jake and winked, "What'd I tell you? There's the start of the back pattin', and the finger pointin' can't be too far behind. You'll notice that the officers aren't flitting about camp. I suspect they're all busy writing reports, foisting the blame on each other. I can't wait until some of newspapers make it up river on the boats. Things will really get interesting, then."

The steamer *Josephine* arrived two days later, carrying rations, fodder, and a large resupply of goods for Sutler Smith. The riverboat was under the command of Martin Coulson, the brother of Sanford Coulson who owned the Coulson Packet Co. The *Josephine* was the newest steamer in the Coulson fleet and had been named after the daughter of Gen. Stanley, the commander of the 1873 Yellowstone Survey Expedition. The previous year it had become the first riverboat to navigate the waters of the Yellowstone, while under the command of Grant Marsh.

The entire command was enthusiastic because Smith and Coleman had also been resupplied with liquor and beer. Later that day, a party of Crows came into camp bringing news that Gen. Crook's Wyoming Column had been in a fight on the upper Rosebud, and been turned back the week before the Custer fight. Rumors and speculation quickly began to circulate about how that may have impacted the 7th's battle. Gen. Terry threw a party for his officers and many of them had continued late into the night. The following morning Pvt. Kellar, who was still Weir's striker, quietly reported to 1st Sgt. Martin that the captain was feeling ill and for Martin to take over for the day. Lt. Edgerly was no longer with the company since being appointed regimental quartermaster and there was no junior officer. That evening after dinner Jake and Tom Russell went to the river to retrieve a gunny sack full of bottles of beer that they'd cached there to cool off. Big George and Hurry were sitting nearby on the bank, fishing.

"Having any luck?" Jake asked.

"Naw, pretty slow. Caught a couple of little mudcats is all." Big answered, then spit a stream of tobacco juice and worked the chaw around in his mouth.

"Well, good luck! If you get a stringer full, I'll help you clean them."

When they got back to camp Morse and Flanagan came over to them where they sat near their dog tent. Jake reached in the sack and handed them beers.

"Thanks!" Pat exclaimed, as he opened it.

"Where have you been?" asked Jake.

"Jimmy and I were over visiting with John Ryan. He just got back from the fort where he was looking to see what he could scrounge up in the way of uniforms."

"Did he have any luck?"

"No, but he found out that Terry has requisitioned them, along with 100 horses. He's also planning on moving the supply camp from down on the Powder to up here. He also overheard a conversation between Lt. Edgerly and Lt. Godfrey. It seems that our captain and Benteen got into a big row last night in front of some of the other officers after Terry's party. Supposedly over some remarks Weir made about Reno and Benteen ignoring Custer's orders. They had to drag Weir away when Benteen threatened him. I'm guessing that they were both in their cups."

"How much longer do you think we'll stay here?" Tom asked.

"Who knows, but we're running out of grazing for the horses. It won't be long."

The 7th was finally moved closer to Fort Pease on July 11. The new camp was made on broken dry ground, dusty with little shade, however there was a large island with good grass nearby. The men were notified that mail could be sent out on the riverboat, and Jake made sure to get his letters in the bag. The second day a thunderstorm popped up in the afternoon, cooling things off and settling the dust. The next night a terrific storm pummeled the area, wreaking havoc with the horses and livestock, flooding the area and uprooting tents. Company D was lucky that the bivouac area assigned to them was on one of the few pieces of ground the water didn't reach. However, Terry and his staff were flooded and he elected to move the whole command below Fort Pease to higher ground. Most of the day was spent changing camps and they had just gotten set up when another storm hit accompanied by a large amount of hail. A boat arrived with mail and dispatches for Terry, who learned that six companies of the 22nd Infantry under Col. Elwell Otis, were being transferred to him from the Dept. of Dakota, and also six companies of the 5th Infantry from the Dept. of the Missouri under Col. Nelson Miles, were on their way up river. The *Far West* was expected to arrive any day with 60 horses, rations, supplies, and replacement troops. Terry had decided to consolidate his men at one location. He made plans to go downriver on board the *Josephine* to the Powder River supply depot, before the boat continued on its way back to Bismarck. The plan was to move all the supplies up from there, to the camp near Fort Pease. Major Moore would be ferried over the river, to march up the north bank with the men and wagons.

Back at the 7th's encampment, good weather set in and the heat returned. The men were settling into almost a garrison routine. Guard duties were rotated along with wood and water details, and the men and horses were almost fully recovered from their exertions. Fresh fish and venison augmented the issue rations in the messes. Jake was able to bag a buffalo along with several prairie chickens. Another boat arrived from Fort Ellis upstream, bearing mail, foodstuffs, and miscellaneous goods, including a load of Jamaica ginger beer. The troopers hurried over to where the trader, Paul McCormick, set up his station. Pat Morse took a detail up to draw rations and brought back some of it for the NCO mess to have evening.

"I can't say as I've ever had any of this. Where I grew up in Indiana we just had regular beer." stated Russell.

"Well, that's getting a little scarce until the next boat comes upriver, so here goes, Gents. Cheers!" Pat exclaimed. "I know it's popular with the Brits."

They all raised their bottles, and Jake took a tentative sip. The ginger made his sinuses tingle and it left a slight burning sensation in his mouth. He raised his eyebrows and said, "Okay, that's a bit different, but not bad, it's got a little bite to it."

Martin laughed, "Oh, it's libel to have a big bite if you drink too much it lad! I remember when I was your age back in Dublin. Me and some fellas got pie-eyed on it and we were miserable the next day. So I'd go easy!"

"I heard that the *Far West* is due any day and that Mr. Smith has quite a consignment coming up on it. I'll wager that he'll have plenty of beer and whiskey." Pat said, "There's a paymaster on her too."

"I hope there's some uniforms on the boat, too." Jake said, "Mine's more patches, than anything else. Most of us look like ragamuffins."

"Well, I'll be sure to gently remind our new Quartermaster, young Edgerly, to see that he doesn't forget that we saved his bacon three weeks back." Tom Harrison ventured with a smile, looking over at Jake. "Perhaps he'll see fit to do us a favor?"

There were several islands along this part of the Yellowstone that could be reached by crossing a small shallow channel along the north side. They were covered with abundant rich grass and the cavalry troops were able to turn out the horses to graze. Feeling that they were relatively secure, the men that herded them over returned to camp. Lt. Godfrey, who was officer of the day, found out and was in the process of making them go back, when Major Reno came by and overruled him. Godfrey was furious and stormed to the officers mess tent. He was just beginning to vent his displeasure when he was told that Capt. Lewis Thompson, Company L, 2nd Cavalry, had committed suicide earlier that morning. Thompson had been struggling with lingering health issues stemming back to his time as prisoner of war in the infamous Libby Prison during the war. Godfrey quickly forgot his grievance and joined the others in mourning the loss of the well liked, veteran officer. The death cast a pall over the officers of the entire command. That night shots rang out after midnight and it was discovered that some Indians had attempted to steal horses off the picket line, one of them being Custer's horse, Dandy. Not having seen any hostile Indians since the battle, it was speculated that the perpetrators may have been some local, so called, friendlies.

Two days later the camp was moved a couple of miles downriver to find fresh grass. As the soldiers were getting the camp set up, some Crow scouts came riding in reporting Sioux on some nearby bluffs. After giving chase, they discovered that it was a party of Ree scouts sent up from the Powder River supply camp. Col. Gibbon was alarmed enough that he ordered Major Reno to post vedettes that night. Reno protested, countering that his men were still recuperating and that the detail should be assigned to the 2nd Cavalry if Gibbon thought that they were necessary. The following day Gibbon, anticipating the arrival of the *Far West*, dispatched two 2nd Cavalry companies, accompanied by Lt. Low's battery and 25 Crow scouts, to ride east along the river to meet it. Gibbon and Reno continued to spar over the necessity of using troopers from the 7th for vedettes, to the point that Gibbon had Reno placed under arrest for insubordination. Heavy rains returned causing the ravines and river channels to flood. One of the 7th's pickets was drowned when his horse threw him while trying to cross over one of them. A party of several men was seen on the south bank and after determining that they weren't hostiles, a boat was sent across to fetch them. They turned out to be some Crow scouts and three couriers that Terry had sent out to find Crook's Wyoming Column, back on the 9th.

Terry finally returned on the *Far West* early on July 26. After encountering falling water levels, he concluded that the Fort Pease vicinity was not going to be a good location for his main supply camp. He immediately issued orders for the entire command to begin moving east towards the Rosebud, and sent couriers to tell Major Moore to notify him of the change in plans. The steamer was quickly loaded with what it could carry and the rest loaded in wagons. Gibbon met with Terry to prefer his charges against Reno, but was rebuffed by him and the charges were dismissed. An exasperated Terry summoned Reno and told them both to concentrate on preparing to fight the Indians and not each other. The two commands were being combined and would now be designated as the Yellowstone Column. Terry left on the *Far West* the next morning hoping to intercept Moore, and found his bivouac 13 miles west of the Rosebud. After informing Moore of the change in plans, Terry continued downriver headed for the Rosebud to locate a suitable site. Meanwhile, the Yellowstone Column marched in that direction along the northern bank. After two hot, blistering days it finally reached the new camp opposite the mouth of the Rosebud. Major Moore was already there with his detachment and the wagon train that had been parked at the Powder supply depot had been. The dismounted 7th Cavalry troops, including the Regimental Band, had also accompanied him. Moore had his men already at work, throwing up earthworks. They had already christened the new depot, "Fort Beans" in a joking reference to it's location between Fort Pease, and Fort Rice

The 7th Cavalry troopers were able to secure the larger tents and the baggage left behind with the wagon train at the Powder River camp. The dismounted detachments left behind there were reunited with their companies. Reno was still deciding how to re-organize the remaining companies into battalions. His plans would be contingent on how many replacement mounts the regiment would receive as the resupply steamers arrived. In the mean time, the men and officers enjoyed the relative luxury of adequate supplies and rations, including access to the Sutlers. Between the retrieved baggage and the new uniforms that were being issued, the 7th was beginning to look less like a band of brigands. Rumors were going round camp that a large contingent of infantry was due to arrive any day. Terry was waiting for news from Gen. Crook's Wyoming column.

"Well, it hardly seems possible that we were camped over there across the river just over five weeks ago." Morse stated emphatically. "Little did we know what we'd be getting into, eh, Jake?"

He, Jake, and Tom Russell were walking towards the river, where the *Far West* was pulled in, to visit the Sutler's tent.

"It's almost mind boggling if you stop to think about it." Jake replied. "How long do you think we'll stay here?"

"Oh, I'd think maybe a week or so. I'm sure Gen. Sheridan will be prodding Terry to resume the chase. I'm sure that the people back east are clamoring for answers and wanting retaliation.

"Yes, I'm hoping to get my hands on a couple newspapers."

As they got closer, a soldier on the upper deck of the riverboat began waving at them, calling out "Jake, Jake, over here!"

Jake looked up at him in surprise, "Mike Caddle, well I'll be damned! What are you doing up there?"

Mike scrambled down the stairway to the main deck, and motioned for them to come up the gangway.

"Come on guys, it's okay! Hell, I'm a sort of a marine now, horse marine that is. I've been aboard for almost a month." Caddle stated with a big grin. "Follow me!"

Mike led them through a maze of crates, barrels, and piles of bags to a small alcove where some bunks were set up.

"Here we go, take a seat!" Mike said, "I'll be right back." He went to the railing , and hoisted up a dripping sack, then after retrieving some bottles of beer came back and offered them around.

"Sutler Smith and his partner Joe Leighton take care of us for helping them out. Cheers!"

"Okay, now let's hear about how in the blazes you came to be here?" Pat asked.

"Well, when the wounded were brought downriver last month to the Powder Depot, Capt. Baker's infantry company was serving as escort. Major Moore decided that he needed all of his soldiers and took them off the boat. That's when many of us found out we no longer had a company to go back to. So having nothing better to do, some of us cavalry troopers went to Capt. Marsh and volunteered to take their place. We've been onboard ever since. Marsh calls us his horse marines. Apparently, he's been allowed to keep us, as no one in the regiment has seemed to object. I suppose cavalry troopers without mounts aren't much in demand right now."

"So you made the trip back down to Ft. Lincoln and Bismarck?" asked Jake.

"Oh yeh! And what a run it was. I heard that this boat set some kind of record getting there. We helped out with the wounded. Some of those boys were shot up pretty badly, but a few of them weren't. I heard about Reno and Benteen's battalions getting surrounded, and the fight that went on. Mike Madden from Company K, told me how you and John Ryan helped drag him to cover after he was wounded."

Jake nodded his head, recalling the incident, "Well, it wasn't that big of a deal. He'd have done the same. So, what happened back at Lincoln?"

"Man, everyone was flabbergasted by the news when we got to Bismarck. And then when we went down to the fort, it was like a bomb went off, everyone was shell shocked! Luckily, Capt. Marsh didn't tarry, we got loaded and came back upriver as fast as we could."

"So, what do you do?"

"Pretty much anything. There's sixteen of us, besides me. We cut wood and haul it, help with the loading and unloading. We guard the boat at night and watch for Mr. Lo. Hell, one of the lads got to tinkering with a disabled Gatling gun that was left on board and got it working. Lordie, you should see the game that we've been able to bag with it, buffalo, elk, geese, ducks. That thing has amazing range, you just shoot and keep cranking. Any hostiles looking to pick a fight with us will be in for a rude surprise!"

"Well, it sounds like you got lucky. It sure beats what we're doing." Tom said.

Mike looked at them, and asked, "So what's the plan? Is Terry going out?"

"That's what we'd like to know. I heard that Crook's Wyoming Column is supposed to be coming down the Rosebud towards us, but last time he tried it the Indians forced him to turn back. I'm guessing that we're waiting on more troops, horses and supplies. The 7th Cavalry may be able to field seven, or eight fully mounted companies, at best."

At the mention of the battered condition of the regiment, Caddle looked down at the deck and said solemnly, "Yes, I heard bits and pieces about the fighting. I'm hoping that you fellas will tell me what you know about it, and what happened to my boys in Company I."

Jake and Pat slowly related what they knew, and suspected about what had transpired at the Little Big Horn battle. When they got to the details of the bodies and burials of Company I, Mike had tears streaming down his face. He wiped his eyes and asked, "So where's Milt DeLacy and the other lads that made it?"

"Well, they're still sorting that out." Morse answered, "I've heard that the men left from companies that were with Custer might be combined into one, temporarily. There's a lack of officers, and the new recruits have no horses, so won't take the field. I'll tell Milt to come see you."

"Good, I'd just as soon stay where I'm at. I feel that I'm doing more good, then hanging around camp."

Jake saw a man in civilian clothes that he recognized as the *Far West's* captain, Grant Marsh, coming down the stairs. When he saw them sitting with Caddle, he waved and walked over to them. They all stood as he neared.

"That's not necessary, men!" Marsh said, motioning for them to sit. "I suppose that you're some of Caddie's friends that he's always talked about. Glad to see that you made it."

"Aye, we are too, sir! We were just catching up with Sgt. Caddle, here. He's been telling us about his travels with you on the river."

Marsh grinned and asked, "So, Caddie, are you wanting to go back to being a cavalryman, now? Are you tired of being a Horse Marine?"

Mike grimaced a bit and replied, "Well, there's not much of my company to go back to, sir, and if it's all the same to you, I think that I'd like to stay aboard, I feel useful here."

"Good, I'm sure that Gen. Terry won't mind me keeping you and your lads. By the way, I've just learned that we'll be leaving to go downriver the first thing in the morning. It seems that Major Moore was unable to haul much of the forage supplies from the Powder camp, and we're taking a detail to retrieve it."

Caddle nodded his head, "I'll let my men know, Sir!"

"Well, I'll not interrupt you any longer." Marsh said, tipping his hat. "You men take care."

After he left Jake commented, "He seems like an amiable sort, eh Caddie?"

Mike laughed, "He's called me that since I came aboard, I kind of like it. Marsh treats us well."

"We can see that. Now, have ya got any more of this beer cooling?" Morse asked.

The next morning Aug. 1, shortly after the *Far West* left, the steamer *Carroll* arrived carrying Lt. Col. Otis and six companies of the 22nd Infantry. There was also a Paymaster and several newspapermen. Major James Forsyth, Gen. Sheridan's secretary, was also onboard carrying new orders for Terry to begin construction of two new forts along the Yellowstone. He met with Terry that night and left the next day when the *Carroll*, loaded with sick, wounded, and men with expiring enlistments, started downriver to return to Fort Lincoln. Shortly after it departed, two more riverboats, steamed into view. The *E.H. Durfee* was carrying Col. Nelson Miles and six companies of the 5th Infantry, plus 150 cavalry recruits. The *Josephine* carried supplies, two Rodman 3" artillery pieces, and 64 horses. Terry directed them to unload on the north side of the river. As the 5th unloaded, a sharp contrast was apparent between the disciplined ranks of infantry men in their uniforms fresh from garrison duty and the scruffily dressed men of the Yellowstone column, who wore a mix of patched, faded uniforms blended with some newer items, black, white, and straw hats, plus a sprinkling of buckskin jackets. Col. Miles stood watching, as his men formed up in ranks and marched away to make camp.

****

Colonel Nelson A. Miles

Nelson Miles was born near Westminster, Massachusetts on 18 August 1839. He moved to Boston at age 17. He worked at a crockery shop while attending school at night, and also became a student of a retired French colonel who gave military instruction. When the War broke out, Miles helped recruit men for the Massachusetts 22nd Infantry, and was commissioned as a captain in September 1861, but due to his young age was assigned to the staff of Gen. Oliver Howard. Promoted to Lt. Col. in May 1862, and then Colonel of the 61st New York Infantry in September. He was wounded at the Battle of Fredericksburg and later at Chancellorsville, where he was breveted to Brig. Gen. of Volunteers in May1864. By the end of the war he was in command of the 1st Division, II Corps, and promoted to Maj. General in Oct. 1865. He was then appointed as a Regular Army Colonel in command of the 40th Infantry, a black regiment, and placed in charge of Fort Monroe, Virginia, where Jefferson Davis was being held. Miles married Gen. Sherman's niece, Mary Hoyt Sherman in 1868, and shortly after assumed command of the 5th Infantry in March 1869. His regiment had participated in the Red River campaigns down in Texas, against the Kiowa, Comanche, and Southern Cheyenne where he gained valuable experience fighting Indians. Physically imposing, he was considered somewhat as a maverick and martinet by some of his fellow officers, but was well liked by his men. He had a reputation as a tough, fearless, and competent commander, and was known to embrace innovative tactics and ideas. Sherman had the 5th Infantry ordered up to Montana, from Fort Leavenworth, Kansas, after news of the Custer debacle reached him.

****

Jake stood with several other NCOs watching the riverboats while troops and supplies were being disembarked. He was impressed with the huge quantity of boxes and other items that were accumulating. Nearby, Sutler Smith was setting up shop in a large tent.

"I hear we're going to get paid tomorrow." Morse said, "It sure looks like Smith knows it, too. Things will be hopping around here."

"Well, I for one am ready to sample his wares." Harrison said emphatically.

"Will ya look at those artillery pieces!" Flanagan exclaimed, "I remember those Parrot Rifles from the War. Those things can send a 10 lb. shell out a mile. Mr. Lo is in for a surprise."

"I heard that the 22nd Infantry had a brief scrap with the Sioux as the *Carroll* passed the Powder River. They were seen swarming around our old depot and fired at the boats. Major Moore was sent with 3 infantry companies and a field gun, back down on the *Far West* to retrieve the forage left there. "

Jake wondered our loud, "Why everything is being unloaded on this side of the river? The Sioux and Cheyenne all headed south, shouldn't we be over on the other side? It seems to me that most of this will all have to be moved across for us to go after them. We have enough firepower now that the Indians wouldn't dare attack us."

"Yes, I've heard that Col. Miles of the 5th, has already been critical of Terry's plans." offered Flanagan, "It's gonna be interesting to see how all of these officers get along, many of them were Brevet Generals during the war, lots of egos in the mix. And it does seem that Terry is prone to dither a bit, ever since Custer went off and got his self killed."

"Oh, we'll be moving all right, you needn't worry on that. But it won't be quick. I heard Terry is determined to take a train of over 200 wagons along." Morse said.

Jake raised his eyebrows in astonishment, "Hasn't anyone told him how difficult the Rosebud Valley was for the pack train when we went up it with Custer? It'll be a damn sight worse with wagons."

"I guess he figures that he has enough manpower to blaze a road. Just be glad that we've got plenty of foot soldiers to serve as pioneers." Pat replied.

"Well, at least we won't have to worry about catching the hostiles." Flanagan said disgustedly, "I'm pretty damn sure that they won't be sitting still waiting on us."

Morse's statement turned out to be prophetic. The next few days were spent jockeying soldiers, horses, wagons and supplies in camps on both sides of the river. Reno reorganized the 7th Cavalry so it could field eight companies, in two battalions: Benteen with Companies H, G, M, & C. (C had been reconstituted with the veteran remnants from the other companies) and Weir would have Companies A, B, K, & D. Company D had a new lieutenant, Edwin P. Eckerson, who was a retread from the 5th Cavalry, so he at least had some field experience. The remainder of the dismounted men, including the fresh replacements, were used to fill out the ranks of Companies E, F, I, & L, and would be left at Fort Beans. The regimental band was being sent back to Fort Lincoln on the *Josephine,* along with the men whose enlistments were expiring, this included Sgt. Tom Harrison. Morse's platoon had a going away party for Harvey Fox and the Kentuckians Tom Stivers, Billy Harris, and George Scott. Surprisingly their fellow corn cracker, Jimmy "Peaches" Hurd re-enlisted, claiming that he'd still rather soldier than go back to plowing tobacco fields. Two new men, John Quinn and William Sadler, who had been at the Powder River Depot were assigned to the depleted "set of four". Sadler, a German, ironically was actually a saddler, and replaced the late unfortunate Vincent Charlie.

The riverboats brought newspapers in addition to reporters. The articles were the first that any of the officers and men of the 7th Cavalry had a chance to read, and revealed how the fight on the Little Bighorn was perceived back east. It quickly became apparent to them how controversial it already was. Reno in particular felt that he was being unfairly blamed for Custer's demise. He asked to be interviewed by James O'Kelly, from the New York Herald, and issued a pointed letter of rebuttal. Benteen was also interviewed but downplayed his role, deferring to Reno, his commander. Many campfire discussions by both officers and enlisted ranks, speculated about what had actually transpired, with many partisan theories and perspectives espoused. As the days drag ged on the weather was hot, dry, and the wind deposited dust everywhere, which did nothing to improve the dispositions of the men. The ready access to alcohol and lack of activity exacerbated the situation and discipline was deteriorating when finally on Aug. 6, the 7th Cavalry the last regiment to be ferried across the Yellowstone went into camp about a mile up the Rosebud. The following day was spent finalizing plans and getting the wagon train organized.

At 5:00 AM on Aug. 8, the Yellowstone Column consisting of over 1,700 officers, men, packers, and scouts moved out of camp heading south. The scouts and the 2nd Cavalry led the advance, with the infantry securing the flanks on both sides of the wagon train, and the 7th Cavalry serving as rear guard. The terrain immediately proved to be an obstacle. The wagons struggled to make progress and it was 6:30 before the 7th cleared the camp perimeter. The day warmed quickly as the wagons crept forward along the route, waiting for bridges to be thrown up, or banks to be cut down by the pioneer parties. In the mean time most of the soldiers sat motionless, baking in the merciless sun which had caused the temperature to rise to 111 degrees in the shade. After traveling an arduous 9 1/2 miles, Terry decided to call a halt at 2:00 PM, when a decent bivouac area with shade was reached. He sent out a party of Crow scouts to attempt contact with

Gen. Crook. During the afternoon, clouds began building on the horizon and that night heavy rains fell. Dawn brought chill temperatures, and after breaking camp at 4:45, the column resumed its advance with the Benteen's battalion of the 7th out front. In addition to encountering the same terrain obstacles, light rain began falling later in the morning and a fierce north wind sprang up. The pace was so slow that small fires were lit for the men to warm by as they crept along, the temperatures having dropped by over 60 degrees from the previous day. They reached the vicinity of one of the abandoned Indian encampments that the 7th had found on their way up the Rosebud with Custer, seven weeks earlier. It was late afternoon when the Crow scouts that Terry had dispatched came galloping back, bearing news that a large body of hostiles was coming down the valley towards them. Benteen sent two of his companies forward, while the wagons were closed up and the rest of the command prepared for an attack. When no Indians materialized, Terry elected to go into bivouac and instructed his officers to take defensive precautions. After a cold, nervous night, the Yellowstone Column resumed its march again, with Weir's battalion out front. Terry had been unable to persuade any of the Crows to carry a message through to Crook, but they did agree to screen the trail immediately ahead. The column found a few more of the abandoned Sioux and Cheyenne campsites later that morning. The valley was beginning to widen when the Crows came dashing back crying out that the Sioux were coming. A large cloud of dust could be seen behind a hill to the south. Weir made a quick decision to deploy his men in a mounted skirmish line and the order was passed back along the column. Commands rang out as the companies began to deploy

"Okay, lads, you know the drill, check to see that you're loaded and have your ammo handy!" Morse called out to his platoon.

Jake quickly looked over to his section, making eye contact with Holden who gave him a reassuring nod. He saw that the rest of them were checking their weapons, and tightening their reins in preparation. Charlie Welch nervously settled his hat down on his head.

"Make sure the men maintain intervals and stay on line!" Morse called over to Jake and Tom Russell.

Weir spurred his mount forward, Company D and the battalion spread out on both sides of the trail behind him. As they moved to a gallup and advanced on the hill ahead, a lone figure appeared on top of it, stopped and began waving a big white hat. Weir signaled for the rest of the battalion to halt, and then rode slowly forward as the rider came down the hill. Waves were exchanged as they got closer to each other and Jake saw them both lean over to shake hands as they met. Weir wheeled his horse and they both came riding back. When they got closer, Jake saw that the strange rider was dressed all in buckskins, with tall knee high boots. The wide brimmed hat that he'd been waving sat atop his shoulder length hair and a long flowing mustache with a neatly trimmed goatee adorned his smiling face. He was having an animated conversation with Weir.

"Well, damn me if that ain't ol' Bill Cody!" Morse exclaimed.

When they reigned up, Weir stood up in his stirrups, waved his hat and shouted, "Boys! Here's Buffalo Bill! He's scouting for Gen. Crook!"

A call for three cheers went out, and Jake joined in. Cody eased his horse forward and called out. "How ya been, Pat? Glad to see you still got your hair!"

Morse grinned broadly, "You too, Bill, although mine ain't near as pretty as yours! Good ta see you! What's it been, 6 years ago, back down in Kansas? I heard that you'd given up bein' a scout and were a showman now."

"Oh, I came back west needing a break from all that. Somehow I got persuaded to sign on with Major Carr and the 5th Cavalry. Col. Merritt took over from him back in July, and we just hooked up with Gen. Crook last week, so now I'm scoutin' for him."

Jake, who had read many of the dime novels featuring Buffalo Bill, was surprised to see how young the man appeared. He took note of the heavy Sharps rifle in its elaborate beaded scabbard, and the shiny Scofield .44 revolver in the fancy holster that he carried.

Cody noticed Jake eyeing his weapons and said. "I see that's a fancy rifle you're totin' there, Sarge. You must be a good shot if they let you carry it."

"Well, I'm sure that I'm not in your class, Mr. Cody, but I most generally hit what I aim at." Jake replied, slightly in awe of the man.

Bill laughed, "Nothing wrong with that. What's your name?"

"Jake Rogers, Sir!"

"Oh, you just call me, Bill." Turning back to Pat, he asked. "I'm bettin' that you might know where a man might find some whisky in that big wagon train, eh Pat? That damn Crook runs a lean outfit."

Pat laughed, "I'm sure that we can find a wee drop somewhere, Bill!"

"Well, let me go see your General Terry. Crook's camped about 6 miles up ahead, and I'm to guide you boys to him. I'll come look you up later!" he called, as he turned his horse to follow Weir back towards the main column.

Crook's column consisted of 1800 soldiers, 250 Indian allies and 200 packers and volunteers, had taken the field five days earlier after the arrival of the 5th Cavalry from Nebraska. Crook stripped his entire command down to the bare essentials. They had no tents and his men carried only blankets, overcoats, and few personal effects. When Terry rode in with his staff and found Crook having a lunch of bacon and hardtack, he was invited to join him. When Crook's men saw the Yellowstone column's huge wagon train as it went into bivouac below them they looked on in envy. Many of the officers of both columns knew one another and quickly made plans to dine together that night in the luxury of field tents, many of them with carpets. Terry and Crook dined together and discussed their plans for combining the two columns.

Bill Cody had shown back up, along with his side kick Jonathan White, and was entertaining Pat and everyone gathered around a large fire later that evening. He regaled them with stories about his journeys and adventures as several bottles were shared around. Bill had just finished telling the story of the fight with the Cheyenne at Warbonnet Creek three weeks earlier, and how he had personally killed a young warrior, Yellow Hair, when two other scouts showed up, Bill introduced them.

"These here gents are Buckskin Jack Russell and Captain Jack Crawford, two of the finest scouts roaming these parts, 'ceptin' for me o'course! Captain Jack just now caught up with us carrying dispatches for General Crook from Fort Fetterman. Come on boys, take a seat!"

"Damn, you drug out all the old hands for this shindig, Bill. Where's Bill Hickcock?" Morse asked.

"Ah, I heard that he got his self killed, back in Deadwood last week." Crawford stated somberly. "He was in a card game and some deadbeat named, 'Crooked Nose' Jack McCall, snuck up and shot him in the back of the head."

A brief silence hung in the air for a minute, until Bill broke it, by saying, "Well shit fire! At least he went out playing cards, he surely enjoyed gambling! Let's have a drink to Bill!"

The storytelling soon resumed and Jake found their stories fascinating, marveling at the exploits that these men had experienced, and even if you discounted half of it as embellishment on their part, it was still apparent that they were well traveled across the frontier. Cody and the others finally wandered away when the whiskey was gone. Jake retired to his tent and was sound asleep when he was roused by the sounds of a few gunshots, and many pounding hooves off in the direction of Crooks camp. He and Tom Russell jumped up out of their tent and stood listening. Eventually word reached them that some of the 2nd Cavalry mounts had stampeded, but were being pursued, so they went back to sleep.

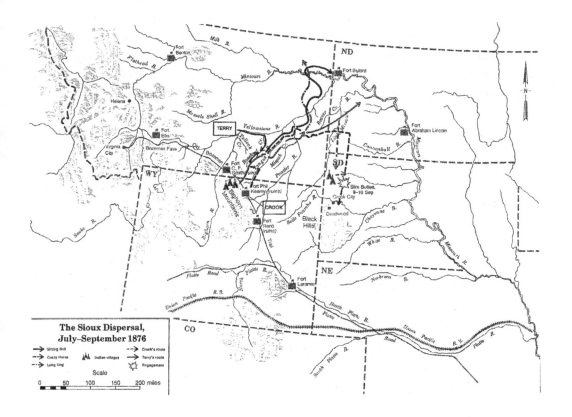

The Sioux Dispersal,
July–September 1876

Scale
0   50   100   150   200 miles

CHAPTER 36

Yellowstone River, North Bank below Wolf Rapids - Montana Territory, August, 1876

General Terry, finally conceding the futility of bringing along the wagon train, had a pack train fitted out again using wagon mules with similar results to his previous efforts. This elicited much derision from Crook's men, who in contrast had a pack train that was a model of precision. Terry detached Col. Miles and the 5th Infantry to take the wagons back up to the Rosebud depot. Once he arrived there, he was tasked with patrolling the fords along Yellowstone, seeking to prevent the Indians from crossing over and going north.

The next three weeks of maneuvering by the combined commands had turned into be a fiasco. The two columns were commanded by almost polar opposites, Terry, the senior in rank, and Crook, a reluctant and stubborn subordinate. Believing that the hostiles were headed east and north they crossed over to the Tongue River attempting to follow the trails back down it. The weather took a turn for the worse shortly after the march was resumed, when cold driving rains arrived. The route was churned into a mass of glutenous mud by the combined command of twenty-five Infantry companies and thirty-six Cavalry companies, accompanied by hundreds of horses and mules. The rains continued to plague them for several days. Expecting the Indian trail to go back up to the Yellowstone, it instead turned east and they reluctantly followed it. The Ree and Crow scouts tried to convince Terry of the futility of following the trails which they assured him were over two weeks old, but Terry, determined to prevent the Indians from crossing the Yellowstone, stayed in pursuit. The weather finally turned better on the 13th as the heat returned, but then they reached the difficult terrain of the Lower Powder River Valley and another deluge caught them that night. Terry had ordered his men to emulate Crook's bare essentials only campaign style. The exhausted soldiers and troopers suffered miserably through it all with no shelter. They made camp on the 16th, near Locate Creek, where the 7th had bivouacked back in May. Desperately needing rations, supplies, and forage for the under nourished animals, Terry directed them to head up to the old supply depot location at the mouth of the Powder. Meanwhile he had dispatched scouts with instructions for the *Far West* to meet them there with supplies. They finally arrived there, stumbling and staggering into camp. The list of sick, many with scurvy and dysentery, was appalling and morale hit rock bottom when the anticipated riverboat was no where to be seen.

Fortunately, Col. Miles arrived with the steamboat later that afternoon, returning from a quick reconnaissance up stream to the Tongue River ford. A quick inventory of the supplies he had on board was taken and they were found to be woefully insufficient for the needs of the weary soldiers. After unloading, Miles proceeded downstream to check on the garrison he had posted on the north bank at Glendive Creek, then ran back upriver to the Rosebud depot to close it down and bring back the remaining supplies. The wagon train was already making its way down the north bank trail. The two columns hunkered down in primitive, separate bivouacs on opposite sides of the Powder, where both were assailed by a series of thunderstorms, strong winds, and grassfires while waiting to be resupplied. Terry and Crook continued to bicker about how the campaign should be renewed and where the hostiles were to be found. Meanwhile couriers continued to trickle in bringing news that the trail of the Sioux and Cheyenne indicated that they had splintered into several bands, heading in opposite directions. The *Carroll* arrived on Aug. 21, followed by the *Josephine* and the *Yellowstone* on the 25th. The latter two were also loaded with construction materials for a stockade that Sheridan had ordered to be built at the Tongue River confluence.

Fortunately, the arrival of the riverboats and their supplies alleviated the lack of rations for the soldiers and several traders also came downriver from Fort Ellis, in Mackinaw boats loaded with goods and liquor. The wagon train arrived across the river from the Rosebud on the 23rd, and Terry's men were able to collect their tents and extra gear. The mail brought up by the steamers was also distributed.

1st Sgt. Martin had scrounged up a tent to use as company HQ and was passing out mail, after morning formation.

"Rogers! You have several letters here!" he called out.

Jake stepped forward and took them, "Thanks Top." he said as he tucked them under his rubber poncho then headed back to his tent to get out of the drizzle and cool wind. He was thankful to have a tent again after the rigors of having to endure the miserable conditions, since leaving the

Rosebud, with only his blanket, poncho, and overcoat. He'd been fortunate to buy a new shirt, underclothes, and socks from one of the traders, so even though his uniform was faded and patched, he was relatively clean.

Once he got settled on his cot he took the letters and laid them out.

He had several from Holly, and they were filled with her concern for him. The post at Leavenworth was all abuzz waiting for news about the 5th Infantry that had been sent up to the Yellowstone. She related little anecdotes about her travails at school, and her frustrations over boarding with the Goodfellow's snippy daughters. She closed as always with a declaration of her love and that she was praying for his safe return.

His mother's letter expressed her relief in receiving his letter, assuring her that he was safe. She detailed the news around home and how his Father was getting ready for the harvest. He did note that she made a special point to say that Frank and Colleen were going to get married, and also that he should write more often.

There was also a letter from Vanessa. She disclosed that she had contacted Capt. Hale who let her know that Jake was not on any of the casualty lists, and expressed her pleasure and relief in finding that out. She noted some of the interesting reactions that she'd overheard from some of the railroad people and politicians that she encountered. She ended with a cryptic comment about the possibility of making a trip west, later in the fall. Jake was reflecting on all of this when Tom Russell ducked his head in.

"Hey, Jake! I just heard that Milt DeLacy is being court-martialed this afternoon. That new Lieutenant, Garlington, is the Judge Advocate and he has assigned Capt. Weir as to preside over it."

"What in the hell did Milt do?"

"Well, it seems that he left the camp at the Rosebud without permission and has been aboard the *Far West*. He's charged with being AWOL, along with conduct against military order and discipline."

"Let's go see Top and see if he knows anything about it." Jake said, stashing the letters in his haversack.

Jake, Tom, and Pat, walked over to where the proceedings were to take place under a large cottonwood and saw Milt sitting on a barrel, under guard. He waved at them to come over.

"What's all his about you being AWOL, Milt?" Jake asked.

DeLacey replied, "It's all bullshit! When Col. Miles came back to the Rosebud depot and got things moving, I was onboard the *Far* West visiting with Mike Caddle. I was tired of sitting on my ass nursing recruits, so when they cast off, I stayed. George Gaffney, the Quartermaster Sergeant is in charge of the Company I troops, stayed with Mike to help out. That damned

DeRudio was the only officer from the 7th in camp. He was commanding Company E, and got pissed when he found out what I'd done. He said that I didn't clear it with him and he's the one that filed charges."

"That damn jumped up little Italian prick! He's always stirring up shit. We'll go talk with Capt. Weir." Pat stated firmly, "He'll be on your side. I'm sure that he'll remember that you and your lads pitched in with us up on that damn hill, while DeRudio was hiding down in the bushes."

The court-martial turned out to be a farce. Pat had been correct in his assessment of Weir's position. After the proceedings began, the charges were read, then Weir called an adjournment, taking DeLacy aside and questioning him. After hearing DeRudio and the other witnesses, Weir ruled that DeLacy was guilty and fined him $10, recommending that the sentence be suspended. After DeRudio stalked away, Capt. Weir, who had purchased a demi-john of whiskey from one of the traders, invited DeLacy and his NCOs to share a drink.

"Well, DeLacey, you'd best go see Capt. Nowlan, he's to take over Company I as soon as we get in from the field. Tell him your side and have him come see me if he has any questions." Weir advised.

The recent rains had raised the level of the Powder to where it was impractical to ford, hampering communications between the two commands. Resupplied with 15 days rations Crook, who as commander of the Dept. of Wyoming was more concerned about the hostiles headed south, decided to go back up the Powder to pick up the trail. Unfortunately, his Shoshone and Crow scouts, dissatisfied with the course of the campaign elected to depart for home. Bill Cody had left him earlier and was being utilized as a messenger up and down the river working for Gen. Terry, leaving Crook with only with a few civilian guides. Suddenly on Aug. 24, Crook, dissatisfied with what he considered Terry's indecisive plans, took the opportunity to head back up the Powder and his column floundered through the mud for 9 1/2 miles. Terry was taken by surprise, but determined to follow Crook. He used the riverboats to transfer the cavalry across the mouth of the Powder to follow Crook's trail, and the next day started south with the infantry on the east bank. Terry was only three miles from catching up with Crook when Bill Cody arrived bearing dispatches. They warned of the presence of a large number of hostiles threatening the 5th Infantry detachment downriver, at Glendive Creek. Terry rode to Crook's camp and informed him that he would take his column overland to try and intercept the Sioux there, while Crook continued his pursuit to the south. The next day Terry's column made a quick oblique march of 28 miles across a grassy plateau and arrived back at the Yellowstone near O'Fallon's Creek. Terry and his staff returned to the Powder Depot where four riverboats were tied up there waiting to ferry the wagon train back to the north bank. The next day, Aug. 27th, Terry used the riverboats to cross his entire command over the Yellowstone, and took them 7 miles downstream to an area of low hills with good grass.

Company D boarded the *Carroll* about 7:00 AM, to be ferried across the Yellowstone. Jake tied Ajax to a picket rope, then moved over to the railing to watch the passing river bank. He saw Captain Michaelis standing nearby using a crutch and went over to him.

"Good day, Sir! I see that you've been injured. Nothing too serious I hope."

"Ah, Sgt. Rogers! I'm glad to see you again. Yes, I had a slight incident with a rattle snake and my horse threw me. Nothing that a little rest won't hurt. Gen. Terry is sending me back to St. Paul to get it looked at." Michaelis replied.

"Well, I hope it heals well, Sir. I still have your rifle and I have to say that it came in handy on an occasion or two. It's on my horse over there. Do you want me to go get it?"

The captain was silent for a bit, as if considering Jake's question, then said, "You know Rogers, that rifle was sent to me for evaluation by Sharps. I will send them an excellent report about it, thanking them. You're still in the field and it'll be of more use being carried by you, so why don't you hang on to it. If it creates a problem, I know where to find you."

Jake smiled, and said, "Thank you, Sir! I don't know what to say other than I'll take good care of it."

"I've no doubt about that, Sergeant. Gen. Terry told me that he intends to try and intercept the Sioux to prevent them from going north. It may come in handy again."

The troopers spent the rest of the day tending their mounts and enjoyed a meal of fresh beef. However, Terry, anxious to get the column moving, ordered a march late that afternoon by the 7th. Lacking knowledgeable scouts familiar with the countryside, and after 6 1/2 miles of moving in the dark across a featureless, rolling terrain, the command went into a dry camp on the prairie. The next day an early start found them seeking water along Bad Route Creek, and the next several days were spent blundering across the hills with the few remaining scouts, including Cody, more intent on seeking out water than Indian trails. Fortunately, wild game was in abundance and the column encountered a large buffalo herd, managing to kill over 50 of them, along with a dozen antelope. Unknowingly, the shooting alerted a band of Sioux, led by a chief called

Long Dog, which they inadvertently passed to the north of by only a couple of miles. The Sioux then quickly slipped away to the west. When the soldiers reached the headwaters of the Bad Route, Terry had the column swing northeast until they came to Deer Creek. He sent Reno and the 7th to scout down towards the Yellowstone and in the direction of Fort Buford, searching for river crossings. Terry, accompanied by the infantry units, followed Deer Creek back down to the Yellowstone and went into bivouac just across from the Glendive Cantonment. Several riverboats had just arrived there and were carrying supplies for the new Tongue River Cantonment that Col. Miles and the 5th Infantry were building. Major Moore and the wagon train also arrived from Powder River and when Reno returned on the Sep. 2nd, the original units of the Dakota/Yellowstone columns were reunited. Finally, on the 5th, Terry made the decision to terminate the long, disastrous and fruitless summer campaign. Col.Gibbon, the 7th Infantry, and the 2nd Cavalry left to return to their western posts. Col. Miles and his 5th Infantry loaded their own wagons and headed back to the Tongue, along the south bank. General Terry and the remainder of his staff including Bill Cody, boarded the *Josephine* to go downriver to Fort Buford accompanied by the *Far West*. Major Reno and the 7th Cavalry, along with three companies of the 6th Infantry, were assigned to march along the north bank of the Yellowstone towards Fort Buford watching the river crossings. On Sep. 9, a belated report reached Terry, at Fort Buford, that Long Dog's band had been sighted near Wolf Point up on the Missouri River. He sent a courier with orders directing Reno to head north across the divide to investigate. The courier arrived just as the 7th was breaking camp on Sep.10. Reno delayed leaving while he conferred with his remaining scouts and found that none knew the overland route.

Jake and Pat were checking out the platoon's saddles and tack while they waited.

1st Sgt. Martin called out. "Morse, Rogers, the captain wants to see you. He's over talking to Major Reno."

They found Weir with Reno and several scouts, poring over a map spread across table behind one of the ambulance wagons.

"You wanted us, Sir?" Morse said.

"Ah, Sgt. Morse, Sgt. Rogers! Yes, we've been ordered to cut across to the Missouri River at a place called Wolf Point. It seems that there's no one that knows the route."

Reno stood and looked at the two NCOs, "As I recall, you two spent some time pathfinding with Lt. Greene when we were on Boundary Escort Duty, the year before last."

Morse replied, "Yes, sir!" then nudged Jake towards the map.

"Well, come look at this map, though there's not a lot of details on it. I want to head on the most direct route." Reno said.

They moved to the map, and Jake saw that most of the finer details were closer in to the actual river courses, but the spaces in between were relatively blank. He studied it closely, moving his finger to where someone had marked a location as Wolf Point.

"We don't know how accurate that is." Weir stated.

Jake took out his compass and checked the maps orientation, he picked up a nearby ruler and laid it down to designate a direct course towards the mark. He laid his compass down and orientated it.

"Well, there's our azimuth if this map was to scale, but we could come out miles from where it actually is, depending on how closely we can hold our direction on the march. We passed near there, on our way up to the Milk River along the north bank of the Missouri. There's some rough country on the south bank, as I recall. This map shows some creek branches flowing in that direction. Our best bet would be to find one of them, follow it and hope it comes out close." Jake said tracing the route with his finger.

Reno studied the map then looked up at Jake, "It seems that you picked up a trick or two from Lt. Greene, Sergeant."

"Yes, sir!" Jake replied, "I also learned a lot from our main scout, Val Wheeler."

"Yes, I seem to recall that name. A half breed, wasn't he?"

"Irish and Gross Ventre, sir!"

"Very well, you can go now. Weir, your company has the advance until we get up there. I want these two men out front."

Jake and Pat Morse led the advance party across a burned over prairie, courtesy of the fleeing hostiles. They came to a creek about 10 miles out that had halted the grass fire, and after crossing it, they followed it north until they found a bivouac area with good grass and plenty of wood, just below two pointed buttes. The following morning, clouds and heavy mist blocked the view of any points they might use to sight a compass, so they blundered forward in the rain, using a rough map they'd traced off, and a compass bearing. The route led them across a featureless plain with few trees. After making several attempts to find a suitable campsite, they settled down for a cold rainy night in a small grove of trees along a dry creek bed. The next day the rain and mist lingered as the march was resumed. Mid-morning, the prairie turned into badlands and the column struggled through them. Fortunately the fog lifted and the timbered banks along the Missouri River could be seen in the distance ahead. After reaching the bottomlands, they went west to the confluence of the Redwater River, which according to the map put them east of Wolf Point, and made camp. Retracing their steps, they marched west 16 miles the next morning and finally arrived at the Wolf Point Agency. There the agent, a Mr. Thomas Hughes, told them that Long Dog and his band had crossed over the previous week, and were headed to Canada. The only Indians there were peaceful Assiniboines, who were busy hunting buffalo. It turned out that Joe Leighton, the trader and agent, was at the agency making arrangements with Hughes. He informed Reno that Gen. Terry was due to arrive on the steamer *John M. Chambers*, probably the next day, so Reno directed his weary soldiers to make camp along the river, to wait for its arrival. Some of the men fished, while others were sent out hunting to help supplement the dwindling rations.

"Damn, that was a good steak, Jake!" Pat sighed, as he patted his belly, "I couldn't hardly see that deer and you dropped him dead in his tracks."

The NCOs were gathered around the fire where the buck that Jake had shot had been cooked, enjoying some coffee.

Jake grinned, and replied, "Well, I knew I had to or you would've let me hear about it for days."

"None the less, that was some fine shooting today, Rogers." 1st Sgt. Martin said

"Maybe when we get across the river, we'll run on to some buffalo."

"So, do you think that we're done chasing after the damn Sioux now, Top?" asked Flanagan.

"Aye, we aren't ever gonna catch 'em anyway, they'll be across the Medicine Line by now. We've a fair piece of marching to do to just to get back to Fort Lincoln before the end of the month, and I'm expecting a frost any day."

"So what do you think will happen when we get back?" Jake asked.

"It'll be the same old routine for us. But the officers will be jockeying for promotions. Hell, they already are, Henry Bender, the new First Sergeant of Company L told me that Lt. Godfrey is hot to get command over Company L."

"Well, that's not all bad." said Pat, "He showed well during the Washita fight, and again on the Little Big Horn."

"Indeed!" said Martin, "But there's many slots to fill and you know how those officers are. I've heard Reno is after the Lt. Colonelcy, and Benteen maybe his Majority."

"God! I hope not!" Tom Russell swore loudly.

"Oh, I think that our Major Reno hasn't yet realized that someone has to be blamed for the whole fiasco." Pat stated, "Col. Sturgis lost his boy and I'm sure he'll be will be wanting some answers. I expect we'll see him when we get to Lincoln. Things will get lively then."

Jake spoke up, "From the newspapers that I've seen, the press back home is busy stirring the pot. Gen. Rosser, who was Custer's old classmate and friend, has already gone on record blaming Reno in one article that I read."

"Well, at least they can't point fingers at Capt.Weir." said Pat. "He tried to follow Custer's orders."

The next day was Sep. 15 and around noon the riverboat arrived with Gen. Terry and badly needed supplies. Learning that the Sioux were long gone, Terry declared that the campaign was now officially over and arranged for the steamer to transfer all of the soldiers to the north bank of the Missouri. Reno originally intended to march as soon as the supplies were distributed, but when it was discovered that Joe Leighton had a load of goods including food and liquor on board, he changed his mind. The next morning, a light frost heralded the coming change in season. The companies of the 6th Infantry soldiers were embarked on the boat to return to Fort Buford, where they would winter. The 7th Cavalry began its march back down along the Missouri and made about 30 miles before bivouacking . They were pleasantly surprised when they met the steamer, *Benton* coming upstream and it stopped to drop off mail. The *John M, Chambers* which had gone aground on a sandbar earlier, also stopped and moored by them that night. When the regiment set out the next morning, they were surprised to find that Weir was now in command. During the evening, Reno, along with his new adjutant Lt. Wallace, had gone on the riverboat and somehow finagled his way aboard to accompany Terry and his staff down to Fort Lincoln.

After reaching Fort Buford, on Sep18, they exchanged the pack train for wagons, and were able to visit the post traders store. Jake and Pat were familiar with the overland route along the Missouri on over to old Fort Berthold, and then down to Fort Stevenson from their time returning from the Boundary Survey two years earlier. Weir had them roam out along the trail ahead, looking for game and scouting out campgrounds. The regiment, accompanied by a well supplied wagon train, proceeded at a comfortable but brisk pace. The entire command was anxious to get home as the occasional morning frosts reminded them that the fall equinox was already upon them. Except for a few showers, the weather held and they made it to Fort Stevenson on Sep 23, to re-provision and visit the post traders store. Weir and some of the other officers had an impromptu get together at the fort and some of them, including Weir, got so inebriated that they had to be hauled back by an ambulance wagon. The next morning the column struck out for Bismarck and Fort Lincoln, 60 miles to the south. The trail cut across a big bend in the river then ran along the edge of the river bluffs the rest of the way. They bivouacked on Turtle Creek just below the old Fort Mandan ruins and the next day began to encounter a few ranches and farmsteads where some men were able to buy fresh milk and chickens. Weir decided to camp short of Bismarck to allow the men to freshen up, clean their uniforms as best they could, and take extra time grooming their mounts in preparation for their arrival.

"We should be in Bismarck by early afternoon, tomorrow. It will be interesting to see what kind of reception we get." said Tom, as he hung his tattered uniform blouse on a bush to dry.

Jake was sitting on his saddle near their tent re-reading a letter from Holly, and said as he looked up. "I expect that most folks will be happy to have us back, at least the merchants and bar keeps."

"Well, I for one will be glad to have a solid roof over my head. Just think, we only have to walk a short ways to get to your friend, Mr. Seip, and a cool beer."

Jake frowned and pointed to Holly's letter. "It seems that Bob is no longer the Post Trader, at Fort Lincoln and isn't doing too well. According to what she's heard from her Aunt Kate, he was replaced because of the scandal. They are still in Bismarck, and he's having trouble selling his inventory and paying off his partners."

"Well, whoever replaced Bob, I'll bet having us back will boost his business. Especially when we receive all of the new recruits that are rumored to be on their way to us."

"I'm having a hard time imagining what things will be like at Lincoln without the Custer's and their clique. I met Col. Sturgis, in St. Louis last year, he's a bit older and didn't strike me as much of a socializer."

"Yes, I'm sure the pecking order, is going to be quite different." Tom stated.

CHAPTER 37

Fort Abraham Lincoln, Dakota Territory - September 26, 1876

The return of the 7th Cavalry to Fort Abraham Lincoln was in marked contrast with its departure back in May. There was no band or crowd of spectators on hand to welcome them. The citizens of Bismarck watched in silence as the column of eight companies rode through town. There were a few locals that waved at them from the sidewalks as the worn and dusty troopers made their way down to the riverfront, where they would wait their turn to board the ferry over to the fort. Major Reno and his acting adjutant Lt. Wallace were waiting at the Fort Lincoln riverboat landing where Capt. Weir formally reported the regiments return. Reno ordered the companies that had been in garrison at Lincoln, to return to their barracks, and the balance of the regiment went into the encampment just south of the fort from which it had departed back in May.

The returning men were pleasantly surprised to find that barracks and stables had been cleaned up by the dismounted detachments who had returned from the field on the riverboats. After overseeing his section as they cared for their horses and watching them get settled into the barracks, Jake headed to his own room over in the NCO quarters. He slung his battered haversack over his shoulder and started down the company street, surveying the parade ground and surrounding buildings as he walked. The houses along Officer's Row had all of their window and door frames painted black and the Post flag was at half mast. He looked north towards the Post Trader buildings and wistfully noted that the house had been painted a different color. He wondered what had become of Bob and Kate, and made a mental note to inquire as to their whereabouts. He saw several men sitting on the porch of his quarters and as he drew nearer, one of them waved at him, and called out.

"Lookee here! If it ain't ol' Jake Rogers!"

Jake saw that it was Mike Caddle, and grinned, "Mike, when did you back?"

"I've been back about a week. Captain Marsh brought in the *Far West*, and us horse marines had to come back to the cavalry. I'm glad to see that you finally made it back okay. Hey, why don't you get cleaned up, and after supper, we'll go up to the bar and drink some beer?"

"You bet! It'll probably take me about an hour to get these layers of dirt off, and I need to find some clean clothes."

"No problem, Jake! I saw to it that you and Tom's footlockers were put up in your room."

"Thanks, I'll see you in a while."

The post trader's bar was doing a booming business for a Tuesday night. Tom had decided to join them also, and when they arrived, they had to shoulder their way through the crowd, to get to the bar. Jake recognized the bartender, Joe, who had worked for Bob. He waved at him and called out.

"Hey Joe! How about a round of beers ?"

"Hey Jake! Glad to see you made it back okay."

As Joe began drawing the beers, Jake leaned across the bar and said, "I hear that you've got a new boss."

"Yeh, all that Belknap business that Custer helped stir up cost Bob his appointment as post trader. The new man's name is William Harmon, he's an ex-Army officer and well connected. He worked for that Durfee & Beck outfit, running the trading post for them down river at Standing Rock. His wife Zoe Lulu is half Sioux, and her mother is said to be very influential with the tribes."

"That's interesting, is he around? I'd like to meet him."

"Not right now, he just left to go over to the Officer's Club. They're having a big get together tonight, most all of the officers will be there."

Jake nodded his head, "Okay, I'll catch him another time. Any idea where I can find Bob And Kate?"

Joe pushed the foamy mugs of beer over to Jake, and replied, "They're over in Bismarck staying at the Merchant's Hotel. Bob is still settling up with Mr. Harmon over the merchandise inventories. He told me that once he's he done that, he's thinking about partnering up in a hardware store, selling goods to the miners bound for the Black Hills."

"Thanks, Joe, I'll have to go see them."

Jake carried the beers over to a table that Tom had secured for them, and they spent the next hour or so comparing their stories from the campaign with Mike, who had seen other perspectives from aboard the *Far West*. They all agreed that the worst thing about the end of the campaign would be the reinstitution the grinding garrison routines. After several rounds, they called it a night and started back down towards their quarters. As they walked along the road, they heard a commotion coming from over by the Officer's Club. The door burst open, illuminating several figures who emerged on the porch, and there was loud shouting going on.

"Looks like the officers are having a little ruckus. Let's sneak over there and see what's going on." Mike suggested.

They left the road and crossed over behind the hospital, to where they had a clear view of the well lit club entrance, and could see a disheveled Major Reno swaying drunkenly and cursing at Lt. Varnum. The lieutenant was standing between Reno and an Infantry officer, who was shouting back at Reno, while being restrained by several others. Varnum appeared to be trying to mediate the situation.

"I want Lt. Manley out of here!" yelled Reno, "Don't you try and intervene on his behalf, Varnum, that will make it a personal matter between us!"

Capt. Weir emerged from the doorway and went over to Reno, put his hand on his shoulder and said, "Look now, Marcus, just settle down and shake hands with Varnum."

Reno shrugged off Weir's hand, and when Varnum proffered his, Reno shouted, "I'll not shake hands! Manley has insulted me, and now Varnum is taking his part! Let's send for some pistols and we'll settle this right now!"

One of the other officers stepped forward and called out loudly, "There will be no guns here. If I see you with a pistol, Major Reno, I will be obliged to place you under arrest!"

Reno glared at the officer, and asked haughtily, "Who the hell are you?"

"I'm Lt. Robinson, posted as the Officer of the Guard for today, Sir. I just transferred in from the 3rd Cavalry."

Weir quickly drew Reno aside and persuaded him to go back inside, and the rest slowly followed. Jake, Mike, and Tom quietly retraced their steps back towards their quarters.

"Well, that was interesting." Tom said when they were out of hearing range.

Mike replied, "The newspapers, are full of different scenarios and speculations about what happened to Custer, some of them are placing the blame on Reno for not going to his aid."

"Yes, I suppose that a case may be made for that, but it was a bit more complicated, eh Tom?" Jake stated.

Jake and Pat broke out their civilian clothes and went over to Bismarck to meet up with Murray Johnson that weekend. The railroad man was anxious to hear their version of the campaign, and had sent over an invitation for them to meet him for supper at Forster's. When they arrived they found Murray ensconced at his usual table and he waved at them as they came through the door.

"Well, I'm glad to see that you two came out unscathed, although you both look like you lost some weight. Have a seat, I'm buying!"

"Thanks, Murray! You look the same. How's things on the railroad?" Pat asked.

"Busy, busy! Particularly with all the Army traffic coming this way. Nothing like a little war to stir things up!" Murray smiled, and waved to the waitress, "Sadie, fix these two up with what ever they want."

Over the next couple of hours, and the best meal that they'd had in months, Murray plied them with questions about their experiences. They went over the events of the campaign, while Murray listened thoughtfully.

"It sounds like you were damn lucky that Benteen insisted that he wanted your company to go with him that morning." Murray stated.

"Aye, twas a near thing, it was. When I think about how we found Custer and the others, I shudder to think." Pat exclaimed, and quaffed the rest of his beer.

"So what went on back here, Murray?" Jake asked.

"Pretty much business as usual. The miners headed for the Black Hills have been a bonanza for the local merchants. They've been pouring in since you left, even when the news broke about Custer, it didn't slow them. Funny ain't it, if Custer hadn't found gold down there, he'd probably still be alive!"

"So, have you heard any good rumors about what the Army is planning?" Pat asked.

"Well, Grant is said to be furious, and has given Gen. Sherman free rein to mobilize all available troops. Col. Miles is building two new forts along the Yellowstone River and will stay in the field all winter. It's rumored that Sherman and Sheridan are planning a massive campaign to subjugate the Sioux and Cheyenne. I've heard from a very reliable source that there is a plan in the works to confiscate the ponies and firearms down at the Standing Rock and Cheyenne River Agencies. It's been reported that some of the bands that you boys fought at the Little Big Horn have returned to them. Hell, a minor Sioux chief named Kill Eagle, even gave an interview to the Tribune about it this week!"

"You're kidding!" exclaimed Jake.

Murray pointed to a newspaper laying on the table near him, "Read it yourself, it's on the front page." Then slid it across the table to him.

Jake picked it up and scanned the newsprint, he saw that a Commission had reached an agreement with Red Cloud and Spotted Tail for the Black Hills, and that they were discussing the relocation of the Sioux and Cheyenne to the Indian Territory. He also noted that the notorious James/Younger Gang had been shot and captured after trying to rob a bank in Northfield, Minnesota two weeks earlier and read the article to Pat.

"Huh, what do you know? I remember tangling with those boys back during the war." said Pat, "Your Pa and I rode against them, at Little Blue River, during Gen. Price's raid back near the end of '64. They were riding with Todd's guerrillas at the time, after he split from Quantrill. They were some mean sons o' bitches! I wonder what they were doing so far from Missouri?"

"Who knows, and the authorities are pretty sure that Jesse and Frank James got away." Murray said. "They're still scouring the countryside looking for them. They think that they were headed for the southeast Dakota territory."

"Well, they'll be lucky to catch them, those ex-bushwackers are hard riders. We chased them all the way back down to Texas and the Indian Territory, and never caught up with them! " Pat exclaimed.

After they finished eating, Murray suggested that they go over to the new Morton's Club for drinks and cigars. As they entered the saloon Murray lead the way through the dim lighting and cigar smoke back to a sitting area. He gestured to Jake with his head towards one of the tables and commented, "There's Alvin Leighton, and his erstwhile partner John Smith, over there, talking to Bob Seip. I wonder what they're up to, they're all in cahoots you know?"

Jake nodded and said, "I'm going to go over to say hello to Bob. I'll be right back."

As he approached he called out, "Hello, Bob! Good to see you!"

Bob looked up in surprise, "Hello Jake, I'm glad to see that you made it back okay. Kate was watching the casualty lists in the paper, and we never saw your name."

"Yeh, I was lucky and never got a scratch. How is Kate?"

"Kate's fine, she's gone back to Ottumwa, Iowa to see her family. By the way, this is one of her uncles, Joseph Leighton." Bob said, pointing at the man across the table.

Jake looked at him and said, "Good to meet you, sir, and I've met Mr. Smith before, up at the Powder River Depot as I recall." nodding his head at Smith, who nodded back at him in acknowledgement.

Bob looked at Leighton and said, "This is Sgt. Rogers from the 7th Cavalry, Kate and I got to know him over at Fort Lincoln, last year. He became a good friend of your great niece, Holly, and I believe they still maintain a correspondence." Bob added.

Leighton studied Jake for a moment, then said, "Ah, little Holly, I haven't seen her in a couple of years. She's off to school somewhere isn't she?"

Bob answered, "Yes, down at Fort Leavenworth."

"That's good, she's better off down there, she's well placed I trust?"

"Yes, she's staying with Hiram Goodfellow and his daughters."

"So, Sgt. Rogers, did you see any of the fighting that took place?" Smith asked.

"Yes, I was with Capt. Weir, in Benteen's battalion."

"Well, you were fortunate, I saw many of the wounded being loaded on to the *Far West,* at the Rosebud."

"Yes, we were lucky that Capt. Marsh got them back down here so quick."

"I see that you're with Murray Johnson, do you know him well?" Leighton asked, curiously.

"I've known him for a couple of years, we met when he was the railroad agent over at Jamestown."

"He's an interesting fellow, always seems to be very well informed about things."

"Yes, well, the Northern Pacific, connects us all with the East, doesn't it, so he hears a lot of things." Jake stated.

Leighton said tersely, "Yes, I suppose he does. I'm more of a river man myself."

"So Bob, what are you up to these days?" Jake asked.

"I'm just waiting to get settled up with Bill Harmon, over the inventory from the fort. Then, I'm thinking about getting into the hardware business."

Jake noticed Alvin cast a frown at Bob, and sensed that he was intruding. "Well, good to see you Bob, tell Kate hello for me. Nice meeting you Mr. Leighton!" Then turned and went back to join Murray and Pat.

"Leighton doesn't seem to be very fond of you, Murray." Jake said when he sat down."

"Yes, the river men know their days are numbered. Once the Northern Pacific starts building west across the river, and the Indians are subdued, the steamboat business will slowly wither away."

Pat asked, "When do you think that they'll start laying track again?"

"Probably next year, Tom Rosser, who did the survey with Custer back in '73, is rumored to be coming back as head engineer to get things ready."

Pat leaned forward and said, "Any chance that a man like me might come in handy?"

Jake stared at Pat and exclaimed, "What? You're gonna leave the Army?"

"Yes, this last campaign did it for me, I'm getting too old for soldiering! Plus, I suspect that this business with the Indians is going to get uglier. The greedy Indian agents and traders like Leighton over there, have done nothing but lie to them and cheat them. The government has been breaking signed treaties, and is stealing their lands. I don't want to be part of it all, it reminds me of how the British treat the Irish, and why I left home."

Murray said, "I think that you may be right, Pat. Just let me know when your enlistment is up and I'll have a job waiting for you as my field superintendent."

"I didn't know you felt that strongly about it, Pat. I just assumed that you'd re-enlist." Jake said.

"No lad, I'm done! Tis time for me to do something else, and I think working for the railroad will suit me. Come December, I'll take you up on your offer, Murray."

"Consider it done!" Johnson smiled and raised his glass, "Cheers!"

The regiment spent the next several weeks getting re-acclimated to garrison duty, meanwhile 500 new recruits and 500 horses arrived at Fort Lincoln. There was also an influx of new junior officers fresh out of West Point, as the vacancies in the regiment were refilled. Company D received several new men and horses, but the majority went to reconstitute the five companies that had followed Custer up to that ridge above the Little Big Horn River. Capt. Weir had suddenly been ordered east to replace Capt. Benteen on recruiting duty. Benteen was rumored to have lobbied Col. Sturgis to make the switch, siting his separation from his family as a reason. Sturgis was blaming the loss of his son on Custer, and Weir was one of the few surviving Custer favorites, so the switch was made.

Weir called for a meeting with his NCOs to notify them. Jake noticed that he looked haggard and bleary eyed, as he addressed them.

"Well, it looks like I'll be gone for a year or so. 1st Lt. Eckerson will be taking over the company for now, and you'll be getting a new young 2nd Lieutenant named Brewer. I expect that you men will give them your full cooperation."

"Aye, Sir! You can depend on it." 1st Sgt. Martin spoke up. "We'll see that the lads stay in line."

"I'm told that Col. Sturgis will be here in a few weeks, and that he's planning some type of operation, so you'd best get the new men up to speed." Weir paused, then said solemnly, "I expect that the Army is not done investigating what happened up on the Little Big Horn. Company D has nothing to be ashamed of. Tell the truth if you're asked about what I did, or didn't do. You did your duty and followed my orders."

As the sergeants filed out, Weir shook hands with each one of them and exchanged goodbyes. When it was Jake's turn, he shook Weir's hand and looked the captain in the eye.

"Thank you, Sir. I hope that I never disappointed you."

"Rogers, it's been a pleasure watching you mature into a fine soldier. You always seem to exceed my expectations, I hope that you'll continue that progress while I'm away."

Jake was called to the orderly room several days later to find a man from the telegraph office waiting for him, holding an envelope.

"I have a telegram here for Sgt. Jacob Rogers, Company D, 7th Cavalry."

"Okay, I'm Rogers." Jake said, holding out his hand for an envelope.

He opened it and took out a slip of paper that read:

> *Will be in Bismarck, Oct. 6*
> *The Merchant Hotel*
> *Come see me!*
>
> *V. B.*

"Everything okay, Jake?" asked 1st Sgt. Martin.

Jake nodded his head, "Yeh, no problems, Top. Some good news! Say, can I take a couple of days off, later this week? I'll pull extra duty if I need to."

Martin looked and him and smiled, "Oh, I think that I can spare you, but don't wander off too far. I'm hearing rumors that something is in the wind, but your section seems to be looking good."

"No problem, I'll be over in Bismarck."

Merchants Hotel, Bismarck Dakota Territory - 1876

Jake borrowed a valise and made sure that his civilian clothes were cleaned and presentable. He caught Dietrich's afternoon omnibus over to Bismarck at the Post Traders, reaching Bismarck within the hour, then went to Forster's looking for Murray and found him.

"Well, look at you Mr. Rogers! All clean and shiny, what's the occasion?"

Jake sat down and ordered a beer, "I'm sure you remember my lady friend, Vanessa."

"Oh yes, she's hard to forget." Murray grinned.

"Well, she's here, in Bismarck. She sent me a telegram to come see her."

"I see! Hence, you are here."

Jake smiled.

Murray looked at Jake, "Generals Sheridan and Terry arrived here on Wednesday, and left this morning. Sheridan and his secretary, Col. George Forsyth went back east, while Terry left on the *Key West* to tour the Indian Agencies down stream. Something is up!"

"What's that have to do with Vanessa being here?"

"You know what she does for a living, Jake?"

He nodded his head, "Yes, I do. So, you're saying that's why she's here."

Murray looked at him closely and said. "Sheridan just got married last year to Gen. Ruggles' daughter. However, Forsyth is a bachelor, and he makes a good cover as they both enjoy companionship during their travels, particularly when it comes courtesy of the railroads."

Jake replied, "I see."

"Just a word of advice, I would be very circumspect if I were you. Don't go taking her out around town, or to The French Restaurant. She was just there last night, and was seen in their company. It would be best for both of you if maintain a very low profile, Generals tend to be very possessive."

Jake nodded, "Thanks for the heads up Murray, I'll try and be the soul of discretion."

As Jake walked towards the Merchant Hotel, just west of the railroad depot, he looked up and noticed someone standing on the second floor balcony with an umbrella. It was Vanessa, dressed in a pale blue dress, waving at him. She motioned for him to go to a stairwell at the far end of the balcony and waited at the top of the stairs as he climbed them, watching him with a smile.

"My dear Jacob, I'm so glad to see you alive and unhurt!" she exclaimed.

"Hello Vanessa! How are you?" Jake replied.

"Oh, I'm fine, even better now!"

"It goes with saying that I was pleasantly surprised when I got your telegram."

"Well, I was presented with an opportunity to come here, so I took it. Now look how well it worked out. Let's go inside, shall we? I've arranged to have some refreshments up to the room."

Jake followed her down a hallway and as they went through the doorway to her suite, she tossed the umbrella, then twirled into his arms, and hugged him in a fierce embrace. Jake used a foot to push the door shut, then picked Vanessa up and carried her over to the bed. They took turns frantically disrobing each other, and Jake marveled at the sight of Vanessa's exquisite body as she pushed him onto his back."

"Just lay back, I have some particular ways that I want to show you how glad that I am to see you."

"Yes, Ma'am! I'm at your command!"

Later, Jake sat back in bed, while Vanessa brought him some of treats that she'd ordered, and they sampled them while sipping champagne. Jake found her total lack of self consciousness while naked arousing and they soon resumed their lovemaking while Vanessa introduced him to some interesting new positions. Finally spent, they cuddled and Vanessa quietly quizzed him about his experiences during the recent campaign. Jake related some of them without going into the more gruesome details.

"So, what do you think will happen now?" she asked.

"Well, we're waiting for Col. Sturgis to arrive. Then, I think that there are plans being made. Some of the Indian bands that left to roam this summer are being reported by the Agencies, and even in the newspaper. A friend of mine, who is in a position to know, says that the Army is planning to confiscate their pony herds and guns."

Vanessa squeezed him, "Well, your friend is right. Your Gen. Terry has gone to reconnoiter, under the guise of advising the Treaty Commission that finished last week. Now that the tribes have signed over the Black Hills, moves are planned to ensure that the Indians will never be a major threat, again. Particularly, as the Northern Pacific gets ready to move west. Resources are already being marshaled to facilitate that."

"You always amaze me on how well informed you are, Vanessa." Jake said.

"Well, dear boy, it's not like you don't know what I do."

"Yes, but I'm puzzled about why you seek the company of a lowly soldier like me?"

Vanessa sat up, her raven tresses cascading around her shoulders, and let the sheets fall away. Smiling, she reached under them to grasp him.

"Dreary old officers and business men just like to talk most of the time. You, in contrast, are enjoyable. You're a sort of holiday for me, a guilty pleasure if you like." she laughed. "I'm also drawn to you by your innocence, you don't judge me or try to take on airs, you're just Jacob."

"Well, I'll not plead to being totally innocent, but I enjoy being guilty with you. How long are you staying?"

"This is all paid for until Monday, then I'll board the train to head back to St. Paul. Can you stay until then and see me off?"

Jake felt himself responding to her manipulations, and replied, looking down, "That's up to you, My fate is in your hands, so to speak."

Vanessa responded by kissing his chest, working lower as she did, chuckling softly, "I have many ways to convince you."

Jake escorted Vanessa over to the depot Monday morning, carrying her bags. When they got there, Murray was waiting to greet them, and tipped his hat at Vanessa.

"Ah, Miss Blake, a pleasure to see you again!"

"Why thank you Mr. Johnson! St. Louis last year as I recall, wasn't it?"

"Yes, Ma'am, I'm here to see you get aboard and settled in. We have a suite in a Pullman for you. I'll see that your bags are taken on. Is there anything else that I can do for you?"

Jake followed along as Murray escorted Vanessa to her railcar. When they got there Murray said, "I'll leave you to say your goodbyes, Miss Blake." He looked at Jake, "Come look me up before you head back to the fort, Jake." then turned and strode away.

Vanessa watched him walk away, and asked Jake, "I suspect that Mr. Johnson and you are acquaintances, Jacob"

"Yes, we are."

"Excellent, he's a valuable contact, and very well regarded by his superiors."

"Murray is a good friend. He has many connections, and is always well informed about current events."

"Ah! Your well positioned friend! I'm glad to know that. Now I will have a better way of contacting you." Vanessa said grinning, "That is if you still want me to, you've not mentioned your intentions regarding your young friend Holly."

"Whatever they are, I've got a year and a half to figure out." Jake stated, then drew Vanessa to him, and looked her in the eye, "You're here and I count it a blessing to be with you!"

After a long embrace, they kissed and Vanessa drew away, then dabbed her eyes with a kerchief. "Go now dear Jacob, and do be careful, and write me when you can. I watch the newspapers daily and fear for your safety."

Jake walked back along the rail platform, looking for Murray, and found him directing a couple of men towards some railcars. He stood and waited for him to finish up with them, then walked over.

"So, I take it that you know a bit more about Vanessa than you're letting on, Murray?"

Murray looked a Jake with a serious expression, "Well, she's employed by the railroad, so to speak. I was notified to make arrangements for her trip back. I didn't anticipate that you would be part of her itinerary."

"That's okay. It was a surprise to me also."

"Miss Blake is highly thought of in some circles, and is also very intelligent. She provides a valuable service in helping the powers that be to influence clients and make sure investors view the railroads in a positive light. Miss Blake is also rumored to own stock in several of those railroad companies. You probably don't appreciate how extremely fortunate you are in having gained her affections."

"She says that I remind her of her fiancée who was in the British Army and killed down in New Zealand." Jake said.

"Well, count yourself lucky my friend. Now, let's go have lunch and I'll tell you the latest rumors I've heard.

On October 18, Col. Sturgis forwarded orders to Major Reno to prepare the 7th to move south to the Standing Rock Reservation, along the Missouri River. Sturgis, accompanied by Gen. Terry would move south along the east bank with eight companies of the 7th, two infantry companies, and an artillery section, while Reno with the remaining four companies of the 7th, would move rapidly south staying on the west side of the river to block the potential escape routes on that side. The columns moved rapidly south on the 20th and 21st then spent the next several days at Standing Rock Agency scouring the villages for firearms. What guns were found were mostly old flintlocks and trade rifles, leading to suspicions that the tribes had known of the plans to seize the guns, and hidden their more modern firearms. However, the plan to confiscate the pony herds took the Sioux and Cheyennes completely by surprise, and under the threat of gunfire, they could only watch angrily as they were rounded up. Reno returned to Fort Lincoln on Nov. 3 with 900 ponies and several wagon loads of the seized firearms. In the mean time, Terry and Sturgis had continued south to the Cheyenne River Reservation, where they disarmed and demobilized the Indians there, before returning to Fort Lincoln on Nov. 11. With the threat of the nearest Indians neutralized, the 7th was dispersed to winter quarters. Capt. Bell and Company F were sent to escort the captured pony herd to Fort Abercrombie, Company C was sent back to Fort Totten, and Companies A, D, H, & M were assigned to Fort Rice, while Companies B, E, G, I, K, & L were stationed at Fort Lincoln.

"Well, I'll be damned!" exclaimed Charlie Welch, "Here we are back where we started, three and a half years ago.

Welch had just been promoted to sergeant to replace Tom Rush, who had elected to take a furlough, before considering whether to re-enlist. He, Jake, and Tom Russell were just moving into the NCO quarters on the lower floor of the company barracks at Fort Rice.

"I think Ol' Rush just didn't want to spend the winter stuck down here, so he got out." Welch opined, "The same as Morse is doing."

Pat had informed 1st Sgt. Martin that he didn't intend to re-enlist, so he had been left back at Fort Lincoln on detached duty, assisting the post provost sergeant. That way he could stay in his quarters there and wait on his separation papers. However, Jim Flanagan had decided to re-enlist and took over the platoon.

"I can't see that I blame him." Jake agreed. "This place is a dump!"

It had been a complete surprise when 1st Sgt. Martin had informed Company D, that they were reassigned to Fort Rice. There was a lot of grumbling in the ranks by the veteran troopers at being sent to the aging installation. They'd arrived to find that the barracks to which they were assigned, had been used by an infantry company that had stripped it of most of its furnishings before leaving. The structure itself was sadly deteriorated, and the pine planks used for the outer walls were warped and cracked. The inner walls had been lined with clay bricks and covered with bits of canvas, which insured that a layer of dust was always in evidence.

"Well, I'm going to see John Ryan over a Company M, he's been posted here for a couple of years." Jake stated. "I'm sure he'll have some ideas on how to fix this place up."

Jake made his way over to the Company M barracks and found Ryan in the orderly room. Ryan listened as he related his issues with the condition of the barracks.

"Okay, the first thing you need to do is let me introduce you to Captain Scully, the Post Quartermaster. He's the man that can help the most. It wouldn't hurt to have your company commander go see him also."

"Well, I'm not sure if we can depend on Lt. Eckerson to get anything done. He's one of those officers that likes to let us NCOs run the company. He didn't impress me much while we were down at Standing Rock, a few weeks back. He's a bit too fond of a bottle."

"Yes, I know all about that, Capt. French seems to be getting worse at that as well. That's the main reason that I'm not staying in when my enlistment is up at the end of December. He let Benteen bust me back to the ranks, back in April, and now that Benteen is back, he'll be gunning for me. French is usually drunk every day, and I suspect that he is taking too much laudanum, too."

"You're leaving the Army?" Jake queried.

"Yep, I'm going back to West Newton, Massachusetts where I grew up. It's a little town just west of Boston and my folks still live there. I've seen enough of this country, and I'm ready to settle down."

Jake said nothing for a minute, "Well, Pat Morse is getting out too, at the first of the month. He's going to work for the Northern Pacific."

"See, there you go, Pat and I both joined the regiment at Fort Riley, back in '66, about the same time. Many of the officers were up from the ranks, but these new ones that we're getting are all snot nosed youngsters full of that West Point nonsense. Hell, that new Lt. Gresham, we've got in Company M, had the company ride through a buffalo wallow on the way back from a patrol, because he didn't want to lose his compass bearing. I don't have patience left to play wet nurse to them, any longer."

"Well, I'll appreciate any help and advice that you can give me about this place before you leave." Jake said.

"Sure thing, Rogers, let's start by going to see Capt. Scully." Ryan said clapping Jake on the back.

Pat came down from Fort Lincoln on the last Saturday of November, and they had a goodbye party for him. He brought a keg of beer with him to share. Top Martin had sent Jake back up to Bismarck with money from the company fund, to procure some fresh rations of potatoes, onions, and canned vegetables. He managed to bag a nice deer on the way back, so they were well fixed for refreshments.

After they ate, they took turns toasting Pat and telling stories about him. Martin and Jake had taken up a collection, and when he was in Bismarck Jake had purchased him a gift. Martin stood and called for everyone's attention.

"Hear, hear! I call for a toast! To Patrick Aloysius Morse, May the roads always rise up to meet you, and the wind always be at your back"

Jake laughed, exclaiming, "Aloysius! Really, I never knew that.!"

Morse replied, "Tis nothing wrong with it! My Da was an Aloysius."

Jake handed him a small wooden box, "Here you go, Pat. We all pitched in and got you a little gift."

Pat opened the box and then displayed a large silver railroad watch. "Thanks Lads! I'm sure that it'll come in handy. I won't have a damn bugle reminding me what time of day it is!"

The party began to break up as 1st Sgt. Martin admonished the other NCO's that Major Tilford, who had returned as post commander, would be conducting the Sunday dress parade. Before he left he told Pat, "I've your papers on hand and you can collect them on Monday morning."

Before they turned in, Jake and Pat sat and talked for a while.

"So, when do you start working for Murray, Pat?" Jake asked.

"Right away. He's taking me back to St.Paul next week, and introducing me to the other people working along the line. Then I can have a few days there to relax. I'm really looking forward to it." Pat said.

"Well, tell Murray hello for me. I intend to volunteer to go up that way every chance that I can. I'll be sure to come see both of you."

"Make sure that you do. You be careful when you're out and about down here. The Sioux aren't happy, and there's still a lot of them still away from the agencies."

"I will, Pat, don't worry."

Pat looked at Jake and said, "You're a good soldier Jake, and I'm proud of how you turned out. Just remember, once the fighting is done, there's not much of a future for soldiers. The Army's role here is changing, and I think that you'll be spending most of the time policing the tribes. You just got a taste of that."

"Yes, I'm starting to realize that. The Indians are being made to give up the ways they've lived by for centuries. They're losing their land and resources so that the railroads can bring in more people, penalizing the Sioux as they're forcibly civilized. Once my time is done, I'll be getting out." Jake reflected.

"I'm planning on traveling a bit, chances are that I may get down towards Springfield. If I do, I'll look in on your folks." Pat said.

Jake smiled, "Be sure to give Ma a hug for me, if you do, and let them know that I'm doing well."

Pat looked at Jake intently, then said, "There's still some smaller bands out there. Sitting Bull and the Hunkpapas are rumored to be up close to Canada, and Col. Miles is said to be pursuing Crazy Horse and the Oglalas. I don't think that there's enough of them to cause a major problem, but they can damn sure be a nuisance come spring. The Army will be out for vengeance, and won't rest until they're all gathered on reservations. You'll do well to remember that Mr. Lo usually only resorts to fighting, when he can't run, or he thinks he can ambush you."

"I will, Pat."

"See that you do, lad! I'll not care to hear that you suffer harm."

CHAPTER 38

Fort Rice, Dakota Territory - December 10, 1876

Light snow was falling, covering the parade ground as the temperature hovered just below freezing. The Sunday dress parade had been cancelled and most of the garrison was ensconced inside. Jake and Cpl. Holden were playing chess in the Orderly Room when they heard horses ride up outside.

"Who do you suppose is out and about in this?" Holden wondered.

They heard the clomping of footsteps on the porch outside, and they both stood up as the door swung open, revealing two bundled figures in officers overcoats, one much taller than the other.

"Ah, Sgt. Rogers!" exclaimed the tall one, as he unwrapped a scarf.

Jake recognized him as Capt. Hale and said, "Hello Sir! This is a surprise, what brings you to Fort Rice on a day like this?"

Hale pulled off his gloves and pointed at the shorter officer, who had moved towards the wood stove. "I rode down from Fort Lincoln with your new commanding officer."

The other man turned and Jake saw that it was Lt. Godfrey. Surprised, he asked, "I'm a bit puzzled, Sir. What about Capt. Weir, has he been re-assigned?"

Godfrey took off his overcoat and Jake saw that he wore shiny new silver captain's bars on his epaulettes. He looked back at Jake with a solemn expression on his face. "I'm sorry to be the bearer of ill tidings, Sgt. Rogers, but Capt. Weir died yesterday. I've been promoted and assigned as your new company commander."

Jake was stunned, "Capt. Weir is dead, Sir? May I ask how he died?"

"I'm not completely sure, the telegram mentioned congestion of the brain, whatever that is. Sergeant, please send a messenger to Major Tilford and inform that I'll be reporting to him, directly"

"Yes, Sir! Henry, please see to it, and you'd best send someone for 1st Sgt. Martin and also over to Lt. Eckerson's quarters." Jake said, as Holden headed for the barracks stairs. He turned back to the officers, "Well, it's good to see you both, Sirs. I wish the circumstances were better. I have some hot coffee over there on the stove, I'm sure you both could stand a cup."

"Excellent, Rogers!" Hale exclaimed as he shed his overcoat.

Jake found a couple of mugs and proceeded to fill them, then said. "If you don't mind, sir, I think I'll go see to the men, you know how rumors can fly about a barracks."

"Go ahead, Rogers. I'll be formally taking over in the morning, and I'll have a meeting with all of the NCOs."

Jake answered, "Very well, Sir." As he was leaving he overheard Hale say, "This place looks the same as it did two years ago, eh God?" Hale stated.

Godfrey replied. "There may be a few more houses and buildings toward the river. But no, it hasn't changed much. My Mary isn't too thrilled about having to come back here and give up living near Bismarck."

The next day, Godfrey was formally announced as the new Company D commander, by Major Tilford. That afternoon he held his meeting with the NCOs, and later Martin, Flanagan, Jake, Welch, and Holden headed over to the post traders.

"So Top, what do you think happened with Capt.Weir?" Jake asked. "You served with him a long time."

"Well, the man always had a weakness for the bottle, and it got worse after Custer and most of his other officer friends were killed. He had no real family that I know of, except a sister somewhere, so the Regiment was his home. He used Army discipline to keep himself somewhat in check, and had Kellar, his striker, to help him. I'm afraid that without them, and bereft of any friends, the man may have drank himself to death."

Jake was impressed with how his new captain had taken an interest in overseeing the daily workings of Company D, even Lt. Eckerson became more involved. The company was also assigned a new 2nd Lieutenant, Edwin Brewer, fresh from West Point, who seemed content to take Godfrey's lead. The veterans of the Little Big Horn fight all respected Godfrey and Jake remembered his calm demeanor during the fighting on what was being called Reno Hill, by the newspapers. As Christmas approached, the garrison made preparations to cerebrate. Jake wistfully remembered the previous year's celebrations at Fort Lincoln, and sadly reflected on the contrast. Over across the parade field, the officers and their wives seemed full of holiday spirits, but in the individual company barracks the men just went about their daily routines. There were some efforts were being made to stock the messes for a big holiday meal. Jake saw John Ryan off on the 19th and wished him luck, as he left the post on his way up to Bismarck.

Jake received some packages from home which spurred him to spend his spare time to catch up on his letter writing, sending missives off to Holly, his mother, Frank, and even Vanessa. The notes inclosed in the packages were full of the usual local news and anecdotes. However, Holly's letters made it clear that she was becoming increasingly frustrated with the Goodfellow family, and Fort Leavenworth in general. Jake put some thought on the matter and sent a letter to Frank inquiring about Drury College, in Springfield, and the possibility of Holly getting enrolled there. He would wait to hear back before broaching the matter with Holly. The holidays passed and as winter descended in full force on the plains around the fort, the soldiers hunkered down, only engaging in outdoor details vital to the livestock and well being of the garrison.

In the middle of January, he said his goodbyes to Henry Holden, George Horn, and Joe Green, as their enlistments expired, and they elected to become civilians once again. Jake and Henry had several conversations before he left on the Jan. 9.

"So, what will you do Henry?" asked Jake.

"I'm not sure, Jacob. I do know that I'm getting too old for the cavalry, this last campaign was a rough one. I'll be 40 soon, and I've been soldiering half of that, it has taken it's toll on me. It's a young man's game. Perhaps, I'll go back east and get used to living in a city."

"Not back home to England?"

Henry paused for a second before replying, and had an introspective expression on his face, "Well, I suppose there's always that option, though I'm a bit hesitant, it has been over 20 years. I'm sure things have changed. I admit that it's something that I have contemplated. How about you, are you considering another hitch?"

"No, when I joined the Army I thought I would just see some other places, and seek some adventure. Now, after having been faced with cold, hard reality of combat, I'm ready to be done with it."

"Good, you've come a long way, since I first met you, Jacob. I told you back then, that you'd change once you saw the elephant."

"I'm going to miss you, Henry. I hope you find your way home."

"Oh, I suspect that I will. I left it suddenly, so perhaps I will return the same way."

Jake was beginning to notice that there were getting to be fewer and fewer faces in the ranks from his early days up on the Boundary Survey. Although, it was amusing to watch some of the new men as they stumbled to learn the daily routines. He found time to catch up on his correspondence. Jake heard back from Frank, who wrote that he was now working for the Saint Louis & San Fransisco Railroad which had taken over from the A & P. and had even been promoted. He also wrote that Colleen said that it would be relatively easy for Holly to enroll at Drury College. Frank even offered to let Holly board with he and Colleen, if she chose to come down to Springfield. That posed Jake a challenge to find a way to facilitate that. He wrote Holly to see if she was interested, and let him know her thoughts. He got a response from her in a couple of weeks that she thought it was a wonderful idea, and was in total agreement, but was at a loss how she could arrange it. She said that she'd sent a letter to her Aunt Kate about it, but hadn't gotten a reply, and suggested that it would help if Jake went to see her.

Jake, in order to escape the boredom and routine details, had volunteered to help provide escort for the wagons that plied the trail, back and forth between the two forts, hauling supplies and mail. Top Martin and Flanagan readily agreed to let him, sending special shopping lists along with him. When he overnighted at Lincoln, he bunked at the NCO quarters. He ran into Mike Caddle and Jake was flabbergasted when Mike informed him that Milt DeLacy had been busted back to the ranks, put in confinement, and was awaiting court martial. It seems that Milt had gotten drunk, gone AWOL, and then swapped some bags of Company I forage from the stables, for turkeys and potatoes over in Bismarck. Mike contended that Milt had done it intending the items for the company Christmas mess, but also added that Milt was guilty of other drunken episodes, prior to being caught. Capt. Keogh's old friend, Capt. Nowlan commanded Company I, and Caddle was trying to intercede with him on DeLacy's behalf, but Milt was still locked up.

"It just don't seem fair after all he went through!" Mike exclaimed.

"Sounds like someone has it out for him." Jake said.

"Yeh, it does. I just haven't figured out who. It may just be that Col. Sturgis is making an example out of Milt. And, I'll grant you that Milt hasn't been the same since we got back. Hell, he and I, we had both been hitting the sauce hard. Fortunately for me, I had been looking in on my old bunkie's, Archie McIlhargy's, widow. He'd asked me to watch over her and his two kids if anything happened to him. Well, Josephine, she took note of it, then sat me down and convinced me that if I got my drinkin' under control she might not mind spendin' time with me."

The winter was not as severe as the previous one. Due to the high demand of goods brought on by the opening of the Black Hills, and the new forts being built to support Col. Miles' winter operations along the Yellowstone, the Northern Pacific had continued rail traffic between Bismarck and St. Paul. Jake soon got word that Murray and Pat were back in Bismarck, and went to meet with them on his next trip. He found them at Forster's and was amazed at Pat's transformation into a nattily dressed civilian.

"Well, I hardly recognize you, Mr. Morse!"

"Ah, heavy on the Mister, Jake!" Pat laughed, "I'm quite pleased to be one. How's life down at Fort Rice these days?"

"Just the same old dreary routine! I try to get up here as much as I can." Jake replied, "I suppose you heard that Godfrey got promoted and took over Company D?"

"Yes, I heard about that. Wasn't it damn shame about Capt. Weir!" Pat said.

Murray spoke up, "Yes, and a writer Frederick Whittaker, has just published a biography about Custer. In the chapter called *The Last Battle* there are some interesting claims about the actions, or inactions, of your Major Reno, and Capt. Benteen. Whittaker maintains his information is based on a source from someone who was at the battle. I speculate that it could only have been Weir."

Jake raised an eyebrow, and replied, "Is that so? I'll have to see if I can find a copy."

Murray reached below the table and produced a book. "I just happen to have one for you."

"Have you read it, Pat?" Jake asked.

"Oh, you know I'm not big on reading much beyond newspapers, Jake. But Murray here, has given me the highlights about the accounts of the fighting. He says the rest of it is just a glorified account of Custer's career."

"So, what do you think about Whittaker's account of the fighting?" Jake asked.

"Well, we were both there, and we know most of what happened. I think that there were a lot of mistakes made, but that's the nature of a battle. Some mistakes were more serious than others, and Custer paid for his with his life. Do you remember what I told you that night on the Little Bighorn after we buried Custer and the others?"

"About finger pointing and who would be blamed?"

Pat nodded his head, "Indeed! Now, there's lots of questions being asked, some that only the dead can answer. This book doesn't change a damn thing for you and me, but there's always a price to be paid for failure. I'd speculate that as the senior surviving officers, Reno and Benteen will be paying it."

"And, from what I've heard." Murray interjected, "Reno has other worries. I've heard that he's facing a court martial for trying to seduce Capt. Bell's wife, Emily, while he was commanding Fort Abercrombie. It seems that during the holidays, when Bell went home to see his sick father, Reno was observed on several occasions making inappropriate advances to her"

"Is that so? Well, I'll still read the part about the battle." Jake said. "Just to see how it's being portrayed. Now, I've something else to discuss and need some advise from you two."

They both looked at him expectantly and he told them about his plans concerning Holly, and his dilemma in getting her moved down to Springfield.

"Well, I can tell you Bob Seip won't be a factor. Kate has divorced him." Pat stated.

"Really, I hadn't heard about that." Jake said.

"Bob has been spending all of his time attempting to get re-established in a business, and has partnered up with a fellow named James Douglas, who owns Old Pioneer Hardware. It seems Douglas and his cronies are business rivals with the Leighton's."

"Oh, I can see that wouldn't please Kate."

"Well, there's that, and then she found out that he was seeing another woman while she was back in Iowa." Pat said, raising an eyebrow.

"Well, I wonder where I can find her?" Jake asked.

Pat gave Jake a huge grin, "Oh, I may be able to help you with that!"

The Dakota Territory had enacted divorce laws, in 1867, that required the approval of the territorial legislature and signature of the governor. These laws were very specific, and a case based on the grounds of adultery was relatively easy to get for residents of the territory. Kate had used her uncles' connections to get hers fast-tracked, and had received her decree from down in Yankton, in less than thirty days. She remained in Bismarck, staying at the Capitol Hotel, while she waited on Bob to honor the terms awarding her half the proceeds from the sale of the inventory that he'd received. She frequently dined at Forster's and when Pat and Murray had returned to Bismarck it wasn't long before Pat ran into her.

"You know I always thought that she was too good for the likes of Bob!" Pat said, after relating what had transpired. "And, she and I always got on well, if you recall. So, we've been sort of keeping company for several weeks."

Murray laughed, "Well, that's an understatement! Pat's hard to find after he's done at work."

Jake looked at Pat, "It's hard to picture you, playing the gentlemen, Pat. That probably accounts for your nice clothes, eh?"

Pat grinned sheepishly, "Aye, I suppose Kate has influenced my wardrobe a wee bit!"

They spent some time discussing the logistics of Jake's plans and what arrangements had to be made. Once they felt that they had a workable model, Pat suggested that he and Jake had better go get with Kate.

They went over to the Kate's hotel, and Pat led Jake up to her room and knocked on the door. When it was opened Kate looked at Jake and Pat with a surprised smile.

"Jake Rogers! This is a surprise! Where did you find him, Pat?"

"Oh, he found me, Kate. We thought that we'd come get you, then go get something to eat. We can catch up over dinner."

"Well, okay, let me get my coat." Kate replied.

They went down 3rd Street, to Henry Sagnier's restaurant just down from the hotel and got a table. After a waiter came to take their order, they exchanged pleasantries, and Kate wanted to know how Jake was faring down at Fort Rice. Jake got Pat to tell him about his job on the NPPR, and then Kate gave him a brief summation of her breakup with Bob. Jake noticed that Pat was surreptitiously holding Kate's hand under the table as she did, which he found a bit amusing.

After they finished eating, Jake looked at Kate and said, "I'd like to talk to you about Holly."

"I suspected as much."

"I'm sure that you must be aware of how dissatisfied Holly is with her situation down at Fort Leavenworth."

"Yes, she's made it quite plain in her letters. But, until I finish getting my financial matters settled, I won't have the means to get her into a school elsewhere."

Jake nodded, and said, "I may have a way to resolve that." He went on to discuss his correspondence with Frank, and how Colleen had connections at Drury. He emphasized to Kate how close friends they were, and how Springfield and Drury College was a better environment for Holly, as apposed to a military town like Leavenworth.

Kate sat listening intently, then asked, "Jake, so what exactly are your long term intentions towards my niece? I can also move her back to up here, to live with me."

"Yes, you could, but there are no good schools here, and admit it, Bismarck is still pretty rough around the edges with all the miners and river men passing through. My enlistment is up in a little over a year, and I intend to go back to Springfield. This way Holly can see if she likes living there, if we are to get married."

"If?"

"Well, that's if something doesn't happen to me. I expect that the Army will send us back out come spring. Pat can help you appreciate what hazards that come with that."

"Let me think about it. How would I get her down there?"

Pat spoke up, "Murray, says that the Missouri, Kansas, and Texas Railroad has a line running from Olathe, Kansas, near Leavenworth, down to a new town called Vinita in the Indian Territory. There is a connection there, where the railroad from Springfield merges with it. Probably just a two day trip, Murray says that he can arrange it, and we can get her down to Vinita, where Frank and Colleen could meet up with her for the trip to Springfield."

"Well, it sounds like you two have given this some thought. In her last letter, Holly seemed quite excited about the prospects and I suppose that I have no objections. I'll be expecting you men to insure her safety."

"You can depend on it, Kate." Pat assured her. "We'll have it co-ordinated on both ends."

"So, when do you propose to do this?" she asked.

"As soon as we can, you should probably inform Hiram Goodfellow. Once we have a date we can use the telegraph to notify everyone." Jake said, "Once spring gets here and the riverboats can navigate, I anticipate that the 7th will return to the field. I'd like to get it done before then."

Jake went back over to Fort Lincoln that evening, to prepare for the return trip back to Fort Rice the next day. He ran into Mike Caddle and invited him to the post trader's bar for a beer. As they walked over, Jake was reminded of how he'd first encountered Holly there. He and Mike began to reminisce about their early days at Fort Lincoln.

"So Jake! Have you stayed in touch with Holly?" asked Mike.

"I have. It just so happens that I saw her Aunt Kate over in Bismarck today." Jake replied, and went on to explain about his plans to try and get Holly down to Springfield.

"I may have a way to help you with that, Jake. We have a new, young 2nd Lieutenant, Hugh Scott, he's one of those West Pointers, but fortunately he's not as bad as most of them. He and I have developed a good working rapport, particularly since I've kept him from stepping on his dick several times, since he joined the company."

"So how does that help me out?" Jake asked, puzzled.

"Well, it just so happens that Col. Sturgis has assigned Lt. Scott to be in charge of a detail taking 10 prisoners from here, down to the new Army prison at Ft. Leavenworth. Scott's asked me to volunteer, and help him pick men for the escort. He's authorized to take men from other companies in the Regiment, including another sergeant. That could be you!" Mike said grinning. "I'll explain to him how we traveled together with Capt. Michaelis as escorts, and I'm sure that he'll agree to take you."

Jake pondered that for a minute, trying to work out a scenario where he could bring together all the parts of his plan.

"Okay, but I need dates, and I'll need a set of orders to take back to Capt. Godfrey. Then I have to get back with Kate, Pat, and Murray, to start the ball rolling, and get some telegrams sent out, also."

"We'll go see Lt. Scott first thing after breakfast." Mike stated.

The prisoner detail left Fort Lincoln on, Feb 20. One of the prisoners, a man named Williamson, was a known trouble maker who had been sentenced for several stabbings, and had vowed that he would escape somewhere along the way. The train made overnight stops, in Jamestown, Fargo, Brainerd, and Omaha before reaching Fort Leavenworth. Each night the prisoners were escorted to the local lockup, except for at Brainerd, where they were locked in a hotel room. Lt. Scott assigned Mike and Jake to oversee Williamson and they shackled him to another prisoner.

Mike stood in front of them and pulled his pistol, "Sgt. Rogers and I are pretty fair shots with these. If you boys try and escape, the lieutenant has told us that we could shoot either of you to prevent it." He pointed his barrel at Williamson's crotch, cocked it, then pointed it at the other prisoner. "I'd probably aim for one of your legs, but who knows? Best that you don't test us, eh?"

Williamson glared back at Caddle, "Ya, Mick bastard! You'd better hope that I don't get loose. I'll have your guts for garters!"

That night, Jake and Mike took turns keeping watch. Mike was sitting near the doorway while Jake was napping on a cot. Some faint rustling roused Jake, it was coming from the direction of where they'd stashed Williamson, and his shackle mate. The sounds seemed to be moving ever so slightly. Jake, in his stockings, rose silently and crept towards them until he could make out some faint figures, he cocked his pistol and whispered quietly. "It's a good thing that I'm not an Indian, or you boys would soon be missing your hair."

"We was just lookin' for the chamber pot. I gotta take a piss." Williamson hissed.

"It's over in the far corner, behind you. Now, head over that way, or piss your pants."

Caddle stood and came through the doorway, "You'd best listen to him. I've a mind to talk the Lieutenant into keeping you two trussed up the rest of the trip. Our job is to get you delivered to Leavenworth, and it makes me no never mind if you're comfortable."

CHAPTER 39

Fort Leavenworth had been established back in 1827, and was the oldest fort west of the Mississippi. It was the Headquarters of the Department of the Missouri, and a major supply center for the frontier Army. Located on bluff along the west bank of the Missouri River, The fort had a central parade ground which was surrounded by a sprawling complex of buildings, officers quarters, barracks, corrals and stables. Stone storehouses were lined up along the railroad tracks that ran along the river front down to the fort's railroad depot. The prison, which had opened in the summer of 1875, was on the north side of the post, and occupied several old commissary and quartermaster buildings surrounded by a tall fence. Compared to the frontier forts, it was a paradise, with solidly built frame barracks and officers quarters, brick headquarters and hospital buildings, paved streets with trees, two churches, a bakery, and a school. Water was pulled from the river by a water works, with a steam driven pump that fed the water tanks and cisterns located around the post. The Department Headquarters. where Gen. Pope was in command, was located a few blocks away from the other buildings, in an enclave on the southeast corner of the fort.

Fort Leavenworth - Circa 1870s

Once the prisoners had been delivered to the prison, Lt. Scott left to check in with the fort adjutant and on his return, he called Mike and Jake over to talk with them.

"Well, that's over with. Thank you two for making sure things went smoothly. That was my first independent command, so to speak."

"You're welcome, Sir."

"Okay, there's a space in a barracks arranged for you and the men to stay in, and you can eat in the mess. We'll be here for several days, and I'll be conducting morning roll calls. As long as everyone is present and passes my inspection, and if no one gets in trouble, I'll be inclined to be very lenient until it's time to leave."

"I'll see to it, Sir!" Mike stated. "By the way, Sgt. Rogers here has some personal business to attend to."

Scott looked over at Jake, and asked, "Personal, Sgt. Rogers?"

"Yes, Sir! I'm arranging for my prospective fiancée to move down to Springfield, Missouri. I'd like to be able to escort her as far as Vinita, where some friends of mine will meet us to take her back to Springfield."

"How long will that take?"

"I should be back in three days, or less. We'll take the train from here to Olathe, and then on to Vinita, then I'll come right back. My friend, Murray Johnson, who works for the NPRR, and another friend that works for the Frisco Railroad, made all of the arrangements for me in advance. I have vouchers for the rail tickets."

"I'm impressed, Rogers, I take it that she's here at the fort?"

"Yes, Sir! She's been going to school here, and staying with Mr.

Goodfellow, the post trader, and his family."

Scott grinned, "I'm sure there's a story there somewhere, Rogers. You can share it with me when you get back."

Once they got the men settled, Mike told Jake to take off, and he bundled up in his greatcoat. The road in front of the barracks ran along the west side of what must have been the original parade ground, but was now covered with trees and served as a central park. When he came to an intersection there where signs posted indicating the direction to: the Post Hospital, the St. Ignatius Catholic Church and School, and the Post Trader. Turning west he passed the hospital and church, then came to a row of officers quarters facing a large open area to the south, where soldiers were drilling in formation. Just south of the drill field, there was a large lot with a house and a big two story frame building, surrounded by a split rail fence. The building bore a large 'Post Traders' sign, and there were a couple of rows of chicken houses across from it along the eastern side. Beyond, lay low rolling hills and fields dotted with haystacks and trees. Farther off in the distance, Jake could see the chimneys and rooftops of the town of Leavenworth.

"Well, Fort Lincoln has a ways to go before it'll be this nice." Jake thought, "I'll bet it's really pretty in the spring."

As he approached the complex, the front door of the house flew open and Jake saw Holly scramble down the steps of the porch, then run towards him. As Holly got closer, and Jake could see the huge smile on her face. "It's about time!" she declared.

Jake opened his arms wide and she rushed into them, hugging him fiercely.

"I've been watching out the damn windows for the last several days and you finally showed!" Holly exclaimed, "I thought you'd never get here!"

Jake laughed, "Well, I couldn't get the train to go any faster!"

Holly grabbed him around the neck and he lowered his head as she kissed him, passionately.

When they finally broke for air, Jake looked up and noticed a curtain moving in a window at the house, and he said, "I think someone is watching us."

"Oh, it's probably Mrs. Goodfellow. She's such a busybody, this will give her something to gossip about. I don't give a hoot now!"

"Well, are you packed up?" he asked, "As we came through the depot I checked on the train schedule, we can catch the local train to Olathe in the morning, and then change over to the M, K, & T. to get down to Vinita."

"Oh, I've been packed for days!"

Jake looked towards the house, "I suppose we should go see your Mrs. Goodfellow."

"Yes, she's been very curious about all of this since Aunt Kate's letter came explaining what we were doing. She's made it plain that she thinks it's borderline scandalous that I'm going away, escorted by an enlisted man."

"Only halfway, then you'll have a proper married couple to chaperone you the rest of the way."

"But that doesn't give us any time to be alone." Holly pouted, then smiled coyly and said, "If you know what I mean?"

Jake grinned, "Well, we will have to stay the night down in Olathe, and also Vinita. I also arranged to have an extra day to get back. So, I'm sure that somewhere along the line we can arrange something. If know what you mean?"

"Oh, you do, do you?" Holly laughed. "That's one of the things I love about you, Jake. You always seem to have a plan!"

Martha Goodfellow insisted that Jake stay for supper, and he had to endure a minor inquisition from her the rest of the afternoon. He was introduced to her two daughters when they came home from teaching school. They were quite homely, and on the plump side, which was probably the reason they weren't married. Jake could see that they were quite envious of Holly. Eventually, he and Holly were able to break away to go over to the store to see Hiram Goodfellow. He seemed affable enough, but Jake sensed that he was a bit henpecked. Later on that evening, after enjoying a good home cooked meal, Hiram invited Jake to join him for a cigar out in the parlor.

"So Sgt. Rogers, being as you've just come from the Dakota Territory, what are your thoughts on the solution to the Indian situation up there?" Hiram asked.

"Well, sir, I think that there is no easy solution." Jake answered. "I worked with a guide who's half Indian a couple of years back. He explained to me that the Indian way of life is one that they've pursued for generations. Some of them have no concept of the so-called civilized world that you and I live in, and just want to continue living according to their customs. These are the bands that are considered hostiles. It's unfortunate for them that they don't realize that that way of life is coming to an end.

"Yes, well, we can help them learn a better one if they'll let us. That's what the reservations are for." Goodfellow stated. "Personally, I'm a staunch advocate of 'Manifest Destiny' and that it will ultimately benefit them."

Jake looked at the man and replied, "That's one point of view, but they don't see it that way. What they see are broken treaties and promises, the poor quality and quantity of promised allotments that fail to arrive timely, and intact at the reservations. I was at the Standing Rock reservation back in October, when the Army confiscated their guns and ponies, taking away their ability to hunt. They lived off the land and were self sufficient, and now we are forcing many of them to turn into beggars and thieves, in order to survive. Quite frankly, I have to question if that is help."

"But I understand that you fought at the Little Big Horn? I figured that someone like you would want revenge."

"Those of us that survived, know that it was a near thing. I lost friends, fellow soldiers and almost my life. I helped bury mutilated bodies that I'll never be able to forget, and yes, at some level I want revenge."

"Well, I understand that Col. Miles is having some success in his winter campaign pushing them towards the reservations"

"But, why are we forcing them to the reservations? Some of us have spent the last three and a half years roaming the plains and hills all across the Dakota, Wyoming, and Montana territories. Most all of it was treaty designated reservation land for the various tribes that live in them. Now, much of it has been has been taken from them, and what land they have left is ill suited for farming, yet we tell the Indians to learn to survive that way. So, most of us are not entirely unsympathetic to their plight."

"Well, once we educate these heathens, they'll begin to see the advantage of learning our ways." Goodfellow said, puffing on his cigar.

"Perhaps, if they are able to survive that long." Jake said wryly.

Jake bid the Goodfellows goodnight and Holly followed him out onto the porch. The temperature had dropped along with the sun, and she had wrapped herself in a shawl, but still stood shivering. Jake pulled her to him.

"I'll be so glad to leave this place!" Holly sighed. "I doubt that I'll sleep tonight."

"Well, Hiram has volunteered to bring you to the train depot in the morning. I'll meet you there."

Holly tilted her head, seeking his lips, which met hers hungrily.

Jake reluctantly broke the embrace. "I'll see you in the morning." then turned to make his way back to the barracks.

Olathe, Kansas was originally a way stop along the Santa Fe trail which began at Westport, Missouri. Primarily a farming community, after the War it received a significant in traffic along the trail until the coming of the railroads. By 1877, three railroads served the town of 2,200. The M, K, & T Railroad, briefly known as the Southern Branch of the Union Pacific, had been the first to complete tracks down to the Indian Territory in 1872, winning a competition against two other lines. Originally, tracks were laid to connect Fort Scott down to Fort Gibson, but by 1877 had reached all the way across Indian Territory and down to Galveston, Texas. The A & P Railroad, which had been acquired the previous year by the St. Louis and San Fransisco Railroad, connected at Vinita, a small town on Cherokee Nation land.

Murray Johnson had given him a letter stating that Jake was acting in an official capacity for the NPRR, and inter-railroad ticket vouchers. When he and Holly arrived at Olathe depot the next afternoon, Jake went inside looking for the local M,K,& T agent. After asking around, he was directed to a small office. He knocked on the door.

"Come in. Can I help you, soldier?"

"Yes, I was told that you are the MK&T agent here."

"That's right, my name is Mark Walsh, what can I do for you?"

Jake presented the man with the letter and vouchers. He had worn his best uniform for traveling, and as Walsh took the papers from Jake, he took note of the 7th Cavalry emblem on his hat.

"7th Cavalry, huh? You know anything about the Custer fight?"

Jake nodded his head, "I do, I was there. I fought with Benteen's battalion."

"Well, I'd sure like to hear about it from someone that was actually there. I lost a cousin, Pvt. Tom Connors, he was in Capt. Keogh's Company I."

"Sorry to hear that. I came down from Fort Lincoln with a sergeant named, Mike Caddle, from that company, he probably knew your cousin. He's at Fort Leavenworth until the end of the week."

Jake nodded to where Holly was standing, and said quietly, "I'm escorting my fiancé down to Vinita. I have a friend who works for the Frisco Railroad. He is going to meet us there to take her on back to Springfield where she's going to go to school, while I head back up to Fort Leavenworth, and then on up to Fort Rice."

"What's your friend's name, I know some of those Frisco fellows?"

Jake answered, "Frank Armstrong, he works out of Springfield."

"Really? I've met Frank several times, I'm responsible for our depot down in Vinita also. I go down there a couple of days a week, and I run into him every so often when he happens to be there. He's a fine fellow."

Walsh looked down at the paper work, and then over towards Holly, "I tell you what, Sgt. Rogers." He said with a smile, "I have a new combination caboose on this route, The front half of it is set up to accommodate a few overnight travelers when necessary. I use it myself when I go down to Vinita. As far as I know, there's nobody booked on this run so I believe that you'll have it to yourself. In fact, I can let you stay in it tonight if you like, it will save you having to find a room in town."

Jake looked at Mark and replied, "You don't know how much I appreciate that, I think that will work out nicely, Mr. Walsh!"

"Then perhaps you and the lady would like to join me for dinner. Let me help you get settled in, and we'll go grab a bite to eat. I'll have one of my men light the heating stove and make sure the lamps are full of kerosene, while we're gone."

"Well, I can't say no to that. I don't know how to thank you, Mr. Walsh."

"Don't worry about it. Just be sure to tell Frank that I took care of you, I may need a favor from him sometime. And, perhaps on your way back through, I can go back up to Fort Leavenworth with you and look him up your Sgt. Caddle. We can go have a couple of beers and I can ask you about the Little Big Horn. I'm sure my Aunt Bertha would like to know more about how her son came to be killed."

When they returned from eating, Mark saw them over to the railcar and bid them good night.

"The train will pull out at 8:00 O'clock in the morning. I'll probably be too busy to come by, so I'll say my goodbye's now. It was a pleasure to meet you, Holly, and I hope you like it over in Springfield." he said, then looked at Jake, "Come see me when you get back from Vinita, Jake."

"I will Mark, thanks for taking care of us. I'll be sure to tell Frank."

The passenger section of the railcar, had a seating area up front and several sleeping compartments along a hallway behind it. The stove had warmed it quite comfortably, and the lamps cast a pale glow. One of the sleeping compartments had been prepared for them and the beds were made up. They discarded their coats and Jake moved to embrace Holly. After several passionate kisses, Holly stepped back, pulling away from him.

"At ease there, soldier!" she laughed, "Just you wait here a couple of minutes, I've been preparing for this for weeks." Then she turned and headed for the compartment, looked back over her shoulder at him, and said in a teasing voice. "We have all night, and I mean to make the most of it."

Jake went over to a window, where pale moonlight illuminated the surrounding countryside. The low rolling hills and leafless trees were a distinct contrast to the flat barren winter plains up in Dakota, and he stood there in nervous anticipation, contemplating different scenarios, when Holly called out softly. He turned to find her standing in a sheer blue silk nightgown that did little to hide the curves and contours of her body.

"How do you like it?" She asked as she spun around. "I stumbled across this in a shop, over in Kansas City, several months ago. I babysat some officer children to save money for it."

"Oh, I like it just fine!" Jake smiled, "It's the same color as your eyes."

Holly beckoned him with a finger. "Well, then, why don't you come see what's underneath?"

Jake woke to the jostling of the railcar as the train made ready to depart. Holly snuggled against him and sighed. "Damn, it can't be morning already."

"I'm afraid so, dear." Jake replied. "We'd best get dressed."

Holly reached around and grasped him and began softly stroking. "I have several more of those lamb sheaths. There's no use wasting them." Then began softly kissing his neck.

"Damn! How many did you bring?" Jake exclaimed.

"I hope enough. We have another night."

The train rolled into the Vinita depot around 6:30 that evening just at dusk. The trip down had been uneventful, with brief stops at Fort Scott and Parsons, Kansas. Jake and Holly had gone up to the dining car, but spent most of the trip back in the caboose. They'd spent the day chatting and exchanging stories about the months that they'd been separated. Jake told her a little about his exploits during the campaign last summer, focussing on the daily challenges presented by negotiating the various terrain that the Dakota Column had to cross. Finally, Holly broached the subject about the Little Big Horn fight.

"I didn't want to read the casualty list when it came out, I was afraid that your name would be on it." She stated, grasping his hand tightly.

Jake patted her hand, "Well, I didn't get a scratch, darling. I'm still here!"

"Was it terrible?"

Jake closed his eyes, vividly recalling the sights, sounds, and smells, "It was, but let's not dwell on it. Let's talk about Springfield."

When the train came to a halt, Jake and Holly stepped down from the railcar to find Frank and Colleen waiting on the platform.

"Hello, Jake. Mark Walsh sent me a telegram to let me know you were on your way." Frank stated. "We thought that we'd come meet you. This must be Holly."

"Yes, Holly Walker" he said grinning, then turned to Holly and gestured, "These are my friends Frank and Colleen Armstrong."

"I've heard so much about both of you, it's a pleasure to finally meet you." Holly said smiling.

Colleen reached out and took her arm, "Come dear, let's get out of this noise. We'll let the men fetch the bags. Frank has arranged rooms for us at the railroad hotel. You can get freshened up there, and we can get acquainted over a nice supper."

As they followed the women to the hotel, Jake noticed that Colleen and Holly were having an animated conversation, with much laughing and hand waving. He was relieved that they seemed to have taken an immediate liking to each other.

"She's pretty." Frank said, "I don't know what she sees in you though!"

"I could say the same about you and Colleen." Jake jibed back.

"So, you gonna marry her?"

"Probably, we'll see next year. I want to finish my hitch in the Army, then come home and see what happens."

"Good, Springfield is growing and there's lot's of opportunities to be had."

They chatted all through supper, and afterwards when the girls left to go to the powder room Jake and Frank moved to the hotel lobby, where they found an alcove with some chairs.

"Thanks for getting us rooms, Frank, and I appreciate everything else that you're doing. Holly's Aunt Kate, will be sending her some money, and I have some for you."

"Don't worry about it, Jake. We'll figure things out. Colleen has arranged for Holly to work at the college, with her."

Jake nodded his head, "That's good, Holly worked for her uncle when he was the post trader at Fort Lincoln, and also for the post trader up at Fort Leavenworth. She's not afraid of hard work."

"So what do you figure on doing after the Army?" Frank asked.

"Well, you know I worked with the Boundary Survey up on the border for a couple of seasons. I learned a lot, and thought I might try my hand at surveying."

"I think that's a great idea, Jake. The railroads are fixing to expand. The Frisco is poised to start laying track in several directions. We're just working out negotiations with Washington and various Indian tribes for the right-of-way. A man with your experience could do well."

Frank had arranged for Jake and Holly to have rooms next to each other, and shortly after bidding the other couple good night, Jake slipped over to her room. Jake found that Holly was already under the covers, and quickly shed his clothes to join her. They struggled to stifle the sounds of their lovemaking, and afterwards lay entwined, whispering quietly.

"So, you seem to have hit it off well with Colleen and Frank."

"Oh yes! She's sweet, and has some funny stories about you. Frank is so polite, he reminds me a little bit of you."

"He should, we were practically raised together."

Holly hugged him and sighed, "I just wish you didn't have to leave."

"I know, me too. But I'll be back next spring."

They lay silently, holding each other and soon drifted off to sleep. Jake woke at first light, and started to slip out of bed, when Holly pulled him back for a quick frantic coupling.

"Once more, Jake! This will have to last me a year." She whispered as she squirmed on top of him.

Later that morning they all went to the train depot where the MK&T train was boarding for the return north. While he and Holly said their goodbyes, she put on a brave face, only occasionally dabbing here eyes.

As they broke their final embrace Holly whispered in his ear."Come back to me safely my love! I'll be waiting. And write me more often, please!"

Frank and Colleen were standing nearby, and Jake waved at them and said. "I'll see you all next spring." then turned and climbed the steps. He stood on the railcar platform watching and waving as the train pulled out.

Upon his return to Olathe, Jake carried through with his offer to Mark, who went with him up to Fort Leavenworth where they found Mike Caddle. Mark treated Mike and Jake to a fine dinner over in town, and they told him what they knew about the demise of his cousin, and Company I, at the Little Big Horn. Jake was careful to not go into too many details about the conditions of the bodies. The next day Lt. Scott gathered up the guard detail for the return to Fort Lincoln. After an uneventful rail journey, they rolled into Bismarck on the March 10. Jake had already received permission from Lt. Scott to stay over at Fort Lincoln for a couple of days, so when they got to the depot he went to Murray's office, knocked, then poked his head in the door.

"Hey Murray!" Jake exclaimed.

"Well, Jake! I see that you made it back. Everything work out?"

"Yes, things went very smoothly. Thanks for all of your help. Between you, the MK&T agent in Kansas, Mark Walsh, and my friend Frank, we were able to get Holly over to Springfield without a hitch. It's good to have friends in the railroad business."

"Excellent! So, how long before you have to go back to Fort Rice?"

"I'm heading back Monday morning with the weekly supply wagons."

"I'll send word to Pat that you're back. We can meet, he and Kate, for supper over at Forster's. I'm sure that she'll want to hear all about Holly."

Jake relayed the details of his trip over supper and reassured Kate that Holly was enthusiastic about her change in schools. Kate informed him that Bob Seip had finally settled their finances and was still rumored to be partnering with the owner of Pioneer Hardware. Jake learned that Kate had rented a house, and from the sound of things, Pat seemed be spending much of his time there when he was in town. Then the conversation turned to local news. Several officers from the 7th Cavalry, including Cap. Benteen, had been summoned to St. Paul to testify at Major Reno's court martial and rumors were rife that he would be found guilty. Pat commented that Jack McCall, Wild Bill's murderer, had been found guilty and hung down at Yankton at the beginning of the month. Murray confirmed that another expedition to the Yellowstone was in the planning stages, and that his new boss was coming to Bismarck to announce the new daily train schedules that would be implemented. It was speculated that the entire 7th Cavalry would be leaving by June, to support Col. Miles and the new forts being constructed up on the Yellowstone at the Tongue and Big Horn Rivers. Many more new recruits were arriving to swell the ranks of the 7th and Pat told Jake that the veterans had derisively dubbed them "Custer Avengers". Regular stagecoach mail and express routes were now in service down to Fort Rice and Standing Rock, and also up to Forts Stevenson and Buford. Pat mentioned that Company L was throwing a St. Patrick's Day ball the following Friday.

"Kate and I will probably go over, Johnny Mullen is the 1st Sergeant and I know him from our days down in Kansas." Pat said. "Maybe you could come up for it?

"I'm heading back to Rice, tomorrow." Jake replied, "I expect Top Martin will have me plugged back into the detail rotation, so I doubt that I will be able to."

CHAPTER 40

Fort Abraham Lincoln, Dakota Territory - April 27, 1877

The four companies of the 7th Cavalry stationed at Fort Rice spent several weeks preparing for the field early in the month. On April 18, Major Tilford led them north to Fort Lincoln, where they went into bivouac in the area just south of the fort upon their arrival. Col. Sturgis would command the entire 7th in the field on this campaign, minus Company C, which would remain behind to help provide security for the Black Hills route. Based on the experience of the previous year, several major changes were implemented to increase the mobility of the regiment. The *Far West* would accompany the regiment as it made its way along the Missouri River route up to Fort Buford, carrying rations, supplies, ammunition, and forage. Each man was told to pack a spare uniform and a few personal items in a duffle bag that would be stored on board. A complete change of underclothes and socks went in their saddlebags. Officers were authorized a small trunk to be placed on the riverboat. Only one wagon was allotted to each company, and two for Headquarters and the medical detachment. Each wagon would carry three 'A' tents per company, along with four days rations, and axes, spades and picks. No personal baggage was allowed to accompany the column. Pistols would be issued when the regiment reached Fort Buford. Every company would receive twelve Springfield Infantry rifles, to be assigned to the best marksmen in each one. Those men would not have to carry sabers.

Capt. Michaelis had set up a table in one the Commissary warehouses where he issued the rifles. 1st Sgt. Martin had assigned Jake to pick the men for Company D, and sent him over to meet with the Ordinance officer.

"Ah, Sgt. Rogers! I sensed that you would be putting in an appearance. I trust you still have my rifle." Michaelis said when he spied Jake.

"I do indeed, Sir! And, I was interested to hear that we were getting the infantry rifles." Jake replied.

"Yes, well, I was able to persuade the powers that be, to experiment with this program. Unfortunately, the extra expense of Malcolm scopes was deemed too expensive and impractical. I'm assuming that you don't want to exchange the Sharps for one of these Springfields."

"Not unless I have to, sir."

"I think that I can spare it again this year, Sgt. Rogers. After reviewing the campaign reports from last year, several issues became very apparent and I've been able to persuade Col. Sturgis to let me address them."

"Might I ask what they are, Sir?"

"Well, first off, we've determined that the men, in general, were poorly trained in marksmanship, and not accustomed to firing their weapons very often."

Jake nodded his head in agreement. "I think that's very true, sir. We were rarely allowed to target practice."

"So, it's been decided that I'm to issue ammunition for the men to practice with. I'll be looking forward to seeing you at the target range and helping me correct that." Michaelis stated. "In addition, there's been some speculation that there was a problem with some of the Springfield carbines jamming."

"I saw it happen a few times." Jake said, "I think that most of them were caused by corrosion on the cartridge cases. The copper cases have a tendency to turn green in the leather cartridge belts, particularly when they get soaked with sweat."

"Precisely, that green is technically called verdigris!" the officer exclaimed. "It's important that when the men are issued ammunition out in the field, it is inspected frequently."

Jake nodded his head, "I had an old guide who showed me a trick to remove it. Just mix a little urine and salt to wipe them with, then rub them with a dab of oil."

"Yes, well that would work. Ammonia, or vinegar would be a little bit more sanitary I suspect." Michaelis frowned.

"Hey, both were easy to come bye out on the trail." Jake grinned.

"Lastly, the cavalry carbines don't have much range advantage over the Henrys and Winchesters that the hostiles favor. However, the infantry rifles are effective at over twice the range. By augmenting the firepower of each company with a dozen rifles in the hands of the best marksmen, we should be able to make Mr. Lo duck and stay farther away."

"I like the way you think, Sir!"

Jake went over the muster rolls with 1st Sgt. Martin, and they picked over it, discussing who would be chosen for riflemen.

"Besides being good marksmen, I want proven veterans. Men that we know are steady under fire." Martin stated.

"I think Sgt. Welch, and Sgt. Cunningham, along with Cpl. Kipp, and Cpl. Cox would be good candidates." Jake said, "Then I've picked these privates."

Martin reviewed the list "Eh, well that damn Little George, he's a hot head, I grant that he's a scrapper. But if he bows up on me again, he'll get more than fined and put on shitty details! And his mate George Dann ain't exactly on my good side either."

Little George Hunt had clashed with Top Martin, along with his bunkie, Big George Dann. The loss of the veteran presence of Henry Holden, George Horn, and Joe Green had meant that the two Georges were the only original members of Jake's old section, and left them feeling a bit disenfranchised.

"Well, the Georges and Jimmy Hurd are the only ones left of Pat's old platoon. They just need to be around some old hands. I'll get them squared away."

"Okay, but you let him know that I'm giving them a chance to make it right with me. I like Dawsey, Deetline, Fox, and Kipp, they're steady lads. Best you include a couple of the new boys also, to give the some of these 'Custer Avengers' some incentive to show what they can do."

Jake took his selected marksman over to exchange their carbines. In addition to being issued the Springfield rifles, the designees were also issued the Model 1873 Trowel bayonets, to replace their sabers. These 10" long blades were almost 4" wide at the base, and had a reinforced spine. Col. Miles and his Infantry units had them, and they'd been proven particularly useful in the field for entrenching.

"Damn, I wish we'd have had these last year, when we were surrounded up on Reno's hill!" commented Pvt. Dave Dawsey.

After moving to the target range, Capt. Michaelis came over to watch as the groups from each company fired the rifles, keeping track of the ammunition expended and noting the results. The added recoil from the larger powder charge of the 45-70 cartridges resulted in many sore shoulders for the less experienced troopers.

Mike Caddle came and invited Jake to have supper at he and Josephine's house on Suds Row. Afterwards, they sat out on the porch discussing the up coming campaign, when the subject of Milt DeLacy came up. He had been given a dishonorable discharge earlier in April and sentenced to two years at Fort Leavenworth.

"That just ain't right!" Mike declared, "Capt Nowlan has appealed to Col. Sturgis. But, with the regiment preparing to take the field, I don't know if Sturgis will do anything before we leave. I hate the thought that Milt would get stuck in Leavenworth."

"Yeh, that'd be a damn shame." Jake said.

"Do you remember when Rain in the Face escaped from the guardhouse last year?" Mike asked.

"I do."

"I've been thinking about that. No one ever figured out how he and those other prisoners got away."

Jake looked at Mike and said, "Not that I recall."

Mike just looked back at Jake and nodded his head slightly. "I'm gonna go see him tomorrow. Maybe he'll have heard something."

On May 9, Colonel Sturgis led the two Battalions of the rejuvenated 7th Cavalry Regiment, across to Bismarck. There was a minor stir the morning they left. The prisoners, including ex-sergeant Milt DeLacy that were being held in the stockade, broke through a wall and escaped during the night. Sturgis assigned the officer in charge of the rear detachment to try and apprehend them, then left to accompany the column which headed north along the Missouri towards Fort Stevenson. Lt. Col. Elmer Otis, who had taken Custer's regimental position, commanded the 1st Battalion, consisting of companies H, M, K, E, G, and L. Major Lewis Merrill commanded the 2nd Battalion consisting of companies A, B, I, F, and D. The Missouri River route was well traveled now and they encountered several stages and wagon trains, hauling people and supplies along it. The battalions alternated back and forth, with the individual companies rotating as the advance party each day. With no huge, trailing train of wagons strung out behind, the regiment made good time up to Fort Stevenson. They paused there to resupply, then struck out for Fort Buford. The weather began to deteriorate and the command struggled through pouring rain and thunderstorms. It wasn't until May.17th when they reached Fort Buford, where the *Far West* was waiting to ferry them across to the north bank of the Yellowstone River. Miles had sent orders for Sturgis and the 7th to head south towards the Glendive Cantonment, and then proceed up to the mouth of Cedar Creek where a supply camp had been established for them. A messenger reached them on the 23rd bringing news that Miles had tracked down and attacked the camps of Lame Deer, a Minneconjous chieftain, and a minor Cheyenne chief, White Hawk, along a tributary of the Rosebud. Lame Deer was killed and his followers scattered, leaving no large bands of hostiles south of the Yellowstone. Worried about the continuing presence of Sitting Bull's band somewhere off to the north, Miles directed Sturgis, who had reached Cedar Creek on the 28th, to send out patrols along the Yellowstone to watch for any hostiles attempting to join Sitting Bull.

Jake stood under the fly of Top Martin's orderly tent watching the rain come down in sheets, as another torrential downpour inundated the 7th's bivouac area. He huddled in his poncho, sipping from a tin cup of coffee.

"That's a god damn toad strangler out there, ain't it!" exclaimed Charlie Welch.

Jake nodded his head in agreement, "Glad it's not our turn to patrol."

Besides Sgt. Flanagan, Jake, Tom Russell, and Charlie Welch, the other sergeants on the company rolls, were two older veterans that had been recently promoted from corporal, Al Cunningham, a taciturn Englishman on his third enlistment, and Bill Oman, a quarrelsome Indianian with a checkered past, but who had performed well on Reno Hill. Another was, Jimmy Alberts, a no nonsense, steady ex-farmer from Illinois, whom Lt. Edgerly had promoted to corporal for his bravery on Reno Hill. Tom Russell was leaving in a few weeks, his enlistment was expiring on June 23, and he'd decided to go back home and try civilian life. There were also two corporals, George Wylie, a Cajun from New Orleans and Civil War veteran, and John Quinn, a Connecticut Yankee and blacksmith, who was a good friend and ex-bunkie of Alberts. 1st Sgt. Martin had worked over the roster to sprinkle the newer men among the more experienced, and rotated his NCOs among the various guard and fatigue details.

The rains and even some wet snow had plagued the area for a week. Jake had heard rumors that the Tongue River Cantonment, where Col. Miles kept his Headquarters, was flooded. Fortunately, Capt. Godfrey had remembered the flooding that had happened to the camps along the Yellowstone, last year, and insisted that Company D be located on higher grounds away from the river. Some of the new men had grumbled about the extra distance that they had to take the horses for watering, but now realized how fortunate they were as they watched some of the other companies scrambling to find high ground.

"Well, one good thing, the riverboats will have plenty of water to come up stream."

It was rumored that Gen. Sherman and Sheridan would be coming out in a few weeks aboard the new Coulson steamer *Rosebud*, commanded by Grant Marsh. There were also several other boats shuttling supplies and building materials to the new forts being built at the mouths of the Tongue Riven and Little Big Horn River. The heavy rains having made the overland route along the Yellowstone impassable.

"Capt. Godfrey told me that we're going to patrol all the way to Sunday Creek and then north to its headwaters towards Fort Peck." 1st Sgt. Martin called from inside the tent. "That's getting pretty close to our old friend, Val Wheeler's stomping grounds ain't it, Rogers."

"Maybe, he was talking about starting a cattle ranch somewhere up in that area."

On June 16, Col, Michael Sheridan arrived on the steamer *Fletcher*. He had been dispatched by his brother to supervise the retrieval of Custer's remains, and those of his officers, from the battlefield site on the Little Big Horn. Sturgis designated Capt. Nowlan and his Company I to accompany Sheridan, and Col. Miles sent along Lt. Doane, 2nd Cavalry and his new Crow scout contingent, Miles in the mean time, left on the steamer *Ashland* to confer with Gen. Terry at Fort Buford. On July 6, Col. Sheridan plus Company I returned from their battlefield expedition. Col. Sheridan left immediately accompanying the coffins on the riverboat, after dropping off the cavalrymen,

Jake and Charlie were at the sutler's tent that evening when Mike Caddle came strolling up.

"Hey Mike, I heard you were back. Let me buy you a beer, and you can tell us what you found up on the Little Big Horn." Jake called out to him.

Caddle grimaced and shook his head, "Aye, but you'd best make it two beers, Jake, I've a sad tale to tell you."

It seems that when the burial party got up to the battlefield, most of the bodies were laying exposed to the elements. Rains had washed and eroded the skimpy graves, and many had been dug up by animals, and perhaps Indians. Mike said they spent ten days trying to identify the remains and rebury them.

"Capt. Nowlan personally led us to where he said Custer and his brother, Tom were buried. But, I can't say for certain."

Jake said, "Well, Nowlan was there when we covered him up, and he made a list. He should know!"

"Yes, but I thought that I recalled you telling me that the grave was covered with a piece of canvas and some kind of basket."Mike replied. "We found nothing like that, just a few rocks. The first body we dug up had corporal's blouse in with it."

Jake frowned, "Well, I wasn't there when they put the bodies in, I just helped cover them up."

"Well, the captain, and Col. Sheridan had me dig next to it and we found a skull, ribcage, and some leg bones. Anyway, we put them in a coffin and marked it as Custer. Colonel Sheridan remarked that it was good enough that people thought it was Custer."

"I suppose that's right."

"Anyway, we went on to dig up the other officers. I found one of Keogh's boots, near where he was buried, and saw the graves around him. It looked like my Company I lads made a stand there, before they went down."

Jake nodded his head as he remembered the grizzly scene. "I know they did, Mike." he said quietly.

Caddle went on to relate on how they had scoured the whole field for bodies, and then went over to Reno Hill to retrieve the bodies of Lt. Hodgson, Lt. McIntosh, and Dr. DeWolf. All told, they retrieved all the officers, except Lt. Crittenden, whose family requested that he stay buried where he fell.

"I've not much confidence that the graves will hold up, though. That soil is so poor that the rains will wash it away."

Upon his return from conferring with Gen. Terry, Col. Miles led a column consisting of nine companies of the 7th Cavalry, two companies of the 2nd Cavalry, and five companies of his 5th Infantry mounted on captured Indian ponies, north to examine the country between the Yellowstone and Missouri. Miles was seeking to block any attempt by the remnants of the few roaming Sioux and Cheyenne from joining Sitting Bull. Along with a scout contingent, cattle herd, artillery piece, and wagon train, it was the largest expedition fielded so far that season. A base camp was established near the site of the Cedar Creek fight, the previous October, where Miles had driven off Sitting Bull and his band of Hunkpapas. And then had intimidated the rest of the Hunkpapas, Minneconjous, and Sans Arcs chieftains into agreeing to head for the reservations. He sent out patrols and scouts in all directions, scouring the countryside. After 12 days, Miles was satisfied that he'd succeeded in scattering the remaining hostiles south of the Missouri River. After receiving dispatches from Generals Sherman and Terry, who were coming upriver on the *Rosebud* to inspect the construction of the new forts. Miles took his personal escort and headed for the Glendive Cantonment to meet up with them, he directed the rest of the column to return to their Yellowstone camps, near the Tongue River fort.

On 16 July, Miles returned to the Tongue River aboard the *Rosebud* to find that his wife, Mary, and some of the other officer's wives had arrived on the *Josephine* the week before. A review and dress parade by the 5th Infantry was held the next day, and then Sherman and Terry proceeded upstream to the Bighorn Post, to meet with Generals Sheridan and Crook who had traveled overland from the south. They went on to tour the battlefield near the new fort and were appalled to see the condition of the graves. Lt. Col. George Forsyth was immediately tasked with making the field presentable. The generals met to discuss the impact of the new forts on keeping the Sioux and Cheyenne in check. Against Terry's wishes, who still blamed Custer for not following his orders, Sherman and Sheridan decided that the Big Horn Post was to be renamed Fort Custer, and the Tongue River fort was to be called Fort Keogh. The next day, Crook and Sheridan left on the *Josephine* to inspect Fort Custer, before going on to Fort Buford. Terry followed two days later on the *Rosebud*, while Sherman headed west for a tour of the new Yellowstone National Park accompanied by his son, a couple of staff officers, four soldiers, a guide, and three light wagons. When Terry reached Fort Keogh, Miles persuaded him to leave the newer *Rosebud,* which was built specifically for navigating the shallower channels of the upper Yellowstone and captained by the redoubtable Grant Marsh, for him to use the rest of the season to shuttle between the two new forts. Terry switched over to the *Far West,* which had just unloaded building materials, and continued his way downriver to Fort Buford. The 7th Cavalry continued to bivouac near the mouth of Cedar Creek on the north side of the Yellowstone. Miles, now headquartered at what was already being called, Fort Keogh, continued to send out patrols and escort parties for the supply trains.

Several weeks went by as the weather warmed. The regular passages of the riverboats insured that mail came frequently, and Jake received several letters from back home. Holly wrote that she really enjoyed living in Springfield and about how nice Frank and Colleen were. She added that they had taken her over to Henderson with them and introduced her to his parents, explaining that Holly was staying with them while she attended Drury College. She had taken a job working at Jackson's Grocery store, and was able to save enough money to open a bank account. His mother wrote telling him the usual anecdotes about the farm and local affairs. She did mention that Frank and Colleen had brought a delightful young women named Holly to see them. Then she mildly scolded him for not keeping her apprised of their relationship. Colleen also wrote him and explained how Sarah had grilled her relentlessly about Holly, during their visit, and was pretty sure that his mother had a fair idea of Jake's relationship with Holly, but also stated that Sarah was quite taken with Holly. Jake thought to himself and reflected that all in all, things were working out down in Springfield quite nicely. He also got a letter from Kate, letting him know that she and Pat had gotten married in St.Paul, back at the beginning of July, and just returned from their honeymoon. Pat sent his regards and Jake smiled at the thought of the inveterate bachelor succumbing to Kate's charms.

Jake was leading his section on a patrol. They were returning from escorting a wagon train to the mouth of Sunday Creek, across from the Tongue River Cantonment. They had been out a week, and after the heat and dust, he was looking forward to a bath and visit to the sutler's tent for a cold beer.

"So, do ya suppose we're gonna spend the rest of the summer just ridin' around up here, Sarge? Shit fire, I signed up to fight some Injuns!" complained Pvt. Curran.

John Curran was one of the few new replacements that Company D had received, most having been assigned to restore the rolls of the decimated companies that had accompanied Custer.

"Well, I'm afraid that you're too late to the party, Curran. You should have joined up earlier, Ol' Mr. Lo ain't around these parts anymore." Pvt. Dawsey commented wryly.

Jake chuckled and said. "I'm afraid that Dawsey's right. We can't find any to chase, let alone fight."

"Where'd they all go?"

"Sitting Bull is rumored to be up in Canada, Crazy Horse and most of the other chiefs, including the Cheyenne, have already surrendered and are on reservations. Col. Miles spent all winter running them to ground. The only Indians that you're likely to see, are scouting for us."

"Yeh, but a year ago some of them were shooting at us." interjected Dawsey.

"Maybe so,

"So why do we have to guard these supply trains if there's no Indians?"

"We're just making sure that the supplies get through to where they're supposed to go without some of them disappearing. There's all kind of characters roaming up the river looking to get rich. Miners, wood hawks, buffalo hunters, and just plain thieves." Jake replied.

"Shit! I didn't sign up to watch over a bunch of wagons!" Curran groused.

"Neither did any of us!" Jake stated, "But that's the way it is."

That evening, Jake and Charlie Welch were sitting under a tree near the sutler's drinking a beer and watching a game of horseshoes, when Mike Caddle walked up and sat down.

"Hey Jake! How've you been?"

"Just out enjoying the countryside, don't ya know. I've been doing a little hunting when I can, bagged some nice prairie chickens the other day." Jake replied. "What have you been up too?"

"Just playing nursemaid to a bunch of baby face youngsters. Bob Murphy took Milt's place as first sergeant, and he has me trying to turn them into cavalry troopers."

"How's that going?"

"Slow! Were we ever that helpless?" Caddle asked.

"I wasn't, but I remember a few times back in the day that you were pretty raw. Say, speaking of Milt, has there been any word on if they caught him?"

Mike shook his head, "No, and I don't reckon that they're gonna. I suspect that he's long gone from these parts."

"You sound pretty sure about that, Mike." Jake said.

Mike looked at Jake and held his gaze, "Yep!"

Jake nodded his head. "Good!"

"Anyway, I came over to tell you that Capt. Nowlan has just come back from over at Bighorn Post. Col. Miles just received some dispatches and it seems that several bands of Nez Perce Indians broke away from their reservation back in June, and may be headed for Montana. General O. O. Howard, the commander of the Department of Columbia, set out in pursuit with a few units of the 1st Cavalry. They have fought several engagements with them, but he's been unable to stop them. There is speculation that the Nez Perce could be headed to Canada to join Sitting Bull."

"So how does that affect us?" Charlie asked.

"Col. Miles is worried that this would be undermine to his efforts to secure the border. He and his staff are already working on contingency plans.

On August 3, Miles dispatched Lt. Doane, 2nd Cavalry, along with 30 Crow scouts, and Company E, 7th Cavalry under Lt. DeRudio, to patrol up the Yellowstone and look for the Nez Perce. Doane who was very familiar with the area having been stationed at Fort Ellis for several years, had served as an escort for the survey that had resulted in the creation of the National Park. In the meantime, Miles had Sturgis and the 7th relocate their bivouac to Sunday Creek, opposite the Big Horn River from Fort Custer. On the 10th, he sent Col. Sturgis and two battalions under Major Merrill and Capt. Benteen containing the six strongest companies of the 7th to head off and engage the Nez Perce. Miles kept a battalion of the 7th under Capt. Hale, which consisted of Companies A, D, and K. Then a messenger reached Miles and he learned that Col. Gibbon and a mixed force of regular infantry and volunteers had attacked the Nez Perce camp on the Big Hole River on Aug. 9. After initially surprising the camp, Gibbon had been forced to retreat, losing a third of his men and an artillery piece in the process. Gibbon and his surviving men were pinned down, surrounded, plus were low on ammunition and rations. Fortunately Gen. Howard had advanced towards Gibbon with several companies of the 2nd Cavalry and reached the scene of the fighting on the 11th, only to find the Nez Perce long gone. Miles quickly dispatched orders to Col. Sturgis, warning him to maintain vigilance and to move in the direction of the Musselshell River and block the Indians path.

The next several weeks a continuous stream of messengers roamed between Howard, Fort Ellis, and the forts on the Yellowstone keeping Miles apprised of the status of the pursuit of the fleeing Nez Perce. On Aug. 20, the latter surprised Howard at a place called Camas Meadows and in a daring raid made off with the most of the mules of his pack train, forcing Howard to detour to Virginia City for supplies. The Indians bands then detoured south and east through the new National Park, easily maintaining a two to three day lead on their pursuers. Meanwhile, Sturgis had met up with Lt. Doane's detachment and his scouts, who informed him that the Nez Perce had been reported as being in Wyoming. Sturgis wanted Doane to join with him, but Doane had orders from Col. Gibbon to report back to Fort Ellis. Sturgis forded the Yellowstone on the 25th, and needing scouts familiar with the area, went south to the Crow Agency on the Stillwater River. While there, a courier from Howard reached him, directing Sturgis to head south along Clark's Fork of the Yellowstone to try and intercept them. Sturgis sent out his new scouts and when they returned on Aug. 31, he moved to the Clark's Fork Canyons. On Sep. 8, one of his scouting parties was ambushed and another reported seeing the main body of the Nez Perce from a mountain top, headed east towards the Stinking Water River. Sturgis, not realizing that this was a ruse, attempted to push cross country. The wily Nez Perce maneuvered and laid a false trail that led south, then doubled back letting Sturgis pass them to the east, then resumed their track to the north, along the Clark's Fork where once out on the plains, they struck straight north towards the Yellowstone.

When Howard's scouts discovered the presence of Sturgis and his column, he rode to meet Sturgis and they realized that they had been outfoxed. On September 12, Howard sent a dispatch to Miles notifying him that the Nez Perce had slipped by, and urged Miles to make an effort to try and block the Nez Perce from escaping. Howard then sent Sturgis and the 7th, along with a re-enforced company of the 1st Cavalry and about 100 scouts to aggressively pursue the Indians. Howard would follow as quick as his exhausted infantry could manage.

The second week of Sep., Miles dispatched a battalion of the 2nd Cavalry under Capt. George Tyler, and Capt. Hale with his Company K of the 7th, to head north to the Missouri River where they were to catch a riverboat up to Fort Benton. Once there, they would accompany Gen. Terry who was heading up a peace commission to cross into Canada and meet with Sitting Bull. On Sep 17, Miles received Howard's dispatch and immediately set plans in motion to assemble a column on the north bank of the Missouri to strike northwest towards the Musselshell River and attempt to intercept the Nez Perce. Working through the night, wagons, mule teams, horses, and two pieces of artillery. (One of the new 2" Hotchkiss breech loading mountain guns that could be broken down and packed on a mule, and a larger caisson drawn Napoleon cannon) were ferried across. The column would consist of over 500 men with three companies each of the 2nd, and 7th Cavalry, five companies of the 5th Infantry, (four of which were mounted on captured ponies and one escorting the two artillery pieces), scouts, teamsters for the 36 wagons, and packers for the mules. Departing at sunrise, Miles led the column up to the high mesa above the camps heading for the headwaters of Sunday Creek, and on towards the divide between the Yellowstone and Missouri Rivers. A courier was immediately dispatched to Capt. Tyler informing him of the change in plans.

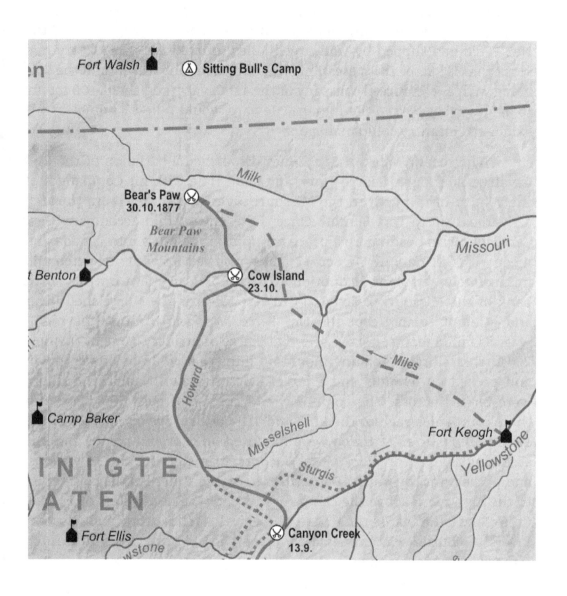

US Army Column routes during the final stages of the
Nez Perce Campaign - Fall 1877

CHAPTER 41

Missouri River, near the mouth of the Musselshell River, Montana Territory

Monday, Sep. 24, 1877

It had been a rough six days since Miles had led the column north along Sunday Creek. The terrain was mostly arid badlands with little water. The column had traversed 35 miles the first two days across the difficult and barren landscape, encountering only stagnant pools of water. The wagons were always a couple of hours behind when they made bivouac, and the impatient Miles made plans to leave them when he reached the Missouri River, where he would resupply from a riverboat that he had sent his Adjutant, Lt. Baird, to bring down from Fort Peck. Wednesday evening a group of twenty-five Northern Cheyenne caught up with them, after having been recruited to scout for Miles. A courier from Gen. Howard caught up with the column informing Miles that Sturgis and his troopers had been in a running fight with the Nez Perce at a place called Canyon Creek. The Indians had gotten away, but Crow scouts had captured over 400 ponies the following day. Howard was stopping at the Musselshell to recuperate, his men and mounts utterly exhausted. Hopefully, his halt would cause the Nez Perce to slow their pace also, giving Miles' column more time to head them off. Determined to detect the Nez Perce before they reached the Missouri, Miles threw out a screen of scouts, searching to the northwest. After crossing the divide near Big Dry River, the column reunited with the Tyler's cavalry detachment to which Miles had sent a messenger, telling him to halt and patrol. Saturday, herds of buffalo lay across the route and the winding arroyos and dry stream beds marked the beginning of the tributaries of Squaw Creek, and on Sunday the bluffs of the Missouri were in sight. The smoke from a riverboat was spotted several miles upriver and Miles sent out a party to flag down the steamer, then followed with the entire command. When it arrived at the river, the *Fontenelle* which was en route from Fort Benton bound for St. Louis was waiting. Miles used it to ferry Tyler's 2nd Cavalry battalion and 12 wagons across to the other side of the Missouri, to continue on to Fort Benton, then left the remaining wagons and prepared to march west along the south bank. That evening the rest of the column crossed the nearby Musselshell, at a ford three miles below the Missouri and then made its way back to the banks of the Missouri. There, Miles found Lt. Baird and the riverboat, *Benton,* had just arrived and was unloading supplies, before steaming on to Fort Benton the next morning. The *Fontenelle* finished transferring supplies and left soon after heading downstream.

1st Sgt. Martin, Jake and several other sergeants were eating breakfast huddled near a campfire. The nights had turned chilly, and Jake remembered how quickly the fall equinox had precipitated the weather that descended on them back on the Border Survey two years earlier.

"I think that we should make sure that the men carry their overcoats, fur caps, and an extra blanket, Top. Especially, if we stay out here with just a pack train." Jake said.

"Aye!" Martin replied, "Make sure you each see to your sections. Check that their ponchos and shelter halves ain't ripped up, too. Odds are that we'll be seeing snow pretty damn soon."

"Oh, you can count on that!" called out a gravely voice from behind Jake. "Hope you soldier boys remember what I showed you about beating the Hawk."

Jake's finger's felt under his neckerchief for the wolf fang he'd started wearing again when they took the field, and swore that it was tingling.

"Well, I'll be damned! Is that you, Val Wheeler? Where in the blazes did you come from?" Martin called out.

Jake turned to look and saw Val grinning at them. "I was at Fort Peck selling some beeves and heard that your Col. Miles was lookin' for scouts. I thought it'd be a quick way to get back upriver if I signed on, plus I'll make a few dollars. That Lt. Baird fella told me he had some troopers along from the 7th. I spotted your black horses this morning when you were watering them and decided to mosey on over. Say, I'd be partial to a cup of that coffee!"

Jake stood and said, "Come have a seat, and tell us what you've been up too, Val."

Wheeler sat and looked around, "Where's Pat?"

"Oh, he took a job working for the Northern Pacific last year."

"Ah, smart move on his part. He was getting too old for soldiering." Val stated.

"So, have you signed on to scout for us?" Martin asked.

"I have, Miles is wanting someone that knows the country north of the Missouri to the Boundary Line. I reckon that I know it as well as anyone."

"So, does he think that the Nez Perce have gotten across?" Jake asked.

"He ain't sure, but he's hedging his bets. I tell you that man is a ball of fire, he's cast a big shadow on these parts. Ol' Sitting Bull is making sure to stay on the other side of the Medicine Line. Your Col. Miles wants to keep it that way and doesn't want the Nez Perce to join up with him."

"D'ya know anything about them, Val? We've not seen hide nor hair of them. Just heard stories." Martin asked.

"Oh, I know plenty. They've been coming out here from their homelands over in Idaho Territory, to harvest buffalo for as long as I can remember. They mostly socialize with the Flatheads, and the Crows, over in the Bitterroot Range."

"Well, from what we've heard they've given Gen. Howard fits all summer, and that they whipped Col. Gibbon and his men pretty bad."

"I can tell you, don't be comparing them to the Sioux and Cheyenne. They live in close-knit bands, and are very organized. They've had guns for years and know how to shoot. They don't fight the same way, either. Their warriors are disciplined and they have war leaders in each band, kind a like the way you soldiers have officers and sergeants."

Jake nodded his head thoughtfully, "What got them out on the warpath, Val?"

"They ain't on the warpath, the way I hear it.. The Nez Perce tribe became divided into treaty and non-treaty bands over the last twenty years. While the non-treaty bands were out here on their annual hunt, some of the treaty bands signed away their homelands. When the non-treaty bands returned and disputed the terms, Gen. Howard threatened to use force to move them on to the reservations. Then unfortunately some of the young warriors got all liquored up, killed a couple of whites, and that started the fighting. Joseph and the other leaders decided to head out here where they've hunted for hundreds of years. They've always got on well with the Flatheads and Crows and I think that they were hoping they would be welcomed so that they could settle in around here, but that didn't happen! The Crows saw what happened to the Sioux and Cheyenne, and they ain't about to get crossways with Col. Miles. I heard that the Crows just helped captured a big chunk of their horse herd when they tangled with your other 7th Cavalry boys, down on Canyon Creek a couple of weeks back."

"What do you think is going to happen?"

"Well, I reckon they're headed for the Medicine Line to join up with Ol' Sittin' Bull. I don't know if you boys can catch them before they get across the border, but it'll be close. Losin' those horses had to slow 'em down some. I sorta hope you do, cause that will go a long ways towards keeping things calmed down up here. But then again, the Indian in me kinda hopes they make it!" Val said with a wry smile.

A commotion was taking place down by the river, and a few minutes later Pvt. Dawsey came running up. "A boat just came in from up river." He said breathlessly, "The Nez Perce are across!"

The mackinac boat that had arrived from upstream carried "Yellowstone" Kelly, one of Miles favorite civilian scouts, and also a letter from Col. Clendenin at Carroll Landing, informing Miles that the Nez Perce had crossed the Missouri River near the supply depot on Cow Island on the 23rd. They raided the depot taking provisions and then set fire to it. Clendenin speculated that they would strike north in the direction of the Bear Paw Mountains and then on to Canada. Miles immediately modified his plans and had the *Fontenelle* summoned back by firing several rounds from the Hotchkiss artillery piece. Upon its return, the rest of the day was spent using the steamer to ferry the entire column over to the north side of the river. That evening, he dispatched Kelly and a team of scouts to immediately ride out, then had Snyder's 2nd Cavalry battalion move out behind him, for Fort Benton. The rest of the column would follow in the morning.

Mike Martin invited Val to mess with the Company D sergeants that night and during the coming march. Val showed his appreciation by bagging a young buffalo, and donating it to the mess. That evening after supper, they gathered around the camp fire and he produced some cigars and a bottle of Canadian whisky, along with a bundle of buffalo coats.

"I got this here bottle from some Métis fellas at Fort Peck, along with these buffalo coats. We got to talkin' about the cattle business, and they had a lot of questions. They're getting worried about how far they havin' to go to find the buffalo nowadays. Particularly since there's more competition, what with Sitting Bull and the Sioux staying up around here year round. They're thinking about going in to the cattle business also. There's already some of them in it over towards Bozeman" Val stated. "When the railroads get out here, there'll be an easier way to get 'em to market."

Jake spoke up, "We told you that Pat Morse got on with the Northern Pacific railroad. He seems to think that they'll start laying track again next year, they pretty much know the route now, and with the Sioux out of the way he thinks they'll get the rails down quick.

"See that's what I'm a thinkin'." Val replied. "You tell Pat I said, Hi! when you see 'im agin."

"So, I take it that you're doing okay with your ranching, Val?" Martin asked.

Wheeler nodded his head, "So far, I got a few Gros Ventre cousins working for me, and I'm buildin' up a nice little herd. The market has been pretty good, what with all you Army fellas and your new forts. But, we ain't had a real bad winter for a couple of years, that'll be the test."

"You find you someone to warm your bed at night, Val?" Martin asked.

"Well, you remember that little Chippewa gal that I wintered with back at Fort Totten?"

"Yeh, her name was Shanaya, wasn't it?" Jake said.

"Yep! I'll be damned if she didn't fall in with some of my Métis friends and follow me way out here. We been hooked up for a while. I even built her a nice cozy cabin, up a creek valley along the Milk River, about twenty miles north of the Bear Paws."

"I remember that country being pretty nice." Jake said. "You worried about the Nez Perce bothering your place if they head that way?"

"Yeh, that Kelly fella was saying that the Nez Perce have been plundering most of the farms and ranches they come across." Charlie Welch added.

"A bit, but I don't think that they'll bother my place, cause there's no white folks there." Val stated, "I used to hunt and trap with a fella by the name of Joe Hale for a couple of years. He's half French, and half Nez Perce, and goes by the handle, Poker Joe. His Indian name is, Lean Elk, and according to the news that reached Fort Peck from Fort Ellis, he's been leading the Nez Perce on the trail, and has saved a bunch of white people from being killed by the young warriors. He knows this country pretty well, and that the best route up to the Medicine Line is along the valley of East Fork of the Milk River, well east of my place. You followed it up there with those supply wagons back in '74, Jake."

"Yeh, as I recall once you get in the river valley, the going is pretty easy."

"Well, if Poker Joe gets them there first, we won't be able catch them." said Val.

Martin stated, "You can bet Col. Miles will be going hell for leather to keep that from happening."

"He ain't tangled with the likes of these Nez Perce warriors, before. That messenger from Cow Island told me that they appear to have a lot of guns. Spencers, Henrys, Winchesters, and even some Springfields that they took off Col. Gibbons men after the fight over in the Big Hole Basin, last month. I reckon that it'll be a hell of a fight if he does manage to catch them." Val replied. "You'll do well to remember to keep your eyes peeled and your heads down, if I ain't there to remind you!"

The mention of rifles prompted Jake check out his own. He reached for it and the oiled metal and shiny brass scope gleamed in the firelight as he slowly extracted the Sharps from its scabbard.

"I been wonderin' about that fancy big rifle that you're totin' around, Jake. What's the story on it?" Val asked.

Val listened as Jake explained how he'd come to be in possession of the rifle, and raised his eyebrows when Jake related how accurate it was at long ranges.

"I've seen a few of them Sharps used by some Métis, but none with that fancy lookin' glass contraption. A man can put down a lot of buffalo from a long ways away, and the critters don't know to run."

Jake checked it over and wiped it with an oily rag , then slid it back in the scabbard. "Yes, I'd hate to think how many a man could kill pretty quickly."

"Too damn many!" Val exclaimed. "I've seen it with my own eyes, and the same people wonder why the buffalo herds are shrinking!"

As the fire began to die down and they wrapped up in blankets, Val tossed a buffalo coat over to Jake.

"Here! Speakin' a buffalo, you may as well take this. You're gonna be needin' it before too long. I reckon we'll be seein' snow a'for the weeks out."

"Thanks Val! I imagine you're right. The fall equinox was few days ago."

For the next two days, Miles led his column through low rolling hills and gradually ascending terrain onto a plateau near the east side of the Little Rockies Range. A vast grass covered prairie stretched out ahead of it, with plentiful herds of buffalo and antelope roaming in all directions. Towards the end of the second day, they caught up with the Tyler's 2nd Cavalry Battalion, and merged it back into Miles command. Impatient with the pace of the wagons, Miles decided to leave them, the larger Napoleon cannon, and the unmounted infantry to follow in his wake. He set off that evening taking all the mounted soldiers and a pack train carrying the Hotchkiss gun, staying on the prairie below the foothills of the Little Rockies. Later that night, Friday, Sep. 28, the weather turned cool and windy, as the column ascended the foothills working its way around to the northern slopes, and following a pass along a creek that led to the west through the range. After a march of 28 miles, they went into bivouac along a clear graveled creek with wood and grass for the horses.

"These Little Rockies are sacred to the Gros Ventre. Their medicine men come up here where they fast, and visit with the spirits." Val Wheeler told Jake. "It is said that they can only stay three days or they will receive terrifying visions."

"Do you believe that?"

"Oh, I don't know." replied Val. "My mother used to come up here and collect shiny pieces of colored agate stones. She claimed that they had great healing power, and could be used to talk with the spirits."

"Maybe we should look for some."

"It wouldn't do you any good. The patterns in the stones have to be interpreted by one who can read them. He reached into his pocket retrieving a small pouch, Jake assumed it was tobacco until Val shook a couple of colored stones into his hand. He selected a gray one and held it up to the light, then tossed it to Jake.

"Here, put that in your pocket and don't lose it. My mother gave them to me. Powerful medicine!"

Jake looked at the patterns and spots that seemed to dance in the reflection of the firelight. "Hey, you sure?"

"Yeh, besides, we won't be here long enough to look. This is called, Peoples Creek, and it leads down towards the broken plains to the west, towards some hills called Three Buttes. From the tallest one, a man should be able to see the Bear Paws and the faint outlines of the Wood Mountains across the Medicine Line. If we're gonna catch the Nez Perce, we'll have to do it in the next two days, or they'll get across."

"What do you think?"

"Miles sent a detail with a Lt. Maus, plus some civilian and Cheyenne scouts, ranging out to the south and west. I think that's the direction of the route that the Nez Perce will be using if they're headed for the Bear Paws. They should cut across their trail if they're ahead of us."

The following morning Miles had them up and on the march before dawn. When they reached the Three Buttes, several officers climbed the highest one to survey the country side but saw no movement. Later that morning a cold rain began to fall and soon turned to snow. A courier arrived from Gen. Howard advising Miles that he had reached Carroll Landing, on the Missouri, and would keep Col. Sturgis and the remainder of the 7th Cavalry with him. Miles sent back a reply urging Howard to come up in case the Sioux came across the Medicine Line to help the Nez Perce. Moving on to the foothills, while still following Peoples Creek, the troops went into camp. Lt. Maus and some of his men rode in and informed Col. Miles that he and the scouts had had a clash with a party of Nez Perce warriors leading a small herd of ponies. Maus reported possibly wounding a couple of them and capturing a dozen or so ponies. Miles immediately dispatched Kelly and some other scouts to try and track them, before dark. Meanwhile the troops huddled together in their great coats and under ponchos and canvas shelter halves. Most had started wearing the muskrat fur hats with ear flaps that had been issued . They gathered around smoldering fires of buffalo chips, trying to heat rations and sipping tepid cups of weak coffee.

Early the next morning, Val Wheeler appeared out of the pre-dawn at a weak fire that Jake and Charlie were hunkered over, trying to coax more flames from a fresh batch of chips.

"I'll see you boys later. I'm headed out with that fella Louis Shambo and some of the Cheyenne scouts. He claims he was following a trail to the northwest late yesterday, and saw some Indians running buffalo. He said that he could make out that they were wearing striped blankets, which is a sign that they could have been Nez Perce. That sounds likely to me, so I guess I'll tag along with them."

"I thought Lt. Maus and Kelly said that they were southwest?"

"There ain't usually buffalo off that direction, but north of here, closer to the big hills where there's good water and grass, they'll be thick. There's some good places for the Nez Perce to make camp, too. I'm thinkin' that's where they'll be. We're close to 'em, I can feel it." Wheeler stated, as he fingered the wolf fang necklace around his throat. As he turned to walk away, he said quietly, "Stay on your toes, Jake. There's lot's of cover for them to hide in."

Charlie asked, "You think Val's right, Jake?"

Jake nodded his head and felt the wolf tooth pendant around his own neck. "He was raised in these parts, I reckon that he knows what he's talking about." He tossed the dregs from his coffee cup and said, "We'd best get the men up to feed their horses. You need to make sure that they check their weapons and cartridges, too."

"What about breakfast?"

"They can choke down whatever they can afterwards. I expect Col. Miles will have us on the move before light."

The clouds had lifted overnight, and as dawn began to break Miles led the column southwest to intersect the trail that had been spotted the day before. The 5th Infantry battalion mounted on ponies was in the advance, with the two battalions of the 2nd and 7th Cavalry following trailed by the pack train and its escort. The breaths of the men and their horses could be seen in the frosty air, as the morning turned sunny and clear. They made their way across the broken ground and defiles as the mist on the hills slowly dissipated, their peaks starkly profiled on the horizon. A halt was called about 6:30 to allow the horses to rest and water along side a clear running stream. Miles dispatched 2nd Lt. Oscar Long, his acting Engineering Officer, to ride ahead to make contact with Kelly and his scouting party. About 8:20 the scouts caught up with Miles, informing him that the trail led north, and that the Indian encampment was several miles away. Miles quickly halted the column and issued orders to his officers to prepare the men for battle, then they would follow the scouts up the back trail. To save time he reversed the marching order, putting Hale's battalion of the three 7th Cavalry companies now in the advance. A few of the Cheyenne scouts were already headed up the trail.

After returning from meeting with Col. Miles, Capt. Hale called his officers together while the extra ammunition was being drawn from the pack train and the men were checking their weapons. Capt. Myles Moylan was in command of Company A. His veteran 1st Sgt. George McDermott had lost most of his experienced NCOs to detached duty and expired enlistments. The company's ranks consisted of mostly "Custer Avengers" and the official muster was only 30 men. Hale's own company was commanded by 2nd Lt. John Biddle who had taken over Lt. Luther Hare's spot, and 1st Sgt. Otto Wilde who was new to the regiment. Most of the veteran sergeants were on detached service back at the Tongue River and their sections were being overseen by corporals. Its official muster was 44 men with over half of them veteran troopers. Capt. Godfrey's Company D was fortunate to have only one sergeant on detached service, while half of its muster of 40 men were seasoned veterans.

1st Sgt. Martin summoned Jake and told him to report to Capt. Godfrey, pointing to where he was standing with Hale and the other officers. The temperature was still frigid and sunlight was sparkling off the surrounding snow and frost covered hills. Snow crunched under Jake's boots as he walked up. The tall, ruddy faced Capt.Hale was regaling his officers with some story when Jake approached. He noticed Jake and called out in a hearty voice. "Ah, Sgt. Rogers! This is quite a change from when we first met down in Louisiana isn't it? I thought that I'd never miss the heat and mosquitos, but now I'm not so sure!"

"Yes, Sir! I'd welcome a little heat right now."

"Godfrey tells me that 1st Sgt. Martin informed him that you're familiar with this area from your time up here a couple of years ago."

"Yes a bit, sir, I did some hunting around these Bear Paw Mountains back then, but we were bivouacked over to the north and west of here."

"Yes, and I seem to recall Tom Weir telling me that you have a good eye for terrain." Godfrey spoke up..

Jake smiled, at the thought of his old captain paying him a compliment, as if from the grave. "Then I'll try to live up to his assessment, sir."

"Well, I want you out front Rogers, we're to lead the advance. Pick a few men and find us a good route. Col. Miles wants to move quickly to attack the camp that the scouts found." Hale stated. The other officers, Capt. Moylan, Lt. Biddle, and Lt. Eckerson nodded their heads, casting nervous glances to the north.

Hale smiled as he looked out at the mountains outlined on the horizon. "This is pretty country up here. It's too beautiful a morning to get killed!" he announced and pulled out a locket from under the scarf wrapped around his neck. Hale looked at it, smiled, then patted it against his chest. "There, nothings going to hurt me now!" he laughed. "A certain lady back in St. Louis gave me this for luck."

"Let's hope she put enough luck in it for all of us, Owen." Moylan said, when the others stayed silent.

Jake chose Charlie Welch, along with Privates Dawsey, Deetline, and Cpl. Kipp to ride forward with him. As he was mounting Ajax, Martin came over to him.

"You watch yourself out there, Rogers. Don't get too far ahead, there's still scouts out there, let them do their work."

"Will do, Top! Val's out there somewhere, I expect he'll find us."

After they left the Peoples Creek valley, the terrain was a series of low ridges tapering off downhill to the northwest from the high ground. There were a couple of narrow ravines to negotiate but then the ground ahead became more level. Jake rode up to a high spot on one of the ridges and scanned the area with his binoculars.

"See anything, Jake?" asked Charlie anxiously when he returned.

"I don't see the camp, but there's some riders off to the west, coming this way. It may be our scouts. Let's keep moving, but tell the others to have their guns loaded and handy just in case."

The ground they were riding over was pocketed with little streams and shallow holes full of thin ice, patches of snow also speckled the ground. They rode slowly, picking their way and after covering a mile or so Jake made out a small group of riders approaching. He was relieved to see that one of them was Val Wheeler, who was waving at him to stop.

"We found 'em!" Wheeler called as he reigned up, "They're up ahead camped in a bend of the Snake Creek. You can't see the camp, but the pony herd is on the bench land to the west. Shambo is going to go back and fetch Col. Miles. I'll stay with you until the he comes up and decides how he wants to wants to play this out."

"Are they running?" Jake asked, "Col. Miles is worried about that."

"Well, they saw some of the Cheyenne, so they know there's some other Indians about, but that's not unusual with the buffalo around. I don't think that they know about you soldier boys, yet. We won't be sneaking up on them though, they'll have lookouts posted."

Jake and his men dismounted waiting for Miles to come up. When he arrived with his staff, he was shown the lay of the land in the direction of the camp and quickly summoned his battalion commanders. He directed Capt. Tyler and his 2nd Cavalry companies to follow the Cheyenne scouts and charge the camp, while Capt. Hale and his 7th Cavalry companies would come in behind them. Capt. Snyder and his mounted 5th Infantry companies would follow as a close reserve.

As the various units moved to comply, Val walked over to Jake and said, "I reckon there's gonna be some kind of fight. These Nez Perce are crafty fighters and will probably try to get the drop on you fellas. You'd best use what cover you can find when they do. I gonna be riding with Shambo and the Cheyennes when they go after the horse herd. Those spotted Palouse horses have the Cheyenne boys in a tizzy!"

"What's a Palouse horse?"

"It's a special bred spotted horse with striped hoofs. The Nez Perce have been breeding them for years. They're tall, smooth gaited horses that are known for their staying power. Most all of the plains tribes out here prize them. Your Col. Miles has promised the Cheyennes they can have their pick if they make off with the herd. He'll have the Nez Perce trapped if they do."

Jake nodded his head, "That sounds like a good plan to me. Maybe they'll try and negotiate if they don't have horses and can't get away"

"I don't know about that. What I think is that your colonel over there is seeing a star coming his way if he can make sure they don't get over the Medicine Line. He's gonna attack 'em!"

Jake looked over to where Miles and his staff were busy conferring with Shambo and some other scouts, pausing to aim their field glasses at the terrain ahead. "It looks like you're right, Val."

"Then you'd best remember that a man is most dangerous when he's trapped, especially when he's got his family to protect. These Nez Perce are unlike any other tribe when it comes to fightin' and they're pretty damn handy with rifles." Val mounted his horse and looked to the north, then stated, "I'm noticin' that there ain't a lot of cover out there. Keep your head on a swivel, Jake!"

"I will, Val."

CHAPTER 42

Snake Creek, Montana Territory, south of the Bear Paw Mountains - September 30, 1877

Col. Miles and 1st Lt. George Baird, his adjutant, came forward to ride with the advance. He had them proceed at a trot in a 'columns of four' formation and after a couple of miles increased the pace to a gallop. Once they crested a slight rise and could see the pony herd, the battalions slowed and Miles ordered 'left front into line' with the 2nd on left and the 7th on the right. It was 9:30 when, with pistols drawn, the entire line charged towards the village. The Cheyenne were out front and veered left, intent on capturing the pony herd. Tyler followed their lead and Miles, who was riding in the center near Hale, directed the 7th to charge straight towards the Nez Perce camp. Hale ordered the 7th back into 'columns of fours' and all three companies resumed the advance galloping, with Moylan and Company A on the left, Godfrey and Company D in the center, and Biddle and Company K, accompanied by Hale, on the right. Jake and his detachment had joined back up with the rest of Company D, falling in several files behind Capt. Godfrey, who rode at the head of the column with his guidon bearers. When Godfrey had the trumpeters sound the charge. Jake took up his spot next to the left file and reined in Ajax a bit to keep his interval with the rider ahead of him. He checked to his right to see if his troopers were staying abreast of him, then to his left towards Company A. The ground ahead rose to a crest where the charging troopers encountered a coulee that forced Company K off farther to the right. Jake saw Capt. Hale, mounted on big gray horse, descend into the swale and clamber up the other side followed by his troopers. Company A was riding through a slight depression and veered closer towards Company D as they ascended the crest. Jake looked up just in time to discover that there was no slope on the other side, but instead a steep bluff that fell away down into a valley. He could see the Nez Perce encampment nestled among various ravines along the creek bed and also the figures of Indians and some horses milling about. Both Company A and D, came to an abrupt halt about twenty yards from the edge of the precipice. The startled lead elements reigned in their mounts, struggling to control them. Jake got Ajax stopped and was turning to warn the column behind him when he saw numerous warriors appear from below the edge of the bluff ahead aiming rifles at them. Rapid volleys rang out and bullets began impacting the men and horses ahead of him. The troops milled about in confusion and several horses bolted over the edge carrying their riders with them. He heard bullets ripping the air around him as the column was raked by rapid rifle fire

"Fall back! Fall Back!" Godfrey yelled, as he turned his mount, "We need to regroup, fours left about!"

The Nez Perce warriors, armed with repeating rifles, poured merciless volleys into the confused ranks of the troopers. Jake saw Godfrey's horse struck by several bullets, pitching the officer over its head as it went down.

"Charlie!" he yelled. "The captain is down! Come on!"

As Jake and Charlie dismounted and grabbed their rifles, Jake summoned Pvt. Curran to hold their horses, then they ran towards Godfrey where they saw him struggling to get to his feet. Trumpeter Herwood moved his mount to shield the officer and Jake saw him flinch, then grab his side, swaying in the saddle.

"Get out of here, Herwood!" Jake yelled. "We'll see to the captain!"

Jake ran over to Godfrey, who had managed to regain his feet and said. "Let's go, Sir! We need to get away from here!"

Charlie was laying behind Godfrey's horse, cooly working the action of his carbine, reeling off shots. "Go on, Jake! I'll try and make them keep their heads down. They seem to be moving to the right."

Jake turned and looked that way and saw that Capt. Hale had dismounted his men in a skirmish line. They were shooting down into the creek bottom at the Nez Perce sharpshooters under the bluff. Having repulsing the cavalry in front of them, the warriors turned and concentrated their fire in the direction of Company K, while others began popping up out of the gullies to engage the Company K troopers. Jake looked and saw that Curran was struggling to hold their horses, looking desperately in their direction.

"Come on Charlie! Let's get out of here while they're distracted. I'll grab the captain, we gotta go, now!"

Godfrey had recovered enough to manage a slow run and when they reached Curran they grabbed their mounts, then made their way down the rise to where the slope protected them from the rifle fire. Lt. Eckerson had fallen back a couple of hundred yards with the rest of the company where it had formed a dismounted skirmish line, along with Moylan's company and Snyder's 5th Infantry battalion, which had come up in support.

Col. Miles was riding back and forth behind the lines encouraging the men. Godfrey had recovered sufficiently by the time they reached the company to request a new mount. His orderly went to find one and when he came back leading one with a blood covered saddle.

As Godfrey mounted, Jake looked at it and remarked, "Hey, that's Jimmy Alberts' horse."

1st Sgt. Martin who was standing nearby, replied solemnly, "Well, he ain't gonna need him Jake, Alberts went down in the first volley."

Gunfire continued to crackle and the sound of volley fire from the vicinity of Company K crashed loudly. Jake looked through his binoculars and could see that some of the fighting was hand to hand. He could make out the tall figure of Capt. Hale striding up and down a skirmish line directing fire and shooting his pistol.

Capt. Moylan rode up and called out to Godfrey, "Col. Miles wants us to support Hale! We're to advance on foot in that direction!"

Godfrey nodded his head and looked over at Martin, who said, "Right, I'll get the lads moving, Sir! Sgt. Welch, go get the sections moving and hook up with Sgt. Flanagan. Rogers, you go round up your riflemen and be prepared to have them lay down covering fire."

The two cavalry companies some in their caped overcoats and others in buffalo coats moved clumsily, attempting to double time. The horse holders trailed along behind and struggled to control the nervous mounts. When the leading section reached the ravine, Godfrey who was still mounted, led them across and as he started up the other side he was struck in the side and slid from his saddle, grasping the pommel to keep from falling. His orderly grabbed the reins and led the horse to the rear as the officer grimly hung on. The Nez Perce seeing the approach of the reinforcements, began creeping up the gullies of the ravine and opened fire on them, raking the ranks as they hurried to get across. Jake and Welch gathered up six of the riflemen and took them forward to try and cover their flank. As they were taking position. Jake saw 1st Sgt. Martin exhorting some of the men to hurry. "At the double time now, lads! Get up there!"

"Let's get these bastards!" Jake yelled, "Shoot at the powder smoke, we've got to slow their fire!"

Jake was peering through his Malcolm scope, seeking a target when he heard a loud "Smack!" behind him and turned to see Martin fall to the ground, half his head gone.

"Charlie!" Jake called, "Top is gone! I'm gonna go find Flanagan!"

As he scrambled out of the ravine, Jake saw that Capt. Hale had pulled his men back a from the bluff about a hundred yards and was re-establishing the skirmish line. Capt. Moylan, still mounted, rode over to where Hale was rallying his men and as he was getting off his horse a bullet struck him in the right thigh. Moylan's orderly grabbed him and the wounded officer hopped away with his assistance. Jake ran over to report to Hale.

"Capt. Godfrey got hit and 1st Sgt. Martin is dead, sir!" he yelled. "I don't know where Lt. Eckerson is! Where do you want us, sir?"

"Glad that you made it Rogers! The Indians have been creeping up that gully and picking us off. I've lost Lt. Biddle and my first sergeant, too! Sgt. Rott is senior now. I have him pulling back the horse holders." Hale said as he calmly reloaded his pistol, "We've got some wounded men out there that we need to recover. Try and cover our left flank and we'll see if we can get them out of there."

Jake replied, "Yes, sir! I'll take some marksmen."

Hale grinned, "Damned hot work for such a cold day, eh Rogers?"

Jake heard the high crack of bullets passing near, and saw a couple of clumps of dirt erupt near the officer. One struck Hale under his chin, causing the scarf around his throat to flutter and flinging his head back. The officer crumpled to the ground without making a sound.

Stunned, Jake dropped to the ground and crawled over to where Hale lay. He could see blood soaking the scarf and Hale's head was twisted at an unnatural angle. He heard someone come running up behind him and turned to see 2nd Lt. Long, one of Col. Miles staff officers, who flung himself to the ground next to Jake.

"Is that Capt. Hale?" Long asked, incredulously.

"I'm afraid so, sir. It looks like the bullet shattered his neck."

"Lt. Baird was wounded, so I was sent forward with orders for Hale from Col. Miles! Are there any other officers still alive?"

Jake looked at Long, noting that the officer seemed a bit overwhelmed. "Capt. Hale had just finished telling me that Lt. Biddle is dead. I think Lt. Eckerson is coming up with the rest of Company D, somewhere behind us."

"No, I saw him on the way here and he said that he was going back for more ammunition." Long replied

"That seems odd. Why didn't he send a sergeant or corporal?" Jake wondered out loud.

"I didn't ask."

"Well, then I guess you're in command, Lieutenant." Jake said.

The young officer looked around, "What do you think we ought to do, Sergeant?"

Jake looked back to the south where a low ridge offered some cover, then looked over to where the rest of Company D, and A, were struggling out of the ravine.

"I think we need to move back to that ridge line and regroup, sir. That will get us far enough out of range that at least we're not sitting ducks."

"I think that you're right. Start the men moving!" Long said.

Fortunately, Miles had sent the 5th Infantry battalion up, and they pressed forward to the south bluff of the camp. The firepower of their Springfield rifles forced the Nez Perce warriors to fall back, relieving the beleaguered 7th Cavalry companies. When the troopers gained the scant cover below the ridge, Lt. Long ordered the remaining sergeants in each company to get the men regrouped. Jake did a quick head count and found that he, Charlie Welch, & Sgt. Al Cunningham, along with Cpl. Tom Cox, were the only NCOs in the company left unscathed. His rifle section had suffered four casualties with Pvt. Dawsey killed, Cpl. Quinn, Pvt. Deetline, and Pvt. Lewis wounded. Most of the horses had run off to the rear as the horse holders of the sections got pulled into the fray. Jim Flanagan, who was wearing his left arm in an improvised sling, took over as acting first sergeant and when Lt. Eckerson returned with ammunition, Flanagan called Jake over.

"Jake, see that everyone gets some. Lt. Eckerson is going to talk with Lt. Long."

"I'll see to it. How's the arm doing, Jim?"

"Getting a mite stiff and sore, but the bleeding's stopped. I was lucky that the bullet just grazed me, poor Mike Martin caught one in the head! It was a bit of near thing that we made it across that ravine with as many men as we did. I hear you lost some of your marksmen." Flanagan said.

"They caught us up in the narrow end and just opened up with repeating rifles. It was like we were targets in a shooting gallery, we're lucky we didn't lose more men." Jake replied.

Flanagan shook his head sadly, "Aye! We've two officers killed, and two wounded, along with all three of the First Sergeants killed. Company A, is down to a pair of veteran corporals and the privates left are mostly all new men. Company K took the brunt and they're in the same shape, although they've a couple of former sergeants looking to the men. We lost Jimmy Alberts! Cpl. Wylie and Cpl. Quinn are both wounded so, I've got you, Charlie Welch, Cpl. Cox, and Cpl. Kipp left."

"I think that the Nez Perce were targeting anyone with stripes on their pant legs. Val Wheeler told me to watch out." Jake said, "Now I realize what he meant!"

"As far as I know, your man Dawsey is the only one of our troopers killed so far. I'm still not sure how many of the other lads are seriously wounded. I need some junior NCOs to help out. I think Cpl. Kipp is good candidate for sergeant, and Pvt. John Fox would do okay as a corporal. I've been watching them all summer."

Jake nodded his head in agreement, "I agree, good choices both of them. Kipp showed well last year at Reno Hill, and Fox has been with us two years."

"Right! Although I'll have to get it okayed by Lt. Eckerson." Flanagan stated. "He's the only officer still standing in the battalion."

"Speaking of the lieutenant, it seems odd that he went after the ammunition on his own. Did he know about the captain being wounded?"

"I couldn't say for sure, that was about the time I got hit. Then Cox found me and told me about Mike. That's when I learned Eckerson had gone back."

"Hmm! Okay, I guess it doesn't matter now. What do you want me to do, Jim?" Jake asked.

"Have the men dig some pits and post your riflemen to keep a watch for any movement out there, then help me get the rest of the lads sorted out."

Col. Miles roamed behind the attacking battalions, watching the fighting as it developed. Tylers's 2nd Cavalry had been following in the wake of the Cheyennes and joined them in successfully capturing the bulk of the horse herd. However, a group of Nez Perce warriors, accompanied by some women and children, had been able to escape to the north and east along with a couple of hundred horses. Tyler sent 2nd Lt. McClernand and his Company G to pursue them and he engaged then in a running fight for about 5 miles, until the Nez Perce warriors turned and drove him off while their non-combatants fled. When Miles saw the 7th Cavalry's assault repulsed he sent word to 1st Lt. Romeyn, the commander of Company G, 5th Infantry and his 23 men to join up with the troopers. Romeyn was a veteran officer in his mid-forties and had been breveted Major during the war for his actions at the Battle of Nashville. As Romeyn moved off to reinforce the 7th, Miles directed that the Hotchkiss gun be sent forward to fire on the village. After Romeyn arrived and assumed command of the battered 7th troops, Lt. Long left to report back to Miles. Dr. Henry Tilton and a medical orderly arrived shortly to treat the wounded, but he quickly ran out of bandages and had to send for more.

Jake took a detail to recover the Company D mounts and when he returned found Sgt. Flanagan talking to an infantry First Sergeant.

"How'd you do, Rogers?" Flanagan asked.

"We rounded up enough to mount most of the unwounded men, Jim." Jake replied. "I put Kipp in charge of them, and left them back down the hill aways."

"Good! This is 1st Sgt. Henry Hogan, Company G of the 5th. His Lieutenant Romeyn is senior officer now."

Jake nodded at Hogan, and said, "Jake Rogers."

Flanagan said, "Henry and I both grew up in County Clare back in Ireland, don't ya know! He and his lads used to chase Mr. Lo with us down at Fort Wallace, back in '69."

"Aye! Twas hot, dry, and dusty there, not like this fookin' weather!" Hogan replied. "At least Miles has got us mounted on Indian ponies up here, although it looks like we'll be advancing on foot from here."

"Do ya think Miles will have us go at them again today?" Flanagan asked.

"Oh, you can count on it, lad!" Hogan stated, "His blood is up! He's not one to get punched in the nose and then back away!"

Col. Miles was indeed planning a general assault. With the 2nd Cavalry occupying the high ground north of the Nez Perce encampment, he had them virtually surrounded. Lt. Jerome and his Company H had already been engaged on the west side of Snake Creek. On the south bluff, the barrel of the Hotchkiss gun couldn't be depressed low enough to be effective and the men serving it were quickly driven off by long range firing from Indian marksmen. Lt. Woodruff, who had replaced the wounded Lt. Baird as Miles adjutant, dispatched messengers to coordinate with the units south of the bluffs. The plan was for a general assault at 3:00 PM. Lt. Maus and his scouts would fire into the ravines from the west, while the Companies I & F of the 5th, advanced up the creek valley in the center. Romeyn was to charge forward with his men, and the remains of the 7th, from his position on the ridge on the right. Unbeknownst to Miles, the messenger carrying the order to charge at 3:00 never reached Lt. Romeyn.

Jake was huddled in hastily dug rifle pit trying to keep out of the frigid wind that sprung up, bringing flurries of light snow with it that were beginning to turn everything white. He was grateful for the buffalo coat that Val had given him and had donned a fur hat, also. When he left to retrieve Ajax earlier, he found his colored snow glasses still safely stored in their case in his saddlebag and was glad that he'd had the foresight to bring them. They helped block the wind as he occasionally peered towards the encampment looking for targets. He heard someone behind him and turned to see Charlie Welch.

"Hey Charlie! What's going on?"

"Lt. Romeyn is waiting on word from Col. Miles. We're going to try and make it back up past that ravine, while the rest of the 5th assaults the bluff and puts pressure on the hostiles."

"Damn, that sounds risky! These Indians have Springfield rifles, too." Jake replied with a grimace, "We'll be in their range as soon as we show ourselves!"

"Yeh, I know but Romeyn wants us all to go forward when we do, so come on."

The two scrambled down to where the companies were assembling. Jake decided to leave the Sharps rifle. He secured it in its scabbard tied to his saddle and found a spare Springfield carbine along with full bandolier to carry. He had just finished checking it over when the sound of heavy firing broke out to the west.

"It sounds to me like they started without us!" Jake yelled.

Off in the distance, buglers began to sound the 'Charge' and Lt. Romeyn quickly directed his own to follow suit. He yelled and ran forward leading the ragged battalion up and across the ridge line, advancing at the double time. They surged forward for fifty yards or so before bullets came zipping at them. Romeyn was hit in the chest almost immediately. His 1st Sgt. Hogan stopped to help him and supported the officer as he staggered to the rear. Jake looked towards the bluffs ahead and saw small clouds of gun smoke bloom along the line of the bluffs ahead. All along the ragged line of charging troopers men began to fall. Jake turned his head to check on the Company D ranks and noticed that he couldn't see Charlie. He just raised his arm to wave them on when he felt something punch him in the upper arm and almost simultaneously his head took a jarring blow that knocked him into a black oblivion.

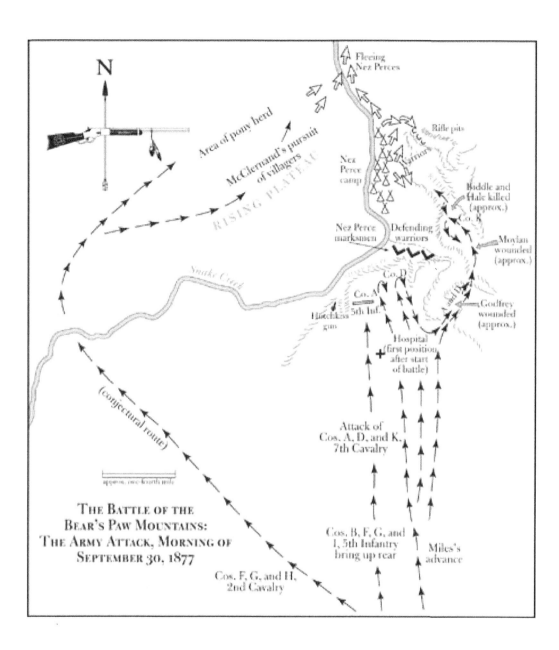

N

Fleeing
Nez Perces

Rifle pits

Area of pony herd

McClernand's pursuit
of villagers

RISING PLATEAU

Nez
Perce
camp

Warriors

Biddle and
Hale killed
(approx.)
Co. K

Snake Creek

Nez Perce
marksmen

Defending
warriors

Moylan
wounded
(approx.)

Co. D

Co. A
5th Inf.

Hotchkiss
gun

Godfrey
wounded
(approx.)

Hospital
(first position
after start
of battle)

(conjectural route)

approx. one-fourth mile

Attack of
Cos. A, D, and K,
7th Cavalry

THE BATTLE OF THE
BEAR'S PAW MOUNTAINS:
THE ARMY ATTACK, MORNING OF
SEPTEMBER 30, 1877

Cos. B, F, G, and
I, 5th Infantry
bring up rear

Miles's
advance

Cos. F, G, and H,
2nd Cavalry

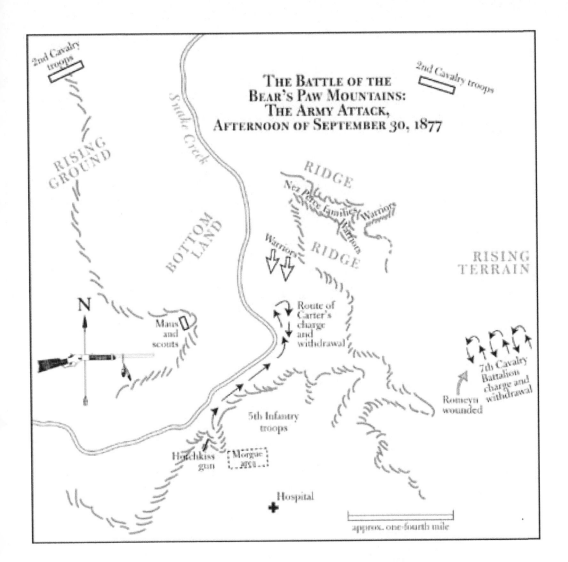

THE BATTLE OF THE
BEAR'S PAW MOUNTAINS:
THE ARMY ATTACK,
AFTERNOON OF SEPTEMBER 30, 1877

2nd Cavalry troops

2nd Cavalry troops

Snake Creek

RISING GROUND

BOTTOM LAND

RIDGE

Nez Perce families

Warriors

RIDGE

Warriors

RISING TERRAIN

Maus and scouts

N

Route of Carter's charge and withdrawal

7th Cavalry Battalion charge and withdrawal

Romeyn wounded

5th Infantry troops

Hotchkiss gun

Morgue

Hospital

approx. one-fourth mile

CHAPTER 43

Snake Creek Battlefield, Montana Territory - Night of Sep. 30 - Oct. 1, 1877

Blowing snow was blanketing the ground and covering the fallen bodies of the fallen combatants of both sides. An occasional moan, or cry for help, from one of the wounded could be heard and sounds of digging emanated from the both the Nez Perce camp and along the soldier positions. A few furtive figures flitted about the fallen troopers, as warriors quietly searched for guns and ammunition. One of them paused to roll over a body clad in a buffalo coat and began to undo the buttons. The man stirred and let out a moan, surprising the Indian who bent to check his breathing. There was a scarf around the man's neck and when he began to unwrap it, a subtle glint from an object caught his eye. The warrior grasped it lightly and peered at it in the dim light, then drew back a bit startled as he realized what it was. Suddenly, he became aware of someone else drawing near and whispered quietly in the Nez Perce language.

"This one still breaths. He wears a pendant with a tooth of a wolf around his neck. I sense powerful medicine in it."

The other whispered back using the same language, "Yes it is, I have one also, it has helped lead me here to find my friend!"

The warrior asked, "Who are you to have a friend out here?"

"My name is Pale Wolf, I was a friend of Lean Elk some years back. I've been looking for this man. How are you called?"

"I am called Hustul, but my white man name is, Tom Hill, and I remember you. You are also called Val Wheeler. I was with Lean Elk back then, also. I followed him when he took our band to join up with the others. Are you with the soldiers fighting us?" he asked.

"No, not fighting, I live near here and came with them to see that my wife and home are not harmed. Leave this one to me, I will see to him." Val replied. "I do not want him to die out here."

"I would like to have his bullets and guns." Tom stated.

Val unbuckled Jake's ammunition bandolier and tossed it. "You can have them. Tell Lean Elk that I said to get away if you can. They have you surrounded."

"Lean Elk is dead! One of our men thought he was a Cheyenne and shot him by mistake."

"My heart is sad to hear that."

"We can't leave our wounded, or the women and children, so we must prepare to fight on." Hill said sadly. "Take your friend."

When Hill left, Val leaned forward and listened to Jake's breathing which was steady. Val took a blanket that he'd brought and rolled Jake in it, noting that blood was matted in his hair, He wrapped Jake's head with the scarf and then retrieved the fur cap, placing it gently over the scarf and tied it. He picked up Jake and hoisted his inert form over his shoulder, then bent to grab his Henry rifle. He made his way across the snow covered ground with slow, quiet steps, heading back to the south. Eventually he got close enough to make out the ridge line on the horizon in front of him where the soldier positions were. He gave out a low whistle and soon Sgt. Flanagan appeared out of the darkness.

"So, you found him!" Flanagan exclaimed, "Is he still alive?"

"Yeh, but he's knocked out. I think he got his bell rung pretty good, but he's still breathin'. Help me get him over to the doctor where we can get him checked out."

"Right, I've got Cpl. Kipp and Pvt. Kellar waiting back there with a stretcher that we rigged from blankets. Let me go get them, they just came back from hauling Charlie Welch over to the hospital? He was hit early on and was close enough to the lines that he managed to crawl back. He got hit in the right leg and its busted all to hell. He'll be lucky if he doesn't lose it."

"Well, it was a cockeyed plan to charge like that, from the git go." Val stated, then spit tobacco in disgust, "Downright stupid if ya ask me! Let's get Jake over to the hospital."

The hospital area was several hundred yards back south from the edge of the bluffs in a depression that shielded it from the fighting. Because the pack train and wagons had still not arrived, there was only one tent and the wounded were laid outside in a row, covered with blankets and ponchos as best as they could be. The surgeon, Major Henry Tilton, his assistant surgeon Lt. Edwin Gardner, and their orderlies were tending to the men by lantern light, while other orderlies worked to keep a small fire of buffalo chips burning hot enough to heat water and coffee. When the stretcher party got there, Val had them set Jake down near the tent where the surgeons could see him.

"Who is this?" Asked Tilton, "I see from his pant legs that it's another sergeant."

"Sgt. Rogers, Company D, from the 7th!" Val stated, "I think he was hit in the head, but he's still breathin'."

Tilton bent to look and gently removed Jake's hat, then peeled away the scarf. "Bring me some hot water, orderly."

After they'd washed away some of the blood, Tilton used his fingers to feel around a small furrow on the left side of Jake's head. "Head wounds always seem to bleed the most. I don't think the skull is cracked, but he's going to have a hell of a headache when he comes round." he stated, then said to his orderly Pvt. Conner, "Let's get this buffalo coat off and see if he's wounded anywhere else."

As they were pulling the coat sleeve from Jake's left arm, they could see blood glistening by the fire light. The orderly said, "The whole sleeve is soaked and it looks like the blood is running down his arm, Sir."

"Let's get his uniform jacket off." Tilton said. After that was done, he took a pair of scissors from his pocket and used them to slit the shirt and long underwear sleeves. "Go fetch some more water to rinse it off, I'll need to probe the wound."

The orderly went for the water and Lt. Gardner brought over a pouch of medical instruments. Once they washed Jake's shoulder they could see the bullet hole clearly, Tilton grabbed some narrow forceps and said, "It's a good thing he's not conscious, we're out of chloroform until the wagons get here. He inserted the forceps in the wound, which elicited a moan from Jake.

"I can feel the bullet, it's lodged against the humerus." the surgeon stated, "I think that I can get a hold of it. Hold on to him, Conner!" He looked up at Val, "You may as well help, too."

Jake groaned and tried to thrash around as Tilton worked to grasp the bullet, finally extracting it. He held it up to the light and said. "Looks like a .44 Henry bullet. That buffalo coat and his uniform slowed it enough to keep from shattering his arm." He dropped it in a tin cup, then said. "I need to see if I can get the cloth and fibers out also, or the wound won't heal properly. Better hold him down again!"

After the doctor was finished and Jake's wounds were dressed, the orderlies wrapped him in a blanket then carried him over and laid him with the other wounded. Val went back and retrieved the buffalo coat that Jake had been wearing, draping it and a poncho over him.

Wheeler walked over to the where the surgeons were working on another wounded man. He asked, "There was another sergeant from Company D brought in earlier, Sgt. Welch. I was just wonderin' how he's doin'?"

Gardner looked up and said, "He's over there, too. A bullet shattered his thigh. We cleaned it up and put a splint on it. But I think he needs surgery to get it set properly. Time will tell! Hopefully it'll mend, but he'll probably never walk straight again. Sorry!"

"Hell Doc! It ain't your fault!" Val exclaimed, turned and looked towards the bluffs where the Nez Perce camp was hidden. "I've known both those boys since they was snot nosed privates. It pains to see them all shot up!"

"Unfortunately, they have a lot of company here" Tilton said, sadly.

Val asked, "So, do you think Rogers will come around soon, Doc?"

"Hard to say, but I think so. Probably when it gets light." he stated. "He's going to be very sore when he does."

"Well, I think I'll go and sit with him. There ain't no scoutin' around here to do now." Val said, "I may as well hang out here til light. Then I'll go see if I can scrounge you up some firewood, Doc!"

It was still snowing as Val walked over to where Jake lay. He sat down, cross legged, on a blanket and opened a soft deerskin pouch. He shook out a half dozen pieces of translucent agate in varying sizes and colors, then sorted through them. He selected the gray one, touching it first to his forehead, then Jake's head, and clasped it in his fist. He settled his wide brimmed slouch hat at an angle, then gathered his own buffalo coat around him.

As Jake regained consciousness, he slowly became aware of an intense throbbing pain emanating from his head, and another from his left arm. When he first opened his eyes they had trouble focusing and there was only blackness. He blinked several times and attempted to raise his head. When he moved it the pain only intensified. He became aware that he was totally covered up with a blanket and used his right arm to move it away from his face. The dim light revealed total whiteness and he realized that he was covered with snow. His feet felt like blocks of ice and he wiggled his toes attempting to feel them moving. A snow covered figure was huddled near him, and Jake recognized the feathers, sticking up from the hat, as belonging to Val Wheeler. He attempted to speak, but it came out as a croak.

"Wha, Wal!"

Val jerked his head up. "Jake? Bout time you woke your lazy ass up! I been sittin' here in the damn snow waitin' on you for couple of hours now." He said with relief, as he stood up, shaking the snow off, then asked "How ya feelin'?"

"Where am I and how'd I get here?" Jake managed to ask haltingly.

"Well, you got yourself shot up charging straight at those Nez Perce bucks right out in the open, like a fool! I had to go out and fetch you to here! This is what passes for a hospital for now. So again, how ya feelin'?"

"Like I got kicked by a mule!"

"Damned lucky ya gotta a thick skull then. That particular mule was a bullet, and another one got you in the arm up near your shoulder. Do ya think that you can stand if help get you up on your feet?" Val asked.

Jake became aware of an urgent pain coming from his bladder and replied, "I hope so. I gotta piss like a race horse!"

Val quickly reached over to retrieve the piece of gray agate that had fallen on the ground next to Jake, then helped him struggle to his feet. He supported him while Jake took a few tentative steps. "Let's go over here a ways. I hope ya can take yer pecker out with one hand. I ain't much lookin' forward to havin' to help ya fish it out!" he wise cracked.

When they came back to the hospital area, Major Tilton saw them and drew Jake over to the tent where he checked on his wounds.

"Good! Your eyes seem be focusing and the bleeding has stopped." he said, "Let's check that dressing on your arm and I'll get the orderly to rig you a sling for it.

When the surgeon was done he helped Jake don his buffalo coat. Jake noticed that one of the orderlies had cleaned up it up a bit, along with his fur hat.

"Careful with that, you have some swelling and try not to move that arm around, I put a couple of stitches in it."

Jake noticed that Capt. Godfrey was laying wrapped up in some blankets nearby, propped up by some ammo crates and holding a tin cup of coffee.

Jake went over to him and asked, "How are you, Sir?"

Godfrey stared up at him listlessly, his eyes slightly unfocused, "Okay, I suppose, how many men did we lose, Rogers?"

"I can't rightly say, sir."

Godfrey didn't say anything and when Jake looked his head was lolled to the side, Tilton reached over and took the cup from Godfrey's hand saying. "Your captain has a big hole in his side, an inch closer and his back would have been severed. I dosed him pretty heavy with laudanum for the pain. I have a little that I can give you if you want it."

Val walked up with a cup of coffee and handed it to Jake, "I'd try and stay away from that stuff, Jake. Here, I put some of my mother's potions in this coffee. Try it, first! It won't make you sick, but it helps with the pain and gives you good dreams!" Val looked at Tilton and explained, "My mother is a Gross Ventre medicine women."

Tilton looked back at Val curiously and asked, "Any idea what it is, I'm always interested in different ways to treat pain and I've heard that the native tribes out here have some unusual ways?"

"Just some seeds and herbs, mostly from what you whites call hemp plants."

The surgeon nodded his head, "That's not the first time that I've heard of that. I may have to experiment with some of it. In the meantime, Rogers, you stay nearby and try to stay off your feet. I suspect that your concussed and I want to keep an eye on you. I'll have one of my orderlies see if he can find you a little hardtack and bacon. I'm told that Col. Miles sent his scout Yellowstone Kelly, to hurry the wagons. We'll be able to get these men out of the weather then."

After he finished the coffee and ate a little bit the pain had eased and settled down to a dull throb. "I'd like to go find Charlie." Jake said. "Will you help me, Val?"

"Okay, it's getting pretty light out. But you let me go find him and I'll come back and get you."

5 inches of snow had blanketed the surrounding countryside and a fitful wind continued to blow, with the temperature hovering near freezing. The three 7th Cavalry companies were down to less than 60 effectives available for duty and had been replaced along the line of rifle pits early that morning by the rest of the 5th Infantry units. Miles felt that the longer range of the infantry rifles would be more effective in engaging the hostiles. The 7th was moved to positions directly behind the Hotchkiss gun, just east of the hospital. Lt. Eckerson was the lone officer and the three companies were temporarily consolidated into one unit with Sgt. Flanagan designated as temporary First Sergeant. The men with shelter halves put up crude tents, propping them up with rifles and carbines as the troopers huddled under them. Details were sent over to the pack train, which was located off to the west where it sheltered under a creek bluff, to draw forage for the horses that they'd gathered up. Miles had also located his headquarters tent near there and was talking with his staff and a few scouts, discussing his plans for the morning. The men detailed as the artillery crew were working on the Hotchkiss gun and breaking open ammunition boxes. Thin streams of smoke blew across the small make shift shelters, rising from smoldering buffalo chip fires as the soldiers attempted to heat coffee and the few rations that they'd scrounged together. While the Cheyenne scouts were out making sure the captured

horse herd was secured, several of the them approached the Nez Perce camp to speak with them. They were told that they were very concerned for the safety of their women and children. Three of the Cheyennes rode directly to Col. Miles and broached the idea of a truce, and the possibility of a meeting to discuss terms of surrender.

Val had found Charlie Welch along with several other wounded men from Company D. He came back and helped Jake over to where he'd found them. Cpl. Quinn, and Pvt. Deetline both had shoulder wounds similar to Jake's. Charlie was well dosed with laudanum and was sleeping when Jake made it over to them.

Deetline, a German who'd served in the infantry before enlisting in the 7th, was one of Jake's marksman. A solid soldier, he'd volunteered to be a water carrier on Reno Hill. When he saw Jake he rose and greeted them, "Es gut to see you, Sarge! Der verdammt Injuns, dey done shot the schiesse out of us, eh?"

"Yeh, I guess they did, Deet." Jake replied, wearily.

Quinn was sitting, wrapped in a blanket and poncho, he noted Jake's sling and commented, "Hi Jake, it looks like we both got hit in the same shoulder."

"Yeh! Lucky us. Who else we got here, John?" Jake asked.

"Privates Clark, Baker, and trumpeter, Herwood."

Jake nodded, "I saw Herwood get hit. Any others?"

"No, we're the worst of the lot. Lewis and Jones had flesh wounds, and Curran lost a finger, but they went back to the company. You can see some of our boys over there, feeding the horses." Quinn said, pointing.

"We need to go see if we can find our saddle bags. I could use a new shirt and I've got some rations in a tote bag." Jake stated, "Maybe we can scrounge up more?"

"You sit down, Sarge. I vill go and get a couple of fellas to help me vit 'em." Deetline said. "My arm is not so bad as you, I tink."

"Yeh, I'll go with him." Wheeler said, "I left my horse over there and I can load your stuff on him."

"By the way, Val, how did you come to be back here anyway? I thought you were over west with the Shambo and his scouts?" Jake enquired.

"Oh, after they captured most of the horse herd, Capt. Tyler saw some Nez Perce gettin' away to the north. He ordered Lt. McClernand and his company to chase after them and Shambo asked me to guide them. We chased 'em for about 5 miles, until I figured out that we were badly out numbered and was able to persuade the Lootenant that it might be a good idea to back off. As we were ridin' back we heard sounds of the firing down where you boys were fightin'. I circled around and came in from the east, then found what was left of your boys about dark. Flanagan told me that he saw you get hit and about where you went down. So I waited a bit, then went out and dragged your ass back to the lines." Val answered, then turned to leave.

"Why, do I suspect that it wasn't quite as simple as that." Jake said quietly to himself, as he watched Val and Deeline walk away.

After Wheeler's return, Jake and the other Company D men rigged a small shelter to block the wind and huddled together underneath it for warmth. Occasional shots rang out most of the morning, as the two sides took turns sniping at each other. The Hotchkiss gun banged out a few rounds, which were largely ineffective.

Just before noon, Johnny Bruguier, one of Miles's scouts who went by the nickname 'Big Leggins' came looking for Val.

"Hey, Wheeler! I heard you were over here. The colonel has agreed to a truce. "The Nez Perce just broke out a white flag and a fella by the name of Tom Hill just came across the lines asking to see you." Bruguier stated. "Miles sent me to fetch you and bring you back to his tent."

Val looked up in surprise, "Hmm! I wonder what he wants me for?"

"Don't know!" Johnny declared, "But I reckon if it gets the shootin' stopped for a while, it's a good thing! Let's go see!"

Miles headquarters tent was located well above the Indian encampment on a sheltered bench in the creek valley.When they arrived, they found Tom Hill sitting at a camp table eating lunch with Miles.

Miles looked up and said, "I'm hoping to arrange a meeting with Chief Joseph, but this fellow wants to speak with you first, Wheeler."

Val nodded at Hill, "Hello, Tom! There's a bit more light now, then when I last saw you."

Hill looked at Val, with piercing dark eyes and spoke slowly in English, "I wish to talk with you, only."

Miles seemed to be mildly surprised at the request and frowned slightly. "Cannot we discuss it together, Mr. Hill?

Hill looked at him, "I know of this man from before. I trust his word and must ask him some things that you would not answer."

"Very well. You two go outside and talk, but be quick about it. My patience is wearing thin!" Miles said bluntly.

Outside, they walked away for a few yards then stopped. Hill turned to Val. "Can we trust this man's words?"

"I do not know him well." Wheeler answered, "He is a brave soldier and fighter. I do know that you cannot defeat him. He has defeated the Sioux and Cheyenne already."

"He wants to see Joseph, who is our camp leader and not a war leader. Most of them are dead. Joseph is worried about the women, children and old ones, but the warriors want to keep fighting." Hill stated. "They want to make a try for the Medicine Line and cross over into the Old Woman's Land. They've come so far and are so close!"

Val considered that for a moment and replied, "I know the route well, but you should also know that the Gross Ventre and Assiniboine tribes aren't pleased about you stirring up trouble on their lands. Don't expect them to help you."

"Yes, we've seen how the Crow and Cheyennes have turned on us, also."

Val nodded his head slowly, "Some can probably make it, but the rest will not. If Joseph can save the women and children, then he should."

Hill looked over in the direction of the Indian camp and made a sign, then said quietly to Wheeler, "We will see. Thank you Pale Wolf!"

Joseph, the Nez Perce camp leader, made his way across the creek in the swirling snow and under a flag of truce, while the fighting men from each side watched. Tom Hill went down to meet him and then led him back up to Col. Miles, where they shook hands and went into the tent. Meanwhile, with a truce in place the soldiers immediately sent parties out to retrieve the dead and wounded. The various bands of the Nez Perce, had hastily abandoned their camp circles to take shelter in a series of narrow ravines along Snake Creek. They'd left most of their supplies, blankets, and other gear. The bodies of their slain warriors were strewn about, still laying where they fell. The Nez Perce crept out of their shelters in the ravine and began to salvage what they could, removing the corpses for burial. On the other side of the creek, the frozen bodies of dead troopers and soldiers were gathered and placed in the depression south of the bluffs and laid out in rows, then covered with a tarpaulin.

About 4:00 PM the wagon train finally reached the Army camp, and the hospital tents were unloaded. The decision was made to relocate the hospital to the sheltered bluff behind Miles headquarters tent, where it would be completely safe from the Indian's fire. A new influx of wounded arrived, due to the truce, with several suffering from frostbite. The lack of wood for cooking fires was still an issue and several of the wagons were broken up for wood. Miles sent a well guarded pack train out to gather wood that morning and it returned fully loaded at dusk. The cooks got busy and before too long the smell of coffee and bacon wafted on the breeze, with portions being delivered to the men on watch along the line of rifle pits. Jake gathered the Company D men in a corner of one of the hospital tents. Just before dark, Jake retrieved his pouch that held his letters and writing materials from his saddle bags. He spread them out on his blankets and had just began reading his last one from Holly, when Val come in

"Well, you boys got it down right cozy here!" Val declared. "I might just bunk with you boys if they don't run me off!"

"That a letter from Holly?" Charlie asked Jake.

"Who's Holly?" Val asked.

"His gal that he's got stashed back home, down in Missouri." Charlie said, "He met her when we were at Fort Lincoln. She's going to school down there and supposed to be waiting for him."

Val laughed, "That sounds serious Jake, if you been makin' plans like that! That's good! You boys need to think about gettin' out of this soldierin' business. It's bad for your health, a man can only dodge so many bullets!"

Charlie had recovered sufficiently to lean up against a saddle and some bags, replied glumly, "Yeh, I guess my luck ran out on me. I just hope I can still walk good when this heals."

Val said, sympathetically, "I know Charlie, but at least you still got two. They'll get you fixed up. When I stopped to talk with Doc. Tilton, he said he would probably end up cuttin' off the legs on those boys that just got brought in. They got frostbite pretty bad."

To change the subject, Jake asked, "So, what's going on out there, Val?"

"Col. Miles is trying to persuade the Nez Perce to turn in their guns and surrender."

"Is he having any luck?"

"No, and then he decided to keep that Chief Joseph as a hostage to put pressure on them, which I think was chicken shit move! Unfortunately for Miles, one of his officers, a Lt. Jerome from the 2nd Cavalry, was over reconnoitering the Indian defenses and when Miles sent Tom Hill back to tell the other Indians to surrender, they grabbed him. Now they have a hostage, too!"

"So now what?" Charlie asked.

"Oh, in the mornin' they'll yell back and forth for a while, then eventually work out an exchange, I expect that'll eat up most of tomorrow. I think that the Nez Perce think this plays in their favor. They're buying time, hoping that the Sioux will come to help them."

"What do you think?"

"Well, the local Assiniboine or Gross Ventre would already have sent word if the Sioux were making a move in this direction. Besides, those Canadian Mounties keep a close eye on Ol' Sittin' Bull and his braves. They tend to look the other way when the Sioux poach a few buffalo or antelope this side of the line now and then. But, I've heard from some of my Métis friends that Sittin' Bull was told in no uncertain terms that if he stirs up any trouble with the U S Army, the Medicine Line would no longer protect his people."

"And in the meantime?"

"Miles will tighten the noose. The Nez Perce ain't got but a few horses, little food, few blankets, and its gettin colder. I 'spect that big cannon that rolled in with the wagons will get some use, too. I don't think that it can get at 'em the way they're hunkered down in that ravine, but it will scare the hell out of the women and children. It's just a matter of time, now."

That night Miles had his men push forward to edge of the bluffs surrounding the Indian camp and dig rifle pits. On the bench to the west, he had an emplacement built for the Napoleon cannon where it could command the creek valley, and surrounded it with more rifle pits. The morning was spent negotiating the hostage exchange and early in the afternoon Chief Joseph was exchanged for Lt. Jerome in full view of both sides. Once that was accomplished, the rest of the day, saw little activity on the part of either side except some sporadic sniping. A crew of soldiers were preparing the Napoleon cannon for use and conducting practice drills.

Jake felt strong enough to walk over to the 7th's camp and visit with Flanagan. When Jake ducked through the tent flap he saw that Flanagan was sitting at a small field table on which a sheaf of papers lay and had a tin cup of coffee in his hand. It reminded Jake of all the times he'd seen Top Martin similarly engaged.

"Hey Top!" he exclaimed.

Flanagan grimaced and replied, "Top my ass! I ain't likin' this one bit! Poor old Mike should've kept his head down, dammit ta hell! How you doin, Jake? Ya look a damn sight better than when I last saw ya!"

"I can't use my left arm much and it's aches like hell. I still get a bit dizzy if I move too quick. But, the Doc says I should be okay if infection doesn't set in. How's your arm?"

"Ah, nothing but a scratch, just a tad sore!" Flanagan replied, then reached behind him, producing Jake's Sharps rifle in its scabbard.

"Here, I held on to this for you when Wheeler drug you in. You good to carry it?"

"Sure, I was wondering what had became of it." Jake said, as he hefted it with his right arm, How's the company doing?"

"Well, Lt. Eckerson is a bit of a pain, but you know that. I've made Fox and Kipp both sergeants. We've only enough men to field an understrength platoon, which is all that we have healthy mounts for anyway."

"How's my horse, Ajax?"

"I've assigned him to Kipp for now, he'll treat'm good. Miles has us out patrolling looking out for the Sioux. There was a right panic earlier today. A scout thought he spotted a long line of horsemen coming up from the south. Fortunately they turned out to be a herd of snow-covered buffalo."

"Val Wheeler seems to think that the Sioux won't come."

"That's good to hear. Have ya heard any good rumors over by the hospital?"

"Just that Miles is going to give them an ultimatum tomorrow. I think that if they ignore it he'll use the artillery guns. I've heard that Gen. Howard is on his way here, also."

"Oh! I'm sure that Miles won't be too keen on that, he'll want to have the Nez Perce in the bag before Howard arrives."

The following day, which was Wednesday, Miles issued orders that if there was no sign from the Nez Perce forthcoming that all units were to consider the truce over and open fire. At 11:00 AM a bugle sounded and almost simultaneously, both field pieces commenced firing with the explosive shells, knocking down the white flag that still flew over the besieged camp. The men in the rifle pits followed suit and a furious fusillade of bullets impacted all around the area of the ravine. The Napoleon's barrel was elevated by lowering the tail of its carriage into a pit, and with a reduced powder charge, the gunners attempted to lob a shell, mortar fashion into the ravine. The cannon fire was sporadic, and over the next two days there was some desultory firing on both sides, but no significant changes in positions or responses to several attempts for parley. The main body of the beleaguered Indians continued to huddle in shelters down in the ravines. Some of the warriors occasionally sent bullets towards the soldiers manning the rifle pits along the bluff. Thursday, the weather continued cold and overcast with a bitter wind. The Napoleon's gun crew finally succeeded in dropping a shell down into the ravine collapsing a portion of one wall, but they were running low on ammunition. Late that afternoon scouts came in and reported seeing a party of mounted men coming up from the south. It was soon identified as Gen. Howard and his escort following the same trail the Nez Perce had taken from Cow Island. As dusk settled in, Miles went to greet Howard and they spent much of that evening in Miles' tent discussing the status of the siege.

Friday morning brought clearing skies and the sun appeared, bringing a little warm as it glistened off the snow covered battlefield. Dr. Tilton, Gardner and the medical orderlies were making the rounds of the hospital tents.

"We heard that Gen. Howard came in last night." Jake said, as Tilton was checking the dressing on his arm.

"Yes, that's correct. I went over to Miles' tent to give an update of the casualty list and met the General."

"Is he taking over command?"

"No, he has deferred to Col. Miles. I think maybe because all of the troops, except the small escort that came up with him, are not from his Department. Miles served under Howard during the War and they know each other well."

"Any idea what they have planned, sir?" Jake asked.

"Howard has two Nez Perce men with him and they each have daughters down in the camp. There's also a white interpreter named Ad Chapman. I think that they are going to attempt to re-open negotiations. I hope it works, we've three men that we're going to perform amputations on this morning. We need to get you wounded men to adequate hospital facilities as quickly as possible."

Later that morning word rapidly shot through the ranks that Howard's Nez Perce emissaries had gone over and had persuaded Chief Joseph to meet with Howard, Miles, and Chapman at a spot between the lines. Terms were discussed and Joseph agreed that he and his band would cross the creek and lay down their arms later in the day. That afternoon Val came over and let them know the proceedings were starting. Jake, along with the wounded men that could move and the medical staff gathered outside the hospital tent to watch. They could see Howard, Miles, and their staff officers waiting nearby on a rise just below them. As they watched, Chief Joseph mounted on his horse and accompanied by five warriors, slowly crossed over and rode up to the waiting commanders. Joseph stopped, slipped down off his horse and went to them. He paused briefly then quickly extended his Winchester rifle to Gen. Howard, who gestured for him to give it to Col. Miles, which he did. The interpreter Chapman was also there, and after a brief exchange Joseph shook hands with all of them and was then escorted to the headquarters tent.

"Well, I guess that's that!" exclaimed Tilton. "Now we can get you men headed back towards a proper hospital."

Val noticed Tom Hill still standing on the other side of the creek and waved at him. Hill saw him and waved back, then turned and went slowly back in the direction of the ravine, rifle in hand

"Maybe so, but it'll be interesting to see if they all come over. I think that some of them would rather die than give up their freedom and way of life." Val said sadly, "I know I would."

For the rest of the day small parties of the Nez Perce filtered across the creek. There were a few warriors, but mostly just old men, women, and children, dressed in dirty ragged clothes and blankets, many were barefoot. The warriors symbolically deposited their rifles and pistols on buffalo robes that were laid out for them. By the end of the day 87 men, 184 women, and 147 children had turned themselves in. The ones that were wounded were taken up to the hospital area to be treated.

Jake and the other soldiers were surprised when they saw the Nez Perce up close. These were the fierce warriors that had shattered the ranks of the 7th, and had held them at bay all week? Surely, there were more of them than these pitiful, starving wretches.

When Val came back around that evening, Jake asked him, "Is that all of them, I thought that there would be a lot more them?"

"No, there's more. They just all ain't made up their minds yet. They're supposed to come across in the morning."

"I thought that they'd all surrendered!"

"Well, see, there's where your general and colonel are mistaken. They don't understand that Joseph, he ain't a war chief! And he ain't the chief over all of 'em! There's five or six different bands that the Army's been chasin' after all summer. It's up to each band, and each warrior, if'n they want to keep on goin'. We'll see in the morning what they decided."

"What do you think's gonna happen, Val?" Charlie asked.

"I think that most of what I seen on those piles of guns, are old trade rifles, flintlocks, and just a few repeaters."

The next morning a few more Nez Perce filtered across. The Indians were allowed to retrieve what possessions they could. They gathered around large fires eating the food and fresh buffalo that Miles provided for them. By mid-day, Miles patience wore thin and he sent out details to investigate. They found that the rest of the Nez Perce, mostly the band led by a warrior named White Bird, had evaded the picket lines on the north side during the night and were long gone. Miles and Howard were furious. They confronted Joseph, who calmly explained to them that only he and the others that came over had decided to quit fighting. He had no power to make the others quit, so the ones that didn't want to, simply left.

Two days later, with over 400 Nez Perce accompanying the Army column, they all set out on the back trail towards the mouth of the Musselshell, on the Missouri River. Riders had been dispatched with orders for the rear detachment left there to flag down any passing riverboats and have them await the arrival of the wounded. Major Tilton had some travois assembled and several wagons padded with willow branches and grass for the wounded to travel on. Jake and the other wounded men were over saying good bye to the rest of their comrades in Company D. Jake was standing near Ajax, stroking the horse's nose and feeding him some sugar cubes that he liberated from the hospital mess. He was giving tips to Sgt. Fremont Kipp on what Ajax liked when Val rode up, leading two other horses, a gray stallion with prominent black spots and striped hooves, and a lighter colored mare with brown spots. He got down off his paint horse and said to Jake.

"Looks like you boys are gettin' ready to roll."

"And it looks like to me like you got a couple of new horses, Val." Jake said, grinning"

"Hell yes! This is pair of those Payouse horses that I was tellin' ya about. When I heard that Miles was lettin' the Cheyenne scouts take five a piece, I figured that I may as well get me a couple to breed for my string."

Jake was still wearing his left arm in a sling and wiggled it. "I still can't use this much and tend to have a bad headache now and then, so Major Tilton has me riding a wagon. He informed me that when we reach the Missouri River they're going to load us wounded men on a riverboat and most of us will be going all the way to Fort Lincoln."

"Well, it's a damn good time! That river will be freezin' up soon." Val said, "Myself, I think I'm gonna head back home to Shanaya. I can be there in an hour or two. I might stop to pick me up a nice buffalo or two. Specially seein' as I got a way to haul 'em." He nodded his head at the horses.

"I don't know if I ever thanked you for hauling my big ass back after I got hit? I was a little out of it for a while." Jake stated.

Val handed Jake the deerskin pouch of colored agates, "Here, take these. They are spirit stones that my mother gave to me. There's two of each that match in color. She says that when you look into one of them, you can reach out to the spirit of the one that you has the other. Mine is gray, that's how I knew how to find you." He looked at Jake solemnly for a few seconds, then said, "You can thank me by gettin' out of this soldierin' thing, like we talked about."

"Oh, I'm pretty sure that I'm about done with it, Val. Come May, my hitch will be up. I got my own gal that I want to get back to!" Jake said with a smile.

"Well, then I guess this is where we part trails again, Jake. If'n you run across that rascal Pat Morse, you tell 'im to come look me up when they get the railroad out this far. I should have a nice herd built up by then and I may want ta do some business!"

Jake held out his hand for Val to shake, "Hell, you never know? I may come look you up one of these days"

Val shook his hand, then smiled and looked him in the eye, "I'd surely enjoy that, Jake. Bring that little gal Holly of yours with you. Who knows? I may even have a house by then for you to stay in." With that he turned and mounted his horse, giving a slight wave as he rode away.

CHAPTER 44

Fort Abraham Lincoln Landing, Dakota Territory - Friday, October 26, 1877

After leaving the Bear Paw Mountains, Gen. Howard headed straight back down to the Missouri River near Cow Island, where the steamer *Benton* was waiting to transport him down to Squaw Creek where he'd sent the rest of the 7th Cavalry to bivouac. Col. Miles took his own column, accompanied by the captive Nez Perce, and returned via the route he taken two weeks earlier, down to the Missouri River and Squaw Creek. Howard had arranged for several steamboats and they were moored waiting on the column. After Miles arrived there on the 13th, Howard left immediately aboard the *Benton,* headed for St. Paul to file his report. Major Merrill had been ordered to put the wounded men aboard the *Silver City* and accompany them downriver, while Col. Sturgis along with his regimental headquarters staff and the wounded officers would leave on the slightly smaller and faster *Big Horn.* Miles decided to leave the balance of the 7th Cavalry regiment to remain camped along the Musselshell under the command of Capt. Benteen, to monitor whether any Sioux attempted to come across the border. The following morning the riverboats left to head downstream, stopping first at the Bighorn Post/Fort Custer site, and then on to the Tongue River Cantonment/Fort Keogh. Jake received permission to take a detail to find the stored footlockers that his troopers had left there. When the *Silver City* arrived at Fort Buford, the more serious cases were left at the hospital there. Jake had to say good bye to a very upset Charlie. The doctors insisted that too much time had already passed and that Welch needed immediate surgery. He spent the rest of the journey, along with the help of Pvt. Pete Hall, who had been detailed to accompany them as a nurse, looking out for the Company D troopers. Jake found himself enjoying the trip downriver. It was the first time that Jake had been a non-working passenger on a riverboat, and he marveled at the passing scenery. He spent some of his time writing letters and reading old newspapers. The sutler had given his bartender instructions to treat the wounded men to free beer at the bar in the main salon. Jake occasionally joined in some card games and even he had a bit of luck at poker. He made it a daily habit to walk around the boat in the mornings and made a few friends with some of the crew. After the first week, he tried helping them stack wood for the boilers to exercise his arm. The headaches and slight vision issues that he experienced from time to time, slowly disappeared.

The riverboat *Silver City* jockeyed in the river current sounding its whistle to herald its arrival, as it pulled in towards the landing at Fort Lincoln. There was a crowd of people on hand waiting to welcome home the wounded men of the 7th, along with the regimental band to add to the occasion. Jake leaned on the railing of the upper deck, where he was pleased to spot Pat Morse, Kate, and Murray Johnson in the crowd and he waved to catch their attention. Presently, the crew got the steamer secured and the ramp positioned to start unloading. Jake stayed where he was watching and waiting for the crowd to die down. After most of the passengers and freight got unloaded, Jake went down to the lower deck where he found that his friends had already came on board to find him. Kate rushed over to him and hugged him tightly, with tears in her eyes, while Pat and Murray stood watching.

"We saw your name on the casualty list, are you okay, Jake?" she asked, stepping back and eyeing him up and down with a worried expression.

"Yes, I took a bullet in the left arm and had one bounce off my hard head. The arm is still a bit stiff, but the doctor says that it's healing well. I'll have a scar on my head to remind me to duck, but that's it." Jake replied with a smile, doffing his hat and tilting his head to show them.

"Good, I've been waiting to send a telegram down to Springfield!" Kate said, "They're all probably frantic and waiting to hear news."

"Hey thanks Kate! I have to go and report to the hospital with my men. Maybe I can get over to Bismarck and see you all this weekend. I don't know if, or when, we'll have to go on down to Fort Rice."

Pat, who had been standing behind Kate, reached out to shake his hand, "Ah, ya look good, Lad! I was worried when Kate read me the casualty list. I've seen some nasty head wounds over the years don't ya know."

Murray came over and patted Jake on his good shoulder. "Come to Forster's on Friday. I've extra rooms that I keep for railroad use and you're welcome to use one of them. We'll catch up over dinner and get some good food in you. You look a mite thin!"

"Thanks Murray! That sounds wonderful!" Jake replied.

After reporting to the Fort Lincoln hospital, the doctors there sorted the soldiers, keeping the most seriously wounded that required beds. Cpl. Quinn and the other Company D privates that were able to fend for themselves, were loaded up in an ambulance and taken to a vacant company barracks. The ambulance driver took them over to a barracks that had been readied for them, then helped them with their bags and footlockers. Jake had noticed that the driver seemed to know Quinn and Deetline, and was watching him intently. He volunteered to take Jake's footlocker to the Orderly Room,   while he was gone Jake said to Quinn, "It seems like I should know him from some where."

"His name is Will Mueller. He came out from Jefferson Barracks with a bunch of us back in late '75. He's a German like Ol' Deet, here."

Deet grinned, "Yah, he is! Vill stayed here to vork the garden, ven ve all leave mit Custer that spring."

"Yes, I vaguely remember him now. There was a whole group of you newbies that joined the company back then."

"Yes, well, it seems that Mueller did such a great job with the company garden that summer while we were out, that the hospital got him re-assigned to stay at Fort Lincoln and take care of theirs." Quinn said, "He drives an ambulance for them during the winter."

"Yes, now I remember! Top Martin was plenty pissed off when we came back. He wanted him for the garden down at Fort Rice!"

Quinn looked at Jake and said, "You weren't around much that winter. You and your boys were running the telegraph lines and fetching the mail."

Jake smiled at the memory of those times. "Yes, that was damn cold work, but it beat hanging around this place."

Quinn stated. "You probably never realized how much we were in awe of you back then, Jake. The daring young sergeant and his band of hardy men."

Jake looked up in surprise.

"No, I mean it!" Quinn said. "We all looked up to you, because you were one of us, not some grizzled old veteran leftover from the War that yelled and cussed at us. We used to gather round Henry Holden back in the barracks and he and Old George Horn would tell us about the days when you all were all together up on the Boundary Survey. You were always doing things the smart, easy way, and then there was your reputation as a marksman."

Jake felt his face flush a bit. "Gee, Quinn, I wasn't trying to be anybody special, I was just trying to do the best that I could at what I was doing."

"Ya see! Thats why everyone likes you, Jake." Quinn grinned. "What say we get Ol' Will to run us up to the Post Traders?"

"He vill! Deetline exclaimed, "Und, I be buyin' the first round, Sarge!"

The next morning, they had to go to breakfast over at another barracks where the mess hall was in operation. After they returned, Jake mustered the men and took roll. With no horses to care for, or other details for them, he just let them stay in the barracks. He went into the orderly room, sat down at a desk and started perusing a stack of old newspapers that was laying on it. The door opened and a fresh faced, young private wearing a clean blue uniform stepped in, then walked over to the desk in front of Jake and came to attention.

"I'm looking for Sgt. Jacob Rogers." he announced.

Jake looked up, slightly amused. "At Ease, Private! There're no officers here. I'm Sgt. Rogers. What's your name and why are you looking for me?"

"Private Billy Smith, sergeant! Captain Michaelis sent me to find you, sergeant. He asked me to tell you to come see him as soon as you can."

"Where might I find the captain?" Jake asked.

"He's over at the Adjutant's Office."

Jake stood up and said, "Well, let's go, Smith! There's damn sure not a thing going on around here!"

As Jake followed Pvt. Smith back over to the Adjutant's Office at the west end of Barracks Row, he saw a lot of activity going on. The rear detachment troops were bustling around the warehouses and vacant barracks. Col. Sturgis and his regimental staff having returned from the field several days earlier, were busy writing orders, reports, and compiling supply lists in preparation for the return of the regiment and it's winter garrison assignments. 1st Lt. Garlington was the current Regimental Adjutant and was engaged in getting Fort Lincoln prepared for the return of the 7th. When Jake went in he saw Capt. Michaelis standing near a wood stove with a cup in his hand. Jake started to come to attention and salute, but Michaelis waved to him dismissively before he could.

"Never mind that, Rogers. Let me start by telling you how glad that I am to see you survived that debacle of a charge at Snake Creek."

"Indeed, sir! Probably not as glad as I am!" Jake replied.

"Want some coffee, Rogers? There's a relatively fresh pot here!"

"Yes, sir, I would. The air is getting a bit nippy already. Winter is just around the corner."

"Well, get a cup, and let us sit down over here. I've something to discuss with you."

"Oh, don't worry, sir! I still have your rifle. I'm afraid that it has a few dings on it, here and there, but I assure you that it's in good working order. I have it secured in the orderly room where Pvt. Smith found me." Jake said.

Michaelis chuckled, "I'd expect nothing less Rogers, but that's not what I want to discuss. The recent engagements with the Nez Perce have rekindled a debate about the overall preparedness of our enlisted cavalry troops. Particularly given the facts that they seemed to have performed quite poorly when comes to marksmanship. Would you concur?"

"Yes, unfortunately, I suppose I'll have to agree, sir. There are very few of us that are proficient with the weapons we have. Most of the better marksmen learned to shoot before they joined. We haven't been able or allowed to target practice very much, in order to conserve ammunition supplies."

"Well, Gen. Sheridan is extremely unhappy about this lack of training, and what he deems an unacceptable casualty ratio over the last two years"

"With all due respect, sir. We would have done better if we'd still carried Spencers." Jake stated. "The Sioux and Cheyenne had Henrys and Winchester repeating rifles, and so did the Nez Perce."

"Well, in some circles it's thought that the superior range of our weapons should over come that advantage."

"Whoever thinks that has never fought against Indians. They don't stand around like targets! They sneak up on our positions and once closer than 200 yards, they have the advantage in rate of fire."

"Ah, this is precisely why I need someone like you Rogers, a proven marksman with combat experience! I've been tasked to evaluate the 7th's weapons training and their performance during combat, by Gen. Terry. I want you to come work for me." Michaelis said emphatically.

Jake raised his eyebrows in surprise, "Hmm, what would I be doing, sir?"

"Well, there'll be some traveling involved. You'll be helping me gather information, shooting and evaluating weapons, and probably visiting a few gun manufacturers." the officer replied.

"What about my present duty assignment?"

"I'll take care of all that. I'll make you an ordinance sergeant and you will report directly to me. For now we will base here, out of Fort Lincoln, but I expect that we'll be traveling back to St. Paul and Fort Snelling before too long. I'd rather spend the winter back there. My family lives there also, and the holidays are coming up."

Jake's thoughts turned to visions of the barren snowy plains and hills surrounding Fort Rice, and the numbing cold and monotony of winter guard duty. He suddenly realized that he had no close friends, and few veterans, left in the company to spend time with off duty.

"You should know, sir, I have plans to leave the Army come May."

"Oh, that's not a problem for me, Rogers! We should be done with my report by then. What say you?"

"I think that would be a good way for me to finish out my enlistment, Sir. It sounds interesting and I might learn some things that could help me after I get out. What do I have to do?"

"Nothing, I'll see to everything. Move your things over to the NCO Quarters, I believe that you're familiar with them. You should be able to pick out a good room before the rest of the regiment gets back"

"Yes, sir! I'll do that today."

"Good, now take the next several days to get settled in and report here next week when you're ready. I'll have all the orders issued, then we'll get you over to see the Post Quartermaster. I'll want you in all new uniforms, including dress. You'll be seeing a lot of higher brass and I want you looking sharp!"

"Thank you, sir! I'll do my best!" Jake stood and saluted.

As he turned to leave Michaelis stopped him and said, "By the way, that Sharps rifle was just declared damaged and surplus. I'll get you a bill of sale for it. You owe me $5. Keep it with you, I may need to have you demonstrate how effective a longer range precision weapon like that is."

Jake spent the rest of the morning getting moved into the NCO Quarters and was even able to get the room that he'd once shared with Tom Russell. He wondered briefly on how civilian life was working out for Tom? He unpacked his foot locker and worked on putting together a presentable uniform to wear to town. He would have to figure out a way to retrieve his civilian clothes and personal effects from the company storage area down at Fort Rice. He was planning on catching the early afternoon ferry over to Bismarck and looked forward to spending the weekend there. The thought of staying in a comfortable hotel evoked memories of Vanessa's visit. He made a mental note to write to her about his new orders. In fact, he needed to post all of the letters that he'd written when he got over to Bismarck, so they could go out that day.

The warehouse area between the warehouses and tracks along the Bismarck riverfront was stacked with piles of railroad construction materials, crates, and barrels. Jake was amazed at how the city had grown over the last six months. He made his way up Front Street and headed towards the railroad depot, where he dropped off his letters at the postal box, then crossed over to Forster's Hotel and Restaurant. Murray could usually be found ensconced there at his usual table, when he wasn't at his office at the NPRR depot. Since it was nearing 5:00 on a Friday, Jake figured that's most likely where he'd be. When he went in the front door, he spied Murray at his usual table involved in an earnest conversation with a tall, well dressed man with dark hair and a prominent mustache. They were poring over a map spread across the table and the stranger was tracing across it with his finger. As Jake drew near the table, Murray noticed him and waved him over.

"Hello, Jake. I was hoping you would show up!"

"Well, everything went smoothly over at the fort and I was able to get away." Jake replied.

The other man stood up quickly, folding the map and said to Murray, "I best be getting over to the Sheridan House, Mr. Stark wants to go over what we saw today across the river. By the way, some of the local businessmen are having a dinner for us there tomorrow night, but I suspect you already know that, so I expect that I'll see you then."

"Before you leave, Tom, you might want to meet Sgt. Rogers. He was with Custer last year, and fought at the Little Big Horn. In fact he's just returned from Miles' fight with the Nez Perce a few weeks ago. He was wounded there."

Rosser eyed Jake, as Murray introduced him, "Jake, this is Thomas Rosser, the Chief Engineer of the Northern Pacific, and also a former General of the Confederate Army. He and Custer were roommates at West Point together. They remained friends even after they fought against each other. Tom accompanied Custer during the 1873 Yellowstone Survey."

"Pleased to meet you, Sir"

They shook hands and Rosser said, "I trust you weren't wounded severely, Rogers. You look fine."

"I got lucky, sir. My wounds were not serious and I'm pretty much healed up."

"So, you were on the Little Big Horn campaign last year?"

"Yes, sir! I was in Capt. Weir's Company D, 7th Cavalry."

"Benteen's battalion! He dawdled when he should have been riding to help Custer!" Rosser said vehemently.

"Capt. Weir took us that way, but we were too late." Jake stated, a bit defensively.

"Yes, Well, I met with Weir briefly back in Chicago last fall and we discussed it. We were going to meet again but he had to hurry on to New York. Damn shame about him dying like that!"

Jake just nodded his head.

"Perhaps when I have more time, you and I could discuss your version of the events of the fight. Why don't you come with Murray tomorrow night! I have to run on now, I suspect that I'm already late. We'll talk again, Murray." He stated, then turned and headed for the door.

As they watched him leave, Murray said, "Gen. Rosser obviously has strong opinions about what happened to Custer."

"Yes, I sense that." Jake agreed.

"Rosser is here to lead an engineering team and lay out the route along the Heart River over on the other side of the Missouri. The plan is to have a line completed as far as the coal fields before winter sets in."

"Aren't they going to go farther?"

"Well, the plans are to lay track all the way to the Yellowstone. It's contingent on funding. Our Vice President George Stark, is out here pursuing some local investors. But enough of that! Sit down Jake, let's get you a beer!" Murray exclaimed, motioning for a waitress, "Pat and Kate should be here, soon."

The couple arrived in a few minutes and Kate immediately quizzed Jake about his wounds. He assured her that they were almost healed and that he felt fine.

Pat interceded, "Now, Kate! Let the lad enjoy his beer. We've all evening to catch up."

Kate replied, "I'm just making sure! Holly telegraphed me and tasked me with verifying that he's okay. Have you written to her Jake? She's very anxious to hear from you."

"Yes, I posted all of my mail on the way here." Jake said, "And I'll see about sending her a telegram tomorrow. I need to send one to my folks, too."

Murray had arranged for a sumptuous dinner of steak and fresh vegetables, and while Jake focused on the food, the others discussed local events. Afterwards, they quizzed Jake about the summer and Nez Perce campaign. Jake gave them a few details about the fighting. Pat became very somber when he heard how Mike Martin got killed.

"Ol' Mike and I, we went back a ways! I went down to Fort Rice to check on Ellen and the kids. She's going to move down to Sioux Falls." Pat added that while they were over at Fort Lincoln, yesterday he had talked with some contacts at regimental headquarters. He said, "There's a battalion of 5 companies from the 7th escorting the Nez Perce down from Fort Buford with Capt. French is in command. They should be here before Thanksgiving."

"Is Company D one of them?" Jake asked.

"No, just B, G, I, L, and M. Capt. Benteen is staying near Buford with the rest of the regiment. It may be close to the end of the year before there're ordered home. "

"I guess it doesn't make any difference to me, I"m no longer in Company D." Jake stated, and then proceeded to tell them about his promotion and transfer to Capt. Michaelis' Ordinance detail.

"That's wonderful, Jake!" Kate exclaimed, "You can spend the holiday with us!"

"Maybe? I get the sense that Capt. Michaelis is planning on being in St. Paul with his family. I can ask him if I can stay here until afterwards." Jake said, then let out a yawn. "Sorry, between the beer and food, I hear may bed calling. I can't wait to sleep in a real bed."

"Oh, let's get you to your room Jake. You need to rest up. Besides, it may be a late night tomorrow over at the banquet." Murray said. "Pat and Kate are going too."

When they got to the room, Jake saw that it was well furnished with a feather bed and sitting chairs. There was a small bar with several bottles of whisky and some glasses.

"How about a quick night cap?" Murray asked. "I have something to tell you."

"Okay."

After pouring the drinks, Murray handed him one and toasted, grinning, "Here's to your hard head!"

Jake laughed, "Amen to that!"

"Have a seat, I need to tell you about the banquet tomorrow night. A certain attractive lady will be attending, one that I believe you know quite well."

Jake thought for a second, "Miss Blake?"

"Not exactly, she is attending as a Miss Jennie White, an assistant to Mr. Stark. He is here to find local investors for the proposed route across the river. It is most important that we get a start as soon as possible. Grading crews are already headed this way. The Northern Pacific needs money to make that happen."

"So, what are you saying?"

"I'm just giving you a heads up. It would be better if you act like you don't know her when you meet. Just be polite and let her concentrate her on attracting investors. I'm sure she will arrange her schedule to see you later. Besides, Kate will be there with Pat, and I'm sure you wouldn't want your prospective Aunt to know of your involvement with Miss Blake."

Jake nodded his head, thoughtfully "Well now, I wasn't expecting this at all. Maybe it would be better if I didn't go."

"No, this will be good for you. Particularly, since you'll probably be rubbing elbows with some wealthy and powerful folks when you travel with Capt. Michaelis. It won't hurt you to watch and learn some social manners."

"Well, I'd feel more comfortable if I had my civilian clothes, this uniform is a bit scruffy and worn in spots."

"I'll tell you what!" Murray stated, "I'll take you over to the St. Paul Branch Clothing House in the morning after breakfast, and I'll introduce you to Sig Hanauer. We'll get you fixed up with some new clothes. I have an account there and you can pay me back later."

The following morning at the clothing store, the proprietor, Sig Hanauer, had been very solicitous when he found out that Jake had just returned from the field wounded. He helped Jake select a three-piece dark, sack suit, with a linen shirt, paper collar, and dark cravat tied bow style, all topped by a black Bowler hat. Jake had also purchased a pair of black brogans to wear instead of his trail worn boots. Sig insisted that Jake complete his wardrobe with new winter weight long johns and wool socks. Altogether, the tab had been almost $50, which Hanauer discounted down to $35 out of respect for Jake's recent wounds. Fortunately, Jake had almost $200 stashed away in the Bank of Bismarck. He also had several months back pay coming, along with the almost tripled pay from his forthcoming promotion to ordinance sergeant. Murray also took him to visit his barber and Jake was clean shaven for the first time since spring.

The Sheridan House which had just opened in September, was the newest building in Bismarck and the largest in the Dakota Territory. It was a three story, L shaped brick building with a tall, colonnaded, double portico with two balconies. It served as the main entrance on the southern side that faced the Northern Pacific rail lines. The eastern side of the structure stretched the whole block of Third Street up to Main Street. The Northern Pacific had partnered with Eber H. Bly, one of its senior employees, at a cost of $50,000 to build it and it was to serve as a hotel and depot for its customers and travelers. The second floor above the lobby had a large ballroom that opened out on a large balcony. It had been designed that way so it could be used for banquets, theatricals, dances, and political rallies.

The Sheridan House - Bismarck 1877

A steady stream of people was flowing along the board sidewalks of Front Street towards the Sheridan House, which was well lit by festoons of lanterns hanging from the entrance portico. Jake and Murray made their way from Forster's which was just half a block west. Jake felt a little self conscience wearing his new clothes, although Murray said he looked quite dapper. They met Pat and Kate in the lobby, then ascended an ornate staircase up to the Ballroom. Murray guided them through the crowd to a table off to the side, that had a good view of the dais.

"Have you met this Mr. Stark, Murray?" Kate asked.

"Yes, just briefly when he arrived. He seems like a no nonsense type. I'm told that he's a seasoned railroad man from back in New England, and is one of several hired by our current president Mr. Charles Wright, tasked to get the rail lines moving again."

"I heard someone refer to him as General Stark." Pat said.

"I believe he was a General in the New Hampshire militia during the War, but was never involved in actual fighting."

Tom Rosser and a tall, distinguished looking man, followed by a small party, worked their way through the crowd. They paused to shake hands here and there with some of the people.

Murray leaned over to Jake and said quietly, "All the local Bigwigs have turned out. There's John McClean, the current mayor, Clement Lounsberry, the owner of the Tribune, and George Peoples, who is favored to win the mayoral election in two weeks. If you recall McLean was one of the men that bought that lot of uniforms and gear that you and Pat got in that auction a couple of years ago. Peoples was in on that deal too, by the way. He and McClain are partners in several enterprises, here in Bismarck and elsewhere. That other man with them is J. W. Raymond, who's probably the wealthiest man in Bismarck."

As they approached the head table, Jake caught glimpses of the others in the party as they took their seats. That's when he spotted Vanessa. She was wearing a black velvet coat trimmed with a brown fur collar and cuffs over a brown dress, and a black hat with white ribbons perched at a jaunty angle on her dark hair which was done up in a bun. As he watched, the man next to her pulled out a chair and proffered it to her. She smiled at him and gracefully sat down.

Murray saw where Jake was looking and remarked. "That's Eber Bly, the man that built this building. He also has interests in some coal mines 40 miles west of the Missouri River, and a sawmill that produces railroad ties. He and Tom Rosser have worked together previously surveying and picking out townsites along the NPRR routes."

Jake nodded his head, "Sounds like a good man to know."

"Yes, now that the Indian threats are diminished, the opportunities for the Northern Pacific are huge. If they can start getting tracks laid down, they can begin selling the land that comes with it, and money starts pouring in."

"You make it sound so simple, Murray." Pat said with a grin.

"It is, if someone will give you the land!"

Waiters entered into the hall and bustled about serving dinner to the guests. Afterwards, Mayor McClean gave a quick speech, then deferred to George Peoples who rose and began making a campaign speech.

"They'll go like this for a while, let's go out on the balcony and have a cigar." Johnson suggested.

Pat said, "Kate and I will stay here, it's too chilly! You two go ahead."

Several other people also sought refuge from the speechifying by adjourning to the balcony. Jake recognized Tom Rosser standing at the railing gazing off to the west, with a glowing cigar in his hand. Rosser turned around and saw Jake.

"Well, Sgt. Rogers! You look to have prospered since we met yesterday." he said smiling.

"Yes, well, a day back in civilization can do wonders, sir. Not to mention having a friend with a few connections." Jake replied, nodding at Murray.

"The resourceful Mr. Johnson is good at that." Rosser stated. "That's been established many times. As I recall, I wanted to discuss your recollections from last year's campaign."

"Yes, sir! I'm at your service when it's convenient for you."

A very pleasant and familiar voice sounded from behind Jake, and they both turned towards it. "Ah, there you are Mr. Rosser! Sorry for interrupting, but I have been tasked with finding you!"

Rosser sighed, "And, Miss White you have succeeded."

Vanessa just stood smiling and said, "Mr. Stark has someone asking questions about what arrangements have been made to accommodate the grading crews when they arrive."

"This is Sgt. Rogers, from the 7th Cavalry. He's just returned from campaigning against New Perce. He also fought against the Sioux last year when my good friend George Custer was killed."

She looked at Jake with concern in her eyes and said, "Yes, I've read about it in the newspapers. They say that some of the wounded men have just returned."

'Yes, Rogers here was one of them." Rosser said.

"But, you look well, Sergeant."

Jake replied, "Yes, I was very fortunate."

"Well, Rogers, it seems that we must delay our conversation once again. How long will you be here in Bismarck?" asked Rosser

"At least until Tuesday, I'm staying with Mr. Johnson over at Forster's. My company is still in the field, and technically, I'm still on the wounded list."

"Very good! I will come by tomorrow and we will discuss it then."

Rosser turned to go, and as Jake stepped back he felt Vanessa touch his arm then slide her hand down into his coat pocket.

"So sorry to hear that you were wounded!" She smiled demurely at Jake, then followed Rosser back inside.

Jake reached in his coat pocket to find a piece of paper. He held it up to the light reflecting through the glass doors and read.

Room #306, Midnight! V

He caught Murray watching him, out of the corner of his eye, and shrugged his shoulders. "What?"

Jake made his way quietly along the 3rd floor hallway of the Sheridan House. When he reached Room 306, he tapped lightly on the door which opened immediately. Dim candlelight revealed Vanessa standing there in a frilly dressing gown with her raven tresses cascading on to her shoulders. She silently reached out, drawing him into her embrace, and he felt her push the door shut behind him.

"My dear, Jacob!" She whispered, as she pulled his head down to kiss his lips. When they finally broke for air, she asked. "Are you hurt badly?"

"No, just sporting a couple of new scars here and there." he said removing his hat.

She reached up to caress the scar above his eyebrow, with her fingers. "I was quite alarmed when I saw your name on the casualty list. Come, let us get comfortable, I want to inspect the rest of you."

Later, as they lay intertwined in the bedcovers, Vanessa traced the puckered scar on Jake's arm. "Does it still hurt?"

"It aches now and then, particularly when I over exert it. I'm still working to get my strength back in it."

"Were you afraid, when it happened?" she asked.

"No, I was unconscious. When I came to, a friend had already rescued me and taken me to the surgeons."

"Thank goodness for friends! Hopefully the fighting will be over for now. I overheard that Chief Joseph and his band are on the way here."

"Yes, that rumor is going round." Jake said.

"Many of the newspapers seem most equivocal concerning them. Does that bother you?"

"No, not now! I saw them up close after the fighting. Most were women, children, and old people that were cold, hungry, and scared after months on the run and far from home."

"You sound almost sympathetic, Jacob."

"I suppose that I am. The friend who rescued me is half Indian. He's shown me that our civilized notions of progress are causing the destruction of their way of life."

Vanessa was silent for a moment, "I can relate to that. When I was child back in India, I was caught up in the middle of a similar dilemma. Ultimately, one has to make a choice or have it made for you, if you're to survive."

Jake sensed that she was reflecting on her own circumstances. He pulled her to him in a tight embrace and kissed the top of her head. "Yes, I suppose so."

"But, one can choose to seize opportunity and gain some modicum of control over ones destiny."

"Yes, that's true!" Jake agreed.

"I have accomplished that. I have reached a point where I am now on retainer with the Northern Pacific, exclusively. My superior reports to Mr. Wright and the six men that he's chosen to re-organize it."

"Okay, what is it that you do, exactly?"

"I find things out for them when they need information and want to be very circumspect about obtaining it."

"Hmm, I understand, I think."

Vanessa chuckled, "I'm very good at it!"

"I know you are. Coincidentally, I'm making a change, also." Jake offered

"And what might that be?" she asked.

Jake told her about his decision to take Capt. Michaelis up on his offer, and explained what he knew of it so far, including the travel and potential re-assignment to St. Paul.

Vanessa sat up and exclaimed, "I like the sound of that! I'm much more comfortable with the thought of you shooting at targets that don't shoot back. Not to mention that you may be in St. Paul on occasion."

Jake admired her profile in the dim light, and said laughing, "I just happen to have a couple of targets in my sights right now."

Vanessa woke Jake in the wee hours of the morning, whispering in his ear. "You should probably get up and get dressed. There's a big breakfast meeting planned for this morning and I need to be ready. I'll make it up to you when we meet up back in St. Paul. We'll have a special holiday season!"

Jake exited the Sheridan House by the side door and walked the short distance to Forster's. Murray had given him a key and he carefully removed his shoes, before quietly making his way up to his room. He quickly removed his new suit and hung it up, then fell on the bed, asleep as soon as his head hit the pillow.

He awoke to the sounds of knocking on the door, and Murray's voice calling out.

"Okay, get up Jake! It's Sunday morning and they serve a great breakfast downstairs. Meet me in 20 minutes!"

Jake got up, washed and dressed quickly, then went down to the dining room where Murray had a pot of coffee waiting on the table.

"Did you sleep good?" Murray asked with a smile and raised

eyebrow.

"Yes, just not very long!" Jake replied, as he poured a cup.

"Ah, you're young! Pat and Kate will be here shortly. So tell me, how was your rendezvous with Miss Blake?"

Jake grinned, "Most enjoyable, as always! She's going back to St. Paul tomorrow, though."

"Yes, I know. Rosser is staying here to get things moving, and Stark will be pushing him to get as much track down as possible before the weather becomes an issue. Pat and I will be working over across the river, getting the materials staged. You probably won't see much of us for a while."

"Well, I'm not sure what Capt. Michaelis' schedule is, but I suspect that he's planning on being back in St. Paul with his family for the holidays. I have to go down to Fort Rice and get the rest of my things this week. Then I don't know what he has in mind for me after that."

"Well, I heard last night that Col. Miles is personally escorting Joseph and his followers to Fort Lincoln. They're supposed to winter over there."

"Yes, That's what I've heard, too."

Pat and Kate arrived shortly in a buggy that Pat rented to drive them around town. The first thing after breakfast Kate insisted that they go over to the telegraph office so Jake could send off messages to Springfield for Holly and his folks. Afterwards, Jake spend the rest of the morning with them as they made their way around town, showing Jake the new buildings and growing business district. They dropped him back at Forster's and he went up to his room for a brief nap before he had to meet with Tom Rosser. He left Murray a note to send a bell boy up to tap on his door when he arrived.

"So, Sgt. Rogers, I'd like to ask you a few questions about the events along the Little Big Horn, on June 25 last year." Rosser stated, as he sat a pad of paper and a pencil down in front of him.

"Very well, sir. I'll try to answer them as best as I can."

"Now, Rogers, having fought in many battles myself during the War, I'm aware that each man can have a perception of the events around him unique to his location and time when they occurred. I'm hoping that I can piece together what happened by interviewing as many men that were there, as I can."

Jake nodded his head in agreement.

"So, in particular, I'm interested in the location of the pack train, as it pertains to the arrival of the messengers that Col. Custer dispatched to find Capt. Benteen."

"Well, as I recall, we'd just reached the mouth of the creek we'd been following, when Trumpeter Martini reached us. The pack train was strung out behind us, probably a half mile back."

"What did Capt. Benteen do, then?"

"He showed the message to Capt. Weir and then we followed Custer's trail that led up the hill ahead. That's where we found Maj. Reno and what was left of his battalion. They'd left the river valley and retreated up onto the bluffs above it."

Rosser asked, "When did the pack train arrive at that point?"

"I can't rightly say for sure, sir. Capt. Weir led our company to the north, looking for Custer. We went about a mile to some high ground where we could see smoke and dust on a ridge a few miles ahead. We knew that there was fighting going on, we could hear gunshots and I saw lots of Sioux riding around through my field glasses."

"Where were Reno and Benteen when this was going on?"

"Well, Capt. Benteen came up to us shortly after, but I never saw Maj. Reno. Benteen spoke with Capt. Weir, then pretty soon he left to go back and we followed him soon after."

"Where was the pack train, then?"

"It was on the hill with Reno when we got back. He'd already made the decision to dig in. I don't know how long that it had been there though, perhaps an hour."

" So, no other attempt was made to go to Custer's aid."

"No, sir! We were attacked soon after we got back to Reno's hill."

Rosser continued making notes, then put down his pen and looked at Jake with an intense expression. "So, Sgt. Rogers, in your opinion, do you think that the rest of the command had the ability to reach Custer?"

"Ability, sir? No, but some of us could have if we'd gone straight through to him. His brother Boston, went by us and he made it, I saw his body."

Rosser stared off, looking out the window in silence.

Jake continued, "I don't know what would have happened if we had. It was poor ground to defend and it was a huge village. Outnumbered as we were, I suspect that we'd have shared the same fate, sir!" he said solemnly.

Rosser turned his head to glare at Jake, "Hmm!"

Jake calmly returned his gaze, "I've learned quite a bit about the Indian tribes out here over the last four and a half years. Most of them don't want to change the way they've been living for a hundred years. Unfortunately, they also don't understand that they are going to have to in order to survive. It's a hard, hard lesson and some of them would rather fight and die, rather than learn it."

"So what are you saying?"

"I was almost killed a month ago, up at the Bear Paw Mountains, while trying to help force the Nez Perce into surrendering. They beat us that first day! That's just the way it was. That's what Custer was doing on the Little Big Horn and he lost that day. In my mind, we under estimated the Indian tribes both times and that's just what happened. This won't end well for them, either. And I've learned that's just the way it is!"

"That's a very cynical way to look at it, Rogers!"

"I apologize for that, I left my rose colored glasses laying busted in the snow somewhere along a bluff above Snake Creek, up in Montana, sir."

"Well, regardless! I intend to continue my criticism of Maj. Reno's actions that day."

Jake let out a sarcastic chuckle, "I won't argue with you on that, Mr. Rosser."

CHAPTER 45

Fort Abraham Lincoln, Dakota Territory - Friday, October 30, 1877

To Jake, it hardly seemed possible that he'd only been back two weeks. When he'd returned from Bismarck after that first weekend, he'd met with Capt. Michaelis who gave him the rest of the week to get his effects in order, before reporting for duty. The Kupitz stage line ran three times a week down to Fort Rice, and Jake caught a seat on it that Wednesday. Cpl. Quinn, and the other men from Company D, had already been taken down in an ambulance by Pete Hall, who was still serving as a their nurse. When Jake arrived he found that they had teamed up with the rear detachment, and were already moved in to the company barracks. He went across the parade ground to visit Capt. Godfrey who was staying in his quarters with his wife and son, while recuperating from his wounds. His wife, Mary, answered the door and showed him into the parlor, then left the room. Godfrey was seated in an easy chair near the fireplace, wrapped in a blanket. Jake could see his long johns and slippered feet resting on an ottoman.

"Pardon me if I don't get up, Rogers. My wound precludes me wearing pants as of yet. I find belts and suspenders to be quite uncomfortable." Godfrey said.

Jake nodded his head, "Well, you look better than when I last saw you, sir."

"I might say the same about you, sergeant." he replied with a tight smile. "You look well."

"Still sore here and there, sir. But, I'm pretty much healed up."

"I'm told that there are several of the walking wounded Company D troopers back, and that they are opening up the barracks. I haven't received any official word about the rest of the Company, but Capt. Benteen's wife, Kate, told Mary that he has been writing her. He is still in camp near Fort Buford, and is anxiously waiting on orders to return here by the Holidays."

"I hope so, but it will be a cold march back down here. Most of the riverboats went south two days ago and the Missouri will soon be frozen over enough for an ice road."

"I can still remember the cold in my bones from that hospital tent." Godfrey said quietly as he watched the dancing flames, the light reflecting in his eyes. "But at least I survived, thanks to you, Sgt. Welch, and poor Herwood. I've heard that they are both still at the hospital up at Buford."

"Welch wrote to say that he's getting better, but won't be winning any foot races soon."

"I can sympathize with that, Rogers."

Jake pulled out a copy of his transfer orders, and handed them to Godfrey then stood silently while the officer read them.

Godfrey looked up and said, "I remember when you came with Capt. Michaelis to help train the men down in Louisiana. He wanted you to work for him back then, so I'm not surprised."

"Well, he convinced me that I could do more good serving out the remainder of my enlistment, helping him with his weapons project. I just wanted to see you before I head back up to Fort Lincoln, on Friday. I wanted you to know that I'll never forget how relieved I was at the sight of you that day, on Reno Hill, standing firm with your skirmish line as we hightailed it back."

"That was a bad day. I fear that there's more controversy brewing. Custer was well liked in some circles, and they are looking to blame someone." Godfrey stated.

"I suspect so, sir. Anyway, I just wanted to say goodbye. It was an honor to serve with you."

"You're a good soldier, Sgt. Rogers! I wish you good luck, and tell Otho Michaelis that he owes me big favor!"

Back at the Company D barracks, Jake went to the orderly room, where he sorted through his stored effects and discarded some of the worn uniform items. He was rummaging through Top Martin's desk looking for some roster forms, when he found a leather pouch. He opened the flap and he found that it contained a folded cloth. He pulled it out revealing a faded US Cavalry guidon. There was a small note, too.

Company D Guidon, carried at the Little Big Horn fight

Jake carefully refolded it and thought to himself, "I may as well keep this, I'm about the only one left that fought under it." Then packed it away with his other things.

On his return to Fort Lincoln, he spent the next couple of weeks getting settled into his new daily routine working with Capt. Michaelis.

Most of his time was spent collecting copies of requisitions and reports related to ammunition expenditures from the various companies.

"I've been going over the Regimental reports of the engagement at Canyon Creek, back in September." Michaelis stated, "And, I've also visited with several of the officers who were involved in the fight."

Jake was seated at a desk across the room and was compiling lists of ammunition expenditures, replied, "Find anything interesting, sir?"

"It seems that our marksmanship was abominable. These reports are blaming gale force winds for it, but it doesn't seem to have effected the Nez Perce warriors. They were certainly able to pin down six companies of our troopers. Col. Sturgis and Maj. Merrill were quite complimentary of the Regiment's performance, while Capt. Benteen's initial report was rather curt, mentioning horses "abandoned in pursuit." However, he did file another report two weeks later that went into a bit more detail, siting several individuals for their conduct under fire."

"Well, I can attest that the Nez Perce had some damn good shots amongst them!" Jake remarked.

"I know that Benteen is a bit of a curmudgeon and is prone to denigrate some of his fellow officers, particularly those he doesn't care for. Still, I'd like to get his views of the engagement. Unfortunately, it appears that we will be back in St. Paul before he returns from Fort Buford."

Jake thought for a second, "I'm hoping be able to talk with some of the NCOs from the companies when coming in with Col. Miles. Several were at the Canyon Creek fight. In fact, one of my good friends is in Company I and I'm hoping to look him up."

"Do that, but Rogers, be very circumspect! All in all, the 7th Cavalry proved to be somewhat less effective than expectations on this season's campaign. There's little glory to go round, and what little there is has some people scrambling to claim their share. Our responsibility is to help make sure that improvements are made, and not to assign blame."

Word reached Bismarck and Fort Lincoln, that over 200 of the Nez Perce, mostly women, children and elders, would probably be arriving by river on Saturday, in mackinaw boats. Col. Miles, with five companies of the 7th commanded by Capt. French, was escorting Joseph with the remainder and was expected a day or two later. The local populous was galvanized by the impending arrivals and frantic preparations were being made, particularly in light of the national attention being focused on the Bismarck area.

Jake heard the booming of a cannon and knew that it signaled the arrival of the mackinaws carrying the Nez Perce. He was working his way up from the ferry, against the flow of traffic, as people streamed towards the river. A crowd had already been gathering, with children scampering along the riverbank to try and catch the first glimpse of the captured Indians. Local officials and members of the press were sitting on platforms erected to give them a commanding view of the river front landing. When he arrived at Forster's he found Murray already there, and seated himself in a chair.

"I think the crowds will be disappointed when they see the Nez Perce." Jake commented. "When I first saw them up in Montana, almost two months ago now, they were a pitiful looking lot. I don't suppose that all the time spent getting here has much improved them, although I'm sure Col. Miles saw to it that they haven't starved."

"I've been reading some of the newspapers from St. Paul and Chicago. Some of articles are touting them as a new and improved type of Indian, much superior to the typical Sioux and Cheyenne." Murray observed.

"It's always interesting how these Indian experts always manage to interpret how Indians out here think and act without ever meeting a real live one, don't you think?"

"None the less!"Murray exclaimed, "Several churches and civic minded groups are preparing to welcome the Nez Perce, and their noble Chief Joseph, with open arms."

It turned out that the Indians in the boats were traumatized by the booms from the cannon and the screech of locomotive whistles. They hunkered down in them and refused to disembark. Eventually, they were sent down to the Fort Lincoln landing, where they were persuaded to get off and allowed to put up tents along the river. Col. Miles and his wounded aide, Lt. Baldwin, rolled in on an ambulance later that afternoon.

On Monday, November 19, Col. Miles rode out to greet the column, accompanied by some local officials. They were welcomed with much fanfare as he led them into Bismarck, riding side by side with Joseph right down Main Street, while the 7th's band played the "Star Spangled Banner". The crowd broke out cheering and waving and some of the women were carrying dishes of food and baskets of bread to give to the Indians. After a time, the Nez Perce were escorted down to the riverbank, south of town, where they made camp and the ones that had come by boat earlier, were brought across from Fort Lincoln to join them. Meanwhile, Miles was feted and invited to a meticulously planned banquet, for that evening at the

Sheridan House, by Mayor J. A. McClean and the Tribune's C. A. Lounsberry. The weary and trail worn companies of the 7th Cavalry quietly boarded the *Union* and were ferried across the river to Fort Lincoln. The companies that had been posted there at the fort back in May, went to their barracks and the others into bivouac at the campground south of the fort.

The balance of that week proved eventful. Miles left the following day for St. Paul and Gen. Terry's headquarters. The city officials, were so pleased with the banquet that they'd thrown for Miles, that they decided to have one for Joseph, on Wednesday. On Thursday, Miles sent word via telegram, to Ad Chapman, Joseph's interpreter. Chapman was to inform the Nez Perce chieftain that his people would not be staying at Fort Lincoln for the winter, but instead would be to be taken by train down to Fort Leavenworth. Friday morning they were loaded onto a special train and left for St. Paul.

That Friday afternoon, Jake went to the Company I orderly room, looking for Mike Caddle, When he went in he found Capt. Nowlan talking with a First Sergeant who he didn't know. Nowlan looked up when he saw Jake.

"Sgt. Rogers, I haven't see you since we left the encampment up on the Yellowstone, back in September. I saw your name on the casualty list and I'm glad to see that you've recovered from your wounds.

"Yes, sir! I was very fortunate. I came to see if I could find Sgt. Caddle."

"This is my new First Sergeant, William Costello." Nowlan said, introducing the other man. "I was just leaving, but I'm sure that he can point you in the right direction. By the way, congratulations on your promotion, Capt. Michaelis is very complimentary of you."

"Thank you, sir!"

Costello spoke up "Mike is over at the storehouse. He's the company quartermaster sergeant now. Come on I'll walk you over, Rogers."

As they headed over to the quartermaster's warehouse, Costello asked, "How's it that you know Mike?"

Jake gave him a brief recap of his history with Mike, and when he finished, Costello said, "Mike's one of the few marksmen that we have in the company. He probably saved my ass during the fight, at Canyon Creek. We had a lot of replacement troopers and they had little training or experience with their weapons. Hell, they couldn't hit the broad side of a barn. Most of the shooting was done at long range and I suspect few of them adjusted their sights."

"Well, according to the reports that Capt. Michaelis let me read, it sounds like the wind and weather conditions were pretty bad that day."

"Hmm! Well, it didn't seem to bother the Nez Perce too much. They had us pinned down from the cliff tops, and I suspect there were only a few of them. One of them in particular had a big rifle that sounded like a cannon going off. Caddle was one of those carrying a Springfield rifle and I'm pretty sure he may have dinged one of them. Other than that, we just wasted a lot of lead."

When they found Mike, he was busy berating a couple of new privates as he was issuing them equipment. Jake grinned, waved to him, and called out. "Meet me at the post traders tonight, the beer's on me!" Mike smiled and nodded his head, then continued with his invective filled instructions.

When Jake and Mike met up at the post trader's bar that evening, they sat down and caught up over several beers.

"Quartermaster Sergeant, eh? Hearing you with those new troopers today reminded me of when I first got to Fort Rice." Jake laughed.

"And, I see that you got have a star over your chevrons. We should've both taken Capt. Michaelis up on it when he offered it, two years back."

"Say, I haven't noticed you at the NCO Quarters, Mike. Are you staying at the barracks?"

Mike's face colored slightly. "Ah, no! Do ya remember me telling ya about Josephine McIlhargy? She's still a laundress here at Lincoln, and I'm sorta looking after her and her kids."

Jake grinned, "You old dog! It's a wonder you found someone to take you in!""

"Me and Josie, we're plannin' a wedding for Christmas Day. I'd be proud if you were to attend, Jake."

"Well, good for you, Mike! But, I'm pretty sure that I'll be in St. Paul by then. Capt. Michaelis has his family there and I'm sure he plans to spend the holidays with them."

Mike wanted to hear about the events that had occurred leading up to the Snake Creek fight, so Jake recounted what happened after they left the Tongue River and headed north to intercept the Nez Perce."

"I remember seeing that Wheeler fella, when we were up on the Survey, but never met him. Sounds like you're damned lucky to have made his acquaintance, though."

"Yes, very lucky!" Jake agreed.

"And, I'm sure sorry to hear what happened to Capt. Hale, he was a fine officer." Mike stated.

"Yes, he was." Jake said solemnly, then to change the subject, he said,

"So, tell me about the fight at Canyon Creek."

"It really wasn't much of a fight. Maj. Merrill had us dismount and form a skirmish line as soon as we spotted some warriors. Personally, I thought that we should have stayed mounted. The few of them that we actually saw, were well out of effective range. They just shot at us enough to make us keep our heads down, then sneaked away. Merrill had us advance on foot for over a mile across the top of this ridge, while the horse holders stayed where they were at. Once we cleared the ridge, we stopped to wait on our mounts. Col. Sturgis ordered Benteen to take Companies G and M and go on ahead to keep pressure on the Nez Perce. We could just see the main body of them off in the distance, making for the mouth of the canyon. Our horses had still not been brought up, so Capt. Nowlan had us double timing on foot to try and help support Benteen. Meanwhile Merrill stayed where he was, still waiting on the horses. By the time we got up to where Benteen was, we were gassed and his two companies were pinned down by Indian sharpshooters. We crept forward through gullies and washes, popping up to fire up at the Indians now and then, but they were well hidden. We finally advanced to the mouth of the canyon, where several more warriors on the clifftops on both sides tried picking us off, fortunately it got dark before too long. We were so exhausted, that we just pulled back a ways and camped right there on the creek."

"So, all of the fighting was with rifles and carbines?"

"Yep! I never unholstered m' pistol, they were too far away!" Mike replied, then took a long pull off his beer. "The head scout, Stan Fisher, found a rock with over 40 shell casings laying around it, where one of their warriors blasted away at us. Just between you and me,'twas a mighty poor showing on our side. The civilian scouts with us were very vocal about it. Particularly, when they discovered the Crows had rifled through our pack train and stolen their saddle bags and bedrolls. They left us the next day, disgusted with Sturgis."

"Your telling of it, is at odds with the official reports that I've read."Jake pointed out.

"I don't doubt that!" Mike exclaimed. "I've heard that Col. Sturgis left for St. Louis two days after he got back, and the rumor is that he'll not be back this year. Merrill is in command here and will be want ta put his part in the best light, before Benteen returns. There's no love lost between those two!" Mike guffawed. "Now, Capt. Benteen and Capt. French they led their men in two separate charges, and Capt. Nowlan was the one that kept us moving on foot. Then, young Lt. Fuller took Company H and tried to force his way down the creek. So, I hope that they were mentioned."

"I'm sure that when the rest of the regiment returns there'll be many recriminations bandied about." Jake offered.

"Yeh, but ya can bet that Benteen will be kept down at Fort Rice, where he can stew in his own juices."

"So, what's your plans, Mike, "Since you're gonna be a family man now? You going to reenlist next year?" Jake asked.

"Naw, I'll be gettin' out. But I'm thinkin' that me and Josie will stick around here. That's why I'm glad to be workin' with the Quartermaster and learnin' how the local contracts work. I figure to make some connections that I can use to get hooked up supplyin' the Army, and maybe even the reservations, too. How about you?"

"No, I'm done. I joined up to travel and see some of the country. I've seen enough of these parts. This new job with Capt. Michaelis will take me back east and I'm ready to see what that's like. Then I figure that come May, I'll head on back down to Missouri."

"There you go!" Caddle laughed, and raised his beer, "Here's to a life without bugles and addle headed officers, it can't come too soon!"

Capt. Michaelis was set to leave for St. Paul the following week. He called Jake into his office to discuss his plans.

"We need to finish up with our work here by the end of the month. I'm going to be presenting some of our findings to Gen.Terry, while we're in St. Paul, then we're going back to New York and Connecticut to visit some firearms manufacturing firms. They had several prototype repeating rifles on display last fall, at the Philadelphia Exposition. I want to look at them more closely, and also let you have an opportunity to evaluate them."

"I was hoping to stay here through Thanksgiving, sir. I think that you'll remember Sgt. Morse. He and his wife have invited me over for dinner. He works for the Northern Pacific under Murray Johnson now, and I'm sure that they can arrange for me to reach St. Paul by the following Monday."

"Yes, I see no reason that you will be needed in St.Paul until then, Rogers!" Michaelis replied. "At any rate, I will be spending time with my family."

"Thank you, sir."

"You can finish up consolidating the individual company ammunition expenditures. I'd like to get an idea of the average rounds fired at each engagement and compare them. I just received the 5th Infantry reports and it will be interesting to see how their numbers look. Most of them were veterans, having much more experience and familiarity with firing their weapons. You can spend your time looking at them, and we can go over the numbers in St.Paul."

"Yes, I'll be very interested in seeing those, also." Jake said, then asked, "When will we be coming back here, sir?"

Michaelis looked at Jake and said, "I wouldn't be surprised if we don't, at least before your enlistment expires. You'd better bring along all of your effects. We can find a place to store them at headquarters, while we're traveling. So, it's good that you'll have time to say your goodbyes to your friends in Bismarck. You should make sure your mail is forwarded to Ordinance, at the Department of Dakota Headquarters, in St. Paul. I will make arrangements for it to be forwarded to us, when we travel."

The following Tuesday, he spent the morning finishing packing his footlocker and an old leather portmanteau Murray gave him that was still serviceable. Jake marveled at how much his wardrobe had expanded since his early days as a private, as he sorted through his old uniforms selecting items to donate to Mike. When he went over to the office, he found some mail waiting for him that had arrived on the stage from Fort Rice that day. He made a mental note to send a telegram to the people in Springfield notifying them about his change in address before he left. He spent the rest of the afternoon reading letters. Most of the news from home centered on preparations for the coming holiday season. He was pleased to read that Holly was going over to Henderson, with Frank and Colleen for Thanksgiving. Noting the time, he gathered his baggage and toted them downstairs to meet Mike. He'd volunteered to help him carry it over to river landing, where the *Union* was making its last crossing of the season. Jake didn't want to get stranded at Fort Lincoln and have to wait for the ice to get thick enough to support stage and wagon traffic.

When they reached the river and got on board the boat, Jake noted large chunks of ice drifting in the current.

"Looks like this old tub, is tempting fate by waiting this late in the season." Mike remarked, as he eyed them also.

"Yeh, at least the trains are still running. I should be in St. Paul, by Tuesday."

"Well, Jake, I wish you the best of luck, though you seem to make your own most of the time."

"Thanks, Mike. I hope things work out well for you and Josie. Good luck with your plans."

They shook hands and as Caddle started up the gangway he called back over his shoulder, "Tell that Miss Holly of yours that Ol' Mike Caddle sends his regards."

It was quite an impressive spread for the Thanksgiving Day meal, at Kate's house. Pat had bagged a turkey and Murray produced a large ham, while Kate had outdone herself with side dishes and desserts. Afterwards, they bundled up and went on a carriage ride about town. As they traveled down Main Street, they passed The Old Pioneer Hardware, that Bob Seip had purchased.

"I don't know if you've heard, Jake, but Bob has been very ill." Kate said.

"No, I hadn't."

"He's consumptive, and not doing well. Dr. Porter has been treating him with laudanum, but I hear that he's steadily going downhill."

"I'm sorry to hear that, I know that he was unfaithful to you, but he always treated me well."

"Oh, I'm sorry for him, too!" Kate exclaimed. "He just wanted to be a big wheel, and let himself be compromised by others. I'm okay with the way things turned out though." She smiled and hugged Pat's arm.

Pat looked at Jake and said, "Aye, me too, I needed to make an honest woman out of Kate." That earned him a punch in the arm from her.

Jake laughed and said, "I think maybe that it was the other way around, Pat!"

"Aye! You're probably right about that." Pat replied. "Any chance you'll be comin' back this way?

"Maybe, I can probably persuade Capt. Michaelis to let me have a few days leave. It'll depend on if the trains can get through,"

"Oh, they'll get through!" Murray stated firmly. "We're only going to run back to Fargo three times a week this winter, but the tracks will be kept clear. We've got an experienced crew running a specially equipped plow train, now."

After touring the downtown area, Murray and Jake had the driver drop them off at Forster's, where he and Murray stayed up talking for a while, over drinks.

"You still planning to head back to Missouri when your hitch is up?"

Jake considered the question, then said. "Yeh, I'm pretty sure, why?"

"I can always use a man with your experience, if you're interested?"

"Well, thanks for offering. But, I'm wanting to get back down to where the temperatures aren't so damn cold. Besides, my friend, Frank, thinks that he can get me on working for the Frisco line. They're getting ready to expand out to the southwest, and I kind of liked surveying. Lt. Greene taught me a lot when I worked with him up on the Boundary."

"My offer stands, if you change your mind. Working for any railroad is going to be a good way to make a living, and being involved in the surveying will insure that you'll be in the thick of things. Always try to work an angle to own some of its stock. That's how you'll make some real money." Murray advised.

"Thanks Murray!" Jake said, "Whatever I decide, I'll stay in touch."

CHAPTER 46

Headquarters, Department of Dakota, St. Paul, Minnesota - Wednesday, Dec. 5, 1877

Jake had seen very little of St. Paul when he passed through it back in '75. He'd seen the waterfront from the train as they went by and the blocks of buildings off to the north. The weather was just above freezing when he arrived at the Train Depot that served the waterfront and downtown. Snow covered the roofs on the sheds and warehouses that lined the waterfront, which showed little activity. He was surprised to see that the Mississippi River wasn't frozen over yet. At the ticket counter he enquired about the address he'd been given and the agent told him that he could catch a horse drawn streetcar out front that would take him right by it. When he went outside he found one waiting and, after checking with the driver, he piled his baggage on board. Jake noted that both of the horses that pulled the car looked to be in pretty ragged condition and needed a good grooming. Fortunately, the ride was fairly short and he got off in front of a red brick, five story building. There were two uniformed privates posted at the entrance, and big bronze letters above the doorway.

U S ARMY HEADQUARTERS

THE DEPARTMENT of DAKOTA.

One of the sentries came over to Jake, noting his chevrons, and asked. "Can I help you, Sergeant?"

Jake nodded his head, "Thanks, I'm here to report in to Capt. Michaelis."

"Here, let me help you get your things inside, where we can watch them." As he picked up the footlocker, he said, "Judging by the scabbard, that's quite a rifle that you're toting there."

There was a vestibule inside that led to a lobby area. A burly, red faced sergeant sat behind a large wooden desk watching them, as Jake's things were placed on some nearby benches. Reaching inside his coat, Jake retrieved copies of his orders and turned to hand them over to the other sergeant.

"Sgt. Jacob Rogers, reporting for duty," he announced. "I'm here to see Capt. Michealis."

The man behind the desk replied, "He told me to be on the lookout for you. You're his new Ordinance Sergeant, the one that's coming from the 7th Cavalry."

"Yes, I just came in from Fort Lincoln."

"Well, you'll like this place!" he said smiling, "I've been to Fort Lincoln in the winter. It's cold as hell there, with nothing to block the wind. It's been unseasonably warm here, this is the first snow that amounts to anything. We've nice cozy billets here, just over a block away, for the itinerant Officers and NCOs. I'll take you over m'self once the Captain is done with you." He got up and held out his hand "Bill Byrne! Nice ta meet ya!"

Jake shook his hand and said, "Jake Rogers, likewise! That's good to hear about a cozy room. I've had my fill of cold."

Byrne led Jake up a flight of stairs and showed him down a hallway until they came to a frosted glass door with painted gold letters.

Captain Otho E. Michaelis
Ordinance Department
Chief Ordinance Officer

"Here you go, I'll be keepin' an eye on your things for ya. Come see me when you finish with the Captain." Byrne announced, then left to go back downstairs.

Jake knocked on the door, then opened it when he heard "Come in!".

Michaelis rose from behind his desk as Jake came to attention and saluted, "Sgt. Rogers, reporting for duty, Sir!"

The officer returned his salute, then said, "Sit down, Rogers. How are your wounds? Any problems with them?"

As Jake grabbed a chair, he noted that the office walls were lined with bookcases filled with Army manuals and many framed certificates. A separate table in the corner contained a chessboard with a game in process, judging from captured pieces around it.

"I'm fine, sir, no issues. My arm is healed and I've almost got full strength in it."

"I'm pleased to hear that! Let's get you settled in, we'll be working here until the first of the year, then we'll be heading up to New York and Connecticut."

"I've never been in that part of the country."

"Well, you'll be spending some time there. We'll be evaluating several different rifle prototypes. I'll want your input as to the practicality of the different designs for use under field conditions."

"That sounds very interesting, sir."

"Until then, you can help me organize my report. There's not much going on around here right now, Gen. Terry just returned from his October Peace Commission trip up to Canada, and has taken a leave to go back to the east. I'll be spending my afternoons with the family until after Christmas, so consider yourself free to explore the area. I feel that you've earned it."

"Thank you, Sir! That's very generous!"

"I've given Sgt. Byrne instructions to get you settled in your billet and show you to the NCO mess. I've already arranged to have your pay sent here. How are you fixed for funds?"

"Pretty well, sir. I finally got all my back pay last month, and I have a bank draft that I'll need to find a local bank to open an account with."

"Excellent! I will have you issued some vouchers for when we travel. Now, take the rest of the week to get settled in, and report back on Monday."

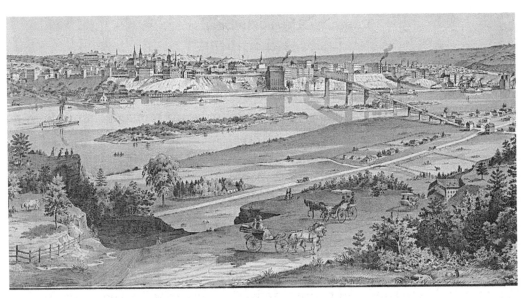

St. Paul Minnesota - Circa 1878

When Jake went down stairs, Byrne was waiting with his coat on. He had a corporal sitting at his place behind the desk.

"Let's go, Jake!" he exclaimed, "Cpl. Dougherty will mind the door for the rest of the day. I've taken the liberty of stashing that big rifle of yours in the arms room. Let's take the rest of your things over to where you'll be staying and I'll introduce you to the landlady. It's a nice boarding house with breakfast and laundry included. Then, we'll go introduce you to St. Paul's wide variety of fresh brewed beers. We've got a dozen or so brands to choose from, my personal favorite is a brand called 'Yoerg'. There's lot's of Germans around here, and they like their beer."

"Sounds like a good plan to me!" Jake exclaimed.

Byrne was expounding on St. Paul and its surroundings while they drank beer and sampled sausages, pickled herring, and potato dumplings, at Otto's Wirtshaus, down by the riverfront.

"Ya see, Rogers, there's two cities here. St. Paul what bein' the older, state capitol and all, but Minneapolis is growin' fast."

"Yes, I remember seeing lots of buildings and the mills off in the distance, when I came through Fort Snelling a couple of years ago. It was in the summer and they were pretty impressive. I never made it up there, though."

"I prefer St. Paul m'self. Course it's handiest to Headquarters, and I find the food and beer to be better. There's lot's of Germans in St. Paul, why they even publish a couple of newspapers in German here. The brewers have dug down into the sandstone bluffs south of the river, to house their breweries. There's a dozen or so scattered along it. There's a fair amount of Swedes and Irish out to the east side, along Phalen Creek and south towards the river. The riverboats still do a thriving business up here to St. Paul, until the rivers freeze over."

"I like what I see of it so far."

"Now, Minneapolis is a major town for the trades. There's lots of jobs to be had, along with lots of noise, hustle, and bustle." There's gettin' ta be many Pole and Norwegian immigrants, in addition to more Germans and Swedes. The milling companies over there, like Washburn-Crosby and Pillsbury, are building bigger mills, using smooth steel rollers to produce finer flour. The Saint Anthony Falls provide ample supplies of water to power them. Then there's the lumber mills and steel works, served by the railroads needed to haul the grain, flour, logs and all that.

Jake took a pull off his beer, "I suspect that I won't be here that much."

"There's another bit of fun a man can have here in St. Paul." Bill hinted.

"What might that be?" asked Jake.

"Brothels! They're sorta illegal, but the madams pay the fines once a month ta stay open. A man can get his ashes hauled when he's got the urge. I know a couple of nice ones where the women are clean, if you're so inclined."

Jake said. "Thanks, but I'm trying to save some money for when I get out. Besides, I've got a girl waiting on me, and I don't want to chance catching a dose of the clap. That wouldn't be too smart at this point."

"Suit yerself! Just giving ya the lay o' the land!" Byrne said with a grin, nodding his head in the direction of their waitress, "There's many a lass working the saloons and beer halls to be charmed, also."

The next week, temperatures hovered above freezing and Jake took advantage of it to tour the city by riding the street cars, which charged a nickel to ride. He sought out a jeweler to mount the agate stones on silver pendants, and bought a pair of heavy silver chains, and a matching watch fob chain. The jeweler assured him that he would have them ready in a week. As he rode the street cars, he had a few conversations with fellow passengers. Many were quite vocal about their opinions concerning progress in what they were calling the 'Twin Cities'. He heard that the population of the St. Paul had just reached 40,000 people, but had been passed by Minneapolis, with just over 46,000. One day, Sgt. Byrne invited him to accompany him to Fort Snelling, where the 20th Infantry Headquarters and Company E were getting ready to transfer down to Texas. Byrne had a friend there who he wanted to see before he left. Afterwards, they ventured over to Minneapolis and Jake marveled at the amount of construction that was going on. He was bit disappointed at the appearance of the St. Anthony Falls, though. They had been tapped by so many of the mills that the limestone cap was in danger of collapsing, and was shored up with a massive timber apron. The new Hennepin Suspension Bridge over the Mississippi River had just been completed the year before. From the bridge there was a panoramic view of the river upstream on both sides. Byrne pointed out the various grain and lumber mills. Nicollet Island, in mid-stream, was piled high with freshly milled lumber that had been cut from logs floated downstream from the northern forests. They caught a street car back down to St. Paul and Byrne kept up a running commentary along the way, pointing out places of interest. As they got back downtown on to St. Peters Street, Bill pointed at an elaborate, four story brick building.

"That's the Greenman House, it's one of the fanciest hotels in the city. People from all over the world stay there, when they come ta town. They've a good bar, with many fine whiskies, but 'tis a bit pricey for my tastes. Mind ya, there's many pretty ladies wanderin' through the lobby to admire."

Jake replied, "Yeh, I think it's over my budget. I'll stick with Otto's, and beer."

Jake was surprised that he'd already received several letters, then realized that he was a lot closer to home instead of being at the end of the line, on the frontier. In Holly's letter, she was quite relieved to hear that he was okay, and that the wounds were not serious. She'd also heard about him from her Aunt Kate. Holly seemed excited about all the local preparations for Christmas around Springfield. She and Colleen were both going to be in a holiday pageant. She hinted that she had a special present for him, but couldn't send it by mail and he would have to wait to open it when he came home. His mother wrote telling him how glad that she was to hear about his wounds healing, and about his new duty assignment. Now she wouldn't have to worry so much about him, and was looking forward to seeing him in the spring. They were ready for winter with well stocked cellars. His father had killed a couple of nice deer, and was looking to bag a turkey for Christmas dinner. She wished that he could be with them. It sounded like Frank and Colleen were doing well in Springfield, and that they would be in Henderson for Christmas. They were supposed to bring that that nice girl, Holly, with them.

His thoughts on the coming holiday were dampened by the rain and heavy fog, that started on the 18th. The roads were in poor condition, and after venturing forth to pick up his items from the jeweler, he decided that travel around the area was almost impractical. He spent more time at headquarters rather than at his billet, just to have someone to talk to. Capt. Michaelis loaned him several books, including one on chess, so Jake began experimenting with the rudiments of the game. Christmas Day was on the next Tuesday, so most of the Headquarters staff, including Byrne, were taking Monday off. A skeleton crew was detailed to guard the building, and even the small mess hall would be closed. He supposed that Otto's might have some kind of special Christmas dinner planned. At least that would be better than staying in his room, alone. Jake wistfully recalled Vanessa mentioning a special holiday just before he left her hotel room, that early morning back in Bismarck. He'd heard nothing from her and wondered if his letters had even reached her. Friday morning, he was sitting at a small desk, in a room across the hall from Michaelis' office, when one of the sentries from down stairs walked in and handed him an envelope. He opened it and read:

Coming in tomorrow and will be staying at the Greenman House, downtown St. Paul. I'm sure that my intrepid pathfinder can find his way to me. Meet me at the lobby bar Saturday evening, around 5:00.

V. B.

Jake grinned and thought to himself, "Well, perhaps it'll be a Merry Christmas after all!"

That afternoon, he hurried back to his room to lay out his civilian clothes. As he was looking for clean socks, he came across the velvet pouches that the jeweler had provided with the agate pendants. He sorted through them, admiring the translucent colors, and decided that the pair of greenish brown agates that were streaked with various shade of brown, with tiny black spots, would look the best for Vanessa. As he put the other away, he stopped to gaze at the grayish one, and was suddenly amazed at how clearly he could recall the exact moment when Val had given them to him, almost as if it was yesterday. The thought of it brought a calm, reassuring moment to Jake.

The rain continued Christmas Day, and Jake spend most of it reading one of the new books that he'd borrowed from the captain. It was titled "The Adventures of Tom Sawyer" by an author called, Mark Twain. Jake was curious, because that was a term he'd heard riverboat men use when sounding the depth along the rivers. It was a humorous book about a young boy in Missouri, and it reminded him of some of his childhood adventures with Frank Armstrong. That afternoon, after washing up and shaving, he carefully dressed in a clean linen shirt with paper collar, before donning in his sack suit. He grabbed his over coat and Bowler hat, then headed downstairs. There was an umbrella stand by the door, and although the rain had eased up, he made sure to take one with him. He quickly made his way along the sidewalks towards St. Peter's Street, which was a couple of blocks to the west, and then turned towards the river. The Greenman House stood at the corner of 5th Street with a dozen wide semicircular stone steps ascending up to a white columned portico topped by a balcony, that framed the ornate wood and glass double doors of the main entrance on the second floor. Jake trod up the steps and went through them to the lobby. Inside, there were many people dressed up for the evening, some standing huddled in small groups, while others strolled around them. The lobby was bathed in light from several massive chandeliers, and he could hear a piano playing quiet music in the background. Most people were holding glasses of wine, or champagne, although he did spot a few mugs of beer, here and there. The front desk was busy, with a few people still checking in. After checking his hat and coat, Jake followed a well dressed waiter bearing a tray of empty glasses through an archway into what turned out to be a gaily decorated dining room. A massive, mahogany bar backed by huge mirrors that ran the length of it, where several bartenders wearing white shirts and vests, bustled to wait on the thirsty crowd. Festive curtains decorated the windows, which let in the weak fading light from outside, while chandeliers that matched the ones in the lobby also illuminated the room. A tall blue spruce tree stood in one corner, festooned with colorful ornaments and ribbons and topped by a large golden star. The murmur from dozens of conversations and gay laughter filled the room. Jake noticed the figure of a solitary woman outlined against one of the windows as she looked outside. He drifted in that direction, until he saw that it was indeed Vanessa. She was wearing a gray dress trimmed in blue with matching feathered hat. Using a small group of people to conceal himself he edged ever closer, but not wishing to startle her, he exclaimed softly.

"They say that if you look hard enough, you'll eventually find what you are looking for."

Vanessa turned around slowly, wearing a wistful smile. "Indeed, then it seems that they are correct. I was watching for you."

"And here I am!"

She stepped towards him, and offered her hand. "It's so good to see you, Jacob. I trust that you have fully recovered?"

"Yes, just left with a couple of scars to remind me of how lucky I was." he confirmed, as he took it. "And, of how lucky that I continue to be. You look beautiful as always, Vanessa!"

"And you look very gentlemanly, Jacob. Not at all like a dashing young cavalryman just back from battling savage warriors on the frontier!"

"Which do you prefer?"

"Now, that's a difficult question. I suppose in this setting, the gentleman is more appropriate." she teased, "But, when it comes time for hard charging, I'm quite sure that I prefer the other."

"Fortunately, I can accommodate you in either case!" he declared, as he offered her his arm, "Shall we?"

They went to the dining room entrance, where there was a small line waiting. When a uniformed waiter came to escort them to a table, Vanessa whispered something to him and he nodded his head. He escorted them to an alcove across the room where they were afforded a bit more privacy. After seating them, he handed them menus and announced that the special this evening was fresh red snapper that had just arrived from the Gulf of Mexico, by rail in a refrigerated car. It was specially prepared by the head chef and accompanied by servings of new potatoes and vegetables.

When the waiter inquired about wine, Vanessa spoke up, "Jacob dear, if you don't mind, please let's have a bottle of good German Riesling. I enjoy it so much with fish."

Jake nodded his head in agreement and as soon as the waiter left, he said with a grin. "Well, it seems that I have more to learn about my role as a gentleman."

"Your role is to be my companion for the next four days, dear Jacob. It's all been arranged and paid for by my employer. Officially you are my American cousin, from Missouri, and you're sharing a suite with me. Separate bedrooms, of course!"

Jake raised his eyebrows in surprise.

Vanessa leaned towards him, and said with a mischievous grin, "So, we'll have to be sure and muss the bedclothes in both of them."

"Okay!" he chuckled. "I'll do my best!"

As Jake studied the menu he was astounded by the variety of items on the menu. Venison, buffalo roast, quail, pheasant, duck and goose were all listed, but the red snapper sounded the most interesting.

"Have you ever had red snapper, Vanessa?" he asked.

"Yes, it is quite delicious. It is a mild flavored fish, I'm sure that you'll enjoy it."

"Yes, it will be something quite different from what I've been accustomed to."

After they finished eating, they sat chatting while finishing the wine.

"There's a local small orchestra playing in the ball room if you'd like to listen to them." Vanessa offered.

Between the excellent food, the wine, and his proximity to Vanessa, Jake couldn't remember the last time had that he felt so good. As he gazed into her dark smiling eyes, it seemed that he was drawn into them, and felt an urgent need to be with her.

"Do you suppose that we might be able to hear the music up in the room?" he asked.

Vanessa stood and held out her hand, "I suggest that there is only one way to find out. Shall we?"

The weather continued to be rainy and unseasonably warm for the next several days, staying just above freezing, even at night. Sunday they stayed in the hotel room for most of the day, only emerging to visit the dining room, and Monday morning they dressed for town. The rain had churned the gravel streets into rutted muddy tracks bordered by sidewalks.

Vanessa arranged for a carriage and driver to take them around the city. They spent the day exploring St. Paul, stopping to shop occasionally, and for lunch. But even the overcast skies didn't dampen the festive spirits of the people that were out and about. Back at the hotel, the lobby was full of revelers, and the bar was dispensing large quantities of Christmas cheer. Jake and Vanessa went upstairs to freshen up, then returned to listen to the carolers and join in the festivities. A buffet was set up in the dining room, and they enjoyed sampling the various holiday delicacies, many of them traditional German and Swedish. Finally, they tired of the crowd and feeling a little tipsy, they made their way back to the suite. Vanessa giggled as Jake fumbled with her buttons as he hurried to undress her, then she fell into bed naked, urging him to join her. As they made love, she shed her normally refined pace, and Jake marveled at her sudden wild abandon. Finally, they reached an intense crescendo and collapsed intertwined, falling asleep in each others arms.

Jake woke Christmas morning a bit blurry-eyed, to find Vanessa dressed in a robe. He noted that his clothes, which he vaguely recalled strewing about, were now neatly hung from various pieces of the furniture.

"Merry Christmas, my dear Jacob!"

"Merry Christmas, Vanessa!" he replied.

"Did you sleep well?"

"Indeed I did! Like a rock. How long have you been awake?"

"Not long. I've just been picking up after our frantic little tete ´a tete last night." She smiled. "Perhaps we should dress and go find some breakfast, I'm famished, how about you?"

The dining room staff were bustling about waiting on the guests as they trickled in. As Vanessa sipped her tea, Jake drew in the aromas wafting from the direction of the kitchens and said, "Something smells good, you wouldn't believe some of the breakfasts we concocted out in the field. There's only so much that you can do with salt pork and hardtack crackers!"

The waiter returned to their table, "Our chef has prepared a special breakfast, this morning. He learned to cook it at Delmonico's restaurant, in New York. It's called 'Eggs Benedict'. Buttered toast topped with back bacon, poached eggs and a creamy Dutch sauce. It's quite tasty!"

"I think I shall try that." Vanessa said.

Jake nodded his head, "I will, too. And more coffee when you can. Thanks."

When they went back to the room, Vanessa went to a closet and retrieved a rectangular package, wrapped with a ribbon, put it on the bed, then said, "My Christmas present to you, dear Jacob."

Jake looked at her, and said, "You didn't have to do that, Vanessa. You are all the present that I need. Besides, you've arranged all of this." He waved his hand around the room.

"Ah, this is just a convenient place for us to spend our hours together. Now, please open it, I had a difficult time selecting it."

Jake carefully unwrapped the box, which was fairly heavy, revealing a walnut wood case with latches on one side. When he opened it, there, laying nestled in blue velvet padding was a Colt revolver, but one like he'd never seen. "Oh, what a beauty!" he exclaimed.

"I ordered this for you after you told me that you were leaving the Army. The gunsmith that I consulted with recommended it. He said it was Colt's newest design, and had special double acting trigger, whatever that means. You've told me that you'll probably not return to the field, but I want you to have it anyway."

Jake gently picked the pistol up to inspect it. The checkered walnut grips had a rearing colt etched in them and contrasted with a bright nickel finish. There was a curious spur on the frame just above where the hand grip tapered at the bottom, with a lanyard ring on the butt, underneath. While he was studying the pistol, Vanessa produced a box of cartridges labeled *.44-40 WCF.*

"The gunsmith recommended this caliber, he says that it's getting to be the most popular round on the civilian market, mostly because Winchester rifles use them also."

Jake looked up at her and said, "I hadn't heard about these new pistols."

"Well, the gunsmith told that he went to some great lengths to procure it for me. It's the new Model 1878, just being introduced. There are very few available."

He put it back in the case, and closed it, "That's a very nice pistol, Vanessa. Thank you!" then bent to kiss her.

He reached into his pocket to find the pouch containing the agates, then pulled her down to sit next to him on the bed. "I have something for you, it's not much, but I hope you'll like it." And dropped the pendants into his hand, then held one out to her. "Here hold this up to the light from the window."

Vanessa gazed at the shimmering stone, and said, "It's very soothing to look at, very unusual."

"Do you remember me telling you stories about my friend, Val Wheeler."

"Yes, the half Indian fellow! I rather like him, though I never met him, I suppose it's because we share that trait," she laughed softly.

Jake went on to relate the story about Val and the spirit stones, particularly the part that they'd played at Snake Creek.

"So you see, these are another pair of them." he said softly, while dangling the other pendant from his hand. "We'll each have one and our spirits will be connected through them."

Vanessa continued to stare at the stone as it glimmered green in the pale light, and Jake saw a tear slowly forming at the corner of her eye, then run down the side of her face. She reached over to grab his hand and squeezed it fiercely, then pulled him back onto the bed, "Let's just hold each other for a while." she whispered. "I want to savor this moment."

Later, they went to the dining room where a special Christmas dinner was being served, and afterwards went for a stroll along the sidewalk, circling the block, chatting quietly as they did. She asked him about his agenda for the coming months, and inquired about his plans after his discharge, listening patiently as he enthusiastically described them. When they circled back to the hotel, they went up to the room, where Vanessa proceeded to make passionate love to him, using some techniques that left him spent and almost gasping for air.

"That was amazing! I can't hardly move."

Vanessa giggled, "That was the rest of your Christmas present."

"I'm almost glad that I have to report for duty tomorrow. That is, if I can find the energy. What are your plans for after the holiday?"

"I've a fair bit of traveling ahead of me, then I will have to see."

"I should be heading back to my billet, pretty soon. That way I won't have to wake you early."

"That's okay, I don't mind !" she said, as she snuggled against him, "I like to up wake in your arms."

"Well, okay. Tomorrow, when I get off duty, I'll come see you before you leave."

Vanessa squeezed his arm in reply.

The following day, as Jake rose and dressed, Vanessa lay under the covers watching him in the dim light. When he bent down to kiss her, she drew him to her and pulled him into a tight embrace and gave him a lingering kiss, then whispered. "Good bye my dear!"

"Oh, I may be able to get away early, it just depends on what Capt. Michaelis has planned."

He hurried back to his billet, and scrambled into his uniform then hurried over to headquarters. He was pleased to see the mess hall open, and ran into Byrne there.

"Well, Jake, how was your Christmas?" he asked.

"Just fine, Bill. I went over to the Greenman House for Christmas dinner. It was quite a spread."

"Ah now! Twas a bit pricy I bet."

"Yeh, I suppose it was, but it beat staying in my room."

Jake met with Capt. Michaelis later that morning, and they went over all of the reports that Jake had compiled the information for. The captain was in a very good mood, and complimented Jake on them.

"This is good work, Rogers. As soon as I get them submitted to Gen. Terry, we will see about scheduling our trip back east. I should think that we will try and leave shortly after New Years."

"Thank you, Sir! I'm looking forward to traveling in that part of the country. I've heard a lot about it from some of the other men, that are from there."

"We'll be staying at the New York Army Arsenal, on Governors Island, in New York. It is a good place for our base of operations, while we are conducting our evaluation of the new rifles being developed."

"Do you have any idea how long we'll be there, Sir?"

"I should think several months, it just depends on how forthcoming the different firearms manufacturers are with their prototypes."

Jake nodded his head, "So, we will be coming back here?"

"Oh, yes! My wife is quite adamant that I return as quickly as I can. We've five young children and another on the way. I'm hoping to be assigned command of one of the Arsenals after this, so I can have a proper home for them and be done with traveling. We should be back in plenty of time for you muster out in May."

When he got off duty, he went back to his room to change, then headed for the Greenman House. He wanted to inform Vanessa about his travel plans and see if she might be able to arrange another rendezvous. As he entered the lobby, the desk clerk called him over.

"I have something for you, Mr. Rogers." Then, reaching down, he produced a package and an envelope, sliding them across the counter to Jake.

Jake recognized the package as the one that held the Colt pistol, but was puzzled by the envelope.

To Jake's surprise the clerk continued, "Your, ah, cousin, Miss Blake, left these with me as she was checking out and asked me to give them to you when you came back."

Jake was stunned momentarily, then said, "Oh, Okay! She must have had to leave suddenly."

"Yes, she did seem to be in a hurry." The clerk replied.

Jake crossed the lobby and found a chair, then sat, opened the envelope and read the letter inside.

My dearest Jacob,

I'm going back to England. My livelihood relies on my looks, and I'm getting of an age that it is getting harder to maintain them. I have been very fortunate to have received generous remuneration over the last few years, much of it in the form of several different railroad stocks which are now starting to perform extremely well. Consequently, I have reached a point where I have enough wealth accumulated to live comfortably where ever I choose to. Back there I can start over, without fear of running into someone that knows anything about me. If the fates will permit it this late in life, I'd like to have a family and hope that I'll find a gentleman that will fill my needs.

I've battled with myself for some time over trying to persuade you to come with me. You remind me so much of my dear Nigel, whom I lost to a Maori spear down in New Zealand, years ago. But I know in my heart that it wouldn't work. First of all there is the difference in our age to consider. But more importantly, I have seen that you are a man that requires challenges in his life, and I'm sure that they lay in another direction.

So, we part ways for the last time. I will always remember you as you are, and hope that you do as well of me. Fate threw us together and we took advantage of it while we could. But, it wasn't love, it was two kindred spirits enjoying the moment. When I gaze at the spirit stone that you gave me, that is what I will see. Go pursue your dreams and Miss Holly Walker. She seems to be your genuine soulmate and I envy her for it. I wish you both only the best. I'm sorry to leave you so abruptly, but I have to make a clean break of it. I didn't want it to be any sadder than it already is, and I hate goodbyes!

Fondly,
Vanessa

Jake frowned then re-read it, totally surprised at the content. He considered briefly about asking the clerk some questions, then decided against it. After carefully folding the letter and tucking it in his pocket, he stood and put the box under his arm. He looked around the lobby, then went out on the portico and cast an eye up and down the street, vainly hoping to see Vanessa. Sensing that it was a futile gesture, Jake headed back to his billet, pondering the words in her letter and feeling a sense of loss.

CHAPTER 47

New York City, New York - Monday, January 12, 1878

New York City & Harbor - 1878

Jake accompanied Capt. Michaelis on a cross country rail journey after departing St. Paul, that included stops and changing trains in Chicago and Cleveland. Jake marveled at the expanse of Lake Michigan and Lake Erie as the rail lines skirted their shorelines. After reaching Buffalo, they boarded the New York Central Railroad which turned south at Albany, following the west bank of the Hudson River. Michaelis pointed out the Military Academy at West Point, along the way. As they drew nearer to New York, the countryside transitioned into increased urban development and then the train passed through Central Park before finally arriving at the Grand Central Depot, on 42nd Street, in New York City. It had been completed in 1871, by Cornelius Vanderbilt, and three different railroads used the 12 sets of tracks that terminated under a huge glass roofed train shed with raised loading platforms. The shed was connected to a three story building that housed the three different depots with separate waiting rooms, four restaurants, several stores, a billiards room, and even a police station. When they arrived, the conductor informed them that their car would be disconnected and drawn by a team of horses down to the old 30th Street Depot.

"Why can't we get off here?" Michaelis queried.

The conductor smiled and asked, "Where are you headed for in the City, Captain?"

"We're going to the New York Arsenal, on Governors Island."

"Well, I can tell it's been a few years since you've been back, Captain. You can, if you wish, but then you'll have to ride an omnibus, or hire a taxi to take you on into the city. However, at the 30th Street Depot, you can catch the 9th Avenue elevated train and ride it all the way south to the South Ferry station then catch a ferry across to the Arsenal."

"Yes, I agree that sounds much better. When I was last here, the elevated train construction had been halted by bankruptcies. It will be interesting to see how they operate."

"They are running well ever since the wealthy Cyrus Field took over as president of the New York Elevated Rail Road last year. He's also building a new route along 3rd Avenue that will connect to the Grand Central Depot by this fall."

As the elevated train made its way south, Jake was astounded by the numbers and heights of the buildings on both sides of the train car. As he watched, a train passed them headed back north on the double tracked system that facilitated travel in both directions. He craned his neck to peer through gaps in the track as the train slowed to stop at stations and caught glimpses of crowded side walks and streets packed with wagons, carriages, and horse drawn omnibuses.

"And I thought St. Paul was interesting, this is all amazing!" he exclaimed.

Michaelis grinned and replied, "New York City is the most modern city in the world! You've not seen anything yet!"

At the end of the line, they stepped off onto the loading platform to claim their baggage and Michaelis took time to point out some local landmarks.

"That round structure off to the west is Castle Clinton, an old artillery battery, and below us is Battery Park, mostly just called the Battery by locals. Over there is Castle Garden, which is now in use as an immigration and customs center. When my family immigrated from Germany we came through there." Then, pointing his finger and fanning his arm in a semi-circle, he continued, "This is all New York Harbor, over to the west is New Jersey. Straight ahead is Governors Island, where we're headed. That round red sandstone structure is another old battery, Castle Williams, and just behind it to the east, you can just see one of the ravelins of Fort Columbus, which was originally called Fort Jay. Off to the east lie Brooklyn and Long Island."

All around the waterfront Jake saw that the docks were packed full of sailing ships, their tall masts and riggings a veritable forest rising above them. Small steamers and side wheel ferries plied the waters creating a patch work, crisscross pattern of wakes, as larger vessels slowly worked their way in and out of the harbor.

"It's all a bit daunting, sir. I don't know that I've ever seen so much activity!" Jake exclaimed.

"Yes, it is a place of constant motion, Rogers. They say it's a city that never sleeps."

After a brief crossing on a ferry, they disembarked on a pier at the East River side of Governors Island and began picking their way through wagons full of lumber and building materials that were being unloaded. As they wrestled with their things, a sergeant and two guards approached them.

"Good day sir!" the sergeant said saluting, "May I be of service?"

Michaelis returned the salute and then replied, "Yes, thank you Sergeant. I am Capt. Michaelis with the Ordinance Department." He turned and pointed at Jake, "And this is Sgt. Rogers, who is assisting me. We're here on an assignment from Gen. Terry. We just came from his headquarters, back in St. Paul. We'll be staying at the Arsenal, so perhaps you can direct us to it."

"Right, sir!" he replied, then turned to the pair of privates, "You two men, grab their bags. We'll show you to the Arsenal office and they can see to getting you quarters, sir."

Following the guard detail up the pier, Jake noted that the Post Trader's buildings were located near the end of it. They continued on in the direction of the fort, but had to halt several times to wait on workers hauling loads of materials.

"There seems to be a lot of construction going on here, Sergeant." Michaelis commented.

"Yes, Sir! The Division of the Atlantic Headquarters is moving here.

Gen. Hancock and all of his staff will require accommodations. In addition, all New York based personnel are being assigned here, including the general service staff, and they'll also need offices and housing. The workers are being pushed to have it all completed a soon as possible. Fortunately for them the weather is cooperating, we haven't had but a trace of snow, and it's unseasonably warm."

"Yes, it was that way back in St. Paul, also." the officer commented. The followed the road for about one hundred yards before the detail came to a large red brick building, which bore a sign,

NEW YORK US ARMY ARSENAL
HEADQUARTERS

"Here you go, Sir!" the sergeant announced, "You'll find things a bit more quiet here. The Arsenal complex is behind this building and is off limits to the workers. There are some nice officers quarters, also. I'm sure they'll take care of you inside."

"Thank you, sergeant." Michaelis said, then looked over at Jake, "I'll go inside and report in, Rogers. Why don't you wait here with our baggage."

"Yes, Sir" Jake replied.

After Michaelis went through the doors, the sergeant left with his men, so Jake began looking around, spotting the massive gates of the fort off to the west. To the south, rows of two story frame houses were in the process of being built along both sides of the large parade ground, and he could see the spire of the chapel rising just beyond. Presently the captain came back, accompanied by a lieutenant and a couple of privates.

"Okay, Rogers, this orderly will show you to your quarters, while Lt. Frasier here will take me to mine. Let's plan on meeting here in the morning, and we'll see about establishing an agenda,"

"Yes, Sir! I'll see you then, have a good evening."

The Arsenal complex lay behind its headquarters in a cluster of red brick buildings. There were a couple of large storehouses, officers quarters and a small barracks for the enlisted men with separate rooms for NCOs, where the orderly showed Jake to a room.

"Here you go Sarge. We have a pretty good mess hall here, down at the end of the building, and a nice bath house with hot water if you've a mind. Anything I can help you with?" he asked.

"No, I'm good, thanks.

Capt. Michaelis had told Jake to meet him at the Arsenal office in the morning, so he unpacked a few things, then went to the bathhouse to wash off. He put on a fresh uniform and made a mental note to enquire about a laundress. Noting that he had some time before finding the mess hall, he elected to go look at the fort. Shaped like a five point star, the fort was built of gray granite stones topped by brick bordered earthen embankments. He could make out dozens of huge guns lining the parapets overlooking the waterways. He stopped to admire the gates, which were topped by a large elaborate stone sculpture of an eagle with spread wings, surmounting a mortar on one side and a cannon on the other. Beyond the gates, a tunnel penetrated the massive casement leading to the interior of the fort, where four long, two story brick barracks with columned front porches formed a hollow square.There was very little activity going on, and Jake mounted some stairs leading up to the parapets. He walked to the nearest massive cannon, which was mounted on a swiveling steel carriage, and looked out across the harbor. He marveled at the size and how it was able to be used to cover the whole channel towards the city. Hearing footsteps behind him he turned around and saw another sergeant coming towards him.

"Hello, I was just checking out this cannon. I've never seen one this big." he stated, "Out west we just have small ones, compared to this."

The other soldier laughed, "Oh, that isn't even our largest, that's a 10" Rodman gun, we have some 15" ones over at other revetments. Where out west where you stationed?"

"Mostly at the Fort Lincoln and Fort Rice, then out along the Yellowstone River."

"I saw the yellow stripes on your trousers and knew you weren't from around here." he out his hand, "Name's Danny Foster, 2nd Artillery."

Jake shook hands and stated "Jake Rogers, 7th Cavalry."

"I see that 7th Cavalry badge on your hat." Foster said, "Were you in the fighting against the Nez Perce last fall?"

"Yes, I was with Capt. Hale's battalion that fought under Col. Nelson Miles, at Snake Creek."

"I read about that in the New York Herald, it sounded like some fight."

"Yes, it was early on." Jake replied, as he recalled the frantic chaos of the morning.

"Well, say, how about I give you a tour, then we go over to the Post Trader's? I can give you the lay of the land, so to speak, over a beer or two."

"Sounds like a plan to me!" Jake said with a grin. "The food any good there?"

"Actually, they have some pretty good food there. Lot's of fresh fish if you care for it?"

"I'm up for that!"

Foster nodded, "Well, let's go then!" and led Jake back down to the barracks level. "Let me stop by the orderly room and tell Top what I"m up too."

Foster nodded, "Well, let's go then!" and led Jake back down to the barracks level. "Let me stop by the orderly room and tell Top what I"m up too."

Governors Island, New York Harbor - Circa 1878

The bar at the Post Traders was doing a booming business as the construction workers waited to catch ferries back across the harbor. Foster led Jake back to the dining room where there were some vacant tables.

"It'll be a bit quieter back here. This move to bring the Department HQ has really disrupted things. I've been here two years, and up until lately, it's been a pleasant posting." Foster commented.

A waitress appeared and asked, "What'll it be Danny, the usual?"

"Right, Tess! Bring us a couple of Yuengling lagers. What's the fresh fish, today? Jake here has been out west, and is craving something besides

610

beef and salt pork."

"We have some nice cod cakes, done up with potatoes."

"There you go, Rogers! We'll have couple of beers first, Tess, then bring us a couple of plates."

When the beers arrived, Danny said, "This is good beer, Yuengling just opened a brewery here in New York, but they've been brewing it over near my hometown, in Pennsylvania, for nigh on 50 years. Most of the breweries around these parts don't last but a few years, and some ain't worth puttin' to your lips. Here's to the 7th Cavalry!"

Jake had to agree that the beer was excellent, and when the cod cakes came, he was surprised how good they tasted.

"Well, I have to admit, I'm taking a liking to this place, already. Thanks Danny!"

"Say, I just remembered something. There was an officer from the 7th Cavalry, back a year or so ago. He died over in the City, pretty sudden like, and they brought his body here for burial. A captain if I remember right."

Jake set his glass down. "What was his name?" he asked tersely.

"I was a short name, started with a W, I believe."

"Weir?"

"Yeh, that was it. I heard he was at the Little Big Horn when Custer got killed. They said that he died from congestion of the brain, whatever that is."

"Damn!" Jake exclaimed, then asked Foster, "Where's the cemetery?"

"Down past the chapel, over by the old hospital on the south shore. Why, did ya know him?"

"Yes, I served under him for three years. He promoted me to Sergeant, and I was with him at the Little Bighorn!"

"Ah, sorry about that, Rogers! Sounds like you liked him."

Jake picked up his glass, drained it, the said. "I think that I'll have another!"

Foster stayed at the bar with Jake while he related his time under Weir, and described the sequence of events leading to the Big Horn debacle. Danny listened patiently, and then consoled Jake.

"It sounds like your Capt. Weir was a good man. You know, I fought in some battles near the end of the War, and recall that some men, officers too, seemed lost when it all ended. Myself, I had nothing better to do. I was an orphan and the Army was a safe home for me. I think that your Capt. Weir probably felt lost, especially when most of the other officers he served with for years were killed."

"I guess you're right, Danny. I sensed that about him, afterwards. He spent a lot of time in a bottle of whiskey."

"So, what about you?"

"Come May, I'm done. I'm going home to Missouri!" Jake said.

When Jake met Capt. Michaelis the next morning, he quickly related what he'd learned about Capt. Weir.

"I remember that day vividly! I accompanied Weir to find Custer and you were with us. I sensed that his world had collapsed and he was prone to melancholy ever after that. I know that he had no real family, other than a sister somewhere down in Georgia. Let us go pay our respects, before anything else."

When they reached the cemetery, a fitful wind blew through the branches of leafless trees, that cast stark shadows across the neat rows of grayish stones and earthen mounds. They stepped through a wrought iron gate and strolled slowly, reaching the headstones. Finally in the last row, Jake spied one of the newer, less weathered ones, and went to it. It was inscribed -

THOMAS BENTON WEIR
CAPTAIN
7TH REGT CAV
DEC 9, 1876

"Ah, there you are, Sir!" he sighed, then going down on one knee, he took off his hat. Michaelis did so as well, and they stayed silent for a moment. When they stood, Jake reached in his coat pocket, extracting a soft leather pouch. Gently opening it, he took a folded cloth from it and shook it out. It was a slightly faded swallowtail shaped flag, with an upper red field with a numeral 7, and a lower white field with the letter D.

"We fought under this guidon that day. Do you think that I should leave it with him, Sir?" he asked Michaelis.

"No, Rogers, I think that he'd want you to keep it." The officer replied quietly.

Jake refolded the guidon and put it back in the pouch. "I suppose you're right." Jake stated, before coming to attention and saluting. "It just doesn't seem right for him to be buried here, so far away from all of the others."

"Well, it's just his body laying here, Rogers, I imagine that his spirit is back on that distant ridge above the Little Big Horn River."

That afternoon, the captain secured an area inside the Arsenal office building for them to use. He also was able to get a civilian clerk assigned to him. He was a compact, middle aged fellow who sported a handlebar mustache and dressed in a dark suit with shiny black shoes. He introduced himself to Jake.

"Good day, Sergeant! My name is Bernard Braun, but most people call me Bernie. I've worked here since the War, and know this place like the back of my hand."

Jake replied, "Jacob Rogers, pleased to meet you. You can call me Jake."

Bernie looked around the empty space that the captain had been allocated. "This won't do. If you'll come with me, Jake, I know where we can find what we need."

As they scoured through various offices and storage area, Bernie told Jake that he lived over in Brooklyn and commuted by ferry daily. He regaled Jake with stories about the Arsenal and some of the weaponry stored there. They were able to find some chairs, desks, and a couple of tables to furnish it. Once they got the office set up, Michaelis returned and sat down with them.

"Okay, now we need to establish our agenda. My instructions are to perform a preliminary investigation into what rifle manufacturers are developing in the way of magazine fed, repeating rifles that can utilize the standard 45-70 cartridge. Based on what I report, the Army may institute a new rifle board and invite them to submit weapons for evaluation and testing. Bernard, let's start initiating a list, and sending out correspondence. I would like to notify the major rifle manufacturers and invite them to present any prototypes, or designs. I should think that Remington, Winchester, Sharps, and of course our own Springfield Armory should be on that list. I've also read that the Whitney Armory has come up with a design."

As Braun began making notes, Jake asked, "What would you like me to do, Sir!"

"Next week, you and I are going to go see Col. William Church, over in New York City. He is one of the founding members of the National Rifle Association. Church and Capt. George Wingate, were instrumental in establishing a shooting range over on Long Island where rifle competitions are held. I am going to ask him if we might be able to use their range to test fire and evaluate any new rifles that we might want to."

"I was wondering about that." Jake replied. "There didn't seem to be any where to shoot here."

"Well, there are some ranges over at the Sandy Hook Arsenal, in New Jersey, that would work. At this point we are just conducting an informal evaluation for the Ordnance Department. My superior Gen. Benet, requested that I keep as low a profile as possible. The NRA is always interested in new and experimental weapons, so we can minimize our involvement."

Jake grinned, "Planning your moves in advance, Sir! Just like in chess."

"Exactly, Rogers! Once we've secured the Col. Church's cooperation we'll begin our visits to the different manufacturers. We can inspect their facilities and talk to their design engineers." Michaelis replied.

For the next several weeks, Jake accompanied the captain to nearby Massachusetts and Connecticut, where they visited several different firearms manufacturers. At the Arsenal Armory, in Springfield, MA, there were several Winchester gunsmiths helping to develop a prototype for a tube magazine fed, bolt action rifle based on a design by Benjamin Hotchkiss. He was the one who had designed the small shell firing cannon that Miles had deployed against the Nez Perce. Hotchkiss was currently focused on developing weapons for the European market, and Winchester, headquartered out of New Haven, had purchased the manufacturing rights for it. The rifle used a tube magazine contained within the butt stock, similar to the Spencer Carbine, but with no detachable loading tube. The rifle was to be manufactured there at the Arsenal at Springfield. Michaelis and Jake were taken on an impressive tour of the main Arsenal building and the surrounding complex of machine shops, forges, and metal working facilities that sprawled around it.

They traveled along the Connecticut coast to the New Haven/Bridgeport area. Jake enjoyed looking out at the water and watching the boats plying the waters of Long Island Sound whenever the train traveled near the shoreline. He found the cool, salt laden winds invigorating. In Bridgeport, they met with the Lee Arms Company. It was a small new company owned by Scottish born gun designer, James Paris Lee and his brother John. Lee had a unique design prototype for a bolt action rifle using a patented removable box magazine, and had contracted with the Sharps Rifle Company to manufacture it. In 1876, Sharps had relocated to Bridgeport, from Philadelphia. Jake enjoyed the tour of the factory and was greatly impressed with Lee, and also the Sharps manufacturing superintendent, Hugo Borchardt. Borchardt showed him the new hammerless Sharps rifle that had just gone into production. Jake shared a couple of anecdotes about his own experience with a Sharps with them, and they made him promise to show it to them if they came down to the

New York Arsenal.

Later, in nearby Whitneyville, they met with Eli Whitney, the entrepreneur son of the famous cotton gin inventor. He had partnered with Andrew Burgess, who had patented a top loading, lever action rifle with a tube magazine under the barrel. They claimed that the rifle action developed by Burgess was strong enough to handle the 45-70 cartridge, which the current production lever action Winchester rifles could not. It was to be built at the Whitney Armory which had been contracted by Colt to build pistols for many years.

After returning to Governors Island, they sat down with Bernie to review their notes, leaving him all of the information provided by the manufacturers. Bernie informed the captain that Col. Church, had sent notification that the Creedmoor Shooting Range would be available the first two weeks in April.

"Excellent! I want you to notify all of them, and ask them to bring any working prototypes."

They set out for Ilion, New York to visit the E. Remington & Sons factory there. Located in central New York State, near the city of Utica, the small village was clustered around the huge Remington complex. Jake was greatly impressed with the Remington manufacturing facilities which produced a variety of products such as farm implements, sewing machines, and typewriters, in addition to firearms. Samuel Remington, one of three sons involved in the company, personally conducted a tour of the buildings and machine shops. The primary rifle being manufactured there was the Remington No. 1, Rolling Block design, a single shot weapon that was being built in various calibers for export around the world. Many of them were designed as sporting rifles that competed directly with the Sharps design. Jake recalled seeing Custer carrying one on many occasions, including the day he was killed. Remington was working on developing a bolt action rifle, designed and patented by John W. Keene. It also had a tube magazine located under the barrel that could hold nine cartridges, similar to the Winchester lever action, but the loading gate was underneath, in front of the trigger housing.

Once they were back at the New York Arsenal, Michaelis had Jake and Bernie develop a report detailing the design features of the various rifles, and compiling a list of discussion points to be addressed. Meanwhile, the officer departed for Washington D C, to consult with his superiors, leaving them to complete their tasks. During his absence, Bernie and Danny took turns showing Jake around New York and Brooklyn. One weekend, Bernie invited him to come over to Brooklyn. Jake dressed in his civilian clothes, then took the ferry over to Hunter's Point where he met up with Bernie. Bernie suggested that they take the Central RR Long Island train out to the Creedmoor Rifle Range to watch a shooting competition. Jake recalled that Mike Caddle had worked for the CRLI prior to enlisting, as a conductor on this very same train. Jake wondered briefly at how Mike was faring with married life back at Fort Lincoln.

The range itself was a wide open field with a series of raised earthen berms stretched across the far end. A tall tower with a clock and large weather vane stood at one end of the firing line. Tall poles sporting pennants were spaced along the side of the range to indicate the direction and speed of the prevailing winds. Bernie went to look up the range foreman, Bob Williams, and after introducing themselves, they persuaded him to take them out to inspect the target area. Inside the berms a long tunnel ran across the width of the range with an opening below each target. The targets consisted of 6' x12' steel rectangles with a 3' center bullseye, having an outer and center ring. Several men took turns monitoring the targets and would raise a color coded paddle to indicate the strike of the bullet: Black for the outer ring, Red for the inner ring, and White for a bullseye. When they got back to the area of the firing line, the shooters were getting settled in. The competition that weekend was between two area shooting clubs and Jake was surprised to see how elaborate their preparations were. They were set up on the 1,000 yard firing line, and some of the participants fired from the prone position, while others used a unique reclining position, crossing their legs and using one to support the rifle barrel. Nearby spotters seated behind tripod mounted telescopes surveyed the targets and tracked the hits. Most of the shooters sported expensive custom rifles, but after watching them, Jake could tell that that wasn't a good indicator of the expertise of the shooter.

"These are two local clubs that are mostly made up of wealthy young men." stated Williams, "A few of them can shoot a little, but most just like to strut around the firing line and then go to the clubhouse to swill beer."

"I can see that." Jake replied.

"Now, when we get military or militia teams, it gets a little more serious. That's when the competition heats up."

Jake smiled and said, "Yes, I bet it does."

"You a good shot, Sgt. Rogers?" Bob asked.

"Oh, I've never shot at a range like this."

"Do you want to try? I've got a Sharps #3 'Creedmoor' Match rifle. It's the same gun that was used by the American team, back in the '74 Match against the Irish shooting team. Col. Church, himself, gave it to me as a reward for seeing everything went smoothly during that competition."

"Well, if you're sure you don't mind?"

"No, I don't get it out and shoot it as often as I'd like. Wait here, I'll go fetch it."

While they were waiting for Williams to return, Bernie asked, "Can you hit anything that far away, Jake?"

"Well, shooting at a known distance, with a good rifle and decent sights takes some of the guesswork out of it. If the wind holds steady, it's relatively easy to compensate. Having those flags at the other end helps to estimate how far to hold off."

"So, does that mean you can do it?"

Jake grinned, "I reckon that I can."

One of the young men that had been shooting came towards them. He was short, nattily dressed in a nice suit, with a fancy vest and a bowler hat. As he approached he called out, "You there, I need a clean blanket over at my spot on Lane 6. The one there is filthy."

"Sorry, sir! We don't work here." Bernie responded.

"Well, then why are you on the firing line? Spectators are supposed to stay in the bleacher area." He said haughtily.

Bob came up from behind him, carrying his Sharps rifle, and said, "These men are with me, Mr. Appleton. We're getting ready to fire a few rounds."

"I thought our clubs had the range reserved for today."

"Yes, you have lanes 1-12, we'll be shooting on the other end of the firing line on lane 20."

"I should think that my club won't welcome the additional distraction caused by your firing."

Jake was incredulous, and started to laugh, then quickly tried to stifle it, but was only partially successful.

"You find that amusing, do you, Mister, ahh?" Appleton asked tersely.

"Rogers, Jake Rogers, and I was just struck by your odd comment. Noise is part of shooting. No offense, Appleton!"

"Well, I take it that you're not from these parts. We take our shooting very seriously around here."

Jake felt his temper begin to perk, and said, "Is that a fact. I'd hate to interfere with such a serious competition."

"I have a Remington #1, 'Creedmoor Special' rifle personally made by Lewis Hepburn, the Remington sharpshooter who designed it."

Appleton stated, "It was very expensive! That's how serious I am about the sport."

"Hmm! I guess that where I'm from, we don't consider it so much as a sport, but a skill, and we don't have too many 'special' rifles."

"Then you obviously don't appreciate the finer techniques that we employ. Perhaps you would like come and demonstrate your skills then, Mr. Rogers? Maybe a small wager would be put on the table?"

"That might make it interesting! I take it that you would be shooting against me."

"Indeed! I will go inform my fellow club members. You can join us when you're ready."

As the man walked away, Bob said dryly, "Bart Appleton is a pushy little prick."

"He a good shot?" Jake asked

"Oh fair, his spotter is damn good and get's him on target."

"I take it that the sights on that Sharps of yours are finely calibrated for this range?"

"Damn straight they are!"

Jake nodded his head and grinned, "Good!"

Williams went over the Sharps with Jake, while he studied the rifle. He was impressed by the fine balance and simple functionality of the weapon.

"She ain't as fancy as that Remington of Bart's, but she's all business when it comes down to it." Williams said proudly.

"I'm used to shooting a 45-70 bullet, but I see this is a 44-90."

"Yes, it was developed primarily for long range target shooting. It's bit easier on the shoulder. The Sharps bullets weighs 520 grains, while the Remingtons are 550 grain, so the Sharps is just a wee bit faster."

"I note that the wind is out of the west."

"Yes, the prevailing winds around here this time of the year usually are. It's not bad today, maybe 4-5 miles an hour. You thinking about how far to hold off?" Bob asked.

"Yep! Say, you wouldn't happen to have some bullet lube, also?"

"I do, but you'll be using paper patch bullets, so it won't be necessary to use any." Bob answered.

"Oh, for the kind of shooting that I have in mind, it'll come in handy. We won't be swabbing the barrel after each shot, if that's okay with you. The lube will help keep the barrel from fouling."

Bob raised an eyebrow, and grinned, "A huh, and just what kind of shooting are you proposing?"

"Buffalo hunt style!"

As they approached the area along the firing line where the shooting clubs were set up, Jake could see that Bart Appleton was haranguing the club members and on lookers and was gesticulating down range. He looked at Jake, then turned, and said something that got a chuckle from the others. When they got closer, Bart called out.

"We can move up to a closer range if you'd like, Mr. Rogers?"

Jake replied, "No, don't bother, I wouldn't want to inconvenience you."

"So, would you like to take a few ranging shots, before we start. Then we can discuss our wager. Do you have an amount in mind?"

"Let's just keep it simple! The loser has to clean all the rifles afterwards."

Bart said nothing for a minute, then barked out a laugh, "Interesting wager, Rogers. Bragging rights versus soiled hands. Done! So would you like to take a couple of shots?"

"No, But since you challenged me, I do want to discuss the format that we'll be using."

"Yes, well what do you propose?" Bart asked smugly.

"Well, you see, out west when we hunt buffalo, we don't have a lot of time to waste when we're shooting at them. I propose that we each get 5 minutes to see how many targets we can hit. Each bullseye constitutes a kill, and anything else is just wounded, and we will also alternate targets from 1 through 12, with Mr. Williams randomly calling out which number to shoot at."

"But that's not how we do it!" Appleton protested, "We have procedures that we follow! We don't shoot that quickly!"

"Yes, I've seen. I just think that my way might inject a bit more realistic shooting conditions into our match." Jake stated, noting that several of the other shooters behind Appleton were grinning at his proposal.

"Well, that may be, but I'm sure it would be against range rules. Isn't that right, Mr. Williams?"

Bob, who was struggling to contain a smile, replied, "I don't see any safety issues with it. Especially since only the two of you will be firing."

"But I won't be able to shift to a different target quickly, it gives Rogers an unfair advantage. I use a reclining position when shooting, my sights are mounted too far back for prone shooting."

One of the others spoke up, "You can use my rifle, Bart. It's a Remington like yours."

"No, I'm not familiar with your rifle."

Jake said, "Look here Appleton. I haven't fired a rifle since the end of October, last year. Bob is letting me use his, and I've not ever shot it, although I am familiar with a Sharps rifle, mine is a 45-70."

"No, I refuse to participate in a such an unorthodox match." He said, then turned on his heels and stormed off.

"Well, I guess he ain't happy." Bob commented dryly. "You still want to shoot, Jake?"

"Sure, why not!"

A crowd gathered behind Jake as he settled on the firing line, in Lane #3. Bob sent a runner to the target butts to let them know what was up, then sat down on a chair nearby. Jake laid out a row of lubed cartridges and took up a prone position, then signaled that he was ready. Bob gave him a go sign and he began firing. His first shot hit just outside the bullseye, and as Bob called out new target numbers, Jake calmly put his following shots solidly in the bullseyes. The onlookers applauded when Jake was done.

Creedmoor Rifle Range - Circa 1878

One of the shooting club members asked Jake, "Where did you learn to shoot like that, sir, and why haven't we seen you around here before?"

Bernie spoke up, "Fellas, this is Sgt. Jake Rogers, of the 7th Cavalry Regiment. He just came from back from out west. While you boys have been shooting at targets, he's been fighting the Sioux, Cheyenne, and Nez Perce Indians for the last two years!"

More applause broke out, and someone called out. "I'd say that calls for a round of beers!"

Later on in the clubhouse, Jake was congratulated several times for his exhibition, and also for showing up Bart Appleton.

"Rogers, if he'd a shot against you, you'd put a whuppin' on that boy!" Bob chortled, as he toasted Jake. "It did my heart good to see him taken down a notch."

Jake grinned, and replied, "Well, he sort a reminded me of some of the officers that I've had to put up with over the years."

When Capt. Michaelis returned the following week, he informed Jake and Bernie that all their plans had been for naught. He had been issued new orders. Gen. Benet had chosen to convene a Magazine Gun Board consisting of several Ordnance officers senior to Michaelis, to take over the rifle evaluations. All of the information was to be turned over to the Board and they would conduct their own trials at the Springfield Arsenal starting on April 3.

"Not that it matters now, Rogers, but I'm curious from your point of view, which design did you consider the best." Michaelis asked.

Jake thought about it and replied, "Well Sir! I think Mr. Lee's design is the most interesting. I always liked the Spencer rifles and you could carry a lot of preloaded magazine tubes for them. His box magazine is the same concept but easier to reload without having to move the whole gun off target to do it. I can see where that it would be a lot more practical during a fight. I liked the Remington-Keene rifle also, the tube magazine loads like the new Winchesters."

"Yes, I concur, but I fear that not much is going to happen. Major Parker, the president of the new board is a not a fan of magazine guns. I saw where they are going to insist that each rifle has a magazine cut off feature added, so that single fire discipline can still be in place."

"Pardon my saying so, Sir. But that's just stupid! The Indians have the advantage of repeating rifles as they maneuver around us. A more powerful magazine weapon would give both the advantage of range and firepower. I suspect that this Major has never fought against them."

"Yes, your suspicions are correct. To my knowledge he's never been even close to any sort of fighting. He's primarily a weapons manufacturer for the Ordnance department. His primary focus will be on what is most economical for the Army budget."

"Then it's just as well that we aren't part of it anymore, Sir!" Jake stated, "What happens now? Do we go back to St. Paul?"

"For now, I'm still hoping for a new assignment."

CHAPTER 48

Jefferson Barracks, St. Louis, Missouri - Thursday, May 2, 1878

Jake looked around his sparsely furnished room in the NCO quarters to make sure that he had everything packed away for the next day. Earlier that day, as Jake was processed his discharge paper work, he had been repeatedly asked if he would consider re-enlisting. Each time he had respectfully declined. He was given a voucher for the train trip down to Springfield and received his final pay. Fortunately, he'd been saving up most of his detached duty pay and had managed to accumulate a nice little balance in his bank account, back in St. Paul. He had a cashier's check for over $500 in his pocket and enough cash on him to get a good horse and saddle once he got to Springfield.

His civilian outfits were packed in the old battered portmanteau that Murray had given him. He sorted through his uniforms, opting to wear his dress uniform on the train. He'd polished up a brass emblem of crossed sabers with a 7 over them on it, and pinned it on a new gray Stetson that he'd bought to wear home. His boots were shined to a high black gloss. The rest of his uniform items he had donated to hand out to new recruits. He reflected on how quickly the last few weeks had passed.

After accompanying Capt. Michaelis back to St. Paul, he had arranged for Jake to be transferred down to Jefferson Barracks to finish out his enlistment time. He'd spent the last couple of weeks, helping out the training cadre with new recruits. He was amazed at the innocence and ineptitude of most of them, and thought to himself, "Surely I was never that bad!" Most of the training sergeants were older, and lived off post, so he only had a few other NCOs quartered with him. He'd made friends with one of them, a young Swiss named Dan Fuss, who happened to be the firearms instructor.

"Say there, Jake! Let's go outside the gate to Louie's Beer Garden and have some beers." Fuss called to him from the doorway.

"I suppose you're expecting me to buy, huh Dan?" he replied.

"Yah, youse da one who is a rich civilian tomorrow, eh?"

Jake grinned, and said, "I don't know about rich, but I will damn sure be a civilian!"

After the debacle of the recent battles out West, Gen. Sherman had instituted a new emphasis on weapons training for his soldiers. Dan, who was a veteran of the Swiss Army, had come over last year and enlisted. When it was discovered that he was an expert marksman, he was promoted rapidly to sergeant and put in charge of firearms training. He and Jake had hit it off right away when Jake had taken his Sharps and Colt pistol to the arms room to store them, when he arrived. Dan had been there working on a training rifle and immediately questioned Jake about his guns when he spotted them, particularly the Sharps with its Malcolm scope. They started talking about rifles and Jake had been very interested to discover that Fuss had been trained to shoot with a repeating rifle, the 10mm Vetterli bolt action rifle. Fuss told him that the Swiss Army had been using it since 1869 and he was puzzled by the American Army's insistence on standardizing on the single shot Springfield rifles and carbines. When Jake told Fuss about his recent assignment up in New York, they quickly bonded. Dan got his training company First Sergeant to assign Jake to help him.

"So, Jacob, you're sure that you are done with soldiering, eh?" Fuss queried, as they were finishing up plates of schnitzels.

"Yep! Tomorrow come this time, I should be down in Springfield. I've telegraphed my friend Frank to pick me up at the train station."

"Ya! Is good to have family and friends. All mine are very far away."

"Why did you come over here, anyway?" Jake asked.

"In Switzerland, ve haven't fought a battle in over thirty years. I read about Custer and his fight with the Sioux. I want to see wild Indians, and shoot buffalo like in the newspapers and magazines."

Jake shook his head slowly, "Well, I've done all that, and I can tell you it ain't all it's cracked up to be."

"Maybe, but I still vant to. 1st Sgt. Hadley has promised to send me after this training cycle." Fuss stated. "I hope to go mit the 7th Cavalry when they take the field dis summer."

Jake recalled the rigors of campaigning, the heat and dust, rain and mud, spoiled rations and foul coffee. Dan's Swiss accent also conjured up a horrible mental image of Farrier Vincent Charlie and the panicked grimace on his face as he dragged his hipshot body through the brush above the Little Big Horn, pleading with Lt. Edgerly not to not be left behind.

"At some point you'll probably find yourself wishing that you stayed here, Dan, but that's your call. Myself, I'm looking forward to a roof over my head and a decent bed to sleep in."

"Ach! I vill enjoy the challenge!" Fuss said emphatically.

The next morning, when reveille sounded, Jake caught himself responding, then realized that he no longer had to attend roll call. Later, downstairs in the NCO mess, the others NCOs congratulated Jake then quickly left to go herd the recruits through their morning drills. He lingered over coffee contemplating the coming changes in his daily routines, then wandered over to the orderly room to say his goodbyes, then claim his Colt pistol and Sharps rifle from the arms room.

"There's an omnibus out by the front gate that'll take you right to the Depot, Roger's." 1st Sgt. Hadley said, "It'll be leaving at 8:30."

"Thanks Top!" Jake said, "I appreciate your hospitality over the last couple of weeks."

"Yeh, I just hope that things work out for you. If they don't, you know where to find a home,"

The St. Louis Depot was even busier than he remembered, with bustling travelers
scrambling to catch their respective trains. Jake made his way over to the Frisco desk and presented his voucher.

"Springfield, huh Sarge? Going home on leave?" the clerk asked.

"No, just going home." he replied. "I'm officially a civilian now."

"Oh, okay, I suppose." the clerk said and looked at Jake's hat, "I see that you're a 7th Cavalry trooper. Did you see any action?"

"A bit."

"Well, lucky for you that you weren't with Gen. Custer, eh?"

Jake considered that for a moment, and said, "Yeh, lucky!"

The clerk sensed his hesitancy, "Well, anyway, good luck back home. You should get there by dark. This is the local run, and the train stops at Rolla and Lebanon along the way, so you can get something to eat along the way."

"Good to know. Thanks!"

Jake sat by the windows and watched the countryside roll by. Sunshine shown on the rolling hills highlighting their brilliant green fresh spring leaves, and here and there neat plots of furrowed fields dotted the bottom lands along the creeks. It was a stark contrast to the barren plains and sparse trees of the Dakota territory. The horizons up there seemed to stretch on forever in the distance. Jake sat back in his seat and reflected on the last five years. It was amazing to think of how much that he'd experienced. He mentally scrolled through images of the places and the sights that he'd seen. He remembered some the people and friends that he'd made, and some others that he'd lost. He also recalled the boredom and drudgery of garrison duty, the rigors endured out on the campaign trail, and lastly the vivid, intense memories of combat. He propped up against his bag and soon the he rocking motion and noise of the train lured him to sleep,

The conductor, an ex-soldier who Jake had spoken with several times when they stopped in Rolla and Lebanon, made his way through the car then stopped by Jake, looked at his watch and said quietly, "We'll be at the Depot in North Springfield in 15 minutes, Sarge."

Jake stirred and replied. "Okay, Thanks!"

Occasionally, over the last 2 1/2 years since he'd been back home, he'd wondered what changes had taken place there, and was anxious to see them. He also felt himself getting a bit nervous about the prospect of seeing Holly. Her letters were full of stories about work and school, and she still expressed her feelings for him, but he wondered if living in a town like Springfield, instead of a frontier Army post, had changed her. And, he was a bit apprehensive about how he was going to make a living. Frank had hinted about the possibility of a job working for the Frisco, but that remained to be confirmed.

As the train began to slow Jake stood, nervously adjusting his uniform, and grabbed his things in preparation. He moved to the platform behind the railcar and stood watching as buildings began to appear and the train whistle began to blow announcing their arrival. When the train finally came to a stop he stepped down on to the platform, looking around. Off towards the front of the train, he spotted a group of people as the steam from the locomotive dissipated. Suddenly a figure broke from them and began walking in his direction. It was Holly, and he saw that she was wearing the same gray dress that she'd worn on their dinner date, before leaving Fort Lincoln. She had a huge smile on her face and when he started towards her, she hurried to fling herself into his arms, burying her face in his neck and hugging him fiercely. He snuck a peek over her head and saw his parents, along with Frank and Colleen, all smiling as they came towards them. Holly broke from their embrace and held him away at arms length, quickly looking him over, then locked her brilliant blue eyes into his.

"It's about damn time, Jacob Rogers!" she exclaimed, then smothered him with a passionate kiss.

EPILOGUE

Vinita, Indian Territory - October, 1878

The town of Vinita hadn't grown much since Jake had dropped off Holly there three years previously. The town had originally sprung up around the intersection of the MK&T and the A & P/Frisco railroads. There were buildings sprawled several blocks in each direction and scattered houses beyond that. The surrounding flat plains began just on the western edge of the Ozark Hills, near the Missouri state line. Located in the Cherokee Nation, which had permitted the building of the railroads, it was still the western terminus of the line for the Frisco, but just a whistle stop for the Katy which ran all the way down to Texas.

After helping Zeb with the farm through the summer, Holly and Jake had gotten married back in September. Kate, Pat, and Murray came down from Bismarck to attend the wedding in Henderson and as a wedding present had arranged for the couple to spend their honeymoon at the Arlington Hotel, in Hot Springs. When Jake and Holly returned the following week later, they spent some time catching up on the events up in Bismarck, before the others had to head back north. Bob Seip had finally died from consumption, back in July and left every thing to Kate in his will. The Northern Pacific was operating a transfer steamboat to ferry railcars across the Missouri River and was ramping up to begin laying tracks west and was stockpiling supplies at Mandan. Fort Rice had been abandoned and the troops sent down to the new Fort Yates. After Pat, Kate, and Murray left Henderson to go back to Bismarck, Jake and Holly moved to town and Jake was able to find a place to rent in North Springfield, on Pacific Street, near Frank and Colleen.

As he'd promised, Frank arranged for some interviews with the Frisco Railroad and was taking Jake to Vinita. They reached Vinita just before noon and were greeted at the depot by Mark Walsh, the Katy agent.

"Frank! Good to see you again, you too Jake! Frank told me you were back."

Jake shook hands with Mark and replied, "Yes, I've been back since May. I helped my father out on the farm for the summer and we just got the harvest in."

"I hear you married that pretty gal that was with you last time you were here."

"Jake nodded his head, "Yes I did. You still the local agent here?"

"No, I actually got promoted last year. I'm in charge of operations all across Indian Territory now. Well, come on you two, we're waiting for you." Walsh said, and turned to walk to the steps leading down.

"Who's waiting on us?" Jake asked, when they reached the rail siding.

"See that Pullman car sitting down there, the railroad provides it to a lawyer named, Elias Boudinot, who uses it to travel back and forth to Washington D.C. where he's a lobbyist for them. He and several others are waiting lunch on us. Hope you're hungry."

Frank looked at Jake, raised his eyebrows in surprise and shrugged his shoulders.

When they got to the Pullman car, Mark stopped and said, "The men that you're about to meet represent a consortium of railroad interests looking to expand across Indian Territory, and beyond. There are plans being discussed for rail lines down to Fort Smith, to McAlester and the coal fields down in the Choctaw Nation, and another west to the Arkansas River to be nearer the cattle trails from Texas."

"Okay, and what I am I doing here?" Jake asked.

"One of them is a man named Otis Gunn. He's one of the leading railroad engineers west of the Mississippi and is being courted by both the Frisco and the Katy railroads. Gunn will be in charge of selecting the routes and is looking for someone to help him scout them. Frank and I think it's something you're perfect for." Mark stated. "Let me do the introductions when we go inside."

A whited jacketed attendant met them at the door and led them to a room farther back in the railcar. Mark went in first, then turned.

"This is Mr. Otis Gunn." He said, pointing at well dressed middle aged man." Then Mark continued, "This gentleman is Mr. B. F. Hobart, he runs the M.K.&T. Coal Company, and this other is Charles Condon a banker and businessman formerly in Arkansas, but now in Oswego, Kansas just across the line from here. And finally, this dapper gentleman is our host, Elias Boudinot. He's an Arkansas attorney with many connections back in Washington, and also out in the Indian Territory. Gentlemen this is Jake Rogers, and I think you've all met Frank Armstrong from the Frisco."

Jake and Frank shook hands with all of them.

Boudinot dressed in a suit, who had long dark hair swept back above his ears and large mustache, spoke up, "Well, I suggest that we have lunch and get acquainted. My cook has arranged for some excellent Texas beef, and has a prepared a special recipe for a rib roast. I think everyone will enjoy it."

They moved to another section of the railcar and took seats around a large table where two white jacketed attendants appeared to wait on them, bringing bottles of wine, and appetizers.

"I'm told that you fought with General Custer, Mr. Rogers. We are all ex-soldiers here and would like to hear what your experience was." Mr. Gunn stated.

"Actually, sir, I never fought with Custer. Which I suppose was lucky for me, else I wouldn't be here. I was with Capt. Weir's Company D and we were in Capt. Benteen's wing during the fighting at the Little Big Horn."

"Please call me Otis, and yes I suppose so, but I'm sure you have some interesting stories about it."

"We'd also like to hear what you have to say about the upcoming Court of Inquiry into Major Reno's actions there." Boudinot proffered.

"I wasn't aware of it, sir." Jake responded.

"Please call me Eli. You see, I just got back from Washington where Reno has been pestering President Hayes to tell his side so he can uphold his reputation. I believe that it's been scheduled for after the first of the year, in Chicago. He specifically wants that fellow Whittaker to be questioned about his book. Have you read it?"

"I have."

"I think we all have too and we'd be interested to get your opinion, since you were there."

Jake was quiet for a moment, then said, "Yes I was, but I can only speak of what went on in front of me. In my opinion, much of that book is hearsay and speculation, I just know that there were many very angry warriors trying to kill us. Personally, I thought that we were damn lucky that Gen. Terry came up when he did!"

"Hmm, still it will be interesting to follow the proceedings don't you think?"Boudinot queried.

"I suppose so, although I doubt anything will change. The Army will not welcome too much scrutiny. Mistakes were made on several levels and they've already been buried along with the bodies."

"I understand that you were wounded fighting the Nez Perce with Gen. Miles at what they are calling the Battle of Bear Paw Mountain." Gunn said. "I know Miles from his time at Fort Leavenworth."

"Yes, I was. Luckily it wasn't serious."

"Are you aware of the fact that those Nez Perce are here in the Territory just a few miles from here?" Condon asked.

"I read something about it." Jake replied. "I hope that they are doing well. "

"You don't hold any ill will towards them?" Hobart asked.

"No, as I recall, they were a pretty sorry lot, mostly women, children, and old men. I thought Gen. Miles promised them that they would eventually be allowed to go home to Idaho as part of the surrender terms."

"Well, apparently not. Their Chief, Joseph, is in Washington right now trying to negotiate." Eli stated. "However, I've heard that they are to be moved down to some land near the Salt Fork of the Arkansas and the Chikaskia River."

Jake nodded his head, "Hmm, that figures."

The lunch, consisted of aged beef prime rib and Jake marveled at the tenderness of the meat. He declared, "This is quite good! 5 years of Army food will make a man appreciate an excellent cut of meat like this."

More wine appeared and Jake deferred, noting that the others, excluding Boudino, did also and asked for coffee instead. "I really enjoy a good cup of coffee that's freshly brewed. You wouldn't believe what passed for coffee when we were on campaign."

After lunch the attendant cleared the table, and Jake was quizzed extensively about his experiences, not only about campaigning against the Indians, but also up on the Boundary Survey. After a while, they asked Jake, Frank, and Mark to step out outside for a few minutes so they could consult in private before calling them back in.

Boudinot spoke up first. "Mr. Rogers, we have a proposal for you. Both the Katy and Frisco Railroads have plans to expand across the Indian Territory. I myself am half-Cherokee and although I was raised and educated with my mother's family up in Connecticut, I have many connections within the tribe. My uncle is the ex-Confederate Gen. Stand Watie and I rode with him as a Lt. Col. in his Cherokee Mounted Rifles during the War. All of us here are working towards advancing the railroads, but it may take a while, even a year or two. We are waiting on an agreement to be reached between the US Government, the Cherokee, Creek, Choctaw Nations, and the provisional Territorial Government in Fort Smith and as you can imagine, this can be time consuming. In the meantime we want to investigate the possible routes we might follow."

Gunn looked directly at Jake, "You appear to be fairly knowledgable about the surveying process and have experience traversing unknown terrain. We are looking for someone like you to discreetly conduct informal surveys along some of the projected routes and report back on any potential obstacles."

Mr. Condon interjected, "Discreetly! That's most important! If word gets out about the routes, it can impede our efforts. We've looked into your background and have been assured by several of our contacts, men such as Murray Johnson, and that you are considered quite dependable."

Boudinot spoke again, "We are prepared to compensate quite handsomely for your time and discretion. If you complete your mission to our satisfaction, we are even prepared to offer you some stocks and continued employment."

Jake took a minute to consider the offer, then stood and addressed them. "Thank you, Gentlemen! I'm honored that you've offered me this opportunity. Let me assure you that I will endeavor to do my best. Just let me know when you want me to begin."

Jake was hired as an independent contractor and they assigned him to work out of Vinita, but also provided him with a rail pass that allowed him to travel back to Springfield as time permitted. His main contact was to be with Boudinot. Frank explained to Jake that Boudinot had many contacts back in Washington, down in Fort Smith, and over in the Cherokee Nation. He was heavily engaged in efforts to re-allocate the lands in the Indian Territory to form a state controlled by the resident Indian tribes that would be called, Oklahoma, based on the Choctaw word for red people. He was also a proponent of opening up the unassigned lands in the Indian Territory to non-Indian homesteaders. Jake learned that Eli and his uncle, Stand Watie, had been a key negotiators in the post war treaties reallocating the Tribal boundaries and were instrumental in persuading the Tribes to agree to permit the Katy and Frisco to lay their existing tracks. It turned out that Eli had also been responsible for naming the town of Vinita after, Vinnie Ream, a talented young sculptress back in Washington of who he was enamored. It was Eli who suggested that an ex-sergeant of his, Ned Walkingstick, should accompany Jake in his travels and help run interference with the local tribes if needed. Ned lived down near Fort Gibson and Eli arranged to summon Walkingsick, while Jake went back to Springfield and made his preparations.

After returning to North Springfield, Jake set about equipping himself for the trail. While he and Holly were over in Henderson visiting his folks, he was able to find himself a good horse. Zeb's hay partner and neighbor, Thurlo Watts, also raised horses and made Jake a deal for a black Morgan gelding. Thurlo assured Jake that the 3 year old horse had a smooth gait, good stamina and was an easy keeper. Jake found that it reminded him of Ajax and was of similar temperament and intelligence. The horse had a single white spot on his forehead, and Holly suggested calling him Ace. Zeb, recalling his own years of riding a rock hard McClellan saddle, insisted that he and Jake go to Springfield and shop for a new saddle. They found a decent 'Texas rig' saddle, with a Cheyenne roll back and a padded seat, which Zeb paid for as an early Christmas present. Back in North Springfield, Jake was able to board Ace at Stoughton's livery just two blocks away from the bungalow that he and Holly were renting. Even though he still had the Sharps rifle, he decided that it wasn't very practical as a saddle gun. He went over to Doling's hardware on Commercial St. where he found a Winchester Model 1873 saddle ring carbine chambered in 44-40, the same as his Colt. It had a 20' barrel and a tubular magazine with a capacity of 12 cartridges.

When he returned to Vinita, Eli introduced Jake to Walkingstick. Ned was tall, thin with a wiry build, and a decade older than Jake. Jake immediately developed a liking for him. Ned who was half Cherokee reminded him of Val Wheeler. But with long wavy dark hair and a flowing mustache, he didn't look much like an Indian, but did have a taciturn nature similar to Val's. Ned recommended that they travel during the winter months, not only so they could better see the terrain, but also avoid the voracious ticks, chiggers, and snakes that infested the wilderness. In addition to his own horse Ned had an extra horse, already provisioned and packed, along with an Army 'A' tent and mess gear.

"It'll be mite chilly, you gotta problem with that, Mr. Rogers?"

"No, I've been up north where chilly is warm." Jake replied. "Besides I was raised over by Springfield, so I'm used to the cold around here.

"Where up north?"

"Up in the Dakota and Montana Territories."

Ned nodded his head, "Yes, I've heard that it gets damn cold up there. Myself, I'm partial to bein' cozy at night, anymore."

"I got no problem with that." Jake grinned.

"By the By! We're likely to run into some two legged critters on the trail, too. You any good with that shiny pistol?" Ned said eyeing Jake's Colt.

"Better with the Winchester, but I generally get by in a pinch."

"You ever been in pinch before?" Ned asked.

"I just spent 5 years with the 7th Cavalry, so I reckon I have. But, if it's all the same to you, I prefer to stay clear of trouble."

"Hmm! Eli said ya had some sand in ya. We might just get along, Mr. Rogers."

"Call me, Jake! I hear you rode with him in the War."

"Yeh some. I was younger than you back then and he talked me into it. We was always on the move, that man does like to be in the thick of things, particularly politics and anywhere else he can get an audience. He comes by it honest though, it's said that his Dad was the same way."

"Yes, it sounds like he gets around." Jake said.

They went out in November and followed the Katy line south. Using the traditional surveying transit was too obvious, so Jake practiced his map skills shooting azimuths with his compass. To help just distance along the routes, Jake showed Ned how to use the stadia range finder and they got pretty proficient at estimating distances. He'd also purchased one of those new Tiffany pedometers and experimented with using from horseback. After the holidays, in early January, Jake and Ned left Vinita to establish a route over to the Arkansas River. Jake soon found that Ned was extremely familiar with the territory and knew the countryside like the back of his hand. Initially the route went west out of Vinita into what was called the Cooweescoowee District of the Cherokees, then it began to dip to the southwest. After about 15 miles and making a couple of bends between some low rolling hills it crossed the upper Pryor Creek and ran straight for about 20 miles down to what was once an old Osage village, but was now called Clermont by the Cherokees. Ned knew a man there named, Clem Rogers, who had established a large ranch there that he called the Dog Iron. Clem was another mixed blood who had served as an officer in the Cherokee Mounted Rifles and was allied to Boudinot's faction. Stopping there for a couple of days, Clem invited them to stay with him in his recently built two story ranch house. While there they consulted with him about the route so far, and what lay ahead. Jake took advantage of the time to post a letter to Holly at the nearby post office, in Clermont. From there, it was relatively flat and open prairie until they reached the vicinity of the Verdigris River. They found a way through and dropped out of the hills onto bottom land, before reaching the Arkansas River near an old Creek settlement the locals called Tulsey Town. Ned knew one the them, a Creek named, George Perryman. He and his brother Josiah, had established a combination store & post office on a creek near the boundary between the Cherokee and Creek Nations. They were also supporters of Eli's, and advised Jake and Ned that being on the Creek side of the boundary line would make establishing a railhead easier, mostly because the Creek Nation allowed non-Indians to own businesses. The route ended up being a total of approximately 80 miles.

Now, they were returning after several weeks on the trail and as the buildings of Vinita came into view, Jake stated, "Well, I don't know about you Ned, but I'm ready for a hot bath and a soft bed!"

"Hmm! A beer sounds better." Replied Walkingstick.

" Yeh well, I'm headed back to Springfield in the morning. I haven't seen Holly in three weeks. You goin' home for a spell?"

"I suppose I ought ta. My Sally will be wantin' me to stay a while, though. How long before we go back out?"

Ned lived down by Fort Gibson about 75 miles away. The Katy tracks ran near it through the new town of Muskogee on a daily route, just across the Arkansas River in the Creek Nation.

"Well, I have to write up my survey report and draw some maps. I'd say a couple of weeks."

"Any idea where we're gonna head next time out?"

"I'm pretty sure Otis is going to have us look at the route down to Fort Smith."

"Hoo Wee! We gonna have to be careful in that eastern part of the Cherokee Nation. There's a fella named Ned Christie lives over there in the Cookson Hills. He and his Keetoowah friends ain't gonna be too keen on havin' railroad tracks run through there." Ned said gruffly.

"What's a Keetoowah" Jake asked.

"They're a secret society and most of them are full bloods. They believe in the old ways of the Cherokee and that the land is sacred."

"Do you know this Christie fellow?"

"Yeh, I've met him. It'd be just as well that we don't run into him." Ned said, then turned his head and spit a stream of tobacco. "He can be a hot head, specially if he's drinkin'!"

"Why do I think that there's more to that story?" Jake asked.

Ned grimaced and said, "Oh, don't worry too much on it. My cousin, Dennis Bushyhead, is the new principal chief. I can get him involved if we need him."

"Okay! Well, I'll send a telegram when I'm ready, probably around the first of March, that work for you?"

"Yeh, let's get it done before it gets hot." Ned replied.

The next morning Jake boarded the train back to Springfield carrying his saddle bags and guns. He'd dropped Ace off at the Frisco stables and stored his tack with them. Jake sent a telegram ahead from Vinita, so when the train arrived at the Depot in Springfield, he saw Holly and Frank waiting on him.

"Hey you two!" He called out, waving as he stepped down to the platform.

Holly exclaimed. "Hey yourself! I was hoping you'd be back soon."

Jake embraced her and said, "Me too, I missed you!

Then after exchanging a kiss, he looked over at Frank. "Thanks for bringing her."

"No problem. Come on I've got my buggy. Grab your things and let's go. Colleen is fixing supper for us."

"That sounds great, but I don't want to put you out!"

"Nonsense! This way the girls figured that you two can have the rest of the evening to yourselves."

Holly squeezed Jake fingers, and smiled demurely at him.

"Well, if you put it like that!" Jake grinned, "I wouldn't want to disrupt any plans."

And the plans that Holly made were quite enjoyable, after an intensive bout of love making Jake drifted off to sleep with Holly in his arms. They slept in the next morning and after a late breakfast Jake walked over to the Frisco yard to where Frank had his office. He knocked on the door and stuck his head in.

"Hey there, you busy?" Jake asked.

"Jake! Come in and have a seat." Frank said, rising from behind his desk. "Want some coffee?"

Jake laughed, "You bet! It's got to be better than that lukewarm mud that Ned's been calling coffee."

They visited for a few minutes, and Jake gave him a brief rundown on his journey west and when he finished he stood to leave. "Well, I'll get out of your hair. Holly has plans for us today and she'll be mad if I make her wait."

Frank turned and retrieved a stack of newspaper from a table. "Here, I saved these for you." And offered them to Jake.

"What are these?" Jake asked.

"They're copies of the St. Louis Daily Globe. It is publishing daily transcripts from the Army's Court of Inquiry, up in Chicago. They're looking into Major Reno's conduct at the Little Big Horn. It started last week and I figured that you'd want to read them."

Jake eyed the newspapers and replied, "Yes, I suppose. It will be interesting to see who they call for witnesses and if anything new has come to light in the last two and a half years."

Jake and Holly spent the rest of day the moving around Springfield, riding on the horse trolley and shopping. They ended up back in North Springfield at Brunaugh's Restaurant for dinner.

"I see that Frank gave you those newspapers about the Reno Inquiry. Colleen and I have been keeping up with them." Holly said to him.

"So what do you think of it?"

"Well, so far, I don't recognize any names and I never met Major Reno, he came after I left Fort Lincoln."

"I don't think that you'll know too many of them. Most of Custer's favorites died with him. Capt. Moylan was one of the few that didn't. We'll just have to see who else they question." Jake replied.

"Regardless, I find it interesting having known many from the 7th."

"Well, I don't think that they'll call many enlisted men."

"Let's you and I read the rest together. I want to get your take on things. Aunt Kate wrote and said that she and Pat are going to do that." Holly looked intently into his eyes, "I want to know what you went through. I worried myself silly about you that whole summer, fearing that you weren't coming back to me.

Jake looked back at Holly and said, "Okay! We'll do it."

For the next couple of weeks reading the Globe's account of the Reno Inquiry became part of their daily routine. Jake was working in a spare office down the hall from Frank, going over his notes and marked up maps, before putting together his report. Frank would bring him the day's Globe so he had it to take home with him for Holly to read. The first 2 weeks consisted of mostly testimony about Reno's attack, then retreat to the bluffs and hill that now bore his name. Jake explained to Holly that all he knew concerning that was based on what he'd heard from some of the men that survived it, most especially from Sgt. Ryan of Company M. The 3rd week's proceedings started with a couple of days testimony from Lt. DeRudio, who'd been left behind at the timber.

"I don't understand why they're wasting this much time on him." Jake told Holly, "He missed all the fighting on the hill."

However, for the next 7 days the testimony included Davern, who'd been Reno's orderly that day, Martin, who'd delivered Custer's last orders, and most of the surviving officers, including Benteen, Godfrey, Edgerly, McDougall, and Mathey. Most of their accounts all seemed straight forward, but Jake got the sense that they were all being careful to not stir up any controversy. The main salient point revolved around the timing of the arrival of the Pack Train, particularly the mules carrying the ammunition packs. There was also varying accounts of who had heard volley firing in the distance from down stream, and when.

"I remember meeting Capt. Benteen one time when he was up from Fort Rice." Holly said, "I thought he was a polite southern gentleman. And also your company officer, Lt. Edgerly, who was about to be married and was very tall as I recall."

Jake discussed his recollections about those two with her, then said, "It's too bad that Capt. Weir died. I know he was extremely upset with Reno for not responding to Custer's dispatch to Benteen and the sounds of the fighting downstream, I'd have liked to hear what he had to say about it!"

Godfrey was one of the last ones questioned and Jake thought that he came closest to criticizing Reno's performance.

"It sounds to me that he's not particularly fond of Major Reno." Holly said.

Jake nodded his head, "I know that for a fact, but Godfrey is a career officer, and he's deliberately couching his testimony in ambiguous sentences. He's been in three different battles with the Sioux, and his coolness and bravery under fire has been proven beyond doubt. His performance at the Bear Paw battle should insure him future promotion, but I detect he's hedging his bets."

The last several days were a rehashing of the testimonies and Reno's attorney's statement was read. Then on Tuesday, Feb. 21 the Court recorder read his summation and after a brief recess the findings were presented. The last paragraph read,

The conduct of the officers throughout was excellent and while subordinates in some instances did more for the safety of the command by brilliant displays of courage then did Major Reno, there was nothing in his conduct which requires animadversion from this Court.

The conclusion of the Court was that in view of all the facts in evidence, no further proceedings were necessary and the case was convened.

,   That Friday night Frank and Colleen met them for dinner at Brunaugh's Restaurant and they exchanged views of the Inquiry.

"I had to have Colleen look up 'animadversion' in the Webster's dictionary at the library over at Drury College." Frank chuckled, "I'd never heard it before."

"Basically, it means that no blame was found. So what happens now?" Colleen asked.

Jake thought for a bit then answered, "Well, you have to remember that this was an Army Court and it is not subject to civilian laws. The court members are all career officers and they did what they thought best for the Army."

"You're saying that it was a foregone conclusion." Frank stated.

"You have to remember that it wasn't a court martial, although I understand that they could have recommended one. There are people higher up that just want this whole affair to go away. The Army wants to hand off most of the responsibility for Indian affairs to the Dept. of the Interior and the Indian Bureau, as quickly as possible."

"I think that the Army just put out a finding that's full of window dressing and is saying that's it, end of story!" Colleen pronounced.

Holly, being a little more attuned to Army protocols, asked "I've always noticed that most officers are very wary of public criticism of each other, but are quite capable of backstabbing in private. What do you think that they're going to do with Major Reno, and by extension Capt. Benteen as the other ranking officer?"

"If you noted, both of them made several disparaging comments about Custer and went on to embellish their own actions. Gen. Sherman and Gen. Sheridan both liked Custer, and I'm sure the they will take note of that when they read the of transcripts. Bear in mind that the debacle at the Little Big Horn was a major black eye for the Army that will not go away soon."

"So what can they do to them?" Colleen queried.

"Murray Johnson, Pat, and I spent a lot of time speculating about this before I left Bismarck. Of course that was well before any proceedings were being discussed." Jake stated.

"And?"

"We felt confident that Reno's career is over. He was already on suspension and one more miss step will find him dismissed. We were around him for some time and know how officious he can be to his superiors. I'll be surprised if he makes it a year, after this." Jake continued, "Now, Benteen is another matter. It's obvious that he played a large role in saving the command, but he will always be associated with his perceived complicity in supporting Reno's actions. But, he was also commended for his actions during the fighting at Canyon Creek last year. So, unless he does something stupid, he should be okay. But, on the basis of his testimony, I think he'll be shuttled away somewhere that he will have minimum visibility with the public."

"So that's the end of it after 26 days?" Holly asked incredulously.

"No! I have a feeling that the controversy surrounding Custer and the Battle of the Little Big Horn will continue be debated for years!" Jake proclaimed.

HISTORICAL NOTES AND PERSPECTIVES

The Forts

Fort Rice was abandoned in 1878. It is a state historic site, but none of it is still standing, with only a few foundations still visible.

Fort Stevenson was abandoned in 1883. The water of Garrison Reservoir covers the original site, but a nearby state park is named after it and has a reconstructed guardhouse building.

Fort Totten was decommissioned in 1880, but in 1891, it was turned over to the Bureau of Indian Affairs for use as an Indian School until 1935. It is a North Dakota Historical Site and the majority of the buildings are still standing.

Fort Ambercrombie was abandoned in 1877. It is a North Dakota Historical Site and has a reconstruction of the stockade and a museum.

Fort Seward was closed in 1877. The buildings were dismantled and taken up to Fort Totten.

Fort Abraham Lincoln was abandoned in 1891. It is a now a state park and has five reconstructed buildings, including Custer's house.

Fort Buford was closed in 1895. It is also a state historical site and has a couple of surviving buildings, along with a reconstructed barracks.

Fort Benton was closed in 1881. It is now a National Historic Landmark District. The partial remains of one blockhouse remain and efforts are underway for more reconstruction.

Fort Snelling was closed in 1965. It is now a National Historic Landmark with several surviving structures.

Fort Leavenworth is still in operation and is the second oldest active post US Army post west of Washington D.C.

Fort Keogh continued to be used until 1924. It was turned over to the Department of the Interior and is used as a livestock and range research station. Only a few structures remain.

Fort Custer was closed in 1898. Many of the building were used to build the nearby town of Hardin, Montana. The original site is now an abandoned golf course on the Crow Indian Reservation.

The Métis

The various bands spread along the border west of the Red River continued to migrate back and forth across the Medicine line pursuing buffalo. After the demise of the herds, the larger percentage settled in Canada where they were slowly given recognition as a First Nations people. In the USA the only recognized Métis belong to the Turtle Mountain Band, which is closely affiliated with the Chippewa tribe, and considered to be Indian under US law. Turtle Mountain Reservation and trust lands are scattered across North Dakota and Montana. Still considered an indigenous people, most Métis are loosely organized without much governmental over sight.

The Lakota Sioux

Sitting Bull and his Hunkpapa band survived in Canada until the decimation of the buffalo forced him into finally surrendering at Fort Buford in 1881. They were then sent south to Fort Yates, near the Standing Rock Agency. In 1884, he was persuaded to go on tour with Buffalo Bill Cody and Annie Oakley for a couple of years. He returned to live near Standing Rock and was still very influential among the Lakota. Sitting Bull was suspected of being a proponent of the Ghost Dance movement and was killed while being arrested by Indian Agency police in Dec. 1890. The rising tensions over his death led to the Battle of Wounded Knee two weeks later.

Crazy Horse and his Oglala band, along with some Miniconjou, Sans Arc, and Brule bands, surrendered in May of 1877 at the Red Cloud Agency. In early September he was arrested on the suspicion that he was planning to leave and join with the Nez Perce. While being taken in custody, he was stabbed by a bayonet and died while being treated by Dr. Valentine McGillicuddy.

The rest of the smaller bands of the Lakota Sioux made their way back to the reservations where they were eventually disarmed and forced to submit.

The Northern Cheyenne

Dull Knife and Little Wolf and their bands of Northern Cheyenne surrendered at the same time as Crazy Horse. They were escorted to

Bismarck by Capt. Benteen and sent by rail down to Indian Territory to join the Southern Cheyenne bands on their reservation. The following year they led 300 of their people on a trek back to Montana. Little Wolf and his band made it back to the Tongue River. Dull Knife and his band were captured and taken to the Red Cloud Agency. After refusing to be returned south, many of Dull Knife's people fled to the Pine Ridge Agency where the remaining Oglala Sioux were located. The next spring Dull Knife and his family slipped away to join the other Northern Cheyenne.

Two Moons and his band of Northern Cheyenne surrendered to Col. Nelson Miles ion April 1877. Due to their participation as scouts in the Nez Perce Campaign, they were allowed to settle in the area of Fort Keogh and the Tongue River basin.

The Nez Perce

Joseph, and the Nez Perce that surrendered with him, were relocated from Fort Leavenworth to the Quapaw Agency in Indian Territory, in 1878. The following year they were moved to the Oakland Agency near what is now Tonkawa, Oklahoma. The tribe named it 'Eeikich Paw - The Hot Place'. Joseph continued to lobby for his people to be allowed to go back to their homeland, and with the help of civilian advocates across the country, they were finally allowed to go up to the Colville Reservation in Washington State. Less than 300 survived by the time they left Indian Territory in May 1885. Joseph continued his efforts to be allowed to return to the Wallowa Valley for the rest of his life. He died, alone in his teepee on the Colville Reservation in September 1904.

White Bird and the nearly 300 Nez Perce that followed him, including Joseph's daughter, made it to Canada and Sitting Bull's camp. Eventually, after negotiating with the Canadian Northwest Mounted Police, they were allowed to settle along the banks of Pincher Creek near the Piegan Reservation. Over the years, small groups began to filter back to the Lapwai Reservation in Idaho. White Bird was killed in a dispute in 1892, and by 1898 the village was abandoned.

The Buffalo

Once numbering in the millions, the coming of the railroad carrying professional hunters, doomed the buffalo and they were systematically decimated, first the Southern Herd in the 1860/70s, and then the Northern Herd in the 1870/80s. By 1889 it was estimated that just over 1000 were left, with over half of those up in Canada. After lengthy conservation efforts to preserve and restore the species, the current population is estimated at just under 400,000 in all of North America. Approximately 70,000 are harvested for commercial purposes each year.

The Department of Dakota

General Alfred Terry - He remained over the Department of Dakota until 1886, when he was promoted to Major General and given command of the Division of Missouri, in Chicago. He retired in 1888 and died two years later in New Haven, Connecticut.

Colonel Nelson Miles - Was finally promoted to Brigadier General in December 1880. He went on to command various Departments across the West and campaigned successfully against Geronimo in 1886. In 1890, was promoted to Major General and went on to become the Commanding General of the United States Army in 1895. He commanded it during the Spanish American War, and was responsible for capturing Puerto Rico. He retired as a Lt. General in 1903, and afterwards the Chief of Staff system was introduced. He died of a heart attack in Washington D.C. in 1925, and is buried in Arlington.

Captain Otho Michaelis - The Ordinance Department promoted him to Major and he was assigned to command the Army Arsenal in Augusta, Maine. He died there in May 1890. Many of his competitive chess matches are still studied to this day.

The Department of Dakota moved its headquarters to Fort Snelling in 1879, then back to downtown St. Paul in 1886. It was discontinued in 1911. It's last commanding officer was Gen. Winfield Scott Edgerly.

Army Weapons

The Army retained the single shot Springfield 'Trap-door' Rifle until 1892 when another Rifle Board selected the Krag-Jorgensen, .30-40 caliber, bolt action rifle to replace it. Designed in Norway, over 500,000 were manufactured under license at the Springfield Armory in Massachusetts. The Army used it until 1903, when it was replaced by the Springfield M1903 30-06 caliber, bolt action rifle closely based on the Mauser design.

Also in 1892, the Army replaced the .45 Colt revolver with the Colt Model 1892, double action, .38 caliber pistol. During the fighting over in the Philippines in the early 1900s, it was found lacking in stopping power and the .45 Colt was re-issued to troops there. Coincidentally, this led to the development of the famous Colt Model 1911 semi-automatic pistol.

Notes on the surviving 7th Cavalry Officers of the 1876 Campaign

Colonel Samuel Sturgis - In 1878 he was assigned to command of the Middle District, Dept of Dakota, where he was responsible for the construction Fort Meade, near Deadwood, South Dakota. In 1881 he was appointed governor of the US Old Soldiers home in Washington D.C.. He retired in June 1886 and died in St. Paul, Minnesota in September 1889. The town of Sturgis in South Dakota is named after him.

Major Marcus Reno - On January 13, 1879, almost two and a half years after the Battle of the Little Big Horn, a Court of Inquiry was convened at the Palmer House, in Chicago. Major Reno, who was still suspended without pay, had been lobbying with President Hayes since the previous June for one to be appointed. After three weeks of testimony by 23 witnesses, the results of the proceedings were forwarded to the Judge Advocate General, in Washington, and Reno was exonerated. At the beginning of April he was restored to duty and reported back to the 7th Cavalry, now garrisoned at the new Fort Meade, near Deadwood, Dakota Territory. That fall, after multiple incidents of drunk and disorderly conduct, including accusations of stalking Col. Sturgis' daughter, he received a court martial. Reno was found guilty of conduct unbecoming an officer and gentleman then dismissed from the service on April 1, 1880. He moved to Washington D. C., where he went to work for the Bureau of Pensions and unsuccessfully lobbied to regain his military rank until his death from cancer, in late March 1889.

Major Lewis Merrill - Was on detached duty as Chief of Military Staff to President Grant and did not re-join the 7th until November 1876. His actions during the Nez Perce Campaign in 1877 were criticized by some. He stayed in the 7th at various posts until he retired in May 1886. In 1890 he did receive a honorary brevet promotion to Brigadier General for gallantry at Canyon Creek. He died in Philadelphia, in February 1896.

Captain Frederick Benteen - While well regarded by the men of the 7th, he continued to suffer from the negative press associated with his perceived lack of action at the Little Big Horn. He remained with the 7th and played a prominent role at the Battle of Canyon Creek during the Nez Perce campaign. A major witness at Reno's Inquiry, he became increasingly contentious in his relationship with the other surviving officers. Benteen was promoted to Major in 1882, and spent the rest of his career with the 9th US Cavalry 'Colored' at various posts in the west. He retired while under suspension for drunk and disorderly conduct in July 1888. He was breveted to Brigadier General in 1890 for his actions at Canyon Creek. He died from a stroke in Atlanta, in 1898, still a controversial figure in the Custer saga.

Capt.Thomas French - He remained with the 7th, but continued to struggle with alcohol and laudanum abuse. This led to a court martial in January 1879 where he was suspended without pay. He retired on February 1880 and died from a stroke, at Fort Leavenworth, Kansas in May 1882.

Capt. Myles Moylan - He continued serving on frontier duty with the 7th around the Dakota and Wyoming Territories until 1892. Promoted to Major, he was reassigned to the 10th Cavalry, the other 'Colored' regiment. He served with it for a year, then retired. In 1894 Moylan was awarded the Medal of Honor for his gallantry at the Battle of Bear Paw Mountain. He died in San Diego, California in December 1909.

Capt. Thomas McDougal - Remained with the 7th until May 1888 when he took sick leave due to complications from malaria, and retired on disability as a major in 1890. He died in Brandon, Vermont in July 1909.

Capt. James Bell - He was on leave when Terry's column left Ft Lincoln, and was promoted to Captain, Company F to replace the slain Yates, in June 1876. He didn't rejoin the regiment until September. Reno's first court martial was for making improper advances to Bell's wife, Emily, at Ft. Abercrombie that winter. He took part in the Nez Perce campaign the following year and fought in Merrill's battalion at the Battle of Canyon Creek where he was commended for bravery. He continued to serve with the 7th and was in charge of the escort for the Northern Pacific construction crews in the summers of 1880-1882. Bell received a brevet promotion to Lt. Col. for his actions at Canyon Creek in February 1890, and in May 1896, he was promoted Major, 1st Cavalry. During the Spanish American War he was advanced to Brigadier General of Volunteers and Lt. Col. 8th Cavalry. He served in the Philippines and following his discharge from the volunteers, in March 1901 he was made a Colonel and then retired as a Brig. Gen. that October. He was under consideration for a Medal of Honor, for his actions at the Washita Fight. (It was never awarded) When he died in September 1919, in Hermosa Beach, California, he was still married to Emily.

1st Lt. Edward Godfrey - After recovering from his wounds he served as an instructor at West Point until 1883, then returned to the 7th. He was in command of Company D at the Battle of Wounded Knee. Shortly afterwards he was injured in a train accident which kept him out of the field. He published his diary from the 1876 campaign and wrote about his experiences during it in 1892. In 1894, he received the Medal of Honor for his actions at the Battle of Bear Paw Mountain. He was promoted to Major in December 1896 and assigned to the 1st Cavalry but transferred back to the 7th the next year. He was with the 7th, in Cuba, during the Spanish American War. He was again promoted out of the regiment in February 1901, serving as a Lt. Colonel in the 12th Cavalry in the Philippines. In 1902, now a full Colonel, he commanded the 9th Cavalry before being promoted to a Brig. General over the Department of Missouri. He died in New Jersey in April 1932 and is buried in the Arlington National Cemetery.

1st Lt. Henry Nowlan - Promoted to replace his good friend , Miles Keogh, in command of Company I, he would retain that position until July 1895. He received a brevet as Major in February 1890 for his actions at Canyon Creek. He fought at the Battle of Wounded Knee, and was recognized for gallantry during that action. He was promoted to Major in July 1895. He was the commander of Fort Huachuca, Arizona from 1896 through 1898. Nowlan died from heart disease at Hot Springs, Arkansas in November of that year, while on medical leave.

1st Lt. Edward Mathey - Also continued to serve with the 7th the rest of his career. He was promoted to the command of Company K following the death of Capt. Hale. He retired from active duty with disability at the rank of Major, in December 1896 and taught ar Baylor University from 1901 to 1903. Mathey received a promotion to Lt. Col (retired) in April 1904 and died in Denver, Colorado in July 1915.

1st Lt. Francis Gibson - He was promoted to Captain of Company H in February 1880 and remained on frontier duty with the 7th until June 1889. He was granted sick leave and eventually retired on disability in December 1891. Gibson moved to New York City, where he was once mentioned as a potential candidate for mayor, by Teddy Roosevelt. He died there in January 1919.

1st Lt. Charles DeRudio - Finally promoted to Captain of Company E in December 1882, and served with the 7th all over the frontier, until retiring with the rank of Major in August 1896. He died November 1910 in

San Diego, California.

2nd Lt. Winfield Edgerly - He was assigned to Company C and served as its 1st Lt. until he was promoted to Captain in September 1883. He commanded it during the Battle of Wounded Knee and received a commendation for his actions there. After the conclusion of the Indian Wars, he was assigned as a Professor and Inspector General at various locations. He was promoted to Major in July 1898, in the 6th Cavalry. However, he rejoined the 7th and fought with it in Cuba the following year. Edgerly was promoted to Lt. Col., 10th Cavalry in 1899, but returned to duty with the 7th in July 1902. Promoted to Colonel, in command of the 2nd Cavalry, he was sent to the Philippines in February 1904. He was promoted to Brig. Gen. in June 1905 and returned to the US in March 1907 to command the Department of the Gulf. He served on various boards, commanded the Department of Dakota, and the Cavalry and Artillery School until he retired on disability in September 1909. He returned to his home state of New Hampshire, where during World War 1, he served on a military board and commanded a mobilization camp in mid 1917. Edgerly died in September 1927 and is buried in Arlington National Cemetery.

2nd Lt. George Wallace - Promoted to 1st. Lt. after the Little Big Horn, he served as the 7th's Regimental Adjutant until June 1877. Reassigned to Company G, he fought at Canyon Creek in Benteen's battalion. He remained with the regiment and was eventually promoted to command Company L in September 1885. Wallace took over command of Company K in September 1890, and was killed at the Battle of Wounded Knee that December. (He was the only Little Big Horn surviving officer killed in action)

2nd Lt. Charles Varnum - He was also promoted to 1st Lt., Company C after the Little Bighorn and in November was appointed Regimental Quartermaster. He remained in that capacity until November 1879. He serving in the 7th at various posts on the frontier and was assigned as Post Quartermaster and Adjutant at Fort Sill when he was assigned to command Company B in July 1890. He played a key role at the Battle of Wounded Knee and was awarded the Medal of Honor for gallantry. In 1895, Varnum went on attached duty teaching military science at the University of Wyoming until the start of the Spanish American War. Rejoining the regiment, he sailed with them to Cuba, where he fell sick. Sent stateside, he was assigned as Adjutant General, Dept. of Colorado. Promoted to Major in February 1901, he transferred to the 9th Cavalry in 1904, and was promoted to Lt. Col., 4th Cavalry in April 1905. He served in the Phillipines and, when he returned, as commander of the Department of Dakota before retiring from active service in 1907. Varnum then taught military science at several posts, lastly at Fort Mason, in San Francisco, where fully retired as a Colonel in April 1918. He died there in February 1936.

2nd Lt. Luther Hare - Was promoted as a 1st Lt., to replace Porter in Company I after the Little Big Horn. He fought at the Battle of Canyon Creek during the Nez Perce Campaign and was commended for bravery. Continuing on frontier duty with the regiment, he served as Regimental Quartermaster at Fort Lincoln from 1886-87 and finally made Captain of Company K, when Wallace was killed at Wounded Knee. He served down in Arizona during the Apache Campaign of 1896, and as a Lt. Col. of Volunteers, with the 1st Texas Volunteer Cavalry during the Spanish American War, down in Cuba. He was appointed a Colonel with the 33rd Volunteer Infantry in July 1899 and accompanied that unit to the Philippines. He took place in several battles and received two Silver Stars for gallantry. Promoted to Brig. Gen. Of Volunteers, he commanded the Dept. of Luzon until June 1901 when he returned to the 7th. Hare was then made a Major, 12th Cavalry in July 1903 and retired from active duty on disability. He was assigned as commandant of the ROTC program at the University Of Texas and taught military tactics there until taking full retirement as a Lt. Col. and returning to his home in Sherman, Texas. He died of cancer at the Walter Reed Army Hospital in Washington D.C. in December 1929 and is buried in Arlington National Cemetery.

2nd Lt. Andrew Humes Nave - Was on medical leave in Tennesee, but was promoted to 1st Lt. effective June 25, 1876. He rejoined the 7th at Fort Lincoln. He was post-adjutant there during the Nez Perce Campaign. He served at various posts until September 1880 when he went back on sick leave due to health issues. He was promoted to Capt. in January 1884, then retired on disability in September 1885. He taught at the University of Tennesee as a professor of military tactics and died in Knoxville December 1924.

2nd Lt. Edwin Eckerson - Originally appointed to the 7th in May 1876, he was granted leave before reporting. He had a somewhat checkered past with the 5th Cavalry and had been dismissed from the service back in July 1875, for conduct unbecoming an officer. He eventually joined the regiment in field, after the Little Big Horn fight, and was promoted to 1st Lt. in Company D to replace Bell. He was stationed at Fort Rice along with Company D, prior to the Nez Perce Campaign. Eckerson was the only officer of Hale's battalion still standing at the Battle of Snake

Creek and assumed command of what was left of three companies. He was commended for conspicuous duty, but there were some who questioned his actions. Eckerson received another court martial at Fort Lincoln for conduct unbecoming an officer while intoxicated and was again dismissed from the service in June 1878. He eventually found employment at Fort Hays as a civilian working for the Quartermaster Dept in 1880. He died there in August 1885, from malaria

Notes on the surviving Company D, NCOs and Enlisted Men

Sgt. James Flanagan - Stayed with the 7th until November 1881 as a quartermaster sergeant and was discharged at Ft. Yates, as a sergeant of excellent character. Died in Mandan, North Dakota in April 1921.

Sgt. Tom Harrison - Discharged as a sergeant of excellent character in August 1876 at the Rosebud encampment. He was recommended for the Medal of Honor by Lt. Edgerly, but it was not approved. He died in Philadelphia, Pennsylvania in December 1917.

Sgt. Thomas Rush - Discharged as a sergeant of good character in November 1876, he eventually re-enlisted in August 1878 and rejoined Company D as 1st Sgt. He went on detached service to Fort Snelling in 1881/82 with the rifle team. He was discharged as a first sergeant of excellent character in August 1883. He died in November 1905 in Elmhurst, California.

Sgt. Tom Russell - After his discharge at the Tongue River in June 1877, he re-enlisted in the 17th Infantry the following April. He was stationed back at Fort Totten for several years and went on to serve mostly in the infantry, stationed at forts all over the west. He fought in the Philippines and retired as a sergeant of excellent character in July 1900, at the Presidio, in San Francisco. He died there in May 1926

Sgt. Albert Cunningham - Discharged with disability due to rheumatism contracted in the line of duty, in October 1879, at Fort Yates. He probably went home to Leeds, England. Death unknown.

Sgt. George Wylie - He remained in the 7th until discharged in March 1883, as a sergeant of very good character. He re-enlisted again in May of that year and served in the various Cavalry regiments for the rest of his career. He went up and down the ranks, from private back to sergeant, due to what the records termed 'occasional sprees', and even spent 2 years in Fort Leavenworth prison. He eventually retired as a first sergeant of excellent character in October 1906. He died in March 1931 in Kansas City, Missouri.

Sgt. Charles Welch - He was discharged for disability in June 1878 at Fort Rice, and that October was awarded the Medal of Honor for bringing water to the wounded on Reno Hill. He bought a farm near LaSalle, Colorado and lived there for 37 years. He died in June 1915 of septic poisoning from bone necrosis, probably the result of his old leg wound at Snake Creek.

Cpl. Henry Holden - After going back to the east coast Holden re-enlisted in July 1878. He was assigned to the 2nd Artillery and posted at Fort McHenry, in Washington D.C.. He was awarded the Medal of Honor in October 1878 for bringing up ammunition under heavy fire on Reno Hill. In November 1882, Holden was discharged for disability after being kicked by a horse and suffering a compound fracture of his right tibia. He returned to Brighton, England where he married a widow with two children from a previous marriage. He died in December 1905.

Cpl. Fremont Kipp - Promoted to sergeant in October 1877 following the Battle of Snake Creek, he re-enlisted in Company D that December. He was discharged at Fort Yates as a sergeant of excellent character in December 1882 and returned to his home state of Ohio. In 1898 he re-enlisted in the 17th Infantry and served as a drillmaster at the Columbus Barracks, Ohio. Kipp was sent to the Philippines where he was commended for capturing an outlaw leader. He was discharged in June 1901 and resided in Columbus, Ohio, before moving to the US Soldiers Home in Washington D.C., in October 1921. He was one of the few enlisted men still living to attend the 50th anniversary of the Little Big Horn fight, at the battlefield in June 1926. He died at the Soldiers Home in January 1938.

Pvt. George Horn - He also went back to the east coast where he re-enlisted in February 1877 and was sent to St Augustine, Florida with the 3rd Artillery. Lt. Edgerly recommended him for a Medal of Honor for helping Henry Holden bring up ammunition on Reno Hill, but it was never approved. He was discharged as private of good character and a sober steady man, in February 1882. His whereabouts after that are unknown.

Pvt. Joseph Green - There is no record of his whereabouts after his discharge in January 1877. Where he went after his discharge is unknown but he ended up at the Old Soldiers Home, in Washington D.C. in April 1918 and he died there in November 1919.

Pvt. George Hunt - There are no records for Hunt after his discharge as a private of good character at Fort Rice, in June 1878.

Pvt. George Dann - He deserted in March 1878 and re-enlisted at Harrisburg, PA as Guy Arlington in December 1879. He was assigned to the 19th Infantry in Fort Garland, Colorado where he deserted in March 1880. He was apprehended that May, then dishonorably discharged as a private of no character and sentenced to 2 years in Fort Leavenworth. While serving his sentence he identified himself as George Dann and was released in January 1882. There are no records of him after that.

Pvt. David Manning - After being discharged as a private of excellent character in October 1878, he went back to Boston where he re-enlisted a month later, and was assigned to the 3rd Cavalry. He remained in the Army where he followed a pattern of being discharged, then re-enlisting a month later in a different unit. After two hitches in the Cavalry, he switched over to the Infantry in December 1888. Manning ended up serving with the 9th Infantry over in the Philippines where he finally made corporal and then retired in June 1902 in San Francisco, as a sergeant. He died in New York City in Oct 1910.

Pvt. Charles Saunders - After being discharged as a private of excellent character in Jan 1877. He was recommended for the Medal of Honor for conspicuous gallantry by Lt. Edgerly, but it was not awarded. He ended up in Brooklyn, New York, where he enlisted in the Marine Corps in February. Sanders deserted a year later, then enlisted back in the Army and was assigned to the 6th Cavalry. After it was discovered that Sanders was a deserter, the Adjutant Generals Office ruled that he could serve the balance of his original Marine enlistment, in the 6th Cavalry. When that was completed, he enlisted in the 8th Infantry and served in the Arizona Territory. Sanders remained in the 8th for the rest of his career and retired as a sergeant of excellent character in October 1897. He died in Lincoln, Nebraska in August 1915.

Pvt. James Hurd - He was discharged as a private at the Rosebud Creek encampment in August 1876 and then re-enlisted in September at Fort Lincoln. He was discharged again as a private of very good character at Fort Yates, in September 1881. Hurd died in Harrodsburg, Kentucky in 1911.

Pvts. Thomas Stivers, William Harris, and George Scott - They all enlisted together at Mount Vernon, Kentucky and were all discharged in August 1876, at the Rosebud encampment. All three were awarded Medals of Honor in October 1878, for bringing water to the wounded on Reno Hill. Stivers was already dead, having been killed in a gunfight while visiting a brothel in Richmond, Kentucky, in June 1877. Stivers cousin, William Harris, was killed in gunfight involving bootleg whiskey in June 1885, in Madison County, Kentucky. No other records of George Scott have been found.

Pvt. Harvey Fox - the other Kentuckian, was also discharged at the Rosebud encampment. He returned to Fort Lincoln and went to work as a hostler for the post quartermaster. Fox married a half blood Blackfoot woman and went to live on the Blackfoot Reservation near Browning, Montana, where he raised livestock for 20 years. He died in the Montana State Hospital in Warm Springs, in March 1913.

Pvt. Frederick Deetline - After recovering from his wounds he returned to duty. He was awarded the Medal of Honor in October 1878 for bringing water to the wounded on Reno Hill. He was eventually promoted to corporal in January 1879, and then sergeant in August 1880. Deetline was discharged at Fort Yates in August 1880 as a sergeant of excellent character. He re-enlisted in St Louis in June 1881 and was assigned to the 5th Cavalry. He was discharged at Fort Reno, Indian Territory, in June 1886. He went up to Washington state and re-enlisted in the 2nd Cavalry at Fort Walla Walla in September 1886. He re-enlisted in the 5th Cavalry in September 1891 back at Fort Reno, and remained with the 5th the rest of his career, serving down in Cuba during the Spanish American War. He retired as a quartermaster sergeant of excellent character, in July 1900. Deetline died in San Antonio, Texas in December 1910.

Of the 24 Medals of Honor awarded for the Battle of the Little Big Horn, all went to enlisted men. 7 of them went to members of Company D.

Other Enlisted Survivors

Sgt. Michael Caddle - He remained at Fort Lincoln in charge of the company garden when the 7th left to the establish Fort Meade near the Black Hills during the summer of 1878. Caddle was discharged that September, at Fort Lincoln, as a sergeant of excellent character. He lived there with Josephine until 1883 when he moved down to a homestead 2 miles north of Fort Rice. He maintained contacts with the quartermasters of the surrounding forts and with the railroad, bidding on various contracts. Later on, he became a commissioner for Morton County, and was also a local mail carrier. He lived in North Dakota for 46 years before his death in May 1919. He is buried in Fort Rice Community Cemetery.

Pvt. Gustave Korn - Was discharged at Fort Lincoln in May 1878 as a blacksmith of excellent character and re-enlisted the same day, with a promotion to sergeant. He spent his entire career in Company I, and was personally responsible for tending to Keogh's horse, Comanche. His exploits at the Little Big Horn were much storied, and it was quietly known that he carried more water to the wounded than any other trooper. He was commended by Major Merrill for his actions a Canyon Creek. Korn was killed at the Battle of Wounded Knee in December 1890, and is buried at Fort Riley Post Cemetery.

Pvt. John Keller - After Weir's death he remained on regular duty in Company D. He fought at Snake Creek and was discharged in October 1878 as a private of good character and reliable man. Keller moved to Helena, Montana and lived there for 38 years, dying there in February 1913.

Sgt. John Ryan - After his discharge in December 1876, he returned to his home town of West Newton, Massachusetts just a few miles west of Boston. He joined the local police force in January 1878 and worked there until retiring in January 1913. He wrote about his experiences in the 7th Cavalry and in 1908/09, several area newspapers published them in a series called - "Ten Years with General Custer among the Indians". He also wrote many letters and was actively involved with other 7th Cavalry veterans. He died in West Newton in October 1926.

The Riverboats

After the surrender of Sitting Bull, the threat from hostile Indians was virtually eliminated. With the most of the various tribes relocated to reservations and the Army closing forts, the riverboat companies struggled to survive. When railroad construction resumed west of the Missouri River the need for steamboats was reduced, particularly along the Upper Missouri and the Yellowstone. By 1884 most of the larger, custom built riverboats were operating south of Bismarck towards Sioux Falls and St. Louis. The fickle nature of the Missouri ice flows slowly decimated these vessels. The *Western* and *Fontenelle* were both lost near Yankton during the massive ice flow of April 1881. The *Far West* was lost near St. Charles, Missouri, in October 1883. The *Rosebud* and the *Josephine* both made over 50 round trips on Montana Rivers. The *Rosebud* was wrecked on submerged pilings at Bismarck in 1890, and the *Josephine* lasted until March 1907, when she was lost to an ice snag near Running Water, South Dakota.

The upper Missouri River is now impounded by fifteen different dams, but the lower portion, a distance of over 700 miles, can still be navigated from Sioux City, Iowa to St. Louis, Missouri.

The main channel of the Yellowstone River is still open to navigation, however there are five major reservoirs along its tributaries. It is still subject to seasonal water flow fluctuations, and is renowned for its trout fishing from the mouth of the Rosebud Creek to the North Dakota state line

Captain Grant Marsh - Continued to work for Leighton and Jordan, captaining the *F.Y. Batchelor* for them until 1882, when he purchased his own boat, the *W. J. Behan*. He was hired by the Army to transport Sitting Bull down to the Standing Rock Reservation. In 1883, when business diminished with the expansion of the railroad, he sold his boat and moved to Memphis, Tennessee, spending the next 12 years as a Mississippi riverboat pilot. In the early 1900s, Marsh returned to Bismarck and went to work for the Benton Packet Company which had 5 steamboats, 2 ferries, and a couple of barges. The company serviced the new homestead communities along the Missouri that had no rail connections. Grant retired in 1907, but continued to live in Bismarck and died there in 1916.

The Railroads

The Northern Pacific Railroad

In march of 1880, the NPRR officially resumed construction west from the Missouri River predominately following the survey route that had been mapped by Gen. Rosser and Custer back in '73. In January 1883, the tracks reached Livingston, Montana and that October a bridge spanning the Missouri was completed at Bismarck. Before the end of 1884 the Northern Pacific's tracks were completed along the entire route linking to the Pacific Northwest, effectively spelling the demise of the Upper

Missouri and Yellowstone riverboat trade. The golden age of railroading had begun and the NPRR successfully operated until 1970, when it merged with three other railroads and it is now called the Burlington Northern Railroad.

The Missouri, Kansas, and Texas Railroad

The Katy continued to expand across Texas in the 1880s, reaching Dallas, Waco, Houston, and in 1901 San Antonio. It acquired and partnered with other railroad companies, running many special passenger trains. In December 1989, it was purchased and merged into the Union Pacific. Many of it urban track beds have been closed and donated to the local cities to be used as recreational trails.

The Saint Louis - San Francisco Railroad

The Frisco was finally able to start laying tracks west, reaching the Arkansas River in 1882 near what is now Tulsa, Oklahoma. It eventually operated across Oklahoma, Missouri, Southern Kansas, Arkansas, and North Texas, with service to St. Louis, Kansas City, Oklahoma City, Dallas, and Memphis. Despite the name, the farthest west it reached was western Oklahoma and Texas. It was acquired by the Burlington Northern in November 1980.

ABOUT THE AUTHOR

James W Mcdonough

    A native of Wichita KS, now living in retirement on Fort Gibson Lake, in Oklahoma, after a 40 year career in the Material Handling business. Also a veteran, I served as a Tank Commander during the Cold War in Germany, in the early 70s. I'm a life long history buff, with an extensive library, including over 100 books on Custer and the Indian Wars. I enjoy reading, target shooting, fishing, boating, and traveling. I am a member of the Western Writers of America.

Made in United States
North Haven, CT
07 December 2023

45319673R10370